THE YOUTH OF CÉZANNE AND ZOLA

BOOKS BY THE SAME AUTHOR

Picasso's Brothel: Les Demoiselles d'Avignon
Freud, Leonardo da Vinci, and the Vulture's Tail
The Ara Pacis of Augustus and Mussolini
The Dirtfarmer's Son (autobiography)
Little Sister (novel/screenplay)
My Self (autobiography)
Scenario for an Artist's Apocalypse
Paul Gauguin: The Writings of a Savage
American Sculpture In Process
Gauguin's Paradise Lost
Cézanne's Portrait Drawings

FORTHCOMING

Cézanne and the Eternal Feminine
*The Picnic and the Prostitute: Manet's
art of the 1860s*

WAYNE ANDERSEN

THE YOUTH OF CÉZANNE AND ZOLA

NOTORIETY AT ITS SOURCE
ART AND LITERATURE IN PARIS

ÉDITIONS FABRIART

ISBN: 0-9725573-5-0 (cloth)

Contents

Cézanne. Self-Portrait. Pencil on paper.
Collection Maurice Gobin, Paris.

FOREWORD

This book opens on the boyhood of Paul Cézanne and Èmile Zola, who managed to become remarkable men. It is about their shared upbringing, schooling, fantasies, loves and hates, frailties and strengths. It is about art and literature at a particular time in two well-defined places, Aix-en-Provence and Paris, about the young Cézanne's obstreperous behavior and his dreadful and wonderful early paintings, about Zola's hotheaded art criticism and trashy but extraordinary novels. I have treated both subjects equally, warranted by the fact that from their shared school years in Aix-en Provence until their maturity they were at most times inseparable and mutually dependent.

It occurred to me only a few years ago, that after some forty years of studying, puzzling, and lecturing on Cézanne's art—not to say that was all I was doing—the missing ingredient in my thoughts and words was Zola. And when, to correct that oversight, I undertook an extensive study of Zola, sure enough the missing ingredient was Cézanne. While every Cézanne monograph and biography includes comment on Zola, and those of Zola bring in Cézanne, no text to my knowledge, not even John Rewald's doctoral thesis at the Sorbonne, submitted in 1936 as *Cézanne et Zola*, allows Zola more than standing room under the sun-worship of Cézanne. When Rewald's book was published in English in 1959, Zola was dropped from the book's title. In academic literature courses, Zola's novels are usually put out with the trash. And for half a century, Cézanne's early paintings were an embarrassment to most connoisseurs and curators. In the 1860s they entered into art history on the shoulders of Freud when, in 1952, Meyer Schapiro introduced into the literature on Cézanne psychoanalytical interpretations of his principal themes, infusing them with father-son conflict and sexual repression.

Psychoanalytical investigations of an artist's imagery cannot avoid looking to family background and youthful works. My own entry into a psychological study of Cézanne began in 1959, head to head with my study of Gauguin that ended with the publication of *Gauguin's Paradise Lost* in 1971. Six years earlier, in 1965, when I taught a summer session course on Impressionism at Harvard University, I devoted a few lectures to Cézanne's art of the 1860s. Jane Cone, a student in that course, who had been raised in a family dedicated to supporting modern art, approached me with the idea of organizing an exhibition of Cézanne's early paintings at Harvard's Fogg Museum. We wrote to John Rewald, who responded with the assurance that he would support our effort to borrow pictures. But the time was not right. The Fogg's directorate was not only disinterested, but also strongly opposed to an exhibition that would diminish the exalted achievements of Cézanne's mature works. I still recall the advice of the esteemed connoisseur of drawings, Frederick Deknatel, who took me aside and said, «Wayne, why do you occupy yourself with Cézanne's awful pictures when he created so many wonderful works of art?»

Twenty years later, when academic deconstruction began dismantling heroes like revolutionists pulling down statues, and post-Freudian polysemy had opened the gates to interpretive pasturing on artists' imagery, weeds and all, Cézanne's early paintings became the subject matter of psychoanalysts—either art historians writing as amateur analysts or analysts as amateur art historians. The earlier myths of Cézanne as a genius, whose art laid the foundation for twentieth-century painting, were transformed into Cézanne as a neurotic—misogynous to the extreme, scoptophilic, paranoid, vulgar, violent if not just chronically cranky. In the name of scholarship, the character diagnoses recapitulated what had been said derisively about Cézanne during his lifetime. Among other examples, Mary Cassatt likened him to a cutthroat with large red eyeballs standing out from his head in a most ferocious manner, a rather fierce-looking pointed beard, quite gray, and an exciting way of talking that positively made the dishes rattle. «He scrapes his soup plate, then lifts it and pours the remaining drops in his spoon; he even takes his chops in his fingers and pulls the meat from the bone.» Soon after Cézanne's death, Cassatt described his paintings as «figures really dreadful, neither drawing nor color. Public taste has been perverted by Cézanne,» she said.

Yet another problem confronting any study of Cézanne's early work is the fact, as I will demonstrate, that a number of the pictures assigned to him are not by him, and others have been so radically mistitled as to have obliterated the subject matter—an erotic painting titled *Lot and His Daughters* that Cézanne did not paint, a canvas titled *Overture to Tannhäuser* that has nothing to do with Wagner's opera. A poem by Cézanne is interpreted as a covert wish for his father's death, when, in fact, it's a poem he sent from Aix to Zola in Paris scolding Zola for having fallen behind in their correspondence. And Cézanne's startled and gruff reaction to a young man who'd come up behind him while out walking, who'd touched him on his shoulder, is interpreted as Cézanne's unconscious fear of homosexual assaults from behind (!).

The extant correspondence between Cézanne and Zola is both a great asset to scholarship and a problem. We have enough letters to understand their relationship, but too few to avoid reductive interpretations. When John Rewald published the first English translations of Cézanne's correspondence, he included only a few truncated letters from Zola to Cézanne. And he left Cézanne's poems in French, saying, by way of justification, that they were not serious. But, as we shall see, they were. Both the letters and the poems are integral to my narrative, allowing Cézanne and Zola to speak to each other in letter writing, prose or paintings, and to their mutual friends. Of the 230 letters written by Cézanne that Rewald located and published, roughly one-third are to Zola. The only letters that Cézanne saved are a few received from Zola when in their late teens and twenties. Cézanne's letters to his and Zola's mutual boyhood friend, Baptiste Baille, about whom we will hear a great deal, were not saved, nor were letters from other companions of their youth in Aix who we will come to know from Zola's letters: Antonin Valabrègue, Gustave Boyer, and Joseph Villevieille.

I have re-translated Cézanne's youthful letters and translated for the first time many of Zola's letters, his newspaper reviews, his treatise on optical screens, the reviews of his early books, and his heated exchanges with editors and reviewers. To represent the wording and spirit of their letters as they wrote and read them, I avoided historically archaic expressions and other pitfalls of literal translation. Considering that they wrote in the modern language of their time, they must be read in the modern language of our time. And I made no effort to imitate the clever rhyming in Cézanne's poems, while remaining alert that at times he selected a word that rhymed even if not the most appropriate word as to meaning. Zola in the early 1860s had to admit that his friend was a better poet than he. Ironic, is it not, that when they were late adolescents, taking art lessons in their spare time, Zola regularly won prizes while Cézanne managed to receive just one, not until he was twenty and in law school, and a second prize at that!

I owe much to the late John Rewald. Throughout my career he had been a supporter, even when we were in disagreement, as we often were. Art history as a discipline may have outdistanced his approach to Impressionism, but his many books nourished everyone of my generation. His masterpiece, *The History of Impressionism*, was first published in 1946, the year I graduated from high school. While not personally acquainted with Frederick Brown, I want him to know that, had he not published his superb biography of Zola, I may not have undertaken this book. My dependence on Dr. Rewald and Professor Brown will be made apparent by the numerous borrowings that enriched my text. No one should interpret my disagreements with either of them as lack of respect. My colleagues at various universities, Professors Paul Barolsky, Albert Boime, Kermit Champa, Bradford Collins, Michael Leja, Peter Selz, Richard Shiff, and the late, sadly missed Mark Roskill, read portions of the manuscript where I am especially disputative. Without committing any one of them to a ratification of my entire text, I am grateful for their encouragement and degree of support that no risk-taking scholar can do without.

TO MY FRIEND ZOLA
PASS THIS ON TO THOSE WHO HAVE
RIDICULED YOUR POETRY

You veritable herd of swine wallowing under the wing
Of a putrefied pendant who stupidly guides you,
Forcing you to admire, without knowing why,
Verses in which you find beauty in his words alone,
When amongst you there now surges like spurting lava
An unrestrained poet, breaking all shackles.
It's as around the eaglet one hears the squalling
Of a thousand puny birds, their wings aflapping.
You chintzy derogators, priests of pettifoggery.
You vomit on him your irreverent slobber—
I hear you, a virtual concert of toads,
Singing your heads off, all out of tune.
Nobody in this world has ever seen frogs
Who like you, Sirs, mumble and sputter so stupidly.
But go ahead, fill the air with your asinine clamor—
The verses of my friend Èmile shall remain the vanquishers!
They will endure your vile small-mindedness,
For they are marked by the true stamp of genius.

Paul Cézanne

THE LOVE OF UGLINESS

A painting depicting the head of a man, dark and bearded, whose cheeks were sculpted with a trowel and who seemed to be the prey of eczema, particularly amused the crowd. The other paintings by this ultra-impressionist named Cézanne all had the air of defying no less directly Corot, Théodore Rousseau, Hobbema, and Ruysdael. Pissarro, Monet and the other eccentric painters of the out-of-door school—those who are called «confetti painters»—are academicians by comparison with this strange Cézanne, whose productions Zola picked up like a hobo collecting trash.

The experts in charge of the sale themselves experienced a degree of embarrassment in cataloguing these aberrational things, and attached this note to each one of them: «Work of earliest youth.»

If Mr. Cézanne was, in fact, still at his mother's breast when he committed these daubs, we can have nothing to say. But what is to be thought of that Zola, the head of a literary school, the squire of Médan, as he fancied himself to be, who propagated such madness? —he who wrote Salon reviews in which he pretended to rule over French art! Nothing remains as supreme symbol of the art dear to Zola than to set fire to the Louvre.

—*Henri Rochefort*[*]

---

[*] Henri, Rochefort, a political adversary of Zola, published a review of the Zola estate sale on 9 March 1903 in *L'Itransigeant,* from which these remarks are taken. The paintings by Cézanne that he castigates were from Cézanne's youth.

TO MY FRIEND PAUL CÉZANNE

With profound joy, my friend, I talk to you alone. You would not believe how much I have suffered during the quarrel I just had with a mob of people unknown to me. I felt myself so little understood, such hatred all around me, that at times despair caused the pen to fall out of my hand. Today I will allow myself the pleasure of one more intimate chat with you, like those we have had over the past ten years. It is for you alone that I write these pages. I know you will read them with your heart, and that tomorrow you will love me with even greater affection.

Imagine that we are alone, in some out-of-the-way corner, remote from battles, and that we talk as old friends that know each other's hearts and understand each other at a glance.

For ten years we have talked of art and literature. We have lived together—do you remember? And often daylight took us by surprise while we were still talking, ransacking the past, questioning the present, seeking the truth and creating for ourselves an infallible and perfect faith. We turned over mountains of ideas, examined and rejected all systems, and after this hard labor came to the conclusion that outside of an active and individual life, there is nothing but lies and stupidity.

Happy are those who have memories. In my life, I see you as the pale young man about whom Musset speaks. You represent the whole of my youth. I find you involved with all my pleasures, all my sufferings. Our brotherly spirits developed side by side. Today, at the beginning of our careers, we have faith in ourselves because we penetrated each other's hearts and skins.

We lived in our own shade, isolated, not very sociable, enjoying each other's thoughts. In the midst of the complacent, superficial crowd we felt lost. We sought personality in everything. In every work, whether painting or poem, we looked for a personal note. We held it to be true that the masters, the geniuses—every one of them—were creators who constructed a world out of many pieces, and we rejected all the followers, the impotent ones, whose métier it is to steal from here and there a few scraps of originality.

Do you realize that we were revolutionaries without knowing it? Now I am able to say out loud what for ten years we have been saying quietly to each other.

The noise of the battle has reached your ears, hasn't it? And you have noticed the reception that has been given to our most cherished thoughts. Oh! Those poor boys that lived so healthily in the heart of Provence under the bright sun, hatching such follies and false persuasions!

You probably don't know this but I am a man of bad faith. The public has already ordered several dozen straightjackets to haul me off to the madhouse at Charenton. They say I praise only my relatives and friends, that I am an idiot and a crook and have a hankering only for scandal.

That is a pity, my friend, very sad. Will it always be the same story? Does one either always have to howl with the pack or be silent? Do you remember our long conversations? We decided that even the smallest new truth could not see the light of day without generating rage and ridicule. Now it is my turn to be jeered and shouted at. You painters on the outside, you are always more irritable than writers.

Here they are, the torn up pages of a study I have not been allowed to complete. For nothing in the world I would destroy them. By themselves they are not worth much, but they were, so to speak, the criteria by which I tested the public. Now we know how unpopular our cherished ideas are. Yet it pleases me to lay them out here a second time. I have faith in them. I know that in a few years the whole world will say that I am right. I am not afraid to that one day they will be thrown in my face.

Èmile Zola, Paris, 20 May 1866†

---

† Zola is referring to his reviews of the Salon, some unpublished, others published the previous month in the newspaper, *L'Événement.*

INTRODUCTION

Setting one's watch by clocks in the clock-merchant's window, which are adjusted daily to the military outpost firing of the noon-time cannon, which the cannoneer adjusts weekly to the clocks in the clock-merchant's window, would not be a good idea for anyone who travels beyond one's home town. But if nothing depends on what time it is at any place other than one's own, to believe the clock-merchant's time, or the cannoneer's time would not matter. Why be concerned with what time it is in Greenwich?

If one were to find in the records of Paul Cézanne and Èmile Zola's boarding school when youths at Aix-en-Provence that one night, while the other boys were asleep, a certain unruly boy ran a cord through the handle of each bed pan under each boy's bed and raced down the stairs dragging the string of clattering, sloshing pans behind him, finding that same event in one of Zola's novels would prove the factuality of one by the other. But if the event is found only in a Zola novel, can it be said it actually happened? To some biographers it would not matter, because true or not, the incident helps to make a good story. Yet, to set a real clock by the hands of a fictional clock is like forging a real person's life to match a character in a novel—a true story based on a fictional one, a fairy tale narrating reality.

A few years ago in Paris, when Robert Altman was making the first cut of rushes for his film *Vincent and Théo*, he asked me to join him one afternoon at Claude Lalouche's private screening theater in Montmartre to critique scenes in which Paul Gauguin figured (one might assume for historical accuracy). Alone in the theater, the two of us in the center of the back row so Altman could yell instructions to the projectionist, we viewed about half the raw film. Along came the scene when Gauguin arrives by train at the sun-drenched Arles where he will spend some time with Vincent Van Gogh. The train grinds to a halt. Gauguin dismounts with the aid of a cane, looks about for a moment, and heads down the platform, limping heavily. The year is 1888. I said to Altman at that point, *Do you know that Gauguin didn't hurt his leg until 1894. He's limping six years too early.* Without a pause Altman said, *It doesn't matter.*

Altman was creating a movie, not writing art history. A man descending from a train car and strolling down a platform would be boring. One must not allow art to be restrained by reality. Mantegna painted thirty arrows shot into St. Sebastian's body while one arrow to the heart would have martyred him. Grünewald's Christ on the cross bleeds from every inch of his body—his flagellates abhorred a vacuum. Novel-like biographies are based on real-life characters and events. But in the case of Cézanne's real-life story, one confronts a life based largely on hearsay and on characters and incidents in Zola's novels that reverberate throughout the Cézanne literature—Cézanne's clock set by the clock in Zola's show-windows. For beyond Cézanne's immediate family members, whose sketchy recollections came very late and were screened through what Cézanne had become rather than what he was, few knew much about Cézanne early youth and maturing years; among those who thought they did, fewer still could serve up more than cocktails of facts mixed with gossip, anecdotes, and dregs of stories they'd heard others tell—even by Cézanne in his late years to Ambroise Vollard, Maurice Denis, Emile Bernard, Gustave Coquiot, and Joachim Gasquet. Contradictions generally outweigh corroboration.

Most everything that hearsay and gossip serve up is to be taken with a grain of salt, so little meat on the bones that a single grain is enough to spice them. And it is usually the case that personal recollections are condensed, polarized, aggrandized, and goaded into being entertaining. Théodore Duret, in his 1878 *Histoire des peintres impressionists*, exposed a conflict between hyped opinion and reasonably true facts about Cézanne, saying that, in the minds of those who'd come to know him only through hearsay, he was a social and artistic revolutionary of the most repellent type, but in fact, says Duret, he was a bourgeois, a rich and conservative Catholic. Gustave Jeffroy, who knew Cézanne as well as anyone, recorded in an essay that from all poorly known facts of Cézanne's life—from his secret productions and his inconsistent imagery, which did not seem controlled by the usual rules of publicity—there came to be nonetheless a sort of bizarre renown.

Paul Gauguin once said, *There is no such thing as exaggerated art, salvation lies only in the extreme.* He might just as well have said there is no such thing as exaggerated life; the live one lives is the life one lives; one must not allow art to be restrained by reality. In the course of conducting his psychoanalytical investigations, Freud admitted that psychic phenomena are best studied in pathological exaggerations that usually take the narrative form. For fashioning stories, the most accommodating conflict is between the desiring self and the denying self. If the two are integrated, nothing of much story-telling interest will be offered—a dampened fire does not work up heat.

To set the reader on the narrative track, the opening lines of a marketable text must grab for attention and uncork bottled-up emotion, like the sudden appearance of a succulent young quarry causing a predator's mouth to water, a belly to quiver, a penis to stiffen. A standard opening describes any dire state of affairs that the author promises to fill out and resolve—what screenwriters call the first act. By reifying the desiring and the denying self, by casting Cézanne, in this case, into a pathological state—timid when not violent, obsessed with sex yet phobic of women—one makes him fit for a gripping biography, like tormenting a lion so when let into the arena it will perform with appropriate ferocity. The opening condition must be a void, emptiness, a humble state, such as born in a manger, the opening line a beginning, a once-upon-a-time: *In the beginning, the art world was void and without form, not an artist was stirring, not even an Impressionist.* A recent biography of Cézanne opens with the most reductive clock-setting I've read in the annals of modern art: *It is astonishing to think that modern art began in 1866, invented by Cézanne armed with a palette knife.*

Let us gather up myths that pullulate like lemmings in the Cézanne and Zola literature and toss them off cliffs. Denial of Cézanne's intimacy with any woman, saying he was unable to tolerate a female presence—allowing his live-in mistress Hortense Fiquet to seduce him, not himself to seduce her, as one biographer concluded—permits the art lover to maintain a sensual, if not covertly sexual, accessibility to Cézanne. By forcing enmity between Cézanne and women, and between him and his father, one is able to establish a personal relationship to Cézanne—to love him, father him, mother him—each art lover wanting him for his or herself, wanting him to be devoted only to art and art history, his potency not in other ways expended. To love is to possess but also to surrender, so as to be one with the other. To possess Cézanne, one must first isolate him, kill his father, refuse him the love of a woman, and assert that he had difficulty making friends. Nowhere in the Cézanne literature is Cézanne allowed to love, not his father, not his mistress Hortense Fiquet (later becoming his wife), only art and his own son, that is, only what he, himself, produces (Hortense will give birth to his son, not to hers and his). Even Cézanne's love for his boyhood companion, Zola, is denied by being displaced from the site of any possible threat, or made abstract as subliminal homosexuality.

Surely Cézanne's father constituted a mortal threat to John Rewald's self-image as Cézanne's *guardien*. Rewald, and a good many other Cézanne worshipers, had a psychological need for Cézanne to remain an ineffable, detached individual. Cézanne was Rewald's subject, almost his life's work. Seeking identity with Cézanne, walking his trails in the hills of Provence, those of Saint-Marc and Sainte-Baume, photographing his motifs in order to see them as Cézanne saw them, was as much Rewald's personal pursuit as an archeology of Cézanne's mind. Only Rewald would be able to share the ineffable experiences of the ineffable Cézanne. And the same could be said for all those authors who perpetuate the myths of Cézanne's terror of women and vehemently promulgate the motif of Cézanne's wishing for his father's death, leading a generation of students astray in psychoanalytic wilderness where clichés lurk at every turn. A recent book on Impressionism continues to spread this mordacious balm: *Paul Cézanne, rejected by the Salon, despised by his father*—-which works just as well in the obverse: *Paul Cézanne, rejected by his father, despised by the Salon*, which comes down to saying that his terrible father no less than the Salon jury, prevented him from getting it in.

Zola's 1886 novel *L'Oeuvre* is the springboard from which most Cézanne lore flows. The hero of the story, Claude Lantier, a flawed genius with tainted heredity, is irresistible as a portrait of Cézanne and his milieu as the topography and sociology of Impressionism. Lantier's artistic experiments and futile efforts to realize a masterful work of art, fusing the real world with the dream world, lead inexorably to the ruination of his sense of reality. The nineteenth-century advance of science and philosophical truths had not yet immunized artists against romanticism's virulence. Non-exorcised demons, having escaped the dragnets of secularization police, derange Lantier's mind and corrupt his vision. He is trapped between the evolutionary benchmarks of romanticism and realism, up to his gullet in romantic sauce—a battlefield Achilles mired in mud. *The real interest in my book*, Zola wrote in a letter to a friend, *would lie in the battle of an incomplete genius with nature and the clash of a resisting woman with the call of art.* Helpless under the passion for female flesh, while struggling like a Saint Anthony to ward off temptation, Zola's doomed Lantier snivels plaintively, *I have no other religion. For the rest of my life I will fall on my knees before it.* Mothered by poltroonery, this flawed artist struggles to separate lust for a woman from passion for art. Ultimately, rather than living to see his masterpiece hung in the Salon, he hangs himself right in front of the canvas—a hung viewer.

But Zola's enhanced recollections of the young Cézanne as literary matter for a novel were not intended to chronicle a singular history but to germinate a character that would take on his own temperament as the story unfolds beyond preparatory notes. Few novelists were more adept at beguiling and arresting the reader's focus than Zola while also seducing one to feel that the novel's settings and characters are concurrently real and fictional. When defending himself at the age of twenty-seven against charges that the spurious exposés he published to gratify reader-lust in the newspaper *Le Messager*—concocted as *Les Mystères de Marseilles*—were true-to-life portrayals of each character, he had the editor print a manifesto of sorts proclaiming his intention:

> *Les Mystères is a contemporary historical novel, in which every fact is derived from real life. I selected the essential documents here and there. I brought together twenty sundry stories into one. I gave to each single character the features of several people whom I chanced to meet and study. Thus I was able to produce a work in which everything is true without any need to follow history inch by inch. I am at bottom a novelist. I do not assume the sober responsibility of the historian who would be exposed to accusations of slander if he disordered a fact or retailored a personality. I did as I pleased with the real events that have,*

figuratively speaking, fallen into the public domain. Any reader who is so inclined may search my sources. As for me, I declare up front that my characters are not portraits of this or that person. The characters are types, not individuals.

Yet biographers have taken up the characters created in Zola's *L'Oeuvre* as not types at all, but as individuals—Lantier as Cézanne with a touch of Manet, and Sandoz as Zola. Zola's predecessor Honoré Balzac, who died in 1850 when Zola was ten, had attained fame as a novelist largely due to a capacity to cause readers to both think and speak of his characters as if they really existed, much like today's soap-opera addicts relate to television personages, experiencing more intimacy with them than with real-life people. Balzac, himself, is said to have interrupted a friend who had gotten carried away discussing one of his characters, saying, *Revenons à la réalité. Avec qui marierons-nous Eugénie Grandet?*

Zola's adaptations of real-life personalities will not figure into my text. Rather than being useful, I have found them misleading. While I enjoy novels based on real-life people and events, I have no interest in real-life people fashioned after characters in novels. At times when I have, it has been at a masquerade party. My strategy will not impose history on Cézanne and Zola; rather it will be to move out from the center of their minds to the society their minds encountered. At no other time than the 1860s, and in no other place than Paris, could either have accomplished what they did. They were too young and too provincial to plan for what lay in store for them. Paris waited for them as if in ambush.

I have listened to reliable documentation, mostly letters between Cézanne and Zola supplemented by correspondence with their mutual friends. I have trusted my common sense to develop a parallel biographical narrative of their early years with the greatest chance of running parallel to the truth. Through the first chapters, the problematic relationship of Cézanne to his father will flow as one stream of thought; another will be Cézanne and Zola's attitudes toward the feminine, as two boys facing the reality of adulthood. I chose not to proceed from the baseline of genius, as if genius was in the germ that generated either subject. I refuse to say that Cézanne was a genius who was misunderstood and not appreciated during his lifetime. Manet, Monet, Renoir, and many other painters shared the judgment of Cézanne's pictures by Salon jurists and critics, including Zola. So if the jurists were wrong, so were they. The genius of Cézanne and Zola can be laid to the nature of all geniuses: they work against the grain, they work very hard. If genius and insanity can be equated by any means, it's because they cohabit in the category of the usefully insane, like Darwinian successful mutants.

Cézanne has become treated less as a painter than an the subject matter of his art, like the completely mad Frenhofer in Balzac's *Le Chef d'Oeuvre inconnu* who was one of the most famous artists of the nineteenth-century even though not a soul had seen a picture he painted. Over the 1860s Cézanne was notorious, garnering as much press as most painters of renown, yet hardly anyone saw one of his pictures except as lampooned in the newspapers and in coffee house nattering. Was Cézanne a great artist or an irascible, intellectually vacuous man who failed to mature as an artist while turning out paintings that in time and due to subsequent events would attract minds historically positioned to make a genius out of him? That could have happened. His greatness is a product of the market that became established for his art, allowing it to survive and be curated. Greatness was aggrandized when critics began to call his art great, when Picasso, Braque, Derain, Matisse began to build their art on his, when critics such as Roger Fry promoted it, when curators gave prominence to his paintings and art historians locked him in his historical place.

The art historian's task is to restructure for the present what transpired in the past, not unlike psychoanalytic practice. Sunday painters and other picture-makers aside, for the true artist, whether painter, poet, or novelist, art making is stressful, a process without product until the moment when the artist must confront it. That's the essential difference between an artist and an illustrator. The true artist works against art, like the explorer works against the wilderness. On the front line, or the cutting edge, artists tend to adopt an artist-type personality, often hiding a true self under a mask. One must look behind the mask that imprisons them. Gauguin said to his wife, *Two persons dwell within me, the savage and the gentle man. The savage moves straight ahead.* When writing *Gauguin's Paradise Lost*, I did all I could short of fictionalizing to get to the gentle man, to expose him in raw light for what he was. I accepted Gauguin as his self-creation and did not distinguish between the facts of his life and the life he had made of those facts, allowing him to be one with his art as one with himself. Gauguin was both his interior and his shell, as I would say also of Gustave Courbet, who was both the heart and the vampire of his sadness, as was Cézanne and to a somewhat lesser extent Zola. A person is what they are and what they say about themselves. One is how one behaves, even if one's persona changes under different circumstances. Zola saying, when age twenty, that after a week's orgy with a pick-up girl, without leaving the bedroom, sperm is all over the place, is no less credible documentation than finding out from direct testimony that he was in the room for only one day and only once had he gotten it up. All fish stories are based on the reality of a small fish.

My interest in the psychodynamics of the young Cézanne and Zola is matched by my interest in the psychodynamics of their critics and historians. My focus is as much on what has been made of Cézanne and Zola in the literature, for it is now impossible for anyone to look at Cézanne's paintings or read Zola's novels, or envision either one as a person, except through a dense screen of what has been written about them. One task of psychoanalysis is to understand why the life of a heroic personage is routinely distorted by exaggerations of fame and infamy. Although my text will not deploy the clinical terminology of psycho-analysis, the alert reader will not miss noticing that this book is a psychoanalytical study of the sort that calls upon the reader's shared experiences in his or her own youthful struggle to mature without losing one's cumulative adolescence.

When writing my previously published books, *Picasso's Brothel*, and *Freud, Leonardo da Vinci, and the Vulture's Tail*, I was more overtly analytical. I engaged the problem of how one is obliged to understand an artist and view the artist's work through what had been written about him—much as, I suppose, how one comes to know God through the books of the Bible, written by many disciples, or to understand the universe through the words and mathematics of theoretical physi-cists and astronomers. As for this book, while interested in how the emotional stresses of adolescence and early adulthood entered into Cézanne and Zola's cre-ative output, energizing their respective arts and conditioning the form their works took under the field conditions for artists and writers that prevailed in the 1860s, I set out to demonstrate how certain artists in Paris after the 1840s achieved status through notoriety; with fame coming later, after their death.

Biography is biography if it achieves a textual replication of the subject-as-lived. I am obliged to admit that lives as experienced cannot replicate lives that are lived, and that biographical truth is not the same as literary truth. That's because factual, objective, verifiable truth often lacks the power of a convincing truth. Convincing truth depends on coherent truth. Only literary truth can be coherent and convincing without being verifiably true—like scientific truths fash-ioned by what current technologies can perceive and by how effectively those doing the perceiving are able to convince others to believe their perceptions. If, as Richard Rorty says, one cannot think of oneself as never encountering reality except under a chosen description of it (interaction with reality being impossible outside language—to which I would add, outside perception, reaction, and thought), then one cannot construct a biography without encountering the sub-ject under a chosen attitude toward the subject in interaction between what the biographer wants the subject to be and what the subject was to himself. This can-not be accomplished entirely in either the metaphysical or epistemological sense, as if the subject was both and at the same moment an observer of himself and subject of his knowledge. Even when supported by documents, such as letters on which I chiefly depend, one risks entanglement in tautologies, for letters have a parallel reality to what the correspondent is thinking when writing, and then another parallel to what is actually being thought about. One cannot read the thoughts and feelings that generated the writing or the subsequent reading.

If language as discourse is a parallel reality to a reality it represents—as sub-ject is to object, or language is to the world—historical biography is another par-allel discourse that should strive to represent reality as it was in the past for the sake of where we are now. By running down the history of a myth, interrogating its underpinnings, making it come clean, one can find the instigating reality and upon it build more relevant myths. Perhaps that is all scholarship can do: refashion myths to be serviceable to one's contemporary culture, like nature making gaily plumaged birds as useful to later epochs as scabby dinosaurs were to theirs. There are enough artists and works of art in the historical world to justify any scheme of art history, or to formulate any theory of aesthetics, just as there is enough organic life in the world to illustrate any theory of biological order. We believe in such orders because our knowledge is built on them. The tautology escapes us. Yet, had organic evolution not been organized in the eighteenth-century by species defined as organisms able to sexually reproduce their kind, we may not have a history of art aligned by artist-sons overcoming father-artists for the right to copulate muses, involving life-cycle reactions and revolutions, rebirths, maturity and falls into decadence at old age. Had the aesthetics of art not converged in ancient Greece with the aesthetics of the female body, we would not have a history of artistic production and perception that throughout the nineteenth century could not distinguish the aesthetic of art from that of a perfectly formed woman and a well-turned pot.

Does the same license permit art historians to fish the same waters where the fantasy of the catch is as valid as real fish? Need art history be subordinated to facts when art imagery and the lives of artists offer matériel for art historians to run alongside art production as a parallel transformation of reality validated by the persuasiveness of the text? Does it matter that Gauguin limped six years before he injured his leg, or that his first Tahitian Eves were modeled not on a Polynesian woman but on the body of a Javanese bodhisattva, and their heads on that of his Peruvian-born mother? Facts stultify the imagination, and signify the autocracy of boredom. Fortunately, art and artists offer very few facts to support their work. One is left with biography and psychological speculation.

In Zola's notes for *L'Oeuvre*, speaking of Claude Lantier, whose personality, phobias, habits, and studio substitute for knowledge about Cézanne's, one reads, *He never brought women to his studio. He always treated them like an adolescent who ignored them in agony of shyness, hidden under brash boastfulness. I don't need women, he said, I don't even know what their use is. I have always been afraid to find out.* Gasquet turns up the heat, adding, *Nude flesh made Cézanne giddy. He wanted to leap at his models. As soon as they came in. he wanted to throw them, half-undressed, onto his mattress.* Yet Gasquet wrote, *Those who saw Cézanne at the time depicted him as terrifying, infested with hallucinations, almost depraved, like some suffering divinity. He despaired at ever being able to satisfy himself. He changed models weekly.* So it is difficult to determine whether Cézanne never brought women to his studio or whether he changed models weekly.

In turn Rewald borrows Cézanne from Zola's *L'Oeuvre* but with a dash of Gasquet: *The girls he chased out of his studio he adored in his paintings. He caressed or attacked them in tears of despair at not being able to make them sufficiently beautiful, suffi-*

ciently alive. And Meyer Schapiro fell in step, saying, *Cézanne's pictures of the nudes show that he could not convey his feeling for women without anxiety...he is most often constrained or violent. There is for him no middle ground of simple enjoyment. It is known that he desired to paint the nude from life but was embarrassed by the female mode—a fear of his own impulses which, when allowed free play in painting from imagination, had resulted at an earlier time in pictures of violent passion.* Schapiro quotes Cézanne saying, *Woman models frighten me. The sluts are always watching to catch you off guard. You've got to be on the defensive all the time.* But the quotation comes third hand from many years later—Renoir's son saying what his own father said that Cézanne had said.

From another Cézanne historian, Theodore Reff, we hear: *Cézanne, jealous of his solitude, fearful even of employing female models; we recall the incident of his terrified flight from his gardener Vallier's daughters and the description of his bedroom at Aix—a bare hermit's cell containing only a crucifix over the bed and a watercolor by Delacroix—his fear of women, who wanted, as he often exclaimed, to get their hooks into him.* From there one descends down the ladder to the depths of the tar pit. Sidney Gist writes: *Cézanne's imagination eroticized everything it touched, and his relation to others is essentially sexual. Cézanne's brushstroke is straight, thus phallic by definition.* And from a psychoanalyst, who took note of Cézanne's reaction to a male acquaintance running up to him from behind, grasping his shoulder, one hears, *Cézanne was in terror of homosexual assaults from behind.*

How then could this man, so terrified of women, enter into a sexual relationship, possibly first with Alexandrine Meley, who Zola would take over and eventually marry, and then with Hortense Fiquet? One biographer has an answer: *Hortense, Cézanne's mistress, a strapping brunette with big hooded eyes and no hint of intellect...by some desperate act of submission, Cézanne allowed her to seduce him.*

Allowed her to seduce him!

That Cézanne rarely used studio models is casually taken as fear of the disrobed woman, as if, had he not been fearful, he would have painted every day from a nude model. No one would apply such reasoning to Manet, who hated studio models, or to the likes of Renoir, Monet, Pissarro, Bazille, Guillaumin, or Sisley, not one of whom painted nudes except on rare occasions. By the 1870s, when this bio-utilitarian lore about Cézanne's terror of confronting a naked woman emerged, as if he were a Saint Anthony fending off lecherous whores rather than a painter of the theme, few artists of any non-academic stripe in the 1860s and '70s employed nude models. Nudes posed in teaching studios and for academic painters. Classical and theatrical poses of professional models, referencing remote cultures and myths, had no place among artists who would be labeled naturalists, and later on, impressionists. Realist painting demanded that portrayed subjects be real people and of the moment. Manet, Bazille, and Renoir's models, for example, were not paid-by-the-hour disrobed women striking hackneyed poses out of art history, but friends and family members.

If Cézanne was so terrified of models that he would change them weekly, other than when studying in Paris at the Académie Suisse where undraped models alternated weekly between male and female, he would have been a greater consumer of modeling hours than the total of all those in his circle. Most of his figurative models were sculptures and nudes in paintings he studied in the Louvre, the Luxembourg, and the Trocadéro, involving direct transfer of imagery from art to art with no live models interposed. And like other painters, including Courbet and Degas, Cézanne also on occasion used photographs of naked men and women called *académies*, which, over the 1860s and beyond, were produced by the thousands, sold in packets at art supply stores and hawked to tourists as pornography.

Then again, had Cézanne been entirely free of sexual excitation when working from a naked model in the privacy of his studio, he would have been a castrate. For a supplementary fee, or just for pleasure, most models were sexually available, then as today. A good number were daytime models and nighttime prostitutes. In his journal, Delacroix offers but one example of this dual use of ambulant women: *I worked so hard on my picture today that I had no energy left for the model.* One of the many lures the young Zola, on preceding Cézanne when moving to Paris, cast down to Aix, hoping to hook his pal Cézanne and reel him in, was a comment from their mutual friend, Jean-Baptiste Chaillon, that Zola passed on to Cézanne (then age twenty-one) in a letter dated 24 October 1861. *Chaillon had said that the studio models in Paris, though not the freshest, are fit to drink, that one draws them during the day and caresses them at night* [the word *caress*, Zola adds in his letter, is a bit feeble]. *So much for posing during the day, so much for posing during the night. It is said that the model are very accommodating; as for the fig leaf, that is unknown in the studios.* Zola will make use of this arousing motif in his first major novel, *Thérèse Raquin*, where the indolent rake Laurent, having given up art, says that what he misses are the women who came to pose, whose favors were within the range of his purse.

Over many months that Cézanne did life drawing at the Académie Suisse in Paris he would have looked upon more naked women than most men would in a lifetime. He may indeed have made the oft-quoted remark: *I paint still-lifes. Women models frighten me. The sluts are always watching to catch you off-guard. You've got to be on the defensive all the time.* But if he did say that—and we don't know his exact words—surely he was not alleging that, if not kept an eye on, the model would sexually assault him, but that the model would get off the pose, causing him to lose his line of concentration. And when Cézanne said in the context of his not using nude models, *I paint still-lifes,* he did not mean other than women but that everything he painted was a still-life; that's how he expected the model to pose, like a still-life. In 1899, when the art dealer Ambroise Vollard sat over many tiresome sessions for Cézanne to paint his portrait, and on one occasion fell-asleep and off his chair, Cézanne chastised him, saying he must pose as if he were an apple. This may have been a peculiarity of Cézanne's mind, but it was also a metaphorical denomination of still-life in common use: the young painter critic Odilon Redon commented on Manet's 1868 *Portrait of Zola*, described as having the qualities of still-life, of items arranged in a timeless moment. Zola, too, would find a still-life quality in Manet's pictures of people, saying, in so many words, *Manet treats figural works as in the art school one treats still-life set-ups.*

What then drives the myth that Cézanne could not bear to look at and would not dare to touch a woman? Could it be that, like Jesus, like Buddha, like Gandhi, he must be kept chaste to justify his sainthood? Why is this passage in a letter to Zola of August 20th, 1885 given no attention in the literature? *As for me, complete isolation; the brothel in town or elsewhere, but nothing more. I pay. I know the word is ugly, but I simply must have rest, and at a price I can get it.* And what about this letter Cézanne wrote to an unidentified woman the same year? Known only as a draft found on a sheet of sketches, he may indeed have finalized and mailed it:

> *I saw you. You allowed me to kiss you. From that moment on I have been besieged by a deep excitement. Please excuse the assumption of friendship I am making in writing to you, but I am tormented by anxiety. I cannot justify this presumption that you must deem so great, but could I remain under the plight, which oppresses me? Is it not better to express a feeling than to conceal it?*
>
> *Why, I said to myself, should I restrain what has become my torment? Is it not a relief to one's suffering when one allows oneself to express it? And if physical pain seems to find relief in the cries of the afflicted, is it not natural, my dear lady that moral sadness seeks consolation in the confession one makes to a beloved person?*
>
> *I know that this letter, the sending of which is hazardous and premature, may seem indiscreet, has as its purpose only my recommendation to you that the goodness...*

This is the sort of letter a woman might be grateful to receive, not as has been assumed, a missive from a man at age forty-six who'd lost his marbles and was gushing libido like an adolescent in rut. The common story that the woman was a young domestic servant in the Cézanne household is intriguing, although that would hardly have merited the extreme formality of Cézanne's letter. The only candidate for the liaison was a maid who had left the family employment a year earlier, but perhaps Cézanne kept in touch with her. On May 14th, the year of the letter, Cézanne exposed his clandestine affair to Zola, asking that Zola do him a favor of receiving a few letters at his own address, addressed to Cézanne, and to forward them to an address he will give him in due time. He added, *Either I am out of my mind or being very sensible. Trahit sua quemque voluptas!* (Everyone is carried away by his passion).

No Cézanne scholar to my knowledge has asked whether at any time Cézanne wept in despair because he couldn't succeed in painting a beautiful woman. He paints an autopsy. Because the examiner is bald, he must be Cézanne.

Cézanne paints a picture of a woman being strangled, so Cézanne's terror of women must have led him to fantasize that he was the one killing her. A man resembling Cézanne's appears in his painting titled *The Orgy*, so Cézanne must have imagined himself participating. The man in his *Modern Olympia* is rather bald like Cézanne, so it must be Cézanne enjoying the visual rape of the woman. The Cézanne literature is permeated with such pseudo-psychoanalytical claptrap that is never leveled on other artists except Picasso. Manet's *Olympia* and *Bar at the Folies-Bergère* are routinely analyzed with every tool short of a speculum to find sexual meanings; yet, to my knowledge nothing discovered or imagined has caused the imagery to be assigned to Manet's own sexuality. In Zola's *Thérèse Raquin*, Thérèse's mouth, as seen by her seducer Laurent, is described this way: *Through her parted lips could be seen the pink flesh of her mouth*. What Laurent was actually seeing, then, was her pink *sexe* through parted labia. But it is not Zola's sexuality that anyone catching on to that simile has looked to plunder his psychic depth. Then why do the reddened lips of a huge conch-shell in Cézanne's still-life, *The Black Clock*, come so easily to mind as a distorted hideous vagina that could clamp right down on you, documenting Cézanne's fear and disgust for female sex? When Zola says that he ejaculates sometimes when struggling with a difficult sentence, does that mean he does that spontaneously when overpowering the sentence, as if forcing a resisting woman? One would not hear that said of Zola, but if, when painting a nude woman, Cézanne had said that he occasionally ejaculated, wouldn't it mean that, so completely had he sublimated his terror of women that only when «making» a woman on a canvas, stroking rhythmically with his loaded brush, could he ejaculate? And if that was the case, could the unfinished state of most of his pictures, their *non-finito*, be because he suffered impotency, an inability to climax?

Beyond such risky speculations on Cézanne's sexuality, one encounters throughout the literature heavy doses of imaginative descriptions of his appearance and quotidian behavior, and as well the appearance of his studio. In Zola's *La Conquête de Plassans*, the father Mouret, who has coagulated in many minds with Cézanne's father, has a fixation on order around the house. When interpreted as a true trait of Cézanne's father, it is made to justify Cézanne's adoption of slovenly bohemianism in order to defy his father. With Louis-Auguste and Mouret blended, one reads:

> *Here we are confronted with the unbending father, his outer life organized so efficiently that he can't bear to see a thing out of place. No wonder Paul's rebellion—the only one he dared to mount against this jeering, scowling ogre—took the form later on of chaotic living quarters and disorderly studios. Apart from the bed, the little washstand, and the divan, the only other pieces of furniture in the place were a dilapidated oak wardrobe and a huge table littered with brushes, tubes of paint, unwashed dishes, and a spirit stove crowned with a saucepan still spattered with vermicelli. Chairs stood about with holes in their seats, sur-*

rounded by rickety easels. Near the divan, on the floor, in a corner which was probably swept out less than once a month, was the candle he had used the night before, and the only thing in the room that looked neat and cheerful was the cuckoo clock, a large one of its kind with a resounding tick, ornamented with bright red flowers.

While those words are by a novelist-biographer, with the ingredients taken from Zola's *L'Oeuvre*—a veritable well-stocked pantry—John Rewald, the art historian, gives the same description, taken as well from Zola's novel:

In Cézanne's studio there was a complete disorder. It was only swept once a month, for fear the dust might cover his fresh canvases. A thousand things were strewn on the floor, and ashes piled up there. The sole big table was always littered with brushes, paints, dirty plates, a spirit lamp. Unframed sketches hung on the wall all the way down to the floor where they piled on a heap of canvases.

That description could fit to most any student's quarters when living away at college, or any artist or writer living on a shoestring and devoted more to art than to personal grooming and good housekeeping. Studios of young artists tend towards disarray, as do their hair and trouser seams. Again coached by Zola's notes for *Le Vente de Paris* and *L'Oeuvre*, Rewald describes the twenty-to-thirty-year-old Cézanne as:

Tall and thin, bearded, with knotty joints and a strong head. A very delicate nose hidden in the mustache, eyes, narrow and clear...deep in his eyes great tenderness. His voice was loud. He wore a battered black felt hat and an enormous overcoat, once a delicate maroon, which the rain had streaked green. He was a little stoop-shouldered and had a nervous shudder, which was to become habitual. He planted himself in laced boots, and his too-short trousers revealed blue stockings. He swore, used filthy words, wallowed in mud, and with the cold rage of a tender and exquisite soul who doubts himself and dreams of being dirty.

In his biography of Zola, Frederick Brown fashioned a similar description of Cézanne, based on Zola's notes and Rewald's elaborations:

Terror-ridden, he found shelter in the thicket of an unkempt beard and in the depth of a huge brown overcoat that turned green with age. Mortified by his body, he dressed as a scarecrow, flung obscenities at the world, and wherever he set up house wallowed in debris. Few people penetrated Cézanne's redoubt, especially when despair held him fast, and models that came, never came back. Indeed, the mess, like his scatological bluster, seemed calculated to prove that for women he could only be an object of revulsion or alarm. Such behavior seemed above all to bolster him as he shuttled beggar-like between Aix and Paris and to help him vent anger accumulated since early childhood.

Hortense Fiquet must have been quite a woman to put up with such a terrorized, insensitive, beggar-like man, and his scatological blusters, to have shared a bed with him, had a child by him, and eventually marry him. As for their first conjugation, considering that no one taped the honeymooning couple with Hortense in ecstasy and Cézanne in post-virginal agony, one might wonder from where any biographer could have found the following information:

The man whom Hortense embraced in the conjugal bed was very probably a virgin. No one had any reason to suppose otherwise. Sensuality had lived within him as something sinister, involving violence, breeding terrible secrets. Sex was like a black sickness, a thing of fear and solitude. Now this girl, who refused to see him as depraved but touchingly foolish, suffering only from a lack of experience, embraced him without conditions. His precious and valuable touchstone of virginity was then no more, broken into like his freedom. Suddenly, and catastrophically, he was the slave of another person.

Cézanne. Sketch of Hortense Fiquet. Pencil on paper. Coll. Benjamin Sonnenberg, New York.

Part I

SHARED ADOLESCENCE

1

As adolescent boys in Aix-en-Provence, Cézanne and Zola came together at the Lycée Bourbon, a civic middle school housed in a former nunnery with dormitories on the upper floors overlooking a courtyard ringed by plane trees. Bonded to one another by complementary temperaments, their fates would depend on being coupled at the brain stem. It is not likely that, without Zola's support, Cézanne would have become the artist recorded by history as having laid the cornerstones of twentieth-century art, and without Cézanne as a kick-block, Zola may not have become the writer known today as the prime innovator of literary naturalism.

As a boy, Cézanne was hesitant but steady, while the one-year-younger Zola's ambitions were out ahead of his capabilities. One pushing, the other resisting, in his notes for his novel, *L'Oeuvre*, Zola summarized this odd-fellow kinship as magnets attracting opposites: *Opposed by nature we were drawn to each other by covert affinities, by the force of a mutual ambition and the arousal of a superior mentality for which mobs of dunces regularly thrashed us.*

At his age of eighteen, Zola's mother moved him to Paris. As catalyst and at times a gregarious nuisance, Zola would eventually convince the slower-moving Cézanne to join him. And even after losing interest in Cézanne as an artist, he would continue to foster him as if, within his share of their common brain, his fatherless psychology had grown a substitutive father-impulse. Zola's father had died when he was seven while Cézanne's father would persist in the ambiguity of supporting irritant. So Cézanne had what Zola lacked, which would prove to be one condition of the difference between them. Compared to the more physical, big-boned Cézanne with parents and two sisters in a stable household, Zola, was raised without a father or siblings by a doting young mother. He was frail but not timid, perhaps the sort of brainy attention-seeker who overreacts at times and finds himself cornered by those he'd provoked, as if growing up was a battle he was destined to win. He recalls having tried to convince a teacher that ancient Greek was a useless language and being persecuted over the rest of the year for

The Zola dam near Aix, with Mont
Sainte-Victoire in the distance.

academic heresy. Cézanne, made of sturdier stuff, was more emotionally volatile
than the physically-at-risk Zola whose survival among rowdy schoolboys depended on wits and diplomacy. While easily ignited, he was also slow-burning. To console their mutual Aixois school friend, Jean-Baptistin Baille, who'd been offended on some occasion by Cézanne's brawny nature, Zola sent a note to Baille: *When
he hurts you, you must not blame his heart, but rather the evil demon which clouds his thoughts.
He has a heart of gold and is a friend who understands us, he being just as mad as we are, and
as much a dreamer.*[1] Cézanne responded to Zola's caution with a jaunty retort: *You
fear that our friendship for Baille is weakening. Oh, no, for he is a fine chap, by Jove. But you
well know that, considering my character, I am not fully aware of what I do; and so, if I did
him wrong, well, then he should just forgive me.*[2]

Cézanne's sister, Marie, would describe her brother as a diligent pupil at
school, rather quiet at home yet subject to fits of temper, as prone to flushes of
rage as to periodic depression—moods found later in a few paintings displaying
melancholy in some and violence in others. It is tempting to amplify Marie's
comments by the emotional disposition of geographical Provence. Even in
ancient times, according to the historian Posidonius, the pastoral Midi was cli-
matically fickle, both a benevolent and a wild and violent country. Writers still
today color its inhabitants with pigment from a climatic palette: repressed people
subject to purple and black moods and choleric outbursts, such extremes in contrast to the self-possessed Virgilian charm of the countryside—temperate, sunny,
yielding to romantic impulses. Yet just a bit to the north of Aix, above the village
of Le Tholonet, the gorge of the *Infernets* opens among giant, randomly strewn
rocks and into a landscape distorted by crags and twisted trees, the soil cracked
and hard, the vegetation scrubby, the weather unpredictably cruel. The indifferent winds of the annual mistral have forever frustrated the contentment of Aix's
citizens. *The greatest drawback to the pleasures of Provence*, wrote the early nineteenth-
century Stendhal, *is the mistral. When the mistral rules Provence, one doesn't know where*

The pine wood above the Zola dam. Frequented by Cézanne and Zola in their youth and where Cézanne would often paint.

to find refuge. Though still in sunshine, the wind penetrates into the most carefully sealed rooms. It aggravates the nerves and exasperates even the calmest people. Decades later, warning a friend who was about to depart for Aix, Gertrude Stein said, *You will find yourself getting very nervous down there...suddenly having a terrific fight with your dearest friend.* So it is not easy to distinguish in Cézanne biographies whether his singular temperament is being described or whether an author is applying clichés, as if Cézanne's personality were patterned on the weather—the common mood that prefaces letters like stage sets at the curtain's opening. Baille, by contrast, was plain, neither lustrous nor neurotic, with a temperament that would be hard to justify if an Aixois' personality depended on geology and climate.

Like most young men courting fame when moving into adulthood, Zola in later years would both romanticize and disparage his youth. To whatever degree his first published stories reflected his schooldays shared by Cézanne, he colored them with the miseries he suffered among schoolmates who, *like all children,* he says—excluding himself, of course—were merciless and soulless. *I must have been a strange creature, capable only of loving and weeping. I sought affection. From the very first steps I took, I suffered. My years at school were years of tears. I had in me the pride of a loving nature. I was not loved because no one understood me, and I refused to let myself be understood.*[3] At times he was teased over the accent he'd acquired from his mother's Parisian tongue, which did not coincide neatly with Provençal pronunciations. And he recalls that, at the age of seven, he was so wretchedly retarded he could not yet write or even spell his name—perhaps a made-up originary state of genius, like Einstein's never having learned to count.

In October 1847, when seven, his mother enrolled him in the *Pensionat Notre-Dame* at Aix, a Catholic school where he remained a pupil until the age of twelve. His classmates included two boys who would figure later in his life: Philippe Solari, the son of a stone mason, who would become a sculptor of technical proficiency, and Marius Roux, a future journalist of no distinction but Zola's supporter when needed. In 1852, then twelve, Zola was placed in the municipal school, the *Lycée Bourbon*. After the second year his near destitute mother persuaded the city council of Aix to grant him a bourse. The mayor read her request into the minutes on July 22nd, 1854: *Mme Zola, widow of the engineer who planned the canal that bears his name* [the *Canal Zola*] *solicits a scholarship to secondary school on behalf of his son and hopes that the council will show its benevolence by awarding it as posthumous compensation for services her husband rendered to the city of Aix.* Awarded the stipend, Zola became a day boarder at the school, and his mother moved into an apartment nearby.

Zola at age six.

According to sporadic testimony, none of it firsthand, Zola was a spoiled, self-indulgent child. A photograph of him as a very young boy suggests that he was plump with baby fat and not robust. One might gather from how he armor-plated himself later in life that he was tender and vulnerable and maybe coquettish enough to radiate femininity at an age when differentiation of the sexes is not yet settled. Recorded on the Marseilles police blotter of April 3rd, 1845 is an incident when a certain twelve-year-old Algerian boy in the service of the Zola family was taken into custody and charged with committing an immoral act with five-year-old Émile. It would be imprudent to say that this incident negatively affected Zola's disposition towards the opposite sex. The gravity of the offense is not known.[4] Most boys, during their cute years, when hormones ordain sexuality and equip them for a future of sexual encounters—before the latency phase sets in at nine or ten—are fooled around with by other, usually older, boys. A thirst for drama on the part of Zola's historians led to translating the police charge made against the older boy, *attentat à la pudeur*, as "sexual assault," while the actual charge was an immoral offense against the boy's modesty, not a rape, not sodomy. It has been said that Zola suffered all his life from the aftereffects of that incident but it's unlikely that it affected Zola as chronically as it has served his biographers.[5] Moreover, had Moustafa been a French boy rather than a dark-skinned North African house servant, most likely the police would not have been summoned.

As teenagers, Cézanne, Zola, and Baille were no doubt boisterous, adventurous, silly, and addicted to forecasting fantastic futures to where their imaginative intelligence would surely lead them. They were town boys, whose regular debaucheries were countryside escapes from parents and studies—swimming, fishing, fanaticizing, and taking potshots at birds, relieved to have missed.

But when night fell and the daylight goblins in their heads slipped off to roam the dark in search of more foolhardy victims, they were content to return to mother-made suppers and a cozy bed. Zola recalls those years:

Le collège Bourbon as it appears today

We were three friends: Cézanne, Baille, myself—three urchins still wearing out trouser seats on school benches. On holidays, on any day we could escape from study, we would run away on cross-country chases. We need-ed fresh air, sunshine. We followed paths that were lost at the bottoms of ravines, of which we took possession as conquerors. In the winter, we enjoyed the cold; the ground, hardened by frost, resounded gaily under our boots. We ate omelets in neighboring villages. In the summer, our meeting place was the riverbank where we were possessed by the water. In the autumn, our passion changed. We became hunters—very innocuous hunters. The hunt was only an excuse for taking long hikes, always ending in the shade of a tree, the three of us lying on our backs with our noses in the air, talking freely of our loves. Above all, our loves at the time were the poets. We always had books in our pockets or game bags. Victor Hugo reigned over us—an absolute monarch. He delighted us with his forceful rhetoric. We knew entire poems by heart. When we returned home in the evening at twilight, our gait kept pace with the cadence of his verses, as sonorous as the blast of a trumpet. His dramas haunted us like magnificent visions. When we came out of school classes with our brains frozen stiff by the classical tirades we had to learn by heart, we went into an orgy, fraught with thrills and ecstasy, and warmed our brains by memorizing scenes from Hernani or Ruy Blas. How often, after a long swim, the two or three of us performed entire acts on the riverbank. Then, one morning one of us brought a volume of Alfred de Musset. Reading Musset was for us the awakening of our own true hearts. We trembled. Our cult of Victor Hugo received a terrible blow. Little by little we felt ourselves grow chilled. Hugo's verses vacated our minds. Musset alone then reigned in our game bags. He became our religion. Over and above his schoolboy buffoonery his tears won us over, and when we ourselves wept when reading him, he became completely our poet.[6]

Hugo may have been suppressed in their collective minds at this stage when Alfred de Musset's sensuously sentimental outpourings in *Les Contes d'Espagne et d'Italie*, such lurid scenarios as *Rolla* or *Les Nuits*, and comedies and hilarious *proverbes dramatiques* produced for the stage inspired them to crown Musset as their pedestaled poet laureate. Musset's confessional style—such scenes as Rollo hiring a near-child prostitute for one last night of debauchery on his departure for the

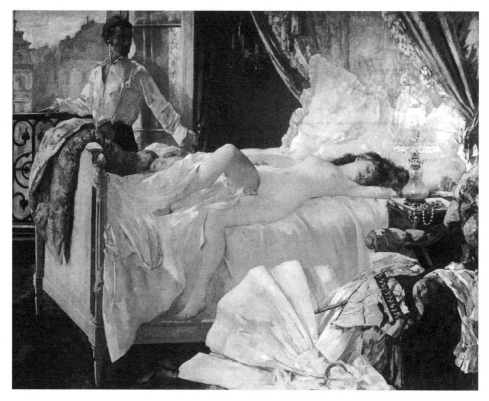

Henri Gervex. The climactic scene from Alfred de Musset's *Rola*. Musée des Beaux-Arts, Bordeaux.

venal world—was fitted to the adolescent psychology that draws to pornography like flies to sweets:

> *With a melancholy eye Rolla looked over*
> *the beautiful Marion asleep in her wide bed;*
> *Knowing not why an unnamable and diabolical horror*
> *Made him tremble to the bone.*
> *Marion had cost him dearly. To pay for the night*
> *He had dispensed his last coins.*
> *His friends knew it. And he, on arriving,*
> *Had taken their hand and given his word that*
> *No one come morning would see him alive.*
>
> *...*
>
> *Rolla turned to look at Marie.*
> *She was exhausted, and had fallen asleep.*
> *And thus both fled the cruelties of fate,*
> *The child in sleep, and the man in death.*[7]

The heavy Romanticism of Hugo, denser than Musset's, would remain on Zola's mind and re-emerge when emotionally he outgrew Musset's romantic memoirs of self-inflicted passions, as in Musset's *La Confession d'un enfant du siècle* (Confessions of a Child of Our Time) in which wine, sex, and prostitution reign as symbols of the times—Paris as a steamy pool of pulchritude. Eight years later, in March 1866, Zola would review Hugo's newly released novel, *Les Travailleurs de la mer* (Seafarers), in the widely read newspaper *L'Événement* (Daily News). Over Zola's torrent of admiration for Hugo's book looms this remark: *My entire being is violently shaken by these strange and powerful pages.* To acknowledge Zola's review, Hugo sent him a note: *Insult rarely touches me, sympathy always does. You have written a fine and noble page on my book, which goes to my heart. I thank you. I am moved.*

Hugo's language in an adolescent's mind that lacks social conscience was narcotic, offering ecstatic highs, like puffs of marijuana or sniffs of glue. Hugo was mystical. He had tyrannized their literary imagination with excesses that justified their flamboyant sense of drama. During their readings on the sly, Zola and Cézanne found the theatrical raging in Musset, too—a dramatic realist, down to earth, an exhilarating contrast to Hugo whose ponderous narratives Musset's impudence would soon push aside. *All that romantic heat blew away*, Zola said, recalling their abandonment of Hugo when displaced by Musset and reinstalled on a remote pedestal:

> We couldn't have said at the time why Hugo's words did not excite us as much as Musset's, but Hugo's mountainous rhetoric was beginning to cool us off. Musset gained our allegiance because the rhetorician in him didn't obtrude but went straight to one's nerves. We adored medieval decor, philtres, and sword thrusts, but we especially adored them in Musset's limber style, with its skepticism and mocking overtones. We exalted over his ballad to the moon because it was for us the gauntlet a superior poet had thrown down to the romantics as well as to the classics—the guffaw of an independent spirit in whom our generation recognized a brother.[8]

This is the mature Zola speaking. It is unlikely that he and Cézanne as adolescents were able to articulate clearly why Musset affected them more than Hugo, who was somewhat of a father image and in tune with the needs of youths moving off from their parents. Musset was like a crafty and verbally adept adolescent himself, someone a boy at the stage of arising sexuality could identify with when father-emulation was no longer needed to secure the boundaries of an ego, like the shell of an egg that the emerging ego must break and then break again to achieve adulthood. It has been said that one always imagines Hugo as old with a white beard while Musset is imagined as perpetually young, the poet of lovers and of adolescent crises. *Musset had no biography*, writes the critic Jean d'Ormesson. *He lived always in the present, was indolent and charming. He loved pleasure. He cultivated insolence. He had passion, which he turned upside down and destroyed.*[9]

For all their pseudo-hatred of school, Cézanne and Zola were attentive, industrious pupils. Zola disdained mathematics but did very well in Latin and literature, while Cézanne excelled in calculus, Latin, Greek, science, and history, and could quote tirelessly in Latin. At the age of thirteen, at the close of the 1853 school year, he was awarded a first prize for general excellence. Late in life, Cézanne described his academic relationship to Zola:

> *At the Bourbon, Zola and I were regarded as prodigies. For two sous I could knock off a hundred Latin verses. By Jove I was smart when I was young! Zola didn't give a damn about anything practical. He was a dreamer, a willful savage, a weedy intellectual—the kind that street kids detest. For no reason they ostracized him. And that is the way our friendship started. Big boys and little, the whole damn school, one day gave me a thrashing because I defied a ban against speaking to Zola and went on talking to him anyway. He was a decent fellow. The next day he brought me a big basketful of apples.*[10]

With a few friends from the *Bourbon*, Cézanne and Zola attended art classes at Aix's *École gratuite de dessins* (the municipal drawing school), where their pre-fate conditionings were oddly inverted. As if Fortuna had set the two boys on roads to a professional future, only to mix them up at a crossing, much of Cézanne's youthful poetry survived, while from Zola's hand we have just one poem. Paradoxically, Zola won a prize in painting each term while not until when he was nineteen and in law school did Cézanne manage a prize—just one, and a second place one at that.

2

Sons of disappointing father

Paul Cézanne was born in 1839 in Aix-en-Provence. His father, Louis-Auguste, a confident, ambitious man, a force to be reckoned with, was a tough model to measure up to. Èmile Zola was born a year later on a parental visit from Marseilles to Paris but shared Cézanne's adolescence in Aix. He too had a self-sufficient, strong willed father—an engineer whose grandiose plans for re-fortifying Paris with remote forts, modernizing the old port of Marseilles, and bringing new water resources to Provence structurally presaged his son's ambitious real-world novels. But just as Louis-Auguste Cézanne disappoints his son by opposing his art career, Zola's father also defaults. His plans for renewing Aix's waterways are thwarted by bureaucratic snarls and money-eyed competitors. Abortively, on the verge of a huge financial success, he neglects a minor bronchial illness and dies of pleurisy, leaving in his wake seven-year-old Zola bereft of a father and fated to grow up in poverty with aged grandparents and an emotionally distraught, twenty-seven-year-old mother. Over much of his early twenties, he would live with his mother in a virtual state of husbandry. To shape himself as an adult, Zola fashioned a figurative father to help him along. Of his school years in Aix, he wrote: *For transforming a child into a man, nothing can replace this communal education in an all-boys school. Let the young boy beat and in turn be beaten, let him suffer and in turn mete out punishment. Let him do what he must to acquire strong limbs and a strong heart. Boys raised at home in their mother's skirts,* he concluded, *remain girls.*[1] Yet the boy who beats and metes out physical punishment was as lacking in Zola's disposition as was a father. Burly young Cézanne—an alter ego who had a strong father—was Zola's fisticuff defender.

Dark tones are typically laid over the picture of Cézanne's relationship with his father. But the father-son conflict, which dominates Cézanne's biographies, goes into solution when mixed with life stories of other artists and writers of his peerage. Few fathers, at any point in history, would be happy over a son's choice of art as a career. During the mid-nineteenth century, a popular dialogue in comedy theater has a father asking his daughter's suitor, who had just asked for her hand in marriage, *And what is your profession? The young man answers, I'm a painter,* at which point the audience breaks out in hysterical laughter.[2]

Even far back in European history one finds cases for scholars to haggle over as to fathers frustrating the genius of sons. Was Thomas More, in the late fourteenth century, actually forced by his father to go to law school, diverting him from more delightful intellectual pursuits; or is his case just another historical myth nurtured through generations by the ghost of Oedipus? Michelangelo's father tried to beat the notion of becoming an artist out of his son's head, only relenting, as the story goes, when Lorenzo de' Medici convinced him of the difference between sculptor and stone mason. Perhaps Leonardo da Vinci was permitted by his father to be an artist only because, being of illegitimate birth, he would have been fettered trying to pursue a proper vocation. The young Gustave Courbet came to Paris from the provinces against the wishes of his family—his father wanted him to be a lawyer—and throughout the 1840s was in conflict with his father over a too frugal allowance. As the art historian T. J. Clark concluded, letters of mutual complaint that passed between Courbet and his father amounted to nothing more than *a typical dispute between a bourgeois father and his son, and were the same whining letters as those locked away in a thousand closets in the nineteenth century by proud, unbending fathers who nonetheless usually paid up.*[3]

Claude Monet's family was an impediment for years, but for a long while young Monet was content to work the Normandy beaches making caricature portraits of vacationers and tourists, displaying them for sale in shop windows. His family consented to finance his art training only if this apparently ambitious but fractious son agreed to take art seriously and study in the studio of an established master. When Monet spurned this admonition, his father refused to pay for a substitute for his military induction, causing his son to serve a two-year term in North Africa, buying him out only when he fell seriously ill. Camille Pissarro was obliged to work in the family store until, after defecting and refusing to return, his father capitulated to what appeared to be his son's inevitable, grievous fate. Édouard Manet's father planned that his son would study law, but yielded to circumstance when Édouard enrolled in the studio of Thomas Couture, an acclaimed and financially successful teacher. Frédéric Bazille was encouraged by his father to go to medical school; after four years of study and having failed his qualifying examinations, he was allowed by default to become an artist. Alfred Sisley was sent by his father to England to prepare for a career in business but returned to France ill-equipped to be more than a picture painter.

Aspiring young writers fared no better. Baudelaire ironically defied his widowed mother's wish that he enter the diplomatic corps and insisted on going to law school. Balzac in 1814 gave up law studies to become a writer, at which point his father reduced his allowance to a pittance. Gustave Flaubert devoted three years to law studies at the University of Paris, supported by his father, but was freed to engage in full-time writing only after failing his bar exams. Paul Alexis,

Zola's acolyte and first biographer, fulfilled his wealthy father's demands that he take a law degree at Aix. But when he had finished and embarked for Paris to join Zola and Cézanne and become a writer, he arrived not with his father's blessings but with a suitcase, a sheaf of Baudelairean-type poetry, and two hundred francs borrowed from a friend.

Not enough is known about Cézanne's father to say much of anything for certain. And next to nothing is known about Cézanne's mother, whose life was apparently given over to the well being of her husband and children. The real-life Louis-Auguste Cézanne, of mixed French and Italian blood, was born in 1798 in the village Saint-Zacherie situated in the rustic, very southern Var area that touches on Italy. He was a branch off a line of artisans. After apprenticing in Paris to a hat-maker during his twenties, he came to the economically tranquil and culturally petrified Aix-en-Provence in 1825 at the age of thirty. The personality of Aix at the time was its courtly and aristocratic past, while its major urban industry was law; on its outskirts, marginally productive wheat, olive and almond farming was supplemented by rabbit-skinning and de-hairing for the production of felt. Soon after arriving, Louis-Auguste established himself as a partner in a profitable firm that wholesaled felt hats, the firm then renamed as *Martin, Coupin et Cézanne*. Deploying steady and noteworthy business sagacity, this model of ambition soon acquired wealth and stepped up to a high place in the local commercial society. In 1837 or early 1838, at the age of forty, he took up with Anne-Elizabeth Aubert, a common girl in his employment who was about twenty-four. They cohabited with the usual results: Anne-Elizabeth gave birth to Paul on January 19th, 1839, and in 1841 to a daughter named Marie. Louis-Auguste and Anne married in January 1844 when Paul had just turned five. Six years later a second daughter, Rose, arrived.

In 1849, when son Paul was ten, Louis-Auguste, having profited over the previous years as a private lender at high interest rates, acquired controlling interest in the only locally chartered bank in Aix. This bank had failed during the economic crisis of the mid-1840s but was not so drained of blood that an astute businessman could not resuscitate it. By the mid-1850s, *Banque Cézanne et Cabassol* was very profitable. Perhaps because of his advancing age—he was sixty-one in 1859—Louis-Auguste desired that one day his son would take over this bank when it would be renamed *Banque Cézanne et Fils*. But son Paul's occasional flushes of ambition to be a businessman were like a forehead's brief encounter with a fickle muse's lips.

In 1858, when Cézanne was nineteen, Louis-Auguste purchased a manor house on a large acreage of olives and grapes, the *Jas de Bouffan*, that was once the residence of governors; although run-down, the estate still had an aura of high prestige. It is of course likely that the old money gentry of Aix that cherished pedigrees, moribund conventions, and hoarded family wealth—the sort of people who die in the same house in which they were born—would have some degree of contempt for this self-made businessman who, by his own wits, had acquired wealth, so conscious were they about Aix's proximity to commercialized and socially odious Marseilles, mutilated by capitalists using immigrant workers as tools, where people spoke with a drawl. It has been assumed that the low-caste beginnings of Louis-Auguste, and his cohabitation with a young working girl

The Jas de Bouffon. The manor house and Cézanne family home in Aix-en-Provence.

La kiosque à musique de la place Jeanne-d'Arc, Aix-en-Provence

La place des Prêcheurs, Aix-en-Provence

leading to an illegitimate fatherhood, were reason enough for the Aixois gentry to keep him at a distance and to condition his son's later tendency to avoid society and experience difficulty making friends.[4] But Cézanne did not have difficulty making friends. He may not have been the life of anyone's party, but he was cordial, loyal, and considerate, and had as many close friends as most anyone has over a lifetime.

Zola's father, Francesco Antonio Guiseppi Maria Zollo, a native of Venice, has been treated more factually in literary studies than art historians have treated Cézanne's father. Zollo's life was sufficiently colored not to need more pigment. He began his career in 1810 as a student in the military academy at Pavia. Two years later he was a commissioned lieutenant in the Imperial Army. But when the Allied Powers at the Congress of Vienna granted Venice to Austria under the rule of the Hapsburgs, Zollo found himself an Italian officer in the Austrian infantry. During this transition that unsettled many Italians in the area of Venice, he took a two-year leave to study mathematics and civil engineering at the University of Padua; his doctoral thesis was on the theory and techniques of land surveying. After graduating, he practiced topographic surveying for a spell while staying alert for other opportunities. Soon enough, in nearby Austria, a vast railroad project was in need of topographical engineers. So, rather than join the Resistance, or flee the rigidly bureaucratic Austrian rule that saved Venice from economic ruin while putting Austrian roughage into Italian bread, he resigned from the military in 1820 to take employment as chief survey engineer on the construction of a rail line between Linz on the Danube and Budweis on the Moldau, which was to be Europe's first railway. This job lasted until 1830 when an economic downturn in Austria brought an end to railway expansion and Zollo's hopes to power the Austrian line's rail cars with steam engines rather than horses or oxen.

At the age of thirty-five, Francesco Zollo came to Paris and joined the newly created French Foreign Legion. Posted in Algeria, he all too soon he got caught up in an amorous affair with an extortionist of some sort, the wife of a German non-commissioned officer. Fifteen hundred francs of Zollo's post's regimental funds were found to have mysteriously disappeared. After returning the money, Zollo resigned his post and retreated to Marseilles, where in 1833 he installed himself as *Engineer Architect Topographer* and sensibly changed his name to its French equivalent, François Zola. At the age of forty-four, the newly christened François Zola met a nineteen-year-old woman of Greek ancestry, Émilie Aubert (the same family name as Cézanne's mother's). On a visit to Paris, he spotted her coming out of l'Église Saint-Eustauche. After a brief courtship, they were wed at the mayoralty office of the first arrondissement in Paris on May 16th, 1839, the year Paul Cézanne was born. They settled in Marseilles but their son and only child, Émile Édouard Charles Antoine Zola (his name derived from his mother's), was born in Paris on April 2nd, 1840 on one of several occasions when the couple took short-term residence there so François could plead his case for Louis-Philippe's central government to approve and finance his visionary engineering projects.

One of François' overtures, proposed in January 1841 and calculated to win approval, though it did not, was to renew Paris' fortifications by the construction of advanced forts. More in keeping with his grand visions for modernizing the European economy was a plan to renovate the old port of Marseilles to accommodate modern shipping; another, to respond to the city of Aix's need to build a dam and new canal for upgrading its historic waterways. His Italian blood may have been a factor in his vision of Aix's ancient Roman water system rebuilt with modern hydraulics to restore the agricultural economy the area had enjoyed when a noble province of ancient Rome. A venerable Roman viaduct near Aix—as weathered and worn as the neighboring old mountain, the thousand-meter-high Sainte-Victoire, at whose feet clayey soil was stained red by the blood of Teuton warriors slaughtered by Caius Marius back in the century before Christ—was still a dignified and imposing image in the Provençal landscape. It stood as a reminder of the city's glorious past when Roman engineering and barbarian labor modernized the economy of southern Europe.

In early December 1838, François' audacious plans to enhance the water resources of Aix by constructing a series of dams in the neighboring *gorge de l'Infernet* and a seven-kilometer distribution canal were approved. But it took a few years to negotiate these projects through bureaucratic brambles and satisfy the demands of private interests, especially those of landowners who sought high profit for rights to traverse their acres. In 1843 he moved his wife and three-year-old Émile from Marseilles to Aix, where they rented a house in the *Cour Ste. Anne* within the old quarter and settled into Aixois social life while retaining an apartment and perhaps also an office in Marseilles. Work on the canal dig finally got underway in early February 1847.

But the hounds of ill fate in pursuit of this man of vast but unrealized ambitions were at his heels for one final lunge. François died of a respiratory disease on March 27th that year, a week before his son's seventh birthday and just when he had started on the road to wealth. Perhaps aware of how precarious his business life had been, he had taken legal steps to protect Émilie from being liable for his debts, and had deeded her his shares of stock in the company he'd formed to construct the canal. Even before Émile's birth, François had been aware of his family responsibilities. In a letter to his sister, dated January 10th, 1839, after a year of marriage to then pregnant Émilie, he wrote: *Over the past five years, I have spent everything I earned in Marseilles. I have now passed three years in Paris without earning a sou and am over 20,000 francs in debt.* By the time the contract for the Aix Canal had been secured, he was thousands of francs deeper in the hole, dependent then on his convincing personality and entrepreneurial prestige to borrow more money. So, despite efforts to be financially responsible for his family in the long run, François' death left Émilie with many debts. The company was not profitable, and was eventually declared bankrupt.

Émilie was entitled to only a 150-franc monthly pension from the Canal Authority, an amount a skilled laborer could expect to earn as a monthly wage. Not yet thirty, lacking financial competence and faced with years of impoverishment ahead of her, Émilie was also racked emotionally by threats and actions of creditors. Legal expenses from her futile efforts to litigate with the Canal Authority added attorney and court fees to the debt load. Even the physician in Marseilles, who had treated her husband but could not save him, sued before the tribunal at Aix asking for payment of his fee. Over the years of his maturity, Zola would be hounded by demands to settle his parents' debts—sins of the father visited on the son. Yet, in 1898, at the age of fifty-eight, he would write an article about his father, published in *L'Aurore*, where he sees his father in himself as an insufficiently recognized hero of great energy and hard work. Cézanne's father, on the other hand, lived to a very old age. Cézanne would say of him that he was *a man of genius, for he left me an annual income of 25,000 francs. Yes, he had the foresight to provide an income for me. Tell me what would have become of me were it not for that? We must love our fathers. I shall never be grateful enough to mine. I never showed him enough appreciation.*

3

My father slaved for Provence, for that unkind
stepmother whom I still love, though she ravaged me
and made me an orphan

For all that Cézanne and Zola had to set aside in order to transform themselves from small town boys into Parisian men, much printing ink has been wasted in efforts to divine greatness in Aixois artistic production at the time of their youth—pictures fashioned by delicate little masters who generated trifles for an audience wanting nothing more than acquiescent emotional luxury. Provençal painters were stuck in their diminished Baroque and Rococo heritage while the regional poets were immersed in medieval troubadour traditions. At the *Bourbon* in Aix, teachers drifted along in the classical routine. Recalling his school days, Zola said: *The machine functioned, and it works today in much the same way I imagine our forefathers were taught. Rambling around in the teachers' cold heads were three or four ideas that were made to suffice from October to July. Immured in their little town, like horses in a riding academy, they turn in the same circle.*

In September of 1852—Cézanne then thirteen and Zola twelve—the emperor Louis Napoleon made a state visit to Aix. He was celebrated by a 101-gun salute, a dazzling spectacle of medieval pageantry, and an appropriate speech by the mayor: *The city of Aix, which you deign to visit, was formerly the capital of Provence, the abode of a king, and the fatherland of valiant knights and troubadours.*[1] Yes, everything about Aix was what it once was, nothing had been added for centuries. *An old capital city*, Zola called it, *living in its memories with nothing to commend it but the beauty of its skies.*

Aix's history was too rich to allow its patriotic citizens to subordinate it to modern culture. They preferred to revitalize its past by revisiting it with pageants and exhibitions. In 1856, a princely effort was undertaken by the Provençal painter, Émile Loubon, a promoter of aged romanticism, to refresh Marseilles' artistic community and re-establish a truly Provençal school of art. But this exalted exhibition of regional art in 1861 was a thousand-work art history display with nothing from the past hundred years that suggested viable response to any forward motion of art in Paris. An association of poets called *Le Félibrige* had been established in 1854 to conduct a poetry festival that might re-awaken the Provençal cultural consciousness. On the festival's stage, some of the poets read pastoral verses in the old *langue d'oc,* a vernacular tongue understood only by old folks. Zola's sentimental description of this event forty years later, when guest speaker at a literary banquet held by the perennially regurgitated *Félibrige* group, may tell us what he felt about it at the time he experienced it. His speech is recorded in Mistral's memoirs, where he is said to have said: *I was fifteen or sixteen, and I see myself again, an escapee from school, in the great hall of the Hôtel de Ville at Aix, attending a poetic celebration somewhat like the one I have the honor of addressing today. Mistral was there, reciting his "The Reaper's Death," and there were others, all those who were then only troubadours.*[2] Mistral meant nothing to Zola other than his representing Aix's past into which he would have been mired had he not left Aix. Nothing in Zola's youthful writing reflects Mistral's poetry. Even the Aixois Joachim Gasquet, in his book of reminiscences of Cézanne, admits that had Cézanne not gone to Paris, he would have been no more than a Mistral of painting.[3]

A few heretics in Aix in the 1850s were not wholly impressed with either Aix's past or its potential for the future. On February 3rd, 1856, in the local newspaper, the *Mémorial d'Aix,* an editorial took a jab at the city: *If one wished to depict with exactitude Aix's spiritual state, our city could be fairly compared to a dead sea where the tide of public spirit flows quiet beneath a leaden atmosphere that constricts blood vessels and dampens the will.* Lucien Prévost-Paradol, whose career in belles-lettres (the humanites) included a brief period at Aix's *Faculté des Lettres* in the mid-1850s, found the sloth-like influence there so powerful that the rejection of a manuscript, which ordinarily would have terribly upset him, left him indifferent; he could imagine himself being led down a mossy path to extinction in perfect numbness.[4] Another visiting writer to the *Faculté des Lettres,* Jean-Jacques Weiss, had this to say: *Nowhere outside the prison walls of Mazas can existence be more dreary than here. I will resign myself to it, but that will require great resignation or potent laziness.* Summarizing his research on the pathologies of Aix during this decade when Cézanne and Zola were students at the *Bourbon,* the Zola biographer Frederick Brown wrote: *Had it been some other city, Weiss might have forgiven Aix's theater, the dirty white walls that had put Prévost-Paradol in mind of an assizes court, and the Choral Society of Apollo—its off-pitched crooning—and the backwardness of an old dame who, to make ends meet, sold eggs from poultry kept in the garden of her eighteenth-century town house where she lived among valuable antiques. As it was, Weiss could only wish himself gone from this mausoleum of the ancien régime.*[5] Even years later, in 1899, when Cézanne was sixty and at the first level of sainthood in the eyes of many, Joachim Gasquet, whose fame rests on Cézanne's shoulders, published a passionate defense against recent accusations that Aix was a dead town. In the *Memorial d'Aix,* to prove its cultural fame, he cited Aix's most famous sons: Marabou, Malherbe, Vauvenargues, Mignet, and Thiers. But they all belonged to the remote past. The only recent name he could come up with was

Mistral.[6] So infected was Gasquet with Aix's cultural antiquity that he neglected to mention either Cézanne or Zola—the latter by then having achieved considerable notoriety in Paris.

The *Bourbon's* pedagogical core was the classics—no modern history, no modern literature. Reluctantly taught was natural history, which could be justified only because, like law and medicine, it employed Latin terminology and was structured like history (*The ruling class will always be the ruling class because they know Latin*, proclaimed the militant bishop and education reformer Félix Dupanloup). The *Bourbon* teachers represented Latin not as a language of historical curiosity or a grammatical discipline fundamental to learning proper French, but as tradition-based pedagogy for modern education. Latin writings had survived through the ages because they were written by men of genius in philosophy, political science, rhetoric, poetry, social decorum: Plato, Aristotle, Homer, Horace, Cicero, Virgil. The classics were superior to contemporary literature for which another two millennia of winnowing would be required to blow the chaff off the few seeds worth planting in young minds. Just as scientific and ordinary trade and artisan words had been denied entry into the official French *dictionnaire*, their being too crude and transient, the classics had bucked infiltration of coarseness. But that sentiment held up only under rigorous control of what young people were allowed to read.

Cézanne and Zola were exposed to French literature at school but only to the seventeenth- and eighteenth-century classics—Voltaire, Corneille, Racine, Fénelon, La Fontaine, Montesquieu, Boileau—and nothing by these authors that was politically improper or racy. The Roman and Greek classics, too, were censored, excerpted for school texts, as was the Bible in catechisms and sermons. It was one thing to have Lot's wife turned into a pillar of salt because she disobeyed, another to have Lot's two daughters get him drunk one night and in an incestuous orgy copulate him to orgasm so they could pass on his seed. And while Shepherd David, with his modest but deadly sling, could symbolize heroic virtue over Philistines who block progress, it was another thing to have him, as King David, abduct and ravish young Bathsheba while her soldier-husband was off at the front serving his king in war. And Solomon's *Song of Songs*, however it may be explained as God's message of love between man and woman, was a voluptuous poem celebrating not just love but downright physical sex.

William Acton, the famous English urologist with a very successful practice in Paris, was one among many physicians exhorting parents and teachers to prohibit children from reading Greek and Roman poetry. Acton's *The Functions and Disorders of the Reproductive System*, published in 1857—often reissued and widely read (not just by doctors)—warned that reading love stories in the classics inflames the imagination and leads to the loss of semen. *And this dreadful loss*, he counseled, *results in loss of vigor and eventual insanity*. Claude François Lallemond's popular books cautioned parents that a boy's loss of semen through masturbation and nocturnal emission causes him to become thin, pale, and irritable, his palms moist and cold—the very characteristics of vital exhaustion.[7] Unaware of how Latin poetry might diminish their brain cells, no doubt Cézanne and Zola were titillated to high passion by passages in Latin poetry read outside of school. *When you have finished translating Virgil's second epilogue, send it to me*, asks nineteen-year-old Zola in a letter to Cézanne. *Thank God, I am not a young girl and will not be scandalized*.[8] This simple tale of shepherd Corydon's love for Alexis, who belonged to someone else, was bluntly erotic in the 1850s because it referenced homosexuality, just as such notorious stories as *Lot and His Daughters* were exciting to read because they implicated highly charged incest.

Natural science, toward which Zola would drift, had by this time threatened the classics as much as it was challenging the church. Resistance to science paralleled reaction against modern literature. Revisionist and progressive educators in Paris had experienced a rough time convincing the central government to authorize a *baccalauréat* in science that would address modern issues in biology, anthropology, and geology. Modernity was a threat to traditions.[9] Politics fell in step with the Church's resistance to science. The French ruling class was threatened by scientific thinking, especially social Darwinism that stirred the people to contemplate progress as a sequence of political and economic reforms. By mid-century, the natural sciences had advanced from the speculative to the experimental. To experiment was to search for new ways. Experimentation undermined certainty, showed lack of faith in absolutes. One does not experiment with godhood or nobility, question divine causality, or put to the test the merits of France's cultural patrimony. At the *Bourbon* in the 1850s, when Cézanne and Zola were students, a physics course came under attack for sinning on the experimental side. Divine absolutes were not to be tampered with. Natural history studies, as a sort of intercourse with nature, posited subliminal connotations as sexual intercourse with animals. Nature studies conflicted with Church teachings. Ascent of the noble features of civilized man was mind over matter, spiritual over animal, intellect over passion. Repudiation of the physical world was a sign of moral nobility, while engaging it was regressive, degrading, and immoral. Zola was deeply affected by this polarization. At the age of twenty-seven in 1868, he would envision a story of a young priest torn between his earthy instincts and theological education. Zola wrote in his notes, *I will address the great struggle between nature and religion*.[10]

Cézanne will not disparage Aix to the extent that Zola did, although Zola vacillated when recounting his Aixois youth, shifting between adolescent sentiments—at times cloying, and always felt in contrasts of attraction and repulsion. Metaphorically both boys will associate love and hate with country and city. *You love pretty women, so you hate ugly ones. You hate the town, so you love the fields*, Zola says to Cézanne in a June 13th, 1860 letter from Paris—Zola then nineteen, Cézanne twenty. On being moved to Paris when eighteen, Zola would envision Aix differently than Cézanne, who would remain embedded in Provençal soil for two more years and, over his lifetime, remain rooted there. Disparaging one's roots was a common affliction among Frenchmen of talent who migrated from the provinces to Paris. Zola will often refer to Aix as small, monotonous, and petty, a city of stale history. At the time Zola first experienced it, the master city planner Baron Haussmann was fully engaged in carrying out Louis Napoleon's plans to regenerate and modernize the city. New industries and social and political conflicts were putting a defining edge on the middle class, while the city teemed with creative individuals in the visual arts.

In Paris around 1860 were some two thousand painters and perhaps as many poets. Eugène Delacroix was contesting with Jean-Auguste Ingres, and Gustave Courbet with most anyone who feared that naturalism would decay the noble foundation of the beaux-arts built on Greek and Roman traditions. Simple-minded rustic rural scenes were competing with simple-minded potboilers in the classical style—peasant girls up against Aphrodites, hamlet goose-girls against Ledas and swans. Manet's scandalous paintings would soon appear and provoke an uproar that, even before his 1863 assault on Paris' official Salon, the testing ground for all painters, had heated up as more and more young artists succumbed to the example of Delacroix's multicolored passion and Courbet's unrefined bitumen realism. The invention of the rotary press made possible mass publications of newspaper and magazines. Novels that appealed to the public could be serialized and books printed cheaply. In 1860, Baudelaire published portions of *Les Paradis artificiels* and Champfleury's scandalous *La Mascarade de la vie parisienne* was serialized in the newspaper, *L'Opinion*, the serial flow straightway interrupted by ministerial order—society was to be protected from such carnal matter. Jules Michelet's *La Femme* appeared, breaking all records for sales, and his *L'Amour* sold 55,000 copies over the first few months. In 1859, the brazen Wagner, cursed by many for injecting insanity into classical music, conducted a concert of his own works at the Théâtre-Italien. Baudelaire published a second edition of decadent *Les Fleurs du mal*, and Alexandre Dumas' ribald skits were played over the summer as vaudeville performances. Year-round festivals and *bals masqués* in Paris permitted rounds of gaiety and sensual liberties, especially at newly created pleasure parks that offset the noisy, dusty disruption of massive renovations in Paris. The city was delightfully sinful.

Aix's simple, homespun, and pious annual *Fête-Dieu* (Festival of Corpus Christi), with its municipal marching band of students and amateurs, could not compete with the 150-piece orchestra playing for the 1859 *Mardi gras* in Paris under the baton of Johann Strauss. *Tell me about the processions*, asked Zola from Paris in a June 13, 1860 letter to Cézanne in Aix, referring perhaps to remnants of the Provençal *Fête-Dieu* parade, for the final grand celebration of that festival took place in 1851, when Cézanne was twelve and Zola eleven. *Those parades*, Zola adds in this letter, *are a sort of holy coquetry. Under the pretext of adoring God in one's most beautiful attire, one offers oneself to be adored.*[11] Cézanne recalled these festival parades, marching in them side by side with Zola when they were just boys.[12]

Zola's adult reminiscences conveyed how he felt about Aix compared to the maturity he had achieved in Paris. The contrast of a world lived and a world recalled summons images of an idyllic childhood, or childhood revisited as negative experience: childhood taking blame when adult life becomes stressful, when one feels that a better childhood would have brought about a better adulthood. Over most of his life Zola suffered the trauma of his father's death and blamed it on Provence: *My father slaved for Provence, for that unkind stepmother whom I still love, though she ravaged me and made me an orphan.*[13] But his own quest for recognition and fame seemed at times to take advantage of the fact that Aix failed to recognize his father's efforts and accomplishments. In August 1868, Zola had an opportunity to vent his anger in a *causerie* (editorial chat) published in the cheap Paris newspaper *L'Événement illustré* and rebutted in Aix's major paper *Le Memorial d'Aix*. As if subconsciously recalling when, as school boys, he, Cézanne, and other school band members, serenaded girls outside their bedroom windows with music that surely must have terrified even the town's wailing tom-cats, Zola opened his essay by deploring the *Cour Mirabeau* debates and gender-biased skirmishes over the misbehavior of students on trial in Aix for having sung ribald verses under the window of two young ladies. Siding with the students against the two women, and against all the town's women for having made such a fuss over it, he wrote, *such scandalous conduct could only have taken place at Aix, a barbarous town. Where else but among stupid, churlish people would respectable women, unfortunate enough to be rich and beautiful, arouse the jealousy of the entire feminine public, and find themselves harassed by young men obeying nasty insinuations.*[14]

Zola would follow up *Memorial d'Aix's* rejoinder with a second, more malignant attack published in *L'Événement illustré*, scolding Aix for having failed to acknowledge his father: *True to form, Aix has striven to forget the very name of someone who compromised his fortune and health on its behalf. I spent fifteen years there, my entire youth, yet of its thirty thousand inhabitants, I can count three at most who haven't stoned me.*[15] The debate then vaulted back and forth over the next few weeks, with Aix's second newspaper, *Le Messager de Provence*, taking up Zola's case. To quell the hostility, for nothing could shut up Zola except victory, the municipal council voted to change the name of the *Boulevard de Chemin-Neuf* to *Boulevard Zola.*[16]

In 1867, to his young writer friend Antoine Valabrègue, who could not complete an intellectual transition to Paris, twenty-seven-year-old Zola wrote, *You are right to stay in Aix if your purpose is to get fully ready before coming back to Paris. Don't forget that to be free, you need to be independent. But hurry. The province is terrible. A two-year stay in Aix must certainly be killing. I have a very opinionated idea about this, which will always make me call you back to Paris. Ask Paul, ask all our friends, and you will see that they all fear the province.*[17] Even in his later years, Zola continued laying insults on the Aix of his youth: *To witness Aix's Fête-Dieu featuring a procession of citizens in the high and pointed hoods of medieval penitents was to see a lame Catholicism dragging itself beneath the blue heaven of old beliefs. Of course one finds serious students who read the papers and new books and wax enthusiastic over new ideas, but they are so utterly lost in the crowd that one must consider them anomalous. I speak here of the majority, this majority that wallows satisfied in complete ignorance: no reading or philosophical passions, no interest in ideas that preoccupy the modern world.*[18]

Yet the themes of Zola's novels will not detach entirely from Aix. As a writer he could create at any distance from his subject matter. Cézanne needed his source material out in front of his eye. He will never become a Parisian, even after spending many years there. The natural primitivism he found in Provence, like Gauguin will find in Brittany and Van Gogh in Arles, would suffice for his artistic needs: the worn-down Mont Saint-Victoire, abandoned quarries, twisted trees, peasants, clay pots with geraniums, and common laborers and domestics. His periodic returns to Aix were not just to visit his family or to placate his father so his monthly allowance would continue, as is often implied. The landscape around Aix, not Paris, was fit for his way of painting. Over the 1870s, he would evolve an isomorphic relationship between his colors, brushstrokes, play of light, and the perceptual tissue of the Provençal landscape, like Courbet in the Jura Mountains or Boudin on Normandy beaches. Cézanne's art would never be of the historical moment, never like Manet, Whistler, or Degas'—artists who did not come from immutable working class stock but from a level of society that advances culture through time. His home will remain *la maison de mon père* (my father's house). Zola, on the other hand, was born in Paris, had spent his early youth in Marseilles, his teenage years in Aix, and his emerging adult years again in Paris, having come full circle, Paris to Paris. Cézanne's full circle was from Aix to Paris and back to Aix, a circular journey he will take time and again.

Paris in winter, about the year
of Zola's arrival. Rue de Rivoli.

4

Young Zola to Paris via
third class carriage

Zola's mother went to Paris in early 1858 (Zola was then eighteen) where she hoped to raise support funds from influential contacts that might still be monetarily viable. Perhaps feeling that life could take a turn for the better there, she decided not to return to the Midi. Aix had been for her a place of disappointment, a battlefield of trials and tribulations. Having nothing to go back to, she sent instructions for her son to sell the furniture not already at the pawnshop and buy a third-class railway ticket for Paris. This move may not have been entirely unexpected by her son, but it was nonetheless abrupt and would require him to give up friends and change schools. At Émilie's invitation, Zola's seventy-two-year-old grandfather, Louis-Étienne Aubert, also moved to Paris. So nothing bearing Zola's family name other than his father's gravestone and waterway system, the Zola Canal, remained in Aix.

Zola and his grandfather arrived in Paris during February when perennially the city is at its bleakest, chilly and dank, when the low arch of the sun furnishes just a few hours of daylight before darkness settles in for the night. Zola would soon mourn the loss of the Provençal sun, easy access to the countryside, and the break up of the convivial triumvirate of Provençal *pitots* (a local expression for scamps). But by then, boys who had grown up together and shared schooling and escapades were leaving Aix to scout out a future in cities or attend universities. Rites of passage into adulthood had been collecting toll on their youth: baccalaureate exams, bodies and emotions maturing and coming into sexuality, parents wanting their fidgety sons to grow up, get out of the house, and make something of themselves. Baille would soon take his exams and go to Marseilles for advanced studies in the natural sciences. Several of Zola's other school friends would be moving to Paris where he would reconnect with them. Cézanne would be left behind in Aix, secure in the creature comforts of his father's estate.

A few years later, Zola would publish his first novel, *La Confession de Claude* (The Confession of Claude), which is set in Paris. He dedicated the book to Cézanne and Baille, and at the time wrote a paean to their blissful youth as he'd recovered it on revisiting Aix during a summer holiday:

Brothers, do you remember the days when life was for us a dream? We had friendship. We dreamed of love and glory—the three of us letting our lips say what our hearts felt. Naively, we loved queens; we crowned each other with laurel. You told me your dreams and I told you mine. Then we stooped to come back to earth again. I told you about my pattern of life, devoted to work and struggle, and about my great courage. With a sense of the richness of my soul, I liked the idea of poverty. Like me, you climbed the staircase to your attics; you hoped to nourish yourselves there on great thoughts. Because of your ignorance of reality, you seemed to believe that the artist, over his sleepless nights, earns the next day's bread. [1]

Over the next two years, Zola would work on Cézanne relentlessly to convince him to come to Paris, where they will climb staircases to their attics and where Cézanne's ignorance of reality will earn his daily bread—lying indolently in bed, nourishing himself on great thoughts—while courageous Zola is devoted to work and struggle. In time, Cézanne will heed his call to arms. And the practical Baille, a paradigm of realism, after taking his university degree in Marseilles will come to Paris, too. The story of their disparate lives, fitted between adolescence and adulthood, will now unfold in the contexts of their letters.

5

Cézanne soon felt lost without Zola. On April 9, 1858, he wrote a long letter opening with *Good morning my dear Zola*, as if their separation had been a long night's sleep. The greeting is followed by a doggerel in loose verse:
*At last I take up my pen,
and as is my custom,
I will report straightaway
on the local weather.*

Cézanne goes on to say that a mighty squall had rained down water that freshened the Arc (a narrow river near Aix where he, Zola, and Baille swam and fished) and the mountain (Mont Sainte-Victoire, which they frequently climbed). The valley of the Arc River senses the advent of Spring, he writes in poetic rhyme: *Buds on plane trees are burgeoning, the emerging leaves take the shape of crowns, and the May trees are white with blossoms.* Then, in ordinary letter-writing prose: *I have just seen Baille, this evening I am going to his family's country house, and so I am writing to you.*

The opening lines of this letter were devised to make Zola homesick, to keep the pleasures they had shared in the environs of Aix on his mind; the attractions of Paris might cause him to forget what he had left behind. A second stanza follows by which Cézanne's mercurial disposition transforms the weather report into his mood at the moment of writing. Now the weather is foggy, somber. The sun is pale. Then, written in plain words, comes the mind that evoked the weather:

Since you left Aix, dear fellow, dark sorrow has plagued me. I am not lying, believe me. I can hardly recognize myself. I am leaden, stupid and slow. By the way, Baille told me that in a couple of weeks he will have the pleasure of causing a sheet of paper to reach the hands of your most eminent Greatness in which he will express his sorrows and grief at being far away from you. Truly, I would love to see you, and I trust that I, we, will soon see you during the holidays. And then we will carry out, complete, those projects we planned. In the meantime, I mourn your absence.

Good-bye, my dear Émile
Not that on flowing water
I leave as lively
As I used to in the past,
When our agile arms
Like reptilians
In docile waters
Swam together.

Good-bye lovely days
Seasoned with wine!
Fortunate fishing
Of monstrous fish!
Whence my fishing,
At the cool river
My annoying line
Wouldn't catch a hideous thing.

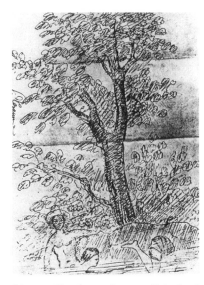

Cézanne. Sketch on a letter to Zola dated June 20, 1858. Cézanne at age nineteen.

Do you remember the pine tree that, planted on the bank of the Arc, bowed its shaggy head above the steep slope at its feet? This pine, which protected our bodies with its foliage from the blaze of the sun. Ah! May the gods preserve it from the fatal stroke of the wood-cutter's axe. We believe that you will come to Aix for the holidays and that then, nom d'un chien, long live joy! We have planned hunts as monstrous and enormous as our fishing trips. Soon my dear, if the weather holds, we will start to hunt and fish again. I am finishing this letter on the 13th, and today the weather is magnificent.

Acidifying nineteen-year-old Cézanne's agony of separation from Zola was his pending baccalaureate exams; his mental virility would soon be tested. At that critical joint in life's long reach, he was not sure of the next move—neither red nor black on a checkerboard played by others, neither boy nor man. Were he to pass his exams, he would be expected to go on to the university. Were he to fail, he would face life as a clerk or businessman. But unlike his friend Baille in the grip of natural science and looking forward to higher education, no great vocational passion had seized Cézanne. His instincts were aiming him nowhere. Art may have been a default position, an activity to pass time while nurturing the growth of a self-pleasing skill. His dabbling at Aix's municipal drawing school had not distinguished him as a future artist, and he would be expected to give up art, as would most of his fellow daubers, to pursue a proper career.

Cézanne was intelligent—his school records so indicated—but neither in his eyes nor Zola's was he an intellectual. His school chum from Aix, Marius Roux, would describe him mildly as *one of the good students our school in Aix has contributed to Paris...an undaunted, conscientious worker.*[1] Joachim Gasquet wrote that, according to the friends he'd been able to question, Cézanne was an excellent pupil, shy, dreamy, a bit reserved, who got on admirably in classics: one called him an *écorché* (flayed man, thin-skinned, supersensitive), and another stressed that he was much more promising at drawing than he turned out to be later.[2] It would seem that Cézanne had managed to get along as a protected youth within a stable family, indulged by a placid mother, an easy-going big brother to Marie and Rose. He had a muscular brain nourished by the energy of stubbornness, but was at times indecisive and vulnerable—rather typical of adolescent boys in that respect. His sisters may also have suffered an emotional slowdown and lack of desire to make decisions as they approached adulthood. Neither sought higher education nor a station in life beyond the conventional. Rose wouldn't marry until the age of thirty-one and then to an ordinary businessman. Marie remained unmarried, controlled throughout her humdrum life by the Church. Cézanne's father would one day lament, *My son is being consumed by art and my daughter by the Jesuits.*

In Aix, Cézanne is not content with how things are going. And Zola is not at all happy in Paris after his first few months there, doing poorly in school except in French composition, hardly justifying the expense his mother chose to bear by enrolling him in the distinguished *Lycée St. Louis*, which boasted a high percentage of pupils from the professional classes and *haute bourgeoisie*. (This was the school from which Baudelaire graduated, having been previously enrolled by a proud stepfather in the *Lycée Louis-le-Grand*, who had said to the headmaster, *Here is a pupil who will bring honor to your establishment*. But Baudelaire was expelled before bringing honor on the school, ostensibly for refusing to give up a note that had been passed to him by a friend, swallowing it instead). Literary composition had been Zola's strength at the *Bourbon* in Aix, but in Paris he was not situated in the division of *Belle Lettres*, but rather in science, in the direction leading towards engineering, the route of his father's profession. In a letter to Cézanne on June 14th, 1858—the second letter he wrote but the only surviving one from that year—Zola lays out his grievances:

> *My dear Cézanne,*
>
> *I'm a bit late in my correspondence and beg you to believe it was caused by a set of outrageous circumstances. I will not try to explain. That would take too long. The weather is terribly hot and humid. And since my poetic fire is in an inverse ratio to the fire bolts the divine Apollo casts down, I will write in simple prose. Anyway, like Mr. Hugo, I love contrasts; so, after a poetic letter I now send you a prosaic one. Instead of making you fall completely asleep, I will only cause you to doze off.*
>
> *My dear friend, I'm going to tell you something, something charming. I have already*

dipped my body into the waters of the Seine—of the broad width of the Seine, of the deep depth of the Seine. But there is no worldly pine tree there, no fresh spring in which to cool the bottle, no Cézanne with his immense imagination, his lively and prickling conversation! So to hell with the Seine, I told myself. Long live the water hole at Palette (a small village on the Arc River between Aix and Le Tholonet) and our celestial parties on its banks.

Paris is big, teeming with amusements, monuments, charming women. Aix is small, monotonous, petty, chock-full of women (may God keep me from bad-mouthing the women of Aix). Yet in spite of all that, I prefer Aix to Paris.

Could it be the pine trees set to undulating by breezes, the dry gorges, boulders stacked one on top the other like Pélion on Ossa; could it be the picturesque nature of Provence that draws me to it? I don't know. My poet's mind tells me that a sheer rock face is better looking than a freshly painted house, a river's murmur sounds better than the humming of a big city, virgin nature is better off than tormented and affected land.

Or could it be the friends I left back in the valley of the Arc who tug my thoughts towards the land of bouillabaisse and aioli? Certainly it is no more than that.

I meet so many young people here who aspire to l'esprit, believing themselves positioned on a more elevated plane than others, and who see merit only in themselves while granting to others an abundance of stupidity. I long to be again with those whom I know truly possess l'esprit and before casting stones take a moment to consider if others might throw the stones back. Well! I'm being terribly serious today! You must pardon the ordinary remarks I just made. But you see, when one observes the world from up close, one can't help but notice how badly it is put together, and then one can't help being philosophical about it. So to hell with reason, long live joy!

This letter moves on in response to Cézanne, who had confessed in a letter to Zola that he had a crush on a girl but had been too timid to approach her:

What about your conquest? Did you talk to her? Ah! you rascal, I swear you could be up to it. Young man, you are about to lose yourself, you're going to make a big mistake. But soon I will be there to prevent that from happening. I don't want anyone to corrupt my Cézanne.

Do you swim? Do you party? Do you paint? Do you play the trumpet? Do you write poems? In a word, what do you do? What about your exams? Do they roll on? Ah! you will sink all the masters [examiners]. Then, by golly, will we have fun. I have convoluted ideas, gigantic ones, you will see.

What does Baille do? What does B [perhaps Gustave Boyer] do? What does Marguery do? What does B [?] do? Those four fascinate me the most.[3] Other than you, they attract my curiosity. They are four fine boys who naturally have their own little faults but of the kind that only add sparkles to their dazzling qualities, as a beauty mark does on a woman's white skin.

I finished my comedy, Enfoncé le pion. A thousand lines or so.[4] You will have to swallow it entirely during the holidays. And you will! Baille will swallow it. Everyone will swallow it. I will be without mercy. No matter how many times you say you have had enough, I will only give you more. I am bringing you a whole supply of words. I won't surprise you with it. I will warn you beforehand. Then you will be able to treat me the same, reuniting us by composing a new Pucelle (metaphor for an unreadable poem of indeterminate length) *to discombobulate my daily life. God almighty! Is it at all possible to find any such insipid creature as me under the canopy of heaven!*

I don't know how I manage to get on. I don't work at all and still can't find time for myself.

I won't tell you a whole lot in this letter because I'm laying in a stock of stories to bring with me to Aix. Today is the 14th, so only two months are left. Time doesn't fly but always manages to walk. Say hello to our friends and to your parents. Send me, if you have time, a pretty piece of verse. That will distract me while at the same time giving me pleasure. As for me, at least for now, I am dead to poetry.

What crowns of laurel you will win! What rousing applause is going to accompany the awarding of prizes! As for me, I can only say that I will not put myself out. I will undertake winning just one prize, the one in narration. Should I win, that will be all I will win. It is not within everybody's reach to be brilliant. There are so many idiots around that, without fear of being disgraced; one can be just another one in their company.

Of what use is it to go on stacking nonsense on nonsense? As I see it, four pages are enough. I'll wait until I'm with you before I set loose my entangled ideas. Never will you have heard so many.

With that I will end this letter, my dear friend. I just wrote a paper on chemistry and am still entirely confused over it. Nothing agitates my nerves more than chemistry [la chemie]. *But then, anything of the feminine gender affects me in the same way. (It is only proper to end on a nonsensical note).*

See you soon. Your devoted friend.

Zola was homesick, looking forward to being back in Aix over the summer holidays. It was not likely that he had plunged his body into the Seine, which anywhere near Paris was a viscous receptacle of human and animal effluvium (in *L'Assommoir* Zola will write of the Seine as covered with greasy matter, bottle corks and vegetable parings, flotsam of filth). In the thick of such melancholic moods, displaced persons, such as the dolorous Zola, typically reflect on happier days and feel urged to write poetically. In a letter of uncertain date but most likely from 1858, Zola wrote to another friend in Aix, Louis Marguery, an eighteen-year-old lawyer's son and writer of stories and vaudeville skits:

Today by chance I saw out the window of my room a cloudless sky, a veritable Provençal sky. Swallows were in the air, and I saw a robber sparrow battling with another over the possession of a straw he was trying to hide in the crack of an old wall. I thought of the evening racket that the city sparrows make in the plane trees of the collège d'Aix.[5]

It would take a while for Zola to come to terms with Paris, to adopt it and be able to say he lived there. As best they could, he, Cézanne, and Baille communicated as if they would be forever the inseparables. When writing, they alternated gaiety and silliness with blue moods and plaintive woes, confidence with heartaches, self-bolstering with self-deprecation. They remained mutually dependent, bonded by complementary personalities and shared growing pains. With whom, other than each other, could they talk of their breakable hearts and burning desires? Not with parents, not with teachers, not with anyone who was not afloat and clinging to the same sodden plank. The amorous crush, which Zola asks Cézanne about, had been divulged in a letter that has not survived. Cézanne's wounded heart still aches in his response to Zola's request for an update on this amatory affair. In an undated letter, Cézanne wrote:

Cézanne. Cicero striking down Catiline. Sketch on an 1858 letter to Zola

> My dear,
>
> It was not only pleasure that your letter gave me, receiving it brought me a higher sense of well-being. Inner sadness still has a hold on me. God's truth, I can only dream of the woman I told you about. I do not know who she is. I see her passing sometimes in the street when on the way to my monotonous school. I am so smitten that I heave sighs, but sighs that do not betray themselves outwardly. They are mental sighs.
>
> The poetic piece you sent gave me great pleasure. I was happy to hear that you remember the pine tree that shades the riverbank at Palette. How I should love—cursed fate that separates us—to have you here. Were I not able to restrain myself, I would hurl long strings of litanies to Heaven: Good God! God's brothel! Sacred whore! etc. But what's the use of getting into a rage? That won't get me anywhere. So I will resign myself to my fate. Yes, as you say in another piece no less poetic—though I prefer your piece about swimming—you are happy. Yes, YOU are happy, but I, miserable wretch, am withering in silence. My love—for it is love that I feel—cannot find an outlet. Ennui accompanies me everywhere. Only for brief moments, when I have a drop to drink, can I forget my sorrow. But then I have always loved wine, and now love it even more. I have gotten drunk. I will get drunk still more, unless by some unexpected luck, ho ho! I should be able to heal, by God! But no, I despair, as I go about stupefying myself.

At this point, Cézanne shows no indication that he longed for a career in art or that his father was frustrating him in any way. Zola asks about his friend's activities in a letter to him of June 14, 1858: *Do you paint? Do you write poetry?* Zola seemed to have no certain idea about Cézanne's thoughts as to a career. It would not be until early 1860 that Cézanne gave an indication that he wished to pursue art beyond it being a pleasant pastime.

As often he will when allowing himself to sink so low and hopeless, Cézanne abruptly stops feeling sorry for himself. After his dolorous opening words for Zola, he pulls himself up. He breaks into a poem associated with an illustration in ink and watercolor sent along with the letter. His poetic narration of this picture is the first known occasion of his describing what sort of art he is making, though the ink-pen hatching suggests that he had copied the illustration from a published etching and then composed the poem. *My friend*, Cézanne says in his letter, *I am unfolding before your eyes a picture representing...*

Cicero crushing Catiline,
after having discovered the conspiracy
of that citizen lost to honor.
Admire, dear friend, the force of language
Cicero deploys to destroy that wicked man,
Admire Cicero whose eyes ablaze
Cast looks of festering hatred,
Overthrowing Statius,[6] weaver of plots
And knocking senseless his infamous accomplices.
Take a good look, dear friend, at Catiline
Falling on the ground, screaming Agh! Agh!
Look at the bloody dagger this arsonist
Wore at his side, bloodthirsty blade.
Do you see the spectators, aroused, terrified
Of having been so close to being sacrificed?
Can you see the banner, the Roman purple
That once crushed Carthage of Africa?
Though I am the author of this famous painting
I shiver seeing such a beautiful sight.
With each word uttered (I am horrified, I quake)
At Cicero speaking, my blood rages,
I can foresee, I am convinced
That you will react to this astonishing effect.
Impossible to do otherwise! Nothing, never,
In the Roman empire was ever so grand.
Can you see the floating wake of battleships
Tossed in the air by the wind's breath?

Regard! look also at the display of pikes
That the author of the Philippics planted there.[7]
Let me give you, now, another spectacle
By explaining to you the signage:
"Senatus, Curia."[8] *Ingenious idea*
for the first time taken up by Cézanne!
O sublime spectacle most wondrous to the eyes
Plunging deep into astonishment.

This poem has been given an entirely different interpretation than the one to be proposed here. The put-down of Catiline, taken by Cézanne from Cicero's *First Catiline Oration*, has been interpreted as a transformation of the classical author's urbane tale into a vehement denunciation in which Cicero stands for the righteous father implicating Cézanne's.[9] But the evidence for Cézanne's identification with Catiline is simply a line in a letter he sent to Zola about six months later, on January 17th, 1859, wherein he blends his name with Catiline's, yielding *Cézasine.* Cézanne and his friends enjoyed this sort of word play. Another of his letters to Zola is signed *Paulus Cézasinus,* and a joint letter to Zola from him and Baille is signed *Bacézanlle,* their friendship fused as one name, as in a letter written by Baille to Zola: *We are all waiting for you: Cézanne and me, me and Cézanne.* In yet another letter to Zola, Baille says, *Give our respects to your mother. I say 'our' for good reason: the Trinity is but a single person,* meaning the Trinity as inseparables—Cézanne, Zola, and himself.[10]

The entire passage in Cézanne's letter reads, *I am in trouble, seeing that in no way do I receive word from you. Upon my word, sacrebleu. I've invented hypotheses, even idiotic ones, in regard to your keeping so silent. Perhaps, I thought, he is occupied with some immenssime work, perhaps he is lubricating some vast poem, perhaps he is preparing some really unsolvable riddles for me, perhaps he has become the editor of some feeble newspaper; but all these suppositions do not tell in reality quod agis, etc. I could bore you much longer, and you could, in your wrath, exclaim with Cicero: Quosque tandem Cézasine, abuteris patientia nostra?* (Why, Cézasine, are you abusing our patience?).[11]

The ink drawing accompanying the letter, depicting the fight between Cicero and Catiline, is captioned with the same Latin line with which Cicero opens his first oration attacking Catiline: *Quous que tandem Catilina, abutere patientis nostra?* (Why, Catiline, are you trying our patience?). This coincidence of names—Catiline and Cézasine—should not suggest that Cézanne would have identified Cicero with his father and himself with Catiline, but that Cézanne is abusing Zola for not having written for so long, trying his patience. Still, fearing he may be upsetting Zola by chiding him when his friend might have a good excuse for not writing, Cézanne gives Zola a number of options and thus allows his friend to be as wrathful as Cicero, with Cézanne (in the letter, not in the poem) as Cézasine beaten into abject submission by Zola's wrath.

After concluding the poem, Cézanne wrote, *This should be enough to reveal to you the incomparable beauties of this admirable watercolor. The weather is improving but I'm not sure that it will go on improving. What I am sure of is that I am burning to go...*

As a daring diver
Plowing through the liquid waters of the Arc
And in this limpid stream
Catch the fish chance offers me.
Amen! Amen! These verses are stupid
They are not in good taste
But they are stupid
And worth nothing.
Good-bye, Zola, Good-bye.

But Cézanne cannot stop! *I see that after my brush my pen can say nothing good and that today I should attempt in vain...*

To sing to you of some forest nymph.
My voice is not sweet enough
And the beauties of the countryside
Whistle at those lines in my song
That are not humble enough.

I am going to stop at last, for I am doing nothing but heaping stupidity on absurdity.

Virile conquest is on Cézanne's mind at this time, whether of a maiden, forest nymph, or victory in combat with baccalaureate examiners. Such topical structures emerge in his letters and poems; later on, they will inspirit his paintings, especially the occasional juxtaposition of violence with placidity and tenderness. Throughout this long and complex letter, Cézanne changes like a chameleon, not just in color but also in shape—self-adapting, not to a background but to shifting moods. Poignantly, he reveals his inner sadness, his mental and spiritual sighing.

A miserable wretch, he makes himself out to be—withering in silent torment, suspended in ambivalence, barely conscious, unable to act, threatening to anesthetize himself against pain by drinking: *I've gotten drunk. I will get drunk still more.* To counter despair, Cézanne calls on chance to save him, to overcome the sorrow that is driving him to drink. But luck cannot be counted on. Fortuna, a woman, will not put out. Betrayed by real life that has usurped his expectations and plots to destroy him, he rages inside and makes of himself an incendiary. His subconscious, always on guard, will take over the dire situation. He will call upon Cicero to destroy the conspirators. In the poem, Cézanne says, *At Cicero speaking, my blood rages.* For those few moments he is Cicero taking command, beating Catiline to the ground with his raging words, overthrowing the whole damn conspiring lot. Zola, too, in a letter to Baille of January 29th, 1859, will call upon Cicero for help when he rashly contemplates going on to university studies: *Help, Virgil and Cicero! It will take only a year...*

Who were these conspirators, these weavers of plots against him? Certainly not his father. They were his examination subjects and the examiners, whose harrowing nature he would express to Zola in a letter of July 26th, 1868, before his first go at the baccalaureate exams:

I tremble when I see all the geography
History and Latin, Greek, and Geometry,
Conspiring against me: I see them menacing
These examiners whose piercing glares
Troubling the depths of my heart.
My fear at every moment doubled once more!
And I tell myself: Dear Lord, of all these enemies
So impudently united to bring about my downfall,
Disperse them, confuse the horrifying band.
My prayer, it is true, is not very charitable
Grant me anyway. I beseech you, my Lord,
I am a pious servant at your altar.

With ordinary incense, I honor your image.
Oh! my Lord, flatten these mean individuals.
Do you see them readying themselves to meet.
Rubbing their hands together, ready to sink us all?
Do you see them in their cruel glee
With their eyes counting who shall be their prey?
See, see, my Lord, how on their desks
They've gathered the fatal numbers!
No, no, do not allow that any innocent victim...
that I should fall under the blows of their rage.
Send your sanctified Holy Spirit!
That it should inculcate me, your servant
From its profound knowledge—the blinding light,
And if you grant this to me, even upon my dying hour
You will still hear me bellowing prayers,
Of which you, all Saints, shall be chilled.
I beg you, please, please, dear Lord, hear me
Also I beg you not to delay
(In the sending of your aforementioned blessings)

May my wishes now rise to the heavenly Eden:
In saecula. saeculorum, amen!

At his second go at the baccalaureate, Cicero will come to Cézanne's aid. He will strike down those menacing examiners, flatten them. In the poem, Cézanne can rant and rage when Cicero speaks, and in imagination he can create a famous painting that will astonish Zola as forcefully as Cicero astonished the conspirators, complying with Zola's encouraging words in an earlier letter to Cézanne, dated the 14th of June: *And your finals? Do they roll on? Ah, you will sink all the masters.*

Impossible to do otherwise, gloats Cézanne. But now he is bragging about the watercolor. When the Cicero/Catiline poem climaxes, one reads: *Oh sublime spectacle most wondrous to the eyes... That should be enough to reveal to you the incomparable beauty of this watercolor.*

The brute force of the subject matter, as typical of much of Cézanne's work from the 1860s, is conveyed by the power of the watercolor as art. After having come through this battle, Cézanne is free to write that the weather is improving, which may just as well be taken to mean that he is improving, coming out of his funk. *I am burning to go*, he writes, *plowing through the liquid waters of the Arc...the limpid stream.*

The poem's final line has the sublime spectacle, the watercolor imagery plunging Zola's eyes deep into astonishment (*qui plonge dans un profond étonnement*). The opening line of the next poem reads: *As a daring diver* (*En plongeur intrépide*). The mind is thus shifted from watercolor to river water, from conqueror to diver. The diver is dauntless, courageous, staunch (in French, *on plonge* is equivalent to the English *one takes a dive into, acts intrepidly*, as in Cézanne's imagination when he encounters a naked nymph asleep in a forest; he will plunge into her, as we will soon see).

Cézanne's subconscious is hard at work in this letter, saving him from sinking into total disheartenment. It is brave Cézanne who takes the plunge and furrows the passive water, making the limpid girl yield to his strokes, his confidence pumped from underground reserves. But suddenly the pump stops pumping: *Amen, amen! these verses are stupid*, he writes. The fantasy that was keeping him up dissolves; his verses are stupid; he is stupid, of no value whatsoever. Only his watercolor has merit. Art will save him. *After my virile brush, my flaccid pen can say nothing good*, he seems to be saying. Having lost tumescence, he then laments, *And yet I should attempt, in vain, to sing to you of some forest nymph.*

Forest nymphs are not supposed to be threatening, but rather sweet and yielding, not like real-life girls with power to tease, reject, and humiliate. In imagination, one can do to a fantasy girl whatever one wishes. But the forest nymph Cézanne encounters, and tells Zola about in another letter, will suddenly transmute from fantasy object of pleasure to real object of terror. She will take over, demand his performance, put his virility to a test, put him to a bachelor's trial more stressful than a baccalaureate exam. Such sudden mood swings—the boy in control of the girl at one minute, but controlled by her at the next—typify the adolescent dilemma. At times such swings do precipitate actual violence, when fantasy conquests fail to discharge pent-up anger, when the sex drive is frustrated by restraint, apprehension, and fear, and has no way to satisfying its needs of expression, leading to despair and at times to assaults, if not to suicide. (*I cannot find an outlet*, Cézanne wails). At their extreme, such swings are known clinically as manic-depression; in Cézanne's time, *la folie de la double forme:* two-faced Janus as the swinging gate, one the face of peace, the other of war—will she say "yes" and exhilarate him, or say "no" and annihilate him. In his letter to Zola, Cézanne laments, *What's the use of getting into a rage? I will resign myself to my fate.* His rage will come and go like the weather, as will his passivity. But Cézanne will never be suicidal or physically aggressive, nor will he display the least symptoms of clinical dementia or paranoia, even when trying to fit the personae of a bohemian artist.

Cézanne. Typical of male youths, Cézanne's early drawing feature subjects that display courage and virility: combatants, war horses, swordsmen, and the like, mostly copied from books and magazines. Whereabouts of this drawing unknown to the author. Photo: Courtesy Jean-Pierre Cézanne.

6

Resolved to seduce her,
resolutely I strode forward

In an April 9th, 1858 letter to Zola, nineteen-year-old Cézanne tells of an encounter with a forest nymph. He recites it as a poem headed *Poème Inédit*, meaning an unpublished poem, fresh from the mind, virginal, meant only for Zola—the sort of verse that he, Zola, and Baille often composed and sometimes set to music by substituting naughty phrases for a song's lyrics. In a postscript to this letter, he says, *I received your letter with the affectionate doggerels we had the pleasure of singing with the bass Boyer* (Gustave Boyer, another shared boyhood companion) *and the high tenor Baille.* Cézanne reciprocates with this poem that finds him deep in the woods where he comes upon a pretty nymph he calls a *mirliton*. During the years of Cézanne's youth, and in some circles still today, *mirliton* connoted a twat or a pussy, and literally referred to a flute of the type that youngsters play by blowing into it while fingering its holes—also a slide whistle, which is blown into and run up and down the scale by pumping an end-plunger. Figuratively, even in English, both slide whistle and kazoo can represent either a vagina, or, when saying, *Up your kazoo,* an adult male rectum.[1] *Mirliton* can refer to any young girl or young pudendum; in common usage it refers a girl apprentice in a bakery shop. *Vers de mirliton* designated "very bad verses" printed by manufacturers on *mirliton* wrappers. It was also the name of a popular satirical magazine. Cézanne's bawdy little poem here follows:

> *It was deep in the woods*
> *When I heard a clear voice*
> *Singing and repeating three times*
> *An enchanting little ditty*
> *With the air of a mirliton, etc.*
>
> *I spied a budding lass*
> *With a neat mirliton*
> *Seeing her so lovely*
> *An ardent shiver shook me*

In want of a mirliton, etc.

Her charms, marvelous
And her demeanor, majestic,
On her amorous lips
A gracious, inviting smile
Gentle mirliton, etc.

Resolved to seduce her,[2]
Resolutely I strode forward,
To have an amorous talk
With this charming object:
Gentle mirliton, etc.

Did you not come,
Beauty beyond words,
From the region of the clouds,
To make me happy?
Pretty mirliton, etc.

Your goddess figure,
Your eyes, your face—all of you,
The subtlety of your attractions,
Everything about you looks divine
Pretty mirliton, etc.

Your aerial bearing
Light as the butterfly in flight
Overtakes with ease, my dear,
The gusty north wind
Pretty mirliton, etc.

The imperial crown
Wouldn't look bad on your head.
Your calves, I imagine
Would be curvaceously formed.
Pretty mirliton, etc.

Thanks to this flattery,
She fell into a swoon,

While she is insentient,
I explore her mirliton.
O sweet mirliton, etc.

When she comes to
Under my vigorous efforts,
She finds herself amazed
to feel me atop her.
O sweet mirliton, etc.

She blushes and moans
Lifting her languorous eyes
As if wanting to say:
"Games such as this delight me."
Gentle mirliton, etc.

At the climax of our puissance
Far from saying: That's enough.
Sensing that I start over again
She says to me: «Ram it! Go deeper.»
Gentle mirliton, etc.

I took my pecker out
After ten or twelve thrusts—
Her butt wriggling for more
«Why do you stop?»
Says this mirliton, etc.

Cézanne's repeated use of "etc." at the end of each stanza most likely asks Zola, *D'ya get it?* He refers to his penis in this poem as a *sapière*, which is either a misspelled word or a cleverly made-up word fusing *sapin*, meaning fir or pine tree, with *sapinière*, a conifer nursery, or tree plantation, where seedlings are nurtured in preparation for transplanting into the adult tree world of lumber forests (the English word "sapling" is expressed in French as *un jeune arbre*, a young tree; metaphorically, a male still a boy). The *sapinière* was most likely linked in Cézanne's mind with the plunger of the slide whistle, a narrow wooden stick. By reducing the girl to a musical toy one plays with, and by poking fun at his penis that is still a sapling, Cézanne dissipates anxiety that would issue from an encounter with an insatiable girl demanding a manly performance from a boy. Cézanne's valor in exerting his copulatory motor to exhaustion leaves the lusty girl calling for more.

She drains his vigor and renders him inadequate. His member has not enough length: *Go deeper*, she yells. And when Cézanne is exhausted, she calls out, *Why do you stop?*

Cézanne's poem is like many of the passages in his and Zola's letters that keep them bonded through reminiscence of mutual secret pleasures. One can imagine Cézanne, Zola, and Baille on hot summer days beside a reedy river, hidden deep in a ravine, naked under the screening head of the giant pine tree that Cézanne mentions earlier in this letter, playing a mirliton, fingering its holes, or, if a slide whistle, making the imaginary girl squeal in pleasure as the plunger goes in and out. The poem abrogates between play and reality, childhood and adulthood, imitating grown up activity while denigrating Cézanne with juvenile silliness. Such self-ridicule is defensive and useful for holding an adolescent's sexual progress in check when in the presence of those who might threaten it. The self is reflexively diminished, as when one drops one's gun belt or lowers one's eyes, as lower-caste canines drop their tails and behave like youngsters in the presence of the alpha-male. Zola, too, participates at his end of the correspondence. About to compose a letter to Cézanne, he first writes, *I am pushing my pen and will tell you beforehand that I am not responsible for the platitudes and spelling mistakes it may commit.* In this way, the two remain bonded, each self-diminishing in order not to be competitive with the other when acting aggressively. The sign-offs of Cézanne and Zola's letters were also meant, subconsciously, to sustain their mutual states of non-dominance. They subordinate themselves to each other by acting silly, while enacting their self-proclaimed genius as self-proclaimed modesty.[3] Cézanne signs off on one letter with, *Permit me to finish this letter, as stupidly finished as it was begun.* Zola confesses in a letter to having stacked stupidity on stupidity, while Cézanne confesses in his letter to heaping stupidity on absurdity. Because stupidity is the foolishness of adults, not of children (little children cannot be stupid), silliness mediates between child-state and adult-state.

Bashful boys can aggressively exploit a *mirliton* without having to contend perilously with a real live girl, just as armchair quarterbacks need not fear the crunch of a lineman's assault. In the poem, it is only when the forest nymph has fainted, is in a swoon, that Cézanne can bring himself to explore her body. A fantasy object, a toy to be played with, but in the semi-reality of Cézanne's imagination, she is transitional from mirliton to real woman of passion. In the poem, when the nymph suddenly comes to and takes command, Cézanne cannot handle her. She becomes the aggressor, demanding a manly performance.[4]

If among thieves there is no honor, among adolescent boys who are intimate friends, there is no shame. By sending this poem to Zola, Cézanne risked shame. He must trust that Zola will not find him shameful, or make him feel embarrassed. He can trust Zola because they are on the same wavelength, as when telling dirty stories or sharing fantasies, just as blue-comedy performers entrust to their audience their off-color jokes, and patients with shameful confessions trust their psychoanalyst not to say, as their mother would, *Shame on you!* In another letter to Cézanne, by way of introducing something he would be embarrassed to tell anyone else, Zola writes, *To you who won't laugh at me.*[5]

As an adult, Cézanne will trust Zola with his secrets and not put him to shame. Only to Zola can he admit to frequent visits to brothels.[6] When deeply troubled over his plunge into an illicit love affair, Cézanne has Zola cover for him, receiving certain letters and forwarding them to a certain post office, and marking an X in the corner of his next letter to signal that a letter is to be picked up at General Delivery. In writing to tell Zola of this affair, Cézanne falls back on the secret Latin aphorisms that appear so often in their youthful letters: *I am either mad or sensible, trahit sua quemque voluptas* (each is carried off by his own passion).[7]

One of Cézanne's juvenile paintings is a copy of the eighteenth-century Nicolas Lancret's *Le Jeu de Cache-Cache* (Hide and Seek) depicting girls and boys in wooded nature.[8] The girls hide themselves, alluding to their secret places, their privates, yet tease the boys into catching them in the manner of satyrs cruising woodlands to catch nymphs. Cézanne's fantasy of the forest nymph is part and parcel of this game of catch—the *mirliton* he comes upon deep in the woods, caught by his seductive words, is overcome, even if turning out to be too hot to handle.

Most of Cézanne's juvenile paintings that survived are copies of such sublimated, sappy subjects, the sort of pictures his family enjoyed: *The Muses Kiss* (said to have been his mother's favorite), *The Visitation, The Virgin in Meditation.* He painted a little girl with an exotic bird; a sweet little boy and girl, too young to be aware of sexual symbolism, fondling a rabbit. The veiled eroticism of Rococo subject matter and style pervaded his pictures, as it did most every aspect of bourgeois society, from etiquette and courtly manners to interior decoration. Most popular were images of antiquated vintage that softened the brains of compliant artists, whose success depended on satisfying middle class sensibilities with pictures that touched the soul only lightly and made no upper brain demands. Such was the sort of imagery that Cézanne confronted in the Musée d'Aix and was encouraged by his art teacher, Joseph Gibert, to copy. Titles alone could convey the cast: *The Little Bird's Nest, First Caresses, The Sugar Plums of Baptism, A Good Mouthful, Grandmother's Friends, First Shave.* For art lovers with a taste for sublimated eroticism and a pretense to high art were such subjects as: *A Woman Tied to a Tree from Which Her Husband Has Been Hanged by Order of the Bastard of Vanves, Governor of Meaux in the Tenth Century, the Woman Being Devoured by Wolves.*[9] Stories that made up Zola's first book, *Les Contes à Ninon,* had the same Rococo flavor, as the astute critic, Jules Vallés, would point out in a negative review referring to eighteenth-century perfume mingling with sniffs of contemporary realism that pervade the stories. Cézanne's *Children with a Rabbit,* referred to above, is a copy of Peter-Paul Prud'hon's painting by that title. Although a painter of the Revolution and First Empire, Prud'hon was trained in Rome. A favorite of both empresses Josephine and Marie-Louise, he was a skilled decorator and painter of heart-touching pictures, known as the Boucher of his time and a bridge between the Rococo of nurseries and boudoirs and the chaste art of the neo-classicists.

The forest nymph of Cézanne's *Un poem inédit* will appear over and again in Cézanne's art—as nymphs set upon by lusty satyrs, maidens abducted, Nereids picked off rocks by tritons, provocatively posed naked women at riverside exciting naked boys on the opposite bank.[10] In his early work also lurks an adolescent ambivalence between tender love and aggression, the opposite sex idolized, ironically denying the ontological split between attraction and repulsion: women embraced and women strangled, adored in one picture and slaughtered in another. And this polarized ambivalence will echo in Zola's writings, as in *Mes Haines* (to be taken up later), where he writes that to love is to hate.

Nymphs and satyrs, classical rapes, voyeuristic encounters, bathing women, all had common presence in Salon imagery, affording painters easy access to crowd-pleasing pornography in an acceptable form—sublimation of voyeurism, rape, and orgies, experienced from a safe distance, either in time, as way back in antiquity, or as culturally displaced Turkish harem women or Greek slave girls, just as ethnological publications could get away with pictures of naked savages who were remote in evolution and, like animals, excused from civilized morality. The typically adolescent ambivalence toward, rather than fear of, the feminine, which was so pronounced in the psychologies of young Cézanne and Zola, was pre-requisite to their romantic, anti-aesthetic. Their psychologies coincided with the social condition of others within their circle who were mostly of the same age. Looking back from mature work and lifetime achievements, the art historian

Alexandre Cabanel. *Nymph Surprised by a Satyr*. Musée de Montpellier. One of hundreds of examples of the nymph surprised. A young man need not have seen such pictures to have that image rise in imagination, as it is a primordial fantasy., rooted in the human psyche—the man a hunter,, the woman quarry. Diana, the Huntress, plays the counterpart. Diana was hated by Venus.

often fails to acknowledge that, with few exceptions, such as Pissarro, Manet, and Degas, the Parisian «avant-garde» painters of the 1860s were in transition from youth to adulthood.

7

Cézanne's letter to Zola of May 3rd, 1858 opens with a rebus: *One must love women*. The French word *rébus* derives directly from the Latin *rebus* as a plural of *res*, meaning "thing" or "event." So a rebus, as in the Latin phrase: *de rebus quae geruntur*, elucidates events that are taking place. During historical ages of illiteracy, the rebus was a standard form of communicating news through pictures in sequence, like the function of petroglyphs or the hieroglyphic texts of ancient Egypt. To read a rebus, one must figure out the meaning of a string of pictures as clues to words. To compose a rebus, one must mediate between having the meaning obscure and accessible. Throughout the ages, the rebus played its role as a game of secrecy, often hiding thoughts about love and sex. Leonardo da Vinci concocted a number of them, including one set to notes on a stave. Following the clef, he drew a fishhook, *amo*, then the notes *re sol la mi fa re mi*, followed by the letters *rare*, then after a bar line, *la sol mi fa sol* and the letters *lecita*. The rebus reads: *Amore sol la mi fa remire, la Solmi fa sollecita*, or "Love alone arouses my memory; it alone stirs my heart." In 1833 Delacroix signed his name with the numeral two (*deux*), followed by the letter *A* on the treble clef, pronounced *la*, and a cross (*croix*), the linkage when pronounced yielding *de la croix*.[1] Gauguin composed his monogram as a rebus: using the English pronunciation of his name, he encircled PG with a O, thus reading PEGO, which was merchant marine slang for penis.

By Cézanne's time, the rebus was popular among all classes as a playful conundrum. French newspapers entertained readers with a regular fare of such puzzles. *L'Événement*, to which Cézanne's family subscribed, offered a weekly rebus with solutions appearing in the next issue. But the word was also current in the vocabulary of anyone stumped by imagery that did not seem to make sense. The art critic Théodore Pelloquet, baffled by Manet's *Déjeuner sur l'herbe* in the 1863 Paris Salon, absolved his chagrin by writing, *I am not asking for a philosophical reading but simply a visible translation of some sort of impression. I seek his meaning and do not find it. The picture is a rebus of exaggerated dimensions that defies understanding.*[2]

Cézanne's puzzle in the letter to Zola is a sequence commencing with the word *Il* followed by a pictured scythe (in French *une faux*). These combine to sound *Il faut*, a common idiom meaning, "It is necessary to" or "One must." Then comes a pictured hedge—in French *une haie* pronounced with a silent "*h*." This combines phonetically with the next picture, a maypole, in French an *arbre de mai*, a May tree. The words *haie* and *mai* fuse as *aimer* (to love). The rebus concludes with the plural article *les*, then female heads giving the noun *femmes*. The May tree is the *aubépine*, the tree of dawn (or *l'aube*, a feminine noun), meaning "the break of dawn"—in Victorian language, "the awakening," the passage of the virgin. Dawn is transitional from night to day; also, from spring to summer. *Aube* is the virginal condition, just before the naked ground is furrowed and seeded, when the May tree's blossoms—virgin-girl colors: pink and white—precede the growth of

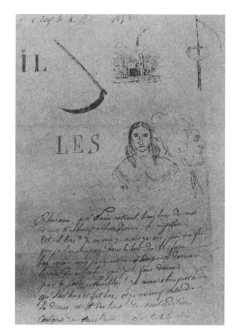

Rebus on a letter from Cézanne in Aix to Zola in Paris, dated May 3, 1858.

leaves. The month of May is *le mois de Marie, la vierge par excellence*, the Virgin Mary. Thus girls do not marry in May but remain virgins until June when one marries— the *aube* having passed. The blossoms having fallen, the ground will now be seeded.

Fantasies of virgin girls were on Cézanne and Zola's minds at the time. And no doubt in Aix and most every town in France, maypole festivals were being celebrated with village girls furnished with necklaces of spring flowers. The maypole tradition survives from medieval rituals of spring. In villages and towns, a pole is installed to represent the tree, streamers of pink and white cloth affixed to its top. Children, proof of previous years' fecundity, encircle the pole, each holding the end of a streamer; alternating boy and girl, the boys hold white ribbons going clockwise; the girls with pink streamers, counter-clockwise; the boys interweave with the oncoming girls, in and out. The streamers are taken up in the windings until the pole is sheathed in a plaited pattern of pink and white.[3] This ceremony is observed during the month of pure love, of violets, lilies of the valley, and lilacs the first of May is when mothers are honored with May baskets as gifts.

If Zola had deciphered the puzzle, it would have reminded him of Michelet's thoughts on love. Cézanne may indeed have fashioned it so Zola would recognize Michelet's admonition that men must return to loving women. Michelet's *L'Amour* had been published earlier that year, and within days had become the most passionately discussed book in Paris. Zola was inspired by it and probably had mentioned it in a letter to Cézanne. But Cézanne was as steeped as Zola in fantasies of saintly, poetic love, and perhaps would not have needed Michelet to please Zola with a rebus saying that men must love women. At the time, love and art had no separate tracks to follow alongside the progression of either Cézanne's or Zola's adolescence. From their exchange of letters, one knows that Zola honestly believed he could consummate his fantasy of writing great poetry only if he could find the girl of his dreams; and that Cézanne dreamed of going to Paris to become an artist, but only if he had the right woman to accompany him—*I had said to myself, if she didn't detest me, we would go to Paris together. There I would make myself into an artist.*[4] No external impetus could match their inner sense of urgency to find a virginal muse to kiss their brow and indulge the single-mindedness of their libido, which, like Cupid's arrow, has but one destiny.

A year and a half after Zola had seen Cézanne's rebus, Michelet's book became the model for Zola's most ambitious fantasy. He speaks of it, rather confessionally, in a December 30th, 1859 letter to Cézanne:

> *What are you up to, you and Baille? I, being bored up here, believe you may be amusing yourselves down there. But, seriously considered, things are the same everywhere, and in these days gaiety is very rare. At that, I feel sorry for you, just as sorry as I feel for myself, and I ask heaven to send down a gentle dove—I mean an amour.*
>
> *You can't imagine what's been going through my head for some time. To you, who won't laugh at me, I will confide it. You certainly know that Michelet, in L'Amour, does not begin the book until after the marriage—only talking about the married couple, not about the lovers. Very well, then, I, the non-entity, intend to depict blossoming love and treat it up to the marriage.*
>
> *You can't imagine the difficulty of such an undertaking: three hundred pages to fill without hardly any plot—a kind of poem for which I will have to invent everything, and in which everything is directed to one goal—love! And what's more, as I tell you, I have never loved, except in a dream, and have never been loved, not even in a dream! But, never mind. In that I feel myself capable of a great love, I will consult my heart and create for myself some beautiful ideal, and then, perhaps, I will accomplish my project.*

Zola had advised Cézanne to accept poetic love as one of the best qualities of youth, for youth must cope daily with the anxieties of chastity. Poetic love would become a debated issue between the two soul mates when Cézanne's quest for the virginal amatory grail slackened a bit under the pressure of real life, leaving Zola still heated up in his visionary pursuit of it. In a letter to Baille, written on January 14th, 1859, Zola went to great lengths explaining his annoyance with Cézanne. While Cézanne had agreed that Michelet's notion of true and noble love *might exist*, he added, *but it is rare.* Upset with this conditional remark, Zola wrote, in this letter to Baille, *I want you to read my response to Cézanne. I hope that reading it will regenerate your heart, now sunk in algebra and mechanics.* Zola's response to Cézanne was curt, as if he had been wounded: *Not as rare as you think,* he wrote in retort. *It was an important task that Michelet started—that a man must return to loving a woman.* The letter here follows:

> *My dear Baille,*
>
> *I will not reproach you for anything. It doesn't help and it's bad manners. You will accuse yourself when you realize that today is January 14th and you haven't written to me, in spite of your word—you'd promised you would. You will never make me believe that work demands so much of your time. I am seriously worried about your health, and your intelligence; nothing gives one headaches, nothing alienates one more, than extended hard work, and it seems to me that you abuse yourself all too gladly.*
>
> *Cézanne, who is not as lazy as you—I should say, not as hard working—wrote a nice long letter to me. Never have I seen him so poetic, never have I seen him so amorous. So that, far from driving him away from poetic love, I dared him to pursue it. He told me that around Christmas you tried to win him back to realism in matters of love. In the past, I had believed that, but I now think it is not a project worthy of our friendship for him. I answered him at length, advising him to always love, and convincing him with facts and ideas I cannot disclose to you here. If by any chance you have become an apostle of realism [Zola at this time was far from being the realist he would later become, while both Cézanne and Baille were slipping off into the real world]—if the advice you gave Cézanne was not dictated by your friendship for him, if you were disparaging about love— I want you to read my response to Cézanne when you can. And I hope that reading it will regenerate your heart, now sunk in algebra and mechanics. I am even going to transcribe a few lines that I intend to send to Cézanne soon. What I say to him will do as well for you. Here are the lines: "In one of your last letters, I found the sentence, Michelet's love, pure and noble love, may exist but it is rare, one must admit."*
>
> *"Not as rare as you think," that's a point I forgot to make in my last letter* [to Cézanne]. *There was a time, not so long ago, when I too said no, when I mocked love, when someone was lecturing me on purity and fidelity. But I thought about it, and I believe I have found that our century is not as materialistic as it may seem. We are like high school runaways fighting among ourselves to find out who has committed the worst crime. We tell each other about our good fortune with as much ego as possible, and yet we also blacken ourselves as much as we can. We tend to reject saintliness, but when we play around with the altar's urns, if we try our hand at demonstrating how worthless we are, I believe it is more due to self-respect than maliciousness. This self-respect belongs to our youth, and since love is, if I may say so, one of the best qualities of youth, one rushes to say that youths do not love, that they only wallow in vice's muck. You went through that phase, so you must be aware of that. The boy who would confess to platonic love at school—that is, a saintly, poetic love—would be considered a fool, wouldn't he? So, I repeat myself: self-respect plays a great role in this matter. As in religion, a young man never admits to praying; in*

love matters, a young man never confesses to being in love. But rest assured that nature never loses its rights. In the days of chivalry, the tendency was to confess your love, and people did confess. Now the tendency has changed, but human beings are still the same. One cannot avoid love. I would bet that love could be found even in the hearts of those wanting to be thought of as the worst criminals. Everyone has his moment. Everyone must go through it.

Now it is also true that there are lovers who are more poetic than others, more passionate than others. To each his own way of loving. But it would be absurd for you—a flower and sunray lover type—to say that one cannot love without writing poetry, without moonlight walks. The rustic shepherd can love the shepherdess. Love is an elevated thing, highly enjoyable. It penetrates each soul. Even the least educated adapts according to the education at hand.

To get back to my point. It is pride, stupid pride that must be dealt with, as I see it. It is society that must be dealt with, and the whole of men all together, not one man alone. A man cannot avoid loving—would it be only a flower, an animal. Why then won't you accept that a man must love a woman?

I know that the case I am pleading is difficult. We are children of this century, of one who has taken care to feed us with definite ideas. We have heard so many lovely pleasantries about women and love that we do not believe much of anything any more. But, if you really think about it, if you look inside your heart, you will have to admit that it is wrong to say that love is dead, that our time is nothing but materialism, considering that you are not put together differently from other men.

It was an important task that Michelet started—that a man must return to loving a woman. He would then have his eyes opened. Because life is short, it would be a way to embellish it. Because the world is engaged in progress, it would be a means to advance oneself further. And I do not think it is just the poet speaking here. And never mind the exaggeration. Michelet considers the woman as a goddess that man worships with humility. For big problems one needs big solutions. If we were to accomplish just half of what he asks, the world would be perfect. My regards to your parents.

Your devoted friend.

From whatever depth Cézanne's rebus emerged, on the surface it is light-hearted, while subconsciously dealing with ambivalence towards the feminine: the need to love women, yet fearing the consequences of rejection, embarrassment, failure to perform (as in his poem telling of his encounter with the *mirliton*). Perhaps Cézanne may also have had a love/hate meaning in mind. The simultaneity of love and hate befits the wily psychology of these two correspondents, so anxiety-ridden over their sexuality while so agile with words. Zola had said to him, in a letter of June 13th, 1860: *Love, as an ideal, calls forth, to a certain extent, the idea of hatred, and vice versa. You love pretty women, so you hate ugly ones.* In contrast with the woman in frontal view with a loose hairdo and in an off-the-shoulder dress, the profiled female head in Cézanne's rebus is imbued with every sign of ugliness. The hag's hair is bound in a granny-bonnet; a fatty ridge of skin projects over her beady eyes in pince-nez glasses; the nose is hooked, the lips narrow, and stiff hairs poke out from her protruding chin.

The meaning may run even deeper. Cézanne illustrates *faut* with a scythe (*faux*), which is the tool of the Grim Reaper, a standard symbol of death. The French word for death, *la mort*, is feminine, and death is associated with the *femme fatalle*. *Faux* also means "false" and sometimes "treacherous." And *haie* (hedge) is similar to conjugations of the French verb, *haïr*, meaning, "to hate." Both hedge and hatred separate one thing from another: what is not on one side of the hedge is on the other; what is not loved is hated. An indecisive person hedges. And then comes the maypole, drawn by Cézanne as a vertical pole within a circle—either a phallic penetration or an enveloping. In the maypole ceremony, the pole is both decorated and bound. The polarity, love and hate, is also a set of coordinates: the opposite sex is an opposition—male opposed to female. In its largest format, this coordinate, like those of latitude and longitude, situates the individual and protects him by putting danger in front of every act of pleasure. Sexual pleasure comes with risk.

In the same letter that opens with the rebus, Cézanne says to Zola (two days later): *My dear, today is the 5th of May and it is raining hard. The gates of heaven are open.* Then comes this shuddering couplet (Cézanne's spellings): *L'éclair a sillonné la nue; et la fordrrre en grroudant rrroule dans l'étendue* (bright flashes furrow the clouds, rumbling thunder rolls in aggressively with outstretched arms). Cézanne deploys *la nue*, which satisfies as a reference to a cloud (*un nuage*) but means, specifically, not a cloud but a naked woman. So what might unwittingly be taken as just a poem on the day's weather in Provence is playfully conveyed to Zola as a thundering assault on a woman stripped naked, furrowed by thunderbolts and about to be ravished by open-armed thunder. This stormy violence, acted upon the woman, may be imbued with Cézanne's anxiety over his pending baccalaureate exams; the examination looms before him as if administered by a wrathful God who has opened the sluice gates and once again is ready to drown all sinners:

My dear, I am studying for the matric. Ah! If I had matric, if you had matric, if Baille had matric, if we all had matric. Baille at least will get it, but I: sunk, submerged, done for, petrified, extinguished, annihilated, that is what I will be.

My dear, today is the 5th of May and it is raining hard. The sluice gates of heaven are half open. Water two feet high runs through the streets. God, irritated by the crimes of the human species, has no doubt decided to wash away its numerous sins by his fresh deluge. For two days this horrible weather has lasted. My thermometer is 5 degrees [Celsius] above zero and my barometer indicates heavy rain, tempest, a hurricane for today and all the rest of the quarter. All the inhabitants of the town are plunged into deepest gloom. Consternation can be read on every face. Everyone has drawn features, haggard eyes, a frightened expression, pressing their arms against their bodies as if afraid of being bumped in a crowd. Everyone goes about reciting prayers. At the corner of every street, in spite of the beating rain, are groups of young maidens. No longer thinking of their rain-soaked crinolines, they cry themselves hoarse hurling litanies to the heavens. The town re-echoes to their indescribable uproar. I am quite deafened by it. I hear nothing but ora pro nobis *resounding on all sides. I myself have let the impudent doggerels and the atrocious hallelujahs be followed by some pious* pater noster *or even* mea culpa, mea culpa ter, quater, quinter mea culpa. *I want to make that august trio that reigns above forget our past iniquities.*

But I notice that a change has just calmed the anger of the Gods. The clouds are disappearing. The luminous rainbow shines in the celestial vault. Good-bye, good-bye.

Cézanne's moods are often conveyed metaphorically. When the skies are less black, things are going better. Zola, too, conveys moods as weather reports: *My future is still the same, very dark, and so overcast by clouds that my eyes search in vain.*[5] On another occasion, he says to Cézanne: *I don't know from which side the storm will break, but I feel that a thunderstorm is hovering over my head.*[6]

Cézanne's mercurial mood now shifts to sunlight; he rambles on in his letter to Zola. Their mutual friend, Gustave Boyer, is with him at the same table:

Are you well? I am very busy. Morbleu, very busy. This will explain the absence of the poem you asked me for. I am, you can be sure, most penitent that I am not able to reply with verve, warmth, and spirit equal to yours. I love your description of the school principal's savage face! (The one in your letter, I mean; there must be no mix-up). By the way, if you guess my fabulous rebus, just for fun write and tell me what I intended to say. Do one for me.

I am sitting opposite Boyer in my room on the second floor. I am writing in his presence and I now order him to add a few words in his own hand:

Then, in Boyer's handwriting:

I warn you that when, on your return, you come to visit Cézanne, you will find on the wall-paper of his room a large collection of maxims taken from Horace, Victor Hugo, etc.

Mid-summer, July 9th, 1858, just before Zola comes to Aix for the holidays, Cézanne assaults him with another long letter complete with doggerels. All the trials and vicissitudes of late adolescence are again represented: final exams, lust dampened by shyness, apprehension of approaching adulthood. The entire letter is worth reading. It opens with *Carissime Zola, Salve*, followed by a few lines in Latin announcing a set of *bouts-rimés* (poems with fixed end-rhymes) that he challenges Zola to use in constructing some poems:

As for the above-mentioned rhymes, you are granted freedom to, primo, *put them in the plural if your most serene Majesty judges it expedient;* secundo, *put them in any order you please;* tertio, *I demand of you alexandrines; finally,* quarto, *I want—No! I do not want—I beg of you, put everything into verse, even Zola.*

Now here are some little verses of mine, which I find admirable because they are by me—the very best reason for their quality is that I am their author!

> *Zola the swimmer*
> *Strikes fearlessly*
> *Through the limpid water.*
> *His sensitive arms*
> *Are spread joyously*
> *In the soft fluid.*

It is very misty today. Listen, I have just made up another couplet. Here it is.

> *Let us celebrate the sweetness*
> *Of the divine bottle,*
> *Its incomparable goodness*
> *Warms my heart.*

This must be sung to the tune: D'une mère chérie célébrons la douceur, etc.
My dear, I really believe that you are sweating when you tell me in your letter...

> *That your brow, bathed with sweat*
> *Was enveloped by a learned vapor*
> *That exhales as far as my horrible geometry.*
> *Do you believe that vilification?*
> *If I qualify, so does Geometry!*
> *In studying it, I feel my entire body*
> *Dissolving in water under my only too*
> > *impotent efforts.*

My dear, when you have sent me your bouts-rimés I will set about hunting for other rhymes both richer and more distorted. I am preparing. I am elaborating. I am distilling them in my alambic brain. They will be new rhymes such as one seldom encounters—morbleau, in a word, accomplished rhymes.

My dear, having started this letter on the 9th of July, it is fitting to finish it on the 14th [French Independence Day]. *But alas! in my arid mind, I do not find the least little idea what or why. And yet, with you, how many subjects would I like to discuss: hunting, fishing, swimming. What a variety of subjects, and love unspeakable (infandum, let us not broach that corrupting subject):*

> *Our soul still pure,*
> *Walking with a timid step,*

Has not yet struck
The edge of the precipice
Where so often one stumbles
In this corrupt age.
I have not yet raised
To my innocent lips
The bowl of voluptuousness
From which souls in love
Drink to satiety.

Here's a mystical tirade. You know, it occurs to me that I can see you reading these soporific verses. I see you shaking your head and saying: It doesn't exactly roar with him, this poetry...

Song in Your Honor!
Here I sing as if we were together surrendering
To all the joys of human life.
It is, as it were, an elegy,
It is vaporous, you will see.
In the evening, seated on the side of the mountain,
My eyes straying over the distant countryside
I mumbled to myself,
When, great Gods, will a companion appear
To deliver me from the misery of all the pain
That overwhelms me today?
Yes! she will seem to me
Dainty, pretty, like a shepherdess,
Sweet charm, a fresh round chin,
Rounded arms, shapely legs,
With a trim crinoline,
And a shape divine,
And lips of carmine.
Digue, dinguedi, dindigue, dindin.
Oh! Oh! the pretty chin.[7]

I am going to stop at last. I see that I am not really in the mood, alas!

But Cézanne cannot stop. He adds one more poem, confirming his unconscious dwelling on the dual cause of his anxiety and self-pity—his pending exams and need for a muse who will accept and love him:

Alas oh Muses! Weep for your foster child

Who cannot even make up a short song.
Oh matric, terrible exam!
Examiners, oh horrible faces!
Were I to pass, oh joy indescribable.

Great Gods, I really don't know what I should do. Good-bye my dear Zola. I keep
rambling.

A week before sitting for his baccalaureate exams, before Zola came to Aix
for vacation, Cézanne had joined with Baille to send Zola the news that Baille had
passed. This letter may reflect that a portion of Baille's examination in the
German language, appropriate for science students. It opens with:

Meine Liebe Freund,
It is Cézanne who writes but Baille who dictates. Muses! Descend from Helicon into
our veins to celebrate my [Baille's] baccalaureate triumph. It will be my [Cézanne's] turn
next week. Then, in his own handwriting, Baille speaks of Cézanne's mood:
This bizarre, original character is quite in keeping with our character, his and mine.
We were going to give you a heap of riddles to guess, but Fate decided differently. I just
came to see this poetic, fantastic, jovial, erotic, antiquated, physical, geometrical friend of
ours. He had already undertaken writing to you yesterday, the 26th of July 1858, and
was waiting for a stroke of inspiration. I gave him one. I wrote the greeting in German.
He was going to write at my dictation and pour out in profusion, together with the figura-
tion of his rhetoric, the flowers of my geometry. Permit me this transposition, else you
might have thought that we were going to send you triangles and other similar things.

By this time, Zola must have broadcast his aversion to mathematics. Baille's
assurance that Zola would not receive triangles is supported by Zola's confession,
in a letter to Louis Marguery, that he had become a lazy lout. Algebra gave him a
headache; geometry filled him with horror; the sight of a triangle sent shivers up
his spine.[8]

But, my dear, continues Baille, *the love that lost Troy still causes much harm. I have*
grave suspicions, believing that our Cézanne is in love. He is not willing to admit it. At which
infamy, Cézanne takes over the pen:
My dear, it was Baille who in bold hand just scribed those perfidious lines. His mind never
conceives of any other type. You know him well enough. You know of his craziness, even
before he submitted to that horrifying examination. How could he not be foolish after expe-
riencing that? What burlesque and misshapen ideas are being hatched at the moment in
his malignantly shocking brain! You know, Baille is now bachelier ès-sciences, and on the
14th of next month he is sitting for his bachelier ès-lettres. As for me, I sit on the 4th of
August. May the all-powerful gods preserve me from breaking my nose in my fall! Which
is, alas, to come. Great gods. I am cracking my head over this abominable work.

And then come the lines that reminded Cézanne of Cicero, who may come to his aid and beat down the conspirators:

I tremble when I see all the Geography
History, Latin, Greek, and Geometry
Conspiring against me: I see them, menacing,
Those examiners with the piercing stare
Which brings confusion to my very soul.
My fear each moment is horribly doubled
And I say to myself: Lord, all these enemies
United here shamelessly to bring about my certain
downfall
Dispense thou them, confound the entire pack.
To be sure this prayer is not too charitable—
But forgive me anyway, have pity, oh Lord
I am a pious servant at your altar.

What a ludicrous digression! What do you say to it? Isn't it totally misshapen? Ah! If I had time to write more you would have to swallow many another. By the way, a little later on I will send you your bouts-rimés. Send up a prayer to the Altissimo [the Almighty] *that the Faculty may decorate me with the much-coveted title.*

Baille, who must have been patiently waiting for Cézanne to complete his long alexandrine, takes over the pen:

My turn to continue. I do not intend to make you gulp down more verses. I have scarcely anything more to say to you, except that we are all waiting for you: Cézanne and me, me and Cézanne. Come then. Only I will not go hunting with you—let that be understood. I will not hunt, but I will accompany you. We will have some good outings. I will carry the bottle, even though it is the heaviest load!

This letter has already bored you. It is made for that. I don't mean it was written with intention to bore you.

Give our respects to your mother. I say "our" for good reason: the Trinity is but a single person.

We clasp your hand. This letter is from two original characters:
Bacézanlle

The pen shifts back to Cézanne:

My dear, when you come to Aix I will let my beard and mustache grow. I await you ad hoc. By the way, have you grown a beard and mustache? Good-bye, my dear. I don't understand how I can be so stupid.

One notes in these letters the coincidence of two fonts of threshold anxiety: the first tests of love and the pending baccalaureate exams. Both enter the late adolescent's life as rites of passage, both will test for virility—failure in either conquest can be morbidly castrating. Teenage suicide is induced at times by the axis of the two: failure in school, failure in love. Zola's first publication, a fairy tale written in 1859 when he was in Paris and Cézanne still in Aix, is titled, *La fée amoureuse* (The Love Fairy). It is a tragic love story of two adolescents, Loïs and Odette, who fail their baccalaureate examinations. Desolated, but protected by the wings of a fairy, they allow death to come as a promise of pure happiness forever. The fairy transforms the distraught lovers into two sprigs of sweet marjoram.

8

A horror story
never before heard

On the 29th of December 1859, Cézanne sent Zola a fantastic poem he had written titled *Une Histoire Terrible* (A Horror Story). This recital may have been seeded by a dream, a nightmare perhaps, elaborated for Zola as a ghost story. Cézanne had been praying that a woman would come into his life—always taking the form of a wispy fantasy, a butterfly with gossamer wings and a sweet and yielding disposition:

When, great Gods, will a companion appear
To deliver me from the misery of all the pain
That overwhelms me today?
Yes! she will seem to me
Dainty, pretty, like a shepherdess,
Sweet charm, a fresh round chin,
Rounded arms, shapely legs...

The woman he encounters in the horror story appears to be this fantasy figure, but only at first. She is ravishing, has mignon feet and shapely legs. When Cézanne's mind shifts from salvation to delight in her curvaceousness, he plants a kiss on her throbbing breast. Then reality strikes with a devastating blow; the beautiful woman transforms into a hideous cadaver, recalling the gentle *mirliton* that converts to a nymphomaniac:

It happened at night—Take careful note that night
Is black, when no star shines in the sky.
So, it was very dark, and even pitch black,
When this gloomy story must have taken place.
It is an unknown, monstrous, extraordinary drama,
Such that no one has ever before heard.
Satan, of course, must play a part in it.
The story is not believable, nevertheless my own words,
That have always been believed, are here to establish

The truth of what I am about to tell you.
So listen carefully: It was midnight, the hour when
Couples in their bed labor without candles,
But not without heat! It was hot. It was
A summer night; a large cloud spread
Across the sky, like a white winding sheet,
From the north to the Midi, announcing a storm.
The moon, now and then, breaking through that shroud,
Lighted up the path, where, lost, I wandered alone—
Some drops falling at short intervals
Stained the ground. Terrible blustering winds,
Ordinary forerunner, an impetuous wind rose,
Blowing from the south to the north, furious;
The dreadful simoon, seen in Africa
Burying cities under floods of sand,
Casually bent the audacious heads
Of trees spreading their branches to the sky.
Stillness was followed by the voice of the tempest.
The whistling of winds duplicated by the forest
Terrified my heart. Thunderbolts, with great noise,
Terrible, shredded the night's veils:
Vividly lighted by lightning's white light,
I could see the elves, the dwarfs, so help me God,
Flying about and sneering up in the rustling trees.
Satan commanded them; I saw him, and all my senses
Froze in fright: his fiery pupils
Shining, bright red; at times sparks
Would come off them, casting a dreadful glitter;
The devil's round was moving along with him.

I fell; all my body, chilled, near lifeless,
Trembled as under the touch of an enemy hand.
A cold sweat inundated my entire body,
Making vain attempts to rise and flee,
I could see Satan's diabolic band
Approaching, dancing its fantastic dance;
Frightful elves, horrible vampires,
Knocking each other down to get close to me,
Darting about in the sky, their looks all threats,
Competing among themselves to make hideous faces.
Earth, bury me! Rocks, crush my body!

I wanted to scream: O place of the dead,
Welcome me alive! But the devilish crowd
Narrowed its nasty spiral;
The goblins, the demons, were already grinding their teeth,
Anticipating their appalling feast—
Pleased at the thought of it,
They cast my way their lustful glances.
My goose was cooked...when, O pleasant surprise!
Suddenly in the distance a gallop resounded,
From neighing horses coming at a brisk trot.
Low at first, the sound of their rapid course
Comes closer to me; the intrepid driver
Laying on his whip, urging them on,
The spirited quartet galloping through the woods.
At this noise, the demons' gloomy troops
Dissipated, as clouds in the wind.
Me, I rejoiced, and then, better off dead than alive
I hail the driver: the alert horses
Stop right away. At once from the coach
Comes flowing a sweet and refreshing voice:
Get in, she says to me, get in. I leap aboard;
The door closes, and I find myself confronting
Face to face, a woman...Oh, I swear on my soul
I had never seen such a beautiful woman.
Blond hair, eyes brilliant with appealing fire,
Who, in no time, captivated my heart.
I throw myself at her feet; mignon foot, delightful,
Rounded leg; plucking up courage, with guilty lips,
I plant a kiss on her palpitating breast;
And at that instant the frigid cold of death seizes me,
The woman in my arms, this rose-tinted woman
instantly disappears, having transposed herself into
A bloodless cadaver with angular contours; its bones
Knocking against each another, its dead eyes sunken...
It was hugging me, Horror!.....A dreadful shock
Wakes me up, and I see the convoy dispersing,
the funeral cortége derailed, I go on, who knows where,
But most likely I will break my neck.

Had the story been a dream, by the act of writing it Cézanne would be taking command of fright, controlling what caused his fear, as happens in the therapy of talking out, of getting one's fears into the exterior world where they can be dispelled. But this story is not just a nighttime dream, in which the psyche is free to operate on its own, but a story that moves between the membrane of Cézanne's unconscious and a fully awake state. By giving the story a poetic structure, making it art, Cézanne buttresses himself against the terrible reality that wrote the story in his psyche.

The poem fits to a type of storytelling that involves terrible things about to happen but ends with one being rescued. Such stories parallel the transition from early adolescence to adulthood, usually opening with some version of Poe's *It was a dark and stormy night*—typical of ghost stories that teenage children tell each other on dark summer nights when clouds, blackened by their own shadow, pass under the moon. Tragedy, murder, or worse, often follow the story's opening, but just as often, the horror is relieved: the mystery is solved, a miracle occurs, rescue comes in the nick of time. Written or told to test listeners' nerves, such stories have the form of secret ceremonies initiating neophytes into adulthood. The neophyte is alone, separated from his family, usually on an unmarked road or deep in a forest. The ritual returns the neophyte to the infantile state of existence, to cosmic darkness where demons and monsters dwell, ruled by Satan. From there the novitiate must find its way back to be reborn as an adult.

Cézanne is severely self-conscious on opening this poem: *Notez bien que la nuit est noire* (take careful note that night is black). He is aware, of course, that Zola knows that night is black when not a single star is in the sky. Cézanne also knows that his opening line is hackneyed, and he wants to be sure that Zola knows that he knows, which is why he refers to the story as *inconnu* (never before told) and why he adds the expression *such that no one has ever before heard*. This tongue-in-cheek seriousness alerts Zola to not take him seriously. What Cézanne actually fears is that Zola will, and if he does, Cézanne will be embarrassed, as when no laughter follows the telling of one's off-color joke.

In the story of the forest nymph, emboldened Cézanne is rendered insufficient by the insatiable *mirliton*; in this story, his bold kiss on the mature woman's breast transforms her into embracing death. He cannot win; his dream to find love in the maternal embrace and bliss at the breast cannot find a place in reality. In the Oedipus story, the father in the coach refuses his son's entry, whereas in Cézanne's dream it's the woman, the mother, who invites him in: *Come in*, she says, *Get in. Come in me,* she may be saying. Cézanne comes in like a man but goes for the breast like an infant.[1]

That this poem was part of a letter to Zola dated December 29th, 1859 does not preclude it having been written earlier. Such lengthy verse took time to write. It may in fact be that the story welled up in Cézanne's imagination, primed perhaps by a dream or by something he'd read back when experiencing anxiety over his pending baccalaureate exams, back in July of the previous year when he wrote to Zola, *I see them menacing, those examiners with their piercing stares, which brings confusion to my very soul—all those enemies united shamelessly to bring about my certain downfall. Disperse thou them, confound the entire pack...*[2] *Disperse thou them* is precisely what the arrival of the woman's coach does in the poem—dispersing the demons. Considering the various causes for anxiety that an adolescent encounters, one should not bring every cause to focus on one conclusion: that this dream-like poem, and others to be presently taken up (*Hannibal's Dream*, and the story of Ugolino and his sons), *conveyed something of the anxiety of the young Cézanne under the strict regime of his father.*[3] Why of his father? Cannot a young man experience anxiety over confronting the feminine without having had a strict father? Male apprehension when approaching a female is biologically almost universal. Were it not, every female would be overrun with suitors.

Both Cézanne and Zola had a remarkable aptitude for elaborating dreams. They probably told each other ghost stories on many nights out under the stars— tales of horror that made Edgar Poe's tales, some translated by Baudelaire, so popular among young people in France (Cézanne's title, *Une Histoire Terrible* gives a conspicuous nod to Baudelaire's title for his book of Poe's poems, *Histoire Extraordinaire*).[4] Their natural competitiveness, their need to impress each other, demanded in storytelling that they go to the limit, as if wrestling before an audience of enraptured girls. Contests in horror-story telling, as in dirty-joke telling and peeing contests, are grounded in the boy's primitive drive to rid himself of sexual rivals, to intimidate the competition, to diminish an opponent's libido by ridiculing sex, which is a way of taking command of virility, of reducing its risky impulse. Surely Cézanne spent many hours composing such long poems—to the envy of Zola, perhaps, whose poems were not fashioned to be entertaining; writing was becoming for him a serious matter. This urge to control will find expression in the way that Cézanne assaults Paris' Salon jury over the 1860s, attempting to diminish its power by ridiculing its feminized aesthetics, like scaring girls with a warty toad in one's hand. In time, this aggressiveness will support Cézanne's fragile ego while almost destroying his chances of maturing into a genuine artist.

Cézanne's *Histoire Terrible* builds on the threshold fear of adolescent boys who, though physically endowed with sexual maturity, are not emotionally capable of measuring up to it. The site of his story is a place of wildness, which is symbolic of alienation: the wanderer is lost, lost in the desert, lost in the woods, an ego lost to itself, as in losing sight of who one is at some terrifying moment of one's being. In classic tales, the wanderer is about to perish when divine nourishment appears: Romulus and Remus, like all castaway infants lost in the wilderness, are suckled by a she-wolf. St. Paul is fed by a raven, Elijah by a flock of ravens, which are ironically associated with death. Cézanne is lost in the wilderness, and like Dante's "deadly woods," it is the domain of the Devil, the chaos of Death, and Cézanne is saved by a beautiful woman whose tempting breast, he hopes, will provide divine nourishment. The story is a psychoanalytical common-place. Dante's *Divine Comedy* opens this way:

Midway along our life's journey
I found myself in a deadly woods;
The right path, from which I had strayed, was lost.
O my! How difficult it is to tell about
The wilderness of that coarse and savage place,
The very thought of which summons my fear!
So bitter was it that death is little more so.

Dante's *midway along life's journey* refers to age thirty-five, but to an adolescent reading his poem, it could be the gap that separates boyhood from manhood. The very thought of it, says Dante, summons fear. En route, Cézanne passes through thoughtful desire and mindless lust that chafe against each other and scramble the adolescent mind: the beautiful woman's blonde hair, her eyes that fascinate, her lissome feet below curvaceous legs. The woman calls from the carriage, *Montez, montez* (get on!), as if commanding him to mount her. Cézanne bows in obeisance, his face at her feet, and gets turned on by her legs. A rush of lust emboldens him—arousing courage is lust's natural function. With guilty lips, he plants a kiss on the woman's breast. The kiss is an entreaty, a pretext: the breasts are tempting, inviting; their pulsation simulates the tempo of suckling and swallowing (in the adolescent mind, swallowing is sustained as taking in words: *I finished my comedy, "Enfoncé le pion." A thousand lines or so,* writes Zola. *You will have to swallow it entirely during the holidays. And you will! Baille will swallow it. Everyone will swallow it. I will be without mercy*).

"Temptation of the flesh" was probably no more on Cézanne's mind than any other warm-blooded youth. Every nineteenth-century child reared under Catholic teachings had heard that expression a hundred times, and as many times had been warned against fleshly sins. It was a favorite story in Romantic writing: the saint tossed into the air by demons, smothered under dirt, his flesh punctured and slit, his limbs dislocated. Saint Anthony's demons, like those that threatened Cézanne, were masters of initiation rites. They destroyed the worldly man, his derelict body, enabling this morally weak, depraved, guilt-ridden monk to be regenerated as a saint. Years before Flaubert's novel *La Tentation de Saint Antoine* was published in its entirety in 1874, the story was illustrated in Catholic teachings and literature—just one such story of sinful saints redeemed when put to demoniac torture.[5]

Once in the 1860s and again during the first half of the 1870s, Cézanne would paint versions of the temptation of Saint Anthony in which the cowering saint attempts to fend off a woman who thrusts her naked body at him.[6] As in Cézanne's horror story, in the 1870s versions of his *Tentation de Saint Antoine*, the

Right: Cézanne. The Temptation of St. Anthony. Ca. 1869. Siftung Sammlung E. G. Bührle, Zurich. One of Cézanne's most enigmatic paintings

Below: Cézanne. The Temptation of St. Anthony. 1877-78. Paris, Musée d'Orsay. This painting comes closer than any other version to Cézanne's *Histoire Terrible*. Venal Venus is often accompanied by amors. There need be no connection between these images and Flaubert's 1874 *La Tentation de Saint Antoine*.

Devil and his entourage is present, the setting deep in a forest. Rather than goblins and dwarfs, the Devil, red as hell-fire, has come with a troupe of amors, suggesting that the woman is a manifestation of the venal goddess, Venus, who never lets up on tempting men to engage in sins of the flesh, for Venus is not the goddess of virgins but of venality. Whether Cézanne identified with St. Anthony, one cannot know, but most men have in one way or another, for all men, in combat with their hormones, must sublimate lust. Baudelaire had no trouble seeing in Flaubert's *La Tentation de Saint Antoine* the author as a *faculté souffrante, souterraine et révoltée* (a suffering mind, subconsciously in revolt).

9

Zola spent the summer of 1858 on school holiday with Cézanne and Baille in Aix. He was back in Paris in September, leaving Cézanne preoccupied with preparations for the second go at his baccalaureate exams. As feared, he had washed out at the first try. Anticipating that failure may repeat with greater certainty than lightening striking twice in the same place, he wrote to tell Zola he was praying to the all-powerful gods to preserve him from breaking his nose in another fall from grace. The more levelheaded Baille had passed his exams at the first try and registered at the university at Marseilles for studies in the natural sciences. By this time, a few of Cézanne and Zola's other school chums had matriculated and gone off for career studies; others would soon follow. Like Cézanne, they were a year or two older than Zola, who languished in pre-university studies for another year.

Passing baccalaureate exams was a sobering rite of passage, marking the end of adolescence and the onset of maturity. Jolted by failure at his first attempt—though many students fail—and experiencing extreme stress over the second try, Cézanne may have been rudely awakened to the plain fact that his adolescent days of merriment were over. Shortly after hearing that the benevolent gods had cooperated to help him endure the torture of interrogation (he passed his exams on November 12th, 1858), he registered for law studies in Aix's *Faculté de Droit*. His father may have settled this decision: by a suggestion, entreaty, bonus, or bribe. But one ought to give Cézanne some credit for being more than a pup on a leash—constrained, as he was, to get a hold on himself.

Aix was a judicial administrative center with a reputation as a litigious town, with law a major industry. The new *Palais de Justice*, facing the *Église de la Madeleine* (Justice and Theology married) across a large square, was a focus of civic pride and a direct link to the central courts of Paris. The law school's faculty and students were spread throughout town. Lawyers, notaries, and law students, all in black suits, gathered like crows at cafés surrounding the church square. A law degree opened doors to careers in industry, commerce, and government, and was regarded as a proper form of higher education. Even the Aixois poet, Frédéric Mistral, was a graduate of Aix's law school.

In a letter to Zola of December 7th, 1858, Cézanne, then nineteen, announced poetically his decision to enroll for law studies:

Alas! I have chosen the tortuous path of law.
I have chosen, that is not the right word,
I was forced to choose!
Law, horrible law of twisted circumlocutions
For three years, will render my life miserable.

The line, *I was forced to choose*, has triggered volleys of shots at Cézanne's father for interfering in his son's choice of career. The Cézanne literature is corrupted by banalities of such Oedipal rubric. Not allowing Cézanne the least control over himself or his future, Rewald says: *After having passed his examinations, Cézanne was forced by his father to enroll in the course of law at Aix University.*[1] But Cézanne does not say his father forced him, only that he was forced to choose. Regardless of what pressure his father may have applied, he had forced himself to choose. This is clarified in Cézanne's letter to Zola: *After being indecisive for some time—as I must confess to you that this pitot was not to my liking—I finally decided to treat him as pitilessly as possible. And so I am putting myself to work.*

The word *pitot* refers to Cézanne, himself; the word is a Provençal bit of slang designating a scamp, scalawag, rascal, an adolescent condition of acting juvenile at too mature an age. In Cézanne's phrase, *le moins pitoyablement possible*, the word *pitot* is embedded in *pitoyable* (pitiable), which is how Cézanne will now treat himself, as pitilessly as possible. He will put the surly rascal, himself, in law school. Zola, too, was at the time a pitiful creature. Just a month later, on January 23rd, 1859, in a letter to Baille, he echoes Cézanne's decision to take responsibility for his own destiny. Zola, too, had law school in mind. He had not mentioned to Cézanne that he was contemplating that course—at least not in any letter that has survived—but in the letter to Baille, he put his thoughts on the table. *My dear friend*, he addresses Baille: *I want to do law. One must have a career, and law is one I can happily square with my intellectual disposition.*

This flush of determination may have been just a passing rainstorm to refresh his spirit. But Zola will soon fail his baccalaureate exams, not once but twice, so advanced education in any field would be out of the question. He was not qualified to attend a university. Yet, to protect Cézanne's biographical persona as a genius thwarted in the germ by his father, Zola's thoughts of enrolling in law school have been left unspoken in the Cézanne literature.

The word that designates a correct course to take, *le droit*—the right angle, as in taking the right turn at a crossroads—is the same word for law (*le droit*).[2] In Cézanne's time, Hercules was invoked at the point of any major decision that

THE YOUTH OF CÉZANNE AND ZOLA—69

involved a course to follow. Cézanne did, in fact, identify his decision-making state with Hercules. The coincidence of the *right* way with going the way of law studies would not have figured other than metaphorically. Wanting to or not, he was forced to choose the *right* thing to do—a sign of maturity, of taking responsibility. Putting an end to self-pity and a stop to the *pitot*'s foolishness, he would put himself to work on the right path. Hercules, the son of Zeus, known for his great strength and courage, came into Cézanne's mind as a model of a man choosing right from wrong. Hercules was a Provençal folk hero. On driving Geryon's cattle from Spain to Italy, he passed through the Midi, founding a couple of cities along the way, including Monaco (*Portus Herculis Monec*). In Cézanne's day, warning signs above the entrance to some Provençal homes read: *The conqueror Hercules dwells here. Let nothing evil enter.*[3] But it would not have taken a literary source for Cézanne or Zola to associate Hercules with Cézanne's wavering over law studies; *Hercules at the crossroads* was an ordinary, commonly used phrase. School children would have found the story in their classics studies.[4]

In his December 7th letter to Zola, Cézanne says: *I will see that I get to know the exploits of master Hercules, and will convert them into heroic deeds of this pitot to the extent that can be possible. I must tell you that my work—should it merit the name, work, rather than muddle—will, for a long time, be elaborated, digested, perfected by me, as I will have little time to devote to the recitals of the adventurous Herculean Pitot.*[5] Cézanne then continues with his poem, but now calls out for pity; self-denial allows him self-indulgence; he avoids having deep feelings by allowing them to surface as silliness:

Muses of Helicon, of Pindar and Parnassus,
Come, I beg you, to soften my disgrace.
Have pity on me, an unhappy mortal,
Torn from your altar against my will.
Mathematician of arid problems,
Your pallid forehead, furrowed, lips as ghastly pale
As the faint shroud of a sickly ghost,
I can see, oh nine sisters [muses, typically nine in number]
You appear distressed!
But he who embraces Law as a career,
In you and Apollo has entirely lost faith.
Do not cast toward me a too disdainful eye
Since I am less guilty, alas! than unfortunate.
Rush up to me, instead, shake off my disgrace
And I will be forever in your debt.

The "work" that Cézanne would now undertake refers to the torturous path of law studies he will have to follow, not a long poem about Hercules, for he will have little time left over to recite the adventures of this *Pitot Herculéen*. In Zola's letter to him of August 1st, 1860, one reads: *On rereading your letters from last year, I came upon your little poem on Hercules between vice and virtue.*[6] Not only do Zola's words *little poem* contradict the assumption that Cézanne would undertake a long poem cataloging the adventures of Herculean Pitot as he undertakes those twelve adventurous labors, but the poem referred to is not, as is said, lost. Surely the verse that Zola came upon was part of Cézanne's December 7th, 1858 letter—a rather disjointed six-part composition of fifty-six lines, of which only the final stanza touches directly on Hercules. Zola says the poem he came upon was in Cézanne's letter from *the year before*. He says this in 1860, but that would not exclude the poem from a late 1858 letter, since it was written in December and Zola's *"l'année dernière"* is a generalization. That stanza would have been the *little poem*, in which Hercules, on awakening and seeing a young wood nymph passing by, would have had to decide between virtue and vice—to close his eyes and pretend he hadn't seen her,

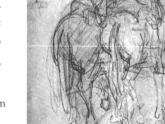

Cézanne. Typical sketches from early sketchbooks dating from Cézanne's age eighteen to twenty.

Right: Atelier Cézanne, Aix-en-Provence.
Below: Paris, Louvre, Cabinet des dessins.

Top: Kunstmuseum Basel.
Lower left: Private collection.
Lower right: Coll. Louis Giniès, Aix-en-Provence.

or take off after her.

Above, I recited two verses of the poem. The remainder now follows. But before Cézanne continues with the poetry in his letter, he interrupts himself, as he often does, to add an aside for Zola: *Didn't you say to yourself on hearing—no, on reading—these insipid verses that the muse of poetry had withdrawn from me forever? Alas, this is what the accursed law has done.* Then the poetry flows again in a playful mood—name dropping, playing with the gods:

> *O Law, who is it that gave birth to you, whose misshapen brain*
> *created you to make me miserable. The deformed "Digest"* [the official law text]*?*
> *And this incongruous code, shall it not remain incognito*
> *In France for another century? that strange furor, what folly,*
> *And what insanity disturbed your quivering brain,*
> *Oh, Justinian, wretched mailman of the Pandects,*
> *Impudent writer of the Corpus Juris?*
> *Was it not enough that Horace and Virgil, Tactitus and Lucien,*
> *presented Law's horror to us for eight years?*
> *Must you join forces with them, the cause of my misery!*
> *If Hell exists, and room remains therein,*
> *My Lord in Heaven, I beseech you*
> *Plunge the editor of the Digest there!*[7]

Once more, Cézanne breaks off, saying to Zola: *Tell me about the entrance requirements for the Academy, as I persist in the intention that we had formed, providing, of course, that it doesn't cost anything.*

It is not likely that Cézanne meant what his message says, any more than Zola had meant for more than a few minutes, perhaps, that he would, himself, study law. Cézanne's request may have been but a fantasy of escape from that to which he had just committed himself—wanting to keep one foot on land while taking the plunge. He even defers this fragile intention to be an artist to Zola, saying, *the intention we had formed.* Then, as an afterthought, comes the fence-straddling coda—*provided it doesn't cost anything.*

The poem continues, a bit out of joint, featuring Nicolas Boileau, the eighteenth-century writer of great fame and durability. In 1767, Boileau published *Art poétique*, where he affirmed in verse the ideal form of classical literature and laid down the laws of good writing as advocated then by the classical school, against which nineteenth-century Romantic writers rigorously fought in yet another quarrel of the ancients and the moderns. Boileau was also historiographer to Louis XIV, the absolute monarch mentioned in Cézanne's poem, whose enlightened reign saw the formation of the French Academy out of which the *Académie des Beaux-Arts* emerged—the fanciful paternalistic chimera.

No doubt Boileau was one of the authors Cézanne and Zola were required to read at the *Bourbon*. Perhaps Cézanne also may have read Boileau's *Dialogue des héros de romans* (Dialogues between heroes in novels), in which the heroic romances of Boileau's day are ridiculed. It might also be mentioned that Boileau studied law at the University of Paris and was a lawyer before taking up writing, before Louis XIV, on hearing him recite, granted him a lifetime pension. Cézanne may have been aware of this piece of history, which might explain why the following stanza comes between his lament over committing to law school and the final stanza where sound-asleep Hercules fails to see the young dryad approaching. And he would have known that Boileau was known as the *legislator du Parnasse*, the founder of literary criticism, even though Boileau's contemporaries felt that his writings lacked passion and imagination. In the poem, Cézanne refers to him as the *rector de Parnasse*:[8]

> *You know that Boileau, his broken shoulder blade*
> *Was found last year in a deep trench*
> *And on digging deeper, the workmen found*
> *All his bones, hard as horn, which they carried to Paris*
> *Where, in a museum, this king of beasts*
> *Was classified with the old rhinoceros.*
> *And these words were engraved, at the foot of his carcass:*
> *Here rests Boileau, the rector of Parnassus.*
>
> *This truth-laden tale*
> *Shows you the fate he deserved,*
> *For having flattered too much,*
> *With his indiscreet verve*
> *The fourteenth Louis, of our kings the most dense.*
> *Then a hundred francs were given to recompense them,*
> *—the ardent workers, who, for this find Received, with*
> *these words, a beautiful medal:*
> *"They found Boileau in a deep trench."*
>
> *Hercules, one day sound asleep*
> *In a wood, where the air was fresh—for really*
> *If he'd not been in a charming grove*
> *Rather exposed to the glare*
> *Of the sun, which cast hot rays as darts*
> *Perhaps he would have had a terrible headache*
> *Anyway, he was sleeping soundly. A young dryad*
> *Passing quite close to him...*

Hercules asleep in a charming grove, a dryad comes by. The usual fantasy of a man coming upon a sleeping wood nymph (the *mirliton*) is reversed. By cutting off the stanza, Cézanne leaves the rest of the poem to Zola's imagination. Comparing a career decision to deciding between this nymph being seduced or not seduced, as a decision between virtue and vice, would indeed at their age have been silly, so Cézanne stops writing, saying *I was about to say something stupid, so I will hold my peace. Permit me to end this letter as stupidly finished as begun.*

Cézanne's deployment of Hercules to elaborate on the decision so heavily weighing him down, like the burden of Atlas on Hercules' shoulders, threatening to break his shoulder blades, as Boileau's were broken in the poem, reflect his anticipation of years of Herculean labor that will prevent his following the muses of Helicon, Pindar, and Parnassus. Cézanne prays that they and Apollo will not entirely lose confidence in him as he toils over the next few years with the brute force of a Herculean rhinoceros.[9]

Zola's letter to Baille of January 1859, in which he states his desire to attend law school, starts with thoughts about getting a job. Here, too, *Hercules at the Crossroads* plays a role in the drama of an unsettled, anxiety-ridden young man trying to make a sensible decision that might promise relief. Whereas Cézanne's dilemma unfolded rather frantically in streams of metaphors in tortuous poetry, the Zola in this letter is the Zola of future novels:

My dear Baille,

I told you in my previous letter that as soon as possible I intended to take an office job. It was a desperate, absurd decision. My future was about to be ruined. I would have been doomed to rot on a wicker chair, to wear myself down, to follow wheel ruts. I could vaguely foresee the consequences, and felt that reflexive quiver that overcomes you when on the verge of diving into cold water. Fortunately, I was prevented from diving as I stood on the edge of the abyss. My eyes opened and fear made me step back when I saw the hellhole, the rocks and sludge waiting at the bottom. Back off, office life! Stay away from me, sewer! I shouted to myself. And then I looked around—calling out for a piece of advice. Only the echo answered, that mocking echo that repeats your words and sends you back to your own questions without having answered them, to make you realize that a man can only count on himself.

I then held my head in my hands and started to think, to seriously ponder. Life is a struggle, I told myself. Let us accept the struggle and not succumb to fatigue or worries. I could take my baccalaureate in science, get accepted at the École centrale, and become an engineer. "Don't do that," yelled a voice in the sky. "The turtle dove doesn't mate with the sparrow-hawk, the butterfly doesn't pollinate stinging nettle. For work to be productive, it must be enjoyed. To make a painting, one first needs colors. Instead of expanding, your horizon is shrinking. You were born neither to study science nor become a clerk. Your mind will always flee algebra to fly off to other places. Don't do that, don't do that!"

And when in anguish I asked what path I should choose...Listen, the voice contin-

ued, my advice will sound absurd and senseless: you will think you are regressing instead of progressing. In this world, my child, there are idols to whom everyone submits, steps everyone climbs, sometimes in vain. Shout loudly that you are a writer and they will ask for your baccalaureate diploma in literature. No salvation without diplomas! Diplomas open the door to every profession. Thanks to diplomas, one succeeds. Even if you are a moron, with this formidable tool, you are thought to be intelligent. If you are a talented man but had never received from the academic certificate proving your intelligence, you are taken as a moron.

To get to work, to work! my dear child. Begin your studies all over again: rosa = the rose; rosae = of the rose, etc. Charge ahead precious talisman! Help, Virgil and Cicero! It will only take a year, six months maybe, of tenacious work. Then with Homer or Tite-Live [Titus Livius, a Roman historian] *in your hand, standing on the edge, surrounded with domesticated translations from one language to the other, you will be allowed to yell, «I am a writer! I am a writer! with glorious resonance, while waving the lucrative diploma.»*

And then, having shouted its last battle cry, the voice in the sky stopped.

My dear Baille. I will forget the epic tone, and repeat in prosaic prose, that I'm going to study literature. And when I have my diploma, I want to study law. It's a career that neatly coincides with my ideas. So I have decided to become a lawyer. Rest assured, the writer's style will show under the toga.

Here is my point: tell me, you who studied literature on your own, how much Latin and Greek should I study; in other words, what is necessary to take the exam? Should I write Latin verses, translate Greek? I plan to study at home (don't laugh, I want to study), and hire a private instructor to correct my homework. You see my point. You can advise me in just a few words what I should study. I'm waiting impatiently for your answer. Drop your book for a moment, tell me how much Latin and Greek you studied, and I will love you even more. As for my baccalaureate in science, I don't intend to give it up. As soon as I pass the bac in literature, I intend to take up science as a second fight at the Sorbonne.

I'm convinced you will approve of all this. There is only one way to succeed, as I have always said—through hard work. Heaven sent me a guardian angel to wake me up, and I will not again fall asleep. It is a difficult task, but I will kiss my golden dreams goodbye for now. I am sure they will come back as a crowd when I call them at some more propitoius time.

I wish you a Mardi-Graz more joyful than mine, which will be, I suppose, one of the quietest. I am fine. My pipe is breaking in nicely. I wish you and your puffer the same.

My regards to your parents. I shake your hand.

Your studious friend.

Zola's grand plan to be studious, to become a classical scholar and lawyer, was a thin-shelled nut that cracked by simply falling off the tree. He will fail even those parts of the examination that, predictably, he should have easily passed.

Confronting professors in academic robes at the Sorbonne, he scored in science and mathematics, but apparently his brain came apart at the seams when assaulted by literary history. He will never admit, however, that this failure was a real failure, that, after all his years at a *lycée*, he would end up with no diploma. He had handy the usual adolescent excuse for it: *I could have done it if I had wanted to.* Fifteen years later, in 1877, he was still making excuses that might justify his case, saying, *the baccalaureate is no more than a lottery. I've seen mediocre students pass on luck alone. In the short time allotted to each student, one cannot make known the full extent of one's knowledge, and anyway, the examiners are restricted to questions on the slips they've drawn by chance.*[10]

After this second defeat, law and engineering were out of the question. He would have to make it solely as a writer. But his schooling had not nurtured him as a poet any more than had the same *lycée* made a poet of Baudelaire, whose only thoughts on matriculating were to go to law school against his family's wishes, for they felt his charming and delicate personality would assure success in the diplomatic corps. Twenty years before Zola's pedagogical demise at the *Lycée St. Louis*, seventeen-year-old Baudelaire wrote to his mother reporting on his progress at school:

All our essays are finished: As for the competition, no news. I can only tell you that, with the exception of the poetry paper, I have no hopes whatsoever. I asked the teacher for my class grades; he replied that my poetry and Latin papers were terrible. So this is the result of one whole year and what school achievements amount to. I feel so bored that I find myself crying without knowing why. I really feel very sad, upset with myself; threatened by failure, I confess that my self-esteem is badly hurt. I can play the philosopher, try to convince myself that school success means nothing.[11]

Too much has been assumed from Zola's December 30th, 1859 letter to Cézanne, in which there is an intimation of Cézanne's father impeding his son from becoming an artist. The words Zola combines in this letter may have been formed in his revolutionary mind, or they may have been in response to a lost letter from Cézanne complaining about his father. Such complaints may have expressed a real conflict, or simply frustration due to Cézanne's indecisiveness about his future. Zola's letter continues:

Forgive me if my thoughts are somewhat confused. We will not talk politics; you never read the papers as I allow myself to do, and you would not understand what I want to tell you. I will only tell you that the Pope is rather uneasy at the moment and suggests that you sometimes read Le Siècle, because these are very strange times.

What can I add to end this letter happily? Should I encourage you to storm the barricades? Or should I talk about painting and drawing?

Damned barricades, damned painting! The one has to stand the test of the cannons;[12] the other is crushed by the paternal veto. When you charge the wall, your diffidence shouts at you: "You won't get very much further." When you take up your brushes: "My son, my son," says your father, "think of the future. One dies with genius but eats with money." Ah! unfortunately my poor Cézanne, life is a billiard ball that does not always roll where the hand pushes it.

Zola's mention of the Pope is really of Cézanne's father, who may have been uneasy at that moment over political events reprinted in the newspaper *Le Siècle*. (A few years later, Cézanne's friend, Antoine Guillemet, would describe in a letter to Zola a portrait that Cézanne had painted of his father. *His father looks like a pope on his throne were it not for his reading Le Siècle.* An early advocate of Second Empire principles, *Le Siècle*, the first mass-published newspaper to gain wide circulation in France, was anti-government in the late 1850s. At the time of Zola's December 30th letter, Cézanne's father—a staunch republican who despised Napoleon III—read journalism avidly, as bankers must do. Perhaps some news or editorial column in the paper connected in Zola's mind as foreboding political revolution, and that, in turn, had painted an image of Cézanne revolting against parental authority. Zola's expression, *damned barricades*, hints of a revolution brewing, implying metaphorically that one must endure a revolt to throw off repression. His expression, *damned painting*, is thrown most likely against the instinctual pressure one suffers in pain when confronting the oppressive reality of what it takes to be an artist in the face of adversity—whether a father's veto or just the over-

Cézanne. This may or may not be the painting referred to in Guillemet's letter. The newspaper here is *L'Évènement*, not *Le Siècle*. The still life hanging on the wall is by Cézanne, suggesting that his parents were happy to have him hang his pictures in the house.

whelming negativity of society toward art. Whatever the case, Zola's expression, *crushed by the paternal veto*, has excessively served biographers as an "eyewitness account" of Cézanne's father quashing his son's dream of becoming an artist. And the *One dies with genius but eats with money* phrase has been taken to be a direct quote from the mouth of Cézanne's father, but if not just a hackneyed expression of the time, it is pure Zola.[13] Anyway, as fate would have it, Cézanne would complete only four semesters of law studies between December 1859 and July 1860, not even enough training to become a *notaire*.

10

*Dreams of the terrible father
who arrives in a chariot drawn
by four white horses*

Concern over Cézanne having been denied the right to become an artist by being forced by his father to enroll in law school has been exacerbated by analyses of a poem that Cézanne inserted in a letter to Zola on November 17th, 1858 (Cézanne then nineteen). It is a long poem of sixty-six lines, which I will presently recite. The poem has been grossly misinterpreted.

Meyer Schapiro said of it: *In Cézanne's Dream of Hannibal, written in mock-classical style, the young hero, after a drunken bout in which he has spilled the wine on the tablecloth and fallen asleep under the table, dreams of the terrible father who arrives in a chariot drawn by four white horses. He takes his debauched son by the ear, shakes him angrily, and scolds him for his drunkenness and wasteful life and for staining his clothes with sauce, wine, and rum. These fantasies convey something of the anxiety of the young Cézanne under the strict regime of his father.*[1]

This poem has been interpreted as an elaborate expression of guilt that projects, in serious but imaginative form, Cézanne's conflicting feelings about himself and his family—*fear of his powerful bourgeois father, and the struggle for independence against an enduring sense of failure in his father's eyes.* The author of that assumption, Theodore Reff, following Schapiro's lead, goes on to say that the central theme of the poem is the adolescent Cézanne's remorse about masturbation and fear of discovery—that almost the entire first stanza [*Excuse, excuse me. Yes, I'm guilty*] can be read as a metaphor for onanism. He interprets Hannibal's wine and rum spilling as sustained symbolism of ejaculation, the spilled liquids a waste of inherited substances— like semen, not to be squandered.[2] Reff says this letter was written the day after Cézanne's graduation and may record a dream fomented by a family celebration of the event at which Cézanne got drunk, made an awful mess, and was scolded by his father. But the letter was *not* written the day after Cézanne's graduation. In it, Cézanne tells Zola of a previous letter, dated the 14th, in which he had told him he had graduated. Having just received a letter from Zola complaining that he had not written in so long—their letters having crossed in the mail—Cézanne is quick to write again on the 17th.

Cézanne's opening stanza is simply this: *Excuse, excuse me. Yes, I'm guilty*. But Cézanne is not guilty over masturbation, rather for not dutifully keeping up with his correspondence with Zola. The next lines of the letter read:

However, for all our sins, there's forgiveness. Our letters must have crossed, so tell me when you next write—there is no need to put yourself out for that—if you did not receive a letter dated from my chamber, rhyming with the 14th of November [chambre/novembre]. *I am waiting for the end of the month so that when you send me another letter you can give me the title for a longissime poem I want to make up, about which I wrote to you in my letter of November 14th, which you can see, if you receive it. If not, I can hardly explain its non-arrival, but, as nothing is impossible, I hasten to write to you again. I passed my matriculation, but you must know that from the same letter of the 14th, providing that it has reached you by now.*

The title of Reff's essay is *Cézanne's Dream of Hannibal*. If any Freudian slip is involved here, it's that Hannibal's dream may be turned subliminally into Cézanne's dream, reinforced by Reff's saying that it was written the morning after the graduation banquet, implying that it had, indeed, been a dream, and written in one sitting—the morning after his successful examination day—rather than copied into the letter from pages Cézanne may have written days or weeks earlier. Favoring its earlier composition is Cézanne's request to Zola for a title for a long poem he has in mind, that he'd summarized in a previous letter. On writing to Zola in mid-January, 1859, two months after he'd posted the poem about Hannibal, Cézanne allows for his friend's delay in responding, saying that perhaps he is occupied with some *immenssime* work, perhaps the lubrication of some vast poem. This would also indicate that lengthy poems they exchanged, such as *Hannibal's Dream*, were not necessarily written on the day they were mailed. The poem follows in my unadorned translation:

Walking out of a banquet in which
rum and brandy had been abused,
Carthage's hero was stumbling and staggering.
Yes, the famous conqueror of Cannes was already
About to fall asleep under the table: O astonishing miracle!
Outrageous debacle of the meal's remains!
For with a great punch of his fist the hero applied
On the tablecloth, the wine gushed out.
The plates, platters, and empty bowls
Rolled tragically in the limpid streams
Of still warm punch, deplorable waste!
Could it be, Sirs, that Hannibal wasted?
Infandum, Infandum, his homeland's rum!

Of the old French soldier, the liquor so cherished!
Could he, Zola, have committed such a horror,
Without Jupin avenging this awful foulness?
Could it be that Hannibal lost his head so completely
That he could forget you totally,
O rum!—Let us move away from such a sad scene!
O punch, you deserved an entirely different tomb!
Why didn't he give you, the fierce conqueror,
An orderly passport to enter his mouth,
And descend directly to his stomach?
He left you lying on the ground, O Brandy!
—And four footmen, irrevocable shame,
Soon take away the victor of Agendum
And lay him on a bed; Orpheus and his poppies
On his heavy eyes let rest come,
He yawns, stretches his arms, and falls asleep on his left side;
Our hero was taking a nap after this debauchery,
When the fantastic swarm of light dreams
Suddenly fell next to his pillow.
So Hannibal was sleeping—The oldest of the troop
Dresses up as Hamilcar, he had the same build—
Spiky hair, projecting nose,
An exceptionally thick mustache;
Add to his cheek a large scar
Making his face look like a shapeless mug,
And you have Sirs, Hamilcar's portrait.
Four large white horses harnessed to his cart
Were pulling him: He arrives and grabs Hannibal by the ear
And strongly shakes him: Hannibal wakes up,
And already angered. But he calms down
Seeing Hamilcar blemishing with
Contained wrath: "Unworthy son, unworthy!
Can't you see what the pure vine juice
Does to you, my son—Blush, dammit, blush
To the roots of your hair. You hang around with no worry,
Instead of waging war, a shameful life.
Instead of protecting your fatherland's borders,
Instead of driving off the relentless Roman,
Instead of gearing up, victor of Tesin,
Trasimene, Cannes, for a battle in the City
That has always been to the Hamilcars the most hostile

And the most biting of all enemies,
That saw all its citizens conquered by Carthage,
O depraved son, you are here partying!
Alas! your new jacket is all stained with sauce,
Good wine from Madeira and rum! It's terrible!
Go, and follow, my son, your ancestors' way.
Keep away that cognac and those lustful women
That hold under the yoke our enslaved souls!
Abjure the liquors. It's very pernicious
And drink only water, you will feel better."
To these words, Hannibal rested his head
On his bed and fell deeply asleep again.

Cézanne then asks Zola, *Have you ever found more admirable style? If you are not impressed, you're not being sensible.*

Evidence for Cézanne feeling guilty, apologizing profusely to Zola, and adding *Yes, I am culpable*, is out of balance with the verdict that Cézanne was guilty over masturbating. I suppose one might fancifully conjure up associations of writing when alone, not conjoined with a real live muse, just playing with oneself, with masturbating. Not sending a letter on time could be associated with not ejaculating, not being forthcoming (in French, to ejaculate is also "to come," as in saying *j'arrive!*). So, if one wished to follow this wispy line of reasoning, out of guilt for not writing Cézanne goes mad, gets drunk, and with an orgasmic shock smashes plates and bowls, as if in his mind he is exploding women's organs. He then ejaculates copiously all over the place, the stream flowing in rivulets across the tablecloth (read *bed sheet*, if you wish)—sort of like Zola's commentary on his garret bedroom after a full week's orgy: *semen all over the place.*[3] (Zola will say also, perhaps during a dirty-joke session, that on occasion when wrestling with a difficult sentence, forcing it to *arrive*, he ejaculates without even having an orgasm).

It would seem that the merchant of onanism was not aware of another poem by Cézanne from six months later (July 1859) in which the debauched character is not Cézanne but Zola. Cézanne is suggesting that Zola had had a strange dream, had been overcome by some young nymph, had gotten drunk (like a Pope's deacon) and fallen asleep under the table:

You who in the past I've seen walking a straight line,
Doing nothing good, saying nothing bad?
In what chaos of strange dreams,
Have you, by chance, seen the Polka being danced
by some young nymph, some actress at the Opera?
Would you not have written, asleep under the table,
After having gotten drunk like one of the Pope's deacons,

Or perhaps, my friend, filled with a rococo sort of love,
The vermouth having hit you on the noggin.[4]

Could the impacted meanings of Cézanne's fanciful *Hannibal's Dream* be intended just to express chagrin over having to apologize to Zola for not writing? It could, indeed. The most relevant lines of the poem expose the motive. The poem is less Hannibal dreaming than of Cézanne talking to Zola: *Could it be that Hannibal lost his head so completely / that he could forget you totally? / Could he, Zola, have committed such a horror?* The "horror" was Cézanne's neglect of their correspondence, and that is what he expresses guilt for, saying *Excuse, excuse me. Yes, I'm guilty.* Then, *for all sins there's forgiveness.*

This would not be the first example of Cézanne's tendency to lay on blow after blow. In another letter, dating two months later, Cézanne does a turnabout and brings hell to bear on Zola for having allowed their correspondence to fall off. In this letter he sketches a frightful scene to punish Zola—an incident from Dante's *Inferno*, which I will presently take up. Referring to that sketch, Cézanne writes: *I am resolved, my dear friend, to terrify your heart, to cast into it an enormous fright by the monstrous aspect of this horrible scene, contrived to rouse the hardest of souls. I thought that your heart, prone to such evils, would cry out: what a marvelous picture you have concocted! I thought that a great cry of horror would exit your chest, on seeing what one can only imagine.*[5]

In the *Dream of Hannibal*, Reff identifies Hamilcar as Cézanne's father (as had Schapiro), while obliged to admit that Cézanne's description of Hamilcar doesn't fit at all—*spiky hair, projecting nose, an exceptionally thick mustache...add to his cheek a large scar, making his face look like a shapeless mug.* To make matters worse, the personage in the poem is not even Hamilcar but a person *dressed up* as Hamilcar (Hamilcar was dead before Hannibal's campaigns had started). In Cézanne's poem, while Hannibal is sleeping, *Le plus vieux de la troupe s'habille en Amilcar, il en avait la coupe*, which translate as *The oldest among the troupe dresses up as Hamilcar, he had the same build.*[6] And Reff's wish to link Cézanne's story with Freud's notions on masturbation, and the *wrongness* of masturbation, with a profound sense of guilt for being caught, leads him to say that Hannibal falls asleep on his left side under the table because "left" symbolizes, according to Freud, wrongness—being wrong, doing wrong. But the line: *Il baile, étend les bras, s'en dort du côte gauche*, was made by Cézanne to rhyme with: *Notre héros pionçait après cette débauche.* Having Hannibal sleep on his right side just would not work with the poem's construction: *gauche* was needed to rhyme with *débauche.* While it is tempting to read complex psychological meanings into these adolescent poems, sometimes the simple explanation based on what the words actually say, such as this rhyming, yields more useful data, bringing one closer to the subject at hand.

11

Death reigns in such places

On the first sheet of a very long letter to Zola on January 17th, 1859, Cézanne sketched a macabre scene with dialogue. At its head, a cartouche reads: *Death reigns in such places*—a paraphrase of the inscription above the gate to Hell through which Dante and Virgil pass on entering the Ninth Circle in the *Inferno* where every coward and traitor must meet death, where sighs and lamentations and loud cries of miserable people who lost the good of the intellect echo across timeless air. In Canto XXXII, the Gate of Hell speaks for itself:

Through me the way into the suffering city,
Through me the way to eternal pain,
Abandon every hope, who enters here.

What follows in Cézanne's rendering is a dialogue between two men at the entrance of a rustic, probably rural, cottage. One man has just pushed open the door with a raised hand while the other points at what they behold. Full-bearded and dressed as Provençal farmers in long coats and high-topped field-worker hats, they are identified in the sketch as Dante and Virgil. Below them are the lines they speak:

Dante: *Tell me, my dear friend, what are*
they nibbling at there?
Virgil: *Good Lord! Yes! It's a skull.*
Dante: *My God! That's appalling! But why are*
they gnawing at that detestable brain?
Virgil: *Listen, and you will know why.*

According to Dante, in the Inferno the Ninth Circle of Hell is reserved for traitors to their homeland or political party. There, Dante and Virgil come upon two traitors—Count Ugolino and Archbishop Ruggieri—who, like all the others suffering damnation, are trapped in an ice field. God had granted Ugolino (who, with his sons, had been condemned to starvation by Archbishop Ruggieri) the privilege to avenge himself by eating Ruggieri's flesh, thus intensifying that traitor's eternal misery.[1] But because he is immobilized, Ugolino can do no more than gnaw at the Archbishop's head. That he *gnaws* at the head, rather than eats it, may explain why Cézanne has Dante deploy the verb *ronger* (to gnaw, or nibble, as rodents do) rather than *manger* (to eat). The dialogue shifts to the characters around the table:

The Father: *Eat heartily this inhuman mortal*
who for so long made us suffer from hunger.
The oldest boy: *Let's eat!*
The youngest boy: *Me, I'm starved, give me this ear!*
The third boy: *For me the nose!*
The smallest boy: F*or me the eyes!*
The oldest boy: *For me the teeth!*
The father: *Hold on! If you eat like that my children,*
what will be left for tomorrow?

The father carves the skull for his four sons—each boy eager to satiate desire by consuming a portion of the head that his father is offering to carve up—just as fathers, as heads of households, carve meat at the table and carve up their estates.[2] He restrains his sons' puerile rush to devour the whole thing in one sitting, advising them to think of the next day's needs—an old moral adage aimed at those who spend money as if there were no tomorrow, at sons who squander their inheritance.

Although Cézanne deploys the word *crâne*, meaning skull, in the first line spoken by Virgil, he deploys *cerveau*, meaning brain, in the second line that Dante speaks. Clearly the object on the table is not defined graphically as a skull but, as in casual French speech, skull, brain, and head are interchangeable in many expressions; skull is favored when referring to the top of the head. For example, in a letter to Zola written a few months later, early in July 1859, Cézanne asks:

Tu me diras peut-être: Ah! mon pauvre Cézanne,
Quel démon féminin a démonté ton crâne?
(You will tell me, perhaps: Ah! my poor Cézanne,
What female demon has scrambled your brain?)[3]

In that passage, Cézanne does employ *crâne*, meaning skull, to rhyme with his name, but he means brain. Skulls are without flesh, they cannot be deranged or scrambled, and they do not have edible ears, eyes, or nose. So, in Cézanne's drawing, Dante would not be asking why those around the table are gnawing at the detestable *cerveau*, meaning not the brain, but the head.

The young man at the left mirrors the father, their postures much the same. Both wear frock coats. They wear the same hairstyle. Apart from the size of their heads, their bodies do not distinguish their ages. Between them, three young boys sit passively; neither one looking at the older brother or their father, who appears to be pushing the platter toward the boy seated across from him, whose hand is stretched out toward it. If that young man is Cézanne, then who are the other three boys?

Cézanne may not have known that only one of Ugolino's so-called sons, the grandson Anselmuccio, was a fifteen-year-old boy. The other three were fully grown men. Yet, in Cézanne's sketch, the three boys at the back of the table appear less than fifteen, while the one across from the father could be Cézanne's age at the time. The father bears not the least resemblance to Louis-Auguste Cézanne. In 1859, he was in his sixties and heavyset, not lean. The father looks more like a schoolteacher than a businessman. The wood plank doors with forged iron hinges, the country-style square-legged table and chairs on a plank floor, establish the setting as rustic, not resembling in the least the bourgeois culture of Cézanne's family.

In his magisterial essay, "The Apples of Cézanne," Schapiro interpreted Cézanne's story as a wish for his father's death so he could inherit wealth and pursue an art career without paternal censure or financial constraint.[4] Schapiro identifies the severed head the sons are about to eat as their father's head:[5]

The original fantasy of the young Cézanne is set in hell like the story of Ugolino. But instead of devouring his children, the bald father is pictured sardonically offering them portions of his own head. One might interpret this image as an unspoken wish for the father's death, which will give the young Cézanne the freedom and means for an independent career. If he addressed this letter to Zola, it was perhaps because Zola was a fatherless boy who could receive with sympathy the play about a grim constraining parent.[6]

Who is this grim constraining parent, identified by Schapiro as bald when he is not? The father in the sketch may be sardonic (how could one tell?), but is he offering his children portions of his own head?

Twelve years earlier than Schapiro's essay, Kurt Badt, in his book *The Art of Cézanne*, also wrote that the picture and the associated dialogue represent a secret wish for his father's death. He offered this description:

Unlike the Ugolino story, the father in Cézanne's sketch is not himself eating but only offering something to his children. In fact, the old banker's opposition [to his son becoming an artist] *did not menace Cézanne himself with starvation, only his spiritual children* [his future paintings]. *The sustenance, which Cézanne needed in order to bring his future children into the world and to maintain them, was money—those few hundred francs of which he spoke in a letter to Zola of 20 June 1859. Had he these, he could live as a painter. The funds could come to him only from his father, but the old man would not give them to him for so long as he lived. If only his father were dead, then he could no longer prevent the son's art from receiving and being nourished by what he bequeathed—by what his head had won through work by his head. Naturally Cézanne did not think it all out with such subtlety; he was following the example of Dante and using the head to symbolize the whole man.[7]*

Cézanne's letter to Zola of June 20th, 1859, to which Badt refers as evidence of this death wish against his father so Cézanne would inherit his money, is a bogus certificate of that meaning. Cézanne was not whining in that letter (written six months *later* than the letter with the Ugolino sketch) about his father's tight purse, but about the passionate crush he had on a girl named Justine, whom he had passed on the street but to whom he had dared not speak. With a few hundred francs in his pocket, he tells Zola, he could live with her contentedly. In that letter, it is Cézanne's bashfulness, not his father meanness, that holds him back— Justine's purse is tighter than Louis-Auguste's. And to Cézanne's debilitating dismay, another boy had anyway laid claim to the maiden:

> *Ah! what dreams I'd built up, and the most foolish ones at that. But you see, it's like this: I had said to myself, if she didn't detest me, we would go to Paris together. There I would make myself into an artist. We would be happy together. I dreamt of pictures, a studio on the fourth floor. I didn't ask in my dream to be rich—you know what I'm like; me, with a few hundred francs I thought we could live contentedly.*[8]

As nicely put by Claude Lévy-Strauss in the introduction to his *Le totémisme aujourd'hui*, Schapiro and Badt's interpretations betray that when one moves off from studying the products of a mind, such as works of art, or even the artist as a mind that produced the products, the investigator's mind plays a large part in interpreting the subject's mind.[9] Both authors overlaid Cézanne with a moving set of associations between Cézanne and his father that are not illustrated by the drawing or dialogue but are grounded in their own social network of 1930s to 1950s psychoanalysis with its heavy pathos of father-son conflict. On promoting Cézanne's drive to be an artist, while basing that drive entirely on the fact that *eventually he became one*, Badt lays down certainties like a soothsayer who knows how the story ends and can aim any origin towards it.

Wanting to say that both the father at the table and the head on the platter are Cézanne's own father, Schapiro says that the seated father is bald, just as the skull on the table is bald. Now, Cézanne's real father had a receding front hairline, but was not entirely bald, and the father depicted in the sketch is not at all bald, but has a crown of hair long enough to be tied by a string-ribbon in the back (to claim that he is wearing a wig will not do). With what evidence, then, did Schapiro state, rather than speculate, that the father is offering portions of his own head to the children? Dante does not document with certainty that Ugolino ate flesh from his dead sons' bodies, thus allowing for the children in Cézanne's sketch to be eating their father's head. He left open the question of whether Ugolino actually ate flesh from the corpses of his dead sons and grandsons, even though the boys, more distraught over their father's suffering than their own, offer him that privilege in repayment for his having given them their flesh. Dante's lines, *Though they were dead, two days I called their names. Then hunger proved more powerful than grief,* implies that Ugolino had partaken of their flesh, but perhaps his grief was cut off by his own death—famine accomplishing what grief could not. Even if Ugolino had resorted to cannibalism, it is improbable that he would stave off his own death by first eating his children's heads. Dante says:

I saw two shades frozen in one hole,
so that one's head served as the other's cap;
and just as he who's hungry chews his bread,
one sinner dug his teeth into the other
right at the place where brain is joined to nape.

It is not the father's head in Cézanne's sketch that the children are eager to consume, but Ruggieri's. And contrary to Schapiro's overlay of father-murder as Cézanne's wishful thinking, the relationship established by Dante between Ugolino and his sons and grandsons, who share the same appalling fate, is tender and loving. William Blake was just one of many artists and poets who interpreted Ugolino as an exemplar of parental affection. At no moment does Dante merit even a glance towards Freud's notion of the first instance of father-murder, the primal horde of sons who kill and eat their father, that motivated Badt, Scapiro and Reff's interpretations.

The story of Ugolino and Ruggieri is part of Italian history and lore that Cézanne and Zola would have encountered in school studies or in casual reading, if for no other reason than that Zola's father was Italian and Aix was connected in many minds with Italy. In the *Inferno*, Ugolino tells his story to Dante and Virgil:

As soon as this sunray had made its way
into that sorry prison, and I saw
reflected in four faces, my own gaze,
out of my grief, I bit at both my hands;
and they, who thought I'd done that out of hunger,
immediately arose and told me: "Father,
it would be far less painful for us if
you ate of us; for you clothed us in this
sad flesh—it is for you to strip it off."
Then I grew calm, to keep them from more sadness;
though that day and the next, we were all silent;
O hard earth, why did you not open up?
But after we had reached the fourth day, Geddo,
throwing himself, outstretched, down at my feet,
implored me: "Father, why do you not help me?"
And there he died; and just as you see me,
I saw the other three fall one by one
between the fifth day and the sixth; at which,

now blind, I started groping over each; and after
they were dead, I called for them for two days:
then hunger proved more powerful than grief.

The Inferno was widely read in over the years when teenage Cézanne and Zola were avid readers. Two French translations of the *Inferno* appeared in the mid-1850s; both circulated widely in France and at times were hotly debated. The literary critic Sainte-Beuve published a disapproving review of the 1854 Mesnard translation in one of his *causeries du lundi* (Monday chats) in the newspaper *Les Temps*. Perhaps inspired by Sainte-Beuve's review, in a long diary entry of August 3rd, 1854, Delacroix took to task an *Indépendance Belge* reviewer's praise of Louis Ratisbone's translation, saying that Ratisbone had flayed the French language and the reader's ears.[10]

Not only had Zola and Cézanne read the *Inferno*, but they knew it well enough to make offhand references to its motifs: in a letter of March 25th, 1860, Zola wrote to Cézanne, *You know the episode in the Divine Comedy: Françoise and her lover Paolo are punished in hell for their sinful luxuriating.*

In Cézanne's sketch, Dante and Virgil, Provençal farmers, are hardly dressed for their rounds through Purgatory and Hell, but perhaps are witnessing a different sort of hell on earth. Surely the sketch is not an original composition by Cézanne out of his imagination but a loose copy from some provincial newspaper or magazine, perhaps a political cartoon dealing with economic problems in Provençal agriculture. Cannibalism is a common metaphor for economic perils and social injustice. The cartoonist would have been invoking Dante's story of Ugolino to illustrate some dire state of affairs. Eating one's own children is psychically linked to destitute farmers eating their seed corn, or slaughtering young calves that should be saved as milkers and breeding stock—concerned about tomorrow but unable to save for it.

Over 1857-1859, prosperity in France reached the peak of the Second Empire boom. Agricultural production had increased on the average by over fifty percent, but not in the area that included Aix, where six years of poor crop yields had put many small-acreage farmers in grave peril. Coded images and stories, and agitation of the populace by caricatures were popular fare at the time (as Cézanne will painfully discover when a few years later he confronts Paris' art critics). Ever since the first publications of *La Caricature* and *Le Charivari* in the early 1830s, in newspapers and magazines throughout the country, caricatures and cartoons of social ills were printed by the thousands.

The story of Ugolino's dreadful fate was well known in France, even before it circulated as translations of Dante's poem. As a simile for government-caused food shortages and farmers' plight, it was on many a tongue as a gruesome allegory of economic injustice, of citizens reduced to bread and water, to eating rats, dogs, cats, and horses after their barnyard fowl and domestic rabbits were gone. In the 1850s, farmers in the Ardèche area just north of Aix were in a dreadful economic state. In 1859, when Cézanne concocted his bizarre drama for Zola, local newspapers, especially those that were anti-Bonaparte, played up the farmer's plight.

So while I cannot offer the newspaper cartoon that I see in my mind, I offer its invisibility as a more tangible explanation for this imagery and text than that Cézanne and whoever else is sitting at the table are about to eat Louis-Auguste's head, as if setting down to a *tête de veau* that fathers, at the head of tables, cut up and serve so that children around the table can call out, "Give me the nose," and so forth. If anything in Cézanne's sketch points to a father dividing his estate, that too can be referred to the economic plight of farmers. The entire southern section of France comprised, by and large, regions of small peasant owner-cultivators on small plots, usually less than two hectares, with larger, but much fewer, spreads controlled by very rich owners. The small farms were the consequence of France's post-Revolution laws on land inheritance meant to distribute farmland to those who actually farmed. The Civil Code prescribed that, on the death of a father, the land must be divided equally among the surviving children. After two or three generations, plots allotted to each child were too small to generate subsistence. So in areas of France other than the great plains of the north and northwest, where communes owned vast acres of pasturage and hay fields, impoverished descendant farmers populated many zones of the nation's agricultural land on non-sustaining plots.

James Gillray. A family of sans-culottes dining. 1792. New York Public Library. It is this sort of cartoon that I suspect Cézanne saw.. *Sans culotte* simply means people without means, at the lowest ebb of poverty, reduced to eating rats and ultimately to cannibalism at the extreme of hunger.

Of books by Dante, the *Inferno* was the most often republished and most widely read. By the mid-point of the nineteenth century no less than ten poetic versions were available in French. Many artists made use of the story. In the 1870s, Auguste Rodin would make several drawings of Ugolino and his sons as studies for their place in his *Gates of Hell*. He said that he had lived a whole year with Dante and become obsessed with the *tenderness* Ugolino had displayed towards his sons, and with the fury of his vengeance against Ruggieri.[11] At the lower left panel of the *Gates*, Ugolino and his dead or dying sons appear, but Ugolino is leaning over them protectively and in anguish, not eating them. Rodin's meaning of the *Gates* fits to his description of Hell as *the martyrdom of all those who are tormented by unrealizable ambitions*—the words befitting the psychology of both Cézanne and Zola at the time of their youthful correspondence, the sort of Hell they were suffering, for which no better description could be offered than the late Rodin scholar, Albert Elsen's interpretation: *Hell is being adrift in an empire of night; born with a fatal duality of desire and an incapacity to fulfill it; damned on both sides of the tomb to an internal Hell of passion.*[12]

Early in the century, the painter Théodore Géricault, in fashioning his Salon entry, *The Raft of the Medusa*, had referred to Ugolino's anguish, knowing that his audience would be triggered to see cannibalism as it had happened on the raft, and which would draw attention to his canvas. The fate of the French sailing ship, the Medusa, and the civilian passengers who'd been abandoned by the crew's commandeering of lifeboats, had been widely featured in the French press. The tragedy was made all the more newsworthy by the fact that, prior to being spotted adrift on the makeshift raft, cannibalism had sustained the few survivors. In the public mind, the sailors had committed treason by abandoning the passengers and deserved the fate reserved for cowards and traitors in the Ninth Circle of Dante's Hell. Géricault depicted Ugolino sitting at the stern of the raft, his demised sons draped over his legs, but their bodies are not even emaciated. Géricault knew that, were he to depict it factually, the imagery would have incited disgust from the public—the level of disgust that Cézanne sought to evoke in Zola's mind when going to great lengths in his letter to make sure that Zola gets the full impact of the drama:

> *I'm resolved, my dear friend, to terrify your heart, to cast into it an enormous fright by the monstrous aspect of this horrible scene, contrived to rouse the hardest of souls. I thought that your heart, prone to such evils, would cry out: what a marvelous picture you have concocted! I thought that a great cry of horror would exit your chest, in seeing what one can only imagine.*

Neither Badt, Schapiro, or Reff accounted for the fifty-six lines of verse by Cézanne that the pictorial stage drama surmounts. And in Rewald's English edition of Cézanne's correspondence, only fourteen of the lines are translated. The missing lines tell more about Cézanne's story than that it references Ugolino, or hides a death wish, or indicates sympathy for fatherless Zola. Cézanne is scolding Zola for neglecting correspondence over an entire fortnight—beating him over the head with a shocking story to get his attention, as he had two months earlier when first apologizing for himself for not writing (when he clobbered Zola with his *Hannibal's Dream*). Now Cézanne offers Zola an array of excuses for his negligence—*for all our sins, forgiveness.* The gesture explains in good part the illustration and dialogue that opens the letter: that boredom may be devouring him, a bad cold may have taken hold of his brain (note the references to devouring and brain), or perhaps that he may have been eating his heart out over some unattainable love, which Cézanne assures him may be lethal in one's mind but at other times a cause of only minor torment and a bit of sorrow. *If it comes today it is gone tomorrow*, he says.

Cézanne's letter goes on with one reference after the other to eating and the suffering it causes, leading all the way to the tomb, the voracious insatiable abyss, to Hell itself, where both the virtuous and the culpable pay due tribute. In this alexandrine one finds references to teeth, to the head, to loss of appetite, to platters of food, to the stomach, to indigestion, to the insatiable abyss, to Hell—all of which must be related to the Ugolino drawing:

If, unfortunately, bad fortune be, it must be said,
If some horrible disease rips you;
However I don't think that malevolent gods
Gave you, for Christ's sake! some terrible toothache
Or some other terribly silly ache
To suffer, for example, a long headache
That from head to toe would take its torment,
That would make you curse terribly to the heavens
It would be stupid—to be sick is,
Whatever, the sickness, extremely boring.
One loses appetite, one doesn't eat.
A thousand dishes would be presented in vain,
All sweet and very attractive; our stomach refuses
The sweetest, the best prepared, the sweetest
Sauce of all: Good wine—for I love it—it is true
That at Baille's, it went to his head
And I make excuses for it: how wine is a good thing!
Of most various aches it can cure the cause.
Drink some, dear friend, drink some, for it is good,
And soon it will cure your ache.
For wine is really good: 'bis ter'.
Did you, by chance, eat too much candy

On New Year's Day? Why Not? For too much
Would have condemned you to keep your mouth shut,
By giving you, alas! indigestion,
And it's enough, by Jove, to indulge with pride
Into silliness: for life cuts, restlessly,
Our life, and our days go by. The tomb,
This voracious and insatiable terrible gap
Is always here, open—Virginity lost, virgin
When our day comes, virtuous or guilty
We will pay our dues to inevitable fate.

Cézanne. Sketches on a sheet of notes concerning the role of bailiffs. «How is this fine to be proportioned? Only the galleys entailed no fine. The fine was to reimburse the trial costs. The penalty of a fine is essetially divisable. 2ndly restorable. If an innocent man has been condemned, his money can be refunded. Equitable and appreciable, that is, it can be proportioned according to the income of the delinquent. How is this fine to be proportioned...»

12

*And if that devil of a Cézanne
would come, we might take a small
room and lead a bohemian life*

In November 1858, just short of age twenty, Cézanne passed his first law examinations at Aix's *Faculté de Droit*. Considering the academic status of this law school, he must have studied diligently. And it might be assumed that he had found satisfaction in the school: new experiences, fresh acquaintances, and subjects of at least some interest. Much has been made of a sheet of notes from a classroom lecture *au sujet des huissiers* (on the subject of bailiffs) on which Cézanne had sketched several heads. It is said that this proves Cézanne was bored with law and thought only of being an artist.[1] But drawing while listening to a lecture, or pausing to sketch while reading a brain-fatiguing textbook, is hardly a symptom of alternative career yearnings. One year later, in Paris, while painting a portrait of Zola, Cézanne carried on for hours with a lecture on economics. Would this have meant that he was bored with art and yearned to be an economist?

Over the months of law school, Cézanne surely had a few altercations with his father over choice of career. Perhaps a protracted battle of wills kept the decision at bay, but at some time or another paternal acquiescence set up the chance for him to go to Paris. Whether the purpose of this first trip was to visit or to study one cannot know for sure. At any rate, the journey was planned for March 1860. It would seem that Zola was either misinformed, kept in the dark about it, or a preoccupied Cézanne was vacillating over the thought of giving up home comforts. In a letter to Cézanne on March 3rd, an exasperated Zola writes:

I don't know why, but I feel a strong foreboding about your trip, at least with regard to the date of your more or less imminent arrival. To have you with me, to chat with you of old—a pipe between our teeth and a glass of wine in our hands—seems to me so wonderful and at the same time so unlikely that there are moments when I ask whether I'm not deceiving myself and whether this lovely dream can really come true. I don't know from which side it will break, but I feel that a thunderstorm is forming over my head.

Zola goes on to remind Cézanne that for over two years he had battled to reach the point where he was now. But Cézanne was not battling to come to Paris or become an artist against his father's wishes. He had been struggling to complete secondary school, pass his baccalaureate exams, cope emotionally with crushes on girls, and feeling pressed to think seriously about what he wanted to be when he grew up. The battle to which Zola refers was not Cézanne's but Zola's—his tribulations in adjusting to Paris were ameliorated by skirmishing to get Cézanne and Baille to Paris where they could restore the blissful union of the Aixois triumvirate. Even over the following year, Cézanne showed neither interest in becoming a professional artist nor a great desire to join Zola—at times he may have, but those times may have been when depressed, when things weren't going well and Paris offered an escape. At Aix he enjoyed a comfortable home life in contrast to Zola's plight, told as anguished tales of poverty, grief, and inability to get down to work. Though from time to time Cézanne complains about law school, or about his family, much of that woe is quintessential adolescent-to-adolescent bewailing and griping, as in letters from college students to friends back home complaining of stupid professors and eleven o'clock dormitory lock-outs, or from green soldiers at camp, grumbling about food, hoodlum sergeants, and idiots in their barracks. Zola rails against Cézanne's apathy, laziness, and inability to make a decision; not for a minute can he accept that Cézanne may be lukewarm about the trip. The lonely and demanding Zola needs Baille, too, to restore the Trinity. On December 29th, 1859, he writes to Baille: *You promised to come to Paris next year, and I count on you. I could see you at least twice a week, and that would distract me a little. And if that devil of a Cézanne would come, we might take a small room and lead a Bohemian life. So we would then at least spend our youth in the right way, while now we are going sour, one like the other.*

In his March 3rd, 1860 letter to Cézanne, Zola speaks of what perhaps he had heard from Cézanne:

There is now this fellow Gibert who is trying to divine your intentions, and is advising you to stay in Aix; as a teacher he obviously does not want to lose a student. At the same time, your father talks about making inquiries and consulting, of all people, this same Gibert. Their conference, which bodes ill for you, would inevitably result in delaying your journey until August. All this makes me tremble, and I fear the arrival of a letter from you notifying me, with many lamentations, of a change in date for your trip. I've become so used to looking at the last week of March on my calendar as the sure end of my boredom, that it would be most painful to find myself still alone—the stock of patience which I've laid in will last only 'til then.

Joseph Gibert, an ordinary portrait painter but dedicated drawing master, was also the museum director. Cézanne's father may have been seeking the art

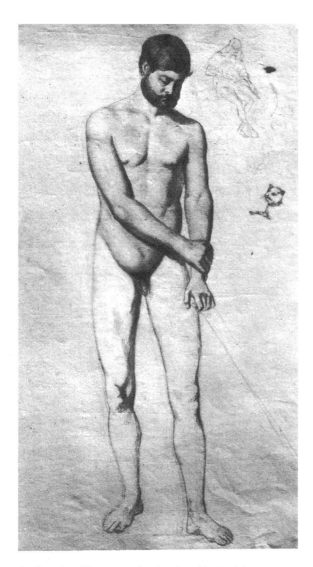

Attributed to Cézanne. A drawing found in the joint reserve of the Musée Grant and the Ecole des Beaux-Arts in Aix-en-Provence, sign and dated 1862 on the verso. Present where-abouts not known.

Joseph Gibert

teacher's opinion on his son's chances of being a serious artist were he to go to Paris, perhaps also asking about admission requirements to the *École des Beaux-Arts*. One gathers from Zola's letter that Gibert's advice was negative. Most likely he hadn't found enough talent in Cézanne's efforts to assure Louis-Auguste that a career in art was a bet to put much money on. With historical hindsight, it is easy to say that Gibert was terribly wrong, but, at the time, given what he had to go on, he'd sized up Cézanne through honest eyes, as had Louis-Auguste.

What art Cézanne had produced when a pupil of Gilbert's remains, to my mind, unknown. Little can be said about Cézanne the artist during the school years he shared with Zola, for it is not at all certain that drawings and paintings attributed to him are, in fact, by him. Art merchants, especially Ambroise Vollard, made a market of misattributions picked up at Aix after Cézanne's death, misleading Cézanne's biographers and historians.

Life drawing classes (male models onl) were held at this tuition-free school early mornings and evenings to accommodate *lycée* students and also *amateurs* who had daytime jobs. Students were also encouraged to copy plaster casts and paintings housed in the Musée d'Aix (now called the Musée Granet) of which the drawing school was a part.

No school drawings by Zola have survived, and those attributed to Cézanne must be interrogated as to authenticity. A few drawings found in the depository of the municipal drawing school are signed "Cézanne," which makes the attributions even more questionable. Drawings had no signatory value in the 1860s, and art students turning out one *académie* after another in teaching studios were not in the habit of recording art history, such as dating a studio assignments by the year when turned out in an hour or less. Surely an interested hand added the signatures and dates.

While living with his parents at the Jas de Bouffan, Cézanne was allowed to decorate the old mansion's salon. It is said that he executed a paravent for his father's study, a folding screen of large dimensions, eight feet high by thirteen feet wide. The subject matter is best described as a pastiche of eighteenth-century French tapestry designs depicting pastoral life.[2] Screens of this type were popular in Aix as interior décor, typically made in arts and craft studios and for sale in interior decoration shops. With considerable detail and elaborate decoration all around its borders and over the entire backside, this screen has all the characteristics of artisan art, which depended on technical skill and no originality, something that advanced art students might make would make to supplement their income (Cézanne and Zola's school friend, Philippe Solari, who would become a sculptor, always struggling to make ends meet, is known to have made such screens).

In addition to the occasional live male model, students at the drawing school copied plaster casts of sculpture. Atelier Cézanne, Aix-en-Provence.

Georges Rivière, an early Cézanne biographer, reported that this paravent was executed with Zola's help. That, too, sounds like a biographical fabrication. All we know is that the screen may have been seen by Rivière at the Jas de Bouffan prior to the manor being sold in 1899, and that it showed up at Cézanne's studio at Les Lauves some time after the studio was built in 1902. The painter Émile Bernard reported that when he visited

Paravent (folding screen) attributed to Cézanne. 8 ft. 2 in. x 13 ft. 2 in. Over its market history variably titled, at one time *Feuillage et scènes champêtre*, at another *Fête à Aix-en-Provence*. At best, a pastiche of typical interior décor based on 18th-century Rococo motifs that were popular at the time and available in home decorator shops. This piece has been heavily restored, with much of it repainted.

Cézanne in the spring of 1904, he saw what he described simply as *un paravent très ancien*. He does not say that Cézanne had painted it.[3]

At some time over 1960-61, four panels allegorically depicting the four seasons were painted on the walls of the Jas de Bouffan salon. The imagery is entirely different from that of the paravent. Most likely Cézanne had a hand in the project but surely it was a group effort. Rivière said that Cézanne's sisters posed for the women depicted in the panels, which is unlikely. Marie was nineteen at the time and Rose was ten; neither had bodies that resemble the women in the panels. Whoever drew the figures in the *spring* and *autumn* panels had a practiced hand for rendering mannered figures in a provincial style of decorative painting that would not have required a model. A likely suspect is the more mature painter among Cézanne's art-school friends, Achille Emperaire, who was nine years older than Cézanne and a rather skilled draftsman. Of the many pictures painted directly on the wall of the salon at the Jas was a painting that Léonce Bénédite, curator of the Luxembourg Museum in Paris, described as the portrait of *an Aixois painter of Aix, a sick little dwarf, named Emperaire*.

The signature "Ingres" appears at the lower right of each panel. The date "1811" is at the lower left of the panel designated by its subject matter as *winter*. The date is a spoof. In the Musée Granet hung a painting by Ingres that the

Aixois community must have treasured—a *Jupiter and Thetis* dated 1811. Rewald's belief that Cézanne signed the panels "Ingres" to advise his father in a mocking way that he, himself, was not inferior to the most famous artist of the age is entirely whimsical. Surely Cézanne, Zola, and their friends, as well as Cézanne's parents had found the attribution very amusing. Gowing's suggestion that the stylistic difference between the awkwardly drawn *Summer* and *Winter* panels and the more

The salon of the Jas de Bouffan. Photograph said to have been taken in 1900. I doubt that. The furniture arrangement, angle of focus, and lighting indicates a professional photographer. I suggest that the photograph was taken after the date when Cézanne's early work came to have market value.

sophisticated *Spring* and *Autumn* panels can be explained by the panels having been painted at different times, the first two when Cézanne's hand was less developed, is not acceptable either. Nothing supports the contention that Cézanne underwent a development over 1860 through 1862. Were one to claim that both the paravent and these panels are by Cézanne's hand, surely one would suffer trying to find any developmental sequence from one to the other.

In a letter from Zola in Paris to Cézanne of June 13th, 1860, Zola tells of an event, half-true, half-fantasy, I'm sure:

The other day, on a beautiful morning, I lost my way in the fields far from Paris. After walking around for two long hours, I had a great appetite. I looked up; everywhere about me were trees, cornfields, and hedgerows. I was in an area completely unknown to me. Finally, beyond an old oak tree, I spied a church tower, which indicates a village, and where there's a village, there's an inn. I walked towards it and soon was installed before a frugal meal in an indifferent café—and that is what I wanted to come to. On entering, I noticed some paintings, which greatly impressed me. They were big panels such as you want to do at home, painted on canvas, representing village fêtes.

The theme of the panels decorating the Jas' salon turned out to be not festivals but personifications of the seasons. Cézanne must have had different thoughts in mind at different times. And in this context, one should realize how convenient it was for Cézanne to remain in Aix in a comfortable home, with a mother and sisters to look after his domestic needs, a neat and cozy niche set in a countryside he loved, and friends who supported his art, however amateurish it was in truth. He had a painting studio in the house and a supporting father, who

Spring

Summer

Autumn

Winter

not only posed for him but allowed his portrait to be painted as the feature panel in the salon. Cézanne may have countered Zola's coaxing that he come to Paris, saying he could work better in Aix. Zola had written:

You pose a strange question. Obviously, you can work here as well as anywhere else if you are seriously determined. Moreover, Paris offers an advantage you could find nowhere else: the museums, where from 11 o'clock in the morning until 4 in the afternoon, you can study the old masters. You could organize your time in the following way: from 6 in the morning until 11 o'clock you could paint from a living model in an art school studio, then take your lunch and from 12 until 4 in the afternoon you could copy a masterwork which attracts you, either in the Louvre or in the Luxembourg [the Musée du Luxembourg, which no longer exists, where works by living artists were installed]. *That would mean nine working hours.*

I believe this is sufficient, and with such a program you can't fail to make progress. You see, the whole evening would remain free and we could use it as we like without doing harm to our studies. And on Sundays, we could make excursions and go somewhere into the environs of Paris. There are charming places, and if you feel like it, you can sketch the trees under which we would have had breakfast. I dream every day about the most wonderful things I want to do when you're here. We are no longer children and have to think of the future. Let us work, work: that is the only way to reach our goal.

Perhaps Cézanne had exaggerated his father's resistance as a way of covering for his hesitation about becoming an artist. Blaming one's father, teachers, society, the weather—it is easy to redirect effects to alternative causes. Perhaps Cézanne had convinced Zola that law studies would make it possible for him to earn income to support himslf as an artist. Perhaps Cézanne and his father had arrived at an agreement. In his letter of March 3rd, 1860, wherein the possibility of Cézanne coming to Paris is implied, it would seem that a monthly stipend of 125 francs had been discussed. Told of this allowance that would deprive Cézanne of his last excuse for not coming to Paris, Zola dangles lure upon lure before Cézanne's indecisive mind, and even proposes a budget:

It is, of course, true that 125 francs a month will not allow you much luxury. I will give you an idea of what you will have to spend: a room for 20 francs a month, lunch 18 sous and supper 22 sous, which makes 2 francs a day or 60 francs a month; with the 20 francs for your room, that comes to 80 francs a month. Then you have to pay for art school. The Suisse one of the cheapest, costing, I believe, 10 francs. In addition I count 10 francs for canvas, brushes and paints. Together that comes to 100 francs. There remain 25 francs for laundry, light, the thousand little expenses that occur, tobacco and similar minor amusements.

As you see, you can just about manage, and I can assure you that I do not exaggerate, rather put everything too low. But that will be a good education for you. You will learn the value of money, and at the same time find out that a resourceful man can always extri-

cate himself. So as not to discourage you, I repeat saying that you will be able to manage.

I advise you to submit this budget to your father. Perhaps the sad frugality of these figures will induce him to open his purse a bit more widely. On the other hand, you can make a little money on the side here. Studies made in the art schools, and copies made in the Louvre, are quite salable. Even if you make only one sale per month, that would pleasantly augment the money available for minor amusements. It means simply that you will have to find a dealer, which is just a question of looking for one. Come to Paris without worrying. As soon as food and drink are secured, one can devote oneself to the arts without danger. I count on you to notify me the day before your departure, of the date and hour you will arrive. I will meet you at the station and conduct you, in my learned company, to lunch. Before then I will write again. I've heard from Baille. Should you see him before your departure, please ask him to promise that he will join us in September.

Zola had every reason to fear that Cézanne would find some reason not to make the trip. His friend seemed at times profoundly discouraged, even before making the effort. Zola would try in letter after letter to assuage Cézanne's doubts. In his letter of April 16th, 1860, in which he says, *You sent me some verses which breathe a somber sadness,* he implores Cézanne to lean on him when depressed: *When you are feeling sad, darken my sky without fear; at times a tear can be sweeter than a smile.* And he points to yet another phrase in a letter from Cézanne that upset him:

Another phrase in your letter has also touched me painfully. It is this: "Painting, which I love, even though I do not succeed, etc." You! Not succeed! You are deluding yourself. I have already told you: there are two men inside the artist, the poet and the workman. One is born a poet, one becomes a craftsman, and you, who have the spark, who possesses what cannot be acquired, you complain when, in order to succeed, you complain when to become a craftsman you have only to train your fingers.

I will not leave this subject without mentioning two more things. I have warned you against realism. Today I want to alert you to another peril: commercial art. The realists still make art in their fashion. They work conscientiously. But the commercials, those businessmen who paint in the morning for their bread in the evening, they crawl along in misery.

I say this not without good reason: you now work at X's studio [this could be Villevieille], *you copy his pictures, perhaps you admire him. I fear for you along this path you are taking, all the more since the one you are perhaps trying to imitate has great qualities but makes poor use of them, which nonetheless makes his pictures appear better than they really are. They are pretty, fresh, well brushed on, but all that is gained from tricks of the trade, and you would be wrong to stop there.*

Art is much more sublime; it is not satisfied with the folds of a fabric, or with the rosy hue of a virgin. Look at Rembrandt. Through a ray of light all his figures, even the ugliest ones, become poetic. Also, I repeat, X is a good master to teach craft, but I doubt if you can learn anything else from his pictures.

As you are financially well off, you no doubt dream of making art and not a busi-ness of it. If I were to advise Chaillon, I would tell him just the opposite of what I am telling you. Beware, therefore, of an exaggerated admiration for your compatriot. Put your dreams, those lovely golden dreams, on your canvas, and try to transfer to the canvas the ideal love you carry inside you. Most of all—and this is the pitfall—do not admire a pic-ture because it has been painted quickly. In one word, do not admire, and do not imitate a businessman artist. I will come back to this subject later. I am offending against some of your ideas. Tell me frankly if I am, so as not to keep hidden any grudge against me, allow-ing it to increase daily.

That Zola would offer their mutual friend Chaillon the opposite advice—that he aims to be a commercial artist—is cause to quote here a passage from another letter to Cézanne. Chaillon was not up to Zola's evolving standards regarding what constitutes a true artist:

Chaillon stopped by last Sunday and spent the entire day with me. We had lunch and din-ner together, speaking of you, smoking our pipes. He is an excellent fellow, but what sim-plicity, good Lord! What ignorance of the world! It seems unlikely to me that he will suc-ceed. He will never be unhappy however, and this is what consoles me in seeing him day-dream this way. His character is no longer young; I suspect him even of being a bit stingy. With both of these faults, which in this case are qualities, he cannot die of hunger, nor become too bitter. He will always retire in time to his village, or content himself with pro-ducing mediocre portraits, which he will sell for as much as possible.

He told me he's staying in a house where twelve young girls are lodging. This bothers him, because they make enough noise, he says, to bring down the walls. So he is going to change his lodgings—the innocent one!

He goes to the Suisse every morning from 6 to 11. In the afternoon he goes to the Louvre. He's a cheeky one! Oh, if only you were here, what a beautiful life we would have!

Zola's letter was well meant but also self-serving. He needed Cézanne. His destitute living conditions and constant anxiety were holding him back; he was becoming increasingly dependent on Cézanne's negotiations with his father. Zola was a struggling poet, but poetry was not his innate talent, rather a state of emo-tion he would later blame on both his youth and Aix, so lethargic a town that one could only dream while there (in his mind Aix was, of course, infused with his youth, for he had experienced no adult life there). He was angry with himself. His entreaties aimed at Cézanne are pompous and overbearing, and the steady stream of paternalistic advice laid on his friend would soon take some polish off their relationship.

By mid-March 1860, Cézanne would have completed the first year of law school. As departure day for Paris drew near, he informed Zola that his little sis-ter Rose was ill; the misfortune would delay his leaving until the first days of

April. But for some unknown reason, by March 25th the trip had been called off. Zola would have to be content with his own visit to Aix, come August, when he would take the customary vacation. He was doubly annoyed by this turn of events, having allowed himself to believe that, unless Cézanne was again at his side, he would produce nothing but stupid poems and false starts at dramas and short stories. In several letters over the next few weeks, Zola will unload his wretchedness on Cézanne's shoulders, while taking him to task for not showing enough confidence in himself.

13

You write that you are very sad
I reply that I am very sad

Zola had in fact become as unrequited a poet as he was a lover, having found it impossible to separate poetry from his amorous cravings. He oscillated between fantasies of finding himself glorified in the literary pantheon alongside Michelet and of finding a woman of ideal virginity, free of cant and pretense, with a chaste soul yet of complete freedom and action, some rare exception to justify her status as unattainable: a virgin essence, like perfume confined by a protective seal that keeps it pure. He cannot find this girl in reality, nor can he write poetry in reality. His sexual encounters would fall in frequency and substance somewhere between self-absorbing masturbation, which is both psycho-biologically transitional to sex with the external world, and fanciful bragging, which is analogous to copious ejaculations. If from time to time in the Latin Quarter he touched a girl less ideal than his dream, it was no different than when from time to time he touched pen to paper. When Zola fashions his first stories and first novel, he plants nauseatingly sentimental innocence and bestial carnality in the same pot—his psyche absorbing the world yet trying to force reality onto it, a pupae struggling to break out of its chrysalis.

On January 14th, 1859, in a letter to Baille, Zola scolded Cézanne for refusing to acknowledge the primacy of pure poetic love in defiance of conventional and practical love to perpetuate family names and properties. He had written then: *We boast about our conquests with as much egoism as we can summon, and blacken ourselves to see who can go one better.* Zola was referring, of course, to the tales of conquest and misbehavior with which boys compete: rushing to confess that they do not love but rummage in the filth of vice.

In this respect, Zola was hardly different from other young men, including Cézanne, who are prone to fabricate sexual conquests when finding themselves in competition with other men. Edmond de Goncourt, in his journal, records bouts of self-revelation among literary confreres, trading confidences with the zeal, recklessness, and braggadocio of adolescents wishing to win approval, score points, or simply talk dirty.[1]

Zola quotes the nihilist writer Ivan Turgenev, a Russian in exile who will befriend Zola in the 1870s: *Do you know that cemetery, Flaubert? I can't remember ever having felt more horny...The woman laid down on a large tomb and lifted her dress and petticoats so that her buttocks touched the stone...I swooped in on her, and in my haste and awkwardness got my rod caught in gravely tufts of grass, from which I had to extricate it.*[2] Edmond de Goncourt noted in his journal that at one of these sessions Zola had said that at the start of his career when toiling with a difficult sentence he would sometimes have an ejaculation without an erection, as if working up the sentence was copulation. He also made note of Zola saying that in his student days he would sometimes spend a whole week in bed with a woman, never getting out of his nightshirt. *The room reeked of sperm*, Zola bragged. And Goncourt adds: *After these orgies, Zola's feet felt like cotton, and in the street he'd grab shutter latches for support.*[3]

Zola at the age of eighteen. Photo: Musée Zola, Médan.

In time, Zola will be able to abandon such fish and pussy stories to embrace lust artistically as a contrast of romanticism with realism. He had conceptualized the essential polarity early on, but it will be two or three years before he comes to terms with the woeful eclecticism of poetic mind painting. The conversion will come along when he also gives up eclectic love, that is, of a dream-girl without artifice, nonetheless made of poetry. He had a crush on a girl depicted by Greuze, a wistful, meditative young girl of the type who reflects the imprint of most every man's desire at some stage. This girl would remain Zola's fantasy in different forms and identities, always elusive, beyond his reach, like nymphs that when grasped for turn into zephyrs and aromas, pond mist, or wispy clouds. Cézanne, too, will find his loves evasive until, in time, he will settle for the solid earthly form of a flesh and blood woman, Hortense Fiquet. In a letter of June 20th, 1859 Cézanne told Zola of yet another failed love:

My dear, yes my dear, it is all too true. I had a fluttering love for a certain Justine, but she always turned away from me. When I cast my peepers towards her, she dropped her eyes and blushed. Now I find that when we approach on the street, she makes a half turn and dodges away without looking back.

One fine day, a young man accosted me—a first-year law student, like myself; it was,

Jean-Honoré Greuze. *La cruche cassée (The Broken Pitcher).* Paris, Musée du Louvre. This was the girl on whom Zola had a crush. Certainly he was one of many boys and men for whom Greuze offered the loveliest of young virgins. Her broken crock intimates her loss of virginity, the hymen broken. Flowers gathered in her skirt bring the viewer back to Prosepina abducted by Pluto while she is gathering flowers. The plucked flower denotes defloration.

William Bouguereau, *La cruche cassée* (The Broken Pitcher). M. H. de Young Memorial Museum, San Francisco. The type of art imagery and type of girl—innocent and impressionable—that Cézanne and Zola, at this point in their lives, fantasized about.

in fact, Seymard, whom you know. "My dear," he said, taking my hand, hanging onto my arm, and continuing towards the rue d'Italie: "I am about to show you a sweet little thing that I love and who loves me."

I confess that suddenly a cloud seemed to pass before my eyes. I had, as it were, a pre-monition that I didn't have a chance, and I was not mistaken, for, midday having just struck, Justine emerged from the salon where she works, and upon my word, the moment I caught sight of her in the distance, Seymard gave me a sign, "There she is," he said. At this point I saw nothing more, my head was spinning, but Seymard dragged me along with him; I brushed against the sweet one's frock.

Ah! what dreams I'd built up, and the most foolish ones at that. But you see, it's like this: I had said to myself, if she didn't detest me, we would go to Paris together. There I would make myself into an artist. We would be happy together. I dreamt of pictures, a studio on the fourth floor. I didn't ask in my dream to be rich—you know what I'm like; me, with a few hundred francs I thought we could live contentedly, but by God, that was a great dream, and now I, who am so lazy, am content only when I have had something to drink. I can scarcely go on. I am an inert body, good for nothing.

My word, old man, your cigars are excellent. I'm smoking one while writing to you. They have the taste of caramel and barley sugar. Ah! but look, look, there she is, she, how she glides, she sways, yes, it is my little one, how she laughs at me, she floats on the clouds of the smoke, see, see; she rises, she falls, she frolics, twirls around, but she is laughing at me. Oh, Justine, tell me at least that you do not hate me. She laughs. Cruel one, you enjoy making me suffer. Justine, listen to me, but she is fading away, she climbs, climbs, climbs until at last she vanishes. The cigar falls from my mouth, and thereupon I fall asleep. For a moment I thought I was going mad, but thanks to your cigar, my mind is recovering. Another ten days and I will think of her no longer, or else I will see on the horizon of the past, only a shadow of what I'd dreamed.4

Cézanne concluded this letter with expressions of joy that Zola was coming to Aix for a visit. But it was not until September 1859 that Zola could make the trip. He was preparing for his baccalaureate exams. Reality would hit hard if he failed. He, too, was a dreamer. The exchange of dreams with Cézanne was, in a positive sense, the only way to make their dreams concrete. Through communication, as in writing or painting, Cézanne and Zola's dreams took on an aspect of reality with potential for justifying what reality was imposing upon them.

On the 25th of March 1860, Zola writes to Cézanne:

My dear friend,

We speak often of poetry in our letters, but the words sculpture and painting come up rarely, if not never. Such a grave omission, verging on a crime. Today I will try to repair that situation.

What follows in Zola's letter is bedrock for an understanding of his notions about art at this point, for they will change, as will Cézanne's. Neither had much to go on. Their experience with art had been confined to studies under a mediocre academician in a school set up for amateurs. Interesting psychologically, though perhaps just coincidental, is that in Zola's attempt to repair the hole in their correspondence—the absence of talk about art—proceeds to his describing Jean Goujon's *La fontaine des Nymphes* (fountain of nymphs) on *Rue François I*^{re} in Paris, which was undergoing repair at the time. He tells Cézanne that the nymphs in bas-reliefs on the fountain's face—charming, gracious, and smiling goddesses—brighten his moods when he feels bored and anxious. *You know the type, those nymphs of Jean Goujon*, Zola says. *You should be able to recall the two bathers I drew so badly one day at Villevieille's* (Joseph-François Villevieille, an Aixois painter ten years older than Cézanne, who from time to time helped Cézanne and Zola with their drawings). Zola continues: *Also, above the fountain's arches are little amours, just as graceful, just as charming; from up there the water falls from basin to basin. I often detour to pass by this fountain to contemplate it and throw it a glance of love.*

But as often occurs in Zola's and Cézanne's letters, talk of soft love becomes uncomfortable and soon shifts to its opposite. In the next paragraph, the tenderness of Zola's words about this fountain transpose to an altogether different emotion: *The other day, while strolling along the Seine, I discovered some very risqué etchings by Rembrandt. As Rabelais said, "I saw behind I know not what bush, I know not what people, doing I know not what, and, I know not how,* [not translatable: *aiguisant je ne sais quels ferrements*], *which they had I know not where, and I don't know how."*[5] *The extremes touched each other; right alongside were hung etchings of works by Ary Scheffer: Françoise de Rimini, la Béatrice de Dante, and so on.*

This leads Zola into a discussion of Ary Scheffer, a history and genre painter whose work spanned the first half of the nineteenth century and was widely known through a proliferation of popular engravings, his imagery a favorite of the bourgeoisie. *I don't know if you are familiar with this genius that died last year. Well, in Paris it would be a crime to say no, but in the provinces it would be only a gross error.* With such finesse, Zola is letting Cézanne know that, by staying the Aix, he will be an unrefined person, a provincial:

> *Scheffer was a passionate lover of the ideal; all his types are pure, aeriel, nearly diaphanous. He was a poet in the best sense of the word, his subjects the most sublime, the most delirious. You will see nothing more poetic, a poetry strange and heartrending, than his Françoise de Rimini. You know the episode in the Divine Comedy: Françoise and her lover Paolo are punished in hell for their sinful luxuriating on earth by a terrible wind which suspends them and makes them turn round and round in somber space. What a magnificent subject! How to render this supreme embrace, these two souls who stay united even while suffering eternal pain.*

Having thus laid out his feeling about great art as great poetry, allowing for his and Cézanne's unity—both to be poets, though one a painter—Zola turns to the subject of realism as opposed to poetry. He is struggling with Cézanne's attitude, which may be resisting the poetic. Zola defines realism by example, locating it where it resides in most minds: on the level of dirt and manure, a farm; the farmer as the realistic base upon which all society rises in levels of sophistication and artifice. *Scheffer the spiritualist*, Zola says, *makes me think of the realists. I have never understood those types.*

Take the most realistic subject in the world: a farm courtyard. Manure, ducks paddling about in a stream, etc., etc. Now that's a picture entirely devoid of poetry. But only if a ray of sunlight scintillates the yellow hay, mirrors light on ripples of water, shimmers on tree leaves...then, if one puts in the background a light and nimble girl, one of those peasant maidens of Greuze, tossing grain to a flock of chickens—at that moment, the picture will have poetry.

Still a near hopeless juvenile romantic, Zola lays into Cézanne for lack of interest in the pure emotion of poetry, as earlier he'd attacked him for his reluctance to agree that love must be as pure as poetry:

What do you mean by this word "realism"? You boast that you only paint subjects devoid of poetry! But everything has its own poetry, the dung heap as well as the flower. Is that because you claim to imitate nature slavishly? But, in that you carp so much at poetry, that is to say, that nature is prosaic, you have lied. It is for your sake that I say this, monsieur, my friend, monsieur the great future painter. It's to tell you that Art is one, that spirituality and realism are nothing but words, that poetry is something magnificent, that outside poetry there is no salvation.

At this stage of awareness about modern art, Zola would not yet have read Baudelaire's 1846 critique of Scheffer: *On Ary Scheffer and Sentimental Monkeys.*

After imitating Delacroix, after aping the colorists and draftsman of the French school, and the neo-Christian school, it dawned upon Mr. Ary Scheffer—a little late, no doubt— that he was not born a painter. From that moment of enlightenment he was obliged to turn to other shifts, and he decided to ask help and protection from poetry.

It was a ridiculous blunder. Poetry is not the immediate aim of the painter. To make a point of looking for poetry in the conception of a picture is the surest way of not finding it. Formerly, Mr. Ary Scheffer enjoyed the public's favor; in his poetical pictures, people rediscovered their dearest memories of the great poets. But his kind of painting is so wretched, so dismal, so blurred, and so muddy that his pictures look as if they'd been left out in a heavy rainstorm.6

Zola's letter to Cézanne of March 25th, 1860 continues:

I had a dream the other day that I had written a beautiful book, a magnificent book, for which you'd done magnificent illustrations. Our two names together in gold letters on the title page, and, in this brotherhood of genius, we went arm in arm to posterity. Unfortunately, this is still only a dream.

The moral of these four pages is that you must satisfy your father by carrying on with your law studies as seriously as you can. But you must also work at your drawings, steadfast and determined—unguibus et rostro [tooth and nail]—*in order to become a Jean Goujon or an Ary Scheffer, not a realist, so you will be able illustrate that special book which struts around in my head.*

As for the excuses you make for the engravings you sent me, or the doldrums you say your letters must cause me, I venture to say your self-criticism is in the worst possible taste. You, yourself, do not believe what you allege—that is, that your letters are too long and too detailed. I always await them impatiently; they fill me with pleasure for a whole day. Therefore, please, no more excuses for not writing. I would rather do without smoking and drinking than give up my correspondence with you.

Then you write that you are very sad. I reply that I am very sad, very sad. It is the wind of the century passing over our heads. We cannot hold anyone responsible for that, not even ourselves. It's the fault of the times in which we live. You add that, even if I have, in fact, understood you, you do not understand yourself. I don't know what you mean by the expression "understand." As far as I'm concerned, I see things this way: I discovered in you a great goodness of heart and a great imagination, the two cardinal virtues, before which I bow my head. And that is enough! From that moment on, I understood you. I've judged you. Whatever your weaknesses, whatever your errors, you will always remain the same person in my eyes. What do your contradictions matter to me? I judged you a good man and a poet, and will always repeat: "I have understood you." So away with sadness! Let us end with an outburst of laughter. In August we will drink, we will smoke, we will sing.

Ary Sheffer. *St. Augustine and St. Monica* (replica). Paris, Musée du Louvre.

Both boys were tussling with *choice*: if one way right, the other way wrong. Contradictions in behavior are a common symptom of indecision, an inability to make a commitment, to grow up, to give one's life determination. Hercules at the crossroads is on their minds, irresolution their predicament. Six months later, on August 1st, 1860, Zola wrote to Cézanne, having come upon his poem about Hercules torn between virtue and vice. After having re-read Cézanne's verses, Zola asks himself:

> *What does he lack, this good and courageous Cézanne, to be a great poet? purity. He has ideas; his form is vigorous, original, but what spoils his poetry—what always spoils it— are the provincialisms, the barbarianisms, etc.*
>
> *Yes, my old buddy, who is more of a poet than I am. My verses are perhaps purer than yours, but certainly yours are more poetic, more real. You write with your heart, me, with my spirit. You think with confidence about what you write, while for me it is just a game of brilliant lies. Do not think for a minute that I am pleased with this, that I am vaunting you or vaunting myself. I've observed, and I'm communicating what I saw, nothing more.*
>
> *The poet has his own way of expressing: with the pen, the brush, the scissors. You have taken up the brush. You have done right. One must follow one's own inclinations. I do not wish to advise you now to take up the pen; in order to achieve something, one must take up a single task. But allow me to weep for the writer that dies within you. The earth is good and fertile; a little culture and the harvest would have been splendid. It's not that you are ignoring this purity of which I speak—you know it perhaps better than I do. It's that, seduced by your own character, worry free, singing just for the pleasure of singing, you use the most curious expressions, most provincial phrasing. Far from me to make this a crime, especially in our correspondence, on the contrary, it pleases me.*
>
> *You write only for me to read you, and I thank you for that. But the mass public, my dear fellow, is quite demanding. To say it is not enough. One must say it well. If a nitwit were to write to me, it wouldn't matter that his style was as raggedy as his ideas. But you, my dreamer—you, my poet—I sigh when I see your thoughts, your princesses, so poorly dressed. They are strange, these beautiful ladies, as strange as young bohemians— their unusual gaze, their feet all muddy and their heads bedecked with flowers.*

Almost three years will pass before Zola gains enough faith in himself to begin writing something other than transcriptions of daydreams—not poetry but short stories. His first published work—beyond the juvenile poetic story *La fée amoureuse* (The Amorous Fairy) printed in the weekly newspaper *La Provence* on January 26th, 1859—was a short piece, *Le Canal Zola* (The Zola Canal) honoring his father, which appeared in *La Provence* the following month. Finding it difficult to produce more—such huge fantasies looming over his fragile talent—Zola transferred his lack of disciplined production to Cézanne, chiding him for having doubts and feeling despair, projecting onto his friend his own miseries, like an ineffectual boy berating his girlfriend because he can't get it up. In this strange way, Cézanne was still being called upon as Zola's defender, this time to absorb the blows of his self-punishment. And Cézanne had always been ready to play his role. On an occasion when Zola tells him that a poem he'd composed and read to classmates, *un pièce à l'Impératrice* [A poem for Empress Eugènie] was far less than appreciated, Cézanne the Defender writes back:

Baille informed me that your classmates—as absurd as it seems to me—criticized your poem to the Empress. It made me livid to hear that, and albeit a bit late, I am dedicating this disapprobation (whose terms are much too lenient) to describe those literary penguins, those aborted, asthmatic banterers of your honest poetry. If you think it is fitting, please pass on my compliments to them, and add that, if they wish to respond, I am here waiting for them, ready to punch out the first one who falls within reach of my fist.

O naughty schoolgirls! Contemptible scabs!

> *You, who dabble along old dusty paths,*
> *Disdaining those who have the heat of passion,*
> *Who arouse even the least sublime impulse in hearts:*
> *What insane obsession pushes you to criticize*
> *The one who laughs off such feeble jolts in the road.*
> *Whippersnappers, little runts, schoolboys! Forced admirers*
> *Of those gloomy flat verses left behind by Virgil.*
> *You veritable herd of swine who walk under the wing*
> *Of a putrefied pendant who stupidly guides you,*
> *Forcing you to admire, without knowing why,*
> *Verses in which you find beauty in his words alone,*
> *When amongst you there now surges like spurting lava*
> *An unrestrained poet, breaking all shackles.*
> *It's as around the eaglet one hears the squalling*
> *Of a thousand puny birds, their wings aflapping.*
> *You chintzy derogators, priests of pettifoggery.*
> *You vomit on him your irreverent slobber—*
> *I hear you, a virtual concert of toads,*
> *Singing your heads off, all out of tune.*
> *Nobody in this world has ever seen frogs*
> *Who like you, Sirs, mumble and sputter so stupidly.*
> *But go ahead, fill the air with your asinine clamor—*
> *The verses of my friend shall remain the vanquishers!*
> *They will endure your vile small-mindedness,*
> *For they are marked by the true stamp of genius.*

Over the months that followed, Cézanne and Zola tended to write to each other, as lovers do, when in a vulnerable mood and in extreme need, projecting the needs of one onto the desires of the other. On February 9th, 1860, Zola wrote to Cézanne, *For several days I've been sad, very sad, and I'm writing to you in order to divert myself.* Typical of the adolescent ennui that coalesces out of boredom, desires, and lack of directed action, Zola blames the cosmos: *We cannot hold anyone responsible for this, not even ourselves. It's the fault of the times in which we live. Boredom is the plague of our century.*

To overcome this dolorous condition, Zola offers the perfect solution: laughter, drinking, smoking, and singing to counter the short span of youth with death over his shoulder on the gritty horizon. At this point no thought of maturity is larger than a pea in Zola's tear-watered mind. He abridges the stages of life with a leap from boyhood right into the abiding grave, welding the faults of his time to his unique psyche, observing himself as diffuse in the condition of the world outside himself. Society's woeful state infects him with woe. During this tremulous phase, he subsists on expectations, postponed fulfillment, his sole pleasure in perpetuating intangible, unrealized daydreams. He organizes his life around fantasies, narrates them in letters to Cézanne with admixed pleasure, while pushing Cézanne towards accomplishment, as if Cézanne the Artist were to be created out of what Zola lacked: a goal in life, a guiding father who re-defines himself in his son. In Zola's womb, in his underbelly nest where his dreams still live in eggs, his poetry throbs, awaiting some auspicious event. *I'm expecting Cézanne's arrival,* he informs Baille on February 20th, 1860. He blames the pleasure-pain agony of this prolonged expectancy on Cézanne's father, who delays his son's move to Paris.

14

Have you never seen in daydreams
as if through a fog
some graceful shapes

It seemed to both Zola and Cézanne that everything they loved went up in smoke—ideas, girls; their dreams float upwards and dissipate into thin air. Muses and anti-muses compete for their souls. *What female demon has scrambled your brain?* asks Cézanne. He had written to Zola in early July 1859:

> *You who in the past I've seen walking a straight line,*
> *Doing nothing good, saying nothing bad?*
> *In what chaos of strange dreams,*
> *Have you, by chance, seen the Polka being danced*
> *by some young nymph, actress at the Opera?*
> *Would you not have written, asleep under the table,*
> *After having gotten drunk like one of the Pope's deacons,*
> *Or perhaps, my friend, filled with a rococo sort of love,*
> *The vermouth having hit you on the noggin.*1

> *Neither love nor wine have touched my sorbonne,*
> *And I have never believed that water in itself was much good;*
> *This statement alone, my friend, must prove to you*
> *That, although a bit of a dreamer, I see, nonetheless, clearly.*

> *Have you never seen in daydreams,*
> *As if through a fog some graceful shapes;*
> *Nebulous beauties whose ardent charms,*
> *Dreamt of at night, are unseen by day?*
> *As in the morning hours one sees vaporous mist*
> *When the sun rises with a thousand fires and lights.*
> *The greenish hillsides where forests rustle,*
> *Waters sparkling with the reflections of the azure sky,*
> *When comes a light breeze,*

Chasing, blowing away the passing mist.
This is how, sometimes, in front of my eyes, appears
Ravishing creatures, with angelic voices
During the night. My friend, it would seem with the dawn
with fresh and new colors, shades them with desire,
They seem to smile at me, and I hold out my hand,
Yet no matter how close I get to them, they suddenly fly off,
Rising up into the sky, carried away by balmy breezes,
Casting back tender glances at me, as if to say
Adieu! In vain, I try to get closer to them
In vain I desire to touch them,
But they exist no more—already the transparent veil
Ceases to paint their bodies in the ravishing shapes.

My dream vanished, reality returns,
Finding me squirming, my heart saddened,
And I see before my eyes, appear a ghost,
Horrible, monstrous, its name is LAW.

I think I did more than dream Cézanne then explains. *I fell asleep, and I must have frozen you with my platitudes, but I dreamt that I held my Lorette in my arms, my Grisette* [girl of easy virtue], *my darling, my saucy imp, that I patted her buttocks, and a few other things besides.*

The magnitude of Zola's projects makes them as easy to evade as his muses find him easy to torment. Knowing that everything is unattainable, he is assured of non-achievement. The epic is beyond his grasp, as is the virgin girl.[2] The courtship of the unattainable allows him not to undertake anything, to protect himself from himself. Had the fantasy of a love saga been just a ten-page poem, he would be obliged to write it. Had the woman of his dreams been an easy woman, or a plain-faced shop-girl down the street, he would have no excuse for not pursuing her. *And what's more,* he had written to Cézanne on December 30th, 1859, *I have never loved, except in a dream, and have never been loved, not even in a dream! But never mind, as I feel myself capable of a great love*— as he feels capable of writing an epic poem on love. Then without even a prayerful nod towards Aphrodite, he converts himself into a Pygmalion and describes the ultimate resolution of love and poetry: *I will create for myself some beautiful ideal woman and then perhaps I will accomplish my project.*

The dream girl haunting Zola's psyche was named the *Aérienne* —whether she is real or imagined, one cannot say, although in either case, she would be based in reality, perhaps a girl he remembers from Aix-en-Provence. As was

Cézanne's Justine, she was beyond the touch of shy Zola. Just as Cézanne had to accept that Justine belonged to someone else, Zola, too, had to admit that he had been bested. Zola had mentioned his dream girl in two of his December 1859 letters from Paris to Baille: *Should you see l'Aérienne, smile at her for me.* The next year, on August 1st, Zola wrote to Cézanne, asking that he speak to him of *l'Aérienne.* This request came in some of the most radiant and picturesque passages that Zola would ever write:[3]

> *Oh! For this great poet—you, who are leaving me—come back to me as a great painter. You, who have guided my hesitant footsteps along the route to Parnassus, you, who have suddenly abandoned me, help me to forget the newborn Lamartine* [one of the four great Romantic poets admired by Zola, along with Hugo, Musset, Vigny] *over a future Raphael* [the High Renaissance painter].
>
> *I want to remind you in a few lines of your old poem, and ask you for a new and purer one, more refined. I want to tell you that I am not satisfied with the few lines of verse you send in each letter. I want to advise you not to abandon the pen completely, and in your off moments, to speak to me of some beautiful sylph.*
>
> *That's all. I don't know why. I lose myself. I waste paper. Forgive me old friend, humor me, speak to me of the Aérienne—of someone, something poetic, and at length. Of course, after your exams, and without interfering with your studies at the museum.*

In 1859 Zola had written a poem to the *Aérienne.* The title means aerial, light as air, vapory, like nymphs in chiffon—airy, like Cézanne's apparitional Justine shaped by cigar smoke:

> *One evening I saw her in a shady lane,*
> *An undulating, veiled, dreamlike form.*
> *Her vague and uncertain glance at times*
>   *sweetly caressed me without appearing to see anything,*
> *Her melodious movement, light-footed carriage*
>   *gave the impression that her figure,*
> *Bending in the wind like a flower, could suddenly fly away.*
> *All of this, made me—a dreamy poet in the shadows—*
> *Take her for a fairy, a serene virgin.*
> *Under my breath I gave her the name, the Aérienne.*[4]

During this period, Zola had been living in close quarters with his mother. Saying he has never been loved helps him disconnect sexually from mother-love, a necessary male condition for love's redirection towards a sexual mate, a girl who is not yet a woman, not yet a mother—a serene virgin, an *Arielle.* Zola seemed remarkably mature about this matter, while also sensitive to feelings his mother must surely have had at times. In his letter to Cézanne of April 16th 1860, reviewing a stage play written by a Mr. Muscadel, Zola writes:

I would be happy if our two opinions were in agreement. I bear no ill will towards Mr. Muscadel, whom I do not know. Nor is it jealousy that pushes me. I read the play with every hope of finding it to be excellent, and I must content myself with translating, as politely as possible, the impression made on me. I'm mistaken in saying that the author had no goal. I think I have found it: that of painting the type of jealousy that a mother experiences against the woman who loves her son. She believes that this woman is stealing from her, that the love belongs to her and her alone—to the one who fed him at her breast and loves him so.

This letter contains many thoughts that Zola has about love and marriage:

I saw Villevieille on Easter Monday. The lazy bones was lolling around the house using the feeble excuse that he was sick. Sick! It's true. Never has any beetle or choirboy been so fat, so rosy, so chubby, so shiny with grease. No matter—he remained in bed. I talked to him for a long time; we spoke of Chaillan, of you, and so on. I did not see his studio where, he told me, no canvasses were sketched in. I'm to return to have tea with him at his home.

Villevieille's wife is very cute, all white and pink. She's almost a child. I feel I could live an angelic life with that little girl. Villevieille didn't flatter her when saying she was adorable: spiritual face just a bit rumpled, a small mouth, small feet—in short, delicious! My God! How foolish of them not to be making love all the time.

I think of our future marriages—yours and mine. Who knows if fate will smile upon us. Will she be beautiful, will she be ugly? Will she be good to us? Will she be mean? Beauty and goodness do not often go hand in hand, unfortunately! Let us hope that we will be lucky in both the material and spiritual sense. All things considered, I think that happiness lies in marriage, as it does elsewhere. They say it's a crapshoot. I don't believe that at all. Luck has a broad back. As soon as a man makes a mistake he blames it on luck, which cannot defend itself. I believe there are as many good numbers as bad ones, that it is the man, not luck, that makes him lucky or not lucky.

Zola carries on in the wake of Michelet's ideas on the education of women, the necessity of the husband to «create» the wife, to awaken her dormant intelligence and arouse her passion:

In any woman there is material for a good wife. It is up to the husband to make the best use of this material. From such and such a master result such and such a valet—or, as goes the husband, so goes the wife. The education of the young woman is so different from that of the young man. At the end of their schooling, even between brother and sister, there remains no common ground. This situation is even worse between strangers, between two spouses. The husband, therefore, is faced with the daunting task of educating his wife. Being married is not just sleeping together, each of the two must think alike; otherwise spouses cannot help but fail at their marriage, sooner or later. This is why the education of girls today seems to me so imperfect. They arrive into this world ignorant—even worse, knowing only things they must forget. I digress greatly, I think.

Here again one encounters Zola's desire to become a great epic poet as inseparable from his desire to find a great love. To accomplish his fantasized project, the epic love story that leads to marriage, his prolegomenon to Michelet's *L'Amour,* Zola needs to connect the ideal love of a woman to his ideal of poetry—sex and art locked in an embrace. So inseparable are they in his mind that one day he will admit that, after a night of love-making, he wouldn't even bother to sit at his desk the next day, knowing that the words he would have written had drained out with his sperm.[5] But the woman of his dreams is insurmountable, and not just a princess cocooned in a turret, but the entire fortified castle. Like Cézanne, his inability to carry out his grandiose dreams protects him from failure. In a letter to Cézanne of January 5th, 1860, he would summarize his daily life in shallow symbols of manhood:

> *I smoke my pipe. I have, ever since New Year's Day—a very nice pipe that I care for dearly, having mastered the art of the pipe* [pipe as muse], *and when smoking I saw in the rising smoke thousands of ideas flying about that I will share with you, hoping you will find them entertaining.*
>
> *You asked me to tell you about my mistresses. My loves are in my dreams. My follies are only to light the fire in the morning, to smoke my pipe, smoke and to think of what I've done and what I will do. You see that these are not very costly, and not detrimental to my health.*

Not until years later, after the marrow in his bones had produced a novelist that could relate to a real woman, would Zola take up life with a woman—the orphaned and penniless Alexandrine Meley, who was not an ideal but an ordinary spirit: half-educated, barely literate, and barren, a good woman for the long haul. She was novelist's material, not a poet's—prose, not poetry, not a Greusian maiden but at least a girl in the farmyard. Years later, Zola would look back to this year of his youth and say that his poems were weak. His fiction would be strong. *The only thing I may still take pride in is the awareness I had of my mediocrity as a poet and the decision to do our country's hard labor with the rough-hewn tool of prose.*

In this dirge for a miscarried genius, Zola was not alone. Many would-be poets capitulate to prose when coming to terms with their poetic mediocrity. In 1830, Saint-Beuve admitted that his passion for an ideal woman had to be abandoned for ordinary physical relief procured from women of the streets, not a virgin in a perpetual love nest but picked-up chippies or whores made use of in a short-stay hotel, a *maison de passe.* And in 1839, Saint-Beuve finally conceded that, after inconclusive attempts, his life ambition to be a poet was not attainable.

Here, too, one finds the association of prose with the ordinary, and poetry with the ideal. In doubt of his capacities even for prose, Saint-Beuve became a critic who accomplished for literary criticism what Zola would for fiction. Like Saint-Beuve, Zola had too much intellectual muscle, too much anger, to excel in poetry. He too will become a critic, a journalist, and then mature as a tyrannical, hard-edged novelist. Forced to confront reality, he had to become a realist. Novelists confront real life, while poets evade it. As a poet, Zola would have remained mired in adolescence, for he was not a strong enough poet to mature out of it. Condescension to being a critic was, in many ways, an expression of anger, of frustration, an attack on himself—an angry confrontation with reality. The savagery of his criticism ran parallel to the violence one finds at times in Cézanne's paintings when he attacks the poetry that had spurned his love.

Over his first four years in Paris, Zola published only five titles, of which four were juvenile poems, such as *Nina* and *Doute* in Géry-Legrand's *Le Journal populaire de Lille*. Risking embarrassment at a last effort to be a poet, on September 8th, 1860, he sent a long poem, *Paolo*, to Victor Hugo, who was then in exile on the Island of Guernsey, having chosen not to swear allegiance to the Second Republic. Zola's cover letter documents his emotional state, and calls to mind something that Cézanne had said to Numa Coste [another boyhood companion, four years Cézanne's junior]: *A poet must always be pregnant with some personal Odyssey.*[6] Zola's sentiment for Hugo, with regard to himself, may have been amplified by Hugo-in-Odyssey, out there on Guernsey island:

> *Sir,*
>
> *It is often said that a man of genius owes himself to youth, that one of his most sacred duties is to encourage those who've received the divine spark and to stop those who've taken the wrong path. The young man writing this letter dares to address his beloved poet, the man of genius, whose paternal solicitude for all things young, free, and loving is common knowledge.*
>
> *When I left secondary school, alone in the world except for my excellent mother, I wanted the opinion I formed in every matter to be my own. Where literature was concerned, the directions one could take were many. I explored every school, and finally, having thought it all through, returned to your ideas on art, those eminently true and relevant ideas that I'd accepted in childhood with faith and enthusiasm.*
>
> *I am now twenty. As I detect within myself a faint echo of the sublime voice that inspires you, I sometimes let my thoughts break into song. But my lyre, still muffled, provokes neither jeers nor ovations. Alone and to this day unknown, I stammer in the darkness.*
>
> *The day has come when this solitude begins to weigh. One understands that one is not ready to face the public, yet has become weary hearing nothing but silence all around oneself. One sits discouraged and awaits the words of praise or criticism that will say whether*

to advance or retreat, assuming there is still time for either. Such is my predicament. Tired of walking in the dark, I suddenly halted and looked about for a torch to guide me. It was then, Sir, that I thought of you, the greatest and most celebrated poet of our time. I see nothing out of the ordinary in this audacity. I come as a student to his master, as a dreamy and passionate young man who bows before the author of Hernani *and* Les Feuilles d'automne, *as a lover of liberty and of love, who pays homage to the sublime cantor of those two divinities. May my feeble voice remind you that the France you love so well still remembers her poet, and that young hearts are obliged to leave the homeland and fly to your land of exile.*

It remains for me, Sir, to excuse myself for entreating you and sending such a long poem. I know how much each of your moments counts for our literature, and can only allege my fervent desire to be better known by you. It is no doubt a very flawed work that I send you, and it has no bearing on present day politics. To excite your interest in my hero, I can tell you that he is not a mere figment of my imagination but has been drawn from life. May he find favor with you. In all events, I'm certain you will winnow the wheat from the chaff. I take this liberty to ask you for your advice.

Fortunately, Hugo did not write back with his usual supporting words for young poets. He was still receiving bags of mail weekly from writers and well wishers, and perhaps reading only a bit of it. Had he read Zola's poem and responded with benevolent kindness, he might have sent the poor boy down a crooked path. Zola did not receive a reply.

As a poet, Zola was entirely out of step with the times, as was Cézanne as a painter. Zola's poem *Paolo* (Paul)—the one sent to Hugo, the third part of Zola's *L'Amoureuse Comédie* (Comedy of Love) drafted in 1860—is an imitation of Musset's *Rolla,* with nothing of the wit and poignancy that distinguished Musset at his elegiac best, as Frederick Brown says correctly. Musset had made classical diction work for him by using it to play up the despair of would-be heroes in a non-heroic age. The noble style as Zola practiced it was simply obsolete. His poetry labored under the dead weight of expletives *(Alas! Ah! Oh gracious friend),* paraphrases and euphemisms that he and every other rhymester deployed, nurtured, as Brown says, by seventeenth-century verse brought down from the attic.[7]

Zola had anticipated that critics would connect him to Musset when reading *Paolo,* although he perhaps was not aware that Musset's style had become historical and no longer fertile for young poets to emulate. Musset's important writings were from the 1830 to 1838 years. On June 25th, 1860, Zola sent a copy of *Paolo* to Cézanne. In an accompanying letter, he told him that no doubt it will be said he had imitated Musset: *As for that accusation, I can only say that Musset is my favorite poet, that every day I read a few pages of his writings. It is not at all surprising that, even when not wanting to, I take on his form and some of his ideas. But I swear to God this is not premeditated crime—I have a horror of plagiarism—on the contrary, I swerve off from Musset whenever I perceive anything that has the look of borrowing.* Here follows a portion of Zola's poem *Paolo*:

For two years, Paolo thus followed Marie;
For almost two years, the sun found him
at the door of the old town house where the cherished one,
In child-like sleep, smiling, dreaming;
And the evening star surprised him there,
Hidden in a gloomy corner, dreaming in the dark,
His eyes fixed on a window where for a moment,
He saw confusedly a vague gliding shape in a long gown.

Now an extract from Zola's *Rodolpho*:
Rodolpho rested his elbows on the stone balcony,
With a tremulous motion parted the curtain,
While, already dirty and whitened with dust,
The wreath of flowers fell to the tiled floor.
«Alas!» he murmured, it was a chimera,
«Oh! Lord, what have I done that you, the Almighty,
Should so let your anger explode
And fall onto a speck of dust
That morning wind will pulverize in passing.
Have pity! Lord, have pity! I am only a child!»
And over there, he saw, in fiery disorder,
Rose, entwined and writhing in the arms of a lover.

And an extract from his *L'Aérienne*:
Ah! be my Beatrice, virgin in modest veils;
Descend, come down here to pull up your lover;
And, your brow crowned with sunrays and stars,
Let us leave this vile silted soil for the blue firmament.
Oh sixteen-year-old virgin, fragile rosebud,
Oh flower still moist from nighttime kisses.[8]

Zola's poetry was excessively internal, typical of adolescent verse and first fiction, nonetheless appropriate for his age and the taste of his time when many young poets imitated the charm and formal perfection of Musset, even while rejecting his romantic lyricism. In correspondence with Cézanne and others, Zola uses many of the same silken phrases and turkey-feather brushstrokes as in his Musset-inspired lines. In letters to Cézanne and Baille from this year of these poems, one finds, *May God guide me...May God protect me...Like the shipwrecked sailor who clings to his plank, I cling to you, my dear Paul...Ah! What a nice fellow you would be to hide for me in this little corner where I, myself, cannot stand.* Some years later, in 1882, the writer J. K. Huysmans will remark in a letter to Zola, commenting on a twenty-year-old poet (not Zola) at how astonished he was that such a young writer, hardly out of school, had avoided being Hugoesque or Mussetian.[9]

Zola's self-consciousness spills over in the cover letter to Cézanne, saying that *Paolo* is his first crime in that genre. And he chooses to be the first to criticize himself for such expletives as *Oh, Alas! etc., etc.* This letter has no greeting or sign-off, as Zola's text was mimicking a preface:

> *It has often been said that one does not read prefaces anymore, that an author interrogates himself twice before writing his useless lines. Never mind, as this is my first crime of this sort—and because I'm sure you will read it—with a few words I will preface the poem I'm enclosing for you.*
>
> *Of course, a preface is a ridiculous thing. The author appears to be saying to you, «I am so obscure, there is such profundity in my work, that you will be stupidly unable to understand me if I fail to explain myself in simple words.» That's good reason for not reading prefaces: the work itself should be enough to judge the author. Now, if it pleases you, continue reading.*
>
> *In writing Paolo, I had a double goal: to exalt platonic love, to render it more compelling than carnal love. Then, to show that, in this century of doubt, pure love can serve as faith, can give the lover belief in a god, in an immortal soul. The poem is basically historic. You will recognize this Paolo adoring his lover as a holy Madonna. As for the details, some are invented, others are true—it being understood that everything in poetic form is in a present that reality itself does not have.*
>
> *The first canto—the most perfect of the three—does not offer a piece that has a sharp edge. As for the other two, much less polished, I recommend to you only the tirade of Don Juan, which ends the second part, and the prayer that ends the third.*
>
> *I'm sending you my work such as it is. Certainly it is in need of correction. But read it slowly, affix yourself to my thoughts without paying attention to the repetitions, the awkward expressions, the oh!s, the alas!es, etc., etc. Perhaps then you will believe that my dreams are truly beautiful. This poem is not my last word. If in a better financial state, with fewer worries over material conditions, I could, and I must, do better. I say this without conceit because I believe it to be so. Forward this notebook to Baille. The easiest way would be, I believe, to give it in an envelope to his father who would deliver it to Baille himself when he goes to Marseilles. Tell me frankly, you two, what you think of my new work.*

Having come to realize that poetry would never sustain his economic needs, on January 5th, 1860, Zola confesses to Cézanne that not only do his loves exist only in dreams, but that the reality of being on his own had forced him to take a job. Soon thereafter, by mid-April, he would be employed as a clerk with the Harbor Administration, at the station in Paris that processed customs at the Saint

Martin canal. In announcing this to Cézanne, he deploys the same justifications for it as Cézanne had when saying he was forced to register for law school:

> *You must be aware that I am anything but a favorite of the goddess Fortuna. It pains me to find myself, a big fellow of twenty, still a burden to my mother. I have, therefore, decided to do something that will earn my daily bread. I intend, within a fortnight at most, to get a job with the Harbor Administration. You know me, how much I love my freedom, so you will understand how much I have to force myself to resort to that. But I think I would be doing the wrong thing, were I not to do it. I will still have time on my hands to do what I like. I am far from letting literature down. One should not let one's dreams go easily. As I told you in my previous letter, life is a ball that doesn't always roll where the hand pushes it, and believe me, with no pleasure do I leave my books and papers to go sit in a chair and write disagreeable documents. But I will always be the same, always a rambling poet. After having shaken off the office dust I will go back to my quill to continue my interrupted poem, or the letter I had started for you.*
>
> *As you see, my friend, I have at length answered your letter. Yet, I haven't said it all, or said it well. Never mind. I only hope it gave you a moment's entertainment.*

Zola knew that his failure to go on to university studies might sink him for good. In a letter to Cézanne on February 9th, 1860, Zola writes in despair: *I'm very downhearted. I think of the future, which is so dark, so dark that I shrink from it, full of horror. No money, no professional training, nothing but despondency. I haven't finished my studies. I can't even speak proper French. I am completely ignorant. There are days when I find myself completely lacking in intelligence, when I wonder how someone worth so little could have entertained such vainglorious dreams.*

Cézanne's delay until August led Zola to bemoan his disappointment in a way suggesting that his blockage against serious work still depended on his friend's presence. Zola's daily life at the time was less aimed toward serious writing than Cézanne's toward art. He worked full days at the Harbor Administration, entering custom declarations, copying letters. He says in an April 16th, 1860 letter to Cézanne, *My new life is rather monotonous. I go to the office at nine. I record customs declarations until four o'clock. I transcribe correspondence, or, even better, I read the paper. I yawn. I take walks all around the place, etc., etc. Pretty sad, really. As soon as work is finished and I go out, I shake myself like a drenched bird, I light my pipe. I take deep breaths. I live. I fashion in my headlong poems, long dramas, long novels. I await summer to give free reign to my spirit. O Virtuous God! I want to publish a book on poetry and dedicate it to you.*

Then, in a May 5th letter: *For a month, now, I've been in this infamous boutique, and I've about had it, by God! I wish only for a cave in the flank of a rock, high in a mountain.*

In a letter to Baille written on March 17th, Zola bemoans his sad state: *If, weary of my loneliness, I call upon the muse of poetry, that gentle comforter, she no longer answers. She has deserted me for some time now, and whenever I compose rhymes without her assistance, I later tear them up in disgust. Even though the last months, with their confusion and disappointments, have done me harm, they have not succeeded in choking all poetry within me. Only some auspicious event is needed for poetry's wings to unfold again. I am expecting much from Cézanne's arrival.*

At the time, Cézanne had put his first year of law school behind him. Zola was hardly justified for his disappointment in Cézanne for undertaking law studies. He had his own trial to judge. Like Cézanne, he was driven by the most basic needs: a career and a live muse. Both were fantasies, in reality unattainable. Zola to Cézanne, June 25th, 1860:

My dear old man,

In your last letter you seemed discouraged. You speak of nothing less than throwing your brushes at the ceiling. You sigh about the solitude that surrounds you. You are bored.

Isn't this the illness we all suffer, this terrible boredom? Isn't it the plague of our century? And isn't the discouragement we share a result of this spleen which chokes us? If I were near you I would try to console you, to encourage you. I would say to you we are no longer children, that the future claims us, that it is cowardly to shrink from the task one has set oneself; that the greatest wisdom is to accept life as it is and to embellish it with dreams while remaining aware that they are only dreams. May God protect me from being your bad genie and landing you in disaster by praising art and dreams.

But I cannot believe this could be the way it is. No devil hides behind our friendship, planning to drag us into the abyss. So, recover your courage, take up your brushes, and let your imagination roam like a vagabond. I have faith in you. If I push you toward evil, may this evil snap back onto my own head. Above all, have courage. Before taking this path think about the thorns you might encounter. Be a man; leave the dream alone for the moment and act.

Now, let me talk a bit about myself. If I show pride and contempt towards the mob, I have none towards you. I know my weakness. As to qualities, I find in myself only love towards you. Like the shipwrecked sailor who clings to the plank floating in water, I cling to you, my old Paul. You understood me; your character is in sympathy with mine. I found in you a friend, and thanked heaven for that. Several times I was afraid of losing you. Now this seems impossible. We know each other too well ever to separate.

I still intend to visit you soon. I need to talk to you. Letters are okay, but one does not say all one would like to say. I am tired of Paris. I go out very seldom. Were it possible, I would settle near you. My future is still the same: very dark, and so overcast by clouds that my eyes search in vain. Truly, I don't know where I'm going. May God guide me. Write often. Your letters comfort me.

I know how much you hate the crowd, so talk only about yourself. And most of all, never be afraid of boring me. Have courage. See you soon.

15

And now I have courage to
touch on the subject of painting

While Zola harbored an excess of talent as a novelist, needing only lust for reality to fuel its faint heart, his outlet for poetry would remain clogged by sexual urges and choked with anger at the world. And like a child, his sexual/poetic excitation was not yet differentiated from gratification. His dreams of writing poetry were still sleep-dreams, his rhyming still infantile rocking:

> *My great pleasures now are the pipe and the dream, my feet in the hearth and my eyes fixed on the flames. Thus I pass my days without ennui, writing not a word, reading at times a few pages from Montaigne. To be frank, I must change my life and shake myself to clean off the dust that is rusting me. I have been meditating too long. It is time to produce...Another sad result of the life I am leading is that I've become horribly gluttonous. Drink, food, everything fills me with desire, and I take the same pleasure in devouring a good morsel as in possessing a woman.*[1]

Cézanne's boredom was much the same as Zola's. His too was normal boredom, arising when what he must not do was what he wanted to do, and from having to do what he didn't want to do, enhanced by the plain fact that he didn't always know what he wanted to do. So at one time what he was doing was gratifying while at another time inhibiting—painting at times painful, at other times pleasurable. And surely work in his father's bank, offering routine tasks and regular hours, was as often enjoyable as miserable. Law school, because it gave him focus and a daily schedule, may have been a great relief.

Typical of their age, Zola and Cézanne deprecate themselves with words a harsh parent would use. Zola lashes at himself, saying that he is lazy, good for nothing, gluttonous, a hardship for his mother. Like a parent wagging a finger, he scolds Cézanne, saying, as if for his own good, *You lack character, you're negligent.* Cézanne calls himself stupid, boring, lazy and slow. Self-punishment takes over parental discipline, becoming self-discipline, an evolving responsibility for one's self to strengthen the ego and prepare for adulthood. To counter the pain of self-discipline, boys tend to indulge in what parental discipline denies. Zola counters parental restraint against excess by being excessive, indulging in food to balance self-pity, giving himself affection of the kind given to children who are hurt and feel downhearted. He laments his loss of childhood freedom, no more outings, fishing, exploring, escapes from school and parents.

In the April 16th, 1860 letter to Cézanne, Zola reaffirms their bond, their affection. For in between the phases of affection, as from one's mother or one's wife, young men look to each other. Zola writes:

You are right to not complain too much about your fate. Because, after all, as you yourself say, with two loves in your heart, one for women and one for beauty, it would be wrong to despair. Time goes by fast, even in solitude, when you occupy this aloneness with cherished ghosts—and what is it to be unhappy if it is not being alone? True, it is not the only curse on the human condition, but between loneliness and the lack of affection stems all our misery. I the isolated, I the disdained, I grab onto your friendship in desperation. As my gaze questions the horizon, it sees only fog, only vague clouds, but at least it perceives you, your figure, in a ray of sunlight. And this consoles me. My poor friend, if ever my thoughts or my actions should displease you, tell me so, frankly: I could then explain myself to you, reaffirming your wavering friendship.

But what am I saying? Are we not already linked? Don't we have the same thoughts? Our friendship is still very solid. What I have just said is no more than exaggerated fears of an imaginary danger.

You sent me some verses in which a somber sadness breathes. The quick flight of life, the brevity of youth, and death over there on the horizon—all this would make me tremble if I were to think about it for a while. But would it not be an even darker picture if, in the hurried passing of existence, youth, the springtime of life, would be entirely missing—that at age twenty; having experienced no happiness, one sees age approaching with long strides, one is unable even to enliven the rough winter days with memories of a beautiful summer? That is the fate now awaiting me.

You tell me that sometimes you do not have the courage to write to me. Don't be so selfish: your joys and your pain belong to me. When you are joyful, cheer me up; when you are sad, darken my sky without fear—a tear can be sweeter than a smile. Also, jot down your thoughts for me from day to day. As soon as a new feeling is born in your soul, write it down on paper. When you have filled four pages, send them to me.

One can infer from Zola's letter that Cézanne had not been conveying every thought that came to him, that he was getting rattled by Zola's pestering him for not taking painting seriously and for not coming to Paris. In Zola's next letter, on April the 26th, 1860, not only is Cézanne berated with a lecture on painting—

given first as words put in his mouth, then by Zola's lecturing on what art is—but is hassled with more advice on how to relate to his father. The letter ends with a postscript: *I just received your letter. It raises sweet hope in me. Your father is becoming a human. Be firm without being disrespectful. Remember it's your future that's being decided, and that your happiness depends on it.* As for the body of the letter, Zola says: *these five pages are the most serious I've written in his life.* This letter contains Zola's first art criticism, going beyond the distinction he had made in his letter to Cézanne three weeks earlier between the naturalist and poetic. Now he makes a great effort to discern a work of art from technique, and from what is merely a picture:

> *My dear old fellow,*
>
> *I will never stop repeating, and I don't think that I've become a pedant. Every time I'm on the verge of giving you advice, I hesitate, I ask myself if it is my place to do so, if you won't tire of hearing me shout: Do this, Do that. I fear that you will become angry with me, that you will find my thoughts contradict yours, and that, as a result, our friendship might suffer. What can I tell you? I'm probably silly to have such thoughts, but greatly fear even the lightest cloud that might come between us. Tell me, tell me again and again that you accept my advice as coming from a friend, that you do not become angry with me if it contradicts your way of seeing. I am no less joyous, the same dreamer, the same friend who so happily stretches out on the grass next to you, pipe in mouth and glass in hand. Friendship alone dictates my words. I live better when involved in your life and affairs. I talk, fill in gaps in my letters, build castles in Spain. But by God, don't think that I want to lay down a path of behavior for you. You must take from my words only what you can use, what you find good, and laugh at the rest, without wasting your time arguing with me.*
>
> *And now, I broach more squarely the subject of painting. When I look at a painting—me, who can at best distinguish black from white—it is obvious that I cannot allow myself to form a judgment about the brushwork. All I can say is whether the subject matter pleases me, whether the overall picture causes me to dream of something good and great, if the love of beauty breathes in the composition. In a word, I can speak only about the thought that is embodied by the work of art without preoccupying myself with studio techniques. And I believe I am acting wisely; nothing inspires my pity more than those declarations made by so-called connoisseurs [critics and aficionados] who, having picked up some technical terms in the studio, spout them with aplomb, like parrots. You on the other hand, you who understand how difficult it is to put paint on a canvas so it matches your intention and imagination, I understand that, in front of a picture, you take the painter's vocation seriously, that you appreciate this or that brushstroke, the color achieved, etceteras. For you, that is perfectly natural. The idea, the spark is within you. You seek the form you do not yet possess, and you admire it openly whenever you encounter it. But beware! This form is not everything, and whatever your excuse, you must put the idea above it. Let me explain: for you, a painting must not be just ground pigment put on the surface of a canvas; one must not be concerned with asking by what mechanical process the effect was achieved, which colors were used. Instead, you must look at the whole and ask yourself if*

the work is what it should be, if the artist who painted it is truly an artist. In the eyes of a layman, there is little difference between a daub and a work of art. In both cases, it is white, red, etc., brushstrokes, a canvas, a frame. The difference lies only in that nameless something that is revealed through ideas and taste. It is that something, that artistic feeling, which must above all be discovered and admired.

Responding to his own boredom and inability to produce, Zola cracks the whip over Cézanne. This letter continues, saying much about Zola's state of mind. At the docks, he is bored, sleepy, and entirely lacking in motivation to do more than sit at a desk, fuss with customs forms, and daydream:

As for me, life is monotonous. Bent over my desk, writing without knowing what I'm writing, I sleep with wide-open eyes, stupefied. At times a flash of memory brings back one of our joyous parties, or one of the places we cherished, and my heart quakes in the most awful way. I raise my head and behold sad reality: the dusty office, crammed with piled-up old papers and clerks who are mostly rather stupid. I hear the monotonous scratching and squeaks of pens, harsh and grating words, some bizarre, others just gibberish. And over there, frolicking on the windowpane, are sunbeams come to announce, as if to annoy me, that out beyond the walls nature is in bloom, birds are singing melodiously, flowers are exuding intoxicating perfumes. I lean back in my chair, close my eyes, and for an instant I see you passing by—you, my friends. I also see women I've loved without knowing it. Then everything vanishes. Terrible reality comes back. I take up my pen and feel like weeping. Oh, freedom! Freedom! The contemplative life of the Orient! The sweet and poetic laziness! My beautiful dream! What have you become?

Zola adds that his letter was written at one sitting, written without taking a break, without snuffing his candle. It is almost midnight, and he is about to put himself to bed. He says to Cézanne, *I feel exalted this evening, so forgive me if my letter is a bit mad, deprived at this late hour of the little bit of reason I have available.*

I could not wait for another letter from you before writing you again, and although I have nothing to tell you, a sudden irresistible urge to blacken some paper overcame me so strongly that I succumbed to temptation.

I shake your hand,
Your friend.

While Zola pines, Cézanne is becoming upset with Baille. It would seem that if only coincidentally Baille and Zola were teamed up to pressure him into resisting his father, to come to Paris and become a painter. In a letter to Baille, Zola shares blame for having ruffled Cézanne's father, perhaps intensifying his resistance to letting Cézanne go. Like Zola, Baille had expressed strong ideas about art that apparently offended Cézanne when he, himself, was indecisive, both whether to be an artist and as to what art was. As the only one of the triumvirate to make a full commitment to practical adult life, he had laid into Cézanne about the tendency for modern artists to indulge themselves in the glory of art without consideration for life's practicalities, just as, earlier on, he'd tried to make Cézanne get realistic about love. As a very practical person, Baille was studying natural science in Marseilles; after moving on to Paris, his first publication would be on electricity—in tune with the growing popularity of practical mechanics during the first age of mass book publication. On visiting Cézanne at the *Jas de Bouffan* in April 1860, he experienced either a cool reception or a difficult encounter. He had told Zola about what had transpired, as had Cézanne. Zola did his best to mend the rift. In a letter to Baille on May 2nd, he says:

> *In his letter to me, Cézanne talks about you. He admits his fault and assures me that he's going to change his character. Since he himself brought up the subject, I intend to tell him what I think about his attitude. It's not necessary to wait until August before attempting a rapprochement between you two.*

Three days later, Zola wrote to Cézanne, determined to reestablish the bond between two of the three inseparables that was coming unglued, while at the same time tactfully favoring his own intimacy with Cézanne:

> *In your two letters you talk about Baille. For a long time I myself have wanted to talk to you about the good fellow. It's true that he's not the same as us; his skull is not from the same mold. But he has qualities we do not possess, and also a number of faults. I don't want to paint a picture of his character for you, to tell you whereby he sins and whereby he doesn't. I would call him neither a wise man nor a fool, because both are relative, depending on the point of view from which one looks at life. What difference does it make to us, his friends? Isn't it enough that we've determined he's a good person, well above the crowd, at least more capable of understanding our hearts and our spirit?*
>
> *I'm aware that the tie uniting you with Baille has weakened, that a link of the chain is about to snap. And, trembling, I now ask you to think back on our joyous parties, of the oath we'd taken, glass in hand, to walk with arms linked down the same path through life, and to keep in mind that Baille is my friend as well as yours, and that, if his character is not entirely sympathetic, he is nonetheless devoted to us, a loving friend, and that, after all, he understands me, he understands you, and is worthy of our confidence and your friendship. If you must reproach him for something, tell me what it is, and I will try to defend him—or even better, tell him yourself what you dislike about him. Nothing is to be feared as much as things that remain unspoken among friends.*
>
> *Keep in mind our swimming parties, the days on the banks of the river when the sun went down in glory; the landscape that perhaps we did not admire so much at the time, but which, in memory, appears to us so calm and smiling. I believe it was Dante who said that nothing is more painful than a happy memory in days of misfortune.[2] Painful, certainly, but also full of a bitter voluptuousness. One laughs and cries at the same time. How unfor-*

tunate we are! At twenty, we already regret the past; we spoil our lives as if for fun; we want to see the past revived; we implore the future with loud cries, not knowing how to enjoy the present. As I told you in my last letter, sometimes a memory, like a streak of lightning, flashes across my thoughts: something which you once said of our excursions, or of a mountain, path, bush, and I long for it and despair—unhappy and mad.

At his menial job, clerking rather than producing literature, Zola was miserable. If only Cézanne were with him, things would change for the better, he thinks. His need for Cézanne exceeded Cézanne's for him, partly because he was displaced from Aix, like a soldier at the front, dependent on memories and letters from home. Zola was single-minded in his quest. The best way to battle was to be offensive.

Over the next exchange of letters between the two, hostility will set in. And when Cézanne does come to Paris a few months later, their reunion will lack the comradeship for which Zola had been praying. Zola writes:

In both your letters, you give me some hope of reunion. «When I've finished my law studies,» you say, «perhaps I will then be able to rejoin you.» May God grant that is not just the joy of a passing moment, that your father's eyes will be opened to your true interest! Perhaps in his eyes I'm a frivolous, mad, or even downright bad friend, because I support you in your dream, your love of the ideal. If he would read my letters, perhaps he would not judge me so severely. But even if I should lose his respect, I'd still tell him frankly, and to his face: «I've thought for a long time about the future, the happiness of your son, and for a thousand reasons, which would take too long to explain, I believe you should let him go to where his inclinations draw him.»

It needs, therefore, some little effort, old boy, some persistence. Que diable, have we completely lost all courage? Dawn will follow the night. Let's try, therefore, to survive the night as best we can, so that when day breaks you will be able to say: «Father, I've slept long enough, I feel strong and courageous. Take pity! do not lock me up in an office; give me my wings, I suffocate, be generous, father.»

I count on coming to shake you by the hand, as I did last year in Aix. True, for a host of reasons, I would prefer that you came to me, but as I still doubt your father's good intentions, I'm about to pack my cases.

Continuing with his effort to patch the rip in their brotherhood, Zola wrote to Baille on May 14th:

As I already told you, I wrote to Cézanne about the coldness with which he received you. I cannot do better than to copy here the few words of his reply to me. Here they are: You seem to be afraid, according to your last letter, that our friendship with Baille is weakening. Oh no! because, morbleu, he's a decent fellow. But you know quite well that, because my character being what it is, I don't always fully realize what I'm doing. So, if I've wronged him, let him forgive me. You know we get on very well together, but I agree with what you say, because you are right, and so we three will remain great friends.

You see, my dear Baille, I was right. This was nothing but a wispy cloud that would vanish with the first puff of wind. I told you that our poor old boy doesn't know what he is doing, as he himself admits pleasantly enough, and that, when he grieves us, we must not hold his heart responsible, but rather the evil demon clouding his thoughts. He's a soul made of gold, a friend who understands us, just as mad as we are, just as dreamy.

I am not of the opinion that he should know about the letters exchanged between us, about your move to make peace. He must believe that I acted without your knowledge. He must, in a word, not know that you complained about him, that you and he were, even for a moment, at odds. As to your attitude towards him until August when our pleasant gatherings will begin again, it should be that way—at least that's the way I feel it should. You should regularly write to him without complaining if he holds off responding, as he probably will. As in the past, your letters should be affectionate, without even a hint of your little rumpus. In a word, it should be as if nothing had happened between you. He is a convalescent we must nurse; if we do not want a relapse let's avoid anything imprudent. You understand what makes me speak like this—the fear of seeing our friendly triumvirate break up. Also, excuse my pedantic tone, my exaggerated fears, my perhaps unnecessary precautions. I'm putting the friendship I feel for you above all else.

In August, I want to show you the number of letters from Cézanne and make you blush when comparing them with yours.

On the 2nd of June, Zola writes to Baille, again on this subject of the rupture, happy that it seems entirely mended:

Good old Cézanne asks in each of his letters to be remembered to you. He asks for your address so he can write to you often. I'm astonished that he doesn't know what it is, and that proves not only that he's not been writing to you but that you've been just as silent. However, as his request shows good intentions, I will satisfy it. And so the little rumpus has become but a legend.

In the meantime, grant yourself some pleasures, as Cézanne says: drink, laugh, smoke, and all will be for the best of all possible worlds.

Letters continued to flow between Cézanne and Zola, and Zola continued to coax Cézanne to Paris. By this time, most of their friends who had taken art seriously at the municipal drawing school had moved to Paris leaving Cézanne with few friends in Aix. On June 13th, 1860, Zola writes to tell Cézanne that he and Chaillan, one of their comrades from Aix's drawing school, now in Paris, were collaborating on a painting, for which Zola is also posing as Amphyon, the son of Zeus and Antiope who'd received the gift of a lyre from Hermes, thus accounting for the origin of music. Of the painting in progress—Zola posing almost naked—Zola tells Cézanne that under brush of Chaillan, Amphyon has the aspect of a monkey in bad humor:[3]

> *My dear Paul,*
>
> *I see Chaillan often. Yesterday we spent the evening together. This afternoon, I will join him in the Louvre. He told me that he'd written to you the day before yesterday, I think, so I don't have to talk about his work in this letter. Combes is also here, as he'll have told you. The other artists I see are young Trumphème, Villevieille, Chautard. I've not yet encountered Emperaire.*
>
> *Before starting the magnificent picture that I mentioned to you, we will wait until I've moved into the room I've just rented. It's on the seventh floor, old boy, the highest habitation in the quarter: an enormous terrace with a view over the whole of Paris; a charming little room that I will furnish in the latest fashion, divan, piano, hammock, masses of pipes, a Turkish narghileh, etc. Then a birdcage, a little fountain—a veritable fairyland.*[4]

Actually, Zola and his mother shared a one-room apartment on rue Saint-Victor in a building that was once a boarding or apartment house in an area almost reduced to rubble as the Haussmann renovations of Paris wore on. Typically such houses had maids' rooms on the top floor, and surely it was one of these rooms, a *chambrette* or a *chambre de bonne*, that Zola moved into—a room probably no larger than two by three meters and not with cooking facilities. The «enormous» terrace, to which Zola refers, was probably a portion of the roof where maids would have strung laundry when the building was, as one says today, *un immeuble á grand standing.*

> *I will tell you more about my garret when all these embellishments have been added. On the 8th of July, we move in. Baille, who will probably come to Paris in September, will no doubt enjoy sharing my retreat. Alas, I cannot say the same for you! Chaillan will tell you all about the felicities which young daubers encounter here.* [Zola is referring to the easy virtue of female models].
>
> *You no longer speak to me about Law. What are you doing about it? Are you still at loggerheads with your father? This poor Law, which cannot help being what it is, how you must rail against it! I have noticed that we always need to have either a grief or a love, otherwise life is incomplete. Anyhow, the idea of love calls forth, to a certain extent, the idea of hatred and vice versa. You love pretty women, so you hate ugly ones; you hate the town, so you love the fields. Obviously one shouldn't push this too far. He who is truly wise is the man who knows only love, and in whose soul hatred has no place. But as life goes, we are not perfect—thank God, that would really be boring—and because you are similar to all others, your love belongs to painting, and your hate, to law.*
>
> *You say that you sometimes re-read my old letters. It's a pleasure to which I often treat myself. I have kept all of yours. They are the souvenirs of my youth.*

16

I have seen Paul! I have
seen Paul! Do you understand the
melody of those three words?

By July 1860, Zola had become fed up with Cézanne. Not only had Cézanne failed him by not coming to Paris, he was not giving Zola the inspiration he needed. Cézanne could not seem to take art seriously. If he wouldn't, Zola would have no way to convince him to leave home. Here follows one of Zola's most aggressive letters:

My dear Paul,

Allow me to explain myself for the last time, frankly and clearly. Everything seems to be going badly in our affairs. I'm in a desperate state of worrying about it.

Is painting for you only a whim you happened to grab by the hair one day when bored? Is it only something to pass the time, a subject of conversation, a pretext not to work at law? If that's so, then I understand your behavior: you are right not to push things to the extreme, and not to create new family troubles for yourself. But if painting is your voca-tion—and that's how I've always seen it—if you feel capable of doing well after hard work, then you have become for me an enigma, a sphinx, someone who is impossible and mysterious. One of two things: either you do not want to, and then you achieve your aim admirably; or you do want to, and then I don't understand anything about you any more.

Sometimes your letters fill me with great hope; sometimes they rob me of hope, and of even more, such as in your last letter where you seem to me almost saying good-bye to your dreams, which so easily you could turn into reality. In this letter, there is this phrase that I've tried in vain to understand: «I'm going to speak in order to say nothing, for my conduct contradicts my words.»

I've built up all sorts of hypotheses about the meaning of those words, but none sat-isfies me. What is your attitude? That of a lazy fellow, now doubt. But what's surprising about that? You are being forced to do work that repels you. You want to ask your father to let you go to Paris to become an artist. I don't see any contradiction between this demand and your actions. You neglect law, you go to the museum, painting is the only work that you accept. All that represents an admirable unity between your wishes and actions. Will I tell you—now don't be angry—that you lack character; you have a horror of exertion, whatever it may be, in thought as well as in action; your principle is to let the water run and to leave things to time and chance. I can't say you are completely wrong; everyone sees things their own way, or at least believes they do. You have already followed this course in love. You were waiting, you said, for the right time and circumstances. You know, better than I, that neither one nor the other has arrived. The water still runs, and the swimmer is one day surprised to find nothing under him but hot sand.

You're a bit negligent—let me say this without making you angry—and my letters no doubt are lying about, and your parents read them. I do not believe that I'm giving you bad advice. I believe that I speak as a friend and according to reason, but perhaps everyone does not see things as I do, and if what I've suggested above is true, I'm probably not very well thought of by your family. To them, I'm no doubt the liaison dangereuse, the stone thrown onto your path to trip you up. All this afflicts me deeply, but, as I've already told you, I've seen myself misjudged so often that one more wrong judgment, added to the others, would not surprise me. Remain my friend, that is all I wish for.

Another passage of your letter grieved me. Sometimes, so you tell me, you throw your brushes at the ceiling when your results do not come up to your ideas. Why this discouragement, this impatience? I could understand that sort of behavior after years of study, after thousands of useless attempts. Recognizing your nullity, your inability to do well, you would then act wisely if you trampled your palette, your canvas and your brushes underfoot. But as up to now you've only had the wish to work—as you have not yet tackled the task seriously and regularly—you have no right to judge yourself incapable. So have courage. What you've done up to now is nothing. Have courage and remember that, in order to arrive at your goal, you need years of study and perseverance. Am I not in the same position as you? Is the form not just as rebellious under my fingers? We have the right idea, so let us march freely and bravely on our path and may God guide us.

You ask me for details of my daily life. I left the docks. Did I do right, have I done wrong? A relative question, according to one's temperament. I can say only one thing: I could no longer remain there so I walked out. What I intend to do now, I'll tell you later, after I've put my plans into practice. For the moment, here is my life: Chaillan and I started the picture of Amphyon in my little room on the seventh floor, a paradise adorned with a terrace from which we can see all of Paris, a quiet refuge full of sunshine. Chaillan comes at about 1 p.m. Pajot, a young fellow I've mentioned to you, follows soon thereafter. We light our pipes and smoke; after a while, we can't see for more than four feet. I don't talk about the noise; these two gentlemen dance and sing, and by God I join in with them. But tumult is only good at the right time—to sing always, to laugh always, is tiring. I don't work enough, so I'm angry with myself. If you come to Paris, we will try to organize our day so as to slog hard—without, however, neglecting pipe, glass, and song.

Amphyon, under the brush of Chaillan, assumes the expression of a bad-tempered ape. Everything considered, I despair more than ever of this fellow as an artist.

Just now, a letter arrived from Baille. I don't understand anything any more. Here is a sentence I just read in his epistle: «It is almost certain that Cézanne will come to Paris:

what joy!» Does that message come from you? Did you actually give him this hope when he was in Aix? Or has he dreamt it, has he taken for real what is only your dream? I repeat, I don't understand what's going on. Please tell me frankly, in your next letter, how things stand. For three months, according to respective letters, I have been telling myself: he comes, he doesn't come. Good God, let us not behave like weathervanes!

My trip is still fixed for the 15th September. When do you have your law exam? Have you passed? Will you pass?

To vent more of his exasperation with Cézanne, Zola writes to Baille on April 22nd, 1861, and takes upon himself some culpability over Cézanne's problem with his father. He indulges himself, as if he were responsible for the entire drama of Cézanne's reluctant exodus:

I thank you for your letter; it makes me despair, but is useful and necessary. The sad impression it made on me has in a way been diminished by the vague knowledge I had suspicion hovering over me. I felt like an adversary, almost an enemy, in Paul's family. Our different ways of looking at life, and understanding it, revealed to me implicitly how little sympathy Mr. Cézanne has for me. What can I say? What you tell me, I knew already, but didn't dare admit it to myself. Certainly I did not believe it would be possible to accuse me to this extent of infamy, and to see in my brotherly friendship nothing but hateful calculation. To be frank, I must admit that an accusation coming from such a source surprises me rather than making me sad.

As Paul's friend I want, if not to be loved, at least to be respected by his family. If someone I'd come across by chance and will never see again would listen complacently to calumnies about me, and believe them, I would let it go without even trying to convince him otherwise. But in this case it is not like that. Wishing, in spite of everything, to remain Paul's brother, I find myself forced into frequent contact with his father. I'm obliged at times to appear before the eyes of this man who despises me, and to whom I cannot return contempt for contempt. On the other hand, I do not want, at any price, to cause trouble in that family. But as long as his son associates with me, Mr. Cézanne will feel exasperated with his son. I don't want this to happen. I cannot remain silent. If Paul is not prepared to open his father's eyes, then I must think of doing it myself.

There is yet another detail I believe I detect and which you hide from me, no doubt out of affection. You include both of us in this reprobation by Cézanne's family; and something, I don't know what, tells me that I'm the more gravely accused of us two, perhaps even the only one accused. If that is so—and I don't believe I'm mistaken—I thank you for having shouldered half of this heavy burden and for having tried to lighten the sad impression of your letter. There are a thousand details, a thousand reasonings that lead me to this thought; first, my small means, then, my more or less openly admitted state as a writer, my stay in Paris, etc...

The problem appears to me as this: Mr. Cézanne has seen the plans he'd formed being frustrated by his son. The future banker turned out to be a painter, who, feeling eagle wings growing on his back, wants to leave the nest. Surprised by this transformation, this desire for liberty, Mr. Cézanne is unable to believe that anyone would prefer the air of the open sky to his dusty office. Mr. Cézanne took it into his head to discover the key to this enigma, but he takes care not to admit that this situation is so because God wanted it so, because God, having made him a banker, made his son a painter. But, had he thought deeper, it was I who made Paul into what he is today, it was I who lured him away from the bank, his most cherished hope... Fortunately, it is likely that Paul has kept my letters; reading them one could easily see what my advice was, and whether I have ever pushed him in the wrong direction. On the contrary, I have repeatedly pointed out to him the drawbacks of his trip to Paris and have advised him to treat his father with consideration.

I wanted to have Paul near me, but when expressing this wish, I never advised him to rebel. Without intending to, I stimulated his love for the arts, and have certainly done nothing except develop seeds that already existed, an effect that any other outside cause could have produced as well. If I ask myself, the answer is that I am not guilty of anything. My attitude has always been sincere and blameless. I've loved Paul like a brother, always dreaming of his happiness, without egoism, without self-interest, rekindling his courage when I saw he was weakening, always trying to lift up his spirit and, above all, to make a man of him. It is true that I have never talked about money in these letters, that I've never drawn his attention to this or that business enterprise where one could gain vast amounts. My letters spoke only of my friendship, my dreams, and I don't know how many noble feelings, coins that have no value anywhere in the commercial world. That is no doubt the reason why I am a schemer in the eyes of Mr. Cézanne.

I am making fun of it, yet I have no wish to. However that may be, here is my plan. Having first agreed with Paul, I want to see Mr. Cézanne alone and have a frank discussion with him. Don't be afraid, I will be restrained and moderate in my language in front of our friend's father; I will behave as I ought to.

I'm telling you all this without really knowing what I will do. I'm expecting Cézanne to come to Paris and want to see him before making any decision. Sooner or later his father will be forced to respect me again; if he ignores the past, the future will convince him.

I interrupt myself, shouting: I have seen Paul!, I have seen Paul! Do you understand? Do you? Do you understand the melody of those three words? He came this morning, Sunday, and several times called my name from the staircase. I was half asleep. I opened my door, trembling with joy, and we embraced furiously. Then he reassured me about his father's attitude towards me; he maintained that over-zealous, no doubt, you had exaggerated a little. Then he told me that his father wanted to see me. I will visit him today or tomorrow. We can only see each other now and then, but in a month we count on living together.

Write when you can. As far as I'm concerned, we will shake your hand in a fortnight, Cézanne and I.

17

I thought that when I left Aix
I would leave behind the boredom
that pursues me wherever I go

L ouis-Auguste Cézanne had accompanied his son to Paris, bringing along for the ride his daughter Marie.[1] This trip was not planned as just a visit for Cézanne, but a move sanctioned by his parents. Louis-Auguste and Marie spent a few weeks with Cézanne, lodged in a hotel on the *rue Coquillière*, seeing the sights, perhaps visiting museums, helping him locate appropriate lodging, settling him in so they could return to Aix knowing he would be reasonably safe and sound. Over those weeks, Cézanne had little time to spend with Zola. In a letter to Baille, Zola mentions that Cézanne was occupied most of his time with his father and sister. And contrary to Zola's puffy premonition, the thought that Cézanne's father despised him would now prove unfounded; all along, Cézanne had advised Zola that it was. Not only was Zola tolerated, but he was asked to join Louis-Auguste and his children for dinner.

Twenty-six months had passed between Zola's relocation to Paris and Cézanne's arrival. Cézanne did not move in with Zola, as Zola had hoped, nor does it appear that much transpired in terms of what Zola had dreamt about as restoration of their youth. Zola was lodged then in the steamy quarters along rue Saint-Victor near the Panthéon, and Cézanne was installed near by, in a furnished room on the *rue des Feuillantines*. A condition of paternal support may have been that Cézanne prepare for the *École des Beaux-Arts* entrance exams, not an unreasonable demand for a father about to lay out years of financial support for what he projected as a dubious future for his son. In time, Cézanne would apply to the École and be rejected. His humble art training in Aix would not qualify him to even take the exam.

The *Académie Suisse*, which Cézanne attended with fair diligence, was one of several open studios where would-be artists could work before a live model. Named after the professional Swiss model that established it, the *Suisse* had no tuition, no teachers or formal classes, no grades or evaluation. Use of this studio in a dilapidated building on the *Quai des Orfèvres* near *Pont Saint-Michel*—known in the neighborhood as the location of a dentist who advertised extractions at one franc per tooth—required only a few sous paid at each session to cover the model's fee and the expense of heating the studio. Models alternated weekly between male and female, mostly professional models who knew how to strike standard poses that admission judges at the *École* would be looking for in applicants' portfolios and evaluating their test sessions before an easel. Courbet and Monet had also made use of the Suisse, and Pissarro, who lived on the outskirts of Paris, could be found there on occasional mornings.

No detailed description of the Suisse has come down through history, but the learning situation there must have been similar to the studio of Gérôme, or that of Gleyre where the young Monet, Renoir, Bazille, and Sisley studied. A friend of Whistler's, who had studied at Gleyre's studio, reported that thirty or forty students worked there daily from the nude model, from eight until noon, and then two more hours after lunch. He describes bare walls decorated with caricatures, palette scrapings all over the floor, a stove, a models' throne, low chairs, dozens of easels; the students varying from graybeards who'd been drawing and painting there for thirty years, a few young men one day to make their mark, others to be singled out for the hospital, the garret, the river, the morgue, or worse, the father's counter—irresponsible boys, all laugh and chaff and mischief; wits, bullies, good and bad, clean and dirty.[12] Gérôme's studio was even more negatively described by the painter Jean-François Raffaëlli: *Wretched young men, most of them coarse and vulgar, telling disgusting jokes, singing stupid obscene songs. Never, never in this assemblage of men called to be artists is there any discussion about art, never a lofty idea; over and over again this dirty and senseless humbug, always filth.*[3] Renoir had this to say about his studio days at Gleyre's: *While the others shouted, broke window panes, martyred the model, I was quiet in my corner, very docile, studying the model, and it was I they called revolutionary!*[4]

On the 1st of May 1861, Zola wrote to Baille, saying that he saw Cézanne often. But the news has a hollow ring to it. Dismal weather intervenes to express the darkness of his disappointment. *Paul works a lot,* Zola says, *but I won't complain about his reluctance to see me. We've not yet had any parties. Those we've indulged are not worth writing about. Tomorrow, Sunday, we plan to go to Neuilly to pass the day on the banks of the Seine, to bathe, smoke, drink, etc., etc. But now the sky has darkened, the wind is blowing, it's getting chilly. So, good-bye fine day. I don't know how we will entertain ourselves. Paul is going to paint my portrait.*

Later, Zola reported that, on occasional Sundays, he and Cézanne would take long excursions by train beyond the city walls to such country places as *Fontenay-aux-Roses,* and from there hike to as far as the border of the Loups Valley. How often this happened, one cannot say. *One morning,* Zola recalls, *while wandering through a forest, we came upon a pond, far from any path, filled with reeds and slimy water, which we called the green pond, not knowing its real name. It became the destination of all our walks. We soon felt for it the affection of a poet and a painter; we loved it dearly and spent our Sundays on the thin grass surrounding it. Paul began a sketch of it, the water in the foreground with big floating reeds, the trees receding like the wings of a theater, draping the curtains of their branches as in a chapel, with blue holes that disappeared in an eddy when the wind blew. The thin rays of the sun crossed the shadows like balls of gold and threw on the grass shining round disks that moved slowly as the sun passed over.*

This may have been one of Cézanne's few days of bliss, and for both of them a restoration of their memories of excursions from Aix. But no sooner had Cézanne settled into Paris and gotten his art studies underway than the process of erosion began. What he had hoped to leave behind in Aix he found waiting for him in Paris. He was not yet ready to invest himself in the serious game of art, not sure how to put himself in the pose of an artist. Raised as a potential bourgeois, he was now a provisional artist among bohemians—pseudo-bohemians, on the lunatic fringe. Boredom, the chronic ailment of the apathetic mind, overtook him within the first few weeks. In a letter of June 4th, 1861, to Joseph Huot, an art-school compatriot in Aix who would become an architect, Cézanne wrote:

Oh, my good Joseph, so I am forgetting you, morbleu! and our good friends at the Bastidon, and your brother and the good wines of Provence. You know it is detestable, the wine you get here. I don't want to write an elegy in few lines, yet, I must confess, my heart is not very gay. I fritter away my petty existence right and left. At the Suisse I'm busy from six o'clock in the morning until eleven.

I thought that when I left Aix I would leave behind the boredom that pursues me wherever I go. I have only changed places; boredom followed me. I left my parents, my friends, some of my habits, that's all this entire move means. I admit that here I roam around aimlessly all day. I have seen—naive thing to say!—the potboilers those admirable monuments enclose: stunning, shocking, knocks you over. I've also seen the Salon. For a young heart, for a child born for art, who says what he thinks, I believe that the Salon is where art is the best, because all tastes and styles meet and clash there. I could give you some beautiful descriptions and put you to sleep. Be grateful to me for sparing you.

But Cézanne cannot resist giving Huot a few descriptions of the pictures in the Salon, which he renders as satirical poetry:

By someone named Yvon, I saw a brilliant battle scene:[5]
In a drawing of an emotional scene, Pils[6]
traces the memory of it in a stirring picture,
And the portraits of those who lead us on a leash;
Large, small, medium, short, beautiful, or of a worse kind yet.
Here there is a river; over there the sun burns,
The rising of Phoebus, the moon's setting,
Sparkling daylight, gloomy twilight
The climate of Russia or the African sky;

Here, a brutal Turk, the figure stupefied, exhausted,
There, by contrast, I see a suffering child
On purple cushions a pretty girl
displays her breasts, dazzling in fresh blooming.
Little armors fly about in space;
A fresh-faced coquette admires herself in a mirror.
Gérôme next to Hamel, Glaise next to Cabanel,
Müller, Courbet, Gudin, disputing for the honor
Of victory...[7]

I am at the end of my rhymes, he continues, *so I shall do well to be silent, for it would be a bold enterprise on my part to give you even the scantiest idea of this exhibition. But there are some magnificent Meissoniers . I've seen nearly everything of his, and I intend to go back. It is worth my while.*

Cézanne's descriptions are not just set to poetry but also poetic—such phrases as *On purple cushions a pretty girl.* By this time he must already have been aware that ridicule of the Salon was a sort of bonding ritual among young and disappointed painters who sustain the raillery until they themselves are accepted by a jury. Journalists and caricaturists wanting to tickle the public subjected the Salon to every form of criticism. The poet Jean Moréas described a Salon—less poetically than the young Cézanne. He drew up a list: *Biblical beggars with blackened complexions, raging Abrahams, Christs as grim-faced shopkeepers, corpulent Cardinals, long-suffering, wilting martyrs, scandalously mammalian and gloomy mercenaries, weeping Venuses, languid nymphs, suburban Napoleons, and an entire carnival-like repertory of the Malaquais quayside all painted in crusted Prussian blue, bitumen, and raw Sienna.*

Ernest Meissonier, Cézanne's favorite artist at this time, was a skilled painter of sweet, sentimental genre scenes meticulously painted in small format and often based on eighteenth-century motifs—an audience favorite at the Salon while the butt of academic painting in the minds of most realist painters and critics. Though still acclaimed for soul-touching imagery of gentle people absorbed in ordinary activities—reading, playing music, cards or chess—he was falling out rapidly by the end of the 1850s. The critic Saint-Victor, writing in *La Presse*, complained in 1857 that Meissonier's *little personages only know how to read, write, smoke their pipe, play the counterbass, and talk between pear and cheese, their elbows on the table—a limited repertoire;*[8] and in the same year, the critic Paul Mantz, also in *La Presse*, asked rhetorically, *Would it be too much to ask of this gifted artist to somewhat renew his choice of subjects?*[9]

Cézanne had not yet grown beyond attraction to such pictures as Meissonier's, just as Zola still adored the bed-pillow poetry of Ary Scheffer's imagery, both having been suckled by such sweetened-milk pictures in Aix's art museum. It is worth noting here that among the two thousand or so pictures in the Salon, the majority mediocre by anyone's creed, the artists that Cézanne mentions in his letter to Huot, other than Hamel and Glaise, were distinguished painters, and, except for Gérôme and Cabanel, who would be elected two years later, were members of the Academy. He also admired, as he says in his letter, *a magnificent picture by Gustave Doré*, whose imagery will also attract Zola; on December 23rd, 1863 the *Journal populaire de Lille* will print Zola's essay *«Cervantès et Gustave Doré: A propos de Don Quiote illustré* [Cervantes and Gustave Doré: Concerning the Illustrated Don Quixote].

Cézanne ends his letter to Huot saying that, aside from his hours at the *Suisse*, he is working every day in Villevieille's studio (Villevieille having moved to Paris for a spell) where the «master» is envisioning huge paintings, as much as four meters tall, with figures above life size:

> *Villevieille, at whose studio I work every day, sends you a thousand good wishes, also friend Bourck, whom I see from time to time. Chaillan sends you his most cordial greetings. Hello also to Solari, Félicien, Rambert, Lelé, Fortis—to all. I should never finish if I named everyone. Tell me, if you are able, the result of the drawing of lots for all these friends* (military subscription depended on one's draw).

Zola's chagrin that Cézanne spent so little time with him arose most likely because Cézanne had made new friends less imposing than Zola and who shared the same routine. In a June 10th, 1861 letter from Zola to Baille, one reads more about this condition:

> *I see Cézanne rarely. Alas! It's no longer as it was at Aix when we were eighteen, free and without worry for the future. Now the demands of our lives and our different work keep us apart. In the morning Paul goes to the Suisse while I remain in my room to write. At eleven o'clock we lunch, each by himself. Sometimes, at midday, I go to his place and he works on my portrait. For the rest of the days he goes to Villevieille's to draw. He has his supper, goes early to bed, and I don't see him anymore. Is that what I'd hoped for?*
>
> *To prove that Paul has lost nothing of his peculiarity, I only have to tell you that hardly had he arrived here when he talked about returning to Aix—to have battled for three years for this voyage and then not give a damn! With such a character, faced with changes of behavior so unpredictable, I admit that I just remain speechless and keep logic packed away. To prove something to Cézanne would be like trying to persuade the towers of Notre-Dame to dance a quadrille. He would perhaps say yes, but then not budge an inch. Age has increased his stubbornness without providing him with anything reasonable to be stubborn about. He is made of one piece, obstinate and hard in the hand; nothing can bend him, nothing can get a concession from him. He doesn't even want to discuss his thoughts; he has a horror of discussion—first, because talking is tiring, and then because he would have to change his view if his opponent were right. So he has been thrown into life with definite ideas, unwilling to change them unless following his own judgment. Otherwise, he remains the best fellow in the world, always agreeing as a result of his hor-*

ror of discussion, but nevertheless following his own little head. When his lips say yes, most of the time his judgment says no. If, accidentally, he utters a different opinion, and you dispute it, he flares up, not willing even to think about it, and shouts that you don't understand a thing about the problem; then he jumps to another subject. How can one discuss? How can one even talk to a fellow of such temper, when you can't gain with him a finger-length of ground, and are simply left high and dry, just observing this very strange character? I had hoped that age would have wrought some changes in him. But I find him much as I left him in Aix. My plan of action is, therefore, quite simple—never to stand in the way of his whims; to give him at most only indirect advice; to rely on his good nature to sustain our friendship, never to force his hand to shake mine: in short, to efface myself completely, to always receive him cheerfully, to seek him out without bothering him, and to leave it to his pleasure how much or how little intimacy he wishes to preserve between us. What I am saying may perhaps astonish you. It is, however, rational. Paul is for me still a fellow with a good heart, a friend who understands and appreciates me. Only, as everyone has his own nature, I must wisely conform to his moods if I do not want to see his friendship fly off. In order to preserve yours with him, I would perhaps try reasoning only with yourself; reasoning with him would mean losing everything. Don't assume there's a cloud between us. We are still close, and what I've been saying has little to do with the fortuitous circumstances that separate us more than I would like.

Zola asked in this letter, *Is that what I'd hoped for?* What Zola had hoped was a Cézanne he could control, whom he could guide like a father. What Cézanne found on coming to Paris was that Zola in the flesh was worse than he had been in his letters over the two years of their separation. Zola's passion was fomented no doubt by his fatherless youth, by being the man of the house when just a boy living with his mother. Eventually he would find a way to build a career on this need to control; his entire Rougon-Macquart series of novels will put him in control of three generations. And even before then, in his book reviews and Salon reviews, he will be the controlling critic, wanting the entire art and literary world to perform to his whip. Cézanne had disappointed him, angered him, because he was not following his tutelage. If Cézanne over-resisted his badgering advice and pushy thoughts about art, it would have been to lessen Zola's imperious jabs.

When Cézanne displays resistance, Zola responds like a petulant child—fretting, smug, self-justifying: *never to stand in the way of his whims; give him at most only indirect advice; never force his hand to shake mine; efface myself completely, always receive him cheerfully, seek him out without bothering him,* Zola writes in self-defense. His letter to Baille tells much more about his own personality than Cézanne's. He had needed Cézanne, yet Cézanne showed no need for Zola. Over the entire period of their separation, Zola had made few friends in Paris. After his disappointment with Cézanne, he again writes to Baille in July, saying that he sees Cézanne infrequently and is now counting on Baille's move to Paris: *Your arrival here will bring about for me greater moral and physical well-being.*

Perhaps still ringing in Cézanne's ears were the tyrannical and castigating passages in Zola's letters to him over the months before he had come to Paris. Swallowing them in letterform may have been easier than hearing Zola haranguing right in front of him:

>—*What do you mean by the word realism? You boast that you paint only subjects devoid of poetry. Is that because you claim to imitate nature slavishly?*

>—*Last time I warned you against realism. Today I want to show you another danger: commercial art.*

>—*Allow me to explain myself for the last time, frankly and clearly. Is painting for you just a whim you happened to have grabbed by the hair one day when you were bored?*

>—*What then is you attitude? That of a lazy fellow, no doubt.*

>—*Shall I tell you? You lack character; you have a horror of exertion. You are negligent. Your guiding principle is to let the water run.*

>—*Up to now, you've only had the desire to work, as you've not tackled the job seriously and regularly. What you have done up to now is nothing!*

Next to Zola, Cézanne's father may have been an angelic sage. In the guise of a loving and caring friend, Zola was abrasive, if not emotionally abusive. A month later, in early August 1861, Zola again writes to Baille. In this letter Zola does an about face, taking back what he'd previously written about Cézanne's character:

>*Should anyone put the question to me, «What do you think of this man?» I would try to politely dodge the question. How can one judge a person who is neither pure matter, like a picture, nor abstract, like an action? What conclusions can one draw from this mixture of good and bad that makes up human existence? That is what I asked myself when thinking of my last letter to you where I expressed my thoughts about Cézanne. I tried to judge him, and in spite of my good faith, I then regretted having arrived at conclusions that are not entirely true.*

>*Hardly had Paul returned from a trip to Marcoussis when he came to see me, and was more affectionate than ever. Since then, we have been passing six hours a day together, every day. Our place of reunion is his little room. There he paints my portrait, while I read or we chat. Then, when work is well above our ears, we usually go to smoke a pipe in the Luxembourg. Our conversations range over everything, especially painting. Our memories also occupy a large space in our conversations. As for the future, we touch it with one word in passing, either to wish for our complete reunion, or to put to ourselves the terrible problem of success.*

>*Sometimes, at his place, Cézanne delivers a lecture on economics, and at the end forces me to go have a bottle of beer with him. At other times, for hours he chants couplets with stupid words and stupid music; in the end, I declare that I prefer a speech about the economy. We are seldom disturbed. Intruders come from time to time and push in. Furiously,*

Paul begins to paint, I pose like a sphinx, and the intruder, put in a state by such hard work, sits for a moment, doesn't dare move or speak, then goes away with a quiet good-bye, closing the door very gently.

Cézanne has frequent fits of despair. In spite of his affected contempt for fame, I see that he would like to arrive. When things go badly, he speaks of returning home and becoming an apprentice in a business firm. Then I have to give him a long talking-to, to prove to him the silliness of returning to Aix. He readily agrees and goes back to work. Yet, the thought of returning gnaws at him. Twice already he has been on the verge of leaving. I fear that he may escape me at some time or another. If you write to him, talk of our next reunion in the most glowing colors. That is the only way we can hold him here.

Cézanne. It cannot be said for certain that this is the portrait of Zola refered to in Zola's letter. If posed like a sphinx, Zola would have been portrayed head on. Zola says that Cézanne destroyed the canvas. This canvas has the aspect of one that had been scraped for repainting. Seoul, Gana Art Gallery.

We have not yet made any excursions. Money holds us back. Paul is not rich, and I less so. However, one of these days we hope to take wing and go off somewhere to dream. To summarize, I can tell you that, in spite of its monotony, the life we are leading is not boring. Work stops us from yawning, and memories we exchange gild everything with rays of sunlight. Do come, and we will be even less bored.

Zola's letter was not completed in one sitting. It is abruptly re-charged by an intervening event:

I re-start this letter to confirm what I said above by something that happened yesterday, Sunday. I went to see Paul, who told me in cold blood that he was about to pack his suitcase and depart the next day. We went to a café. I didn't make a speech. I was so surprised and so convinced my logic would prove useless that I didn't dare raise the slightest objection. But I was looking for a ruse to keep him. I thought I'd found one back when I asked him to do my portrait. He'd accepted the idea then with joy, and for the moment there was no more question of his going back. [10]

This damned portrait, which, according to my plan, should keep him in Paris, very nearly made him leave yesterday. Having restarted it twice, always dissatisfied with himself, he wanted to finish it. He asked me to sit for him for the last time yesterday morning.

So I went to his place. On entering I saw an open trunk, half empty drawers. Paul, with a dismal face, pushed things around and shoved things without any order into the trunk. Then he said quietly to me: «I leave tomorrow.» - «And my portrait?» I said. - «Your portrait,» he answered, «I have just crushed it. I worked at it again this morning, and as it became worse and worse, I annihilated it. I'm going.»[11]

Cézanne at about the age of twenty-one.

Apparently, Cézanne did not destroy the portrait—perhaps he scraped it off—for we have a portrait of Zola that fits this event. It disappointed him, as had its subject. Destroying or defacing the portrait was, as in any style of personage effacing, most likely an attack on Zola, to be rid of him. To return to Aix, Cézanne would have to put Zola out of his mind. Zola's letter continues:

I refrained from reacting. We went for lunch together. During the day, Paul became more reasonable, and in the end, when he left me that evening, he promised to stay. But this is only bad patchwork. If he doesn't leave this week, he'll leave next week. From one minute to the other I expect to see him go. I even believe that he is right. He may possess the genius of a great painter, but he'll never have the genius to become one. The slightest obstacle makes him despair. I repeat, if he wants to avoid a lot of sorrow he should leave.

Zola tried to talk Cézanne into holding fast until September, but Cézanne may have been back in Aix a month before that, thoroughly disillusioned and feeling like a prodigal son. Welcomed home by his family, he took a job in his father's bank.

And so it came to pass that at his first stay in Paris, Cézanne did not arrive at being an artist. His determination may have been too weak; he was without a proper teacher to push him along, and he had fallen in with a lot of mediocre art students. It is said that his efforts at drawing from the model were ridiculed by fellow students, but that should not have affected him. He was not that tender.[12] He may have missed the attention he had received at the municipal drawing school in Aix. He may just have been homesick. Zola, too, pined for Provence, but he had no home for which he would be heartsick; if he had one, perhaps he, too, would have fled Paris to attempt recapturing adolescence under the benevolent Provençal sun.

But not too much should be made of Cézanne's retreat; in the broad category of immigrants, he was one of thousands who came to Paris from the provinces to be painters, poets, dancers, and when up against hard knocks return home to take up a trade or work in their father's business. If against all odds they remain in Paris, when the allowance runs out they fall into bohemia, the river, or on a cold morgue slab. Only a few survive. The Parisian architect Eugène Viollet-le-Duc, an acerbic critic of art education in France, had this to say the year of Cézanne's retreat, 1862, when in March a special commission had been established to study means of improving the curriculum of the *École des Beaux-Arts* (the very year Cézanne will return to Paris and fail the entrance requirements):

> *A young man shows an inclination for painting or sculpture. This young man has first to overcome the distaste of his parents for this profession, who would rather see him enter the school for engineers or make a merchant's clerk of him. His capacities are doubted, proof of his abilities are looked for. And if he is not crowned right off with some sort of success, he is considered misguided or lazy—no more allowance. So it is necessary for him to pursue this success by entering the École des Beaux-Arts. Then he can win medals. But at what price? —by keeping precisely and without deviation within the limits imposed by the corporation of professors, by submissively following the beaten path, by having in his head only ideas that are permitted by the corporation, and by never displaying that he has any ideas of his own.*
>
> *The student body naturally includes more mediocrities than talented people, and the majority aligns itself with the routine. Then there is no ridicule sufficient for the person who shows inclination towards originality. How is it possible, then, for a poor fellow, despised by his teachers, chaffed by his companions, threatened by his parents, if he does not follow the middle of the marked-out highway, to have enough strength and confidence in himself, enough courage, to withstand the weight of this yoke and to walk freely?*[13]

The painter of sheep and cows, Constant Troyon, also spoke of the plight of young artists in Paris in 1862: *The situation is very grave; the artists in general are little satisfied; the poor young folk have a right to complain.* And in the same year, the young Fantin-Latour wrote in a letter to his friends in England, *Paris! that's free art. No one sells, but there one has freedom of expression, and people who strive, who struggle, who approve; there one has artists of like mind setting up a school; the most ridiculous as well as the most glorified idea has its ardent supporters. At bottom, Paris is an atrocious place to live.*[14]

18

*Muses and virgins have little
to do with a writer's success*

Not much is known about Cézanne's life from his return to Aix in the late summer of 1861 to autumn 1862 when he again moved to Paris. Between late January and the end of September of 1862, no letters written by Cézanne have survived, and after September, no letters survive from Zola to either Cézanne or Baille. And no art by Cézanne can be dated with certainty to this year. One can only assume that over the months back in his hometown, living with his parents and sisters, he experienced routine interaction with relatives or friends—a grown-up boy still at home, with friends undergoing the vicissitudes of maturation and coming of age.

A few months of estrangement would pass before correspondence flows again between him and Zola. Cézanne may have felt embarrassed over being unable to cope with Paris; he had failed Zola and proven that his father and his art teacher Gibert were correct in their assessment of his brittle commitment to art. Still, even though his first serious go at becoming an artist was a failure, he most likely resumed studies at the municipal art school in Aix—penitent, perhaps, but no wiser—in the company of friends: Solari, Huot, and Coste. Baille had left for Paris in the autumn of 1861 for advanced study at the *École Polytechnique*.

Cézanne had brought too much ill-packed emotional baggage to Paris on his first trip, or perhaps had left too much of himself in Aix. What's more, Zola had expected a lot from Cézanne: a renewed intimate friendship and a commitment to art. But Cézanne had had all he could take of Zola's pestering and intrusion into his family life. Bonded through the trials of adolescence, maturity was ungluing their relationship, like a love affair going sour when reality sets in. But if Cézanne's first effort to take art seriously was a failure, Zola, too, would have to consign his fantasies to the bulging dead-file of youthful dreams and hope to avoid the yawning abyss by keeping on the move. *What I'm looking for is simply the first job I find*, he tells Baille, leaving the choice up to Fortuna who, thus far, had treated him only with ill fortune. And when he speculates on who he might marry, now that the girl of his dreams had given him up as hopeless, he writes to Baille,

The fast woman is beyond speculation, the widow frightens me, the virgin is non-existent. Like taking a job, he would have to take what came along—no preconception, no dream girl.

To recover from this dire state, he details this litany of woe for Baille: *You may think I'm denying love. But it's just that I'm waiting for some good angel, some rare exception to the rule. I know perfectly well that I'm daydreaming, that my wish may never be fulfilled.* Now it was no longer the case that if Zola had only found true love he would be able to write remarkable poetry, as if believing that if only Cézanne and Baille would come to Paris he could produce epics. By 1861, at age twenty-one, his dreams were fading into drab reality. His visions were changing; he was becoming jaded, like a pair of aging work pants getting immune to dirt. Forced to abandon job-hunting for his bed to keep warm during a frigid winter, he writes to Cézanne, back in Aix, *If my stove were lit I could work so well.* His hot passion for an inspiring muse had been reduced to the warmth of a hot stove.

But the Zola he would soon become was stirring. His self-fathered ego would be put to the task of converting fancy into reality. *I've been thinking long enough*, he wrote to Baille. *Now is the time to start producing. An entire book is taking shape in my head, episode-by-episode, chapter-by-chapter. I believe and hope that I've regained faith in myself. I laugh and no longer feel in the slightest bit bored.* The long period of expectancy was over. Two years later, in a letter to an Aixois friend, Antoine Valabrègue, Zola tells of correcting proofs on this book, the novel *La Confession de Claude*. This book, a potent shot of reality, must have come into his mind as a mystical impregnation. He signs off the letter with, *A poor man who is expecting his first child.*

Making the first attempt to rekindle their relationship, Zola writes to Cézanne on January 20th, 1862:

It's been a long time since I wrote to you. I don't quite know why. Paris did our friendship no good. Perhaps to live merrily it needs the sun of Provence. No doubt an unhappy misunderstanding brought coolness into our relationship—some ill-judged incident or mischievous word taken too willingly. I don't know, and I don't want to know. Stirring up filth, one soils one's hands.

Never mind, I still consider you my friend, by which I mean that you believe me incapable of being mean and that you think as highly of me as in the past. Should that not be so, it would be good if you would explain why and tell me frankly what you reproach me for. It is not a letter full of explanations that I want to write now. I only want to answer your letter as your friend, and talk to you a bit, as if your voyage to Paris had never taken place.

You advise me to work, and you do that with so much insistence that one would think work repelled me. I assure you that my most fervent desire, my thought every day, is to find a job. Nothing but the impossibility of finding one keeps me nailed down in my room. Baille did not mislead you when saying that definitely and soon I will join the house of Hachette as an employee. I'm waiting for a letter to tell me there's a vacancy. I see Baille every Sunday and Wednesday. We do not have much to laugh about. It is wolfishly cold and the pleasures of Paris, if there are any, are crazily expensive. We are reduced to talks about the past and the future simply because the present is so frigid and barren. Perhaps summer will bring back gaiety. If you come in March, as you promise—if I have my job, if fate smiles on us—then perhaps we will live a bit in the present without too many regrets, without desiring too much. But those are many ifs. Only one of them has to fail and everything tumbles down.

Don't think I am completely benumbed. I'm quite ill but not yet dead. The spirit is awake and does wonders in spite of everything. I even believe that I am growing through my suffering.

And you, what are you doing? Have you gotten your life together? Do we have to say good-bye to our dreams? Will absurdities come and thwart our plans?

Librarie Hachette. The leading publishing house in France. This photograph taken about the time of Zola's employment.

On the first day of March 1862, Zola started work at the Librarie Hachette, a conglomerated publishing house and bookstore with innovative skills in production and marketing of books and periodicals. Just twenty-two years old, his entry-level job ranked slightly above that of the store's mouser cat. Over the first months he was the stock boy and shipping clerk at a monthly salary of 100 francs—twenty-five francs less than what Cézanne's father had provided as his son's allowance (During the 1860s, the average monthly pay for a common male worker was a bit less than 85 francs, and many workers were supporting families at such wages on the level of marginal poverty).

If Zola's previous job at the docks recalled his father's profession involving canals and harbors, his employment at Hachette's would open him up to his future; his father's aspirations would no longer figure in his life. His four years at *Librarie Hachette* would be apprenticeship years, an opportunity that comes the way of few young writers. Hachette's was a stage to act upon, offering real characters to relate to, the right backdrops and props, an empire built over three decades by a visionary capitalist who would inspire Zola to stop dreaming and make things happen.

Hachette's occupied almost an entire block near the intersection of

Boulevard Saint-Germain and the Boulevard Sébastopol. It published textbooks, classics, novels, dictionaries, travel guides, children's books, popular science books, illustrated magazines, professional journals, and newspapers; the *Journal pour tous* boasted 100,000 subscribers. Hachette's branch stores spread as far as French-speaking Algeria and Morocco and the French West Indies. As railroad passenger travel blossomed in the 1850s, Louis Hachette recognized a need for books to read while traveling; he established kiosks at every train station, promoting what would one day be called airport novels: diversionary popular romance and adventure books to engage the masses, requiring little effort to read. During the 1862-1864 years, when Zola's eyes were opening to the real world of publishing, Hachette had reached another phase of expansion embracing every aspect of modernity and progress, publishing even more books on science and technology, and promoting a line of books and journals on progressive education, not only for schools but for the general public. The success of the publishing industry, made competitive by cheap printing costs, had come to depend on the rapid growth of literacy and thirst for practical knowledge. Even the architecture of Hachette's dispatch office where Zola started working signaled a commitment to modern life; the building was constructed of steel and glass rather than the typical limestone of Paris' past glory.

The firm's interests in promoting books on science and technology would help to condition Zola's thoughts about realism and scientific writing; his future novels would be based on extensive research into the mechanics of life and the chemistry of human interaction. Zola's closest friends in Paris—Baille, who had finally arrived, and Pajot, who had befriended Zola at the *Lycée St-Louis*—were keen on scientific modernity and popular mechanics. In 1863, Baille, now closer to Zola than to Cézanne, would graduate from Paris' *École Polytechnique* with degrees in chemistry, mathematics, and physics. His dissertation, *The refractive Indices of Lenses Used in the Construction of Optical and Photographic Instruments*, would win the 1866 prestigious National Institute of France's Bordin Prize. The Hachette editor in charge of the series *Bibliothèque des merveilles* had asked Zola for Baille's proposed text, *L'Électricité*, which summed up theories on electricity and their practical applications—the first book devoted to the popularization of the electrical branch of applied physics. Hachette published it in 1868.

A few weeks after taking employment, Zola conceived of an opportunity to impress Louis Hachette. He handed him a memorandum proposing a new magazine, a *Bibliothèque des Débutants*, specializing in the writings of young and promising authors.

> *I can tell you that every young man who writes, being intimidated by the reputation you enjoy, regards your editorial department as an impregnable sanctuary, and hesitates before daring to submit his work. Is it not, Sir, a project meritorious enough to tempt a powerful publisher, with great wealth and great credit? He would in this way place himself up front*

in the literary movement of the young generation, would revolutionize established ideas and expose to ridicule mediocrities who complain about going unrecognized. I venture to say that such an initiative would make him even more powerful and assure him a unique place among his confrères. He would be loved, and people would praise him for extending this helping hand to the young.[1]

Louis Hachette was not inclined to follow Zola's suggestion but must have been impressed by the young man's well-conceived plan and zealousness to promote the Hachette enterprise. He offered Zola the position of head of publicity and sales promotion at double the salary he was then earning. It did not take long at this job for Zola's illusions and fantasies about literary life to dissolve into hard reality. He soon came to recognize that writers are not born and that muses and virgins have little to do with a writer's success. Only a paying readership counts.

Readers are the oxygen the writer breathes; if not oxygen, one inhales only dreamy gases, aromas without vigor, aspirations without remuneration, like wispy cigar-smoke virgins that cannot be caught in one's hands or put in the bank. To reach the reader, one needs a profit-motivated publisher, and the publisher needs booksellers just as motivated. It would stand to reason then that, to be successful as a writer, one must believe that money is the substance by which success is measured. To his yearning writer friend in Aix, Antoine Valabrègue, Zola wrote:

I can now give you a few bits of advice. I'm in a position to pass on to you what experience has taught me. When you are here, we will take the bull by the horns. If you only knew, my friend, how negligible talent is when it comes to achieving success, you would abandon your pen and paper and study the true ways of the literary world, the little chicaneries that force open doors, the art of pulling strings, and the necessity to pitilessly step over the bodies of your dearest colleagues.

Unable to indulge the pleasures of Paris for lack of money, Zola and Baille, who were getting together a couple of times each week, awaited summer when gaiety out of doors is free. But when summer did come, Baille went off to spend the months in Provence while Zola still worked day in and day out at Hachette's. *The sun shines and I'm shut in*, Zola laments in a September 18th, 1862 letter jointly addressed to Cézanne and Baille. He'd been at Hachette's for over seven months, and about a year had passed since Cézanne had returned to Aix. *What are you doing?* Zola asks in this letter. *And why the silence? I expect a response. Will you make me wait long? I'm also still waiting for the copy from you, Paul* (the reference must be a copy of some painting that Cézanne had promised him).

Yesterday a bird coming up from the south passed over my head, and I shouted, «Bird, my little friend, did you notice down there on the road below you an errant picture?»

«I saw nothing of the kind,» answered the bird, «only the dusty road. Be sad,» the bird then said, «they have forgotten you.»

The bird lied, didn't it?

A few days later, on the 29th of September 1862, Zola wrote again to Cézanne:

> *My dear friend,*
>
> *Faith in life has come back to me—I think, I hope. I've set to work with a will. Every evening I shut myself up in my room and write or read until midnight. The most important result is that I've recovered some of my gaiety.*
>
> *I plan to pile manuscript upon manuscript on my writing desk. Then one day I will turn them loose on the newspapers. I've already written three short stories, about thirty pages each, since Baille's departure.*

The three stories mentioned in this letter, *Le Sang, Le Carnet de danse, Les Voleurs et l'âne*, were written over August and September. They would be included in Zola's book of short stories, *Contes à Ninon*, to be published in October 1864.

Zola had given his boss a few pieces of verse to read. Apparently less impressed with the poetry than with Zola's ability to write, Hachette advised him to abandon poetry for prose and suggested he write a story for one of the reviews his firm published for children, the firm's popular *Bibliothèque rose illustré* series—illustrated books with red covers denoting them as children's books, separate from the *Bibliothèque bleue* series, which were romance novels for women.[2] Over 1863, Zola published a few short pieces in the *Journal populaire de Lille* and the *Salut public* of Lyons, both controlled by Hachette. Five years later, in a letter of May 29th, 1867, Zola finally confesses his complete abandonment of poetry with words of advice to Valabrègue. Having no sweet thoughts about Provence, he blamed Aix for having seduced him into poetry in the first place.

> *Well, I just want to tell you to stay in Aix long enough to conquer your freedom, and to beware of that dead town. There you think you're walking and you find yourself sleeping. You can't realize that because you're sleeping, but I can see when I read your letters that you are immobile and stuck in Aix, for I live in Paris, the feverish city. Do you need proof? If you had stayed in Paris, you wouldn't have gone back to poetry. What drives you to poetry, to dreams of rhythmic rhymes, is that dreadful atmosphere weighing down your shoulders. In the quietness of your retreat, your mind is seized by that sweet sleep necessary for the flowering of verse.*
>
> *Of course I don't blame you for being a poet, but I don't believe it represents your true character. As soon as you set foot in Paris again, the frightened Muse of poetry will abandon you once more. I think your current verses are a good exercise. Besides, unless I'm terribly mistaken, if you are truly made for poetry and are the poet our time awaits, your fame will be great. I will know what to think when you come here: if the Muse doesn't flee*

from you, it will be the sign that your verses are not the sons of the Provençal sleep. And then Paris will expand your poetic horizons.

Maybe we sacrifice too much to the present here. We make hay while the sun shines, with all our energy and all our power. We write according to the demands of time, which is why our work is not strong. One should at the same time breathe the air of Paris and write at one's convenience. The works then would be lively and durable. Your lucky situation will help you have this life of work and study. If your will is strong, your place awaits you.

19

*The sun has just put its head
through the garret window*

Give Baille the good news, Zola asks Cézanne in a letter of September 29th, 1862. *Tell him your return to Paris will help to heal past wounds. The past played a great part in my despair; it nearly annulled the future. I find myself completely outside all that now. A hope that may have contributed to chasing away my depression is that soon I will be able to shake your hand. I know that is not entirely certain yet, but you have given me reason for hope—that, in itself, is a lot. I approve completely of your idea of coming to Paris to work and then retiring to Provence. I think it is a good way to escape the influence of the schools and to develop some originality, if one has any. So, if you come to Paris, so much the better for you and for us. We will arrange life to suit us, spending two evenings a week together and working on all the others. The hours we are with each other will not be time lost. Nothing gives me as much courage as to talk for a while to a friend. So, I await your arrival.*

Zola may not have wholeheartedly approved of Cézanne's plan to alternate between Paris and Aix, but at this point he would not risk raising a fuss over it, aware that Cézanne was vacillating over a decision to come to Paris at all. Keeping one foot in Aix may have been for Cézanne a vital compromise (he was not unhappy with life at the family hearth), and there was a ring of truth in Zola's mention that, in favor of developing originality, periods away from Paris would help him escape the influence of schools. The young Claude Monet, who was also a student at this time, would justify his occasional absences from Paris with comparable judgment: *One is taken up too much with what one sees and hears in Paris, however firm one may be about oneself. What I am painting here will have the value of not resembling anyone—at least I think so.*[1]

Cézanne came to Paris the following November of 1862. Two months later, in a January 5th letter to Numa Coste, a friend he'd met at the drawing school in Aix, Cézanne tells of being back at the *Académie Suisse,* settling down to being an artist and spending off-time with other painters to whom he'd quickly become attached: Armand Guillaumin, then twenty-one, two years younger than Cézanne, and Antoine Guillemet, four years younger. Both were landscape painters, as were most of the painters who made use of the *Suisse* during winter months to keep in touch with each other while sharpening their eye-hand coordination working from a model. On occasion, the gentle-hearted Pissarro, who will become a constituent figure in Cézanne's life, showed up at the *Suisse*. And in time, Guillemet, a former student of Corot's, would introduce Cézanne to a loosely tied group in the Batignolles area near Montmartre—the painters Henri Fantin-Latour, Édouard Manet, Claude Monet, Edgar Degas, Alfred Sisley, Auguste Renoir, and Frédéric Bazille, as well as a few writers and critics. But Cézanne would have little contact with them over the early years and almost none at this stage. In the company of other students at the *Suisse*, as he'd been at the municipal art school in Aix, he would be more at ease, able to think of himself as a special type of painter authenticated by others on his level. He will undergo much the same development as Zola does in searching out a theoretic base to structure what intuitively he felt was right. Zola will call it «science,» while for Cézanne it will be «nature.» Both were coming to know that their respective arts would depend on some new and specific view of the world.

Cézanne would arrive at his controlling viewpoint with great difficulty. He lacked a day-to-day mentor with ability to help him focus, either in the style of a teacher or in opposition, and the negative charge of his personality often dispelled positive advice. He would be held back also by the company he kept. At the *Suisse* he was in a corps of non-cerebral, run-of-the-mill painters who resisted the authority of strong teachers; their view of the game was from behind the fence, and their ride through art history will be on Cézanne's shoulders. Not too young by any means at age twenty-three, but still a neophyte, Cézanne would not be courted by painters the likes of Manet or Degas—two well-born and highly mannered young men who'd had extensive art training in major studios: Manet, who was thirty-one in 1863, in Couture's studio; Degas, age twenty-nine, in Lamothe's. They were in league with painters well in advance of Cézanne and with intellectuals and writers a good cut above Zola.

Monet and Renoir were about the same age as Cézanne—Renoir his age, Monet a year younger—but they too were out of Cézanne's peerage, for they had been studying for a few years, most recently in Charles Gleyre's studio. It would not have been a personality shyness that kept Cézanne remote from Monet and Renoir and other painters in Manet's circle. His novitiate years as a part-time student at the drawing school in Aix had not prepared him for sophisticated company. Manet was an imposing figure, not by size or physicality like a Courbet, but intellectually. The English writer and golden-haired fop George Moore, who hung out with Parisian artists and writers and was close to Manet, described Manet as an elegant man with finely cut features, a strong chin, bright eyes, who spoke with the clarity of bottled water, though often harshly, his words at times bitter or imperious.[2] Cézanne, a provincial lad, was more at ease with less cultivated company. He would take to Pissarro, a competent landscape painter, who was devoid of academic romanticism other than towards the rustic, bucolic— more naturalist than realist, an adult personality easily liked. Pissarro, himself, was outside of Manet's circle. He was thirty-two, nine years older than Cézanne, when they became acquainted at the *Suisse*. Born in 1830 at Charlotte Amalie in the Danish West Indies, both of his parents were Jewish bourgeois—his father a storekeeper who had immigrated to the colony from Bordeaux. At the age of twelve in 1842, Pissarro was sent to France and enrolled at boarding school in the Parisian suburb of Passy. There an interest in art found support among his teachers. He was encouraged to draw and taken by a teacher on museum visits. He returned to the Indies five years later to work in the family business, but when thoughts about being an artist grew serious, he ran off to Caracas, Venezuela in 1852 with a Danish topographical painter friend, Fritz Melby. After two years there, he returned home. Agreeably, his parents financed a trip to Paris where he visited the 1855 World's Fair and was taken in emotionally by the art on display, especially Corot's landscapes. Soon thereafter, with a family allowance reluctantly granted, he dedicated himself to art. His first art guide in Paris was Fritz Melby's brother Anton, also a topographic illustrator, who introduced him to Corot, Daubigny, and Courbet. Pissarro then moved among various private teaching studios, studying under masters who also taught at the *École des Beaux-Arts*.

In 1863, Cézanne and Zola were not as far beyond their Aixois adolescence as their age would suggest. Cézanne's father remained on the distant horizon like a sun that simply will not set, a constant reminder of Cézanne's alternative route to a materialist adulthood. The «rowdy dunces» at the *Bourbon* in Aix had been replaced in Paris by boisterous *rapins* (rascals) at the *Suisse*, the baccalaureate examiners will soon resurface as menacing Salon jurists with the same piercing stares, conspiring to bring Cézanne down; soon again he will be *sunk, submerged, done for, petrified, extinguished, annihilated*, not once, as he feared he would be with the baccalaureate exams, but annually.

For Zola, the conspirators will be competitive newspaper critics sneering at the pluck of his immature writings, as had fellow students at the *Lycée Saint-Martin*, whose ridicule of his poetry had brought Cézanne to such a wrath that he doubled up his fists.

No letters addressed by Zola to either Cézanne or Baille over the balance of the 1860s survive. No letters from Cézanne to Zola survive from the period December 1859 to the end of June 1866. And from 1863, we have just one letter by Cézanne, addressed to a friend in Aix he'd met at the drawing school, Numa Coste, a cobbler's son and amateur artist, four years younger than Cézanne, who will give up painting and, after military service, becomes a law clerk. From 1864, again only one letter survives, again to Coste, and from 1865, we have one letter addressed to Pissarro. But from 1866 come several surviving letters between Cézanne and Zola

If appraised by the single surviving letter from 1863, written on January 5th to Numa Coste, Cézanne was coming around to feeling self-confident in Paris, finally on the right path. He had only to recognize how many others were on the wrong one—the path he had come to know well, having been on it for a few years. Continued training under Joseph Gibert in Aix would have led to low-caste academic mediocrity; at best he would become a confined and provincial picture-painter. He was not a Manet, who had the mental strength to study for six years (1850-56) under the disciplinarian Thomas Couture, or a Degas, who applied himself dutifully at the *École des Beaux-Arts* and the Academy in Rome, both knowing, perhaps, that academic discipline would structure their departures from it. Cézanne was without a worthy teacher. Judging from the letter to Numa Coste it would appear that he had rationalized his teacherless position by saying that to copy a teacher's style is to remain forever behind him. But this insight wouldn't leave him with guidance for moving ahead:

My dear Coste,

This letter that I address to you is meant for both you and Mr. Villevieille (Joseph-François Villevieille, an Aixois painter ten years older than Cézanne, who occasionally corrected Cézanne's efforts). *I should have written to you long ago. It is already two months since I left Aix. Should I talk to you about the fine weather? No. Except to say that the sun, until now hidden by clouds, has just put its head through the garret window, and wanting to end the day gloriously, it tosses, on departing, a few pale rays. I hope that this letter will find you all in good health. Hang in there. Let us try to be together again soon.*

As when here before, I go to the Suisse in the morning from eight until one o'clock and from seven to ten in the evening. I work calmly, and eat and sleep that way too. Fairly often I go to see Mr. Chautard [a painter, talent unknown] *who is kind enough to correct my studies. The day after Christmas, I had supper with him and his family, and tasted the mulled wine you had sent them. Now, Mr. Villevieille, and your little girls Fanny and Thérèse, are they well? I hope so, and you as well. Pay my respects, I beseech you, to Mrs. Villevieille, to your father and sister—to yourself too. By the way, is the picture for which I saw you making sketches going well? I spoke to Mr. Chautard about it. He praised the idea of it, and said that you should be able to make something good of it.*

Oh Coste, Coste the younger, do you go on annoying the most reverend Coste the elder? Are you still painting? And the academic soirées at the school, how are they going? Tell me, who is the miserable wretch who poses for you like an X, or holds his belly? Have you still got those two apes from last year?

It is nearly a month since Lombard [a fellow art student from Aix] *came back*

to Paris. Not without distress, I found out he is attending the Signol studio. That worthy gentleman makes his students learn a hackneyed style that leads them to do exactly what he does himself—that's all. And they do that very well, though not admirably. Just think, this young, intelligent man had to come all the way to Paris only to lose himself. Still, the novice Lombard has made great progress. I also love Truphémus' fellow student Félicien. The dear boy sees everything through the eyes of his illustrissme [most illustrious] *friend and only judges his own after his friend's colors. According to him, Truphéme has dethroned Delacroix. Truphéme alone can create color, he says. And also, thanks to a certain most favorable letter, he attends the École des Beaux-Arts. Do not think for a moment that I envy him.* [Auguste Truphéme, a fellow pupil at the Municipal Art School at Aix, had received a grant from the city of Aix to study at the Beaux-Arts in Paris].

I just received a letter from my father announcing his impending arrival on the 13th of this month. Tell Mr. Villevieille to give my father any request for what he may need from Paris, and that, as for Mr. Lambert (my address for the moment being Impasse Saint-Dominique d'Enfer), he should write down instructions, or have them written, about what he wants, the place where it's to be bought, the best way of sending it. I am at his service. Meanwhile I yearn for:

The days we went to the fields of the Torse
[a small river near Aix]
To eat a good lunch, and with palette in hand
Traced on our canvas a luxurious landscape:
That place where you nearly sprained your back,
When your foot, slipping on the ground,
Caused you to roll to the bottom of the ravine,
And «Black» [a dog with an English name], *do you remember him!*
Now the leaves, yellowed by the breath of winter,
Have lost their freshness.
On the edge of the stream, the plants are wilted,
And the tree, shaken by the fury of the wind,
Waves in the air, like some enormous cadaver,
Its leafless branches swayed by the mistral.

I hope that this letter, which I could not finish in one sitting, will find you in the best of health. My respects to your parents. Hello to our friends. I shake your hand.

The doggerel that Cézanne embodied in this letter is remote from his poetry of previous years when the Holy Trinity—he, Zola, and Baille—were still dreamy boys. Silly verses and dependence on stupidities and absurdities to mask anxiety and trepidation was now up against hard-edged reality, which punctures bubbles inflated by fantastical minds. Now he had to come to terms with art as a profession, to recognize the stakes of the game, to take art seriously or admit once again he was a failure worth no more than evolving into an ordinary banker, a free-swimming tadpole becoming a squatting toad behind a counter.

No works by Cézanne can be recognized with certainty as from 1863, or the previous year, or, for that matter, the following year, so not a word about his art can be said without lapsing into speculation. No picture associated with this period in dealer or exhibition catalogues justifies a date, and some are probably not by Cézanne anyway but by friends he painted with, or by others of the time who happened to paint the way he did.[3] An oil painting in the Church of Saint-Jean-de-Malte at Aix, said to have been by Cézanne, was found after cleaning to be signed by his Aixois friend Antoine Marion.[4] And a drawing, related to this painting, signed with Marion's initials, has reappeared on the market with the initials erased. Other examples will be taken up later.

As for Cézanne's day-to-day life, not much can be said of that either. He may have taken up this year, possibly the next year, with a girl his age, Alexandrine Meley, the illegitimate daughter of a teen-aged couple, a hatter and a florist. Over her vagrant youth, shifting from one caretaker family to another, earning her way as a flower vender and seamstress, perhaps also an itinerant artist's model, Alexandrine fell in with the bohemian lot. Chances are good that she posed off and on for Cézanne in 1864. A likeness of her is one of several portraits by Cézanne from about this time (perhaps he thought that proficiency in portrait painting might lead to augmenting his allowance with commissions. In 1877, the writer Joris-Karl Huysmans would describe Alexandrine as a tall, olive-skinned, dark-haired woman with the astonishingly coal-black eyes of a Valasquez princess.[5] If she was Cézanne's *petite amie* for a time, then Zola was her next in line (Cézanne's portrait of Alexandrine was found in Zola's collection). At some time between 1863 and 1866, Zola met her, probably at Cézanne's studio. After a few years of cohabitation, she and Zola married in 1871.[6]

Zola will struggle through the year financially stressed, even though his salary at Hachette's had elevated his daily life from wretchedness to the level of just plain poverty. He was contributing to his mother's support and sharing an apartment with her. To Marius Daime, now in Paris, who had been his mother's supporter in Aix, and perhaps her lover, twenty-three-year-old Zola dispatched the following message on December 2nd, 1863:

> *Dear Sir,*
>
> *My mother must have told you about a 100-franc loan I want to contract. My salary this month was not sufficient to pay a few small debts that have piled up. She told me you might be so kind as to give her hope that you could loan us this amount. Unfortunately, the need is urgent. The bills are due tomorrow, Thursday, and if I do not get a loan before tomorrow evening it will be too late.*

Please give us, dear Sir, a definitive answer. I must say that we have not asked this of anyone else, as we are counting on you. My mother is rather ill. She will nevertheless go tomorrow to the place she usually finds you. If you could let us know even sooner, that would reassure us. It is of course understood that I will agree to any conditions of repayment: cash or whatever. We greatly need this small sum. I am looking forward to your answer.[7]

Zola was now up against the contradiction that pits literature as art against writing as a way of making a living. Throughout 1863 and the following year, he would add a few francs to his salary from Hachette's by reviewing books for newspapers, while also trying to get stories published. In June, he sent two short stories to *L'Universe illustré* with a cover letter to Jules Claretie, a critic and future novelist the same age as Zola, imploring him to read them: *I beg you not to condemn me without reading me. For me it is a question of life and death.* During this year he managed to publish seven short pieces, having lucked into a friendship with Géry Legrand, founder of the *Journal populaire de Lille* and the *Revue du mois*. These newspapers printed most of his output: two short stories, *Simplice* and *Le Sang*, were published in the August and September issues of *Revue du mois*; in late December, *Journal populaire de Lille* printed his essay «*Cervantès et Gustave Doré: A propos de Don Quiote illustré* (Cervantes and Gustave Doré: Concerning the Illustrated Don Quixote). In January 1864, his revue of *Comte Cosia* by Cherbuliez appeared in *L'Athenaeum.* He tried to publish the little story, *Perrette*, in *Revue des deux mondes*, but was rejected. And he managed to write a few stories, *Celle qui m'aime* (Those Who Love Me) and *Soeur-des-Pauvres* (Sister of Poverty) but had no luck getting them in print. Desperate, he assembled eight stories under a collective title, *Contes à Ninon*, and sent them to publisher Albert Lacroix, saying in his cover letter: *Just read one of them at random. I assure you that I have talent.*

His efforts at short story publication were well timed. In this era before radio shows, when newspapers were proliferating and competing for readers, short stories, as *contes*, or tales, or novellas, greatly aided in marketing papers. Publishers favored using them; they were easy to get into circulation and easy to read. For writers of any age, an occasional printed story supplemented income and provided an opportunity to engage a variety of plots in short spurts, considering the length of time required to generate a full-length novel. A few published stories helped establish name recognition, and if reader response was very strong, it augured well for a story's expansion into a longer format and publication as a book.

The government kept high surveillance on published short stories; they could also be vehicles for undermining the ruling body. Most of the stories were moralizing; a clever writer could plant subversive ideas into his writing and alter the social and political beliefs of readers already conditioned by the tales of La

Fontaine and church homilies delivered as allegories of social and moral conduct. One of Zola's pieces included in *Contes à Ninon*, *Les aventures du grand Sidoine et du petit Médéric* (The adventures of Sidoine the giant and Médéric the dwarf), written in early 1864, was, for this reason, refused for publication. In this story, Sidoine and Médéric join into a battle raging between two armies, the Blues and the Greens. On behalf of the Blues, Sidoine makes a bloodbath out of the Greens, and as a result, a plebiscite grants him the royal crown. He then makes speeches and issues proclamations debunking the myth of providential man and criticizing, through parody, the politics of the Napoleonic regime of the Second Empire.[8]

In the tale *Carnet de danse*, a young girl engages in a dialogue with her first dance instruction book. In *Celle qui m'aime* (Those Who Love Me), Zola builds on the mystical lore of the *foraine* (fair), promoted as a place where one sees what one loves. *Soeur-des-Pauvres* features a young girl who is terribly mistreated by an aunt and uncle. The girl's entreaty to the Virgin leads to her receiving a magic coin that will perpetually reproduce itself and thus provide a comfortable life. But the modest girl believes that money is pernicious; she cannot bring herself to achieve wealth without earning it, so she gives back the coin and continues to earn wages performing menial labor. *Le Sang* (Blood), as moralizing as *Soeur-des-Pauvres*, features four roguish soldiers on the eve of a battle who are set upon by horrible nightmares—rivers of blood, slaughters, murders, every crime that man has accumulated since creation bears down upon them. This story ends with a leap into Utopia: the soldiers abandon their weapons and turn to dirt farming. Zola's admiration for those who work hard is embedded in the character of those who choose to devote their lives to honest labor, such as the young woman in *Soeur-des-Pauvres* and the soldiers in *Le Sang*.

A few of the tales comprised in Zola's *Contes à Ninon* bring to mind motifs in Cézanne's juvenile poetry and in their exchange of letters. *La fée amoureuse* fuses the anxiety of the baccalaureate examination with the threshold fear of maturity. *Simplice* recalls Cézanne's engagement with the *mirliton* in the woods. The difference between this poem and Zola's story is as much a difference between the two young men. While Cézanne's nymph is anything but pure, in Zola's tale, a young man enters into the heart of the woods in search of original purity (as if searching in the Garden of Eden), falls in love with a water sprite named Fleur-des-Eaux, and dies in her embrace. In the comedy *Les voleurs et l'âne* (The Robbers and the Donkey) four young men and a young woman are having a party on the banks of the Seine; robbers set upon them, the consequences are amusing. In the late 1860s, Cézanne will paint a picture titled *Les voleurs et l'âne*, which has been associated ineptly with the medieval story, *The Golden Ass*, by Apulius.[9]

Zola's output during these first years in Paris was hardly a measure of his ambition. Nor was Cézanne in any position to be assertive. Not until after 1863 would circumstances bear down upon them and stoke their fires. The Salon of

1863 would be a momentous event in Paris, galvanizing the art world and allowing both Zola and Cézanne to position themselves in the conflict of an emerging avant-garde with an establishment that young artists felt was oppressive. They needed something to fight for, or against, some context into which their energy could be transformed from dream to action. Both were tough-minded. Unable to find a seducible muse of poetry, Zola would now face reality and force it to submit, while Cézanne, by nature aggressive, adapts his personality to a way of art making. Soon they will come to understand that it is easier to build a career out of one's faults rather than to waste life in efforts to correct them. Faults, when thrown at the establishment, or at the public, incite notoriety. As a critic will soon say of Manet, *If Manet would just do something right, no one would notice him.* The route to fame was too long a route for the impatient and uncertain. Courbet and Manet had achieved notoriety. They were famous. It mattered not what they were famous for. Newspapers could make a person notorious, while it took books to establish an enduring fame. Things were moving fast in Paris. There was no time to become famous. Notoriety was a shortcut. One remembers not fair weather but the most powerful and devastating storms, like history measured by wars. In both Zola and Cézanne, a storm was working itself up to a mighty discharge. As usual, Cézanne images himself in metaphor:

> *Now the leaves, yellowed by the breath of winter,*
> *Have lost their freshness.*
> *On the edge of the stream, the plants are wilted,*
> *And the tree, shaken by the fury of the wind,*
> *Waves in the air, like some enormous cadaver,*
> *Its leafless branches swayed by the mistral.*

Part II

CÉZANNE AND ZOLA ASSAULT THE ESTABLISHMENT

20

*Numerous complaints have
reached the Emperor
concerning works of art refused
by the exhibition jury*

1863 was a matchless year for a provincial art-minded lad such as Cézanne to come to Paris and for Zola to get acquainted with the visual art scene. It would have been difficult for any aspiring artist to be bored this year of the infamous *Salon des Refusés*, a massive exhibition of painters, sculptors, and etchers whose works had been refused by the Salon jury. Like big boulders in a usually slow river, this jury may have foreseen but couldn't block the raging flood of entries from lusty springheads with its amassing of badly painted flotsam. The tumultuous event splashed over newspaper pages with the zest of a political sex scandal.

To the Salon of 1863, about five thousand paintings, sculptures, and etchings were entered by some three thousand artists, which meant that almost every artist in the country had submitted—the maximum submissions allowed (a new rule that year) was three. The count of entrants bears out how dramatically the population of artists, especially in Paris, was on the increase. The jury's resolve this year was to stem the flow of badly painted pictures that had converged on the *Palais de l'Industrie* and nettled the juries of 1859 and 1861—presenting a judicial challenge as dreadful as if five thousand prima donnas, ages six to ninety and in all shapes and costumes, had shown up to audition for the *Corps de Ballet*.

In an effort to maintain the status quo, which so many young artists were resisting, the jury dismissed a vast number of entries. Over a period of roughly ten days, the jurists hacked their way through the pile-up of oils and watercolors, etchings and sculptures, separating the appealing from the nauseating. About three-fifths of the entries were rejected, leaving the installers with more than two thousand works representing nine hundred and eighty-three artists, three hundred fewer than had been selected the previous year. Among the two thousand, eight hundred rejected artists, mostly daubers, only a handful would figure importantly in modernist art history: Whistler, Jongkind, Bracquemond, Fantin-Latour,

Legros, Renoir—also Manet, even though two years before, in the Salon of 1861, he had received an honorable mention; a medal would have allowed him to exhibit in 1863 without having his works reviewed by the jury, for previous medallists were *hors-concour*s (not subject to the jury), as were the jury members themselves to prevent self-rejection.

The refused artists raised a storm of protest so impassioned and clamorous that it reached the ears of Louis Napoleon. Concerned not to let any public demonstration get ignited in politically volatile Paris, especially by a mass protest from artists and sympathetic writers, who as a body were anti-royalist and not amenable to reason, the emperor came forthwith to the *Palais de l'Industrie* for a personal look at the heaps of rejected art. Most likely he agreed with the jury's criteria, but would nonetheless have to make a conciliatory gesture towards the rejected artists, but not in his right mind would he reverse the jury's decisions, for the *Institut* was a small but powerfully noisy block that needed stroking—its humanist factions ridden with heretic intellectuals. With Solomonic wisdom, the emperor met with the ruling eminence of the fine arts, Count Nieuwerkerke, and negotiated orders to be published two days later in the official newspaper, *Le Moniteur*:

> *Numerous complaints have reached the Emperor concerning works of art refused by the exhibition jury. His Majesty, wishing to leave the public as the judge of the legitimacy of these complaints, has decided that the rejected works of art be exhibited in another part of the Palais de l'Industrie. This exhibition will be elective; artists who do not wish to take part need only inform the administration, which will promptly return their works to them. This exhibition will open on May 15th.*[1]

Thus befell the first exhibition of rejected artists, a grand show of losers: the «Salon of the Refused,» the *Salon des refusés*, debuting two weeks after the official Salon's opening.

The visual arts in France were governed by the *Académie des Beaux-Arts*, a division of the *Institut de France*. Select members of the Academy were teachers at the *École des Beaux-Arts* (School of Fine Arts) and also directors of the French Academy at Rome, a finishing school for exceptionally proficient graduate students. Headed by the Director of Fine Arts, the *Académie* was responsible for appointing the juries that passed judgment on entries for the Salons, which were held annually after 1863. The ultimate goal of the professional artist, after winning medals at the Salon, was to win a *Pris de Rome* and spend a few years at the Villa Medici in Rome, then be appointed to a professorship at the *École* or the *Académie Française*, and, finally, to complete one's career in the noble ranks of the *Légion d'Honneur*.

Jean-Baptiste Colbert, the minister of culture during the Reign of Louis XIV, initiated the Paris Salon far back in 1667. In the nineteenth century, under Louis

Opening day of the Salon at the Palais de l'Industrie

Philippe the Salon became a bi-annual event. These massive exhibitions of three to four thousand works at the *Palais de l'Industrie* lasted for months as the only sure venues for artists to display works before a large audience, gain professional recognition, and obtain commissions from the State. Attendance at this *Champs-Élysées* trade center, built in 1853 to house industrial exhibitions, could run three to four thousand over a single day. The admission charge was one franc and reproductions of previous Salon favorites—with royalties paid to the artists—were sold at a busy counter.

Not all of the notable painters deigned to show their work in the Salons. Many had developed steady customers and didn't wish to demean their art by subjecting it to judgment or risk rejection—jury members were typically biased, political, and some were malicious enough to overlook quality, seizing an opportunity to stone a personal enemy. For this reason, the juries were very large in number, composed of academicians who would represent a range of stylistic and thematic preferences in order to maintain a just balance between religious and history painters, mythology addicts, portrait painters, and landscapists.

Some artists who enjoyed conspicuous status (such as the ardently conservative and politically powerful Jean Dominique Ingres, who by 1863 had been an eminent member of the *Académie* for thirty-eight years) would not exhibit in such

The *vernissage* (varnishing day). On a special day before the Salon opened to the public, artists were allowed to retouch and and a layer of varish to their paintings. Ladders were provided. Artists' invitees and special guests were invited to view the exhibition on this day. While varnishing is no longer done today, the tradition of the *vernissage* is maintained.

a department store environment, just as couturiers of high fashion would eschew such huge general stores as *Bon Marché* and *La Belle Jardinière*. Baudelaire had summarized Ingres as a despotic, stubborn man who had tacked onto himself the exceptional glory of obliterating the sun. Ingres openly discredited the Salon: *The Salon stifles and corrupts feeling for the great and the beautiful. Artists are driven to exhibit there by the attractions of profit, a desire to get themselves noticed at any price...a picture shop, a bazaar, in which the tremendous number of objects is overwhelming and business, rather than art, rules.*[2] His was not the only voice bemoaning the commercialization of the Salon—due largely to the rapid increase in private collecting that encouraged artists to submit smaller, more sentimental and anecdotal pictures appealing to people with modest funds.

The psychology of élitism was working against populism in the usual fashion. Works by the exalted masters were beyond the purse of the ordinary bourgeois, while affordable art—for the most part small-scale, mediocre, and easy to understand—was as segregated from true art as lower from upper classes. The art critic Étienne Delécluse had written as early as 1831 that the average level of artistic talent, like the average income, had risen enough in the last quarter of a century to promote purchases of pretty works by prolific little masters. *Nothing is more mediocre than such banal items of bourgeois luxury*, he wrote. *One must recognize these works for what they are.*[3] Eight years later, Delécluse would again raise this issue, saying that the Salon had degenerated into a merchandise bazaar, where people looking for a bargain could not tell the difference between the work of true artists and trivial amateurs.[4] He was, of course, not the only referee calling fouls. Like many others, he failed to recognize that since State and Church patronage of the arts had declined, the clientele for paintings, small sculptures, and prints was a population in need of cultural objects that could be possessed and treasured, of which original art was the exemplary sign.

The seashore painter Eugène Boudin, a vital influence on Monet and other painters of contemporary values and casual life, was one among others to call for painters to respect the bourgeois as clientele and their leisure as worthy subject matter. In a letter to the art dealer known as *père* Martin, Boudin wrote that he'd been complimented for having put down on canvas the objects and people of his own time, for having found a way for people to gain acceptance as artists' subject matter wearing contemporary dress: *The peasants have their painters. That's fine. But those middle class people strolling on the jetty at sunset—have they no right to be fixed upon canvas? They are often resting from strenuous work, these people who leave their offices and cubbyholes. If there are a few parasites among them, there are also people who have fulfilled their tasks.*[5] Realizations such as Boudin's would help generate an audience for the new art as painters gave representation to the bracket of society that eventually would become Impressionism's support body—the no-longer shocked (*épaté*) bourgeoisie.[6]

Since 1848, the Salon had been open to every sort of artist. Acceptance by the Salon jury meant the possibility of sales, for the Salon jury's decisions were stamps of approval, guarantees of quality. Jury acceptance and being favorably hung in the galleries was also the best way to attract the attention of private dealers scouting the Salons for additions to their stables, and of critics who might say a few words of praise in the press. Dozens of newspaper critics covered the event. During the Second Empire years (the reign of Napoleon III), the government census listed almost one hundred art critics, the vast majority located in Paris. Newspaper art critics embodied a mix of academics and part-time writers, some doubling up the visual with the theater arts, few knowing much about either.[7] Honoré Daumier's cartoons of rejected artists, *View of a Studio a Few Days Before the Opening of a Salon*, and *The Influential Critic Walks Through*, with gentlemen removing their hats to gratefully acknowledge the critic's advice, illustrate how careers were fashioned or shattered by the domino effect of the Salon judges' decisions.

The Salon was invariably under attack by one or another faction of the art world, no less than the National Assembly was by disgruntled oppositionists, or Louis Napoleon's regime by left-leaning republicans. The Academy had rigorous standards universally applied, like academic standards that control theses and journal publications. Principles of art lay at the basis for jury selections, with individuality encouraged only after mastering hand skills in rendering and the appropriate iconography of subject matter as subjugated to rules of decorum and good taste. (The vigilant poet of the early phase of *art for art's sake*, Théophile Gautier, once reproached an imprudent artist for having painted a swineherd with pigs, whereas, he said, the painter could have decorously rendered the theme by portraying instead the *Prodigal Son Driving Swine*).[8]

In the 1850s, when such painters as Courbet challenged the rules, the sameness of Salon pictures was made more evident. Powerful deviations exposed the contrast. Then Jules Champfleury—author of novels and essays and known for a while as the chief of the realists—could speak of *the mediocre art of our exhibitions in which a universal cleverness of hand makes two thousand pictures look as if they'd come from the same mold.*[9] Even Delacroix, who'd departed from the canons of academic painting by abandoning the perfect human figure and the superiority of antique accouterments—favoring individualism while supplanting reason with sentiment—was called before the Minister of Fine Arts and cautioned to change his attitude or forsake any prospect of his work being purchased by the State. The indomitable Ingres, who had inherited from Jacques-Louis David the pastoral staff to keep the tribe's fine arts lineage in the fold, hated Delacroix for his transgressions of academic standards. The battle of Ingres the Classic versus Delacroix the Romantic stimulated one of the period's most well-known cartoons: Ingres armed with his exacting fine-point brush, and Delacroix with his soft and weak brush, jousting in front of the *Institut de France*. The cartoon is annotated with Delacroix shouting, *Line is color,* and Ingres retorting with *Color is Utopia. Long live Line!*. Such conflicts easily found their way into the discord-hungry press, which helped to stimulate public awareness and interest in the Salons. For many people, attending the Salon was like a visit to the insane asylum or the zoo.

It might be assumed that Nieuwerkerke was fiercely unsettled over the turn of events that estab-

Delacroix (left) and Ingres jousting in front of the Institute.

lished the *Salon des Refusés*. Previously, in 1861, the protest of disgruntled artists had not amounted to more than a group of them chanting like irritable schoolboys under his window. Now the situation was very grave. Still, one should leave open the thought that he and other conservatives saw the disruption as a chance to prove the correctness of the jurists: the public would plainly see the refused works as grievously unfit for display. He might also have predicted that the better and academically loyal artists among the rejected would not wish to see their works in the *Salon des Refusés*, where most certainly they would be maligned and in every other way punished by an audience that delighted in freak shows. Further, influential members of the Academy would lobby right-wing newspaper editors to assure that the press in the worst possible light portrayed the rejected artists.

The respected critic Ernest Chesneau took a dim view of the entire matter. In his *Salon de 1863*, published two weeks before the *Salon des Refusés* opened, he wrote:

> *When the notice announcing the emperor's decision appeared, great excitement broke out among the refused artists. And that part of the public having interest in such questions about art received the news with joy. Although the Salon des Refusés is regarded as a very liberal gesture* [on the emperor's part], *at the same time, the public sees in it a lesson to be taught those excessive and boastfully proud artists without talent who are always the loudest to complain. But will this lesson have any effect?*[10]

The salon jurists assembled and about to undertake their arduous task of winnowing wheat from chaff..

Jules Castagnary, a thirty-three-year-old writer, critic, and leftist politician of sorts, who earlier on, and at some risk, had championed Courbet, gave a more reasonable analysis of the problem now facing the refused artists. They would now have to choose whether to exhibit among the rejected or to remain unnoticed:

> *To exhibit in the Salon des Refusés means to decide, perhaps to one's detriment, the issue that this Salon raises. It means delivering oneself to the mocking public should one's work be judged definitely bad. Or, it means siding with the Institute, not only in the present case but also for the future. Not to exhibit would be to condemn oneself, to admit one's lack of ability. From another point of view, withdrawing one's work would only accomplish glorification of the jury, admitting that its decisions were correct.*[11]

Artists who preferred not to be noticed withdrew more than six hundred of the rejected works. The catalogue of the rejected listed 781 works on exhibit in the *Salon des Refusés*, but there may have been a thousand—the catalogue was incomplete; haste and last-minute decisions retarded its printing. It should not be assumed that more than a few represented «modern art» as other than art of the moment; the general state of the massive majority was mediocrity; the jurists, after all, were excellent painters and qualified judges. It is a mistake often made by champions of the avant-garde to depricate the juridical competence of the jurists.

The installation, in a separate zone of the *Palais de l'Industrie*, attracted a substantial flow of viewers, three to four thousand on a Sunday. About one hundred of the voluntary exhibitors signed a letter to the emperor applauding his decree.

The instigator was the rural landscape painter Charles Daubigny, a persistent thorn in the *Académie*'s side and a bothersome traitor to the conservative cause. Juries usually accepted his works, nonetheless, and he had won a medal or two. If a new Moses were among the desert-weary artists straggling to the Promised Land, it would have been this nature-loving Daubigny breaking trail with his rustic walking stick. Cézanne may have wished to be identified with the refused, which had the aura of youth against the establishment. It has been said that, although he had not offered anything to the Salon, he did put a painting or two in the *Salon des Refusés*, an option left to anyone by the emperor's decree. His name does not appear in the catalogue of the *refusés*, but perhaps that list included only those who had been officially condemned, not those who came to the lynching party carrying their own noose.

Writing for a London newspaper, the respected English critic Philip Hamerton had this report on the *Salon des Refusés* sent across the Channel on the Folkstone boat: *Every spectator is immediately compelled to abandon all hope of getting into that serious state of mind necessary for a fair judgment of works of art. That threshold once past, the gravest visitors burst into peals of laughter. This is exactly what the jurymen desire.*[12] And the writer Zacharie Astruc, soon to be a Manet supporter, had this to say: *One has to be doubly strong to keep on one's feet against the tempest of fools who bear down on one by the thousands and scoff outrageously at everything.*[13] Astruc was so agitated over the publics and journalists' jolly mockery of the *Salon des Refusés* that he founded a daily newspaper to run for the duration of the show in support of the artists. His hero of the event was Courbet. Even though *hors concours* this year, which meant that his offerings would bypass the jury, one of his pictures was rejected anyway as pornographic, not to be hung even with the refused.

Not all of the pictures in the *Salon des Refusés* were derided: Whistler's *Symphony in White* (which had been rejected by the Royal Academy in London in 1862) was the crowd's favorite among the *refusés*. Manet's case was the worst. He'd submitted three canvases: *Young Man in the Costume of a Majo, Victorine Meurand in the Costume of an Espada*, and the *Luncheon on the Grass*, as the latter came to be

Rejected paintings sorted by size, waiting pick-up by disconsolate artists.

Èdouard Manet. *Le Bain* (*Le Déjeuner sur l'herbe*). oil on canvas, 1863. Paris, Musée d'Orsay. Photo: Bulloz

Honoré Daumier. Caricature of connaisseurs, published in *Le Boulevard*, April 20, 1862. «Goodness me! Amazing! For Heavens sake! Superb! It speaks!»

called (*Déjeuner sur l'herbe*), though he had entered it with the title *Le Bain*. This painting, for which friends had posed, would come to represent for future art history the famous ruckus over the Salon of this year. Few paintings over art's entire history had been so murderously condemned yet so critical to defining the art of a period.

Manet's pictures had a small number of supporters among critics writing for newspapers. Zacharie Astruc had this to say: *One of our greatest artistic characters! I would not say that he carries off the laurels of this Salon, but he is its brilliance, inspiration, surprise. Manet's talent has a decisive side to it that startles, something sober, trenchant, energetic, and reflects his nature, which is both reserved, exalted, and above all, sensitive to intense impressions.*[14] But other critics, with the public's

Alexandre Cabanel. *The Birth of Venus*. Salon of 1863. Gold medal winner, purchased by the State. This was the sort of fused aethetic of the female bodt with the aesthetic of art that such painters as Courbet and Manet were up against. when asserting naturalism rather than idealism.

scandal-loving ears in mind, seized the opportunity to ooze vocabulary when describing the *Déjeuner sur l'herbe*. The minor critic Louis Étienne wrote of the subjects portrayed, *An ordinary women of the demi-monde, as naked as she can be, lolls shamelessly between two overdressed fops looking like schoolboys on a holiday doing something naughty, playing at being grown up. I search in vain for any meaning to this indecent riddle.*[15] Théophile Thoré, looking at the woman in the picture as if she were blood and flesh, an object of sexual attraction being wasted on the man she's with, said: *Unfortunately the nude hasn't a good figure, and I can't think of anything uglier than the man stretched out beside her, who hasn't even thought of taking off his horrid padded cap.*[16] Jules Castagnary could hardly believe what he was seeing: *I see garments without feeling the anatomical structure that supports them and explains their movements. I see boneless fingers and heads without skulls. I see side-whiskers made of two strips of black cloth that could have been glued to the cheeks. What else do I see? Lack of conviction and sincerity.*[17]

Hoping to deter any future debacles, such as the massive protests causing him to ordain the *Salon des Refusés*, the emperor called for reforms in the *École de Beaux-Arts'* conduct and a comprehensive review of selection criteria. This directive provoked much debate among the academics. Eugène Viollet-le-Duc—the architect, academician, and influential author on art and architectural education—held out that originality, the most important of qualities, was frustrated by the *École*'s systematized curriculum and the jury's criteria for artistic judgment. Even before the emperor's call for reforms, Viollet-le-Duc had argued that the critical purpose of art education was to develop the neophyte's originality and permit personal expression. Pointing to the Grand Prix winners in the official Salon, he said it could be plainly seen that they had lost every semblance of originality. As if speaking for the rejected, he argued that *each individual, having yielded entirely to spontaneous feelings, sees nature in his own way, experiences a different emotion, and discovers his own way of expressing it. Nothing could therefore be more perfect than this for giving scope to genuine feeling and developing an individual personality, that is, true originality.*[18]

Ludovic Vitet, another educator, wrote in favor of originality, saying that, if properly addressed, the reforms would *come to the aid of those poor pupils who have lived under the yoke for so long, and rescue them from the tyranny of an immovable power. At last they are free, and the age of originality has dawned.*[19] But Vitet's assertion that personal originality could not be attained in school simply because it was innate and naturally endowed entangled him in cacophonous arguments over the distinction between *originalité véritable* (true originality, which, being personal like instinct and intuition, eludes pedagogical systems) and *originalité secondaire* (acquired originality), which seduces through clever or audacious appearances and requires rigorous art school training to integrate with personal originality. Sincerity, then, would be called upon to settle the issue of how originality could be measured, for sincerity does not submit to traditional studio-painting as taught in the Academy. Théophile Thoré will take up this point in 1863 when asserting that the *Salon de Refusés* only widens the gulf between academic artists and *sincere* artists, for whom originality is the only touchstone of genius.[20] It would also be at the core of Manet's 1867 essay «Reasons for Holding a Private Exhibition»: *It is sincerity which gives to works of art a character which seems to convert them into acts of protest, when all the artist is trying to do is express his own impressions.* Manet himself would say in 1867, *There is a traditional way of teaching form, techniques and appreciation, and because those who have been brought up to believe in those principles will admit no others, a fact which makes them childishly intolerant. Any works not conforming to those formulae they take to be worthless; they not only arouse criticism but also provoke hostility, even active hostility.*[21]

This argument over the status and definition of originality would vault back and forth over the years as a struggle between natural and acquired skill, inborn and inculcated originality. The coincidence of the innate and the learned, like heredity to nurture, is common to every form of performance, as between technical excellence promoted by Classicists and the free-style expression favored by the Romantics. In 1878, the pioneer of realism in the 1850s and naturalism in the 1860s, Edmond Duranty, would write a lengthy and important essay attacking the *École des Beaux-Arts*. He concluded with an insult to its graduates: *As artists you have nothing to be proud of, receiving an education that only turns out a race of sheep.* Duranty, too, had placed sincerity and natural originality ahead of academic skill and decorum: *After entire years devoted to such exercises* [daily repetition of banal studies of the model and assigned compositions], *what can possibly remain of the most valuable qualities? What becomes of the naive, the natural, and the sincere?*[22]

Sincerity soon became the mantra and merit badge of young artists in the 1860s, most of whom could play it off against their mediocrity—a pathetic picture, yes, but painted with sincerity. For others, it was a way to assuage the chagrin of viewers whose eyes were reflexively tuned to seeing faults. Even Manet would say in 1867, *Today the artist is not saying, «Come and see some perfect paintings,» but «Come and see some sincere ones.»* Zola and Cézanne will depend on sincerity as justification for the commonplace faults of their own inadequacies until, in time, like other excuses for not facing up, sincerity wears off and is replaced by rigorous critical judgment distinguishing between artistic faults and such just plain faults as lazy thinking and poor execution.

The aesthetics of the sketch had been promoted by the Romantics, who felt that the artist's true feelings were in the sketch rather than the work *à sa fin* (at its finish), in which emotion was sublimated for public exposure.[23] The first impression, *la première pensée*, had become widely accepted in studios as the generative phase, action without pre-meditation, the spontaneous condition of an original idea (often applauded in Manet's pictures).[24] *La première pensée* was the childhood of the finished painting. Thus, debates within the *Académie*, centering on the value of the sketch, were congruent with sympathy for the young artist. The sketch then would be the youthful stage of a painting, while the finished work its maturity. By then, genius had become associated with the power of first impressions (the stroke of genius), while maturity and skill would come only after years of practice, a structure that coincides with notoriety as quick fame—otherwise known as infamous. As pressure on the Salon juries increased and criteria weakened, both juries and critics sought to offset the decline of professionalism and degeneration of standards. Pressure was put on artists to bring their pictures to a high degree of finish, thus creating a conflict between the sketch and the *oeuvre à sa fin*.[25] Delacroix had this to say back in 1831:

> *The artist, closeted in his studio, at first inspired by his work and buoyed by that supreme confidence which alone produces masterpieces, arrives by chance to cast his glance outward on the stage where it will be judged, and on the judges who await it as soon as his ardor is drained. He looks back sadly on his work. Too much contempt awaits this chaste child born of his enthusiasm...He modifies it, he spoils it, he overworks it—all this civilizing and polishing in order not to displease.*[26]

In Cézanne's case, as I will argue, his motive was not *to displease* but to arouse displeasure. His thrust of originality could be associated with lack of constraint, sudden inspiration, freshness, simplicity, like the mental and emotional impulses of children, of adolescents before their development and finish. Like democracy, novelty and singularity endorsed individuality as release from patriarchal sovereignty (and here begins the sagas of young artists thwarted by their fathers). Such romantic notions of the agony of individuality—the liberation of benign spirits from the bonds of tyranny, with a premium put on youth, and such heroes as Victor Hugo in exile—were not just the motifs of Romantic poets but the psychology of the post-revolutionary industrial age that lead such profound thinkers as Nietzsche to call for re-evaluation of all past values. With Christ now dead as a god (fathers, emperors, and kings now dead as gods), one had to look to Darwin and psychically suffer the travails of progress—not determined by divine plan but motored by natural laws, human industry, the rebellious energies of youths.

In a letter to Baille of June 2nd, 1860, Zola wrote of his fascination for the times, his epoch as ravenous for activity. He mentions motion in commerce, in art and science, evident above all by railroads and steamships, applied electricity, and the telegraph. *Religion is in shock*, he says, *and in the political domain it is even worse. The world is precipitating itself into the future, pressing on to see what will be confronted at the end of the course.* Even older artists were caught up in this awareness of how far matters had changed from the paternal French traditions. In 1859, at the age of sixty, Corot said, *This is for me a new world, which I no longer recognize, but I am still too attached to the past. I want to make a new art, just for myself.*[27]

As with Zola, so with thousands of others caught up in the flow of modernity, which was a medium of perpetuating youth: new ideas, innovations, and fresh outlooks. The prevailing circumstances for art in Paris in the 1860s perpetuated this state of juvenility among young artists and writers, and were the historical grounds of support, sprinkled with political revolution as the way to progress (France had had over twenty governments and several emperors since 1800). Darwinian theory, which supported the idea of progress through industrialization, fed the common notion that the moment belonged to youth. Having nothing to lose, youths could be fearless and take risks with originality. To the successful mutant belonged the future.

Throughout the 1850s and 60s, the physical and cultural renewal of Paris attracted thousands of students and apprentices from provincial towns and cities. They flowed in a steady stream into the city's schools, factories, and shops. By 1850, Paris' population had doubled to over a million; during the 1860s, another half-million would be added. The highest percentage of immigrants was under the age of thirty. With this immigration came an increase in crime and vice—the very subject matter of public entertainment. Alexandre Dumas, whose popular theater plays during the 1860s suffered from preachiness, demanding reforms of the vices his plays so picturesquely portrayed, blamed the railways for bringing daily trainloads of newly enriched young people from the provinces, most of whom had arisen from the lowest classes, retaining their animal appetites for sensual indulgence.

Baudelaire had both acknowledged and disparaged juvenility in his review of the 1859 Salon, not scorning young painters in particular but the attitude he attributed to the spoiled child:

> *The first time I set foot in the Salon, I met on the staircase one of the most subtle and best regarded of our critics. To my first question—to the usual question—he replied, «Flat, mediocre. I have never seen so dismal a Salon.» I saw that he was right. At all times, mediocrity has dominated the Salon, but that now it should be more than ever enthroned, that it should have transformed into an absolute triumph—this is as true as it is distressing. After having passed my eyes over so many successfully completed platitudes, so much carefully worked drivel, so much cleverly constructed stupidity, I was lead by the natural flow*

of my thoughts to think of the artist in times past, and to place him face to face with the artist of the present. And then that terrible, eternal question reared its ugly head. It would seem that smallness, puerility, lack of curiosity, and leaden fatuity has taken the place of ardor, nobility, and ambition...The artist today, and for many years past, is a spoiled child. How many honors, how much money had been showered on men with neither soul nor education?

After noting a few exceptions—Chenavard, Daumier, Préault—Baudelaire continues:

Apart from them, you will hardly find anyone there but spoiled children. I implore you to tell me in what tavern, in what social and intimate gathering you have heard a single thoughtful remark uttered by a spoiled child—a profound, brilliant, acute remark, to make one ponder or dream—in short, a suggestive remark? If such has been thrown out, it may have been by a politician or philosopher, rather by a hunter, or sailor, or taxidermist—but by an artist, a spoiled child, never! The besotted businessman pays extravagantly for the indecent little flurries of these spoiled children.[28]

Against this background—better said, within these surroundings—Cézanne and Zola would establish their positions. They had come to Paris at the right time, timing being everything, if one is with the right people in the right place.

21

While Cézanne toiled at the *Académie Suisse* and in his garret, no doubt anticipating the day when he would be obliged to confront the Salon jury and the critics, Zola was encountering the writer's equivalent to the Salon jurists—editors and publishers. His few published works to date were sketches, like the student work Cézanne was turning out at the *Suisse*. He, too, would have to submit more serious efforts and face tougher judges. And should he manage to get past the editorial perusals, he would then see his efforts praised or mauled by the public.

More than could Cézanne in his cloistered studio, from his crow's nest at Hachette's Zola could at last see beyond his nose. He was in daily contact with worldly people: professional writers and editors. Most likely, he was aware of the advantageous position of youth in a period of rapid change. Emphasis on youth in the 1860s paralleled general notions of evolutionary social and scientific progress. Progress could be made only from a youthful to an adult state, as expressed by popular expressions: The Ages of Man, The Age of Science, The Childhood of Art, and so on.

By 1863 the master printer Nicholas Serrière had perfected the rotary press, which greatly increased printing speed and reduced costs. By the end of that year at least six more newspapers appeared in kiosks: *Le Petit Journal, Le Grand Journal, Le Journal populaire de Lille, Le Courrier français, Le Public, Le Nain jeune*. The rapid increase in rail lines allowed Paris papers to be distributed throughout the country, cutting into the territories of localized publishers. Cheaply produced, newspapers were easy to inaugurate and quick to fail. As their number increased, younger publishers entered the arena, and with them came younger editors, columnists, and critics. In any previous decade, the young Zola may not have had such an easy route to notoriety. The Salon of 1863—the protests and the exhibition of the rejected, most of them young—had raised a flagitious commotion. Facing bitter competition for readers, editors pushed their columnists to further agitate the news and excite the public to howl, jeer, and salivate lustfully in anticipation of the next issue.

The proliferation of newpapers, especially in Paris, prompted Honoré Daumier's cartoon of a man trapped in a surf of papers, with geese overhead, apparently fleeing. Titled *La presse in 1868*, published in *Actualities* that year.

The proliferation of newspapers would continue over the next few years, spurred by the fact that literacy among young adults was a profitable percentage higher than among the generation of their parents and grandparents. The generation of readers coming of age had benefited from an adjustment of the Civil Code to require every township with a population exceeding five hundred inhabitants to maintain a public school with competent teachers; from the 1830s on, for the first time in France's history, even children from farming and mining towns were being taught to read. Because youth identifies with youth, daily news had to expand its appeal beyond the politician and businessman to reach the less moneyed classes and young readers. This great expansion of literate newspaper readers cannot be underestimated when looking for an expanded audience for the avant-garde. Then as today, journalists' jabs at artists and politicians effectively sold newspapers: artists were cartooned as juveniles, monkeys, and idiots—not entirely new points of view: Balzac's paradigmatic *Chef d'Oeuvre Inconnu*, the story of the crazy artist Frenhofer, isolated in his attic garret, painting an incomprehensible *tableau*, had been widely read, and the association of adverse artists with naive daubers and monkeys had been a commonplace since the 1830s.

On April 16th, 1864, Zola published in the newspaper, *Le Journal populaire de*

Lille, what may have been his earliest understanding of himself as fitted to progress. His piece was titled, «*Du progrès dans les sciences et dans la poésie*» (On progress in science and poetry). He called for a violent separation of poetry from the 1830s lyrical school that looked to history and mythology. Now Zola would set aside the transitional passions of the adolescent heart. His ardor for Ary Scheffer-type poetic paintings would turn to loathing, and no longer would he dream of the unsullied virgin as a lifetime muse. The poet of tomorrow must draw upon his real world, in which the virgin does not exist and a muse's kiss is redeemable in cash:

> *Let us bid farewell to the lovely lies of mythology. Let us respectfully bury the last naiad and sylph. Let us spurn myths and make truth the one and only reality. In a de-populated Heaven, let us show the Infinite presiding over immutable laws that flow from the world itself, not from above. Stripped of its cute adornments, the earth will then be a harmonious whole through which life flows toward some mysterious goal. Need I add? I would be a scientist and borrow from science its broad horizons, a new Titus Lucretius, and commit the philosophy of knowledge to our verses.*[29]

Titus Lucretius Carus was the Roman natural scientist of the first century B.C. on whose book, *De rerum natura* (On the Nature of Things), many Roman poets depended back when secular life and popular imagery were splitting off from the Greek. The advent of Roman realism, undergoing rebirth in Zola's era, would dampen mythological traditions during a similar age of industrial expansion and capitalist risk. Zola's manifesto embodied the words of many who had sensed the expanding rift between academic painting and the naturalism of Courbet and Barbizon-type rural landscapists.

Good-bye to the woman's body treated as if it were a vase, Duranty would say in 1876.[30] This was also a wave good-bye to Venus, for the ideal proportions of a woman that drove the economics of the corset and couture industries was the vase-like shape, the proportions of Venus that many women resisted. Daumier captured this sentiment much earlier, in a cartoon twitting the 1865 Salon—two women in the crowd of spectators, naught but nudes on the

Octave Tassaert, *Exactly the Right Proportions*, engraving, ca. 1830

wall, one of the women throwing up her hands, saying in disgust, *Venus again this year...Venus and more Venuses!...as if there were any women like that!*[31]

While it would have been possible for an artist to paint an angel behind a plow horse or nymphs doing their laundry on a riverbank, the result would be as hilarious and illogical as judges condemning criminals to serve a term on the police force. One of the most widely read art writers of the 1850s, Paul de Saint-Victor, had drawn a sharp line on the playing court, setting rural, rustic images on one side, and imagery appealing to people of refined sensibilities on the other:

> *We prefer the sacred grove through which fauns make their way to the forest in which wood-cutters are at work, the Greek spring in which nymphs are bathing to the farm pond in which ducks are paddling; and we prefer the half-naked shepherd with his Virgilian crook, driving his rams and she-goats along Georgic paths, to the peasant, pipe in mouth, climbing the back road.*[32]

It would take but a few substitutions of words to apply Saint-Victor's paean to the art of Manet's circle. Realist painters were as bound to logical relations among elements of subject matter as were tradition-bound academics. Nymphs may bathe regularly, but not because their bodies need washing, and they never need to launder their chiffons. And one cannot paint real ducks in an unreal pond any more than one can paint unreal ducks in a real pond. A flushed pink, perfumed Aphrodite can wash ashore on an unreal beach, but on a realist beach, any nude woman washing ashore would be a puffed up, rather smelly cadaver.

Cézanne would never give up the naiads and sylphs; they will become, by way of transition, his famous bathers. Nor would he have the least interest in science. But Zola would gain much confidence associating with science, which was the banner topic of the avant-garde in social thought at the time. Literature and art were pulled along with the advance of science, just as artisanship was motored by industrial mechanization. In 1868, in a short-lived socialist newspaper, *Le Globe*, Zola would promote demystification of the supernatural, demanding that one find what underlies, for example, the ecstasy of Santa Teresa. He exhorted dramatists to look for the truth rather than the fanciful, to dramatize life in its reality, with all the virtues and vices that one encounters in the streets.[33] For Zola, sirens on the rocks calling out to sailors would hereafter be beckoning whores on seaport docks.

Baudelaire tells a story he had heard about Balzac (*and who would not listen with respect to any anecdote, no matter how trivial, concerning that great genius?* Baudelaire adds): *One day Balzac found himself in front of a beautiful picture—a melancholy winter scene, heavy with hoarfrost and thinly sprinkled with cottages and mean-looking peasants. After gazing at a little house from which a thin wisp of smoke was rising, he cried, «How beautiful it is! But what are they doing in that cottage? What are their thoughts? What are their sorrows? Has it been a good harvest? No doubt they have bills to pay?»*[34] Without relinquishing the romanticism that would have Baudelaire preferring Balzac's delectable *naïveté* (the suggestive dream in a picture, an evocation or magical operation), Baudelaire was sensitive to Balzac's down-to-earth «naturalism,» expressed not as some dreamy gesture towards reality, such as the *Who are we? From where did we come?* sort of questions, but *What are they doing in there? Has it been a good harvest? They must have bills to pay!*

Like those peasants of real life, mulled over by Balzac, Zola had bills to pay. Nothing will bring a poetic soul up from the heart to the brain and into reality as deftly as the need to face the fact that one's soul will never know how to make a living. *One eats with money*—if Cézanne's father had actually said that, then Louis-Auguste's wisdom had taken over Zola's mind. As head of Hachette's advertising department, Zola had learned the tricks one needs to promote a book, as well as whom to flatter. When writing reviews of public lectures on culture in Hachette's *Review de l'instruction publique,* he had nothing but good things to say when summarizing lectures by Émile Deschanel, whose book *Physiologie des écrivains et des artistes, ou, Essai de critique naturelle* (The Physiology of Writers and Artists, or, An Essay on Naturalist Criticism) was published by Hachette in 1864. Deschanel commanded great respect. He had been exiled in 1851 and repatriated in 1859. He co-founded in 1860 *Les Conférences de la rue de la Paix*, and would become a professor at the *Collège de France.* Zola was interested in Deschanel's ideas on the style of one's writing as an expression of one's natural self, but he was also aware that Deschanel was a friend of the publisher Jules Hetzel, whom Zola was courting and who would subsequently publish his first book, *Contes à Ninon.*

As an unproved author, Zola had to cover promotional expenses for his first book. In his letter of agreement with Hetzel, he had committed to matching printing costs with placement of notices and advertisements in newspapers. So even if he had wanted to, Zola could not just sit before the fire fondling his muse, smoking his pipe, waiting for reviewers to pounce on *Contes à Ninon.* He preempted them, writing his own news release, contriving his own puffs and sending his own words of praise to editors he had come to now through his publicity work at Hachette's. Many in the trade owed him good will, and he exploited them all: he even provided ready-to-print reviews written by a friend of his, his best friend, himself. One of his self-written press notes reads:

> *The author, Mr. Émile Zola, belongs to the literary family of free spirits, of passionate and astutely taunting temperaments. He comes forward from Mérimée, Voltaire, Alfred de Musset, Nodier, Murger, Heine. He is a storyteller who converses with his muse as his capricious nature dictates. That explains this strange book in which each narrative is born of a distinct inspiration. Les Contes à Ninon is sure to prevail with people of savory taste.*

As for me, wrote Zola in a long letter (wherein news of *Contes à Ninon*'s acceptance for publication appears) to Antoine Valabrègue on July 6th, 1864, *I*

*have scored my first victory. Hetzel accepted my book of stories. It will appear around the begin-
ning of October. The battle was short, and I'm astonished that I was not slaughtered. I am on
the threshold; the plain is vast, and I'm still very much at risk of breaking my neck.*

The result of Zola's media blitz was as disastrous as gratifying. A rash of flattering reviews appeared by compliant critics who hadn't read the book—and better they hadn't, for the short stories comprising *Contes à Ninon* were juvenilia
through and through. Zola's novitiate impatience and rush to fame had put him
at risk. The only honest reviewer was the hard-hitting, uncompromising Jules
Vallés, who owed nothing to Zola other than thanks for a free copy of his book
that Zola had handed him at Hachette's one day (when Vallés casually dropped by
to peruse Charles Dickens' books, which Hachette had just published in translation).[35] Later, Vallés recalled this first impression of Zola as a short man with
olive complexion, very black hair, and a disdainful, supercilious mouth. Appended
to his published opinion of *Contes à Ninon*, Vallés pointed out:

> *The newspapers are awash with the author's name and everywhere one reads nothing but
> complimentary remarks. But the adjectives smack of advertising, and Mr. Zola ought to
> be wary of such spurious ovations. Let him, as I imagine he is able to do, silence all those
> sycophants who for the most part have not read his book, and let him depend for success
> only on his energy and talent, of which he has enough not to need hired applauders and
> flatterers. He will be better off without them, and literary criticism will benefit too.*

Unabashed, energized by conflict and with no self-restraint whatsoever, Zola
managed to publish thirty-four articles, reviews and stories in 1865. Most of them
came out in the *Le Petit Journal* and, under the general title *Les Confidences d'une
curieuse,* in *Le Salut Public.* He also placed works in *Le Courrier,* the *Revue Française,
La Vie parisienne, Le Figaro, Le Grand journal,* and *Le Journal des villes et des campagnes.*
Happily for him, this opportunity to publish was spread over a year of historic
events favoring the rapid pulsation of sensational journalism: the abolition of
slavery in the United States, the assassination of Abraham Lincoln, an epidemic
of cholera killing four thousand (three hundred and fifty people in Paris alone),
the installation of a telegraph line between Paris and Lyon, and no end of political intrigue and society scandals that cheaply produced newspapers could serve
up daily. The expansion of railroad service permitted papers to be at distant
kiosks the morning after the ink had dried, and daily news was becoming as essential to people's lives as fresh baguettes for breakfast. Newspapers were not taken
for granted back then: daily news was too recent a nutritional commodity, the
novelties too startling and fresh.

Now Zola was positioned to court acceptance and to assault negativity, and
by any means to take command of criticism, to control the critics, make the mur-
derous beasts perform to his whip. To become notorious enough, he fed himself
to the hungry critics so they could defecate the daily shit-ration (his words) the

public craves. And he was prepared to say that if his publications were criticized, it was because he had set up critics to respond to his cues. Six weeks after his *Contes à Ninon* appeared, in a letter to Valabrègue dated February 6th, 1865, he says:

> *I am satisfied with the success of my book. Already a dozen reviews have appeared, of which you say you have read a few. All in all, the press has been benevolent: a concert of eulogies except for two or three sour notes. Those who slightly wounded me thought they were the ones most agreeably tickling me. They hadn't read my stories yet spoke about them tenderly but falsely, so their readers must think of me as the most insipid and mawkish person in the world. Such are one's friends! I would have preferred a complete beating down. I'm feeling rushed to publish another volume. I have every reason to believe that the next book will secure my reputation.*

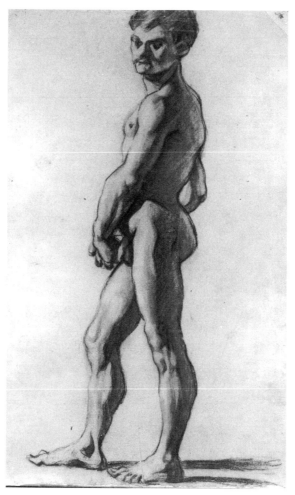

Typical of Cézanne's studies from the nude that would have been made at the Académie Suisse. Collection Fitzwilliams Museum. Cambridge. Photo: Courtesy Adrien Chappuis.

22

A tale of blood and tears that has Fall and
Redemption as its lofty and pure moral

Zola's next publication, the one meant to secure his reputation, was his first novel, *The Confession of Claude*, published in late November 1865. As he had a year earlier, when *Contes à Ninon* was coming off the press, he embarked on a self-propelled promotional campaign, composing his own press release and writing his own review:

> *Mr. Émile Zola, whose maiden work, Les Contes à Ninon, was so well-received, has just published a new book: La Confession de Claude. This one is a physiological and psychological study. Embodied in the work is a tale of blood and tears that has Fall and Redemption as its lofty and pure moral. The frightful narrative relates a virgin heart's passion for one of those girls to whom poets have given the sweet names Mimi Pinson and Musette. The author bares himself therein with a strange talent that combines exquisite delicacy and mad audacity. Some will applaud and others will jeer, but this drama, fraught with anguish and terror, will leave no one indifferent. Emanating from the work are an inexpressible pride, passion and strength that herald a writer of unusual energy.*[36]

The Confession of Claude is a fictional and much elaborated reconstruction of Zola's affair with Berthe (a *grisette*, a lower-class harlot usually attached to students and artists), with whom he'd suffered some non-quality time three years earlier when his emotions were fragile and prone to overdramatize any thought about love. And just as people have read Zola's *L'Oeuvre* (published in 1878) and found Claude Lantier biographically Cézannesque, one might read into *The Confession of Claude* some qualities of character describing Zola. The theme is true to Zola's adolescent fantasies of pure love, virgin girls, poetry, and bucolic nature, but in *The Confession* such sugarplums dancing in his head would convert to horrid realities, like the woman in the coach fantasized by Cézanne. On March 9th, 1859, when still eighteen, Zola had written to Baille about an earlier attraction to a young woman who had failed in his eyes: *I have even made the acquaintance of a young girl, a factory worker—rosy pink, mignon, very sweet, and with a charming name, one of those names a poet would choose. She is called Espérance [Hope]. Alas! she goes dancing and she wears crinolines. Alas! she smokes, she drinks. Alas! this sylph is losing her wings and becoming a reveler.*

These lines are embedded in a long letter to Baille. Since it reveals a great deal about Zola's adjustment to living in Paris, I will provide the bulk of it:

Dear friend,

I am writing to you the morning after Mardi gras, which is a way of saying that I'm exhausted. I can find nothing better to rest my wearied body and dull mind than to chat with you a bit. But I have nothing very interesting to tell you. I've found here only lassitude where I sought to find pleasure. As I told you over the vacation, I feel blasé about everything.

For the past two nights Houchard [a visiting friend] *and I have not slept at all, wanting to see everything, everywhere, from the Opéra* [where a masked ball, *le soir de Mardi gras,* was held] *to public dances about town. If I were not afraid that you would laugh at me, I would tell you of the thoughts which crossed my eighteen-year-old heart upon seeing all those people so stupidly jumping around, one in front of the other, deafening their ears with their own shouts in order to persuade themselves that they were having fun. I thought about (do not laugh at me, now) that young Spanish girl, whom you know as well as I, who, according to the poet's expression, lay down to die in a casket lined with flowers. I wouldn't dare tell you all this stuff if I didn't know that you were so much like me—but you see, like those who seek to forget their troubles with drink, the ball seems to me a Léthe* [the ancient river of forgetfulness] *where the unhappy come to dive in with furor and flail about in the water as much as possible so that all their troubles may be washed away. One must look upon such things with poetic vision. One would laugh heartily if, in the midst of the joyous throng at the dances, one might hear me call out loudly for my woods and valleys* [still missing the environs of Aix]. *I didn't do that. I just watched and pretended to enjoy myself.*

In this letter, Zola tells Baille, who is now studying the natural sciences in Marseilles, about having met a girl named Espérance (Hope). Perhaps Espérance is not a real girl but a figure of speech, a fantasy—hope personified. Or possibly she was a real girl, but the name Zola gave her was poetry. When Zola finds that she smokes, drinks, and dances, he deems her hopeless—his dreams hopeless. *Poor poets,* he goes on, *we have good reason to say they are all dreamers!*

No matter! Espérance is pretty, and if I were Marguery, I would tell you that I had hope [now comes the play on her name] *for an entire night. I don't know if I will see her again. She told me where her workshop was. Will I go or won't I? Good heavens, it's only that Espérance is very pretty!*

I've had better times at the carnival in Aix in previous years. I was younger. I had more illusions. And you, what did you do last Tuesday? [Tuesday in French is *mardi,* the day of the Mardi gras, which would also have been celebrated in Aix]. *Did you go to Aix? Did you wear a costume? Did anything fantastic happen? Tell me every-*

thing in your next letter.

Marguery wrote me a second time. He will, he says, try to put together a vaudeville show in Aix. I don't wish to get involved by giving him advice. He is very young, but as you know, audaces fortuna juvat [good fortune befalls the audacious]. *He is not lacking in good reason: if he feels his vaudeville is solid on its feet, he can perfectly well try to make it work, and if I were in Aix I would go to see it and applaud with all my heart.*

What are you doing? Are you still working? By Jove it is perhaps a good way to live, if not a little too common and prosaic. The Gospel forgot about happiness for those who can work. In my case, my entire being revolts when I have to benumb myself by working. I like work, but in my own way, doing what I want, when I want to do it. You and I have taken different paths. Which is the right one? Life will tell.

You still haven't told me what program you are in and at what level. Don't be modest; it's the prerogative of idiots. Tell me what I suspect, that you've proved to the humdrum people of Marseilles that the people of Aix are the Athenians of Provence.

I saw Guignan and Trouche, who say hello. They are still the same closed-minded people they were, only they weigh more now—two good fellows in every sense of the word.

Espérance as Hope was no Berthe, who turned out to be Despair. Not much can be known for sure about Zola's actual affair with Berthe. For a short time, early in 1862, Zola lived separately from his mother in a boarding house (*un hôtel garni*) on *rue Soufflot*, one of the Latin Quarter's most squalid pre-Haussmann-demolition streets, along which students, shop girls, and prostitutes populated the building's small rooms; through thin walls, sounds of laboring passion passed osmotically. On February 5th, 1862, twenty one-year-old Zola wrote to Cézanne telling of his escapade with Berthe—not the physical details but what he'd learned from its sordidity: *Now I can speak from experience about women of easy virtue. Sometimes we get it into our heads that one can restore to goodness some wretched creature by loving her, by lifting her up from the gutter.* He adds that one's vanity, meaning one's narcissism, is at stake in such matters, and he confesses that such high-flown phrases as *love washes away all blemishes* sound charming but are harshly false. Having been baptized by the fire of passion, Zola had experienced first hand what he would soon propose as realism. While the experience with Berthe had re-shuffled his thoughts about pure love, it had also given him a useful literary structure. Rescue of a fallen woman is as familiar to men's psyches as dreams of flying; by the time Freud took up this structure it was a literary commonplace.[37]

Zola's narcissism, his identification of himself with the unsullied virgin found in his earlier letters to Cézanne and Baille, now shifts from its internalized, juvenile state to an externalized adult state. He splits the bad from the good, retaining the good in his own image and projecting the bad onto others. His juvenile idealism, allowing for all to be good, converts into a sort of grandiosity of self. Rather than allowing his idealism to dissipate, he takes control of reality by internalizing a whole society, which he, himself, will re-fashion in his novels—a contrast of the pure and righteous with the aggressively deleterious bad seed. In 1871, when he publishes the first of his twenty-novel series, *La Fortune des Rougon*, he announces in its preface that, after dissolving the duplex question of temperament and environment, nurture *vs.* nature—*after having every thread gripped in my hands* [like a master marionettist], *I will show the complete social group in action and investigate not just the will power of each member but the comprehensive proclivities of the whole.*

Since early youth, Zola had been the rescuing, situation-controlling type, perhaps in part because the lack of a father left him with a sense of responsibility for his mother and the need to be his own counsel, a parent to himself. In his September 8th, 1860 letter to Victor Hugo, he had written that the man of genius owes himself to youth, that one of his most sacred duties is to nourish those who have taken the right path and constrain those headed down the wrong one. In this spirit, Zola had tried tirelessly to rescue vacillating Cézanne from his father's grip (less tight than Cézanne's grip on himself, perhaps), and to liberate his dreamy friend Valabrègue from the deadly embrace of Aix's sap-sucking muse of poetry. Zola will always be a sort of Darwinian augur with a positive charge, an evolutionary determinist who sets a goal and makes sure that all events lead to it—a fail-safe prognosticator who sees a human in every monkey, a reconstitutable virgin in every streetwalker.

Zola wrote much of *The Confession of Claude* shortly after he and Berthe went their separate ways. Like an unborn child, the manuscript remained unfinished in a womb-like drawer. Success at getting *Les Contes à Ninon* published encouraged him to take it out and complete it. The plot of the *Confession* is Balzacian: an idealistic young man comes to Paris from the provinces where he encounters squalor and depravities and, like the prodigal son, retreats back to the sanctity of the parental den.

Claude is a student lodged in a boarding house. An old prostitute calls upon him to come upstairs and look after a girl named Laurence who has taken ill. Though just in her teens, this girl is already a soulless whore. Claude looks at her half-naked body laid out on the sickbed, the sheet folded down to her waist—the first time since a suckling infant he's seen a woman's breasts. Of this raw witnessing Claude says, *The peaceful sleep of vice, of washed-out features imbued in their repose with angelic sweetness, cast a strange spell over me. I was ashamed for the young woman. I felt my virginity fly away from me.* It was as if Claude had encountered a sleeping nymph whose sweet image was overlaid by a debauched harlot, like Cézanne's *mirliton,* and not wholly unlike the experience viewers would encounter this year at seeing Manet's *Olympia*—aghast at her dubious identity; anticipating a Venus, a luxuriating courtesan, they will confront a plain-looking whore.

After Laurence recovers, she invites Claude to her bed, and then invites herself to live in his room where, while expending his passion, Claude undertakes to reform her, pursuing the Romantic notion of love redeeming a lost soul. But Laurence is hopelessly depraved and sexually his superior. Claude can neither amend her ways nor teach her anything. In the priestly effort he, too, degenerates. So the two of them, cut off from the outside world, wallow in carnality. They hock the last of their meager possessions to buy scraps of food, and Claude is soon down to a single blanket as clothing. Finally, the last of his worldly holdings, the only thing left in his hands—this mistress who has mastered him—shamelessly betrays him. While dirt-poor Claude is ministering to yet another fallen waif, he sees in shadow play his brazen boyhood friend Jacques interlocked passionately with Laurence. Claude's confession then wells up from the bottom of a cesspool: *My suspicions became flesh. At last I knew and I saw. In my imagination I found certain truths that were fraught with painful delights. I thought I was mature enough for the battle, but I was only a naked and feeble child. Perhaps I will always be a child.*

Doubtless aware that he was deploying emotions from his own childhood—the struggle between the internal self and the external world as confrontation with harsh reality—Zola feared his book would not be accepted among grown men, that the text would be read as a childish book. On sending a copy to Ernest Chesneau in mid-November 1865 for review in *L'Opinion Internationale*, he pleaded like a child: *This poor unknown writer needs you in order to succeed in this world. Treat him as a grown-up boy, I mean seriously, and not with the banal lenience that is granted to children.*

Chesneau responded on November 19th, with thanks for the book: *As an anatomist,* he wrote, *you have dissected the body, the soul, and the subject you had at hand. However, the portrait you draw of this youth is very sad. You scared me, and I will remain scared if Claude doesn't prove to be the exception. What cure will suffice, socially, for such twenty-year-old appetites! It is likely that I will mention your book soon.*

Unfortunately for Zola, or perhaps fortunately, considering that Chesneau didn't think much of the book, no review appeared in *L'Opinion Internationale*. But Zola had also written to others, including Jules Claretie at *Le Figaro*, the critic who had called Manet's *Olympia* a vile, yellow-bellied odalisque:

> *Dear Sir and Fellow,*
>
> *You were kind enough to introduce my first book to readers of Le Figaro; you may also be kind enough to introduce them to the new novel I have just published. The book is thin, so you probably won't have the opportunity to fall asleep reading it. But I insist on it being read before being judged, as I prefer a sincere bad critique to a few complaisant remarks. Grant me a little space in your next review column. I thank you profusely beforehand.*

Back on December 15th, 1864, Jules Claretie had made a few complaisant remarks about *Les Contes à Ninon* in his column *Échos de Paris* in *Le Figaro*. He ended that column on a note about one of the stories, *The Adventures of Sidoine the Great and Médéric the Little,* inspired by the outrageously self-promoting words that

Zola had asked to be inserted into Claretie's review: *The public, the publisher and the writer should be enchanted by this book, the strike of a young master in which some satirical speeches of a king named Médéric would make Messrs. Voltaire, Henri Heine, or the author of Les Contes Bleus smile.* But in his *Échos de Paris* column on November 19th, 1865, Claretie only mentioned *La Confession de Claude*, saying that, contrary to the estimations of his colleagues, he did not find in Zola's novel even *the smallest atom of morphine.*

To the reviewer Philippe Dauriac, Zola had written: *I'm not eager to be known by everyone. I wouldn't dare tell you in which newspaper I want to see your review of my book printed. Still, Le Monde Illustré would be the best newspaper for this kind of ad.* And to the critic, Charles Deulin, Zola wrote: *Here at last is La Confession de Claude. It belongs in part to you since you found the title. Might you be able to mention it somewhere, wherever you want, and as you like. Should I send a copy to Sarcey? I don't dare, knowing we don't have kind feelings for one another. I await your answer, trusting you in this matter. Do not write until you have read my book. Then share your opinion with me. P.S. Do you know that the printer first refused to print it? He thought I was too immoral. I finally demonstrated that the book is highly moral and filled with rare innocence.*

Francisco Sarcey, the powerful theater critic for *Le Temps,* was indeed a critic to avoid, though he wouldn't take bites out of Zola's buttocks until the early 1870s when he reviewed Zola's play, *Les Héritiers Rabourdin.* Then, Sarcey wrote, *Zola's Rabourdin is insufferable with his eternal whining, his feigning mortal illness and herbal infusions. The thing that especially displeases me in Émile Zola's manner is his pretensions. Each of his characters always seem to be saying to the public, «See what an abyss of perversity I am.»*[38]

Gustave Frédérix, a journalist at *L'Indépendance Belge,* whom Zola had met at Hachette's, wrote to Zola: *I just received La Confession de Claude which you graciously sent me and will soon mention it.* He did, on November 20th, 1865, quoting extensively from Zola's foreword and summarizing the plot. He also added a few words of advice:

> Mr. Émile Zola mixes skillfully refined style with disgracious stiffness. There is not enough attitude and tension in his style. One can be sure that all this will work out in time when Mr. Zola treats a less bitter subject, when he lightens his distinguished and very personal qualities. Then he should be able to deliver rigorous and careful analysis with knowledgeable precision and poetic emotion.

To one F. Morel at *La Gazette des étrangers,* Zola wrote: *It is to be understood that I would rather be ripped to pieces with sincerity than compliantly praised. Don't worry, hit me, and have your readers hit me harder.* Signed by Dorante rather than Morel, this entreaty struck ink in the November 22nd, 1865 edition of *La Gazette,* in the column *Courrier de Partout*—a laudatory account of *La Confession de Claude,* employing much of Zola's own blurb:

This book is the terrible story of the passion of a virgin heart for one of these girls to whom poets gave two names: Mimi Pinson and Musette. Delicate people will no doubt be revolted, for the author reveals his strange talent made of exquisite thoughtfulness and wild audacity. One will applaud, or even boo, for one cannot remain calm before this drama full of anguish and terror. There is an inexpressible pride in the book, a passion and a strength announcing a writer with rare energy.

Had Zola been less desperate to publish something other than reviews and short stories, he may have listened to his own critique of *The Confession of Claude* before it appeared as a book. In a letter to Valabrègue, who had over-praised it, Zola wrote, *It still contains too much that is puerile. And here and there it sags. The novelist retreats into the background while the poet comes upstage, a poet who has drunk too much milk and eaten too much sugar. The text is not virile. It is the crying of a rebellious, petulant child.*

So Zola as author had arrived at the same conclusion about himself as Claude had in the novel, behaving like a naked and feeble child stuck to the breast. Perhaps this identification explains why Zola adopted the pen name Claude when wishing at times to disguise himself as an art and book reviewer, and why Zola, as much as Cézanne, may be infused into the deranged artist (also named Claude), the subject of *L'Oeuvre,* who hangs himself directly in front of a painting he can't salvage as a work of art any more than Zola could salvage Berthe's virtue—or Claude, the virtue of Laurence. Zola had also sent a copy of the *Confession* to Georges Pajot, his friend from the *Lycée Saint-Louis.* Pajot's letter acknowledging the book is dated November 19th, 1865.

My dear Émile,

I received your book recently and wanted to read it before answering your letter. You know how much I enjoy such correspondence. You should never doubt that I would do the same for you. I am your friend and nothing related to our friendship is unimportant.

I devoured the pages that told me much about our burning life back when we were twenty. I found myself immersed in that life again, in the middle of those painful events.

I would like to give you an informed opinion about your work, at least an impartial opinion, but strangely I'm prevented from doing so, as I did not so much read your book as dream it. I lived it. For a few hours, I found myself before the great wall—rue Soufflot. Berthe was with me in her torn dress. It was truly this woman with her negative qualities, waiting for an alien force to break her inertia and help her make a move. I was confronted again with your own poverty and pain. Therefore, I cannot be both judge and third party to the text; I will read it again and think about it some more.

I have never been able to bear the sight of an open wound. When confronted by any wound, I have looked away, not in disrelish but perhaps out of cowardice. Pain scares me. I feel it, but don't like to see it depicted in vain. If an unfortunate, wounded man were to beg for my help to save him from dying, I might not, under those conditions, be upset by the sight of blood, and would be as happy as one can be for having performed a good deed. But if a physician chanced to show up, I would welcome him as a savior for the wounded as well as for myself.

So I almost hated you when you traced and retraced the pain and poverty. I was ashamed of this poverty so close to disgrace. I told myself that modesty forbade one to expose in the open a body stripped naked by pain. And then I told myself that the physician doesn't fear to probe wounds, to dissect, to cut into living flesh in order to learn and know our body and thus to heal its wounds.

Then I understood your work. But I scolded myself for reading it in the way I was, and when my reading was painful, I blamed it on myself. However—and this is our strange human nature—I could not stop reading before the last page.

It is a fine dramatization of the three types of women. The horrible truth about their character is the warrant for their originality. You are a frightening daredevil. Your gilded dreams about oriental luxuriance harshly contradict the excessive poverty. It looks like a sculpture under a crude light: the bright colors cut harshly and with no penumbra through absolute blacks.

The drinking scene is good and well observed. You are almost sublime when you describe the promenade in the countryside, when close to the sewer of Bièvre, you feel like kissing Laurence. Your style is serious; it seems filled with love and mysticism. In your study of the human heart, you are closer to Lamennais than to Montaigne. You often neglect—too often maybe—material details about life and keep to only the psychological details. One can easily see how, during this long year, you were able to always think, but one does not know how you ate.39

I will stop here for today. By tomorrow I might have modified my critique. I will let you know. If you think I am being inflexible, remember this definition of friendship: it is—I can't remember who said it—the privilege that two men who admire each other have to tell each other unpleasant things without arousing anger. Please excuse me then, and answer me without fear. No matter how far apart we are geographically, our old friendship is unaltered.

It is not fair that Laurence makes us forget about the present. Old pain doesn't bother today's happiness. My best regards to Gabrielle [Zola's mistress, at other times called Alexandrine]. *If she inspires a novel, it won't be as sad as this one.*

I shake your hand. Your friend, Georges Pajot.

Not to be defeated, never to back off, Zola spent the final day of 1865 mounting a counterattack on a critic who'd assaulted and poked fun at *The Confession of Claude*. The day before, in *Le Nain jaune* (The Yellow Dwarf), the militantly royalist novelist and critic Barbey d'Aurevilly had published a short review meant surely to wound rather than simply insult. D'Aurevilly said: *Zola indulges in the most disgusting details a realist quill had ever written. Through three hundred and twenty pages, one's reading churns up voluptuously what Cambronne so concisely threw in one word at his enemy's face!* This reference to General Pierre Cambronne would have been recognized back then by every French reader: in the Napoleonic War, Cambronne was the French commander who came up against Wellington's army at Waterloo. Assured that his disciplined ranks would overwhelm the French, Wellington politely offered Cambronne the right to fire the first volley. Cambronne obliged him, throwing at him one word—*Merde!* [Shit!][40] Just as offensive to Zola was that d'Aurevilly slipped up and gave the name of Hachette as the book's publisher rather than Albert Lacroix. Outraged, Zola dashed off a protest letter to the editor, which was printed in the January 6th issue. But to crank up the torture rack another notch, the editor of *Le Nain jaune*, or someone, printed Zola's letter, more or less as follows, with nonsensical typesetting, some words and phrases in all caps and others in different fonts:

> *Sir,*
>
> *It is customary for writers who are mutilated not to respond to INJURIES aimed at them. SO, I do not intend to defend myself against the attacks one OF YOUR editors thought he could afford to mount against me.* That your columnist calls *The Confession of Claude «a pretty Reine-Claude plum»,* my hero a «toad», *and grants ME THE ART OF «churning up voluptuously,* through three hundred and twenty pages, *what Cambronne, more concisely, threw in one word at his enemy's face!» This IS NOT JUST A MATTER OF bad TASTE—of which I couldn't care less and will pass over*—but I cannot let a publisher be given credit for a work it didn't publish. Your columnist calls my novel the *«little Hachette book.» If that is maliciousness, or simply a joke, I must say that I DON'T GET IT. If that is a mistake, I demand rectification.*
>
> *Your columnist's prose calls to mind an article I published last May in the Salut Public. It was about a novel entitled, I believe, «Un Prêtre marié»* [*A Married Priest* by Barbey d'Aurevilly, the critic Zola is here castigating], *the work of AN HYSTERICAL CATHOLIC, reeking of young flesh. I treated that work badly in my review*—without mentioning Cambronne, to be true. *So now we are even, and that must have BEEN WHAT your editor had in mind. Oblige me, sir, and publish THIS LETTER in your coming issue of* Le Nain jaune.

In response to Zola's letter, the editor-in-chief Jules Castagnary of *Le Nain jaune* had Barbey d'Aurevilly correct his error—identifying the wrong publisher—in the same issue as Zola's spitefully typeset letter. D'Aurevilly's correction was written rather snippily, with couched apologies:

> *Apparently I thought, with an excess of good faith, that Hachette had published Mr. Zola's book. It was a serious error and an important matter. Contrary to what is usual, alas, I was wrong to look more at the book than at its cover, and now I have cause to regret it. The cover, however, is cleaner than the book's contents, and I mistook Hachette with its employee.*[41]

On reading this, and seeing how atrociously his letter had been set in type, steaming Zola blew his lid. He fired off another letter to *Le Nain jaune*, but it was not published in the January 13th issue. Zola wrote with acidic malice afore-thought to editor-in-chief Villemessant of *L'Événement, Le Nain jaune's* rival paper, and asked if he would be willing to print his letter of protest.

Sir,

Would you have the kindness to save an honest man the trouble of hiring a bailiff? [to sue Le Nain jaune]. Here is the story. Following some violent language that a columnist of Nain jaune laid on one of my books, I thought it was my duty to protest. His review wasn't critique. It was downright defamation. My protest letter, addressed to Mr. Grégory Ganesco of Le Nain jeune, was printed, but printed in such a strange and ridiculous man-ner that I immediately wrote to Mr. Grégory Ganesco the second letter which I include here-in:

Sir, I am responding again and ask—no, I demand—that this new letter be pub-lished as follows:

I thank you for publishing my letter to the editor in Le Nain jaune. But I do not thank you for letting your editor, who couldn't alter the text, ridicule my letter by printing it with italics, small capitals, and large capitals. I dare hope that it happened without your knowing it, and that you were as amazed as I was this morning when you saw a private letter transformed by a secretary you most certainly didn't even know.

Should I believe that the mail addressed to Mr. Grégory Ganesco is given to anybody reaching out a hand for it? This is a serious matter, Sir. My thoughts are harmed as to decorum and good manners. I would like to have your opinion in this matter. As you can see, I am incorrigibly impudent.

And I have one more demand. I have been hurt by the way I was treated, and now I dare speak up and ask if it is normal practice for a director [directeur de journal] to have his private mail published with alterations and typographical emphases added by one of his editors.

L'Événement by this date was a daily tabloid. Villemessant would print any-thing that tickled the public or bedeviled his competition. So, by bringing this piece of dirty laundry to him, not to wash but to hang out unwashed in public, Zola was able to attack and demean, as well as prolong the publicity. Grégory Ganesco had no idea how maladroitly he had fallen into Zola's chamber pot. Zola continues with his explanation of the affair for Villemessant's use.

This letter, as to savoir-faire, must have embarrassed Mr. Grégory Ganesco, and he wise-ly decided not to publish it, hoping that I would weary and back off from that unpleasant affair. But I owed him a last warning, and I sent him that warning in the following words:

«Since I wrote to you with a determination to have my letter made available to your

readers, I must tell you that I will at least expect you to print it in the January 17th issue if I don't see it in your January 13th issue.»

I must say, Sir, that I thought myself more courageous than I am. Le Nain jaune being silent, I was overcome with disgust at the thought of my prose being put on legal paper, so I drew back from hiring a lawyer. Could you spare me such a writer/lawyer collaboration by publishing this letter in L'Événement? If you can't, I will go on with my first idea, which is to sue, as I feel my honor is at stake.

Ganesco's letter of rebuttal was printed on January 18th 1866 and included a chronological rundown of the facts and ended with the accusation that Zola's outbreak was only to seek publicity: *Here are the facts*, he writes, *which Mr. Zola alters out of ignorance and for the sole pleasure of having his name once again in the public eye.* The letter Zola had sent him, he says, was opened in his absence by editor-in-chief Jules Castagnary, not by a secretary, as Zola implied. Castagnary forwarded the letter, which seemed logical, to Barbey d'Aurevilly, *«the very author of the article incriminated by the claimant.»* Ganesco ends his rebuttal with: *In spite of the hospitality Mr. Zola's letters received in the pages of L'Événement, I still cannot take seriously his way of recouping his losses.*

On January 18th, Zola followed up with a second letter to Villemessant: *Sir, Grégory Ganesco's letter responds so badly to mine that I would be obliged if you would let me set forth the facts more clearly.*

I will treat the matter in terms more general than personal. I wish to clarify once and for all the appropriate way adversarial letters should be treated in a literary controversy. Journalism, it would seem, is interested in knowing how to properly behave in such matters.

I never complained about the nasty comments that were contrived to annotate my protest letter, and I believe, as does Mr. Grégory Ganesco, that it was proper form to send my comments directly to the columnist who originated them.

What I cannot tolerate—what no one would tolerate—is the grotesque manner in which my comments were printed. Imagine, Roman words, italic words, words in small caps, words in large caps. The worst thing is that some people believed I was the author of that bizarre typography—some have approached me and asked why I so misused the font.

I ask you clearly: Should letters to the editor be published as written? Or is the editor allowed to print them with whatever capricious typography he might wish to use? The answer doesn't require much thought. Grégory Ganesco had no right to alter a private letter addressed to him, even less to allow a third party to alter it, even if that third party was involved in the matter. Do you not sense the meaning of this? And do you not understand why I speak of decorum and literary fairness?

Mr. Grégory Ganesco says he was out of town. Why should that matter to me? There is no fundamental difference between him and the person in charge of opening his mail. What this person did was done in Mr. Grégory Ganesco's name, so he is the only one to be held accountable. In short, although Mr. Grégory Ganesco felt it necessary to argue the situation, I believe he didn't thoroughly look into it. He seems to have ignored the facts in order to avoid the obstacles to truth. Besides, the case has already been tried— and to my advantage, I was told. It would have been unpleasant for Mr. Grégory Ganesco to lose a case, had he defended himself. He cannot bring himself to take me seriously, as he said. What is the least serious in this matter are Grégory Ganesco's answers, which do not answer to anything.

It's may seem obvious, according to the staff at Le Nain jaune, that I write this latest letter only to have my name put once more in the public eye.

So please accept, Sir, my thanks for your loyal hospitality, which some are tempted to consider as a crime.

This drawn out flap over *The Confession of Claude* was augmented by the fact that the book had come to the attention of the public censor, the Director General of Printing, Publishing, and the Press. The text was subjected to scrutiny, as was Zola himself. The investigation came to naught when the *Procureur Général* (Prosecuting Attorney), in a letter to the *Garde de Sceaux* (Attorney General), dismissed the text as simply causing young people to become disgusted with the impure relationships into which they allow themselves to be drawn by poets who glorify bohemian love affairs:

The scope of the book is not immoral. The author only tried to dissuade youths from those impure liaisons into which youths are drawn by their faith in those poets who idealize smut in their bohemian love stories. Mr. Zola strongly disagrees with these poets: «Their mistresses,» he says, «are infamous; their affairs have all the horrors of debasing affairs; they are deceived, hurt, insulted; they never encounter a pure heart, and each of them encounters his own Laurence who turns his youth into desolate solitude.» Laurence must therefore be murdered, since such Laurences kill our flesh and destroy our love. To those who cherish light and purity, I would say: «Beware; you are entering the night, the muck.» To those whose hearts are sleeping and who are indifferent to evil, I would say: «Since you can't love, try at least to keep your dignity and honesty.» This is the moral that Claude himself draws from his confession. Therefore, I don't think that the book should be put on trial as being contrary to public morality.[42]

The Goncourt brothers, Edmond and Jules, may have found all this critical fuss over Zola's novel gleefully amusing. They would spurn any notion that Zola's *La Confession de Claude* was an invention of realist literature, claiming that they had already published the first and best of it with their novels *Soeur Philomène* (1861) and *Germinie Lacerteux* (1864). Intent on faithfully picturing life with the exactness of an historian as to existing conditions, they had portrayed in *Germinie Lacerteux* a female domestic who'd served them for years and yet, all the while, had been living a secret side-life of vice and debauchery—the story based on documented scenes and happenings investigated by the authors in Rome where the unfortunate woman had previously lived. The Goncourts also disliked Zola. They would describe him in their 1868 journal in this fashion:

> *Our admirer and pupil came to lunch today. It was the first time we had ever seen him. Our immediate impression was of a worn-out normalian, at once sturdy and puny, with Sarcey's neck and shoulders and a waxy anemic complexion. The dominant side of him, the sickly suffering, hypersensitive side, occasionally gives you the impression of being in the company of a gentle victim of some heart disease. In a word, an incomprehensible, deep, complex character—unhappy, worried, evasive and disquieting.*

23

For Cézanne we have an empty chronology along the road from 1864 to the summer of 1866. It will be difficult to chart his progress alongside Zola's. On April 7th, 1864, he registered at the Louvre to copy Nicolas Poussin's *Shepherds in Arcadia* (the copy lost to history), and in late 1864 was at work on a copy of Delacroix's *Barque de Dante*. From that time span only two Cézanne letters survive: one to his friend Numa Coste dated February 27th, 1864, and one to Camille Pissarro dated March 15th, 1865. In both, one finds a buoyant, confident Cézanne moving steadily along the path of his chosen profession. But they reveal only how he felt at the time they were written.

Coste had drawn an unlucky number in the conscription lottery and would have to serve seven years of military duty. Cézanne empathizes with his friend in the February 27th letter. He, too, had passed his required fitness tests and was a candidate, but, as was the custom for the well-to-do, his father paid for a substitute to take his place. Zola, being a widow's only son, was exempt from service. My dear Coste, Cézanne writes:

You must excuse the paper on which I am answering your letter. I have nothing else to write on at the moment. What can I say about your unhappy lot? It's a great calamity that has befallen you, and I understand how distressing it must be. You tell me that Jules, too, has been hit by this misfortune, that he is anticipating the call-up.

Baille was with me yesterday when I received you letter. If by chance you are actually called up, you could come to Paris to enlist in a corps here. Baille might be able to put in a good word for you with the lieutenant of the company here because, so he tells me, he knew a great number of cadets who came from the same training school as he did. What I'm telling you is only in case it occurs to you to return to Paris, where even as a recruit you would have more facilities of all sorts, both as regards leave and easier duties. So you could still devote yourself to painting. It is up to you to decide whether this appeals to you. If you happen to see them, remember me to good old Jules, who cannot be very happy, and to Penot, who really should give me news of his family and his father. As for me, old man, my hair and beard are longer than my talent. Still, no discouragement from painting. One can easily make one's little way here, even as a soldier.

For two months I have not been able to touch my galette after Delacroix. I will, how-ever, touch it up again before leaving for Aix, which will not be before the middle of July, unless my father recalls me. In two months, that is to say, in May, there will be an exhi-bition of painting like the one last year; if you were here we could look it over together. Well, may everything turn out for the best. Give my affectionate respects to your parents.

The *galette* after Delacroix (*galette* meaning tart, or any tasty morsel) that Cézanne says he had copied and not yet touched up, was most likely Delacroix's *Barque de Dante*, which hung in Paris' Luxembourg Museum. It was a very early work by the master that Baudelaire hailed as the priming-charge of the revolution in modern painting. The young Manet had copied the *Barque* twice in the mid-1850s. In the 1880s, Gauguin would copy it as well.[1] Having said that two months had passed since he thought to touch up his copy, Cézanne would have been twenty-four, exactly the age Delacroix was when he painted the *Barque* in 1822.

In the January 5th, 1863 letter to Coste, Cézanne said that Delacroix is enthroned. He had chided a fellow student who arrogantly thought the esteemed master could be deposed. That Cézanne would copy both Poussin and Delacroix over a short span of time gives at least some information about his activities and state of mind then. Those venerated painters were antithetical; in the thoughts of many as irreconcilable as a church and a brothel. Poussin was historical, a French painter of the first half of the seventeenth century who worked mostly in Rome but was regarded, nonetheless, as the founder of the French Classical style. The principles that Poussin generated for the phase of pure classicism that followed—clarity of conception appealing to the mind rather than the eyes, moral solemni-ty, obedience to rules of decorum and style—became as integral to the dictates of the *Académie des Beaux-Arts* as were those of Jacques-Louis David that had endured into mid-century as principles of art advocated by Ingres. Delacroix and Ingres had the same antipodal kinship as had Poussin and Rubens. David's sub-ordination of color to line and emotion to the austere virtues sustained Poussin's emphasis on design and controlled emotion, while Delacroix's vibrating, uncer-tain, dissolving lines, and imagery structured by color, sustained the painterly style of Rubens, the vibrant brushstrokes, luminosity of color, and audacity in juxta-positions of complementaries.

Back in 1855, when Paris sponsored the largest international exhibition of art ever staged—over 5,000 paintings by artists from twenty-eight countries—the feature attractions were a gallery of Delacroix's paintings setting off a gallery of Ingres' paintings, or vice versa. Aside from the stylistic contrasts, while Ingres chose to show his best work regardless of date, Delacroix grouped his paintings to demonstrate stages in his development. Professional excellence was thus set apart from evolution, clearly marking the contrast of Ingres' static values (all

Eugène Delacroix. *Barque de Dante*. 1822. Paris, Musée du Louvre.

Nicolas Poussin, *Shepherds of Arcadia*. Paris, Musée du Louvre.

things created by God in perfect form) with Delacroix's evolutionary values (sustained creation en route to perfection). The notion of modernism as progress with an avant-garde in the lead could not have been more effectively demonstrated to a generation at the crossroads between the path to academic glory and the path of adventurous experimentation. By the 1860s this contrast permeated thought in every field, from political science to medicine. Zola's April 1864 essay titled, *Du progrès dans les sciences et dans la poésie* (Progress in Science and Poetry) was not an individualist's whimsy but a timely examination of relevant cultural issues most clearly articulated by one of Zola's mentors, Hippolyte Taine.

If within the same few months Cézanne did copy Poussin's *Shepherds of Arcadia* in the Louvre, and also Delacroix's *Barque de Dante* in the Luxembourg, he had, knowingly or not (and probably not), emotionally metabolized the polarity of sentiment dividing artists' loyalty at the time. He was also engaged in sketching nudes in academic poses at the *Suisse* and natural landscapes out of doors. This mix of Poussin and Rubens, *académies* and landscapes, was not unlike taking different courses in school—mathematics one hour, philosophy the next. Cézanne was a student at this time, not yet an artist in his own right. Temperament thus becomes a difficult basis upon which his style of the 1860s would depend. The mix of the restrained and the exuberant may be a description of his weather-like personality—periods of clarity overtaken by black moods, timidity offset by insolence, doubts by boastfulness—but can one make an art history out of a history of temperaments coinciding at propitious times with the temperament of his milieu?

Such an art history, which may be conceivable, would surely cause Darwin to smile in his coffin. The first problem such an art history would encounter is that neither the personalities of artists nor the disposition of their social environments are level. Over-compensation and sublimation at any given moment are rarely synchronized, and the suppression of an impelling force can be as artistically productive as an effusive outpouring of an inspiration. From the very beginning, certainly by 1867, the variability of Cézanne's production thwarts any effort to put it in order, which explains in good part why so many speculative notions are forged as materialist myths in disguise, and why the chronology of his extant pictures from this period is so bootlessly debated, especially when keyed to pictures attributed to Cézanne but just as likely by a different hand. The problem of coping with the simultaneity of passion and repression will also confound Zola's first art criticism when he tries to explain Manet's *Olympia* in the 1865 Salon. Accustomed as he had become to sublimated subject matter, he will have no way to describe the non-sublimated woman on display, or the maid, or the cat, except to deny that they exist as anything other than colors, as if Manet had simply added colors to a color book.

The worn-out notion that Cézanne's great accomplishment in art was due to his suppression of the romantic temperament by the classic—a sort of conquest of good over evil, like St. George slay-ing the dragon, or St. Anthony warding off temptresses—starts right here, at the moment when Cézanne copying Poussin's *Arcadia* is juxtaposed with his copying Delacroix's picture of Charon's barge headed down river to the Inferno—a heaven for Poussin, a hell for Delacroix. But contrast itself is a qualitative entity, an enduring potential that does not always split into parts. The cross-roads encountered by Hercules would remain a cross-roads, regardless of which road he chose to take. If at any time Cézanne was at the crossroads between the romantic and the classic, then remaining there, casting his eyes down one road, then down the other, could be as stable a position as rejecting one road and heading down the other.

Works by the masters that Cézanne's chose to copy, like books one chooses to read, may have been subject to his vacillating state of mind, at times shy and restrained, at other times rambunctious and erotic. Zola's short stories assembled at *Contes à Ninon* are similarly mixed: some melancholic, some frivolous, some philosophical. Each is a product of a mood, and especially with the young, moods alternate frequently and at times violently. Each mood serves as a trial for the young writer groping along an unmarked route. Speculative looks at Cézanne's psychology as emotionally unstable lead easily to arid generalizations about his art of the 1860s and early 70s. Roger Fry engraved this epitaph on his tomb: *Here lies Cézanne, a Romantic overcome by a Classic*, akin to a victory of virtue over vice, or a clean-shaven Greek warrior over a scruffy Barbarian—as Cézanne saying mirthfully in his letter to Coste, *My hair and beard are longer* [romantic] *than my talent* [classic].⁹

In Cézanne's mind, the team of Delacroix, Rubens, and Courbet will continue to wrestle with Poussin and Ingres-types. Unlike Zola, who could lay down an absolute rule that true naturalism must deny romanticism and display no presence of the artist in the work, Cézanne did not sublimate his art to an entirely fictitious world but remained embedded within it. At his death, a print of Poussin's *Shepherds of Arcadia* will be found hanging in his studio, along with a reproduction of the most erotic of Delacroix's paintings, *The Death of Sardanapalus*. And in Cézanne's wallet, which I came upon when searching closets in his grandson's apartment in Paris, would be found a photograph of Courbet's erotically charged *Woman with a Parrot*—photos of which were hawked as pornography well into the twentieth century—and a membership card for the *Société des Artistes*, signed by the president Charles Bougeureau, the shrewd painter of disguised pornography whom Cézanne supposedly despised.[44] Cézanne's psychology in the 1860s, *vis-à-vis* society, is no easier to schematize than are his paintings in the later context of Impressionism. Nor can a picture by Ary Scheffer on the mature Zola's studio wall—while hidden in a triple-locked vault were pictures by Cézanne and others—be handily explained, considering the style of Zola's 1860s art criticism.

　　Hippolyte Taine comes to mind for his critical methodology applied for the first time in a famous essay, his 1853 doctoral thesis on La Fontaine's fables—*Tout écrivain s'explique par une faculté maitresse et trois facteurs: le milieu, le moment, la race* (the coincidence of social environment, moment of time, and race). Louis Hachette was a close friend of Taine's as well as his principal publisher. Zola had met Taine at Hachette's. Responsible for the Hachette promotional catalogues, *le Bulletin du*

Gustave Courbet, *Woman with a Parrot.* 1866. New York, Metropolitan Museum of Art. H. O. Havemeyer Collection.

libraire et de l'amateur de livres, Zola presented and promoted Taine's books: *Nouveaux essais de critique et d'histoire* and *Voyage en Italie.* In *Mes Haines,* Zola says he considers Taine *a contemporary of the telegraph and the train: The new science, made of physiology and psychology, of history and philosophy, had its first moments in him. He is, for our epoch, the highest manifestation of our curiosity, of our needs to analyze, our desire to reduce everything to the pure mechanism of the mathematical sciences.*

Intellectuals such as Taine, and artists like Delacroix, force polarities onto society rather than just adding something to it. Most everything in modern thinking depends on one or more fundamental contrasts—left or right, democrat or republican, line or color, Ingres or Delacroix—Cézanne copying Poussin and Delacroix in the same year. And the polarity will show up as early as 1867 in Zola's contrast between the Rougons and the Macquarts when a corrupting single gene takes its own course through the generations, affecting one individual on one branch off the crotch of the genealogical tree, then another on the other branch, the legitimate Rougons on one side, the Macquart bastards on the other.

24

The notion that one saw the world only through the screen of one's own *tempérament* made naturalism acceptable to a romantic. It preserved the emotional privacy and mysterious psychiatrics of one's self. In a very long, witty, tongue-in-cheek letter to Valabrègue of August 18th, 1864, Zola boastfully lays out his shift from being a romantic to being a realist. With this letter comes his essay on *les Écrans*, the screens that transpose Creator-created reality into the lived reality of the individual mind, the basis for Zola's statement that art is but an aspect of Creation seen through a *tempérament*:[1]

> *My dear Valabrègue,*
>
> *I don't know what this letter will be like, if I will pussyfoot around or show my claws. You must admit that you provoked my anger. Why on earth did you say to me so brutally, and without warning, that you have become a realist? You must break this kind of news gently to people. I have always found the kind of jokes that consist of hiding behind a curtain, and then howling like some kind of a werewolf when someone passes by, to be in poor taste. I am a high-strung person and was frankly hurt that you did not take pity on me.*
>
> *My Lord, once my fear had subsided, I could not deny that you were within your rights to fraternize with Champfleury* [considered to be the head of the realist school, who wrote *Le Réalisme* in 1857, and had said that man is always carried along by his particular *tempérament*, which makes him render nature according to impressions he receives of it]. *My opinion is that one must know everything, understand everything, and admire everything, according to the degree of admiration each thing requires. Only let me pity you for the depth of the disturbances which each new idea causes you. You were a classic youth from the time you were very young, and that tender and pure soul allowed you to live your youth peacefully. At the time of your first trip to Paris, a demon—an enemy of your delay in coming—suggested romanticism in a whisper, and you became a romanticist, astounded, surprised with your new way of seeing—in short, completely upset.*
>
> *Do you remember? You used to say to me: «I have lost my peace of mind, I've burnt*

what I've accomplished, and now don't know where to begin.»

Because I am a naïve and good fellow, I waited for you to set aside your romanticism. What a laugh! You did not have time to be romantic, and now, here you are becoming a realist, stunned at being able to do so, looking at your reflection in the mirror and unable to recognize yourself, writing me with words that reveal your grievous angst: «I will need some time before I can take my usual place,» you say. Well! Good Lord! It is fine to change one's place, but if one does not want to lose a lot of time one must, in literature, always eat at the same place—at that table setting which is yours. Do you understand what I'm saying, and the meaning behind my remarks? You have gone from Voltaire to Champfleury by way of Victor Hugo. That proves you are on the move, but don't you think it would be better to stay in one place and create—become yourself—without worrying about the others?

I prefer it when you make your spacious spirit open to all forms of art, but I would love you even more alone with yourself, rhyming away without worrying about the various schools, giving your temperament free reign, and above all not allowing yourself to be stopped miserably by ridiculous discoveries, those of unknown worlds visited by all. Would you like me to continue with my frank and slightly brutal tirade? If you do not take up your pen heartily, writing about anything and everything, if you do not feel the strength to understand nature yourself, you will never have even the slightest bit of originality—you will only be a reflection of reflections.

Now, let me congratulate you on having understood a school I love. To tell you the truth, I do not believe that your nature is at ease within it, for you were not born a realist (don't take this in the wrong way but I repeat, it is good to understand everything).

Make me out to be a liar, my dear Valabrègue. Write a second Madame Bovary, and you will see how I will applaud you.[2] I could even forgive you, but only then, the terrible fear your realism caused me to experience, causing me to tremble still. Once I received your letter, after having read it, I was swept away into a long reverie. I shall, as I write you, tell you what my thoughts were. In this way clarifying for myself my own ideas, and sketching the first draft of an extensive study I wish to undertake someday on the subject. Judge the idea and not the form. I am expressing myself as I can, in haste.

THE SCREEN AND CREATION
The Screen Cannot Provide Real Images

I allow myself to start with a slightly daring comparison: all works of art are like an open window on creation; there exists, mounted in the window frame's recesses, a sort of transparent screen through which one perceives objects in a more or less deformed manner. These objects are variably impressionable in their line and color, and depending on the nature of the screen they undergo perceptible changes.

We no longer possess a precise and real world-as-created but one that has been modified by the mediums through which its images pass [medium is here equivalent to milieu].

We see «the created» in a work of art as having passed through a man, that is, through a temperament, through a personality. The image which is produced on, or through, this screen is only a facsimile of things and people which are projected onto the screen—and this projection, or replication, cannot be a faithful one, because it will change as many times as a new screen is placed between our eye and the creation, just as lenses of different colors give the objects we see different colors, just as concave or convex lenses deform objects, each in their own way.

Precise reality is therefore impossible in a work of art. We say that we demean or idealize a subject. Basically, they imply the same thing. There is some deformation of whatever exists—a lie, whether demeaned or idealized. It matters little whether this untruthfulness beautifies the object or renders it ugly. I repeat. The deformation, the falseness produced by this optical phenomenon, is linked to the nature of the screen.

Now, in order to resume the comparison, if the window were open and the objects placed beyond it, they would appear as they really are. But the window is not open—it does not even know how to be open. All images must pass through such a medium. This medium changes them, as pure and transparent as the medium may be. Is not the word Art the opposite of the word Nature [nature on one side of the window glass, art on the other]?

Any time an artist gives birth to a work of art he must place himself in direct contact with the object of creation, see it in his own way, allow himself be penetrated by it, and send back its luminous rays after having, like a prism, refracted and colored the object according to his nature.

As for this idea, only two elements must be taken into account: the external world [as pre-created] *and the screen. The external world is the same for all. All pre-created objects send to the eye the very same image. The screen alone provides a subject for personal study and contention.*

THE SCREEN—ITS COMPOSITION

Speculations on the screen involve major points of philosophical controversy. Some thinkers—and there are many of them in our time—affirm that the screen is made of flesh and bone and reproduces images materially [meaning anatomically determined]. *Among them, Taine considers the screen first within himself. He attributes to it the qualities of a mistress. And then he attributes it to every possible nature, subject to three major influences, race, the environment, and the moment.[3] The others philosophers, without denying entirely the flesh and bone notion, swear that the images are reproduced on an immaterial screen. All of the spiritualists find themselves in this group—Jouffroy, Maine de Biran, Cousin, and so on.[4] Finally, and as everything needs a middle ground, Deschanel wrote in one of his last works, «In so far as we call certain things works of spirit, not everything can be explained by spirit: but also and for all the more reason, not everything can be explained by matter.»[5] Here is a lad who shall never compromise himself. One could say it better by not saying anything. What is, after all, the spirit?*

At this point I am not going to investigate the nature of the screen. The mechanism of the phenomena matters very little to me. What I wish to establish is that the screen produces the image and that by some mysterious property of the translucent being, whether material or immaterial, this image belongs to the screen.

THE SCREENS OF GENIUS AND
THE SMALL OPAQUE SCREENS

The leader of a school is a very powerful screen that gives images with great vigor. A school is a troupe of small opaque screens with very thick grain. Not having the strength to emit images themselves, these small screens take the image from the powerful and pure screen, which they have placed at the point, at the head of the line. The small screens' way of proceeding is shameful. It will always be allowed for an artist of genius to show us creation— in green, blue and yellow, or any other color he likes. He can depict circles as squares, straight lines as dashes and we will have no cause for complaint. It will suffice that the images reproduced have harmony, splendor and beauty. But what we shall not be able to bear is any obfuscation or deformation of the work. It is blue, green, or yellow, and the square, or the straight line, is fashioned according to precepts and laws.

Because genius-made nature undergoes certain deviations in its outlines, certain changes in its nuances, these deviations and changes become articles of faith! Each school is monstrous, in that it makes nature tell lies in order to fulfill certain rules. The rules are the instruments of the lies, which are handed along from teacher to student, reproducing in this way false images which are nonetheless grandiose or charming, and which the genius-screen has given with all the naïveté and vigor of its nature. Arbitrary laws, highly imprecise ways of reproducing creation, are prescribed by folly and foolishness as the easy way to arrive at any truth.

Genius is the sole raison d'être for rules, according to the works of art that formulated them. Except that, in the case of genius, these were not actually rules but the genius' personal vision, the natural effect of the screen.

Schools were founded for perpetuating mediocrity. For those who do not have the strength of audacity and freedom, it is good to have rules. It is the schools who provide the paintings and the statues for grand buildings and public monuments, the tune for each song, who satisfy the needs of several million readers—all of this can be summarized by saying that society requires a certain more or less artistic luxury. In order to satisfy this need, the schools produce, for better or worse, an agreed-to number of artists per year.

These artists carry out their métier, and all is well. But genius has nothing to do with any of this. It is by nature not linked with any school, and creates new ones as needed. Genius is satisfied to place itself between nature and us, and to provide us innocently with images. We are served by its products, and by the freedom of its allure to prohibit disciples from exhibiting any originality. A hundred years later another screen gives to us yet another proof of the eternality of nature; a new set of disciples draw up new regulations, and so on and so forth. Artists with genius [esprit] are born and grow freely. Disciples follow in their footsteps. Schools, however, have never produced a single great man. It is great men who have produced schools. These in turn, provide us in good years and in bad, with the handful of artistic movements that our civilization needs.

(Here I am forced to leave a blank. I would need to prove the major rules, common to all genius, reduced to the simple use of common sense and innate harmony. It is enough to refer to the fact that what I understand to be a rule is any particular process applied by a school.)

ALL SCREENS OF GENIUS MUST BE UNDERSTOOD, OR, AT THE VERY LEAST, LOVED

Certainly, one is allowed to prefer one screen to another, but that is a matter of individual taste and temperament. In the absolute point of view, there does not exist any reason in art for the Classic screen to have an advantage over the romantic and realist screens, and visa versa, since these screens transmit images which are all equally false. They are all, almost as far from their ideal, creation, and given this, they must, for the philosopher, have equal merits. All the screens of genius must be accepted as such the instant in which their creation cannot but give it to us with its precise color and line, it mattering little that it is rendered in blue, green or yellow, in square or circular form.

In addition, I wish, in judging the screens for myself, to make up for what this opinion may have by way of exaggeration. But I must not fail to establish beforehand that, if any epigram should escape me, it is not the genius-screen, the leader of the School that I address, but the school itself, which mimics and mocks the beauty of the master's works. Furthermore, I am only expressing my personal opinion. And I state in advance that, despite everything, I understand and accept the genius-screens, which my own organic structure nonetheless leads me to dislike. (Here once again I leave a blank. I know that the beginning of this paragraph will not convince you of anything. You would like to classify the schools and list them by order of merit. I do not feel that this should be done, since each has its failings and its merits, extreme delicacy [tact] would have to be used in order to make such a classification. If they must be placed in order, let us do so in order of their degree of truthfulness).

THE CLASSIC SCREEN
THE ROMANTIC SCREEN—THE REALIST SCREEN

The classic screen is a beautiful sheet of very pure talcum powder of a fine and solid grain and a milky white color. The images are drawn clearly with a simple black line. The colors of the objects are muted, and by going through veiled limpidity are at times completely effaced. As for the lines, they undergo a marked deformation, tending to bend or straight-

en, becoming thinner and stretching out with slow undulations. The created work loses its abruptness, its lively and luminous energy; it keeps only its shadows and reproduces itself on the polished surface like a bas-relief. The classic screen is a lens that augments and develops lines while impeding all colors from passing through it.

The romantic screen, on the other hand, is a mirror without silvering—clear, although a bit unfocused in certain places—and colored with the seven nuances of the rainbow. Not only does it allow for colors to pass through; it enhances their strength, at times transforming and mixing them. Outlines also undergo some deformation—straight lines tend to break, and circles become triangles. The creation this screen provides is a tumultuous and active one. Large sheets of shadow and light vigorously produce the images. The lies told about nature are more striking and seductive—no peace but life, a life more intense than our own. The pure development of lines and the sober discretion of colors are lacking, but the creation contains all the passion of movement and the flashing splendor of imaginary suns. The romantic screen is a prism with a powerful refraction that breaks all luminous rays and decomposes them in a blinding solar spectrum.

The realist screen is a simple glass pane, very thin, very clear, which pretends to be so perfectly transparent that the images pass through it and are reproduced in all their exact reality. Therefore no change in line or color, rather an exact reproduction, honest and naïve. The realist screen denies its own existence. It really does! It has an exaggerated belief in itself. For no matter what it claims, it exists, and therefore it cannot claim to give us the creation in all the beauty of its truth. For as clear, as thin, as similar to a pane of glass as it may be, the realism screen has nonetheless its own color and is not without thickness. It colors objects, refracts them, just as any other screen.

I do not disagree that the images it provides are the most real, that it achieves a high degree of exact reproduction. It is certainly difficult to characterize a screen which has, as its primary quality, that of almost not existing. I believe, however, if judging it fairly, that a fine grayish dust clouds its limpidity. Any object passing through this medium loses its brilliance, or rather, is slightly blackened [recalling here that realism in the 1860s was often associated with dirt, dirtiness, the color black—see later, p. 000]. Also, lines become more abundant, are exaggerated, so to say, in their direction and width. Their life is spread out thickly—a material and slightly heavy life. Finally the realism screen, the latest of those produced in contemporary art, is a unified pane, very transparent without being too limpid, providing images which are as faithful as any screen can provide.

MY FAVORITE SCREEN

It now remains for me to declare my personal taste, to declare my preference for one of the three screens described here. As I detest the role of disciple, I would not be capable of accepting any one of them exclusively and in its entirety. All of my sympathies, to be honest, are for the realism screen; it satisfies my raison d'être. I feel in it the immense beauty of solidity and truth. But, to repeat, I cannot accept everything it wishes to present to me.

I cannot admit that it gives one true images. And I affirm that it must have its own properties that deform images and consequently make works of art. I fully accept its procedure, which is that of placing itself in all frankness before nature, rendering nature in its entirety, without exclusions. The work of art must, it seems to me, embrace the entire horizon, which includes at one and the same time the screen which rounds and develops the lines, mutes the colors, and also the screen which brightens colors and breaks lines. I prefer the screen that hugs reality, which is content with lying just enough to make me feel like there is a man in the image of a creation.

Having completed his lecture, Zola's letter to Valabrègue continues:
Well, my dear Valabrègue, this is all now said but not without effort. I have just reread my writing and do not know how loudly it will cause you to scream. There are many nuances. It is rough and materialistic. I feel however that I am on the right track.

Thank you for your congratulations regarding my success with Hetzel [the pending publication of *Contes à Ninon*]. *I think that printing will begin shortly. Its publication is scheduled for the first half of October, unless any unforeseen events should transpire. In any case, I have my contract in my pocket and any delay would be nothing more than a business obstacle.*

Mr. Hachette is dead, as you have heard [he died on July 31st, 1864]. *You asked if his passing did not compromise my position. In no way did I. I am thinking of remaining at the bookstore for a few more years in order to broaden my circle of acquaintances more and more.*

Since I wish to answer all of the questions you asked me, I need to bring up this phrase in your letter: «I ask you if your poem must be realistic.»[6] *Although the few pages you have just read must generally inform you on this point, I insist on repeating to you formally that my poem (since there is such a poem) shall be what it can be. Hadn't I already mentioned to you that the poor child* [the poem] *is deeply asleep in one of my drawers and shall no doubt never awake? I need to walk fast these days and rhyming would hamper me. We shall see if the Muse is not angered, and if she has not taken another lover more naïve and innocent than I.*

I am now with prose and find myself content. I have a novel underway and hope to publish it within a year [*La Confession de Claude*]. *You know that I have little time for myself, and that I work slowly. I do not want to tempt your faithfulness, but would inform you, just between us, that I approve of your having, for several months, placed there that great big gal of a Muse (so stupid and so embarrassed about her hands and feet, when not being gracious and pretty) to compromise her virtue. Should I continue?*

Try to have, upon your return here, a manuscript in each hand—a poem in the left, a novel in the right. The poem shall be refused everywhere, and you may keep it as a relic in the bottom of your desk. The novel shall be accepted and you shall not leave Paris with a heavy heart. Too bad if the Muse is angered and holds it against me. I tell you truthfully that away from prose there is no safety. Don't believe that the immortal virgin and I have said good-bye to each other. But I will admit to you that there is now great disagreement between us. All the articles you will send me will be welcome. I do not know you well enough as a writer of prose, so I wish to get to know you better.

Has my letter been cruel? No: my whip—far from slashing anything to shreds—only knows how to tickle people. It makes them laugh and nothing more. It is true that I accused you of not being a realist. For a realist of yesterday, this is indeed a great insult. Please forgive this insult and think of how many others would take it as flattery.

Work! Work! Work! and Write! Write! Write!

Sincerely yours.

25

Z ola's intention to remain at Hachette's for a few more years was abruptly blocked. Hachette's administrators were not as merciful and risk-taking as their adventurous founder. They decided that the Public Prosecutor's attention to *The Confession of Claude* and too many bad reviews of the book had compromised the firm. Zola was dismissed on the last day of January 1866.

The *Confession* had attracted about everything but revenue, so Zola's only hope of income was to turn promptly to hack journalism. He wrote feverishly to several newspaper editors and publishers. Top on his list must have been the estimable *Le Figaro*, while next may have come the purveyor of gossip and other marketable news, *L'Événement*. He had already made inquiries with editors several months earlier when hoping to supplement his salary at Hachette's. On April 11th, 1865, he'd written to Alphonse Duchesne at Le Figaro: *Allow me to introduce myself, as I have no one to do it for me, and I prefer not to make you distrust me by implying the protection of someone else.* Zola's fatherless self surfaces here, as at other times when he promotes himself as all alone in the world. One recalls him saying, *I am only a fighting critic who clears the path in front of him, since there is nobody else to clear it for me.* In time, his overuse of this lament will induce accusations of being a pity-seeking whiner. The letter continues:

> *Recently I published a volume of short stories with some success. I write a literary review for Le Salut Public and contribute articles to Le Petit Journal. This sums up my creden-tials. I wish to increase and surpass them as soon as possible. I gave first thought to your newspaper as one that could attract attention the most quickly. I trust you will not mind my speaking candidly. I am taking the liberty of enclosing a few pages of prose, and I ask you, with complete candor: Is it all right that I did? If my humble personality does not please you, let us not discuss this matter any further; if it is only the enclosed article that does not, I can send you others.*
>
> *I am young, and yet must admit that I have great faith in myself. I know you like to try out new people in order to find new contributors. Try me. Discover me. You can always fire me later.*

Please consider my offer and let me know your decision, either by publishing my article in Le Figaro or asking me to come and retrieve it from your office.

Zola's letter to *Le Figaro* did not produce an immediate response, but by May 1866 he would become a regular contributor—not particulary liked by the editors, but his reviews drew readers like flies to carrion. More providential and potentially renumerative was a positive reply from *L'Événement*. Editor Hippolyte de Villemessant, ignoring the commotion that Zola had aroused over Barbey d'Aurevilly's critique, accepted Zola's offer to write a bibliographical column several times a week, a rapid-fire series of short book reviews mixed with gossip and previews of books not yet published. What the public wants, Zola had said in his letter, are brief notices: the news served like canapés, tidbits on small plates. He pointed out that this sort of column would increase the paper's revenue; the large number of reviews, even if very short, would generate more advertisements. He proposed to title his column *Livres d'aujourd'hui et de demain* (Books of Today and Tomorrow). After settling remuneration terms, on January 31st, 1866 (the very same day that Zola left Hachette's), Villemessant, who had no love for Zola but liked his spunk, put a rather crude note in his newspaper announcing the appointment: *If the new voice in my choir succeeds, that will be for the good. If he fails, the situation is simple enough. He himself has told me that, if that should become the case, he will cancel his engagement and I will cross out his name.*

Zola plunged ahead with his innovative column, reporting on three to five books daily. Over ten hyper-productive months (early February to early November) he wrote more than one hundred and twenty-five reviews in his *Books of Today and Tomorrow* column, perhaps reading only a few pages between the covers of each splayed victim. *I must produce almost an article per day. I must read, or at least leaf through, the writing of every contemporary imbecile*, he lamented in a letter of July 26th to Numa Coste. In addition, Zola published a few articles in *Le Figaro* and *Le Grand Journal*, two short stories in *L'Illustration*, and some thirty-eight pieces in *Le Salut Public*, where longer essays were welcomed. In those he gave critical and favorable attention to books by Balzac, Michelet, Vallès, the Goncourts, Prévost-Paradol, and Sainte-Beuve. Imitating Sainte-Beuve's popular *Causeries de Lundi* [Monday chats], he followed a format of detailed analysis combined with global ideas on the virtues and vices of literature. And he tortured academic writers mercilessly and without respite: Edmond About, Jules Janin, Désiré. On the first of September appeared in *L'Événement* the first episode of Zola's *novel en feuilleton* (serialized), *Le Voeu d'une morte* (The Dead Woman's Wish), over which turnabout became fair play when critics put Zola to the rack while his readers yawned. The series was canceled after a short run.

By this time, Zola had come to terms with the nefarious reality of the writing and publishing business. In a letter to Valabrègue, he admitted with utter candor that the only trustworthy sign of literary success was enough money to promote one's own name. No poetry left in his soul, he was now willing to write for the most degraded tabloids:

> *The question of money is in part a factor in all this. But at the same time, I consider journalism to be such a powerful lever that I am not at all reluctant to use it as a way of producing a larger number of readers for me one day. This explains my contributions to Le Petit Journal. I am well aware of the low literary level of that newspaper, but I also know it will quickly develop a popular reading public for me.*[1]

Financial success as a professional writer came to those who prepared a readership in advance, best done with the serialized novel—each weekly installment a short but prolonging chapter, leaving readers in suspense and propelling them with accelerating heartbeats to the next issue, like radio soaps would do decades later. Newspaper publishers had discovered this strategy by the 1840s when serialized novels caught on as an essential aspect of mass marketing. Issues could be cheaply sold, even given away as promotion when newspapers turned to advertising for revenue. Then literature had to be brought down to the level of the masses, a cheap commodity for quick consumption, easily digestible to make room for the next episode. The serialized novel fitted to the times. By the 1860s, life was moving fast; railroads shortened distances and telegraph communication was instantaneous. Short episodes appealed to mass readers who were neither book buyers nor accustomed to reading long texts, and though literate, were indifferent to literary quality, wanting instead a gripping story with as much sex, violence, and scandal as the public censor allowed. Weekly newspapers became daily newspapers, with the Sunday paper taking over what weeklies had provided: editorials, serialized novels, book and theater reviews.

Writers who solicited a mass audience—such as Balzac in the 1840s—had applauded the serialized novel as a symbol of free-market competition, while Sainte-Beuve held out and disparaged serial novels as industrial literature. Balzac cheered the rivalry among newspapers trying to outbid each other for the most profitable authors: *Le Constitutionnel* cut its subscription rate to a few francs and acquired Eugène Sue's *Le Juif errant* (Wandering Jew) for the enormous price of one hundred thousand francs. Alexandre Dumas even hired assistants to help him quickly turn out *Le Compte de Monte-Cristo* and *Les Trois Mousquetaires*. Though committed to the journal *Les Débats*, Balzac watched with franc-shaped eyeballs the bidding wars between *Le Soleil*, *Le Constitutionnel*, and *Le Siècle*, for he was perpetually in debt to publishers; charges for his excessive emendations of printer's proofs often exceeded his royalties. *It's a money tournament*, he admitted. *I'm a free agent and will do all I can to exploit the situation.*[2]

Louis Napoleon's government levied a stamp tax on serial novels in 1848 in an effort to counter mass circulation of social views expressed in the serializations that were subversive, often ridiculing government institutions and dignitaries in the guise of fiction. The Academy of Moral and Political Sciences promoted statistics that the sexuality and violence of the *romans-feuilleton* stories were responsible for the rapid increase in crimes of passion, suicide, assaults on women, and adultery. Especially disturbing to the male society was the prevalence of novels centered on women and sexuality, and especially that women were reading them. Other than educating each other, women's access to knowledge about physical love came largely from reading novels and how-to manuals. The traditional and very popular novelettes known by blue covers—the *bibliothéque bleue*—were simple romances and tales of chivalry that appealed to the young and the chaste. More sophisticated women, readers of Alfred de Musset, Gustave Flaubert, and Eugène Sue had been raised on the *bibliothéque bleue* (which would retain its color into the twentieth century as blue movies and blue laws.

Although the tax on newspaper novels dampened royalties, the profitable practice of serializing continued under protest. By the 1850s, realistic, low-life stories, recounting torrid romances and infidelities without guilt, started to hit the market. Zola's *La Confession de Claude* and *Thérèse Raquin* would fit to this category. More and more women were reading about love affairs and hypersexual blandishments they could put in contrast to their own love life. Book-derived fantasies of enflamed lovers satisfying hidden desires through illicit, artful sex marked the first stage in the revival of *les liaisons dangereuses* among the bourgeoisie. A rash of novels with plots depicting a husband murdered by his wife's lover fanned the embers of repressed hearth-and-home women. Zola's *Thérèse Raquin* was one of the best of these formulaic stories, but also one of the most moralizing (although not everyone agreed that it was). Thérèse and her lover Laurent do in Thérèse's boring and impotent husband, and marry in a state of lust, but punishment rains down on them: their marriage is haunted by the husband's bloated corpse that they drowned and then saw fished from the Seine; their passion for each other transforms into loathing; in a fit of terror they commit suicide.

The critic Louis Ulbach, writing for *Le Figaro*, summed up the realist school and located Zola and the Goncourts at its core:

> Over the past few years a monstrous school of novelists has replaced carnal eloquence with eloquence of the charnel house, invoking the weirdest medical anomalies, making pus squirt out from one's conscience, mustering the plague-stricken so we can admire their blotchy skin. Germinie Lacerteux, Thérèse Raquin, La Comptesse de Chalis, and many other works that do not deserve special attention will prove my point.

Ulbach was a serious republican who had opposed Napoleon III and positioned himself with the socialists. He criticized Zola and the Goncourts, not for immorality but because their writings subverted their own ends: their brand of realism aroused lewd thoughts rather than passion for redressing social wrongs.

Ulbach was able to defend Balzac, saying that a Madame Marneffe, in *La Cousine Bette*, did objectify every corruption but was never put in a position that would provoke laughter or offend taste, and thus fit for the public to know through theater. On the contrary, the Goncourt's and Zola's characters had no redeeming social value that would allow their portrayal on stage before the general public: *I defy you to portray Germinie Lacerteux, Thérèse Raquin, all those impossible ghosts who exude death without having breathed life, who are nothing but nightmares of reality.*

Ulbach is reminded of Manet's *Olympia*. He writes, *Zola sees women as Mr. Manet paints her, mud-colored under pink makeup.* Ulbach then returns to *Thérèse Raquin*, saying:

> As for the nuptial night, which Thérèse and Laurent spend in their torture chamber, if this represented some individual fantasy I would have said nothing, but the disease is epidemic. Let us force novelists to display their talent rather than their pickings from the law courts and the city dump. Mr. Zola is said to be a young man of talent. All I know is that he has ardently been courting fame. Enthusiastic about smut, he published La Confession de Claude, the account of a student and a harlot. Intolerant of criticism, Mr. Zola himself criticizes with intolerance, and at an age when desire is one's only rule, even the harsh sentence he has meted out to the adulterous couple served no moral purpose, for remorse seen as a physical affliction was pornography in another guise.[3]

Zola reacted quickly, using his rebuttal as an attack on the Parisian stage. He bludgeoned Ulbach with Jacques Offenbach (composer of *opéras-bouffes*, comic operas, including *La Belle Hélène*), mocking the idea that propriety forbade Germinie Lacerteux to show her work-worn face where chorus girls bared their gartered thighs.[4] *Pornography*, wrote Zola, *thrives not in the studios of realist painters but in the make-believe of Salon art and Boulevard Theater. It would not displease you too much, Sir, if Germinie Lacerteux wore tights, provided she had well-turned legs. I am beginning to understand what you desire: silken skin, firm and rounded contours, transparent gauze that barely veils treasures of voluptuousness.* (One is reminded of the adulatory review of Alexandre Cabanel's *The Birth of Venus* in the 1863 Salon—the *Salon des Refusés* year—the painting purchased by the State: *Though wanton and lascivious, she is not at all indecent, cleverly rhythmical in pose, curves agreeable and in good taste, the bosom young and alive, the hips with perfect roundness, the general lines of her body harmonious and pure*).[5]

Still, Zola had learned that he would never be recognized as a serious writer, or garner more than pittances if moving, like a wandering minstrel or huckster, from one newspaper to another. For all his defensive railings, he knew, as did his critics, that no idealism fueled his progress.[6] Having cast his lot with writers of *la littérature putride*, Virgil could just as well come down off his mountain and wallow in a swamp for all he cared.

Honoré Daumier. Landscape Painters At Work. Published in *Le Boulevard*, August 17, 1862.

Pissarro had been nudging Cézanne into landscape painting; in turn, Pissarro had trudged alongside landscapist Corot and slyly submitted to the jury in 1964, and again the following year, as a student of Corot, the better to have his landscapes accepted. Unlike Manet, Degas, and even Monet, Pissarro was a non-aggressive painter who tended to take the easy, untroubled road with landscapes. In the 1850s and 60s, landscapists were generally looked upon as too lazy to paint anything that wasn't right there in front of them, making no demands on imagination or intellect. In the 1860s, Cézanne was not ready to be supple and submissive in front of nature, and certainly not in front of the Salon jury. When it came time to challenge the Salon, his entries would be figurative paintings, calculated to provoke a violent reaction. It is not known what he chose to offer the 1865 Salon. The sole evidence for his having submitted a picture or two is a March 15th letter to Pissarro in which he says that he and the Puerto Rican friend he'd met at the Suisse, Francisco Oller (six years older than Cézanne), were about to bring their canvases to the Salon:

> *Forgive me for not coming to see you, but I am leaving this evening for St. Germain and will only come back on Saturday with Oller to help take his pictures to the Salon. He has painted, so he writes, a biblical battle scene, I think, and the big picture you've seen. The big one is very beautiful, the other I have not yet seen.*[1]
>
> *I should have liked to know whether, in spite of the misfortune that befell you, you have completed your canvas for the Salon. If you wish to see me, I go every morning to the Suisse and am at home in the evenings. Give me a rendez-vous that suits you and I will come and shake your hand when I return from Oller's.*
>
> *On Saturday we are going to the barracks of the Champs-Elysées to bring our canvases that will make the Institute blush with rage and despair. I hope you will have done some fine landscapes. I shake you warmly by the hand.*

Submitting to the Salon was yet another contest against an institution about to pass judgment, an entire committee of judgmental fathers, another ghoulish

Cézanne. *Portrait of Antoine Valebrèque.* Oil on canvas. Submitted to the Salon of 1866.

examination board, another horde of devils lusting to consume his flesh. But, were Cézanne to be accepted by the Salon jury, he would be sorted among hundreds of ordinary painters and sculptors who go unnoticed, not reviewed, their entries hung in back rooms and dark corners, or so high up as to be out of view—»skyed,» as that predicament was called. Nothing could be gained by submitting acceptable works that would be hung with a thousand other acceptable pictures and seen by no one but one's friends. As a critic sympathetic to Manet said, *If Manet would just do something right, no one would notice him.*[2] Ulbach's assessment of Zola was correct: Zola was flat out courting fame, and in his own clumsy way, Cézanne would follow his lead.

Zola had found out that publishing agreeable reviews makes friends but disagreeable ones make a living. Cézanne, too, had recognized by 1865 that an artist in a hurry to become known should not placate the jury by pre-selecting what the members would react favorably towards, but what offered jurists the greatest cause for outrage. This could not be done with landscapes or still lifes, only with atrocious figurative art that would insult the academic traditions. Then one could mobilize an audience by loudly protesting one's rejection and gain even more notoriety in the press, as had Zola when rampaging against Barbey d'Aurevilly (neither had heard the advice offered by photographer Nadar to Courbet in 1853: *Coarseness is not strength, nor is scandal the same as renown*).[3] Under the circumstances Cézanne had gotten himself into, a *succès de scandale* would do just fine. This would involve the intentional production of bad paintings. Not just half-bad. Hundreds of painters did that while trying to paint well. To garner the attention of journalists, one needed to produce very bad painting, so atrocious that the degree of negative response would equal in decibels the applause for an astonishing masterpiece, like the unruly schoolboy getting the most attention.

Having his entries trashed in 1865 was what Cézanne had expected and most likely hoped for. Bleeding-heart art lovers have no grounds whatsoever for pitying this young man with a father paying his bills and at his side the art critic of the moment. One of Cézanne's submittals to the 1866 Salon was a portrait of Antoine Valabrègue painted in heavy impasto, mostly with a palette knife and without dramatic posing or much mentality on the subject's inarticulate face. Cézanne knew the canvas would kick up a storm. Valabrègue's friend, Antoine Marion, had written to Heinrich Morstatt (a young German musician he'd met in Marseilles and recently introduced to Cézanne): I just received a letter from my Paris friends. Paul hopes to be rejected at the exhibition. The painters of his acquaintance are preparing an ovation in his honor.[4] In turn, Valabrègue wrote to Marion to tell him the Salon jury's deliberations: *On seeing my portrait, a philistine on the jury blurted out that it was painted not only with a knife but with a pistol as well. Daubigny said a few words in defense of my portrait, saying he preferred pictures brimming over with daring to the nullities that appear at every Salon, but he hadn't succeed in convincing anyone.*[5] Marion followed up with another message to Morstatt about the Salon rejections, which he interpreted as victories. Having himself never tendered a canvas to the Salon, Marion was like a fly perched on the oxen's horn, pretending that he, too, was out plowing in the field:

> *The whole realist school has been rejected: Cézanne, Guillemet, and the others. But actually we have triumphed: this mass refusal, this vast exile, is in itself a victory. All we have to do now is to stage an exhibition of our own and put up a deadly competition against those bleary-eyed idiots. We are in a period of conflict: youth against old age, the present against the past, that black pirate. Speaking of posterity, well, we are posterity. It is said that posterity judges. We trust in that future. Our adversaries can, at best, trust in their own death. We are confident. All we want is to produce.*[6]

Marion's narrow-focused, incognizant vision of art in Paris, which prompted his sentence *The whole realist school has been rejected*, hadn't allowed him to see that

Cézanne. Letter to the superintendent of the Salon, Count de Nieuwerke, April 19, 1866, demanding another Salon des Refusés. Nieuwerke's comments appear at the upper left of page one.

the jury had accepted Courbet, Monet, Degas, Morisot, Sisley, and a host of other realists whose names don't appear in art history books. Manet had submitted mild pictures, *Le Fifre* and *L'Acteur Tragique*, perhaps playing it safe after being so thoroughly abused in 1865 over *Olympia*. He was rejected anyway. So apprehensive was Renoir over impending rejection that he waited outside the Palais de l'Industrie for the jury to depart. On recognizing two of the jurists (Corot and Daubigny) coming out the door, too timid to identify himself, he asked about the fate of a friend of his named Renoir, He was told: *We are very disappointed on your friend's account. We did everything we could, we asked for that work to be considered ten times over, but there were six of us in favor and the others opposed. Tell your friend not to be discouraged. There are great qualities in his picture. He should make a petition and request an exhibition of the refusés.*[7]

Renoir was just one among many artists hanging around the exhibition hall, anxious to know the fate of their entries. Jacques-Emile Blanche tells of jury meetings dragging on for weeks, the jury members seen passing under close escort from one gallery to the other, of hundreds of artists pestering clerks for any word that might relieve their agony—rejection no more painful than prolonged trepidation.

Avant-garde art usually emerges during times of great social change, when society is more porous, especially alert to the present and highly energetic. At such times, acceptances and positive criticism are of little use to deviating artists. Positive words on the part of a critic are most often limited to expressions of the critic's personal feelings about the work. Well meant explications of the art under review are invariably reductive and more often than not, misleading. Negative criticism, on the other hand, typically represents a broad coverage of public reaction and response. It formalizes what bothers a large number of the public who are unable to articulate their distress (which is why demagogues can be so quickly successful). The negative critic is usually of the same mind as the general public—catering to public sentiment, generalizing, formalizing, and giving negativity a format.

Rejection gave Cézanne the opportunity to protest in Zola-like style. He remonstrated in a letter to the superintendent. Receiving no reply, he followed up with an angry second letter:

To Mr. de Nieuwerkerke
Superintendant of Fine Arts
Paris, 19 April 1866

Sir,

Recently I had the honor to write to you about two pictures of mine that the jury has just rejected. As you have not responded, I feel I must stand firm about the motives that led me to appeal to you. You have certainly received my letter, so there is no need for me to repeat

the arguments I thought necessary to make. I am content just to say once again that I can-
not accept the judgment of those I have not authorized to evaluate me.

Therefore, I am writing to insist that you respond to my petition. I wish to appeal to
the public, not to a jury, and to be exhibited at any cost. This wish seems to me not at all
unreasonable. If you were to question all the other artists who find themselves in my posi-
tion, they would reply that they too disavow the jury and want to participate in one way or
another in an exhibition that is open to all serious artists.

Therefore, let the Salon des Refusés be re-established. Even if I were the only one in
it, I would still want the public to know that I no more desire to be mixed up with those
gentlemen of the jury than they want to be mixed up with me.

I trust, Sir, you will not continue to be silent. Every well-meant letter deserves a reply.
Sincerely yours,
Paul Cézanne

Cézanne's appeal to have the public, rather than a jury, judge his work was to
remind the superintendent of a phrase in Napoléon III's proclamation, published
back in April 1863 when the Salon des Refusés was held by royal command (*His
Majesty, wishing to allow the public to judge...*). Nieuwerkerke read Cézanne's letter and
wrote in its margin: *What he asks is impossible; it has been recognized how unsuitable the
exhibition of the rejected was to the dignity of art. It will not be re-established.*

Zola may have helped Cézanne compose his letter. But by this time, Cézanne
was capable of handling his own campaign, having become as opportunistic as
his feisty friend. He, too, had a predator's nose for weak quarry. He'd perceived
that the Salon was becoming vulnerable, having made one reform gesture after
another without gratifying any faction of the grumbling mass. The government
was listening to artists' protests; dissident artists were no longer hollering in the
dark with no chance of someone switching on a light. And, as newspaper editors
had come to realize, infamous artists and spurious rejections were more attractive
to readers' taste than dreary painters and bloodless acceptances. Condemnatory
art criticism was marketable space in day-to-day journalism alongside nefarious
crimes, social infamies, and political chicaneries. Zola's most blatant assaults on
reader-sucking authors so delighted *L'Événement's* subscriber-hungry editor that
on occasion a Zola *causerie* would be printed on the front page.

As the Salon days approached, Zola talked Villemessant into assigning him
as the paper's art critic. Given the go-ahead, Zola set to work. Just a few days after
Cézanne's protest letter, the first of Zola's seven critical articles in *L'Événement*
appeared. On the 27th and 30th of April 1866, Zola attacked the twenty-four
Salon jury members by name, ridiculing them for incompetence. As had Cézanne
in his letter to the superintendent, he challenged their mental capacity to judge.
Considering that he was but twenty-six years old and had never before written art
criticism, he displayed egregious insolence in that first critique rushed into print

a few days before the exhibition opened. His final review came on the 20th of May, after an outrage from readers over his ferocity caused Villemessant to break up his quills.

Sitting on the jury that year were a dozen of the most celebrated painters of the nineteenth century on whom Zola beat on recklessly: *Before I pass judgment on the artists who were admitted to the exhibit, it seems only appropriate that I should first pass judgment on the judges.* In announcing this assault, he wrote:

> *I have a violent suit to bring against the jury. No doubt I will annoy many people, as I am resolved to speak monstrous and terrible truths. But I will experience much inner satisfaction in getting off my chest a heavy weight of accumulated rage. The Salon today is not the work of artists but of a jury...a mass of mediocrity...two thousand pictures and yet not even ten real men represented...the jury only hacks away at art and presents the crowd with an exhibition that's a mutilated corpse...[8] The Salon is not a whole and complete expression of French art in the year of grace, 1866...rather it's a ragoût prepared and fricasseed by twenty-eight cooks.[9]*

A week later, on May 4th, Zola interpreted the «artistic moment» as the art of the moment, the *maintenant*. This was not a new idea. Baudelaire and others had already put it into currency.[10] This «art of the now» was based on nature rather than fancy. It demanded a true representation of the artist's tempérament. Art was never to look back, only forward, at each moment the now renewed. Manet was the perfect artist to illustrate this point. In his essay, *M. Manet*, published three days later, Zola defended this arch-refusé in the oratorical style of Cicero beating down Catiline and the conspirators:

> *I will make myself as clear as possible about Manet. I do not want any misunderstanding between the public and myself. I do not admit, and will never admit, that a jury has the right to prohibit the public from seeing the work of one of the most potent individuals of our time.*
>
> *It appears that I am the first to praise Manet without reservation, if only because I have no interest whatsoever in boudoir paintings, those colorful but empty pictures, those miserable canvases on which I see nothing that's alive. As I have stated before, I am interested only in artistic temperament.*
>
> *Those jurists, artists themselves, are Manet's colleagues who should be able to understand this entire matter, but they do not dare take a stand. Some, and I am speaking of the fools among them, laugh without looking, and gloat over Manet's canvases. Others talk about his lack of talent, willful brutality and systematic violence. In short, they let the public laugh at their jokes without thought of saying: «Don't laugh so loud if you don't want to be taken one day for imbeciles. There is nothing funny about this art. There is only a sincere artist following his own bent who passionately seeks the truth.»*
>
> *A Salon is only an account of the artistic moment. As juries change, must the art of the moment change? Is it not ridiculous, utterly absurd, to accept Manet's art one year and reject it the next?[11]*

Manet's colleagues, to whom Zola craftily refers, were the jury members, three-fourths of them elected by artists who'd won medals in previous years, as had been the rule since 1861. The 1866 jury included such preeminent painters as Charles Gleyre, Léon Gérôme; the fashionable Alexandre Cabanel and the sweet Ernest Meissonier; Baudry (the favorite at the 1863 Salon), Corot, Daubigny; and the fading romantics, Isabey and Fleury. Of these, Gleyre was off-and-on sympathetic to the proto-impressionist naturalists, Monet, Bazille, and Renoir, who had studied in his studio. Meissonier, the painter Cézanne most admired when he first came to Paris, was now Manet's *bête noire* and one of the most hated by Zola, who called him the god of the bourgeoisie. Concluding his series of boiling critiques, Zola called for a new Salon des Refusés: *I beg all my colleagues to join with me, as I would like to amplify my voice to the level of supreme power and force the opening of those exhibition rooms where the public would judge the judges along with the condemned.*

Èdouard Manet, *The Fifer.* Salon of 1966. Paris, Musée d'Orsay.

When castigating the jury, or anyone who didn't agree with him, Zola never lacked for words. But he didn't have much to say with regard to painting. He lacked studio jargon and technical terms. His interest was in the artist as a personality, a character, like those he would create for his novels. He was less a critic of art than of the circumstances in which artists were embedded. Of Manet's *Le Fifre*, the most he could say was: *Against a luminous gray background stands the young musician, in uniform, full face, with red breeches and a garrison cap.* His interpretation of Manet's *Olympia* in 1865 had been no more astute. Having weak insight into artistic form, to rebuff hostile reactions over Manet's content, he glossed over it, allowing for the subject matter only as a pretext for painting.

As if speaking to Manet, Zola wrote in his review: *For you, a picture is nothing*

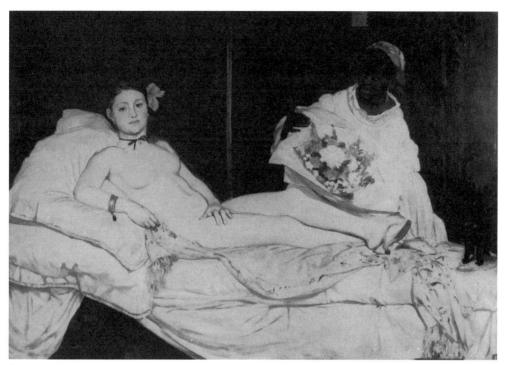

Édouard Manet. *Olympia.* 1863. Paris, Musée d'Orsay. Photo: Musées Nationaux.

more than an opportunity for analysis. You wanted a nude, and you took Olympia, the first to come along. You wanted bright, luminous passages, and the bouquet served your purpose. You wanted black patches, so you added a black woman and a black cat. His words reduced Manet's artistic process to an operation, a nearsightedness that was enough to raise the wrath of those who understood art as excellent renditions of significant themes.[12] Zola wanted to see in Manet's art only a translation of reality by an individual rather than a school.[13] What eluded him was the problem of how to project any imagery of the now into a future, for if the picture's imagery were fixed in time, as time moved on the imagery would stay transfixed and then be in the past, like a footprint or yesterday's news. By abandoning the density of metaphor and allegory that transcends the moment—which Manet had not yet done, but Zola thought he had—one is left with an artifact frozen in a moment of time, which is, of course, the fate of real people and events.

Behind Zola's views on art were the ideas of Eugène Sue, Sainte-Beuve, Flaubert, and Baudelaire, among others. That the realist novel seemed to have abandoned both morality and form disturbed Sainte-Beuve, who could not entirely separate content from form, or content from style or the art of writing. By contrast, in defense of the novel as art, Baudelaire held that the true beauty was not to be found in life but in the way artists looked at life. The nature of beauty should be the true artist's concern, not the beauty of nature; therefore, any subject matter is appropriate for art or literature; social morality need not be the artist's concern.[14] To maintain distance between art and subject matter, one cannot allow the subject matter, itself, to be art. If it were art, then ugly subject matter would generate ugly art.

In academic art, the subject matter and its portrayal were congruous: the beauty of art and the beauty of the subject one and the same quality—beauty is art, so art generates beauty.

Bertall (Charles-Albert d'Arnoux). Caricature of Manet's *Olympia*. Published in *Le Journal amusant*, May 27, 1865. Typical of many cartoons that helped establish Manet's public notoriety The commentary reads: «This picture by Manet is the bouquet of the exhibition. The great colorist has chosen the moment when the lady is about to take a bath, which she certainly seems to need.» Dirtiness, associated with blackness, was connected then as today with dirty minds and dirty sex.

Art theory must dominate art's subject matter, just as the art of medicine and its theories must dominate pathologies. If any moralistic objection is to be leveled at the realist novel, then, as Flaubert said, it should be leveled at the way life itself is, not at the writer as a person. Yet, in *Le Moniteur* on May 4th, 1857, Sainte-Beuve said of *Madame Bovary*: *It is first of all a book, composed, meditated, one in which nothing is left to chance and in which the author does exactly what he wants to do.*[15]

Zola's tactics were to beat down opposition with ridicule, while not fully realizing that the avant-garde needed opposition. Without resistance there could not be an avant-garde. Nor did he understand that the public is not a coherent entity—a mass, even a mob, but always and also a mix of individuals providing the same continuity to social life that nature provides to natural life. The commingling that forms «the public» alters over time in response to changes in prevailing social conditions while remaining *le fond*, or background, for every transitory event. Like Nature, the Public is immortal and as natural a background to life as nature itself. An appeal to public taste is like fishing with universal bait.

Identifying «the public» had been a perennial problem for performers of every feather. Most any academician a century later could have expressed Charles Coypel's 1747 lament about the Salon crowd:

Myself, I maintain that in the Salon the public changes twenty times a day. What the public admires at 10 o'clock in the morning is publicly condemned at noon. Yes, I tell you. This place can offer twenty publics of different tone and character in a single day: a simple public at certain times, a prejudiced public, a flighty public, an envious public, a public slavish to fashion. I can assure you that a final count would lead to infinity.[16]

Zola was not satisfied with the academic word «art,» which suggested some absolute, ideal art that had existed throughout the ages (as uniform beauty), insensitive to individual temperaments. The word conjured up absolute ideals outside the nature of man and beyond nature. In his 1866 Salon critique, Zola reduced art to what artists create according to their own eyes and temperament.[17] This bias aligned him with Baudelaire, who proclaimed that art was not to be found in life but in the way each artist looked at life. Neither Baudelaire nor Zola understood that individuality is also alienation, which explains in part why artists of a feather tend to cluster around some common denominator or powerful style, such as Delacroix, Courbet or Manet's. Intolerant of this propensity for artists to group, Zola would avow in *Mon Salon* that he was not for any school but for the truth of humanity that excludes cliques as it does systems.

Not happy with the word «realist» either, Zola proclaimed that in both art and nature these nonsensical common ideals simply do not exist.[18]

What I expect from the artist is not to give me tender visions or appalling nightmares, but to give himself, body and soul, and to declare himself boldly as a powerful and individual mind, of an honest and strong nature who can grasp life in his hands and set it before us just as he sees it. A work of art is never anything more than a combination of the totality of a man, as the variable element, and of life as the unchanging element. Yet the word «realist» means nothing to me. I proclaim that reality is subordinate to temperament. When one paints the truth, I applaud. But when one paints what is alive and individual I applaud much louder.[19]

Zola's manifesto calls to mind Delacroix's statement that, for an artist, everything is a worthy subject because the subject is the artist, his impressions and emotions when confronting nature. Thus there cannot be absolute standards for objective realism or universal beauty.[20] This was, of course, only an aspect of Delacroix's theory of art, and such ideas were in the air, not needing assignment to an originary cause or continuity by linkage from Delacroix to Baudelaire to Manet. It was as if the Revolution, then a half-century in the past, was still reverberating in all aspects of democratic life.

Over the next few years, Cézanne and Zola would build their mature work on the blemishes of the right-minded art and literature of their time—coarseness, vulgarity, lack of finish—and for that matter, on the social faults of their own personalities—excessiveness, childishness, bravado, obscenity, disdain for propriety—which were more useful when exploited than corrected. Both would sustain this posture with less thought toward a goal for their revolt than for the thrill of revolting, a trademark for those who refuse to grow up and integrate with a mature society. Courbet and Manet had shown them the method, but in the mid-1860s, neither Zola nor Cézanne had reasoned out the rational motives underpinning the mischief of their masters.

Cézanne will take up Zola's manifesto in his own way. He, too, will remain a negativist, like a cat that fights best when on its back. Rejection will be his badge of honor, proof of his individuality, his unique temperament. If only to win by intentionally losing, rather than be defeated trying to win, he would carry on his battle by offering paintings to the Salon jury that were certain to be ceremoniously rejected, perhaps half-consciously knowing that without rejection, the audacious temperament that kept him aloft would deflate.

He may have gained a bit of confidence this year, having been given a chance to visit Manet's studio. Armand Guillaumin, his friend from the Suisse, had taken it upon himself to promote Cézanne to Manet and had shown Manet a few of Cézanne still lifes that he'd painted in Guillaumin's studio. Manet was kind enough to say they were powerfully handled, which led to the invitation for Cézanne to visit him. Cézanne did visit him in April 1866, which gave him a chance to see Manet's pictures that the Salon jury had just rejected.[21] Zola would not meet Manet until the following month.

27

A mong the assorted trash of negative commentaries on Manet's *Olympia* in the Salon of 1865 were a few reviews by noteworthy critics published in substantial newspapers. The most cutting was Jules Claretie's in the high society journal *L'Artiste*: *What is this odalisque with a yellow belly? This vile model picked up I don't know where?*[1] In the influential *La Presse*, Paul de Saint-Victor also came down hard: *As at the morgue, the crowd jostles in front of this gamy Olympia.*[2] The most literate review was by Théophile Gautier in *Le Moniteur universel*, who had attacked Manet's *Déjeuner sur l'herbe* two years before:

> *Olympia can be understood from no point of view whatsoever, even if you take it for what it is, a puny model stretched out on a sheet. The color of the flesh is dirty, the modeling non-existent, the shadows are indicated by large smears of black paint. What's to be said for the negress, who brings a bunch of flowers wrapped in some sort of paper, or for the black cat that leaves its dirty paw prints on the bed? We would forgive the ugliness were it truthful and carefully studied. The least beautiful of woman has at least bones, muscles, skin, heightened by some effect of color. Here there is nothing, I am sorry to say, but the desire to attract attention at any price.*[3]

Negativity was making Manet's name more recognizable than names of the venerable masters who had dominated the Salon for years. While only a few newspaper readers would bother to read serious criticism, everyone would take to the pelting of the likes of Manet—and soon of Cézanne. The most elegant words of a supporting critic, praising an Ingres, Baudry, or Cabanel, could not compete in reader's eyes with reviews written as caricatures or burlesques. The most delightful burlesque on the proceeding of a Salon jury had appeared on June 15th, 1864. The popular playwright and critic, Louis Leroy, published a satire in the buffoontype daily, *Le Charivari* (a prototype of *Punch*).[4] This popular magazine (its name derived from the verb *chavirer*, meaning something like «to upset the apple cart») was devoted to shocking the public into bewilderment. Leroy despised Manet. His response to Manet's *Olympia* was short and acidic: *If I ever write a single line in praise of Olympia, I authorize you to exhibit me with that piece of writing tied around my neck.*[5]

Perhaps incited a bit by Manet's excessive presence on the 1864 Salon walls, enhanced by Degas' *Portrait of Manet* and Fantin-Latour's *Homage to Delacroix* in which Manet appears, Leroy's elbow poking was directed at Manet's canvas, *The Episode in a Bullfight*, a picture that Manet later destroyed.[6] In a skit written by Leroy, coming upon this picture, the Salon spectators found themselves confronted by a ridiculously small bull, so small and disproportionate, so out of perspective in its failed foreshortening, that it brought to Manet a great deal of waggish attention.

Leroy's skit opens with the young artist (Manet), hoisted on a warriors' shield carried by Messrs. Baudelaire et als. The cortège comes to a halt in front of the jury. Then:

The Jury President: That conquering hero pose is despicable. Get him down from there!

Baudelaire (gnashing his teeth): If we could have found a bronze chariot in the square, we would have hired it to bring to you in proper fashion the one and only true painter of our time. Hooray!

The President: Baudelaire, shut up! It's not your place to speak.

Baudelaire (giving full reign to his emotions): Onh!... ffowt!... rhooh!... fowt!... fowt! [French dog language not translated].

The President: This poet of the *Fleurs du mal* is frightfully cacophonous!

Manet (calm and somewhat disdainful): I would appreciate knowing what my prize consists of.

The President: Then keep that idiot quiet. He is disturbing me with his rude interruptions, borrowed no doubt from the language of jungle beasts (the *et als* calm down the author of the *Fleurs du mal*. A moment of silence follows).

The President: Ah, Yes. We were about to talk about your prize, weren't we?

Baudelaire (escaping from his keepers): Rrauwft!... fowt, fowt!

The President: Must I say it again Baudelaire, shut up! You are not privileged to be so obstreperous here.

Manet: Your Excellency, I am still waiting.

The President: Yes. Now where was I. Ah yes, the Butcher's Union. Now, understandably appalled that you know so little about depicting a horned animal, the Butcher's Union has unanimously decided to reserve a special box seat for you in every slaughterhouse in the city of Paris. The Union hopes by this helpful gesture that in time you will be able to paint a bull with the size and thickness that nature so generously gave this animal—a size which you simply cannot continue to ignore without trampling on the sacred and inalienable rights of the defense, at whose service Justice, Truth, and The Right have put themselves.

Baudelaire (trying to behave like a human being): This prize that you are about to award to this one and only illustrious artist stinks of foul criticism coming from the Awards Committee. And no matter how enfeebled the committee members may be, how corrupt, swinish, and idiotic they appear, I must admit to not expecting from them such a disgustingly filthy decision. So be proud, gentlemen of the Committee. You have just gained an evolutionary advantage over mollusks and other spineless zoophytes. Thank you very much, you stinking beasts.

The President: With resounding joy let the secretary be quick to record that the illustrious poet of the *Fleurs du mal* has protested with tact, impeccable taste, and consummate decorum, that his words cannot be given too much praise. How true it is that a voice so elegant as his could not possibly rest unrefined in the embryonic condition of moral politeness. Gentlemen, this meeting is adjourned.[7]

When met head on by Manet's *Olympia*, rather than face reality when anticipating fantasy, befuddled men on pussy patrol through the galleries of alluring nakedness repressed their surge of lust by ridiculing her, just as in adolescence they'd resorted to giddy-headed silliness when the reality of lust confronted them, when called upon to measure up to their fantasies. Olympia not only appropriated their responses, but their gallery space as well: not wearing a veil of fantasy, she confronted the viewer across a real space between them. Although the maid in the painting directs her attention to Olympia, Olympia relates not to her but directly to the viewer. So the action and tension is not within the picture's frame but projected outward. Zola's reaction to the layers of criticism, elicited by failed expectancies, that were heaped on the picture was not to defend it, for he was ill-equipped to do that. Instead, he took the opportunity to poke fun at those who were outraged by diagnosing the entire body of ridicule with a well-chosen scrap of sarcasm: *She who has the serious fault of closely resembling young ladies of your acquaintance. If only Manet had borrowed Cabanel's powder puff and powdered Olympia's face and hands a bit, the young lady would have been presentable.*[8] Zola meant, of course, that men who are captivated by prostitutes, who fancy them and are prone to visit them, are unable to confront their own weakness for them in public.

The following year, when Manet's nonprovocative Salon entries—Le Fifre and L'Artiste—were rejected, Zola published another article featuring Manet in which he sustained his defense of *Olympia*. On May 7th, 1866, in *L'Événement*, he frosted his acrimony with contemptible insults: Do you know what effect Manet's canvases produce at the Salon?

> *Quite simply they burst open the wall. All around them stretch the sweets of the fashionable artistic confectioners: sugar-candy trees and pastry houses, gingerbread gentlemen and ladies made of vanilla cream. The candy shop becomes pinker and sweeter, and Manet's living canvases take on bitterness in the midst of this river of milk. Also, one must see the faces of the grown-up children passing through the gallery. For two cents you will not make them swallow true flesh with the reality of life, but they will stuff themselves like starving people with all the sickening sweetness that is served them.*[9]

In the same review, Zola aligned himself, not just ideologically but bodily, with Manet, as he had been joined previously to Cézanne. Zola was now positioned to champion an artist in heroic struggle against the crowd. He proclaims that triumph will come, that all victims of his vengeance will acknowledge the abused hero:

> *I have tried to grant Manet the position that belongs to him, as one of the first. You will perhaps laugh at the panegyrist as you laughed at the painter. But some day we both will be avenged. There is an eternal truth sustaining me in my criticism: that temperaments alone will live and dominate the ages. It is impossible—impossible, do you understand?— that Manet will not have his day of triumph, and that he will not crush all those timid mediocrities which surround his paintings in the gallery.*

Manet responded on the very day the review appeared, sending a note addressed to Zola at the paper, for only after Zola's review did they meet: *I don't know where to find you to shake your hand and tell you how happy I am to be defended by such a talented man. What a beautiful article! Thank you a thousand times over. The article before last (on the artistic moment) was most remarkable and had a great effect.*

If not genuine, Zola's identification with Manet was at least a positive act of opportunism. His saying, *Some day we both will be avenged,* granted him equal status of victim and potential martyr. As a tabloid journalist, he was required to attract readers to his column, which meant remarking on miseries, sufferings, hates, disasters, atrocities, murders, scandals—anything that would excite readers and motivate them to buy the newspaper. As fitted for this calling as a hangman's noose to a neck, passionate Zola could write art criticism only in opposition to what was oppressive, only when finding some official power in the act of persecuting an individual. On May 20th, 1866, he wrote one of his most defiant, if not his most pontifical and arrogant statements: *I have defended Manet as throughout my entire life I have defended any original and honestly different individual who may be irresponsibly attacked. I will always be on the side of the underdog.* To drive his point into every reader's brain, on May 27th, he published in *Le Figaro* a sort of manifesto. It was a preface to *Mes Haines,* a collection of articles he had published in *Le Salut public de Lyon* over 1865 plus one essay from *La Revue contemporaine* and two pieces not previously published. *Mes Haines* appeaed in bookstores on June 23rd, 1866.

> *Hatred* [said Zola in the preface] *is sacred. It is not enough to speak well of those one admires; one must speak ill of those one hates. Hate is the indignation of strong and powerful hearts, and the militant scorn of those who are angered by stupidity and mediocrity. To hate is to love. Hate is to express one's own warm and generous soul, to live fully while scorning shameful and unpleasant things.*
>
> *Hatred alleviates, hatred brings about justice; hatred makes greatness. I feel younger and more courageous after each of my revolts against the platitudes of our age. I have made hatred and pride my two keepers. I am glad to isolate myself within them, and in my isolation hate whatever wounds the just and the true. If there is one thing I hold dear today, it is that I am alone and that I hate.*

Zola's hates are accounted for one by one: those who deny the present, those who are stagnated, those who are bound to dogma and follow it blindly, those who are pernicious scoffers, young people who sneer, and those who cry out that art and literature are dying. For all those basking in the light of art as truth and beauty, solace, comfort, aesthetic pleasure, Zola's words must have gathered over their heads like a black cloud spelling art's doom. His denunciations appeared as a rejection of the great traditions:

> *There are no more great masters, no more schools of art. We are in a state of anarchy. Each of us is a rebel who thinks for himself, who creates and fights for himself. I scarcely think about beauty and perfection. I laugh at the great centuries. I worry only about life, its struggles and passions. I am at ease with the present generation. We are on the threshold of a century of science and reality, and yet we are tottering like drunkards before the great struggle that lies ahead of us. We are working, preparing the way to the future. We are about to carry out the necessary demolition. Tomorrow the edifice will be rebuilt.*[10]

> *Genius consists in conveying this object or person in a new, more real sense. For me, it is not the tree, the countenance, the scene that touches me. It is the man I find in the work, the powerful individual who knows how to create, alongside God's world, a personal world which my eyes will not be able to forget, which my eyes will recognize everywhere.*[11]

In his 1867 essay on Manet, Zola proclaimed that it is no longer an issue of a search for absolute beauty. *What this artist paints is neither historical nor spiritual, and for him composition does not exist. The task he imposed on himself is not to represent this thought or that historical event. For this reason, one should not judge him as a moralist or literary man but solely as a painter...He has never been so stupid as to put ideas into his painting.*[12] Going even further, in *Mes Haines,* Zola defined the modern aesthetic as a radical subjectivism—no more literary dogma, each work to be viewed as independent and judged on its own merits. Artistic activity must not be governed by pre-existing rules, or measured by transcendental criteria. Art produces its own rules, and supplies the measure of its appreciation.[13]

The acerbic articles Zola contributed to *L'Événement* resulted in a rash of protests and subscription cancellations. He'd done more than raise the sort of journalistic ruckus that draws the public to read, even what they find repulsive. In many reader's minds, he'd gone haywire, completely mad. One protester implored the editor to raise the standard of art criticism by entrusting it to someone whose daily habits would include washing his hands. Another, adding Manet to his protestation, wrote:

> *Your critic is exasperating—no theories, no aesthetic knowledge, no reasoned thoughts about art, just enthusiasm and insults. He politely calls all those who laugh at Manet's paintings idiots. But why is Manet not satisfied with just being mediocre? Why is he also vulgar and grotesque? Why do his dirty figures seem to have emerged from a sack of coal? For mercy's sake, spare your readers further mental torture, or cancellations of subscriptions will soon follow.*

Publisher Villemessant finally had to heed warnings battering him from all sides. He ordered Zola to back off, to wind down his column with just two or three more reviews. Perhaps he thought that, by allowing more episodes as a sort of disengagement notice, Zola might make an effort to redeem himself by saying something that would pacify his readers. But without flinching Zola acted not as a retreating hooligan with a bent nose but as an insolent child throwing everything in his playpen at those he hated. Continuing his coverage of the Salon of 1866— saying what he looks for above all in a painting is a man, not a picture—he calls attention to Monet, whose Salon entry *Camille: Woman in a Green Dress* had met with favorable reviews: *Ah yes! Now there's a man with tempérament, a real man amidst the crowd of eunuchs!*[14] He came down rather hard on Courbet, Millet, and Rousseau for having lost their vigor, saying that the success they still enjoyed was because the admiration of the crowd is in indirect ratio to genius—the more admired and understood one is, the more banal one's works.[15]

What may have upset Zola about Courbet was that his paintings were selling. If Courbet was becoming accepted, the platform under Zola's podium might crumble. Courbet was sending to the Salon only pictures that would attract sales. In a letter to his parents of April 1866, Frédéric Bazille wrote:

> *I saw Courbet yesterday. He is swimming in gold. This is what fashion can do! Over his entire life he has not sold more than 40,000 francs worth of paintings. It's true that this year he is showing some beautiful works; yet they are certainly not up to his Bathers or his Demoiselles de la Seine. The public, however, has made up its mind to grant him success. Since the opening of the Salon, he has sold more than 150,000 francs worth. His drawers are bulging with bank notes; he doesn't know what to do with them. All the collectors besiege him, rummaging through dust-covered old stuff and frantically competing to buy.*[16]

Perhaps wanting to end on a positive note, in his final Salon review Zola granted his parting words to Pissarro. As if speaking to him directly, Zola says:

> *Thank you, Sir. Your winter landscape refreshed me for a good half hour during my trip through the great Salon desert. You should realize that you would please no one, your picture will be found too bare, too black. Then why in the devil do you have such arrogant clumsiness to paint so solidly, to study nature so frankly? Yours is an austere and serious sort of painting, with an extreme concern for truth and accuracy, a rugged and strong will. You are a blunderer, sir. You are an artist whom I like.*[17]

28

*Cézanne and Zola
at summer camp*

Canned by *L'Événement*, again out of a job, Zola assembled the seven Salon reviews that appeared in that newspaper and in May had them issued as a booklet titled *Mon Salon*, for which he wrote the foreword, «To My Friend Cézanne,» that appears among the front matter of this book. Zola was feeling insecure, again in need of Cézanne the Protector, as he'd been over his first two years in Paris when desperate to have Cézanne join him. But now Cézanne could be of no help. Zola had visited a plague on journalism, sickening the tastes and sensibilities of its majority readership, while Cézanne had plagued the Salon to the extent that just the threat of his submitting a picture would automatically shut the door in his face. One defending the other would hereafter be like two despicable sinners trying to stuff each other into Heaven.

Numa Coste would be encouraging. On June 11th, 1866, after a few months of combat training in modern warfare—no more classical one-on-one, hand-to-hand, but modern warfare as one against the masses, like Zola against the public—Coste wrote to Zola: *Now that you've drawn your weapon, you mustn't hold back but step forward boldly to meet the mass of imbeciles you are up against. The great number of them allows you not to aim at anyone in particular. Just aim at the mob and each shot will hit a target.* But, like others who could neither win nor lose in this battle, and meaning well, Coste was no more a worthy judge of Zola's writings than of Cézanne's paintings, which at the time, if not good were at least sincere.

Cézanne—not licking wounds but gathering energy for his next assault—spent much of the 1866 summer in Bennecourt, a small, rather picturesque village on the Seine near Nantes where a number of artists painted, including, from time to time, Daubigny and Corot. Guillemet probably suggested this site, as he was a friend of Courbet and Pissarro's, who also painted in the countryside.[1] While summertime artist colonies had become increasingly popular, this was Cézanne's first experience living and working within a colony-type environment. Guillemet, Chaillon, and Valabrègue were with him a good part of the time from May to September, either rooming at an inn or with local families who welcomed a bit of income from putting up artists while tolerating their capers. On occasion,

Zola visited the group. His letters and recollections render an animated picture of what transpired there. He summarized this reverie at Bennecourt in an early short story, *La Rivière* (The River).

> *In the evening, after supper, the whole company stretches out on two bundles of straw that generous Mother Gigoux has spread out on the ground in the courtyard of the inn. To the disgust of the peasants, who find it impossible to get to sleep, wild theoretical discussions are held well up to midnight. People smoke their pipes and look at the moon. On the slightest difference of opinion, they call each other idiots and cretins; the famous celebrities of the moment are run down; everybody becomes intoxicated by the hope of soon upsetting everything that exists in order to produce a new art, whose prophets they expect to be. These young people on their bundles of straw, in the stillness of the night, are conquering the world.[2]*

In this text, Zola is recapitulating his youth in Aix when summer evenings were spent with Cézanne and Baille in the countryside, conversing, dreaming, calling their fellow students at the Bourbon idiots and cretins. Of the same mind-set, Cézanne and his friends spent much of the time at Bennecourt out on the water, rowing from island to island, sketching and fishing. On the 30th of June, Cézanne wrote to Zola in Paris, *I have done little work, the fête at Gloton* [a nearby village] *was last Sunday the 24th, and brothers-in-law of the patron* [probably père Rouvel, then seventy years old, whose portrait Cézanne painted while there] *came to visit, a whole heap of idiots. Tuesday and last night I went fishing with Delphin* [a local boy]. *In the pools, I caught more than twenty at least in a single hole. I took six, one after the other, and once I got three at one go, one in the right and two in the left. They were rather beautiful. It's easier, all this fishing, but it doesn't lead anywhere.*

On June 14th, Zola wrote from Paris to Numa Coste at his military post. The letter is informative about the group's recovery from the Salon fiasco: Cézanne rejected, Zola fired from *L'Événement*:

> *I have but ten minutes to respond to your letter. I'm off to the country where I will find Paul. Baille is going with me. We will stay for a week far from Paris. Paul was rejected at the Salon, as were Solari and all the others you know. Now they are back to work, certain that they have ten years ahead of them before they are accepted.*
>
> *Valabrègue is here. He works—slowly. I think maturity is coming over him. I have great hopes for him. As for me, I quit the Hachette bookstore on the first of February* [actually, on January 31, he was let go] *and since then have been attached to L'Événement as a regular job: the book reviewer. Besides that I published a Salon that stirred up a big crisis* [a reference to his articles on Manet]. *Now I have combined my articles into a brochure* [Mon Salon], *and will send you a copy of it along with an exemplar of another work I also plan to publish* [which would have been *Mes Haines*].

Writing again to Coste, on the 26th of July, Zola gave an update of what he and the group were dreaming of, plotting to do, or not do, and just plain doing at their holiday encampment:

Your last letter arrived at my mother's while I was still in the country. But you were mistaken: you thought we were at Fontenay-aux-Roses. Some sixteen leagues from Paris is a country still unknown to Parisians where we established our little colony. The Seine traverses our desert. We live in rowboats. For our retreat we have some deserted islands, black with leafy shade. For three days I've been here at Bennecourt with Cézanne and Valabrègue. They will not return until the first of next month. This place, as I said, is a true colony. We dragged into it Baille and Chaillon, and in time will pull you in too.

Cézanne is working. He affirms himself more and more along an original track with his nature pushing him. I have great hopes for him. He has undertaken several works— large works, of four to five meters. He will go to Aix next, perhaps in August, perhaps at the end of September, and will pass two or more months there.

As for the «second,» Valabrègue has been here since March. He has lost much of his youth, and I no longer know how to take him. He has no need to hurry, and I applaud him for not wishing to publish his first work before age twenty-five at the earliest. He is observing and learning. He will leave for Aix in eight days and stay there for two months.

As for the «third,» there remains for me to speak of myself. I sent you my last two publications so you know what I've been up to since your departure. Besides that, since February 1st, I am no longer at Hachette's, éthe epoch when I was published in L'Événement. I worked on the journal la bibliographie, after a fashions. Add to that a weekly correspondence that I sent to the Salut public, that paid one hundred francs. Voilà revenue, and my ordinary occupations. Beyond that, I began a book of criticism, «L'Oeuvre d'art devant la critique» [not known as to what this was], *that I will publish, no doubt, come November. I also figure on putting two or three months into a novel for L'Événement* [This would be *Le Voeu d'une morte*, The Dead Woman's Wish, which will be published in part over 11 to 26 September 1866]. *You see, work is not lacking. Merci-Dieu!, laziness does not overcome me equally.*

I no longer live on the rue de l'École-de-Médecin. I am now with my mother on the rue de Vaugirard, on the Odéon side. We have a complete apartment: dining room, bedroom, salon, kitchen, guest room, terrace—a veritable palace. We will open wide the doors for you on your return.

In short, I am satisfied with the way things are going. But I'm impatient and would like to move ahead more quickly. You cannot believe how much one is subject to lassitude in this ungracious métier that I've undertaken. I have almost an article a day to write. It requires that I read, or at least peruse, the works of all the contemporary imbeciles. I have little time to work on my own books.

Alexandrine [Zola's mistress] *is getting fat but I am thinning down a bit. There remains only for me to wish for your return. The picture you gave me about life in military camp is not at all appealing.*

Coste had indeed given Zola a sordid picture of military camp life, not unlike the way boys write home from boarding school, their grievances amplified. His letter, dated July 20th, 1866, tells of not being able to live at camp without being somewhat of an animal, that he works only in order to keep himself from falling apart amidst layer upon layer of cretins, idiots, horses, and manure. *You are coming again to Paris,* Coste writes. *The sooner the better. I believe that trips to Paris are essential for one's intelligence to be able to function. Write to tell me of you arrival. We will talk of the future.*

The very large works contemplated by Cézanne and mentioned in Zola's letter may have come into Cézanne's mind after the 1866 Salon rejections. He was again at a crossroads, for he knew what it would take to successfully address the Salon requirements. Surely beneath his contempt for the Salon was a desire to be accepted. The rejected one-meter-high portrait of Valabrègue may have been the largest easel painting he had done to date. Perhaps the Herculean Pitot should now impress upon the jury an ability to perform enormous tasks, to execute huge paintings such as those with which such giants as Gericault, Delacroix, and Courbet had overwhelmed the jury in the past (Zola may have exaggerated the dimensions that Cézanne had in mind, though in a letter to Zola of October 19th, 1866, Cézanne does refer to a picture of one meter as small. But prior to the portrait of Valabrègue, no extant easel painting by him is any larger). No huge works were accomplished by Cézanne at Bennecourt. The only canvas that can be identified as painted while there is the 15 x 24-inch view of the village of Bonnières seen across water from the Ile la Lorionne, one of the river islands the painters rowed to for outings and motifs to paint, a canvas that Pissarro could as well have painted.

A second canvas, this one a portrait, has been assigned to Cézanne's stay at Bennecourt, but the evidence for his having painted a portrait like this one is much stronger than the evidence that the one we have is the one he painted.[3] On June 30th, 1866, Cézanne wrote from Bennecourt to Zola in Paris, *I've begun a portrait out-of-doors of old père Rouvel, which is not turning out too badly, but it still must be worked over, particularly the background and the clothes.* If the painting in question is, in fact, of père Rouvel, then Cézanne may have resolved the background problem simply by cutting down the canvas from its 40 x 52-inch dimension (larger than one meter—the dimensions that Cézanne gives in his letter to Zola, perhaps to impress upon him that he is now working in larger formats) to 20 x 19 inches.[4] Neither of these two small canvases can be linked to Cézanne's strategy to paint Salon-scale pictures of four to five meters, as mentioned in Zola's letter.

It would seem, however, that Cézanne had undertaken at least one huge painting. In the June 30th letter to Zola, he speaks of another picture that is also not going too badly. Neither landscape nor portrait, this painting would depict at least three large-scale figures, one of which he shows to Zola as a small sketch on

Cézanne. Le Père Rouvel (?), c. 1866.
Paris, Musée d'Orsay. Photo: Bulloz.

the letter. Of this sketch he says,

> *I am going to change all of the figures in my picture* [which Zola must have seen in progress]. *I have already given Delphin a different posture—like a* [horse][5]—*he is like that. I think it is better. I am also going to alter the other two. I have added a bit of still life to the side of the stool, a basket with a blue cloth and some green and black bottles. If I could work at it a little longer, it would go fairly quickly, but with scarcely two hours a day* [the typical two-hour midday break when his models, employees of the village smith, were available to him] *the paint dries too soon. This is all very annoying.*

Delphin, the model to whom Cézanne refers, was the son of the blacksmith, Calvaire-Levasseur, in whose house Zola rented lodging while in Bennecourt.[6] Delphin worked at his father's forge, so the setting for Cézanne's picture was perhaps the blacksmith's workshop with the characters depicted at work. The sketch shows Delphin stoking or adding coal to a fire. The still-life elements would have been the workmen's lunch basket and wine or cider bottles.[7]

No subject matter in this large-scale format occurs earlier among Cézanne's surviving pictures, and looking ahead, only one theme—again unrealized and known only from being mentioned in a letter—would suggest a recurrence of the

Cézanne. Sketch on a letter to Zola from Bennecourt, dated June 1866. The subject may be the fourteen-year-old son of the blacksmith, Calvaire-Levasseur, at whose house Zola rented lodging in 1866.

idea: a projected canvas depicting a group of his friends out-of-doors that is mentioned in an 1868 letter from Marion to Morstatt: *Cézanne is planning a picture in which, in the midst of a landscape, one of us will be speaking while the others listen.*[8] So it would appear that Cézanne's plan to paint huge canvases of figures interacting within a cohering theme came to naught. About this time (1865-66), Monet also had a thwarted dream of painting an enormous canvas for the Salon with several figures interacting in a landscape. *I think of nothing but my picture, Monet wrote in a letter to Bazille. And if I thought for a moment that I wouldn't bring it off, I believe I'd go mad.*[9] When finally accepting that completion was impossible, and having gone but half-mad, Monet cut off the salvageable parts, one of which, now hanging in the Louvre, measures 165 x 59 inches.

29

After leaving Bennecourt, Cézanne spent the late summer and autumn of
1866 at his family home in Aix. Unfettered by pecuniary needs, he painted several canvases: portraits of Valabrègue, his father, his uncle
Dominic, his sister Marie, himself, as well as a few landscapes and still lifes—how
many one cannot say, since only a few have survived. His inconstant and unstable subject matter often backslid to his adolescence when at his family home.
Such regressions happen when a mature child comes home for a visit: the context
of the parental home is the setting of his childhood, the props still in place, the
parents forever retaining their role as nurturers and advisors. Still, one must avoid
overgeneralizing Cézanne's relationship to his family from the few scanty remarks
he makes in letters. On one occasion in an October 23rd 1866 letter to Pissarro,
he writes: *Here I am with my family, la plus sale people in the world.*

Cézanne's use of the word *sale*, which translates as meaning most any negative from shitty to just soiled, has been misused by his biographers. Most likely he
was contracting *sale bourgeois*—a common expression used by those who do not
want to be identified with bourgeois values. Rather than assume that is truly what
he felt about his family, one should ask whether he felt the same way about them
the day before, or the day after. Rewald pounces on this opportunity in order to
say: *The obstacles that Cézanne's father had put in the way of his son's artistic career resulted
in such severe negatives towards his parents, and this explains the passage in the letter.*[1] But
saying that his family was *sale bourgeois* would have nothing specifically to do with
altercations over the choice of his career.

During these 1866 months in Aix, at the age of twenty-seven, Cézanne
painted a picture of his sister, Rose. He described the painting in a letter to Zola
of about October 19th: *I have just finished a little picture which is, I believe, the best thing
I've done to date. It represents my sister Rose reading to her doll.* The picture is lost, but in
Cézanne's letter he sketches it for Zola to see, and he writes: *This gives you some idea
of the morsel I am offering you! My sister Rose in the center, seated, holding a little book that
she is reading. Her doll is on a chair; she on an armchair. Background black, her head light,*

her headdress blue, blue pinafore, frock dark yellow, a bit of still-life to the left: a bowl and chil-dren's toys. Rose would have been fifteen or sixteen then, so it is not easily under-stood why she would still play mother to a doll and have toys scattered about the room. Even more puzzling is Cézanne telling Zola that he will send this pitifully naive picture to the Salon.[2]

In the same letter to Zola, Cézanne writes: *I am fairly bored. Work alone keeps me occupied. I am less despondent when someone is around. I see no one here but Valabrègue, Marion, and now Guillemet.* He pens a quick sketch in the letter describing the por-trait of his sister, and also a sketch of Marion and Valabrègue about to set out for a session of painting out of doors, about which he says: *You know that all pictures painted in the studio will never be as good as those done outside. The contrasts between figure and ground is astounding, and the landscape magnificent, when out of door scenes are repre-sented. I will have to make up my mind to do things only outdoors.*

Cézanne. Sketches on a letter to Zola, autumn 1866. Rose readng to her doll, and Marion and Valabrèque setting out to paint in the countryside.

It is unlikely, however, that Cézanne had progressed beyond sketching outdoors with the idea of using sketches to realize large pictures painted in the studio—a common practice for artists of all sorts since the eighteenth century and even more widespread in the nineteenth century when pigment was sold in tubes and easily car-ried in a rucksack, with brushes, small pre-stretched canvases, a collapseable easel and a folding stool. Aside from the problem of transporting large canvases, only a few hours of the day offer con-sistent light, so large pictures over which one would labor could not be painted outside the studio. Even when painting straight land-scapes, highlights and shadows change position as the sun moves across the sky; what is light green and highly detailed over one hour becomes dark green and dense over another, blues become blacks, whites become grays;

when a cloud passes over, everything changes. Moreover, unlike watercolor, oil paint takes hours to dry, so one must work before nature *a la prima* (at the first go, for over-painting results in muddy colors). Brushes stiff enough to spread viscous oil paint tend to drag up underlying pigment that is still wet, while a flexible palette knife smoothly layers one color over another. Art historians not experienced with oil painting tend to associate palette-knife painting with violence, as if the painter is attacking the canvas with a knife, whereas the typical use of the palette knife is gentle, like spreading soft butter.

Cézanne's letter to Zola continues:

I have already spoken to you about a picture that I want to attempt. It will represent Marion and Valabrègue setting out to look for a motif (a landscape motif, of course). *This sketch, done after nature, which Guillemet considers good, makes everything else fall apart and appear awful. I feel sure that paintings by old masters representing subjects out-of-doors were done only with chic, because none seem to have the true and original appearances provided by nature. Pére Gibert* [an affectionate name for the drawing teacher Joseph Gibert] *of the museum invited me to visit the Musée Bourguignon. I went there with Baille, Marion, and Valabrègue. I thought everything was bad.*

Remember me to Gabrielle [Alexandrine Meley, before choosing to use her alternate name], *also to Solari and Baille, who must be in Paris with his fraternity. I understand that the trials of the dispute with Villemessant are over. If you see Pissarro give him friendly greetings from me.*

But I repeat that I have a little attack of the blues, though for no reason. As you know, I don't know what it comes from. It comes back every evening when the sun sets, and now it is even raining. It makes me feel black. I think I will send you a sausage one of these days, but my mother must go and buy it, otherwise I will be cheated, and that would be very annoying [short-weighting by merchants in those days was rampant, hence the expression «thumb on the scale», so experienced housewives did the food shopping].

Just imagine, I hardly read any more.

I don't know whether you share my opinion—and that would not make me change mine—but I am beginning to see that art for art's sake is a mighty humbug. That is strictly between us.[3]

Sketch of my future picture out-of-doors. [Here Cézanne added to his letter the sketch of Marion and Valabrègue on their way to the motif].

P.S. For four days I have had this letter in my pocket and now feel the urge to send it to you. Good-bye, my dear.

In the letter to Pissarro of October 23rd, 1866, after commenting on his «disgustingly bourgeois» family, Cézanne brings his friend up to date, including a mention of an alternative Salon held in Marseilles:

I see Guillemet and his wife every day. They found good lodgings. Guillemet has not yet started on big pictures. As a prelude, he has begun some small paintings that are very good.

You are perfectly right to speak of gray, for gray alone reigns in nature, but it is terrifyingly hard to catch.

The country here is very beautiful, much individual character, and Guillemet did a study yesterday and today in gray weather, which was most beautiful. His studies seem to me much freer now than the ones he brought back to Paris last year. I am delighted with them. I will say no more except that he is going to start a big picture as soon as possible, the moment the weather improves. In the next letter we send will probably be some good news about it.

Cézanne was pushing himself to paint large canvases, to move beyond the sketch. He had had this desire on his mind since the summer at Bennecourt, and possibly before. The letter continues:

I just posted a letter to Zola.

I work a little all the time but here paints are scarce and very expensive—marasme, marasme! [stagnation, deep slump]. Let us hope; let us hope that we will sell. Then we will sacrifice a golden calf.

You don't plan to send anything to Marseilles?⁴ Well, neither will I! I do not want to submit again—all the more because I have no frames. And it causes me to spend money better devoted to buying paint. I say this for myself—damn the jury.

The sun will, I trust, still give us some fine days. I am very sorry that Oller, as Guillemet says, cannot come back to Paris. He must be very bored in Puerto Rico, and then too, with no colors within reach, it must be very difficult for him to paint. And so Oller told me it would be a good thing for him to find work on a merchant ship coming straight to France. If you write to us again, please tell me how to write Oller, the address I must put on the letter and the correct amount of stamps so as to avoid unnecessary expense for him.

I clasp your hand affectionately, and after submitting this letter to be read by Sir Guillemet, and acquainting him with your letter, I shall take the present one to the post office.

Please give my kind regards to your family, to Mrs. Pissarro and your brother. I now say, Good-bye.

Guillemet added a postscript: *Today, 23rd October 1866, year of Grace:*
Dear old Pissarro,

I was going to write to you when your letter arrived. I'm feeling quite well at the moment...I've made a few studies and will soon attempt my big stuff, if autumn helps me. Cézanne has done some very beautiful paintings. He is painting in light tones again, and I am sure you will be pleased with the two or three pictures he will bring back. I'm not sure when I will return, probably when my pictures are finished.

So you are back in Paris, and I expect your wife is better there than in Pontoise. The babies are well, I assume. Should you get too bored to work, send us some news. We often speak of you and will be happy to see you again. My wife and I send a thousand greetings to you all. See you soon.

And on November 2nd, Guillemet wrote to Zola, this time with a postscript by Cézanne:

My dear Zola,

In his two letters, Paul has written more about me than himself. I will do the same thing, that is, to say the opposite, and to talk to you a lot about the Master. His exterior is, if anything, more handsome; his hair is long, his face exhales health, and the way he dress-es causes a sensation in the Cours [the Cours Mirabeau, the main street of Aix]. *So you can be reassured on that score. His mind, although always on the boil, leaves him moments of clarity; and his painting, encouraged by some genuine commissions* [proba-bly portraits], *promises to reward his efforts. The sky of the future seems at times less black. When he returns to Paris, you will see some pictures you will like very much; among others, an Ouverture du Tannhäuser, for there is a very successful piano in it; then a por-trait of Paul's father in a big armchair, which looks very good.. The painting is light in color and the attitude very fine. The father looks like a pope on his throne were it not for Le Siècle* [a weekly newspaper] *he is reading. In a word, all goes well, and in a short time you will see some very beautiful things, you may be sure.* [The *Ouverture du Tannhäuser* mentioned here is routinely mistaken by Cézanne scholars as *Young Girl at the Piano*, which I will take up later. We have no extant canvas that could have been titled by Cézanne, *Ouverture du Tannhäuser*. And the por-trait of Cézanne's father, to which this letter refers, show him reading *l'Èvènement*, not *Le Siècle*].

The people of Aix continue to irritate Paul. They ask permission to come and see his paintings, only to scoff at them afterwards; and so he has devised a good way of deal-ing with them: Merde! [Shit on you!], *he says to them, and those who are devoid of tem-perament flee in horror* [This passage is the one most often cited by Cézanne scholars as evidence of his vulgarity. How silly!].

In spite, or perhaps because of that, there is obviously a flow of attention towards him, and perhaps the time is approaching when he will be offered the directorship of the museum—which I greatly hope, because either I scarcely know him or else we will then see in the museum some successful landscapes done with the palette knife, which would have no other chance of getting into a museum anywhere.

With regard to young Marion, whom we have told you about, he cherishes the hope of being given a teaching job in geology. He excavates diligently and tries to prove to us that God never existed and that belief in Him is a fabricated matter. But we don't allow that issue to bother us, because it has nothing to do with painting.

We received a letter from Pissarro, who is doing fine. We have often been to the

Barrage [the Zola dam near Aix]. *We will return to Paris towards the end of December.*

I have added a second sheet of paper, because I think Paul will want to write to you on this same occasion, so in the same envelope you will have both of our greetings. I clasp your hand.

Your devoted friend.

Cézanne now takes up the pen:

My dear Émile,

I am taking advantage of Guillemet's writing to send you greetings but without anything to add. However, I must tell you that, as you feared, my big picture of Valabrègue and Marion has not come off, and that, having attempted a soirée de famille, it didn't come off at all. I will persevere, and perhaps another shot at it will be successful. We went for a walk with Guillemet. The country is very beautiful. I clasp your hand and also Gabrielle's.

Greetings to Baille, who sent his to me in his letter addressed to Fortuné Marion, geologist and painter.

The several references in these letters to Cézanne painting in light tones may suggest a lightening of Cézanne's black melancholy. But significantly, the lightness, the blond, may have been a gesture towards Zola's criticism. By this time, Manet was Zola's model artist, and often in his writings on Manet, the lightness, the blond, is emphasized as a special and modern quality, an enlightenment emerging from dark ages.[5] This blondness is found in Manet's pictures regardless of his blacks, which reference modernism as much as the «black paintings» of the admired masters: Valásquez, Ribera, and Caravaggio. Manet's blacks marked a departure from the moody, dusky, brown-black tonalities familiar from the painting of Courbet and others of the naturalist schools of landscape painting, who extensively used bituminous pigment.[6] Black was of course associated with Romanticism, dark moods, coal-tar melancholia, dark and stormy nights, black *succubi*, black magic, and negresses as *femmes fatales*. Pissarro's advice to Cézanne to deploy grays rather than black will fall on deaf ears until about 1870, despite Cézanne having acknowledged in his October 23rd, 1866 letter to Pissarro that he was correct when speaking of grays as dominant in nature. Manet's blondness inspired his admirers, but his copious use of black distressed his critics. They translated it as dirt. And inasmuch as dirt and sex were congruous, they considered Manet's inclusion of a black woman and a black cat in his *Olympia* the greatest insult to tonal painting.

Black—as Manet, not Courbet, used it—was, nonetheless, the color that signified modernity. Black clothing defined the urban man; the black frock coat distinguished a bourgeois from an artisan; a black tuxedo was a symbol of social achievement, the black smoking jacket signaled a man of leisure. By the 1860s, black was the appropriate color for businessmen's attire, partly because the black suit was less provocative in a competative urban society, and also as far removed from the natural as a color could get, for, other than underground tar and coal, there is no dominant black in nature.[7] Black was also the clothing color of dandies—as exemplified by Baudelaire's black cravats, boots, capes—and the trim color for sophisticated women of high fashion. Yet black was resisted in official art; as a modern color, it offended traditions. Gill's caricature of Manet's 1868 *Portrait of Zola* fairly well summarized the 1860's critical hostility towards black. Not only is the caricature dead-black with just enough harsh white to indicate the subject, but Gill inscribed on it «1660» in reference of course to seventeenth-century painters of black imagery whose work Manet admired: Valásquez, Goya, Caravaggio, artists admired by Cézanne, too.[8]

30

ézanne was back in Paris by mid-January 1867, once again determined to
assault the Salon. What he would paint this year as Salon entries, *Grog au
vin* (Mulled Wine) and *Ivresse* (Inebriation) may have been stimulated by
Zola having once again climbed onto his back. In his 1915 book on Cézanne, the
art dealer Ambroise Vollard wrote that, in response to Zola's telling him he was
still mired in the muck of romanticism, Cézanne had undertaken some droll and
pseudo-realistic little canvases, like *Woman with a Flea* and a picture of a naked
night-waste collector lying on a cot with his wife bringing him a bowl of mulled
wine. Vollard got this information from Antoine Guillemet, a painter-friend of
Cézanne in the 1860s when both were in their twenties. Here is Vollard's story:

> *On his first visits to the Louvre, the young Cézanne was deeply afflicted by confused
> impressions, bewildered and stupefied. Following his own inclinations, the spectacle offered
> to his eyes appeared as a bubbling over of light and color. Rubens, especially, bowled him
> over. Under his influence Cézanne composed some grand scenes in fiery colors. Zola, who
> earlier had put Cézanne on guard against realism, now found that his friend had gone too
> far exalting the romantic. So, as a way of slackening off, Cézanne set to work on some
> droll and pseudo-realistic quick sketches, such as a Woman with a Flea. That picture has
> disappeared, as has a second one from the same time representing a naked man lying on a
> cot. The model that posed for this académie [sketch} was a night waste collector [un vidan-
> geur], whose wife operated a crémerie were she served a beef soup much appreciated by her
> clientele of young daubers. One day, Cézanne, who had gained the confidence of the night-
> waste collector, asked him to pose. The man spoke of his work.*
>
> *«But it's at night that you work,» says Cézanne. «During the day you do nothing!»*
> *The vidangeur explains that during the day he must sleep.*
> *«So, then I will paint you in bed,» replies Cézanne.*
> *The good man was at first under the covers, coiffed in a cotton bonnet, in order to
> comply with the painter's request. But because between friends there were no restraints as
> to manners, he first removed his bonnet, then tossed off the covers and posed entirely naked.*

His wife figured in the picture, with a bowl of mulled wine that she offered to her husband.

A night waste collector was the most despicable of common workers. At each urban building a barrel, or a cesspool in the form of a small ditch, provided a receptacle for human excrement dumped from chamber pots and manure from stables; each night the *vidangeurs* with horse-drawn carts collected the contents and made their dripping way to La Villette, where canal boats awaited to haul the vile-smelling mass to the disposal plant in the Forest of Bundy. Adding to the story, Vollard tells us:

> *The current opinion of official critics of Cézanne's work was that he created his paintings by aiming at a blank canvas with a pistol loaded with various pigments. They commonly called his manner of painting, «pistol painting». The truth is that no one had more concern than Cézanne with showing the public that in his work there was anything other than the effect of chance. But if he knew how to create paintings he was not up to explaining them, nor even to giving appropriate titles. For the study of the night-waste collector, his friend Guillemet came to his aid by offering this title: An Afternoon in Naples, or The Wine Grog.*

Vollard signs off, saying, «The other studies by Cézanne on the same theme are later than this one, which dates to 1863.» By «the same theme,» Vollard was

One of several versions of the so-called *Afternoon in Naples* or *Night in Venice*, wrongly associated with the *Le Puch ay Rhum* or *The Wine Grog*, mentioned by Vollard. This series was painted in the 1870s.

referring to later pictures that go by the title, *An Afternoon in Naples*—several of them, their history confused in the Cézanne literature because Guillemet was not entirely clear about an event that had occurred some thirty years before telling Vollard about it on some occasion after 1895. The *Afternoon in Naples* pictures, which, in my opinion, date after 1874, are brothel settings with a naked man and a naked woman on a bed. A clothed woman does enter their space with a serving platter, but the item on the platter is not a bowl of mulled wine; in some examples it is tea service, in others wine and either fruit of brioche. Such room service was available in brothels.

In 1863, Zola's thoughts were not yet stewing at the bottom of the pot, and Cézanne would hardly submit 1863 pictures to an 1867 Salon.[1] By offering such pictures as *Grog au vin* and *Ivresse* to the jury to mock its criteria—pictures he knew didn't stand a chance—Cézanne was taking the opposite tack that artists heeded when selecting what to submit, most of them settling for crowd-pleasing imagery, called «Salon pictures,» and keeping their more risky images, if indeed they produced any, for private clients. Moreover, the *Afternoon in Naples*, or, as Cézanne's themes of this sort are also called, *A Night in Venice*, were commonplace in pornography, as was the motif of lovers in a *cabinet particulière* (private room in a cabaret). Such rooms were often thematic in decor, such as to allow one to fantacize being in Arabia, Japan, Egypt, or Venice. We will see such a room when taking up Cézanne's *Une Olympia moderne*.

Most likely by 1867, Cézanne had identified the creative artist as not only a *tempérament* expressed in painting, but had associated individual and especial ways of behaving (ill-mannered) and appearing (untrimmed head hair and beard, workman's clothing) with being an original. Zola had been arguing during the mid-1860s that artists should be exempted from social mores, even from laws. Still purging his juvenile romanticism, Cézanne may have found that painting vile pictures for the Salon was his strongest assertion of individuality, so entirely devoid of «art» were they. Like Zola, who'd come to dislike the word «art», it would seem that Cézanne was on course when thinking that the further one got from art the closer one might get to it, as in the romantic maxim, «to hate is to love». So this popular anecdote, contributed by Vollard, may be true, that, on arriving at the entrance to the Palais de l'Industrie, Cézanne would mount the steps and hold up his pictures for all to ridicule before going in to deposit them before the jury, like a comic with a noose around his neck playing to the crowd from the hangman's platform.

After submittals were in for the Salon judging in April 1867, the journalist, Arnold Mortier, could not pass up an opportunity to expose the folly of Cézanne's effort to get his entries past the jury. Mortier had not seen the two pictures but apparently had heard plenty about them. In an early April press notice in *Le Figaro*, Mortier described two canvases by an artist, Monsieur Sésame, the name intentionally maligned, as if the artist had assumed that he need say only «Open Sesame» and the Salon doors would swing wide for him to enter:

> *I heard talk of two rejected paintings by Mr. Sésame (who is unrelated to the Arabian Nights), the same man who, in 1863, caused an outbreak of merriment at the Salon des Refusés with a canvas showing two pig's feet in the form of a cross. This time, Mr. Sésame has sent to the exhibition two compositions which, though less freakish, are just as worthy of exclusion from the Salon. These compositions are both entitled «Grog au vin». One of them depicts a naked man in bed to whom a fully dressed woman has just brought a cup of mulled wine. The other portrays a naked woman and a man dressed as a lazzarone; in this one the grog is spilt.*

Mortier's description of the first painting fits to *Le Vidangeur*. Yet the subject described by him as a man dressed as a *lazzarone* signals a Naples theme: a *lazzarone* is a Neapolitan good for nothing, vagabond, or street urchin. Ironically, if Guillemet recognized the man as a *lazzarone*, it might have prompted his alternative title for the painting. *An Afternoon in Naples*, which probably fit to what Cézanne had in mind: to debase the artifice of classical love by doing what Manet had—transforming the love goddess Venus into a contemporary prostitute. Guillemet would have known that the seaport of Naples, like Marseilles and Antwerp's, was famous for low-grade whorehouses, a deep cut below those of Venice (named after love-goddess Venus) known for erotic opulence. An afternoon in Naples would be like a few hours spent in a sordid brothel, representing an appropriate companion picture to the nighttime emptier of slop buckets and cesspools. Mortier had erred, however, on the title of the second painting offered to the Salon. According to Zola, who published a correction of Mortier's review in the following issue of *Le Figaro*, the title by which it was registered was *Ivresse*.[2]

Although not one of Cézanne's pictures had been exhibited anywhere in Paris, Cézanne was making the newspapers, gaining notoriety—not among an audience an artist would wish for, but an audience nonetheless. In the April 12th, 1867 issue of *Le Figaro*, Zola's rebuttal was contrived to both sting and amuse. He denied that Cézanne had even the smallest pig's foot in his repertoire, but added that he did not see why a painter could not paint pig's feet as appropriately to art as melons and carrots.[3] (Zola didn't know that the 1863 Salon jury had accepted a painting titled, *Pieds de Cochon*). The pig was of course the lowest creature an artist could possibly portray. In 1865 Thomas Couture maliciously lampooned the «realist» by painting a bohemian artist seated on a classical head, studiously painting a severed pig's head positioned on a still life stand. In 1870, Monet would paint a severed boar's head staring straight out at the viewer, much like a portrait. Pictures of girls tending pigs, such as Courbet's *Swineherdess*, allowed male viewers subtle associations with dirty sex.

Zola wrote to the editor of *Le Figaro* to defend Cézanne and correct Mortier's and the editor's presumptions:

> *My dear colleague,*
>
> *I beg you to be good enough to insert these few lines of correction concerning one of my childhood friends, a young painter whose strong and individual talent I greatly respect.*
>
> *You reprinted a clipping from L'Europe dealing with a Mr. Sésame who was supposed to have exhibited at the Salon des Refusés in 1863 «two pig's feet in the form of a cross» and who, this year, had another canvas rejected, titled «Grog au vin.»*
>
> *I must say that I had some difficulty recognizing, under the mask stuck on this artist's face, one of my former schoolmates, Mr. Paul Cézanne, who has not the slightest pig's foot among his artistic equipment—at least not yet. I make this reservation because I do not see why one should not paint pig's feet just as one paints melons and carrots.*
>
> *Mr. Paul Cézanne has indeed had two canvases rejected this year: «Grog au vin» and «Drunkenness». Mr. Arnold Mortier saw fit to be amused by these pictures and described them with flights of imagination that do him great credit. I know all this is just a pleasant joke, which one must not worry about. But never have I understood this sort of criticism, which consists of ridiculing and condemning what one has not even seen. I insist at least on saying that Mr. Arnold Mortier's descriptions are inaccurate.*
>
> *Even you, my dear colleague, add your opinion: you are convinced, as you say, that the artist may have inserted a philosophical message into his painting. That is an inappropriate conviction. If you want to find philosophical artists, look for them among the Germans or even among our petty French dreamers, but keep in mind that the analytical painters, the young school whose cause I have the honor to defend, are satisfied with the great realities of nature.*[4]
>
> *As you know, a number of painters have just signed a petition demanding the reopening of the Salon des Refusés. So now it will be up to Mr. de Nieuwerkerke to determine whether «Grog au vin» and «Ivresse» will be exhibited. Perhaps some day Mr. Arnold Mortier will actually see the canvasses he so glibly judged and described. Such strange things do happen!*
>
> *It is true that Mr. Paul Cézanne will never call himself Mr. Sésame and that whatever happens, he will never be the creator of «two pig's feet in the form of a cross.*
>
> *Your devoted colleague,*
> *Émile Zola*

Zola's pressure on Cézanne to make the leap from romanticism to realism may have reflected his growing admiration for Manet and Monet, whose paintings he regarded as superior to Cézanne's. In his *Salon* reviews and in *Mes Haines*, Zola wrote of Manet: *Mr. Manet's place in the Louvre is marked out, like that of Courbet, like any artist of original and strong temperament.*[5] In his letter to Valabrègue of May

29th, 1867, Zola would described the brochure he'd just published to support Manet's private exhibition that year at the Exposition universelle. It was a reprint of Zola's January 1st article «Une nouvelle manière en peintre» (A new way of painting) in *Revue des XIXe Siècle*, augmented with a foreword, a portrait of Manet engraved by Bracquemond, and an etching after *Olympia*. Zola had hoped to sell this booklet at Manet's private pavilion, but Manet objected, saying that selling a tribute to himself would not be in good taste.[6]

The letter to Valabrègue continues: *Something else: I am close to an agreement with the publisher Lacroix to release a new edition of my Contes à Ninon, illustrated by Manet. We have only to sign the contract.*[7] Years earlier, Zola had told Cézanne of his dream that they would collaborate on a magnificent book, for which Cézanne would do magnificent illustrations: *Our two names together in gold letters on the title page*, Zola had said to him, *and in this brotherhood of genius inseparable as to posterity.*

One recalls Zola saying in his 1866 *Salon* that one day he and Manet will be avenged. He proclaimed himself inseparable from Manet as to posterity—no longer would it he he and Cézanne. Now Manet would be the one to illustrate his book. Even ten years later, on responding to puerile reviews of the 1877 Impressionist exhibition, Zola praises other artists first, and then says, *Next I wish to add the name of Paul Cézanne, certainly the greatest colorist of the group.* On saying that Cézanne's Provençal landscapes *are so strong and deeply felt as to make the bourgeois smile*, Zola adds: *they nevertheless display the makings of a great artist.* Zola was not willing to say that Cézanne was, in fact, a great artist but only with the makings of one. Surely Zola's praise was in support of the subject matter, the landscape of his and Cézanne's shared youth.

In 1868, Manet's portrait of Zola hung in the Salon. In the 1870 Salon, Zola would appear in the group composition of artists in Fantin-Latour's *L'Atelier de Batignolles* along with Manet, Monet, Renoir, Bazille, Astruc, Edmond Maître, and Otto Scholderer. Notably missing was Cézanne, who could plainly see that he was not only outside the circle but also detached from Zola. Zola had succeeded where

Èdouard Manet. Portrait of Èmile Zola. 1868. Paris, Musée d'Orsay

Henri de Fantin-Latour. Portrait of Èdouard Manet. 1867. The Art Institute of Chicago.

Cézanne had not—had even appeared on the Salon walls: as his portrait by Manet and as a member of the Batignolles group painted by Fantin-Latour. Still, nothing in the letters between Cézanne and Zola indicates a rift between them, even though Cézanne may have harbored jealousy over Manet's success and friendship with Zola. Attention drawn to Zola's reviews and essays defending and praising Manet and Monet had reversed Zola's relationship to Cézanne. Among artists at the Café Guerbois, Zola had been introduced as Cézanne's friend; now Zola's elevated status positioned Cézanne the painter as a friend of Zola the critic. In an April 1867 letter, Valabrègue in Aix writes to Zola in Paris:

Paul wrote to me recently. Your letter told me of his rejection by the jury, which I expected, as did you and he. When will Paul not be rejected? On another note, I learned with pleasure of the vigorous way you answered for him. You are destined to torture his enemies. It is impossible to congratulate you too favorably on this fine role. Paul is a child innocent of life while you are his guardian and guide. You watch over him. He walks by your side, always sure of being defended. An alliance between you to defend him has been signed, an alliance that will even be offensive if necessary. You are his thinking soul. His destiny is to make paintings, just as yours is to make his life.

While defining what was becoming the art critic's role—to make the artist while the artist makes art—Valabrègue had put Cézanne's destiny in Zola's hands. It was Zola's prolonged effort to bring Cézanne to Paris that got

Èdouard Manet. At the Café Guerbois. Dated 1869.

him to write about art in the first place. From his earlier letters to Cézanne, several passages on the subject of painting augur what he would write when undertaking art criticism. If Zola were to move on in the vein he'd opened and was recklessly mining, it would be to such painters as Manet that he would have to attach himself, and that would further weaken his bond with Cézanne. More than merely «realist» paintings, Manet's were highly aesthetic, sophisticated, and abundant in matter for theoretical discussion. Zola wrote of his pictures: *When all the pictures in Manet's exhibition are taken in by a single look, you find that the diverse works hold together, that they complete one another, that they represent an enormous sum of analysis and vigor.*[8] For Zola this sense of the totality of an oeuvre had personal meaning. By this time he may have been reflecting on his projected sequence of novels, the Rougon-Macquart series, which he hoped would hold together as one complete work. What he saw as valuable in Manet's pictures at the time—opening a window on the real world—is precisely what he would do with his series of real-life novels.

Nothing like that could have been said about Cézanne's art up to this point. Cézanne was not connected to the avant-garde but still on its periphery. When in May 1867, Frédéric Bazille mentions in a letter to his family that a few young artists planned to organize exhibitions of their own in defiance of the Salon, Bazille does not say who they were, but the group would not have included Cézanne:

> In one of my last letters, I told you about a plan for a group of young artists to hold their separate exhibition. With each of us pledging as much as possible, we have been able to gather 2,500 francs, which is not enough. So we must abandon our project. We will have to return to the bosom of the administration whose milk we've not suckled and who's disowned us.[9]

Other than *The Night Waste Collector*, none of Cézanne's works would approach in imagery anything like Zola's own musings on social evolution starting at the most debased level, the working class, the cesspool of the social system. Neither it nor *Woman with a Flea*, or even a picture depicting an afternoon in a Neapolitan whorehouse, could measure up to Manet when it came to portraying social types. Moreover, Manet's salon rejections—the way he handled them, the way critics handled both them and him—were enacted on a much higher level than Cézanne's burlesque capers. The rigorous schooling Manet had endured profitably over years of study in Couture's studio showed up Cézanne's mediocre training. Cézanne's back patting and words of approval were coming from friends who knew very little about art, from the amateurs Marion, Coste, Valabrègue—weak judgments colored by friendship. Guillaumin, Oller, Guillemet, Emperaire, Huot, Chaillan, Chautard, and the older Villevieille were ordinary painters with little to say about art other than through their second-rate pictures. Even Pissarro was a lesser figure as both artist and intellectual than those in Manet's circle, such as Alphonse Legros, Whistler, and Fantin-Latour. In a discussion between Marion and Morstatt, Marion held up Cézanne as a better painter than either Courbet or Manet, and foresaw that the moment of Paul's success was looming just a ways off. But neither he nor Morstatt were capable of making such judgments, aesthetically or historically. And surely Zola, although more able, would not have approved of Cézanne's pictures of his little sister Rose reading to a doll, or his dauber friends, Marion and Valabrègue, setting out to paint a landscape. Even the supportive Valabrègue had written to Zola back in October of 1866, confidentially poking fun at Cézanne's poor skills:

> *Paul has written you recently. He has just finished two excellent pictures: one a scene in which music is being played, the other of his sister reading to a doll. At the moment, Marion and I are posing for him. We are arm in arm, and have hideous shapes. Paul is a horrible painter as regards the poses he gives people in the midst of his riots of color. Every time he paints one of his friends, it seems as though he were revenging himself for some hidden injury. Paul made me sit yesterday for the study of a head. I am colored so strongly that I am reminded of the statue of the curé* [parish priest] *of Champfleury when fresh blackberries had coated it. Fortunately, I posed only one day. The uncle is more often the model. Every afternoon there appears a portrait of him, and Guillemet belabors it with terrible jokes.*[10]

In 1868, Marion had to admit that realist painting, such as Courbet's, had veered further than ever from official success, and that Cézanne might never have a chance to show his work in the Salon. Zola would not have associated Cézanne with Courbet, not even with Daubigny. Yet to Marion, Cézanne was already the ultimate revolutionary against which official art was pitted. Marion wrote:

> *Too many revolutionary ideas are connected with it; the painters on the jury will not weaken for a moment. I admire the persistence and nerve with which Paul writes to me:* «*Well! they will be blasted into eternity with even greater persistence.*» *All that considered he ought to think about finding another means of getting publicity. He has*

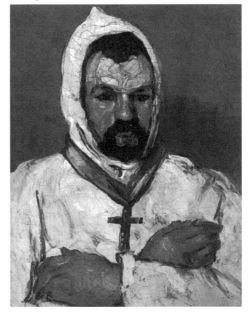

Cézanne. One of several portraits of his uncle Domenique in various guises 1866. New York, Metropolitan Musem. Photo: Bulloz.

reached an astonishing perfection of technique. His exaggerated fierceness has been modulated, and I think it is time that circumstances offer him means and opportunities to produce a great deal.

Cézanne's plight was artificial—revolting, not revolutionary. He was riding on the coattails of Manet, subsisting on notoriety, just as his amateur friends in Aix, such as Marion, were riding on his. Marion was correct only on one point: Cézanne needed another means of getting publicity. No collector in his right mind would have bought Cézanne's night-waste collector lying naked in bed, or the portrait of Valabrègue, or any portrait of his uncle

Cézanne. Portrayal of himself as somewhat mad, perhaps, but in any case as a revolutionary. Private collection, New York. Photo: Galerie Bernheim-Jeune.

Dominic, or the crudely painted picture of a bloody leg of veal reclining on a loaf of bread. Such pictures, seen in retrospect, have value only to document the early work of an artist whose later work significantly affected art history and whose early work was brought into artistic sensibility by art events on the twentieth century. In the 1860s, Cézanne was not being judged wrongly.

Edmond Duranty wrote to Zola, *If this interests you, Cézanne appeared recently at the little café on the place Pigalle, attired in one of his costumes of olden times: blue overalls, a battered old hat, a jacket of white linen completely covered with smudges from his brushes. He had a certain success* [arousing attention]. *But those are dangerous demonstrations.*[11] Doubts about himself as an artist were reflexively manifested as the sort of cynical, offhanded, shrugging-off remarks of the sort that serve as ego-protective devices. According to Vollard, as given in a hypothetical interview, Cézanne said of the Café Guerbois group, *They are all lousy buggers, no better than notaires.* Vollard also said that one day Manet when asked Cézanne what he planned to submit to the next salon, Cézanne responded by saying, *a pot of shit.*[12] Another story tells of an occasion when Cézanne came to the Guerbois where several artists and writers were gathered; after greeting the others with a handshake, on coming up to Manet he said something like, *I would shake your hand, Mr. Manet, but I haven't washed in a week.* If this happened, and it probably did, it was surely a case of Cézanne being boorish with a jocular and common figure of speech, not that he was dirty or hadn't washed in a week.[13] Nor can it be ruled out that Cézanne was getting back at Manet. Perhaps a remark that Manet had made to Guillemet, after seeing Cézanne's *Le Vidangeur*, got back to him: Manet had asked Guillemet, *How can you possibly like that filthy picture?*[14]

Cézanne had set himself in contrast to Manet, who was never seen in public without his cane, silk top hat, and fine leather gloves—impeccably attired at all times, even when occasionally sketching out-of-doors. Manet was a studio painter, while Cézanne was an outdoor painter who wore work clothes and work boots and tramped around the countryside in the company of naturalists. Saying that he hadn't washed his hands in a week—saving Manet's hands from getting dirtied, not wanting to make a naturalist of him—was an acknowledgment of the two prevailing modes of realism: the urban realities of Manet's circle, the rustic realities of Cézanne's. Artists represented by dirty hands would be the naturalists—the line of Millet, Courbet, Daubigny, and so on (or, in literature, the likes of Zola). The usual description of Courbet-like naturalists at the time was that they didn't wash, had straw in their hair from sleeping in barns and smelled

Although this photograph of Cézanne was taken in the early 1870s, he may have looked much the same in the late 1860s.

of manure, like the farmers and common workers they portrayed. Gautier had called Courbet's *Wrestlers* dirty, soot-smeared workingmen.[15] It lent itself to caricature. Several newspaper lampoonists of naturalist pictures recommend that the realists' subjects take a good hot bath. In 1855, Count de Nieuwerkerke expressed disgust for such crude painters as Courbet, who showed neither taste nor refinement. Democrats, he called them, who don't change their linen.[16]

One recalls the protest letter to the editor of *L'Événement* in which a disgruntled reader of Zola's dirty-handed reviews suggested that the paper hire a reviewer who was in the habit of washing his hands. Another reader asked, *Why do Manet's dirty figures seem to have emerged from a sack of coal.* In July 1868, in a postscript to a letter from Marion to Morstatt, Cézanne says, *I press with warm sympathy the hand that no longer dirties itself in philistine occupations* (Morstatt, in this case, was being congratulated by Cézanne for having come into family money, no longer needing to be employed in dirty business). A critic of Degas' *Laundress* asked if the woman featured in it had her arms not in a wash tub but in a coal bin—he wrote, *The first thought that the picture inspires is to make you ask whether the coal vendor is a laundress or the laundress is a coal vendor.*[17]

Manet had heard plenty about how much dirt hostile critics had found in his *Olympia*, not smut-dirt but actual dirt: dirty whites, a black cat with dirty feet tracking on the bed. Against all this background, Cézanne's saying he had not washed in a week was meant to amuse his café acquaintances who would have known how often Manet's pictures had been associated with dirt. Manet and his friends surely got the gist of it, inferring neither an insult to Manet nor an admission of Cézanne's hands actually being dirty. Art students and artists typically disdain the conventions of dress and manners. Even in Baron Haussmann's memoirs one reads of architects appearing unkempt, disagreeable, and difficult to work with. Haussmann adds that it is necessary to overlook such traits out of respect for their professional competence.[18]

In a letter to Numa Coste of July 24th, 1868, where, at Zola's urging, Cézanne mentions that he must soon pay a visit on Alexis, Cézanne says, *I will attempt a descent on his home*—meaning go downtown to the Cours Mirabeau (the main avenue in Aix) *and call on him—but on that day*, adds Cézanne, *I will first change my shoes and shirt.* This pleasantry has been taken to mean that Cézanne wore the same stinking clothing day in and day out, ignoring what Cézanne had just said in the letter: *Since my arrival I've been out in the open, in the country.* Changing one's country shoes and work shirt to go into town, where Cézanne would prefer to appear appropriately dressed, is hardly a sign of disregard for personal appearance.

And a single sentence in a letter from Guillemet to Zola, written on November 2nd, 1866, seems to have formed the only support for Cézanne having a vulgar mouth that spat invectives at people—such as Frederick Brown saying that Cézanne *flung obscenities at the world.* Vollard reported that Carolus Duran's name came up when he and Cézanne were discussing how Duran had turned impressionism into financial profit (inviting Manet's resentment), and that Cézanne had said, *That bloke Duran, he kicked the Beaux-Arts in the ass.*[19] I know of only one other documented example of Cézanne's «vulgar mouth,» and was he any more vulgar than others of his milieu? In Guillemet's letter one reads: *The Aixois get on Cézanne's nerves. They ask to come to see his paintings only to ridicule them. He's found a good way to deal with such people, Shit on you [Je vous emmerde], he says, and those lacking the right temperament flee in terror.*[20] Not cited by anyone making use of this phrase is the sentence that follows in Guillemet's letter and somewhat ameliorates the invective: *In spite or, or perhaps because of this, there is a turn of public sentiment towards Cézanne, and the time is approaching, I believe, when he will be offered the directorship of the museum.* The reader is reminded that *merde* is a common expression, even used by children without reprimand. It does not carry the same weight of vulgarity as in English. Common French expressions as *il est dans la merde* [He's in deep shit], or *il ne se croit pas de la merde* [He has a high opinion of himself], are often heard in ordinary conversation.

Overlooked, too, is Cézanne's letter to Coste, written near the end of November 1868, in which he tells Coste of an amusing event resulting from a conflict between museum director Gibert and the painter Victor Combes who'd been refused permission to copy pictures in the Bourguignon wing of the art museum in Aix. Cézanne writes, *It appears that the Honorable d'Agay* [Combes], *this young man of fashion whom you know, one day enters the Musée Bourguignon, and there Mamma Combes, entering with him, says, «Give me your cane, papa Gibert will be upset»* (apparently canes had to be checked, as perhaps too many pictures had been punctured by viewers pointing out details). *In retribution for Gibert's refusals, the young man refuses to check his cane. Gibert arrives, he makes a scene of it. Shit on you, shouts d'Agay. This truly happened!*[21]

31

*Yes, indeed, imagination certainly avoids
landscape. Perhaps the artists who cultivate
this genre are mistrustful of their memory
and adopt a method of immediate copying
because it perfectly suits their laziness of mind.*
—Baudelaire

Like Zola, Cézanne was motivated to be a provocative sensationalist. Notoriety held out greater promise for success than quest for a future fame. Had he not been ridiculed by critics and caricatured in newspapers, no one would have taken note of him, for painters in the majority were mediocre. Cézanne was newsworthy because he was extreme. He was also compensating for being degraded by becoming hostile. One symptom of this was his attitude towards Manet, who represented what Cézanne would like to be, a dedicated, notorious painter, while Pissarro he could lean on as a man into whose presence he could retreat when the going got rough. Zola was no longer dependable, having lost faith in Cézanne's abilities. It cannot be often enough said that Cézanne in the 1860s was still a student whose maturity would not get underway until the decade's end. History has accommodated his early paintings to characteristics that his contemporaries deplored. His paintings remained the same while his audience changed.

He had aligned himself with outdoor painters, landscapists who tramp about in the countryside and avoid urban life. He was not a Parisian, and never would become one. He had fallen in with companions for whom realism meant vulgarity, which was becoming no less the fate of Zola. Vulgarity was associated especially with landscape painters; many artists regarded that choice of subject matter as an admission of failure to confront art seriously. The natural landscape lacked intellectual or cultural substance. Not even Monet in the 1860s took landscape painting to be a significant art. Manet, Bazille, and Fantin-Latour refused to paint rural nature, and Degas never would. Baudelaire, in his *Salon of 1859*, treated landscape painters with low regard, although he respected Corot's painterly skills, Paul Huet's poetic hamlets, and Boudin's freshness when picturing urban people at seaside resorts. *Allow me*, wrote Baudelaire, *to return once more to my obsession—I mean to my feeling of regret when I see the imagination's part in landscape being more and more diminished. Yes, indeed, imagination certainly avoids landscape! Perhaps the artists who cultivate this genre are far too mistrustful of their memory, and adopt a method of immediate copying because it perfectly suits their laziness of mind.*[1]

Baudelaire's thoughts about Corot in particular were not quite as dismal; he responded defensively to those who castigated Corot as a lowbrow painter. One reviewer of Corot's pictures in the Salon of 1864 wrote, *Corot's figures are the most miserable in the world. And among his followers are those with neither talent for drawing nor gift for coloring, but who hope to find glory with the least effort under art's banner.*[2] (Renoir was to recall later that a crowd of idiots always surrounded Corot).[3] Although agreeing that Corot's pictures were boring, Baudelaire described Corot as a worthy antithesis of the dazzler Théodore Rousseau, tormented by several devils without knowing which one to heed. Baudelaire said that the devil was too seldom within Corot, preventing him from dazzling and astonishing the eye. *We have heard this eminent artist criticized because his color is too soft, his light almost always crepuscular. But the sound of a clear voice, both modest and harmonious, gets lost amid an uproar of deafening or raucous shouts; even the most luminous Veronese would often appear pale and gray if surrounded by certain modern paintings which are more garish than peasant's scarves.*[4]

As for Daubigny's landscapes, Baudelaire admired them for their grace and freshness and the immediacy of feeling conveyed to the spectator's soul, but he regretted that these qualities came at the expense of finish and perfection of detail; lacking definition and solidity, Daubigny's pictures prolonged the flabbiness and impermanence of their improvisation: *In this predominance of an inferior genre, in this silly cult of a nature neither purged nor explained by imagination, I see an obvious symptom of general degradation. Pupils of various masters, they all paint remarkably well, but almost all of them forget that a natural view has no value beyond the immediate feeling that an artist can put into it.*[5]

Zacharie Astruc was also negative about landscape painting, saying that it expects more applause than it deserves. Of contemporary landscapists showing at Martinet's gallery in 1860 (the year before Cézanne's first trip to Paris), Astruc said:

> *Landscape is a spoiled child of criticism, which never ceases to cry out that it is a child genius. No matter what has been said about it, one needs the courage to insist that this special production of our time has established only a meager formula for making art. Within the capabilities of any organized intelligence, it merits nothing more than a bemused look. To laziness, it serves an excuse. We know very well its scope and its complications. To rise to its height, an accurate eye and working at it one or two years are sufficient. I hold that one cannot claim to be a painter, even with solid talent as a landscapist, any more than one is a musician on the strength of a few tunes on a piano.*[6]

While the subject matter of Barbizon-type paintings was steeped in the same shallow sentimentalism as mythologies and folk tales, they were also associated with the quotidian generic simplicity of village dwellers and farmers. (One recalls Zola's early letter to Cézanne explaining the difference between the natural and the poetic: a farmyard is base nature; add a sweet maiden feeding chickens and you have poetry). The socialist-anarchist Pierre-Joseph Proudhon, an idealistic champion of Gustave Courbet, once said, *The peasant loves nature as a child loves his wet-nurse.*[7] Courbet was of course not Millet, his peasants not the same creatures as Millet's. Baudelaire accused Millet of glorifying peasants while making a show of style: *Instead of distilling the natural poetry of his subjects, Millet wants to add something to it at any price. His peasants have too high an opinion of themselves, displaying a sort of dark*

J. F. Millet. Gleaners. Paris, Musée du Louvre. Photo: Giradon.

and fatal boorishness, which makes one want to hate them. Whether reaping or sowing, grazing or shearing their animals, they always seem to be saying, «We are the poor and disinherited of this earth, but it is we who make it productive!»[8]

To a great extent, the debasement of landscape painting had been due to the urban perception of the low social level of rural inhabitants and their culture. Along with still-lifes and homey, domestic pictures, the so-called straight land-scape (the closest to nature, without human figures) were generally thought of as the lowest level of painting. The descending steps were from historical scenes to biblical, classical, mythological treatments, down through nudes, portraits, and still-lifes to raw and rustic nature.[9] Pissarro once recorded his surprise that some-one had actually bought one of his pure landscapes—not a figure in it. In the massive 1855 international exhibition in Paris, when Ingres was allowed to exhib-it forty canvases plus drawings, and Delacroix was allowed thirty-five pictures, neither exhibited a landscape. The romantic landscapist Corot was confined to six canvases; the rural landscapist, Millet, to only one.[10]

As the middle class expanded, suburban dwellers provided a market for non-farm landscapes, supporting a growing number of middling painters who turned out pictures of attractive and flirtatious men and women out of doors on river banks and meadows, healthy children in playgrounds, flowers in beds and vases—an untroubled world of imagery immune to sorrow, pictures that require no thought, just reflection on a view, like easy-to-read novels, popular songs, and entertaining theater. Not delimited by its subject matter, as are portraits, history and religious pictures, landscapes could be like stage scenery without actors or action, an absence of mentality. Having no natural boundaries, the landscapes looseness is associated with the elementary and the unrefined; a landscape painting cannot represent morality or ideologies. Typically neutral on social issues, landscapists were thus not likely to provoke ideological vexation.[11]

The intensification of urbanity, for which Baron Haussmann's upgrading of Paris was in part responsible, had strengthened the polarity of city and country life, making both more describable, hence more real. By the 1860s most of the landscape features in the *Bois de Boulogne* and the *Bois de Vincennes* had been completed—streams, waterfalls, grottos, pleasure islands, wild-gardens, picnic areas, pavilions, restaurants, buffets with outdoor seating, specimen trees labeled like portraits, fields and woods with paths for promenades. Nature, itself, taking on reality, becoming natural—conceptually natural, that is, for nothing on the surface of French soil was primordially natural but in one way or another modified. Every issue of the popular *Magasin pittoresque* was replete with etchings of villages, farm ponds with ducks, groves, grottos, willows leaning over bubbling streams, birds and flowers. And throughout Paris, since the mid-nineteenth century, hand-colored rural and natural landscape prints were promoted in shop windows, kiosks, frame shops, book stores, and such department stores as *Bon Marché*, catering to the large market for prints turned out by wholesalers of pictorial imagery. Changing social attitudes toward the landscape in the 1850s and '60s would condition the bourgeois for eventual acceptance of impressionist painting that, with few exceptions, avoided farmyard and other rustic settings. Impressionism did not achieve artistic status on the ability of artists but on the Impressionists choice of subject matter tendered to the emerging tastes of the suburban bourgeoisie.

Landscape, as a word—as an environment for picnics—derives from the Flemish word *scape*, as does *escape*, meaning *without or beyond boundaries*. Excursions to the countryside could be promoted as escapes from the noise and unhealthy air of a city crowded with worker immigrants—therapeutic for mind and body, a tonic against disease-ridden Paris (in 1865 a cholera epidemic claimed over four thousand victims). Travel agencies, some providing escorts as well as guidebooks, did a brisk business as early as 1855. Picturesque hamlets at railroad stops were dressed up to attract tourists; by mid-century, rustic retreats and even grand country homes in farmlands, hamlets, and Paris' outskirts had become commonplace among the well to do.[12]

What could more effectively illustrate the growing popularity of any social activity than to see it caricatured in newspapers and magazines? Daumier was one of many satirizing the theme of the bourgeoisie engaging nature. His series of cartoons, *Les bons bourgeois*, featured urban dwellers regressing down the social ladder to experience the country—trying in vain to grow flowers on their infertile, badly cultivated plots; uttering inanities about nature; getting stung by bees: an urban couple sitting on the grass observing a butterfly, the punch line, *Don't frighten it, Eudoxie. It's about to land on my nose. It thinks my nose is a rose.* One cartoon depicts a middle-aged urban couple in the forest of Saint Germain, the man sleeping, stretched out on the ground, his wife sitting, wide awake, not feeling pastoral at all, but nervously on the lookout for lizards;[13] another shows two distinguished gentlemen out in the countryside, on a hill, one gazing into the far distance through a telescope, exclaiming, *You want a beautiful view, well here's a beautiful view;* he is looking at Paris' skyline.[14] In most of Daumier's jests on urban bourgeois roughing it in the country, rain ruins their day: Two couples in a rowboat on a scenic river are caught in wind-driven rainstorm. The two women have umbrellas while the two men do not. The cartoon is titled *Un petit grain* (a light squall) and annotated: *Is he ever happy, this Alphonse, for having worn a rainproof hat.*[15]

An output of landscape painting for which little skill was needed helped to promote the sketch as worthy of being exhibited and purchased as art. Casual studios could turn out competent landscape painters in a matter of months. During the 1860s, some twenty art schools opened just for girls, respecting the discomfort woman students felt in the presence of rowdy men when working from nude models in the studio, or when out in the country-side sketching. Some studios mixed genders, offering women as much opportunity as men to draw from the female and male nude. This proliferation of schools reflected the diminishment of professionalism and the opening of subject matter to depiction of most anything pleasing or ardently engaging. Finding how easy it was to be an artist, many, without thought of actually becoming an artist, took painting up as a hobby.

With the demise of history painting, and with little chance for commissions from the State or Church, young painters of the 1860s had limited subject matter to work with. Landscape paintings were the easiest to sell; like still-lifes, the easiest to render. Features of nature—leaves, stems, branches, pebbles, ripples, clouds—are remarkably congruent with the dabs and strokes of a brush; the myriad tones and variations in the light and shades of a natural landscape require less accuracy than is needed to render a human face or the material and ebullience of garments. A natural landscape has few contours requiring exactness of shape-defining lines, such as those that delineate the human figure. To paint landscapes, one hardly need know how to draw, in the sense of Ingres-type or academic drawing. And one was not obliged to engage the imagery with representational knowledge, as when painting historical or religious subjects; or wrestle with perspective and fore-shortening, with how figure relates to ground, or where to position the picture's viewer.

Odilon Redon wrote in a newspaper review, *Let us admit that the best works are to be found among paintings by artists seeking revitalization of nature. Their impulse has been salutatory, has given us some true painters.* But Redon was not about to capitulate entirely to naturalist painting. He missed in landscapes the composition, thought, and philosophy of museum art. After chipping off the absent qualities of art in landscapes, he was left with a core of insight commensurate with what Zola was promulgating: submission to the dictates of nature, no heroes, no evidence of the author in the finished work. Redon wrote, *Since nature is now the master, responsible for the effect it produces in the landscapist's work, the artist must above all be supple and submissive in front of nature; the man must be obliterated so as to let the motif dominate, and the painter must have a great deal of skill to do that without showing off his talent.* This manifesto may not be exactly what Astruc meant in 1868 when he said, *Landscape painting before long will dissolve in a wiser unity, in a more complete artistic formula, but it's close enough.* One might say that a certain yearning would have promoted this prediction, which eventually Cézanne will fulfill, the first evidence for that achievement coming at the end of the 1860s about the time when Zola finds a comprehensive artistic formula for his novels.

One problem with landscape painting, which surely affected Cézanne, was nature's resistance to individuality of expression. Nature's appearance is a given. That was one of Delacroix's chief concerns towards achieving the quality defining the *tableau*: a self-sufficient, aesthetically autonomous picture.[16] Landscapes are difficult to distort. Individuality assumes imperfections and deviations. The old notion of the Ecclesiastical error—that no artistic thing exists without displaying an imperfection—appears in an 1872 letter from the young Degas in New Orleans to Stanislas-Henri Rouart: *The women here are almost all pretty, and many of them have that touch of ugliness without which there is no salvation.*[17]

Uniqueness can only be expressed as faultiness. Any departure from ideal behavior, which, like truth, is unchanging, was a fault when held up to systems of ideal painting. No image can be real if perfect, for perfection is generalization par excellence. Cézanne's problem about this time was an excess of this sort of originality—how one displays one temperament by exaggeration, which could not be done with landscape painting.

This sentiment had been expressed in different ways by others, including Proudhon, who hailed Courbet as a true artist of the people.[18] Proudhon's *Du principe de l'art et de sa destination sociale* (Principles of art and its social destination) was published in 1865. Zola mildly attacked Proudhon's definition of art as an idealistic representation of nature with a view to the physical and moral perfecting of our species. Although Zola had embraced evolutionary progress and social equality, he rejected any sort of idealization that diluted the individual. Against Proudhon's justice, equality, and liberty, Zola pitted his famous phrase that a work of art is neither an abstraction nor a philosophy but an aspect of Creation seen through the medium of an individual temperament.[19] How to apply that to landscape painting, Zola could not say. It would be left to Cézanne in later years to demonstrate how landscape could be imbued with the same display of tempérament that impassioned his portraits and bathers.

32

Landscape painting was not high on Cézanne's mind in the 1860s. Painting out of doors was a pleasant activity but lacked the seriousness of studio painting. Most of the Barbizon painters, including Daubigny and Rousseau, sketched in the fields and woods, but painted in their studios. The open air was too fickle, and what with sunlight changing, appearing and disappearing, rain and winter cold, the plein-air painter was as much at risk as the picnicker.

As for subject matter, it seems that Cézanne was not at all clear on what he should paint—trying this and then that, even falling back on biblical and classical themes, including a *Choice of Paris* and a rape of Persephone, the latter known as *L'Enlèvement* (The Abduction). Like Zola, he was preoccupied with the antagonistic relationship of the sexes—assaults, rapes, murders, orgies, suicides, adulteries, demised virginities—prevailing themes in art and literature at the time. Cézanne's *L'Enlèvement* can be associated with the opening scenes of the novel that Zola's was developing at that time, *Thérèse Raquin*. Although protected by her mother, just as Persephone's mother, Ceres, protected her daughter, Thérèse is seduced by the rake Laurent and punished for her waywardness by death.

The story told in Cézanne's *L'Enlèvement* was a common academic theme. Based on the ancient Greek myth: Pluto's abduction of Persephone, who'd been frolicking and flower gathering in a meadow. Pluto carries her into the underworld of death. Off to our left in Cézanne's canvas, one sees two nymphs, Persephone's companions; in the far distance, a volcanic mountain—heat and smoke of lava, the hot passionate gumbo of Pluto's underworld that would include the morbid unconscious (this mountain references Etna, not Sainte-Victoire as has been proposed). This sort of imagery is still infused with youthful suppuration. The fantasy of *Pluto and Persephone* could have been a sort of overlay on the prototypical simpering saga of *Paul et Virginie*—from the act of saving the distrait girl to abducting her, as one finds in Zola's fantasies, such as *The Confession of Claude*.

Cézanne's paintings from the second half of the 1860s are difficult to deal

Cézanne. The Choice of Paris. Mid-1860s. Private collection, Paris. Probably a copy.

with sensibly. Among them are misattributions and some fanciful titles that obscure meanings—canvases that suffer from an excess of art history laid on by scholars who explain pictures by what they are reminders of rather than what they are. Art historians who drain off an artist's individuality by diluting his or her art in «influences» have brought an avalanche of art history down onto Cézanne's *L'Enlèvement*. From Ovid's *Metamorphose* and the eruptive Mount Etna, one is led to Millet's *Sicilian Landscape* in Marseilles' municipal museum, wherein a mountain just happens to appear. The victim's blue cloak leads to the sixteenth-century Niccolo dell'Abate's *Abduction of Persephone*. One of the nymphs in the background of Cézanne's canvas is found in Nicolas Poussin's *Echo and Narcissus* (that is a fact). It is said that Cézanne was influenced by Piazetta's *Abduction of Helen* in the Musée Granet in Aix,[1] and by Cabanel's *Nymph Abducted by a Faun* in the Salon of 1861, with the nymph's milk-white body set against the bronze arms of her ravisher.[2] It is said as well that *L'Enlèvement* represents «a major venture by the artist into the realm of history painting.»[3] Nothing could be further from the truth. Cézanne never set a foot into the realm of history painting. If anything held him back in the mid-1860s, much to Zola's dismay and to the abashment of those few in Manet's circle who saw anything by him, it was that he still had a foot stuck in mythological sludge. It will take his painting of a cesspool cleaner and a

Cézanne. *L'Enlèvement* (The Abduction). 1867. New York, Metropolitan Museum.

woman with a flea to extricate him, though he will never entirely give up references to ancient allegories. Anyway, *L'Enlèvement* is not a documentation of Pluto carrying off Persephone, but a categorical theme that references Pluto carrying off Persephone. When one labels a picture as a specific event at a moment of time, the imagery is constrained by the traditional boundaries of the subject, and an interpretation of the imagery becomes one of external generalities.

The abduction of Persephone by Pluto was the sort of stock motif that Manet, Monet, and Degas despised. That Cézanne painted it was an indication of how distanced his imagery was from the circle of painters with whom Zola identified in 1867. The existence of another painting of *L'Enlèvement*, similar to Cézanne', would indicate that among Cézanne's painter friends such subject matter was acceptable. Someone in Cézanne's circle painted this canvas.[4] Emperaire is again the suspect. The brushwork in his oil studies of such subjects would have been as loose as Cézanne's in the mid-1860s, and he was more addicted than Cézanne to themes that disguised such erotic imagery as rape, incest, and voyeurism in acceptable, culturally displaced subject matter. Some forty years after his death Emperaire was still remembered in Aix as a poor devil obsessed with sex who sold, as I mentioned earlier, pornographic pictures to students much younger than he. One finds in the *Encyclopédia Départementale des Bouche-du-Rhône* a morose account of his legacy: *Emperaire, comprehensive artist, reasoned better about art than he executed it. His exalted admiration of Titian became a source of his impotence. He produced little. During many years there remained on his easel a scene of a duel and a female nude whose pelvis filled the entire canvas.*

A surplus of meaning and significance has been granted to *L'Enlèvement,* this painting of historical value to us but of little artistic importance to modern art. According to Georges Rivière, it was painted in 1867 at Zola's new residence on rue Condamine the Batignolles

Artist unknown. Perhaps by someone in Cézanne's circle. Photo: Courtesy R. Lipchitz, Paris.

quarter and given to Zola as a gift.[5] The picture is signed and dated, which confirms that it was a gift, says Rewald, for Cézanne would not otherwise have signed the canvas.[6] Of that, I am not at all sure. From about the same time as *L'Enlèvement* dates appears a small canvas by Cézanne depicting a Nereid and tritons (*Néréide et tritons*) and a picture of satyrs attacking nymphs (*Satyres et*

Cézanne. Neireid and Tritons. c. 1867. Private collection, Japan.

Nymphes).[7] The first canvas showed up in the Zola estate sale of 1903, so it's assumed Cézanne had given it to Zola. *L'Enlèvement* bears a signature in bold red majuscules, P. CEZANNE, which would bear out Rewald's conclusion that Cézanne signed only certain pictures.[8] But wariness should be the rule whenever a rule is made. Rewald is at a loss when saying that Cézanne had given Pissarro a related picture, *Women Dressing (Femmes s'habillant)*. Admitting that this picture is not signed, Rewald says, contradicting his generalization that Cézanne signed gifts: *The assumptions concerning Cézanne's signature seem not to hold when it is a question of works offered to other painters.*[9]

Would Cézanne have treated one friend differently than the other, just because one was a writer, the other a painter? Rewald goes on to say that Pissarro might simply have picked up a picture abandoned by Cézanne—just as Renoir did in other circumstances—and that other Cézannes owned by Guillaumin and Pissarro were not signed either. It seems a more sensible conclusion that Cézanne did not make a gift to Zola of either *L'Enlèvement* or the *Néréide et tritons* but simply left them with him, as Cézanne did from time to time when going off to Aix. Just because Rivière said the *L'Enlèvement* was painted at Zola's place and that Rewald agrees does not guarantee that it was. Rivière's testimony, published fifty-six years later than the events he describes, is rarely reliable. Saying that the picture was painted at Zola's place may have been a way to explain why it was in Zola's possession at his death in 1903. In his later years, Zola is reported to have told Ambroise Vollard that his residence was «a house of artists,» but that shouldn't be taken to mean his house was a gallery. While he supported the artists' efforts, he did not hang paintings by his friends—not wanting to risk showing favoritism—but had a vault in which his friends' pictures were kept, as he said, under triple lock and key.[10]

If Cézanne had tendered *L'Enlèvement* as a gift to Zola, one might assume that Zola liked, or at least approved of the picture, but in 1867 this sort of imagery was precisely the sort that Zola disliked. He was adamant about doing away with mythologies, nymphs in chiffons, fantasy landscapes, ecstasies without organic cause, even questioning whether Santa Teresa's seventh heaven experience was a spiritual rhapsody or an orgasm.[11] In praising Manet that year, he wrote that *Manet calmly places a few objects or people here and there in a corner of his studio and begins to paint, while others rack their brains trying to invent a new «Death of Caesar» or «Socrates Drinking Hemlock.»* Zola specifically referred to such sustained reinvention of hackneyed themes as *plagiarism*.[12] Yet with *L'Enlèvement,* if Cézanne meant it as Pluto and Persephone, he was plagiarizing art history. One of the earliest writers on Cézanne, the German art historian Julius Meier-Graëfe, said in 1918 that *L'Enlèvement* was an aberration out of Cézanne's youth. Meier-Graëfe asked how it was possible that Cézanne could so misread Zola's taste as to make this picture a gift to him, so contrary was it to the naturalism that Zola then espoused.[13] Meier-Graëfe may have had in mind Zola's 1867 statement, *Our modern landscape artists stand head and shoulders above history and genre painters.*[14]

The imagery of Cézanne's *L'Enlèvement* fits within the category of men who chance upon women and are aroused to possess them sexually. Throughout history, nymphs of various types have symbolically represented the object of the male urge to seduce women, while satyrs represented men who search for playful nymphs—like Cézanne coming upon the mirliton. Nineteenth-century salons abounded with such ersatz rapes and playful orgies: Alexandre Cabanel's *Nymph enlevée par un faune* (Nymph abducted by a fawn) was a standout at the 1861 Salon, and every year such themes of synthetic passion among the two thousand pictures on the walls were plentiful enough to provide central heating. The classical stories of such «rapes» as the rape of Europa, the rape of Leda, of Lucretia, and of the Sabine women were precedent for any number of nineteenth-century pictures that allowed sensual naketness and over sexuality to be portrayed in an acceptable form.

From about this time, perhaps later, comes another painting by Cézanne that

E. J. Gardner. The Water's Edge. Salon of 1880. A typical sublimated image of a maiden about to submit her virginity. This sort of picture appealed to the more tenderminded viewer, for whom the lily signified purity—until plucked, of course.

Adolphe William Bouguereau. Nymphs and Satyr, 1873. Sterling and Francine Clark Art Institute, Williamstown, MA.

is easy to talk about but difficult to understand. *Le Festin* (The Feast) includes a few motifs of men grappling with women in the context of an orgiastic feast. The canvas is crammed with many figures in a setting stimulated most likely by Paolo Veronese's *Noces de Cana* (Marriage at Cana).[15] The setting is Venetian; at the left side, an architectural elevation of three columns with modified Doric capitals corresponds to the columns in Veronese's picture, even to the placement of a figure in one of the colonnade's bays. Surmounting the entablature is a statue of a figure with its head bent forward, looking down, just as the statue on the more distant parapet is positioned in Veronese's composition. And at the left of Cézanne's picture there is a roughly sketched balcony with figures, a great fabric canopy, draped from the architecture on the

Cézanne. *Le Festin* (Banquet). c. 1868 but reworked at a later date. Private collection.

left, which enhances the *vedute di fantasia* setting for the sumptuous display of naked women and luxurious dinnerware.[16]

This picture is described as an orgy and also as the banquet of Nebuchadnezzar. Both descriptions are as problematical as the date of this work. Nowhere in the Bible does Nebuchadnezzar preside over an orgiastic feast.[17] The feast that is cursorily described in *Daniel* 5:1-31 was Belshazzar's: *King Belshazzar made a great feast for a thousand of his lords, and drank wine in front of the thousand.* That Belshazzar also invited the wives and concubines of those lords, who were his courtiers, ordering that wine be drunk from the gold and silver vessels that his father Nebuchadnezzar had stolen when plundering the Temple of Jerusalem, accounts in good part for the feast's sensual opulence, as well as the mistaken identity of the host.[18]

There is little to contradict the postulate that Veronese's huge *Wedding at Cana* inspired *Le Festin*.[19] Cézanne's picture, however, differs in significant aspects, and the conversion of a wedding feast officiated by Jesus into a sexual orgy is a psychic suppurate that will remain undeciphered. Surely Thomas Couture's highly acclaimed *Les Romains de la décadence* (Romans of the Decadence) provided Cézanne with some of the ingredients for that transmutation. But Couture's pic-

Cézanne. Copy of the semi-nude woman at the center of Couture's *Romans of the Decadance*. Former collection Kenneth Clark.

Thomas Couture. *Romans of the Decadance*. 1847. Paris, Musée du Louvre. Photo: Giraudon.

ture hews more closely to the caprice of an orgy of decadence in that certain participants are senseless, drunk, and the women are as sexually aggressive as the men. In the center foreground of Couture's canvas, the scene is annotated with the stock symbols of hedonistic wantonness—casually strewn fruit, flowers, an overturned pot, and crumpled cloth. When *Le Festin* was with Cézanne's art dealer, Vollard, in 1895, the critic Gustave Geffroy had this to say about it: This picture is a point of departure for the artist. It states clearly, brutally, with fierce affirmation, the passions and loves of Cézanne's youth, his total admiration for Veronese, Rubens, Delacroix—not servile admiration but a profession of faith—and a declaration of a new artist who swears allegiance to painting.[20]

At one time Cézanne's *Le Festin* was more expansive, the picture plane larger, including more than one now sees: a row of columns across the back plane, probably more figures to the right, and surely the feet sticking into the picture plane at the lower margin are not attached to an imaginary body but to a body that in some earlier state was visible. About twenty individuals crowd the composition. Fifteen are women, of which thirteen are white and two are black, six are in service: five carry vessels on their heads or shoulders while one is serving at the table. Towards the far end of the table at the left, a man is seated with his elbow on the table, his head couched in his hand. Facing him is another man. A man in a blue tunic has a half-clad women over his shoulder, and at the right, another man in a blue tunic wrestles with a fully dressed woman.[21] The food service is focused on a single diner at the center of the left side of the table. No one else in the picture appears to be eating or drinking. Either the banquet is over and the woman at the right of the table is clearing plates rather than serving, or the king is dining alone (as he does in Flaubert's *La Tentation de Saint Antoine*). Except for four small plates and a few pieces of fruit on the table, there is no evidence

Details of Cézanne's *Le Festin*.

of banqueting other than by whoever is seated at the table where a woman is serving. This is a very strange banquet, entirely different from Veronese's wedding party—and an even stranger orgy: fifteen women, half of them naked, and four, maybe five, men, two partially naked. By contrast, in Couture's picture there are twice as many men as women, and all of the women are participating as revelers.

What meaning could this picture have had to Cézanne? Nothing up to 1867 predicts it, and not much after 1867 follows on it stylistically. Flaubert's novels, like Musset's, offered erotic material as sort of pre-formed fantasies. In Flaubert's *L'Education sentimentale*, the leading man Frédéric's youthful fantasies are of satin-covered boudoirs where he and his friends will experience orgies with illustrious courtesans. In the same book, the character Pellerin will unsuccessfully undertake a monumental painting titled *The Madness of Nebuchadnezzar*.[22] In Victor Hugo's *Noces et festins* (Nuptials and Feasts) in *Chants du crépuscule* (Twilight Cantos), the orgy signifies the downward plunge of society toward annihilation. It was unlikely that Cézanne had anything like that in mind, however. He was neither literary nor interested in social philosophies. His engagement with the theme would have been personal.

Flaubert's description of this feast in *La Tentation de Saint Antoine* offered nerve tingling imagery. Veronese's *Wedding at Cana* and Couture's *Romans* provided a physical theater and stage on which such fantasies could be enacted. Flaubert's description of Nebuchadnezzar's feast is sumptuous and highly crafted:

Columns in ranks half lost in the shadows, of such great height, beside tables which stretch to the horizon where, in a luminous vapor, appear flights of steps, series of arcades, colossi, towers, all superimposed, and beyond these a vague palatial border, above which black masses formed by cedars soar into the dark sky. Fellow diners, crowned with violets, rest elbows on low couches. Wine from two rows of tipped amphora is dispensed while at the far end King Nebuchadnezzar eats and drinks alone. To his right and left, two rows of priests in pointed bonnets swing censers. On the ground beneath the king, having now no hands or feet, crawl the captive kings, to whom he throws bones to gnaw. Lower still come his brothers, their eyes bandaged, all of them blind.

A continuous plaint rises from the depth of the slave's prison. The sweet slow sounds of a hydraulic organ alternate with the chorus of voices, and one senses all around the hall a boundless town, an ocean of men whose surges batter the walls.

Running slaves carry dishes. Women come around with drinks. Baskets creak under the weight of bread. A dromedary loaded with pierced goatskins passes to and fro, sprinkling verbena to cool the tiles.

Keepers bring in lions. Dancers with their hair caught up in nets gyrate on their hands, spitting fire through their nostrils. Negro conjurers juggle, naked infants pelt each other with snowballs...So frightful is the uproar that it might be a storm. What with all the meats and steamy breath, a cloud floats above the feast. Occasionally an ember from one of the big torches is snatched off by the wind, crossing the night like a shooting star.

With his arm, the king wipes the scents from his face. He eats from sacred vessels, and then breaks them. He makes a mental count of his fleets, his armies, his peoples. Shortly, out of caprice, he will burn down his palace together with his guests. He intends to rebuild the Tower of Babel and to dethrone God.

From a distance, on his brow, Antoine reads Nebuchadnezzar's thoughts. They penetrate him. He becomes Nebuchadnezzar. He is instantly sick of excesses and exterminations, and seized with a craving to wallow in filth. The degradation of whatever is horrifying to men consists of an outrage on their minds, a further means of stupefying them, and since nothing is viler than a brute beast, Antoine drops down on all fours on the table and bellows like a bull.[23]

Nebuchadnezzar was Babylonian. Babylon was synonymous with wealth and excess, intellectual babbling, and prostitution.[24] At mid-century, when Paris underwent urban renewal and restructuring, Babylon could be metaphorically tuned to both its former iniquitous state and the splendor of its modernized one. The touring Bostonian, Edward King, after visiting Paris for the 1867 *Exposition Universelle*, wrote in his travel notes: *The modern Babylon gets improvements, wondrous adornment. Magic palaces rise; glittering promenades are thronged where of late stood only mean and narrow streets, dirty and hideous pavements.*[25]

Babylon was a commonplace euphemism for material and sensual excess, as was Venice for sophisticated orgiastic delight and Naples for low-level whoredom.[26] At least since Martin Luther's *The Babylonian Captivity of the Church*, history has deployed Babylon as a metaphor for opulent cities. Although intellectuals and dispirited politicians most often cite the fall of Rome as the life-cycle prototype for the decadent state of Paris, Babylon was given its share of credit. In Flaubert's *Tentation de Saint Antoine*, Damis describes Babylon to Antony: *What a town, that Babylon! Everybody there is rich! And the temples, the squares, the baths, the aqueducts! The palaces are covered with copper! And the interiors, if you only knew!* Couture's *Romans of the Decadence* was a political statement that touched a common nerve: the decadence of Paris repeating the moral deterioration that had brought ill fate to ancient Rome. Shortly after Couture painted *The Romans*, Alexis de Tocqueville proclaimed his profound conviction that public mores were becoming degraded, and that this degradation would lead to revolution.[27]

Cézanne's picture is not a metaphor but a non-political, private engagement with himself, as was the theme for Flaubert. Both Flaubert and Cézanne were brought up on Catholic teachings and were surely aware of how Babylon figured in moralizing burlesques of contemporary decadence. The *Book of Daniel* was an apocalyptic text setting forth moral lessons, and must have figured in Cézanne's education as a youth. Its stories, which centered around Nebuchadnezzar's bizarre reign—such as *Daniel in the Lion's Den* and *Three Men in the Fiery Furnace*—were told and retold in catechism classes throughout the Catholic and Protestant world, each story teaching how resisting temptations of the flesh and faithful observance of the law is rewarded. One of the most popular illustrators of such biblical themes during the nineteenth century was the English painter and illustrator John Martin, whose imagery appealed to French writers up the line from Sainte-Beuve and Victor Hugo to Huysmans. Among Martin's most popular illustrations was *Belshazzar's Feast*, one among several apocalyptic renderings that included the fall of Ninaveh, the destruction of Sodom and Gomorra, the Deluge, and the fall of Babylon, which was painted in 1819 but its imagery circulated in engravings throughout the century. So well known and admired in France was John Martin that Charles X awarded him a gold medal in 1829; later Louis Philippe honored him. Martin's engravings circulated by the thousands throughout Europe, his imagery pirated and faked to meet an enormous demand.[28]

Perhaps Veronese's orgiastic *Wedding at Cana* figured in Cézanne's venture into copying old masters in order to improve his skills. Copying was part of every young artist's education. On February 13th, 1868, he requested a student card and permission to copy pictures in the Louvre's galleries, perhaps having in mind generating some additional income from making and selling copies of religious imagery, for over the 1850s and into the 1860s, religious themes dominated the art market.[29] During the Second Empire, only about twenty percent of state art purchases were originals (over the 1850s, the government furnished thirty-two churches with copies of Proudhon's *Christ en Croix* and an equal number of his *Assomption de la Vierge*). About mid-century, plans were underway to establish a Museum of Copies in Paris, where expert copies of all the best paintings in the world would be displayed. Over the next year or two, Cézanne would paint as copies of old masters, a *Pieta* after Titian, a *Christ Descending into Limbo* after Sebastiano del Piombo, a rather Venetian *Woman with a Mirror*, and a woman in sorrow thought to be Mary Magdalene.[30]

Le Festin presents a serious problem in chronology. If Cézanne painted it in the mid-1860s, he reworked it at some point later, probably in the mid-1870s. Cézanne's floundering, his searching and inconsistencies, vulnerability to influence, offer little to the art historian in need of an evolutionary development. Over the years leading up to 1866, when some degree of consistency begins to show, John Rewald's catalogue of his lifetime production lists about fifty works: thirty-two landscapes, ten portraits, five still-lifes, one studio interior, and one mythological subject, a judgment of Paris. It would be one thing if these pictures represented a worthwhile sampling, another if they do not. And surely they don't. He painted hundreds more than the few that survived. And among the fifty that did survive are several that he did not paint. His variegated output during his early years has attracted some fanciful market-driven attributions, such as a *Lot and His Daughters* that surely Cézanne did not paint.[31]

Much of the confusion over Cézanne's early work is due to the fact that so little of it exists. He destroyed many canvases and, as most artists do, scraped down many others for re-use of the canvas. Serious artists cull ruthlessly, but they do not destroy pictures arbitrarily: infantalia may be demised at one time; at other times, certain canvases destroyed to improve the quality of one's total production; on impulse, works not fitting one's current style or mood might be slashed. On moving back and forth from Aix to Paris, or from one apartment to another in Paris, some of Cézanne's canvases may have been discarded to avoid the trouble of transporting them. We know that at times he stored canvases with Zola, at other times with Guillemet, and may not have recovered them all.[32] At times he just abandoned pictures, like a tree abandoning its fruit. George Moore, the English writer, who never met Cézanne in person, described him as a wanderer of the outskirts, *in jackboots—no one took the least interest in his paintings, so he left them in the field.*[33] It is often said that Cézanne destroyed paintings because he was subject to emotional tantrums and violently self-destructive, like a tempestuous child breaking up his toys, a frustrated housewife smashing dishes, a blocked poet tearing out his hair. Yet, to my knowledge no one has found it unusual for Zola to rip up his drafts in disgust, or feel at times like throwing his impotent pen to the floor. One can only guess how many sheets of ingratiating, syrupy poetry Zola destroyed after becoming an anti-romantic naturalist by 1864.

The color merchant Père Tanguy tells of having to hide certain pictures from

Cézanne that earlier he'd taken in exchange for pigments and not yet sold, such as a huge painting of a reclining nude, perhaps the infamous *Woman With a Flea*, and the portrait of Achille Emperaire, knowing that, should the artist get his hands on them, they would be annihilated.[34] Surely Cézanne would have trashed *The Muse's Kiss,* a copy he made in the late 1850s of the utterly insipid painting by Felix Frillié, a popular purveyor of gushy sentiment.[35] His mushy *Girl with a Parrot* is another canvas he would have destroyed had his mother not protected it.[36]

If Cézanne was self-destructive, so was everyone in his circle. Renoir decimated a canvas, *La Esmeralda*, that had been accepted and exhibited in the 1864 Salon, simply because he had decided to be more self-critical.[37] That same year, Manet cut to pieces a bullfight painting that had been accepted by the Salon jury but derided in the press.[38] After the Salon of 1865 had closed, Fantin-Latour recovered and destroyed his ambitious canvas, *Hommage à la vérité* (Homage to Truth), which critics had ridiculed. In 1866 Monet, after completing a huge canvas, *Women in a Garden*, done entirely out-of-doors and signaling a new direction, slit and hacked with a knife as many as two hundred canvases that represented his rejected past.[39] For the true artist, the road to achievement is uncertain and tortuous, with disappointments that must be brushed aside like brambles in one's path. For the happy, self-contented, complaisant dauber, picture making comes as easily as whistling.

Misattributions and forgeries are another matter, explaining in part why so few of Cézanne's pictures from the 1860s are discussed in my text. After Cézanne's death, Vollard made several trips to Aix, searching for more of Cézanne's works, approaching people to whom Cézanne may have given paintings. By then it was known in Aix that Cézanne's pictures had some value. No doubt a number of canvases that Vollard bought were promoted as by Cézanne; needing only to see that they *could be* by him, he eagerly bought them up in various states of condition and finish. Vollard felt free to trim canvases to make them look finished at the edges, if not just to fit stock frames.[40] He claimed that Tanguy had given him permission to come by his shop and cut off sections of larger canvases in order to isolate less expensive vignettes, saying Tanguy had assured him that Cézanne had intentionally prepared such canvases—*little sketches intended for collectors who could afford neither one hundred nor even forty francs.*[41] One may believe Vollard's testimony, if one wishes.

Not one of the landscape paintings attributed to Cézanne from the years 1862-1868, and only a few of the portraits, can be proven authentic by ordinary rules of evidence. Whatever may have been Cézanne's novitiate landscape style, it was shared by many painters, young and old, who worked in the manner of Millet and Rousseau, both living at the time in Barbizon village, or of Diaz de la Peña, Charles Jacque, and Corot, who frequented the area. Courbet and Daubigny also painted there on occasion, as did, in the mid-decade, Monet, Guillaumin, and dozens of other pre-Impressionists and landscape painters working in most any style, sharing motifs and a good number deploying the palette knife when painting *a la prima*, layering pigment over pigment that was still wet. In the forest and among Barbizon's picturesque rocks, as well as out in the neighboring farmland, hundreds of painters set up their easels, dotting the landscape with the broad white or green parasols needed to deflect sunlight off their pictures in process. The villages of Chailly and Marlotte at the edge of the Fontainebleau Forest southeast of Paris were also popular artists' colonies, as was the Pontoise and Auvers area north of Paris, where Pissarro, Cézanne, Guillaumin and others would paint side-by-side and from the same motifs between the years 1872 and 1874.[42] At his death in 1909, Dr. Gachet left behind stacks of canvases in his house and studio at Auvers. The fact that he and his son, also an amateur painter, copied many of Cézanne's paintings over the years, should wave a red flag over every canvas the Gachets claimed to be by Cézanne. Gachet was friendly with many run of the mill rural landscape painters in addition to Pissarro, Daubigny, Guillaume, and Corot. He was himself an amateur painter who encouraged artists to share his home, studio, and etching press.[43]

Questions of authenticity apply also to landscape paintings that present views of the *Jas de Bouffan* environs at Aix—the alley of chestnut trees, the pool, the moss and lichen-coated lions at the pool.[44] Cézanne's friends often painted with him at the *Jas* in the 1860s when Guillaumin's landscape style was no more precise than Cézanne's; like Cézanne, he and others painted under the same tutelage and influences.[45] Guillaumin had spent several weeks painting with Cézanne at the *Jas* in 1866, and Cézanne spoke admiringly of his «freer» brushwork. Off and on, the amateurs Antoine Marion and Antoine Valabrègue also painted alongside Cézanne and may have left some of their canvases at the *Jas,* to be later turned over to Vollard as by Cézanne.[46] It does not take much to convert an 1860s landscape painting into one that could be by Cézanne—intensify the greens, add a bit of red, loosen a few brushstrokes. Some of those in Rewald's catalogue display traits of Courbet, others of Daubigny, others of Corot, others of all three, and so on. Antoine Marion's *L'Eglise Saint-Jean-de-Malte* and his *Paysage prés d'Aix* would be known today as paintings by Cézanne had there not been a bit of unavoidable evidence that they were by Marion from about 1866 when he painted side by side with Cézanne. These two pictures, found in a church in Aix, were readily attributed to Cézanne but were found after cleaning to bear the initials of Antoine Marion. A related drawing that floated on the art market with Marion's initials appeared in a Paris gallery some time later with the signature erased, sold as by Cézanne.[47] The canvases *Rochers, L'Estaque* and *Mur de Jardin,* assigned by Rewald to Cézanne, could just as well be by Guillaumin or Marion or most anyone.[48]

33

What at first seems unfamiliar
or even shocking, becomes familiar

Cézanne had made an impression in Paris but as a character actor on the wobbly stage, not as an artist to be taken seriously. His half-boy, half-man condition and indecisiveness kept him in a funk. His working motto was *audaces fortuna* (good fortune befalls the audacious), but Fortuna had proved as fickle as Venus. Back in Aix with his family, he was an adolescent homebody again, emotionally regressive. He had a small studio set up in the family home. His regular companion was now Antoine Marion, the amateur painter with whom Cézanne made excursions into the countryside as he had a decade earlier with Zola and Baille. He and Marion painted side by side at times, but like Baille's, Marion's interest had drifted into science; he was studying geology, and in time would excel in that field. In a letter to his friend in Marseilles, Heinrich Morstatt, Marion says:

> *Here it is almost always the same. In the morning I work on geology; evenings I spend at Paul's in the country* [at the Jas de Bouffan]. *We dine; we take walks; we don't get drunk. All this is very sad. What a generation of sufferers, the two of us here, and so many others among us just as unhappy but with fewer troubles—Cézanne with his living secure and yet subject to the black despair of his emotional disposition.*[1]

Letters are usually written when one feels melancholic. What is «black despair» in one sentence of Marion's letter becomes in a report to Zola that their friend Cézanne was in the habit of forcing optimism to the point of being ridiculous: *He intends to make a gift of the painting of his friends conversing to the Marseilles museum—nicely framed*, Marion writes, *so the museum will thus be forced to display realist painting and our glory.* Perhaps Cézanne was now thinking of museum-type pictures, of *grands tableaux*. He also may have been thinking about how Fantin-Latour's «homages» had forced the Salon jury and the critics to confront artists they despised, hanging not from *les Buttes-Chaumont* gallows like the criminals they were, but hanging on the *Palais de l'Industrie* walls, framed in glory. Unfortunately, Cézanne did not have friends that any critic would notice. While he depended on others for encouragement (and was getting plenty of it in Aix, even from his family), as it had been in Paris, Cézanne was painting in the company of the wrong friends—not an intellect among them, not one of them a talented painter or knowledgeable critic.

As for Zola, over the second half of 1866, once again facing financial destitution, he would have to set aside all principles of literature and write short pieces to generate income. This would remove him from the small circle of serious writers with whom he'd been loosely connected. While Cézanne was short on seriousness, Zola was short on money, and obsessed with a need for notoriety. Shortly after the appearance of *Mon Salon* and *Mes Haines*, he offered yet another idea to the editor of *L'Événement*, another experiment, explained this time as a novel, not to be conceived artistically but written solely to entertain readers, serialized in easy-to-read parts, with calculated suspense at each episode. He submitted an outline. The forgiving Villemessant accepted the idea for publication. Titled *Le Voeu d'une morte* (*The Dead Woman's Wish*), the inaugural episode appeared on the first of September 1866. The project was another unfortunate adventure. Either Zola had misjudged the gutter-level of his audience or had overestimated his ability to write passionately when motivated merely to turn out words. The episodes failed to excite readers. It didn't help to sell newspapers. Villemessant confirmed the series' failure in a letter to Zola: *You asked me to be frank and let you know how the public has received your novel thus far. Here is the truth. It is thought to be colorless, well written, with good intent, but boring. Please, please stop it!*[2]

The series closed after a four-week run, far from the ending. Not one to either accept defeat or fail to publish regardless of quality, Zola recast *The Dead Woman's Wish* as a play. It was performed in Marseilles on October 5th. He also managed to have it published as a book, which appeared in November as another heap of bloody garbage thrown to the laughing hyenas. At Zola's urging, his Aixois friend Marius Roux reviewed the book in the *Memorial d'Aix* in December—Roux having become one of the newspaper's editors. To avoid having to say much about the book, Roux devoted most of his essay to the differences between a novel and the serialized story of interrupted segments that frustrate the narrative. Nonetheless, because his friendship for Zola would require at least a few positive comments, Roux obligingly defended Zola's text as a complete, well studied, strongly styled work of literature.

Also in December, the critic X. de Villarceaux allocated a few dull lines to *The Dead Woman's Wish* in his *Histoire littéraire* column. And a month later, Henry Houssaye compared this new work to *La Confession de Claude*, measuring their good and bad qualities:

> Last year, Mr. Émile Zola delivered up The Confession of Claude. This year he gives us The Dead Woman's Wish. Has he improved? Has he gotten worse? Let us not say at this time. Let his work alone be judged. The Confession's hero was depicted with dark realism;

the Dead Woman's hero is idealized to the point of abstraction. While acknowledging that Zola has the power to give life to his hero, he lacks balance in developing the analytical qualities: conception and composition. His books are essays, not novels. He sacrifices all other characters to the main one. He doesn't look for action, rather for a character, a peculiar nature to observe and render. This results in a lack of interest in the larger topic and lack of harmony in composition.[3]

Houssaye's conclusion that *The Dead Woman's Wish* was only an essay—the hero idealized to the point of abstraction—was about as acute an observation as anyone had made of Zola's pretensions to grand literature.[4] In contrast to contrived image making, non-reflective casualness had been taken by Zola as true realism, the immediately perceived and felt: reality not mediated by traditions, paintings not composed along lines of academic entraining. This approach to subject matter would necessitate a lack of interest in the larger topic and of harmony in composition. It would also confirm Zola's thesis that the artist should be indifferent to subject matter, as detached from it as a coroner from a corpse.

Zola may have been aware that the meaning of realism was undergoing a change. Three years earlier, in 1863, Jules Castagnary, a critic with philosophical sensibilities, took notice that Courbet had narrowed the meaning of realism to a concept and its associated technique—as strictly subject matter infused with social implications. Castagnary had proposed the term «naturalist» to offset the restrictive meaning of realist.[5] Zola would then shift from speaking of realists to speaking of naturalists, then of actualists. The terms cannot be made to overlap, other than that *actuality* is an aspect of *realism*—if expressed as time, the moment, a confrontation *at this instant*—or of *naturalism* if devoid of time, not immediate, vague, dense. A natural disposition confronting reality is like the farmer who is more natural than the urban dweller, but in quotidian life, both farmer and urban dweller face reality in the abstract. This modulation of terminology will surface in Zola's 1868 essay on Manet, where he announces that the *realist* Manet had arrived, his success achieved: *I hadn't dreamed it would be so quick, so worthy.* Zola then switches categorically to Pissarro and to those he called *les naturalistes* as distinct from Manet: *They form a group that grows every day. They are at the head of the modern movement in art; tomorrow one will have to reckon with them. I am selecting one of them, the least known, whose characteristic talent will serve to make known the entire group.* He has singled out Pissarro.

But Zola had a very weak idea as to which artists Pissarro would represent. His list was an aggregate constituting a *genus* rather than a *species*: Corot, Courbet, Bazille, Degas, the sisters Edma and Bertha Morisot, and Boudin. His inclusion of Degas and Corot in this group epitomized by Pissarro betrayed that no coherent theory of modern art as to style or even personality underpinned his critiques. He was ill equipped to formulate a theory of either realism or naturalism. For that

matter, perhaps no one was clear or a difference. The categories were fuzzy-edged and rapidly breaking down, as would the term «Impressionism» over the next decade. Critics and artists alike were confused between the nature of reality and the reality of nature. At no time did either term mean the same to everyone. If naturalism was once thought of as the exact and detailed appearance of non-human nature, at other times it included human nature as one's natural disposition. Naturalism then implied any system of thought that could account for the human condition without recourse to divine guidance or authority, while Realism would refer strictly to human confrontation with the natural and social—the right here, the right now. Reality as a concept was exotic and inspirational but when understood as the ultimate human condition, as the *nature* of life, then the difference between Naturalism and Realism collapsed at the same time when the notion of «the public» was changing.

To defy the officialdom of the *académie*, modernism had gone public. But the demographics of the 1860s no longer allowed one to hold in imagination a coherent notion of «the public.» What is the public, other than, to the artist, poet, and intellectual, what nature is to the farmer? The «crowd» that Zola isolated, as one of the hates he shared with Cézanne, was no longer cooperative or predictable: it was breaking up into fractions, and not every part was hostile to modern art or literature. While modernism was not yet reified, it was invading all levels of society, from the craze of flushing-toilets and newly patented latex condoms to the modernization of dairy farms and the look of the new iron-age architecture.

Zola had to admit that the public might not understand what art was all about but surely he was aware that not as many were laughing. Renoir's *Lise with a Parasol,* a portrait of his nineteen-year-old mistress Lise Tréhot, was described by one critic in an 1868 review as *a fat woman daubed with white,* but by then a good portion of the reading public was becoming immune to such tasteless slander scrawled like toilet graffiti on young artists.[6] The public, too, tends to be romantic, to defend the underdog when the oppressor displays an excess of joy in the prosecution—the whipping man gleefully laying on too many strokes; even tumbrels hauling condemned prisoners to the *Buttes-Chaumont* gallows were halted at times by mobs of law-abiding citizens who sympathized with the vanquished.

The call to let the public rather than official juries judge art issued from both a sense of democracy and Darwinian evolution. It was anti-clerical, akin to the philosophy of private enterprise and capitalism. Any official control of what the public is supposed to perceive is contrary to nature, hence to naturalism. When social control coincides with social realism, it comes up against officialdoms of all sorts. Social restraints imposed by the Church, which had been strengthened over the Second Empire (with governmental policies meant to do the same), were now being resisted in all quarters. The Descartian dualism of the material substance of contained bodies and the immaterial substance of desires and sensations was breaking down as primacy of experience. Sentiment would shift from anchorage in moribund traditions to greater faith in newness and innovation, the fundamental elements of modernism.

Napoleon III's gesture to the rejected artists—that he would allow the public to judge—may have been only a way for him to evade a pesky problem of dissidence, but it was also a tip toward what Zola would call for, a sort of universal suffrage, as in the expression, «taking it public.» Cézanne's letter of protest to Count Nieuwerkerke calling for another *Salon des Refusés* radiated the same spirit: let the public judge. The letter was also a way of saying that art should be released from dogma and allowed to flow with the current carrying society along in its modernist course. By 1865, this was the tactic artists would be obliged to enact with proposals for independent exhibitions, private sales galleries, and the promotion of private collecting nurtured by personal taste rather than official patronage that honors traditions that are motivated by historical patriotism and ancestral devotion.

The unfamiliar becomes familiar after repeated exposure just as vigilant prey becomes less wary after repeated exposure to a threat. Manet was aware that the Salon jury not only controlled what art would be exhibited but also, indirectly, the audience, the selection of what is to be shown tailored to that class of public most profitable to preservation of the academic profession. By 1867, a good segment of the public was ahead of the Academy in embracing modernism because modernism was permeating their daily lives: the telegraph, the railroad, off-the-rack clothing, tourism, and even horseracing at the new hippodrome in the *Bois de Boulogne*. Antiquity was being updated and cast aside as the city modernized. Fashions were of the day, *à la mode*. History was in the day-to-day making, promoted by the daily newspapers. Paris had become increasingly less a city of Ingres' perishing past and more one of Manet's and the painters of modern life. Tuned to this shift in the psychology of the bourgeois, magazine editors adjusted to modernity: the weekly *La Vie Moderne* would soon dominate newsstands along with the less classy *La Mode illustrée*.

A proliferation of nasty reviews, caricatures, and cartoons, inspired by the battles of will between the Salon juries and the dissidents, had brought throngs of otherwise not art-minded people to the Salon exhibitions where they had come to expect ever more daring and transgressive imagery. Hostile critics had generated an audience for Courbet's art.[7] Caricaturists had created his renown, not his qualities as an artist. The same caricaturists promoted Manet, Monet, Renoir, and yes indeed, Cézanne. This sort of publicity was yet another ingredient fomenting a gradual change in viewer demography. A few astute critics were coming around to seeing that modern art was creating its own history out of modernity itself.

On April 4th, 1867, Valabrègue sent Zola news of the Salon jury's actions:

Paul is refused, Guillemet is refused, everyone is refused. The refused would also include Pissarro, Renoir, Sisley, and Bazille. Degas was accepted. Manet had decided not to submit but to stage his own show. As had the self-propagandist Courbet, Manet took his art to the public; he erected a private pavilion at the 1867 World's Fair. As a handout, he wrote a pamphlet titled, *Reasons for Holding a Private Exhibition.* Here follows the complete text:

> *Official recognition, encouragement and prizes are, in fact, regarded as proofs of talent; the public has been informed in advance what to admire, what to avoid, according to whether the works are accepted or rejected. On the other hand, the artist is told that it is the public's spontaneous reaction to his works that makes them so unwelcome to the selection committees. In these circumstances the artist is advised to be patient and wait. But for what? Until there are no selection committees? He would be much better off if he could make direct contact with the public, and find out its reactions. Today the artist is not saying, «Come and see some perfect paintings» but «Come and see some sincere ones.»*
>
> *It is sincerity which gives to works of art a character which seems to convert them into acts of protest, when all the artist is trying to do is express his own impressions.*
>
> *Mr. Manet has never wished to protest. On the contrary, the protest, which he never expected, has been directed against himself. This is because there is a traditional way of teaching form, techniques and appreciation, and because those who have been brought up to believe in those principles will admit no others, a fact which makes them childishly intolerant. Any works not conforming to those formulae they take to be worthless; they not only arouse criticism, but also provoke hostility, even active hostility.*
>
> *To be able to exhibit is the all important thing for the artist, the sine qua non, because what happens is that, after looking at a thing for a length of time, what at first seemed unfamiliar, or even shocking, becomes familiar. Gradually it comes to be understood and accepted. Time itself imperceptibly refines and softens the apparent hardness of a picture. In his search for recognition, by exhibiting, an artist finds friends and allies.*
>
> *Mr. Manet has always recognized talent when he has seen it; he has no intention of overthrowing old methods of painting, or creating new ones. He has merely tried to be himself, and nobody else.*[8]

In response to the Salon jury's rejections, Zola drew into his expansive ego full blame for the jury's decisions: *Irritated by my Salon, the jury shut the door on anyone who has taken the new road.* A year later, he will take full credit for the opposite, for then most of the painters he'd championed would have canvases hanging in the Salon: Manet, Pissarro, Renoir, Degas, Monet, Sisley, Bazille, Morisot. Even Manet's portrait of Zola managed to get past the jury. So Zola, himself, appeared on the walls, while Cézanne' entries were again rejected.

This was the appropriate time for Zola to begin withdrawing from subversive art criticism. The Salon juries of mixed ideologies and convictions were no longer uniformly condemning deviants; as many dissident painters were being accepted as rejected. Artists whom Zola had supported would gain nothing more from assaulting art's officialdom. Better strategy was to invite public participation in their cause, as expressed in Manet's *Reasons for Holding a Private Exhibition*. Conciliatory to the public, his text invited negotiation through understanding. Now it would be up to those Zola had championed to justify their art, to prove that the struggle was worthwhile. *I interrogate the future*, Zola wrote (as if he were a reborn Horace at the death of Caesar asking which god would determine who would rule Rome and bring her to greater glory—Augustus, Lepidius, or Antony), *and ask myself whose personality will emerge broad and human enough to understand our civilization and make it artistic by interpreting it with the magisterial breadth of genius.*[9]

In truth, changes forged by the Independents, as they would come to be called in the early 1870s, had little or nothing to do with either repression of the Salon system or the nature of its reforms. The Salon had been founded on a policy that the subject matter of juried exhibitions was to be public matter, like books in a public library or trees and fountains in a public park—historical personages and themes, biblical stories and subjects, representations of classical heroes, epic events, and universal myths. The function of public art was to offer delight and give consent to sublimation, to bring the common man up to a higher level of culture. Changes in the conduct of the Salon were not the result of assaults by a handful of artists whose names have come down to us as the avantgarde. Like the Chambre des Deputies, the Institute had been assaulted one way or the other since its inception. The stability of government depends on minimum change in its constitution and institutional functions. As a governing institution, the Salon's conduct would never change. What opened the Salon to «independent» artists was not the art of those few that history records, but the massive number of painters that were moving off from institutional criteria. Art of the sort that Cézanne identified with would have to become increasingly private, move away from the public in order to generate its own audience within the mass, like books that find their own readership.

Claude Monet, Camille (Woman in a Green Dress).
Salon of 1866. Bremen, Kunsthalle.

34

Monet would now have his first success at the 1866 Salon with *Camille: La Femme au robe verte* (Camille: Woman in a Green Dress). This event would cause a rupture in Cézanne's friendship with Zola. Monet's success represented a shift in how critics were responding to the avant-garde. Zola went all out in praise of it.

Cézanne was not participating in this shift. For all its audacity his *L'Enlèvement* was still mired in academic silt, and his lost *Le Vidangeur* and *Femme à la puce* were—presumably, in that they do not exist—crude apparitions of old fashioned genre painting emptied of charm. He hadn't yet learned that modernism was not simply perversion of the traditional or defiance of decorum.

In 1868, Cézanne may have begun feeling that, although still a friend, Zola was abandoning him as an artist. Now Monet was someone he should start measuring up to, not just Manet. Attraction to Monet's *Woman in a Green Dress* continued long after the exhibition. Zola favored the painting in his *Mon Salon* column of *L'Événement* on May 11th, 1866, and when he reprinted this review two years later, on May 24th, 1868, in his column *Mon Salon, les actualistes,* in *L'Événement illustré*, he would heightened his praise: *Look at the dress. It is both supple and solid. It trails softly behind her, it is alive, it says beyond anything else: This is a woman. It is not the dress of a doll, one of those muslin chiffons worn in dreams.*

Cézanne may have taken Zola's compliments of Monet's picture as indirect criticism of himself. The gauzy muslin chiffon of dreams, referred to so negatively by Zola, had appeared in Cézanne's pictures of nymphs from the mid-1860s. Zola's reference to Camille's dress as *not the dress of a doll* may have punctured Cézanne's thoughts about his picture of Rose reading to her doll. Zola had referred to Monet as a real man among eunuchs. *Look at the works all around Monet's*, Zola said, *and notice how crestfallen and pitiful they look alongside this window opened on nature. Monet is more than a realist; he is an interpreter both delicate and forceful.* Surely Cézanne was aware by this time that he was not opening a window on nature, as the true realists were. He was still trying to force romanticism onto reality. Even when painting a landscape, he seemed reluctant to accept nature as natural, and unlike Monet, he was not «both delicate and forceful,» just forceful.

In retrospect, Monet's picture was less art that clothing fashion. Baudelaire's symbols of modernity had focused on attire: *That man who manages to snatch the epic side of modern life and make us see and realize, by means of painting or drawing, how great and poetic we are in our cravats and polished boots, will be the true painter. May those who truly seek give us next year that rare delight of greeting the advent of newness.*[1] Baudelaire's words sound trivial when set beside Zola's altruistic socialism that embraced the whole of humankind and the harsh truths of the modern world—not novelties or newness of dress and manners as Baudelaire advocated, but the day-to-day advance of social reality, with modernism overlaying, when not overtaking, expiring social values.[2] Baudelaire's cravats and polished boots were, nonetheless, potent symbols of modernity. Black attire clearly distinguished the bourgeois urban male from the rural peasant and common urban worker. Men who moved to the city from farms or hamlets, wanting to blend with the urban bourgeois, had to shed their country traits and appearance. Adoption of black clothing—trousers black or gray or pin-striped, black frock cloaks and capes, black umbrellas and top hats, black cravats and boots—eradicated the dry grass ochres and bare earth tones of peasantry. As Paris modernized under Baron Haussmann's enterprise, the city's blend of the urban and the rural at its periphery gradually gave way to a greater demarcation of the two orders—the country mouse remaining gray. Montmartre had fingers of rural land penetrating it. Painters could walk to the countryside. When living there, Zola maintained a vegetable garden and a coop of chickens.

T. J. Clark pointed out in his study of Courbet that a certain tension is enacted between urban and rural identity when urban consciousness is heightened by industrial progress and modernization, when the presence of the country *inside* the town became no longer a simple, accepted matter of fact.[3] As for the urban public's reaction to Courbet's paintings of about 1850, Clark wrote:

> *It tells us that cities evolve in a complex and ambiguous way, that men assert an urban identity—call themselves, decisively, citizens or bourgeois—often against the facts. They made sharp distinctions where in fact the edges are blurred; they conceive of the city as separate from the countryside; they conceive of the countryside as different in every way from the city. They find it offensive and dangerous to be told, or shown* [by artists] *the way in which town and country touch, interpenetrate, have classes and institutions in common, imitate each other. Their identity depends on the difference. To be bourgeois, they need a vague but vivid world they have lost or rejected. They need an image of rural society in a way that the countryman or the small-town dweller does not. And if they are faced with an image which contradicts these preconceptions, they are liable to be perplexed and wounded in ways they do not themselves fully understand.*[4]

Whether among birds or people the most impressive pointer to one's identity is the plumage of the individual fitted to a classification. In earlier times, public dress expressed continuity of the past with the present, while not distinguishing the present from the future. To be modern meant to dress for the now, in the mode of the now. Class differentiation had been largely displayed by clothing, from royalty to peasants. By Paris' mid-century, fashion *à la classe* was augmented by fashion *à la mode*. Women's fashions became symbols of urban sophistication, persuasive expressions of modernism. Each season women bought attire that would assert their personality (call it their *tempérament*). At its extreme, this motivation to articulate one's self from the generic populace gave rise to *haute couture*, apparel made strictly for one client and not copied as ready-to-wear. By the 1860s, the economics of women's dress depended on the annual renewal and update of fashion. For women of the higher social class, attire was no longer made to last but to wear for a season and be handed down to the lower classes, consistent with the long tradition of royalty setting the example for the populace, like the trickle-down systems of economics. Only women with wealth could afford to be original, and thus make the vogue; all others had to imitate what was in vogue in order to be *à la mode*. To dress *à la mode* meant to look *of the moment*, like the *now* of realist art.

Not until 1850 did a single shop exist in Paris that both sold cloth and undertook dress-making, making it possible on the same premises for women to choose textures, patterns, colors, be measured, and have a garment made to order that would fit the shape of their bodies. Other dressmakers soon joined the proprietor of this entrepreneurial venture, a Madame Roger, of whom little is known. Some 500 couturiers were operating in Paris by the mid-sixties; some 12,500 workers were employed in the corset industry. The treadle-powered sewing machine was to modern fashion what the rotary printing press was to literature and journalism. Both made it possible for events of the moment to register in the now. Modern art, literature, and criticism emerged during these decades alongside modern fashion. Acceptance of fashion as an abstract system required that fashions change—if only because the principle of fashion mandates change; fashion is always bracketed by time and place. Fascinated by the notion that fashion propelled literature, Stéphane Mallarmé, a great admirer of Zola, would found in 1874 a women's fashion journal *La Dernière Mode: Gazette du mode et de la famille*. It had a short life, September to December, with Mallarmé doing all the writing under several pseudonyms, linking criticism directly with what was *à la mode*: toiletries, jewelry, furniture, on to theater productions and dining menus—all reducible to guidelines for how to seduce a woman, which connected the *à la mode* all the more exuberantly with the aesthetics of art as still infused with feminine aesthetics.[5]

While realism that always verged on decadence gave art appreciation as erotic charge, naturalism would de-feminize aesthetics. The perfumy, sensually feminine landscapes of the eighteenth-century Rococo Boucher and Fragonard were not the natural of mid-nineteenth-century naturalism. Art would be less a matter of seduction than of confrontation. Following Flaubert's lead, Zola's and the Goncourt's de-aestheticizing of the novel reduced seduction to elementary, animal-like sex, an entwining of natural instinct with pellucid realism, like Manet's *Olympia* as a woman who could not be seduced but had for a price. The contrast of the social classes, as between worker-rustic and urban bourgeois, was not as much in the artwork's subject matter as in the relationship of imagery to the viewer who provided the contrasting class. Behind the abstract principle of fashion was the principle of motion—society in motion, superbly illustrated by Balzac's *Peau de chagrin*, a shrinking wild ass' skin. Even a physicist with his powerful machines could not halt the process by stretching it. Balzac speaks:

> *Everything is movement. Thought is movement. Life is based on movement. Death is a movement at which the end escapes us. That is why movement, like God, is inexplicable. Like him, it is profound, without limit, incomprehensible, intangible. Who has ever touched, comprehended, or measured movement? We can feel its effects without seeing them. We can even deny movement, as we deny God. Where is it? Where isn't it? Whence does it come? What is its principle, its end? It envelops us, presses upon us, and escapes us. It is evident like a fact, obscure like an abstraction. Effect and cause all at once. It requires a space as we do. But what is space? Only movement reveals it to us. Without movement there is nothing but a world without sense.*

Baudelaire, to repeat, had had much to say about women's fashions as signs of modernity—by definition transient, in motion:

> *It is easier to say that everything about the garments of a period is absolutely ugly than to apply oneself to the extraction of their mysterious beauty. Modernity is the transitory, the fugitive, the contingent, one half of which is art, the other half the eternal and the immutable.*[6]

Here one encounters the fundamental formula allowing art to be at all times art while being at all times modern, that is, both eternal and transitory. Baudelaire continues:

> *Every painter through the ages was, in his time, modern; most of the beautiful personages in portraits preserved from previous days are dressed in the vestments of their period. They are perfectly harmonious because the costume, the headdress, and even the gesture, the glance, and the smile constitute the whole of a complete variety. This transitory, fugitive element, the metamorphoses of which are so frequent, one has no right to despise or do without. By suppressing it, one forcibly tumbles into the emptiness of an abstract and indefinable beauty.*

In the Parisian newspaper *L'Ordre,* Champfleury had written a review of Courbet's 1850 show in Dijon where Courbet showed his *Stonebreakers* and the just completed *Burial at Ornans*. In the latter, clothing worn by the participants at the burial grounds is singled out as the sign of modernism. Identifying with Baudelaire in this respect, Champfleury wrote:

> *Is it not yet time to say what impression these pictures will make—these scenes of domestic life, as large as history painting, where the author has not flinched from painting a full-length portrait of the modern bourgeoisie in well-brushed provincial costume.*
>
> *Mr. Courbet has understood that painting must not deceive future centuries about the way we dressed. But all the same, has not this much abused garb its own beauty and its own native charm? Is it not the necessary garb of our suffering age, which wears the symbol of perpetual mourning? Note, too, that the dress-coat and the frockcoat not only possess their political beauty, which is an expression of universal equality, but also their poetic beauty, which is an expression of the public soul.*[7]

Against this background, press reaction to Monet's first critical success makes more sense. His *Woman in a Green Dress* had considerable coverage and was admired by critics that counted rather than ridiculed by those who didn't. Théophile Thoré singled it out for praise, adding, for no particular reason other than timeliness perhaps, that Monet had painted the picture in just four days, finishing it the day before the Salon deadline for submittals. Thoré described the picture as *a grand portrait of a woman standing, seen from the back, trailing a magnificent dress of green silk, flashing like the fabrics of Paul Veronese.*[8] Zacharie Astruc gave it a place beside both Manet's *Olympia* and Renoir's *Lise* as high points in the progress of painting toward modern realism.[9] Still, the canvas did not escape Paris' most popular satirists, Gill and Bertall, who recognized unsympathetically its departure from traditional full-figure portraiture and for being more a painting of a dress than a portrait of a woman. On the 12th of May, the day after Zola's review, Bertall placed a caricature of the painting in *Le Journal amusant*. The following day, Gill's caricature of *Camille*, illustrating his *Le Salon pour rire* (Salon for laughs), appeared in *La Hune*.

Fashion plates were useful to artists as examples of clothing types, especially as models for the painting of fabrics. *La Mode illustrée* and the equally popular magazine *L'Illustration des dames* employed highly skilled illustrators of women's wear and accessories; the commercial drawings were prepared for printing by equally skilled engravers. Skill in rendering fabric had always been the high watermark of a painter's rise to competence. In Couture's studio, Manet must have undergone hours of fabric painting—a featured aesthetic of his *Balcony* of 1869 (Berthe Morisot the model) and the portrait of Eva Gonzalès of 1870. Perhaps the only student Manet had in his studio was the twenty-year-old Gonzalès. Among the pointers he gave her was how to convincingly paint fabrics: *The folds will establish themselves*, he told her, *if you place them where they belong. Oh! Mr. Ingres, he was so strong! We are only children. He knew how to paint fabrics!*[10] Vollard quotes

Cézanne as saying almost the same thing. He tells of Cézanne encountering Jean-Louis Forain in the café *Nouvelle Athènes*. After remarking that Forain was very young, Cézanne says, *The bloke, he already knew how to indicate folds in a garment.*[11]

Monet's display of skill in rendering the elegant dress of Camille and of his patroness Madame Gaudibert in the full-length portrait of her from 1868 suggests he'd spent many hours studying and practicing representations of folds, bends, pleating, gathering, stitching, and the play of shading and highlighting that commercial engravers had perfected. Surely these women didn't pose dressed as they appear over the time it took Monet to execute the paintings. And even if Monet had the costumes in his studio to work from—even renting women's garments for such use, as he did on occasion—he would have depended on fashion engravings to achieve such near-flawless execution.

Renoir too would at last achieve critical success with his portrait of Lise, another full-length woman in fashionable dress. On June 23rd, 1868, the journalist critic Marius Chaumelin in *La Presse* wrote of this picture: *Édouard Manet is already a master apparently, since he has some imitators, amongst which must be included Mr. Renoir, who has painted, under the title «Lise,» a woman of natural grandeur walking in the park. This painting has captured the attention of connoisseurs, as much by the strangeness of effect as by the justness of its tonalities. This is what, in the language of the Realists, is called «a fine touch of color.»*

Lise was a modernist nymph in a wood. A lengthy and supportive review of *Lise*, published by Zacharie Astruc a few days after Chaumelin's, on June 27th in *L'Étendard*, aligned this picture with milestones in the track of modern painting while letting the Salon jurists know that modernism was advancing in spite of efforts to suppress it. The official resistance had remained a popular issue, beamed to the public by a rash of newspapers competing tooth and nail to garner the readers' emotions. Astruc wrote:

> The «Lise» of Mr. Renoir completes an odd trinity that started with the very strange, expressive, and notorious «Olympia.» In the wake of Manet, Monet was soon to create his «Camille,» the young girl in green dress putting on her gloves. Here now is «Lise,» the most demure. Here we confront the charming Parisian girl in the Bois, alert, mocking, and laughing, playing the «grande dame,» with a touch of gaucherie savoring the shade of the wood for all the diversions that may be found there: the dancing, the open-air café, the fashionable restaurant, the amusing dining room fashioned from a distorted tree. Let us praise this joyful canvas made by a painter with a future, an observer as responsive to the picturesque as he is careful of reality. The painting deserves to be singled out. By an inconceivable error, which I would prefer to think of as ignorance, she has suffered the fate of the rejected works [meaning, in this case, not awarded a prize]. At the Salon, with its array of marketable objects, such work stands out by its art, its taste and exceptional character, which commands our attention and deserves our study. This was obvious to all the painters, but not to the jury.

Two paintings featuring young women in a garden setting dressed *à la mode* that Cézanne would have done while in Aix at the Jas de Bouffan now come to the foreground within this framework for the realism that will soon characterize Impressionism. The women are not *real* women in a *real* garden, such as Monet had painted earlier, for even at this date, around 1869-71, Cézanne seems not yet prepared to address reality in the manner of either Monet or Manet.[12] The imagery on the canvas illustrated here is copied from a fashion plate out of *La Mode illustrée*, the *Vogue Magazine* of Cézanne's day.[13]

A handy explanation for such out-of-character canvases might be that he painted them as gifts for his sisters, who most likely subscribed to *La*

Auguste Renoir. Lise with a parasol. 1867. Museum Folkwang, Essen.

Cézanne. *La Conversation.* Copied from a plate in *La Mode illustré*, July 31, 1870. Private collection. Photo: Gallerie Berheim-Jeune.

Mode. Pictures by him were hanging throughout the house. More likely, Monet's success with *Camille,* and the attention given to Manet and Renoir's rendering of fabrics, prompted Cézanne to study women's fashions and practice painting fabrics. By 1870, he must have admitted to himself that his painting lacked skill. He was still struggling to be modern while resisting skill, as if skillful rendering signaled commercial art and capitulation to academic criteria. One recalls Zola's letter of March 3rd, 1860 warning Cézanne, still in Aix, about commercial art and also art that lacked poetry: *Art is much more sublime; it is not satisfied with the folds of a fabric, with the rosy skin of a young woman,* and so on. But by 1868 Zola had changed his mind about many things.

35

Apathetic, colorless, academic,
painstakingly executed, nonetheless
highly successful products

A round 1868, the artists most affected by the demographic shift in the art establishment were phasing variably and unevenly into another stage of maturity. Even Manet, whose family wealth supported him in comfort, would say this year, *I want to make money.* Still in dire financial straits, Monet settled into a phase of intense seriousness, as did Renoir. *At the Salon, I ran into Monet,* said Boudin joyfully in a May 4th letter to a friend. *He gives us all a fine example of the tenacity of his principles.*[1] This maturing mood of seriousness will settle on the minds of Zola and Cézanne, too.

I only have the company of painters. There is not one writer here with whom I can talk. Zola had confessed to this quandary in a letter to Valabrègue of February 19th, 1867. A lonely writer with negative notoriety, admired by no one of professional importance, he was indeed without literary friends. The only ones he could count on were mediocre talents, such as Valabrègue and Roux in Aix. The same plight had befallen Cézanne. To this point, neither he nor Zola had produced work weighty enough to magnetize attention from anyone competent to judge artistic or literary quality. Zola had provoked most of the writers and could not count on painters he'd defended as being more than appreciative friends, for there was nothing in his writing that a Manet or even a Monet would esteem as literature, nor were Cézanne's paintings more than testimonies of his being, at best, an engaging and amusing personality.

True to character, in his February 19th letter, Zola offsets his depression and infirmity by bolstering his sickbed, giving advice, taking charge of the fate of others as he had of Cézanne's in their exchange of youthful letters:

My dear Valabrègue,

Just a few words in my rush, so you can't blame me for being lazy or neglectful. I want to comment on a few passages in your last letter.

I absolutely do not doubt you, and I cannot recall what you consider your classical beginnings. As friend and bystander, I see the transformations you are undergoing. I'm *waiting for your first work to classify you in my mind, to arrive at an opinion about you. I know you are a researcher, you think straight, you are young, the future belongs to you. As you can see, I have a lot of respect for you, and you are wrong when you doubt my friendship and my applause. My faith matters to me. You defend yourself vigorously while treating me as a skeptic in your last letter.*

I will hide nothing from you: I have always believed that your life was too contemplative. I would like to see you be more active. At your age, blood beats through the flesh, fever plunders the body. Works made from experienced events have always been superior to works merely dreamt. Admit that you dream yours: the long explanations you sent me about your «Passages d'automne» (Autumn landscapes) proves you are a contemplative person after all. I won't deny that I would have preferred to see you among us, fighting as we do, every day kicking to the right and kicking to the left, always going forward. All paths are good; the path you have chosen may suit your character. My wishes for you may only be egoistic advice dictated by my own nature.

I had hoped to see you at my side. I only have the company of painters; there is not one writer here with whom I can talk. I told myself we would advance together and support each other. And here you are, letting me go it alone, fight alone, triumph and succumb alone. Sometimes, when I think of you, I think: He is falling asleep. Believe me, this is a spontaneous thought that must elude me against my will! Come back with a book, grab life, fight, and you will see I am the first to encourage and applaud you.

When do you arrive? You said March, I believe. Let's say April or May? In your next letter, let me know the date, if possible. Now, if you don't come to fully partake in the fight, it would be better to stay in Aix until the day you believe you are mature enough to put up a fight. Don't forget to bring your landscape book. I am very curious to learn what you have included in it.

Should I tell you a little bit about myself? You must have heard that I am going to begin writing a long work for Le Messager de Provence published in Marseilles. Starting on March 1st, I will publish a long novel: Les Mystères de Marseilles, based on the minutes of recent and important criminal trials. I'm overwhelmed with documents and I don't know yet how I will extract a whole world out of this chaos. This task pays little, but I expect loud repercussions in the Midi. It doesn't hurt to have a whole region on your side. Besides, I have accepted the offers that were made to me, pushed forward by this will to work and fight that I mentioned earlier.

I love difficulties, impossibilities. I love life above all, and I believe that work, whatever it might be, is always better than rest. These beliefs will push me to accept all the fights I might come up against, fights against myself, fights against the public. I was told that the advertisement of Les Mystères de Marseilles created some reactions down there. Flyers will be passed around, posters will be displayed. If you hear something said about my novel, would you let me know?

Paul works a lot, he has already finished several paintings and he dreams of immense canvasses; I shake your hand in his name.

Baille progresses rapidly. His career is soaring, no doubt. Guillemet awaits summer to start a new campaign. Solari got married four days ago. I conclude with all this monumental news, and shake your hand with affection. Gabrielle [Zola's girlfriend Alexandrine Meley, who for a while used the name Gabrielle] *asks me to say hello.*

Zola's *Les Mystères de Marseilles* was patterned after Eugène Sue's celebrated *Mystères de Paris* published in 1842. By now, Zola had transformed himself into a writing machine, a mechanical author. Like a single-piston engine he could knock out seven to eight pages an hour as long as he sustained the beat. The subject matter of *Les Mystères de Marseilles* was enriched fuel for mechanical writing—inflamed appetites, financial crimes, the thirst of the powerful for more power, and the sensual pleasures that animated the city. It was his first social history. The novel opens expectedly with an unequal relationship between the sexes, each sex representing a social category: Philippe Cayrol, a handsome young republican of the *petite bourgeoisie* seduces Blanche de Cazalis, the niece of the very rich and powerful *haute-bourgeois* deputy of Marseilles. Soon pregnant, Blanche flees with Philippe. They are pursued, arrested, and Philippe is condemned to five years in prison. From then on the story builds over a few years towards a duel that brings Philippe to his death; his protagonist Cazalis (Blanche's uncle) has no time, however, to relish victory, for he and his vile colleagues are struck with cholera, while the good people in the novel move on to enjoy a long and prosperous life.[2]

Journalism, publications in newspapers, had been Zola's only source of income to date. So while backing off from art criticism, he would now find it necessary to expand his cause beyond artists and writers to take in politics and social issues. In January 1868, he found employment with a socialist newspaper, *Le Globe*, which had joined dozens of new journals in kiosks, feeding on France's social ills, bank failures, the sudden halt of Haussmann's overhaul of the city, which left 100,000 workers unemployed. And apprehension over the ambitions of Prussia, which two years earlier had crushed Austria and dispirited Napoleon, was blurring eyes then fixed on restoring France's legacy of territory to the eastern bank of the Rhine.[3] After several years of near excessive prosperity, in 1867 France fell into another economic slump, while an entire Europe feared the reunification of the German empire. Within France, anti-royalist sentiment was becoming not just a threat, but as modern and fashionable as Baudelaire's cravats and polished boots. Not until 1871, however, would war with Prussia shake up the entire government of France and bring down yet another Napoleon.

Le Globe survived for hardly a month but had given Zola a platform for espousing political views through the pretext of reviewing books and plays—true to his dictum that art is a negation of society, an affirmation of the individual outside all rules and social imperatives. His reviews, which defended naturalism, carped on the same issue—that the true must vanquish the fanciful. And about this time he proclaimed that all supernatural phenomena must be de-mystified; free minds must discover what lays behind the ecstasies of Saint Theresa and Léonie the somnambulist; novelists and especially playwrights should dramatize life in its reality, with all the virtues and vices that one encounters on the streets.[4]

Zola wouldn't have known that the naturalism he espoused would justify literature being published in newspapers and magazines, for it was not just a literature of ordinary life but literature written for those who lived ordinary lives. The further one descends down the social ladder, the closer one gets to basic reality, for higher orders of society are elaboration on reality—embellished, ornamented, institutionalized. Every runged ladder rests on the ground of being, on dirt. What can be more natural than dirt? *La vie en-bas est sale*—low life is dirty. Unfortunately *Le Globe's* publisher Mille-Noé was more adept at rabble-rousing than running a business. After the newspaper folded, Zola searched for other employment. By April (1868) he had received an offer from the publisher of a cheap daily, *L'Événement illustré* that had superseded *L'Événement*. He was asked to write art reviews. Knowing Zola's reputation, the editor reserved the right to follow up with reviews by others of a different mind.

Zola agreed to write in generalities and not insult anyone by name. Forbidden to write ill of specific artists he hated, his acrimony and sarcasm were constrained, which allowed more lines of support for artists who'd been accepted by a more lenient jury that year—artists the Salon visitors would otherwise have passed by with little notice: Pissarro, Jongkind, Renoir, Bazille, Monet. Not once did Zola mention Cézanne. Perhaps by this time he had concluded that his dearest friend was not the painter he'd so promiscuously promoted. In any case, Cézanne's paintings offered so little to talk about in the context of Zola's thoughts at this time, which were more political and social, anti-Bonaparte and anti-Church, than about aesthetics. Zola preferred even such banalities as his childhood friend Philippe Solari's large sculpture, *Nègre endormie*, about which he had written in *Le Globe, Solari has put behind him the dream of absolute beauty, he does not carve idols for a religion.*

It was less his harsh criticism of the Salon jury that was turning the tide as the sociology of the tide waters washing over old shores. Most of the harshness of so-called avant-garde art and literature was being ameliorated by imitators who moderated between being modern and remaining traditional. Intellectuals less concerned with reality than with social philosophy had softened the hard edges of radical socialism. A vote of deputies on the 9th of March 1868 relaxed the government's restrictions on the press, resulting in a flood of new newspapers. That year, Daumier illustrated the proliferation of street and kiosk journalism with a cartoon titled *La grande marée de 1868* (Spring tide of 1868), which depicted a man struggling through raging surf of newspaper sheets. Lamenting in a let-

ter to Valabrègue of May 29th, 1868, Zola complained: *There are many new newspapers in the air, and I am trying to get a stable position in one of them. My biggest problem is
being twenty-seven years old; if I were fifty, barely alive, bored and fed up with life, I would have
already found a steady position in journalism with an income of ten thousand francs a year.*

Zola's excuse of being too young to succeed in journalism fell short of reality. Even at the age of twenty-five he had been getting his reviews published. Had
he been less caustic, he might still be writing his columns. As for the bored and
barely alive journalists to whom he refers, they were aging beyond their fifties and
making way like winter for the springing of a new generation that would support
younger artists and writers. Over twenty years had passed since twenty-five-year-
old Baudelaire had written that *a great tradition had been lost and a new one not yet
formed.*[5] For a while, Baudelaire thought he had found it in Delacroix, who proved
too romantic and exotic. Courbet he found too crude and materialistic. In Manet's
art, Baudelaire may have felt groundswells, but there would be no new great tradition. Society was no longer cohesive. Great traditions come about only when
fashioned by the mechanics of great and stable societies. Odilon Redon, not yet
established as a painter in the 1860s, was the same age as Zola when he published
his own *Salon of 1868* in which he said: *We are witnessing the end of an old school, just-
ly condemned, while here and there some forceful personalities try to impose themselves.*[6]

While the Gautier-Goncourt days would soon be over, the undercurrent of
Baudelaire's thoughts had seeped into Zola's, particularly his precepts on the sociology of aesthetics: the quality of art as no longer a universal beauty but a different beauty for each culture and each individual. If Darwinian theory had split
the *vrai* from the *beau*, truth from beauty, then, for minds like Zola's, truth was no
longer beauty, and art could answer only to truth, which resides not with the adju-
dicator but with the individual. *The true artist, the true poet*, Baudelaire had written
in his *Salon* of 1859, *should only paint what he sees and what he feels. He must be realisti-
cally faithful to his own nature—his products in relation to himself and not to some so-called
reality.*[7] The sociological matching to this proclamation would be the Goncourt's
call for a new history, a social history of private life, with the historian's raw material not found in academic chronicles, war annals, and government archives but in
newspapers, novels, and paintings.[8] Baudelaire died in 1867. With him went the
esoteric aspect of *art for art's sake* as promoted by the likes of Gautier, Flaubert,
and the brothers Goncourt. The respected Gautier had declared back in 1835 that
art should serve no other purpose than its own aesthetic.[9] And the Goncourts in
the 1860s would insist that painting exists solely to delight the eye and the senses, and that artists should not aspire to beyond stimulating the optic nerve.[10] But
these were contractions and generalizations—alternative ways of looking at subject matter and pictorial relatedness of imagery to life.

The doctrine of being faithful to one's own nature—by the mid-1860s fairly
widespread—appealed to the young who typically regarded the world of their

parents as an homogenous reality, classified as the *bourgeoisie*, the Establishment, even as «the society» of which the young were not yet a part—what Baudelaire had described as *that vast, impersonal and monotonous unity, as immense as boredom, effacing variety from life.* Baudelaire had called for individuals to evade the consolidating rules of the school in order to produce the *ever new.*[11] One recalls Zola saying of his school days: *The machine functioned, and it works today in much the same way I imagine our forefathers were taught. Rambling around in the teachers' cold heads were three of four ideas made to suffice from October to July. Like horses in a riding academy, they turn in the same circle.*[12] And in this sense, the young Baudelaire was like any adolescent who suffers under the rules of dominating parents or schoolmasters—being homogenized, one's individuality being trimmed off so one will fit to the shape of society.

The shock of surprise, which is one of the great joys produced by art and literature, is due to this variety of individual types and sensation—to temperaments, Baudelaire had said, and what Zola took up as his organizing principle of criticism—what Cézanne had deployed in defense of individuality: the shock of surprise, of non-conformity, even when expressing it only through shocking subject matter.[13] The shock of surprise can only be experienced in the now, though at times only vicariously, as Manet surely had in mind when painting his *Nymph Surprised*—the shock of surprise, forcing the viewer into the position of the nymph's encounterer—and the surprises he had given the Salon visitors with his *Déjeuner sur l'herbe* and *Olympia,* forcing an encounter with art.

Viewing nymphs or geographically displaced naked women, such as ancient Greek slave women, or Turkish harem women, allows for the beholder's sexual responses to remain internalized, within the viewer, just as the female imagery stays within the pictorial context—back in ancient Greece, far off in Turkey, at a safe distance. Manet's *Olympia* and the woman in the *Déjeuner* force the viewer to project his responses outside himself, just as the women in both pictures project their attention outward to engage the viewer. Of Gérôme's *Trial of Phryne*, Zola had this to say:

> First, the artist will choose the dramatic moment when in defense of Phryne the lawyer thinks it will suffice to undress her. This female body, so prettily posed, will make a nice centerpiece for the picture. But that's not enough! The nakedness must be underlined by making the «courtesan» react with shocked modesty, by giving her a gesture like that of a little modern mistress surprised while changing her chemise.[14]

Redon was among the first to associate «the real moment» with «the impression» as the non-contemplative «immediately felt.» He had focused first on Corot, then on Daubigny, whom he called *the painter of a moment, of an impression.*[15] This notion of the moment (the *maintenant*) was fairly widespread by the 1860s. Sometimes emphasis on the *now* is credited to Hippolyte Taine, whose *Histoire de la littérature anglaise* was published by Hachette in 1864 and his *Philosophie de l'art* in 1865. Perhaps these books did have special meaning for Zola. Taine proposed that all schools of art are the product of a set of circumstances dominated by heredity, environment, and moment of time (*race, milieu, moment*).[16] The idea of unique temperament as, in part, inherited, and the moment of time as a «now in motion,» would help Zola formulate the structure for his *Rougon-Macquart* series of novels that track heredities, but the formula Taine proffered was simply an abstraction of evolutionary notions that had fed Darwin's theories.

On March 2nd, 1866, Taine wrote to thank Zola for an article Zola had sent along to show what a great influence Taine's writing had been on him:

> *Dear Sir,*
>
> *There are five or six pages at the beginning that I am proud to have occasioned. Thank you very much.*
>
> *When a man is born he brings into the world his own soul, his distinct personality. The more intensely, the more completely this personality reveals itself, the greater in proportion his work will be. But since he belongs to a race, the characteristic features of his soul are also found in the other men of the same race. In the long run, the sum of physiological forces develops the constituent qualities that define this race, producing a high proportion of men called great men. Therefore, Individuality is itself produced according to certain rules. This is Darwin's law. The external milieus, education, the prevailing pressures, develop all the great individuals in this fashion.*[17]

It is risky to pinpoint *first* instances and *direct* influences—as, for example, who was the first to conceive of *the art of the now*—especially during periods of rapid social, ideological, and philosophical change, when ideas are as lively in the air as insects. No one can ever know the originary use of *tempérament* to describe the artist's personality as represented and manifested by his art. And everyone should admit that it's easier to find sources in an outside reference, such as a book, than to search for relevant meaning while sustaining a state of openness and uncertainty. Daubigny was indeed a painter of the moment, but more than that, he was a man of the hour all along the early trail of modern painting. The frustrated Superintendent of Fine Arts, Nieuwerkerke, blamed Daubigny as a Salon jurist for intervening in the selection process, for opening the door to so many young newcomers who were assaulting the status quo and permitting youth to bring art up to date while ignoring traditions. Daubigny was fifty-one in 1868, a modest painter who remained true to the appearance of landscape—perhaps the most influential advocate for painting out-of-doors. A medal winner in 1867, having won several such honors before, he was a strong voice on the jury with no fear whatsoever that a surge of young artists would lessen the integrity of French painting. Castagnary, in his *Salon de 1868*, tipped his hat to Daubigny:

> *If the Salon this year is what it is, a Salon of newcomers; if the doors have opened to*

almost all who present themselves; if it contains 1,378 more items than last year's Salon; if, in this abundance of paintings, official art cuts a rather poor figure, it is Daubigny's doing. I don't know if Daubigny did all that Mr. de Nieuwerkerke says he did, but I shall gladly believe he did, because Mr. Daubigny is not only a great artist but also a fine man who remembers the miseries of his youth and would like to spare others the ordeals he himself underwent.[18]

Zola: «Now let me finish my novel on springtime: *A pile of manure steaming in a sewer.*»
Alexis: «What about the woods, the flowers, the sunshine?»
Zola: «That sort of springtime won't do anymore. It doesn't make money»

One of many newspaper cartoons featuring Zola the naturalist.

The poet and critic, Théophile Gautier, also fifty-one that year, who hadn't had much of anything good to say since 1861 when he managed to admire a picture by Manet, had to admit, after viewing the 1868 Salon, that, for each age of one's life, one understands only what is contemporaneous—art which is twenty when one is, oneself, twenty. *Confronted with these startling examples of new art, one must consider that paintings by Monet and Manet, and tutti quanti, contain much that escapes one when at an older age than the art one is confronting.*[19] (In like spirit, Zola will plea to editor Arsène Houssaye when promoting his *Thérèse Raquin, You are, I believe, the editor I need, young and open-minded, an unselfish lover of all exciting things*). Perhaps important, too, for promoting this attitude were such publications as the Goncourt brothers' 1867 novel, *Manette Salomon*, in which the principal characters are artists, one of whom recites a pithy statement about the congruity of the viewer's age with the prevailing qualities of the art being viewed:

> *All ages carry within themselves a Beauty of some kind or another, capable of being grasped and developed. It is possible that the Beauty of today is covered over, buried; to find it one needs analysis, a magnifying glass, new psychological processes. The intuitive feelings for the contemporary, for painting that rubs shoulders with you, for the present in which you sense the trembling of your emotions, and something of yourself—everything of this is there for the artist to use.*[20]

Seen from all angles, the aging of establishment figures was a significant ingredient in the mix of reasons for the avant-garde gaining acceptance. Like stones in the path of progress, the old men of oppositional influence were wearing down, losing their sharp edges and sharp tongues. The November 1863 reforms, imposed by imperial decree on the Institute of Fine Arts following the debacle of the *Salon des Refusés*, had abolished the Institute's supervision of the *École des Beaux-Arts* and lowered the minimum age of applicants for the *Prix de*

—»J'envoie des photographies du pays à M. Zola, pour lui prover qu'il y a aussi des fleurs dans la nature,»

—I am sending photographs of the countryside to Mr. Zola, to prove to him that there are indeed flowers in nature.

Rome from thirty to twenty-five. This prejudiced loss of parental control over young would-be artists had disheartened many of the older, iron-hearted members of the Institute, notably the principled and idealistic Ingres, who vehemently protested the reforms.[21] But Ingres' status had been declining, and in 1864 he was humiliated over not receiving enough votes from former medal winners to sit on the Salon jury, even though he had spurned participation on the jury for many years.

After reading the list of reforms and thoroughly aggravated by them, Thomas Couture, who had been Manet's teacher, closed his studio. Gleyre closed his, too, for health reasons (failing eyesight but more likely financial depletion) in May of 1864. That left Monet, Renoir, Bazille, and Sisley without a teacher, yet also free to paint out-of-doors. Other luminaries were exiting the stage, by choice or circumstance. Delacroix died in 1863, the dispirited Ingres in 1867. Baudelaire, who hadn't written criticism after 1863, also died in 1867. Sainte-Beuve and Jules de Goncourt would die in 1869. Meissonnier, though only forty-three in 1868, when the tide was most dramatically changing, had become utterly boring to all but a few; his trivial pictures, which Baudelaire had described as having *popularized the taste for littleness*,[22] had sopped up their share of an aging audience for warm-hearted, sentimental kitsch. Recent appointments to the *École des Beaux-Arts* had included Alexandre Cabanel and Léon Gérôme. (One recalls that Cabanel's *Venus*, the freshly born, fully fleshed virgin lolling in a benevolent foamy surf like an 1858 Cézanne dream-girl fashioned of cigar smoke, had taken the top prize in the 1863 Salon—the year of the *Salon des refusés*—and was purchased by the emperor). Gérôme's presence with Cabanel on the 1869 jury—both hostile to any departure from academic decorum—would be singled out by Bazille as the root of animosity that had led to many artists being rejected. *Mr. Gérôme has treated us as a band of lunatics*, Bazille said.[23]

The text of Zola's brochure for Manet's private retrospective at the Paris World's Fair in 1867, written in part as a sarcastic review of the official art section, opened with tongue-in-cheek approval of medals handed out to *the flowers among our painters, the exquisite masters who honor France. Yes, the jury was not in error, so in speaking of those bemedaled painters, I will present to my readers the resplendent personalities of the art of our time, in the order of their merit and grandeur.* Zola then proceeds to condemn Cabanel, Gérôme (as mentioned above), and Meissonnier for their *apathetic, colorless, academic, painstakingly executed, but, nonetheless, highly successful products.*[24]

Such derision of the Salon jury and its medal-bedecked favorites was about as commonplace among journalists as ridicule of the artists the jury had refused. As is the case for umpires in sports and politicians in the Assembly, mockery and jeers came with the job. In a short 1860 novel, *Friends of Nature*, Champfleury describes a session of a Salon jury in which a painting of a cheddar cheese by an English artist has just been accepted. Next submitted is a canvas by a Northern painter portraying a Dutch cheese. This cheese has hardly been admitted when there arrives a third painting, this time French Brie by a Parisian artist. By then the jury has had enough cheese, so they decline the Brie.

The French artist's grief in this story is particularly intense because he considers his rivals' cheeses as not having the quality of true realism. To calm this agitated artist, a philosopher acquaintance of his explains the actual reason for the jury's rejection. *In France,* he says, *painting with ideas in one's head is not liked. There is an idea in your painting, and that's what got you excluded. The members of the jury accepted the cheddar and the Dutch cheese because neither contains anything subversive; but they judged your Brie to be a demagogic picture. The very idea of it must have shocked them. It's a poor man's cheese; the knife, with its horn handle and worn blade, is a proletarian's knife. So the jury took note that you have a fierce liking for the utensils of poor people. Therefore, you are judged a social demagogue, and so you are. You're an anarchist without knowing it.*[25]

36

This will be the
masterpiece of my youth

Zola had become aware that writing reviews for newspapers was not just the lowest level in the hierarchy of literature but a corrupted and obsequious profession. Newspaper reviews, like daily-news items, are both short and short-lived—like the cheap paper on which they are printed, put to the next day's use as fish wrapping or toilet paper, for kindling a fire. Weary of battling out of ambush, in thrusts and onslaughts, he longed for serious work. He knew that serialization of novels made it difficult to hold together a large text destined for recasting as a book. To extricate serious novel writing from journalism, he would have to elevate it from the compromising status of a serial to that of a true book and risk that his readership would be greatly diminished. His motivations were caught in the usual bind—monetary success with low integrity pitted against prestigious success with low earnings. On January 30th, 1867, he wrote that he'd been running right and left under the whiplash of necessity, promising his correspondent that the day he received an independent position allowing him to stop running he would try to satisfy him by writing a worthy novel.

On February 12th, 1867, Zola gave Fortuna a shove by writing to Arsène Houssaye, then publisher of the newspaper *La Revue du XIXe siècle*, to say that the prolonged suspense of serialized stories was no longer what he needed. He needed a larger format. In a letter to Valabrègue of February 19th, Zola said a few words about Cézanne, who was thinking along the same lines, working hard and envisioning immense paintings. Dreaming of his own large projects, Zola now awaited providential dispensation. Here follows his letter to Houssaye:

> *I've been dreaming up some news that I could write for La Revue, and now in my head it has become a novel. Would a novel, in just a few parts, scare you? You've already published such pieces and I don't think it was a bad experience for you. The suspense of serialized stories, the breath cut off each day, as in daily newspapers, is not what I need. I want to deliver large fragments each time. So, I am offering you a novel in six parts, in six equal pieces, each as large as my study on Édouard Manet.*
>
> *Here is my proposition. For some time, I've been contemplating a collection of works*

in which I would completely reveal myself. My topic would be the story I briefly told a while back in Le Figaro: «Un Mariage d'amour.» I'm convinced that this outline has the potential of becoming a masterpiece. I would like to undertake that story, to write it with my heart and soul, to turn it into an animated and harrowing narrative. Would you like to help me give birth to it? You are, I believe, the editor I need, young and open-minded, an unselfish lover of all exciting things.

To write real-life stories with free literary style, I need to be pushed by the publishing criteria. I may never write «Un Mariage d'amour» unless I find an intelligent man ready to accept this novel on my word and ready to publish the six parts as they are now composed. Around the 9th of each month, I would send you the fragment that should be published the following month. And in that way, thanks to you, I will give it birth.

Agree and I shall start working. I feel this will be the masterpiece of my youth. The topic has invaded me. I live with the characters. Both of us will benefit from this publication. As for the price, if you agree, you shall give me for each fragment what you gave me for my study on Édouard Manet.

Answer me quickly. I will consider your agreement an opportunity to satisfy my literary appetite. If you believe in me, open your door widely.[1]

To promote the publication of this novel Zola doused Houssaye with flattery while putting the rush on him. His need for a major accomplishment was not exaggerated; he was still sharing meager lodgings with his mother and Alexandrine, and again facing life with only driblets of income. This new project would also help to erase his embarrassment over the serial thriller *Les Mystères de Marseilles,* which, unfortunately, was still in print, and the even cruder hackwork of the aborted *Dead Woman's Wish.* In a letter to Valabrègue, he says, *I won't tell you anything about Les Mystères de Marseilles. The series bothers me so much that I'm fed up just writing its title.*

In the same letter he announces his new project with typical optimism: *I am very happy with the psychological and physiological novel I am about to publish in La Revue du XIXe siècle. This novel, which is almost finished, will undoubtedly be my best work. I have put my heart and soul into it. I fear however that I unveiled too much of my heart, and that may worry the procurer impérial* [the imperial prosecutor of moral offenses]. *But the thought of a few months in jail won't intimidate me.*

Zola's proposal to Houssaye came down to the expansion of the short story *Dans Paris: Un Mariage d'Amour* that he'd published six weeks earlier in *Le Figaro.* As a long novel titled *Thérèse Raquin,* he wanted it printed one segment each month rather than the usual weekly issues. Houssaye agreed. Serialized in several parts, Zola managed nonetheless to structure the story in the standard three acts: an opening to set up tension (an incestuous marriage leading quickly to an adulterous affair) followed by fully developed continuity (a gruesome murder with dreadful consequences) and an ending to resolve the plot (a double suicide).

Much of Zola's time over the year of 1867 was occupied by this project while also meeting unwelcome deadlines for the serialized *Mystères de Marseilles*.

Thérèse Raquin would become Zola's first major work, even though many critics greeted it as out-and-out pornography, a disparagement that contributed, of course, to the story's success with the general public. A crush of readers taking in breathy draughts of Zola's putrescent swill called for a quick printing of a second edition. The re-publication generated Zola's first substantial income and gave him a private platform on which he could ridicule his critics with outpourings of malice while adding fuel to his flaming notoriety. The new edition was furnished with a preface, as bumptious a text as anything he'd written in promotional self-defense, which all along his crooked path had proved the best offense. As described by the excellent translator of the *Thérèse Raquin*, Leonard Tancock, the novel can be summarized as a saga of *adultery, murder, and revenge in a nightmarish setting—a cautionary tale on the sixth and seventh commandments*, with Zola's preface to the book rendered *in the style of the debating society with its brilliant undergraduate wit and use of such tricks as false naïveté, feigned astonishment, injured innocence, crushing sarcasm, and heavy irony*.[2] Still, aside from all his self-embellishment, Zola's preface is the best vehicle for getting into his mind at this time, and indirectly a way into Cézanne's, for not only does it betray the utility of their sustained adolescence, it defines a creed of naturalism more completely than any of Zola's, or anyone's, writings. He was feeding slop to the piggish public while conning his audience into believing that what they were reading was not pornography but authentic literature:

> *I was simple enough to suppose that this novel could do without a preface. Being accustomed to expressing my thoughts quite clearly, and to stress even the minutest details of what I write, I had hoped to be understood and judged without preliminary explanations. It seems I was mistaken.*
>
> *Critics have greeted this book with churlish and horrified outcry. Certain virtuous people, in newspapers no less virtuous, made a grimace of disgust as they picked it up with the tongs to throw it in the fire. Even the minor literary reviews, the ones that retail the nightly tittle-tattle from hideaways and private rooms, held their noses and talked of filth and stench. I am not complaining about this reception; on the contrary I am delighted to observe that my colleagues have such maidenly susceptibilities. Obviously my work is the property of my judges, and they can find it nauseating without my having any right to object, but what I do complain of is that not one of the modest journalists who blushed when they read Thérèse Raquin seems to have understood the novel. If they had, they might perhaps have blushed still more, but at any rate I should at the present moment be enjoying the deep satisfaction of having disgusted them for the right reason. Nothing is more annoying than hearing worthy people shouting about depravity when you know within yourself that they are doing so without any idea what they are shouting about.*
>
> *So I am obliged to introduce my own work to my judges. I will do so in a few lines, simply to forestall any future misunderstanding.*

In Thérèse Raquin my aim has been to study temperaments and not characters. That is the whole point of the book. I have chosen people completely dominated by their nerves and blood, without free will, drawn into each action of their lives by the inexorable laws of their physical nature. Thérèse and Laurent are human animals, nothing more. I have endeavored to follow these animals through the devious workings of their passions, the compulsion of their instincts, and the mental unbalance resulting from a nervous crisis. The sexual adventures of my hero and heroine are the satisfaction of a need, the murder they commit is a consequence of their adultery, a consequence they accept just as wolves accept the slaughter of sheep. And finally, what I have had to call their remorse really amounts to a simple organic disorder, a revolt of the nervous system when strained to the breaking point. There is a complete absence of soul, I freely admit, since that is how I meant it to be.

Zola was up against critics who found the unrelieved ugliness of *Thérèse Raquin* utterly pitiless, as Sainte-Beuve had found Flaubert's *Madame Bovary*. Sainte-Beuve's judgment of Flaubert's novel appeared as one of his *causeries* [Monday chats] in *Le Moniteur* on May 5th, 1857, and shortly thereafter as a book. As the first and most influential reviewer to characterize the so-called scientific approach to creating literature, Sainte-Beuve may have colorfully influenced the vocabulary that Zola would deploy in his preface to *Thérèse Raquin*. Sainte-Beuve had written: *The ideal has come to an end; the lyric source has dried up. People have forgotten it. A severe and pitiless truth has entered art as the last word on experience. Science, the spirit of observation, maturity, strength, a bit of hardness. Such are the characteristics the leaders of the new generation seem to prefer. Flaubert wields the pen as others the scalpel. Anatomists and physiologists, I find you everywhere.*[3]

Zola's preface now continues:

I hope it is becoming clear by now that my objective was first and foremost a scientific one. When my two characters, Thérèse and Laurent, were created, I set for myself certain problems and solved them for the sake of the story. I tried to explain the mysterious attraction that can spring up between two different temperaments, and I exposed the deep-seated disturbances of a sanguine nature brought into contact with a nervous nature. If the novel is read with care, it will be seen that each chapter is a study of a curious physiological case. In a word, I had only one desire: given a highly sexed man and an unsatisfied woman, to uncover their animal side, and after seeing only that side alone, to throw them together in a violent drama, and record with scrupulous care the sensations and actions of these creatures. I simply applied to two living bodies the analytical method that surgeons apply to bodies.

You must allow that it is difficult—on emerging from such toil, still wholly given over to the serious satisfactions of the search for truth—to hear people accuse one of having had no other objective than painting obscene pictures. I found myself in the same position as painters who copy the nude without themselves being touched by the slightest sexual feeling, who are astonished when a critic says he is scandalized by the lifelike bodies in their work. While I was busy writing Thérèse Raquin, I forgot the world and devoted myself to copying life exactly and meticulously, giving myself up entirely to a precise analysis of the mechanism of the human being. I assure you that the ferocious sexual relationship of Thérèse and Laurent meant nothing immoral to me, nothing calculated to provoke anyone's indulgence in evil passions. The human side of the models ceased to exist for me, just as it ceases to exist for the eye of the artist who has a naked woman sprawled in front of him but is solely concerned with getting onto his canvas a true representation of her shape and coloration. How greatly surprised I was on hearing my work referred to as a quagmire of slime and blood, a sewer, garbage, and so forth. I know all about the fun and games of criticism. I have played at it myself. But I confess that the unanimity of the attack disconcerted me a little. What! Is not one of my colleagues prepared to explain my book, let alone defend it? Amid the concert of voices bawling, «The author of Thérèse Raquin is a hysterical wretch who revels in displays of pornography,» I waited in vain for one voice to reply, «No, the writer is simply an analyst who may have become engrossed in human corruption, but who has done so as a surgeon might in an operating theater.»

Note that I am by no means asking for the sympathy of the gentlemen of the press towards a work that offends, we are told, their delicate sensibilities. I am not so ambitious. I am merely astonished that my colleagues have turned me into a kind of literary sewer man, for they are the very people whose expert eyes should recognize a novelist's intentions within ten pages, and I must content myself with humbly begging them to be so good as to see me in the future as I am and to consider me for what I am.

And yet it should have been easy to understand Thérèse Raquin, to take up a position in the realm of observation and analysis and show me my real weaknesses without picking up a handful of mud and flinging it in my face in the name of morality. That would have required, of course, a little intelligence and a few general notions about real criticism. In the world of science, an accusation of immorality proves nothing whatsoever. I do not know whether my novel is immoral, but I admit that at no time did I go out of my way to make it more or less chaste. What I do know is that I never for one moment dreamed of putting in the indecencies that moralizing people are discovering therein, for I wrote every scene, even the most impassioned, with scientific curiosity alone. I defy my judges to find one really licentious page put in to cater to readers of those little rose-colored books [les bibliothèques roses], those boudoir and backstage disclosures, which run to ten thousand copies and are warmly welcomed by the very newspapers that have been nauseated by the truths in Thérèse Raquin.

Up to now all I have read about my work are a few insults and a lot of silliness. I say this here quite calmly, as I would to a friend asking me in private what I thought of the attitude of the critics towards me. A very distinguished writer, to whom I grumbled about the lack of sympathy I am finding, gave me this profound answer: «You have a tremendous drawback which will close every door against you; you cannot talk to a fool for two minutes without making him realize he is a fool.» That must be the case. I see the harm I do myself in the eyes of the critics by accusing them of lack of intelligence, and yet I cannot help showing the scorn I feel for their narrow horizon and groping judgments totally devoid of method. I refer, of course, to current criticism, which judges with all the literary prejudices of fools, being incapable of taking up the broadly humane standpoint that a humane work demands if it is to be understood. I have never seen such ineptitude. The few punches aimed at me by petty critics in the matter of Thérèse Raquin have as usual missed and hit the air. This criticism is essentially wrong-minded; it applauds the capering of some painted actress and then raises a cry of immorality about a physiological study. It understands nothing, does not want to understand anything, but always flails straight out in front. It is exasperating to be chastised for a sin one has not committed. At times I'm sorry that I haven't written obscenities, for I feel I should be happy to receive a well-merited whacking amidst this hail of blows senselessly pelting my head like falling roof tiles, without my knowing why.

At the present time, there are scarcely more than two or three men who can read, judge, and appreciate a book. From these I am willing to take lessons, because I am satisfied that they will not speak before they have grasped my intentions and appreciated the results of my efforts. They would take good care not to pronounce great big empty words, such as morality and literary decency, and in these days of artistic freedom, would acknowledge my right to choose my subjects where I see fit and require only conscientious work on my part, knowing that just being silly endangers the dignity of letters. Certainly they would not be surprised by the scientific analysis I have attempted in Thérèse Raquin, for in it they would recognize the modern method of universal inquiry, the tool our age is using so enthusiastically to open up the future. Whatever their own conclusions, they would approve of my starting point—the study of temperament—and of the profound modifications of an organism subjected to the pressure of environments and circumstances. I should be standing before genuine judges, men seeking after truth in good faith, without puerility or false modesty, men who do not think they are obliged to look with disgust at the sight of naked living anatomical specimens. Sincere study, like fire, purifies all things. Of course, in the eyes of the tribunal I am choosing to envision at the moment, my work would be a very humble affair, and I should invite the critics to exercise all their severity upon it, indeed I should like it to emerge black with corrections. But at any rate I should have had the deep satisfaction of seeing myself criticized for what I have tried to do, and not for what I have not done.

I think I can hear even now the sentence passed by real criticism. I mean the methodical and naturalist criticism that has revived the sciences, history, and literature: «Thérèse Raquin is the study of too exceptional a case; the drama of modern life is more flexible and not so hemmed in by horror and madness. Such cases should be relegated to a subsidiary position in a book. The desire not to sacrifice any of his observations has led the author to stress every single detail, and that has given still more tension and harshness to the whole. Moreover the style lacks the simplicity that an analytical novel demands. In short, if the writer is now to write a good novel, he must see society with greater breadth of vision, depict it in its many and varied aspects, and above all use clear and natural language.»

I mean to devote a score of lines to answering attacks that are irritating by the very naïveté of their bad faith, and I see that I am embarking on a chat with myself, as always happens to me when I keep a pen in my hand too long. So I desist, knowing that readers do not like that sort of thing. If I had had the leisure and the will to write a manifesto, I might have tried to defend what one journalist, referring to Thérèse Raquin, has called «putrid literature.» But what is the point? The group of naturalist writers to which I have the honor of belonging has enough courage and energy to produce powerful works containing their own defense. It takes all the deliberate blindness of a certain kind of criticism to force a novelist to write a preface. Since I have committed the sin of writing one because I am a lover of light, I crave the forgiveness of men of intelligence who do not need me to light a lamp for them in broad daylight to help them see clearly.

Zola knew he had written a piece of trash. Every aspect of his novel was contrived to fish passion from murky waters, using as lures sticky ribbons of abhorrence the public would be drawn to as flies to a privy. The opening events in *Thérèse Raquin* are told here to demonstrate Zola's style and also to reveal that certain aspects of Cézanne myths, taken from Zola's writings, pre-existed *L'Oeuvre.*

Just after opening the story of Thérèse's horrid life, Zola has the young woman and her feeble cousin Camille marry at the instigation of a mutually shared aunt, not because they love each other but because they'd grown up together. Soon thereafter, Camille brings home a young man, Laurent, whom he had chanced upon at his place of employment and who'd been a childhood school friend. Laurent is described by Zola as *a lazy man at bottom, with animal appetites and very clear-cut desires for easy and lasting pleasures: all his great powerful body wanted was to do nothing, to wallow in never-ending idleness and self-indulgence.*

He would have liked to eat well, sleep well, and satisfy his passions liberally, without stirring from one spot or risking the misfortune of fatigue. His father had pushed him to become a lawyer, but he rebelled. He threw himself into art with the hope of finding a lazy man's job, for the brush seemed a nice light tool to wield and he thought success would be easy. He dreamed of a life of cheap pleasures, a fine life full of women, of lolling on divans, blowouts, and boozing. The dream lasted as long as Laurent Senior sent the cash. But when the young man, who was already thirty, saw starvation on the horizon, he began to do some thinking; he felt his courage fail in the face of privation, and he would not have gone a day without food for the greater glory of art. So, as he said, he chucked painting to the devil as soon as he saw that it would never satisfy his large appetite. His first attempts never even rose to mediocrity; his peasant eyes saw nature clumsily and messily, and his muddy, badly composed, grimacing canvases defied all criticism. Not that he seemed particularly vain as an artist, and he was not unduly depressed when he threw down his brush-

es. All he really missed was his old school-friend's vast studio in which he had lazed so delectably for four or five years. And he also missed the women who came and posed there, and whose favors were within the reach of his purse.[4]

Thérèse's husband Camille, a young man whose soft limp body had never felt the slightest tremor of sexual desire, has boyish visions of the studio life his friend tells him about. He thinks of the women displaying their bare flesh—such a thought never before having entered his mind—and he interrogates Laurent:

«*So you mean that there have really been women who have taken their clothes off in front of you?*»

«*Why not?*» Laurent grins and looks at Thérèse, who turns very pale.

«*That must make you feel ever so funny,*» Camille goes on, giggling.

«*I should feel awful...The first time it happened you couldn't have known where to look.*»

Laurent opened one of his big hands and examined the palm attentively. His fingers tremble slightly and a flush comes to his cheeks:

«*The first time,*» he says, as though talking to himself, «*I think I found it quite natural...It's great fun, this art racket, only it doesn't bring in a sou. I had a lovely red-head as a model—firm white flesh, gorgeous bust, hips as wide as...*»

Laurent looks up and sees Thérèse sitting in front of him silent and motionless, looking at him with burning intensity. Her dull black eyes are bottomless pits, and through her parted lips can be seen the pink flesh of her mouth, caught by the light. She seems cowed, drawn into herself, but is listening.

One evening Laurent shows up with an easel and a box of paints, as he'd proposed to paint a portrait of Camille. He sets up his easel in the couple's bedroom, and over several evenings, works on the portrait. Thérèse never leaves the bedroom-turned-studio when he is working; always serious and subdued, pale and quiet, she sits there and watches the brush move. She comes to this room as if drawn by force and stays as though nailed to the spot. Occasionally, Laurent turns around and smiles at her, asks if the picture is to her liking. She scarcely answers a word, but trembles and relapses into her solemn ecstasy.

«*That young woman,*» Laurent tells himself, «*will be mine whenever I like. She is always there, right on top of me, scrutinizing me, measuring me, and weighing me up. She's all quivering; her face is strange, quiet but passionate. What she wants is a lover, that's a certain fact; you can see it in her eyes.*»

Laurent must wait the right moment. It comes when the portrait is at last finished, when the whole family gathers around to admire the perfect likeness—a miserable daub, dirty gray in color with large bluish patches. Even the brightest colors went dull and muddy when Laurent used them and in spite of himself he'd overdone the pallid coloring of his model, making Camille's face take on the greenish look of a drowned man. And this sinister resemblance is rendered all the more striking by the grimacing draftsmanship that contorts the features. But Camille is delighted with the picture, saying that on the canvas he looks distinguished.

To celebrate, Camille goes off to buy champagne. Laurent and Thérèse are left alone in the bedroom. Thérèse seems to be waiting, tense. Laurent hesitates, looks at the canvas, and plays with his brushes. Time is short. Suddenly he turns and looks at Thérèse. For a few seconds, they look at each other. Then, with a violent movement, Laurent stoops, takes up the young woman and holds her against his chest, pushes her head back, crushing her lips beneath his own. She makes one wild, instinctive effort to resist, then yields, slipping down onto the floor. Not a single word is exchanged. Zola finishes off the seduction with, *The act is silent and brutal.*

Cézanne is implicated in the story—not Cézanne, himself, but those biographers who got hooked on Zola's notes for *L'Oeuvre* taken as true aspects of Cézanne's personality, particularly the anecdote that, unable to confront a naked woman in the studio, he would seduce the woman on the bed of his canvas— painting her with bold and violent strokes. Certainly among artists meeting in cafés or gathered in each other's studios, many stories of exploits with studio models were told, as are stories at men's gatherings of all sorts. In *Thérèse Raquin,* Zola has the roguish cuckolder Laurent seduce Thérèse by painting a portrait of her ineffectual husband. So this motif of seduction on a canvas was on Zola's mind sometime before giving thought to *L'Oeuvre,* in which Claude Lantier's studio would be infused with the banalized eroticism of the love-struck sculptor Pygmalion fashioning his dream girl, and Claude's suicide by hanging, like the luckless Cézanne's fate in his *Histoire Terrible,* suffering a broken neck.

37

I'm sick of popular journalism
with its sleazy stratagems

T hérèse Raquin did not generate the income Zola had thought it would. Despite his efforts to break out of it, he would remain imprisoned in journalism. His tactics, his caustic and lurid anecdotes, had served to establish him as a voice one might despise but still read. In 1868, he was offered another chance to write his own column, this time with a new newspaper, *La Tribune*, which published its first issue in June. Théodore Duret helped Zola secure a contract to write a weekly chronicle about books, plays, and literary events.

La Tribune was the child of two political dissenters, Eugène Pelletan and André Lavertujon, who for some time had supported the more liberal side of the republican objective. It would take many weeks for their newspaper to emerge from the planning stage. In mid-April, Zola wrote to Marius Roux, *I saw Duret at Manet's yesterday. The Tribune venture is limping along. I suspect that Pelletan may be as inept as Mille-Noé. No one is sure when La Tribune will appear, or whether it will appear at all.*[1] But by May, Zola's prospects had improved. On the 8th, he wrote to Duret, *I'll be doing a causerie for the Tribune. We didn't discuss salary, so I hope you will be on hand when that comes up. Please see to it that they hire neither an art critic nor a bibliographer nor anyone who might tread on my turf.* Soon Zola followed up in another letter to Duret, asking if the salary matter had been decided, telling him it was of great concern: *I miss working for a daily which permits me to earn enough to live peacefully. I am sick of popular journalism, with its sleazy stratagems that diminish and destroy people.*[2]

His job secured after weeks of doubt, Zola filed suit against every facet of France's officialdom, its institutions, policies, and politicians, while denouncing France as a nation with no pride, like men of high station who grovel before prostitutes, waste patrimonies, loosen family ties, tear apart society's moral fabric, cheapen people's lives.[3] *Ah! how many sinister dreams unfold in secret, how many men who cast off their black habit as if it were merely a costume, roll on the carpet like a trained dog, and beg for punishment.*[4] Zola raged against the comic operas of Offenbach: *La Belle Hélène amounts to nothing more than a sneer of convulsive gaiety, a display of gutter humor.*[5] As for the play *La Grande Duchesse de Gérolstein*, he wrote: *The day some woman conceives the brilliant idea of running around the stage naked on all fours, acting the part of some stray bitch, that will be the day Paris cheers itself sick.*[6] Chastising Princess Eugénie, he wrote: *Walk around our working-class slums, strictly incognito. You will see what behooves a queen to see: poverty yet courage, muffled rage against the idle and wanton. There you will hear the great voice of the populace, snarling for justice and bread.*[7] He also attacked the Prefect of the Seine, Paris' master planner Baron Haussmann: *I know Mr. Haussmann doesn't like popular festivals. He has forbidden almost all that once took place in the communes annexed to Paris. Relentlessly he harasses street peddlers. In his dreams he must see Paris as a giant chessboard, with geometrically perfect grid lines.*[8]

Closer to Zola's heart was the matter of censorship: in July 1868, *Thérèse Raquin* had been judged indecent and an insult to public morality. Rather than defend his book, Zola doubled-up topical issues by reviewing favorably a different and mediocre novel, also officially condemned as immoral, in which a heroine rebuffs her politically ambitious husband.[9] This was both a convenient and a timely topical issue: just this year the Minister of Public Instruction had opened public secondary schools to women, with the Church protesting vehemently. Ever since the Revolution, the Church had been losing power; the populace of male parishioners had fallen off, leaving principally women under the Church's control, anesthetized with Mariolatry (idolatry of the Virgin). The issue of a woman interfering with her husband's political aspirations was rich fodder. It also fed into Zola's stipulations for the secularization of society, though he did not dare to endorse women in employment or politics at this time, when the huge unemployed male work force was quaking with fear of female competition.

Many of the sixty or so *causeries* that Zola published in *La Tribune* would provide free grist for grinding out his novels. And soon he would have a real war on his hands—the war he himself would celebrate as the critical goal towards which his novels would lead. In 1866, when the Prussians defeated Austria at Sadowa, the threat of German unification unsettled Napoleon, who was ill—if not organically then over fear of King Wilhelm's forces. Nationalists in France were spoiling for war against Prussia, while the republicans, with whom Zola was aligned, advocated pacification of the Kaiser. With Paris embroiled in such debates as to whether women belonged to Science or to the Church, whether the German nation should be tactfully accommodated or heroically attacked, Zola was positioned to espouse most any thought about sociology and politics that came into his head. With this new focus of attention, the petty struggles of the art world no longer occupied his raging mind.

Over September and October 1868, Zola's novel *Madeleine Férat*, dedicated to Manet, appeared serialized as *La Honte* (Shame) in *L'Événement illustré*. The text throbbed with passion and violence while verging on child-porn in its opening: a sixteen-year-old orphan girl, impregnated by a forty-year-old man, gives birth to a girl and dies in the effort. At age six, the offspring girl, Madeleine Férat, is abandoned by her father and handed over to a guardian, Lobrichon, who puts her in boarding school. When Madeleine turns fifteen and is sexually ripening, Lobrichon takes her out of school and bides his time while lusting for her until she turns nineteen. Then he proposes. Madeleine is shocked. She runs off and wanders through Paris until taken in by a young doctor (Guillaume de Viargues) to whom she makes love in gratitude. From then on, as with *Thérèse Raquin*, it's all down hill; everything done becomes undone. *Madeleine Férat* has been called a novel of the Oedipal situation—the essential triangle of one man who is tender and feeble, an older man who is strong and virile, and a sensual woman.[10] Frederick Brown aptly summarized the book, saying for an opener: *With all its melodramatic flummery and psychological humbug, Madeleine Férat translates the horror Zola saw in regression to a primitive state. Yearning for adulthood, Madeleine and Guillaume struggle against a force that pulls them backward or downward.*[11]

Zola deploys a device here that will structure his entire set of integrated novels, the *Rougon-Macquart* series. He sets good against bad, and builds all other contrasts on that fundamental one. *Where Madeleine and Guillaume suffer for sins they didn't commit, Hélène and Tiburce,* an adulterous couple, *fornicate without scruple*—the one couple's actions governed by lust, the other's by ambition.[12] Where history weighs upon Zola's guilt-ridden protagonists, his guiltless couple are a pair of savages unconscious of the past, trampling underfoot class distinctions and generation barriers as they dance naked before the aged cuckold (the cuckold, an aristocrat; his wife, the adulteress, twice the age of the adulterer, who's a vulgar young man).[13] Of the scornful cuckold, the aristocratic Rieux, Zola writes: *Long contemplation of his wife had persuaded Rieux that humans are mean, stupid marionettes. When he searched the wicked doll, he discovered beneath coquettish mask infamies and fatuity that led him to consider her a beast good for whipping. But instead of whipping her, he amused himself by despising her.* The novel ends with Madeleine taking poison. Her lover dances around her corpse, stark raving mad, while the devout old housekeeper Geneviève mutters, *God, the Father, had not pardoned.*

The serial run evaded the eyes of the Public Prosecutor, but the censor caught up with it and issued a writ enjoining Albert Lacroix, who was purchasing the manuscript from *L'Événement illustré,* from publishing it as a book. In his usual state of fury when anything impeded him, Zola refused to make any cuts. He got the public vicariously embroiled in the fracas. He hung his dirty laundry outdoors, exposing the censor's contention in *La Tribune* (he was by then one of the editors). Finally, the Prosecutor had to yield to get Zola off his back, for Zola simply would not come to terms. *What has been sanctioned on the streets cannot be cast out of the bookstore*, Zola informed the editor-in-chief of *L'Événement illustré*, whose difficult task it was to come up with a solution. *I will therefore not approve the cuts. Self-respect requires that I go forward and face the danger now threatening me. If necessary, I will recite the entire story out loud.*[14]

Zola and his publishers made great efforts to sustain the conflict in the press. Every throb of the scandal increased public anticipation and the promise of sales. Staging quarrels and planting words fabricated publicity. Lacroix had in hand a legal writ forbidding him to publish the book. Zola took advantage of that to furnish words for sympathetic journalists. To Lacroix he wrote: *Attached you will find the note that was supposed to run in Le Figaro. I find it so complete, so felicitous, that I cannot just file it away. Try then, for God's sake, to get it published somewhere, anywhere. Feyrnet is back, I think. He could plant it in Le Temps. If he refuses, look elsewhere.*[15] When *Madeleine Férat* was finally published as a book on December 19th, Zola held up the entire run of gossip as evidence of his martyrdom and called on fellow book reviewers to take revenge: *As you undoubtedly know from what you've read in the newspapers, the imperial prosecutor threatened my book's life even before it was born,* he wrote to the book review editor of *L'Artiste. I hope that its misadventures will engage your sympathy.*

But Zola, himself, claimed that it was founded on the theories of Hippolyte Taine and Dr. Lucas, though including as well the theory of impregnation he found in Michelet's *L'Amour*—the theory that the woman's first impregnation will determine the genetics of any child she bears over her productive lifetime, even if impregnated by other, successive men. This theory of impregnation had been given published formulation by Prosper Lucas, the theoretician of heredity, whose monumental corpus of work was published in two volumes, the first in 1847, and the second in 1850. Michelet popularized the impregnation theory in his novel *L'Amour*, which may have led Zola to Lucas, as Michelet's *L'Amour* depended on Lucas for a scientific basis of heredity more sophisticated than simply the transit of seed and the imprinting of one generation's sins on the next (as associated with the passage of royal blood and venereal diseases). Zola wrote, *The few lines they* [the editors] *would expurgate contain the book's central thesis, which I took from Michelet and Dr. Prosper Lucas. I dramatized it austerely and with conviction. Good morals are not endangered by a medical study that serves, as I see it, a high purpose.*[16] Zola's central thesis, with some justification, was the acceptance of the marriage bond as eternal from the physiological viewpoint. *While religion and morality tell man, «You shall live with one woman,» and science says in turn, «Your first wife will be your eternal wife.»*[17] One can see how easily the impregnation theory could be interpreted as a devious way of covering up infidelities, as the offspring of any woman would always resemble her husband and never her lover.

Zola's bow to Taine for the help his ideas provided to formulating the novel acknowledged that Madeleine was a victim of her physiology, heredity, and milieu.

Taine was interested in the novel, and had a few comments for Zola: *If the objective of your novel is to paint a picture of contemporary social values, you must admit that these moral deteriorations, these persistent nightmares, these surrenders to carnal instinct and the idée fixé are rare. To my mind, the future of the novel lies in the story of voluntary combats and victories over social helter-skelter and the feebleness of the fatigued animal. You have a sense for the truth, and I believe that just by casting your eyes all around you, as I do, you will recognize the truth of that.*[18]

In a significant way this notion of the first impregnation corresponds to the prevailing theory of original art in the 1860s: that regardless of what art the painter produced, each work would bear the personal imprint, the original mark, *la première pensée,* of his *tempérament.* And that unique temperament would be the unified result of an individual being born at a particular time and into a matrix of heredity and social environment.

Part III

CÉZANNE AND ZOLA TAKE CHARGE

38

*Noré is a dunce. They say he is
doing a picture for the Salon*

Two letters to Numa Coste are deployed here to fill out what Cézanne was up to following his return to Aix in the summer of 1868. The correspondence he had with Zola is lost, as are his letters to others over 1867 and the first half of 1868. So from this eighteen-month period, Cézanne is a blank canvas. We cannot even determine beyond guessing what he painted over those months. So the two letters to Coste will have to do:

> *Aix, in the first days of July 1868*
>
> *My dear Coste,*
>
> *It's been several days since I had news of you, and I'm hard put to tell you anything new about your homeland, so far away from you. Since my arrival I have been in the open, in the country* [at the Jas de Bouffan with his family]. *I have certainly been on the move several times, one evening after another. I ventured to the house of your father whom I did not find in, but one of these days, right in the middle of the day, I hope to discover him.*
>
> *As for Alexis, he was kind enough to pay me a visit, having learned from the great Valabrègue of my return from Paris. He even loaned me a little revue by Balzac from the year 1840 [Balzac was then editor of* Revue de Paris, *and had published in the 1840 issue an essay on Stendhal's* Chartreuse de Parme]. *He asked me if you were continuing with your painting, and so on—all the things one says when chatting. He promised to come back and see me, but I haven't seen him for over a month. For my part, and particularly after receiving your letter, I directed my steps in the evening towards the Cours* [Aix's main street], *which is a little contrary to my solitary habits. It is impossible to meet him. However, pushed by a great desire to fulfill my duty, I will attempt a descent on his home. But on that day I will first change my shoes and shirt. I have had no more news of Rochefort and yet the noise of* La Lanterne *has penetrated even here.*

La Lanterne was an opposition paper edited by the political journalist Henri de Rochefort, who had started his career as a theater critic for *Le Nain jaune.* Villemessant, as editor of *Le Figaro,* hired him, but when Villemessant recognized Rochefort's natural capacity to whip journalism into polemics with much violence and wit, he financed a separate newspaper, *La Lanterne*, to print what readers of the more dignified *Figaro* wouldn't tolerate. Rochefort was opposed to the regime of Napoleon III. His most famous editorial statement was *France has 36 million subjects, not counting the subjects of discontent*. In Paris at this time, Zola was moving with the tide, aligning himself with left-wingers, as the European political situation was becoming very grave, verging on the Franco-Prussian War.

Cézanne, on the other hand, couldn't care less about politics. Whenever back in Aix with his family, his mind reverted to his boyhood days. The letter to Coste now continues in a stream of reminiscence:

> *I did see a little of Aufan* [a friend, identity not known], *but the others seem to hide themselves and a great empty space seems to surround one after being absent from the country for some time. I don't know whether I'm living or simply remembering the past. I wandered alone as far as the Barrage* [the Zola dam] *and to Saint-Antonin* [a village at the base of Mount Ste. Victoire]. *I slept there in the Miller family's hay barn—good wine, good hospitality. I remembered our attempts at climbing Sainte Victoire. Should we not try again? How bizarre our life, how dispersed and how difficult it would be for us at this hour when I speak, the three of us and the dog, to be where we were only a few years ago.*
>
> *Here I have no amusements but the family and a few copies of Siècle where I find unimportant news. Being alone, with difficulty I take my chances at the café. But underneath all that, I'm always hoping.*[1] *Do you know that Penot* [another mutual friend] *is at Marseilles? I was not lucky enough to see him nor was he to see me. Each time when he came to visit me in Aix I was at Saint-Antonin. I will try to go again to Marseilles one day, and we will then talk about absent friends and drink to their health. In one letter to me, Penot wrote, «And the beer mugs will fly.»*
>
> *P.S. I left this letter unfinished when, in the middle of the day, Dethès and Alexis dropped in to see me. You can be sure we talked literature and refreshed ourselves, for it was very hot that day. Alexis was kind enough to read to me a piece of poetry, which I found very good indeed; then he recited from memory a few verses of another poem called «Symphonie en la mineur»* [Symphony in A-minor]. *I thought those few verses were more unusual, more original, and I complimented him for that. I also showed him your letter. He told me he would write to you. In the meantime I send you his love, also from my family to whom I showed your letter. Thank you very much for it; it is like dewdrops in the glowing sun. I also saw Combes who came out here to the country.*
>
> *I shake you vigorously by the hand. Yours from the heart, Paul Cézanne.*

In the second letter to Coste, Cézanne again displays a casual indifference to the date, as if feeling torpid and slumberous, a grown child at home in lazy surroundings (yet John Rewald interprets the lack of dates to Cézanne being so distressed with his father that he can't remember what day it is):[2]

Aix, towards the end of November, 1868
It is Monday evening.

My dear Numa,

I cannot tell you exactly the date of my return [to Paris]. *It will probably be during the first days of December, about the 15th. I won't fail to see your parents before my departure and bring you whatever you want.*

I saw your father some time ago, and we went to see Villevieille. Speaking about this to you reminds me to go and see him, and above all not to forget him at the moment of my departure. I will write down on a piece of paper all the things I must do and the people I must see, and cross them out as I get them done, so I will forget nothing. You've given me great pleasure by writing to me. That rouses one from the lethargy into which one ultimately falls.

The lovely expedition we were to have made to Sainte Victoire has fallen into the water this summer because of excessive heat, and also the one in October because of the rains. You can see from this what softness has begun spreading through the willpower of our little comrades. But what can we do, that's how it is; it seems that one is not always fully responsive, in Latin one would say semper virens, always vigorous, or better, always strong-willed. As for news from here, I won't give you any...I don't know anything new. And yet, Gibert Pater, mauvais pinter, [«bad painter,» Cézanne's pejorative word play on Gibert's name] *has refused Lambert permission to photograph some pictures at the Musée Bourguignon, thus cutting off his work—refused also to Victor Combes to copy, etc.*

Noré is a dunce. They say he is doing a picture for the Salon.

All this is goitrous. Papa Livé has been sculpting for 58 months a bas-relief of one meter; he is still working away at the eye of saint XXX. It so happened that the Honorable d'Agay [Combes], *the young «fashionable»* [in English] *whom you know, one day entered the Musée Bourguignon, and there Mamma Combes said to him, «Give me your cane, papa Gibert will have none of that.» «I don't care a fig,» says the other. He keeps his cane. Gibert pater arrives; he wants to make a scene. «Shit on you,» shouts d'Agay. Truly!*

Paul Alexis, a boy who, by the way, is far superior to others and, one can safely say, still not stuck up, lives on poetry and other things. I saw him a few times during the fine weather; only recently I met him and told him of your letter. He is burning to go to Paris with paternal consent. He wants to borrow some money, mortgaged on the paternal cranium, and escape to other skies, drawn, by the way, by the great Valabrègue, who gives no sign of life. Alexis thanks you for thinking of him; he does the same for you. I've scolded him for his laziness. He replied that if only you knew his difficulties (a poet must always be pregnant with some Iliad, or rather with a personal Odyssey) you would forgive him. Why don't you give him a prize for diligence or something similar? But I am in favor of forgiving him, for he read me some verses of poetry that give proof of no mean talent. He already possesses in full the skill of the trade. I clasp your hand from a long distance, while

waiting to clasp it from nearer, ever your old—Paul Cézanne.
    P.S. I am still working hard at a landscape of the banks of the Arc, it is always for the next Salon. Will it be that of 1869?

The Alexis who dropped by to see Cézanne, as mentioned in Cézanne's letter to Coste, was Paul Alexis. Alexis was a friend of Valabrègue's from the *Bourbon* days, who had just completed his law studies in Aix but aspired to be a poet. Now twenty-two, he was at the appropriate level of maturity for infatuation with Zola's *Contes à Ninon,* which had become underground reading among the generation of teenage youths in Aix that had succeeded the Holy Trinity of Cézanne, Zola, and Baille. Alexis was determined to come to Paris and meet the famous Zola, about whom he'd heard a great deal from both Valabrègue and Cézanne, perhaps also from Marius Roux. Alexis' father, a wealthy *notaire,* had supported him through law school but refused his leaving Aix for Paris to pursue a fancied literary career. The headstrong Alexis borrowed two hundred francs from Valabrègue and came to Paris in mid-September 1869, apparently severing his ties to his father. Valabrègue, who had accompanied him on the trip, took him forthwith to see Zola. Alexis would recall this first meeting as if he'd met a Confucius on the path to enlightenment:

> *After arriving in Paris to do literature, but still rather young and with some verses in the style of Baudelaire as my only baggage, I was about to meet the Émile Zola about whom I had heard much said since my fourteenth year. The first words out of Zola's mouth were, «Ah! There you are, Alexis! I've been expecting you.» I felt that our initial handshake sealed a pact that I could count on the solid friendship of a sort of older brother.*[3]

Alexis would figure importantly in Zola's life, becoming his first biographer, taking over his mentor's role as an art critic in the early 1870s. Six months after his arrival in Paris, along with Cézanne, Marius Roux, and Philippe Solari, Alexis stood as a witness to the marriage of Zola and Alexandrine Meley on May 31st, 1870. He would not mature into a writer of any consequence. As had Zola, he soon had to admit that he lacked talent for poetry. He, too, would undertake other forms of writing: criticism and biography. One of Cézanne's most successful paintings depicts Zola and Alexis together on a garden terrace of the Montmartre pavilion where Zola was living in 1869. Alexis is reading to Zola, perhaps his own poetry, for at this time Zola was enjoying the role as counselor to an adoring acolyte.

39

Not everything about a painting
can be reduced to symbolism

G one was the day when Zola had told Cézanne of his dream that they
would collaborate on a glorious book for which Cézanne would have
done magnificent illustrations. *Our two names together in gold letters on the*
title page, Zola had said to him*, and in this brotherhood of genius inseparable as to poster-*
ity. Now Zola's identity was wedded to Manet in a brotherhood of genius, both
men courting abuse and looking forward to sweet vengeance.[1] Yet it was to Manet
that Cézanne, no less than Zola, looked after 1865. But Cézanne's look was not
admiring. He would paint at least two versions of an *Olympia* that burlesqued
Manet's picture. The earlier of the two, which now bears the title *A Modern*
Olympia, dates from about 1869. The label was not given the motif until 1874, the
date of the second version, which was included in the first Impressionist exhibition that year against the objections of other exhibitors who feared that
Cézanne's imagery would prime the pump of critical adversity.

The 1869 version features a burly, heavily bearded man wearing a Turkish-
type hat ensconced in a bedchamber furnished with an immense display of flowers and a table holding fruit, bread, and wine. A prostitute's chamber, probably an
alcove in a sumptuous brothel, the curtains are drawn back like those of a theater
when action begins. In the style of *les grands maisons de plaisir,* every prop in
Cézanne's picture is exaggerated to dislodge reality and transport the client into
some one or the other realm of fantasy, supplanting the routine of homespun
sex. A curtain figured also in Manet's *Olympia,* where the maid proffers a gift of
flowers from a gentleman who waits behind it, anticipating a fleshy return on his
floriferous offering. The drawn-back curtain, or drape, associated with sleeping
compartments, was a commonplace convention for intimate settings, with precedent in Ancient Rome, if not in Paleolithic caves, and a future in Picasso's
Demoiselles d'Avignon.

To fulfill the client's anticipation of salacious delight, a black chambermaid
rips the covering off the woman, exposing her naked body now curled into a protective cringe as if surprised out of her sleep and horrified by what she sees. The

Cézanne. *Une moderne Olympia* (also known as *The Pasha*). 1869-70. Private collection, Paris.

rapacious exposure allows the man to experience power over the woman, converting her paid-for service into subjugation, like certain specialist prostitutes who feign being ravenously raped in order to satisfy a man's need to act out the extremes of sexual possession. The action, and the relationship between the man and woman is in polar contrast to Cézanne's *Temptation of St. Anthony* where the saint cow-

Below: Cézanne. *Une moderne Olympia.* 1873-74. Paris, Musée d'Orsay. Photo: Bulloz.

Jean Louis Forain. *Gentlemen's Choice.* A modern version of the Choice of Paris.

Édouard Manet. *Nana.* 1877. Hamburger Kunsthalle

ers protectively before the sudden appearance of a woman who thrusts at him her full-body nakedness

Cézanne's *Modern Olympia* falls out of the historical tradition that supported Manet's *Olympia*. One would have to look ahead to Manet's *Nana* of 1877 for a remote comparison of a well-dressed man with top hat in the boudoir of a woman—Nana the courtesan dressing rather than undressing. But no man needs a script for such dramas. It would be easy to say that Cézanne motif enacts childhood acts of peeking—the child in quest of solutions to puzzles, the solutions usually coming with punishment. Non-pathological voyeurism in such imagery as Cézanne's «Olympia» being exposed was surely on his mind, but not as perverted psychology. Art history bulges with such motifs in many forms: nymphs spied upon and seized by satyrs, the elders peeking at the bathing Diana, comely Bathsheba at her bath spied by King David from his palace rooftop, ordered to be brought to him, ordered to disrobe. At about the time Cézanne painted the later *Modern Olympia*, he also made a copy of Rembrandt's *Bathsheba* and rendered a prostitute being washed by a maid while the client looks on, which represents the collapse of a

Cézanne. A prostitute being prepared, perhaps. Last known location of this watercolor, Waddington Galleries, London.

Cézanne. So called, *Déjeuner sur l'herbe* (Picnic). 1868-69. Private collection.

traditional motif onto a modern one, like that of *The Choice of Paris* onto a motif of a man in a brothel choosing among alternative women.[2] The «voyeurism» implied by the prevalence of such themes must be understood within the biological scheme of human sexual reproduction but also, and especially, in the context of the art history that artists must deal with daily. All art making involves looking. When the aesthetics of art are fused with the aesthetics of the female body, as they were in Cézanne's time (and largely still today), a young painter, such as Cézanne, under pressure and feeling assertive, will make little distinction between subject matter and way of painting. It is as difficult to isolate the pleasurable (even if sadistic) aspect of *seeing* from art making as it is to separate violence from boxing or danger from mountaineering.

As if modernism were to be understood in contrast to the unsophisticated, sylvan, and rustic, Cézanne painted, perhaps in 1969-70, a small but ambitious *Déjeuner sur l'herbe*, hereafter referred to as *The Picnic*. This painting and a similar canvas from about the same time, *An Idyllic Day*, are psychologically loaded and complex, as was the caprice of urban people going out in the countryside to commune with nature. The temporary disengagement from a regiment of comforts

Cézanne. *An Idyllic Day*. 1868-70. Paris, Musée d'Orsay. Photo: Bulloz.

and civilized customs to experience physical contact with the bare earth, like sleep releasing one from reality, sanctions and gives consent to primitive associations including sexual arousal, recalling Cézanne and Zola's naked swims and hours on the Arc's sunny bank reading spicy texts, fantasizing what their capabilities could only promise. Cézanne rendered the picnic and an idyllic day, the latter infused with dreamy and mythical inferences, the imagery more personal than how Manet had evoked the mythical realm by subliminal references to Giorgione's *Concert*

Giorgione, *Concert Champêtre*. Also attributed to Titian. Paris, Musée du Louvre. Photo: Bulloz.

Champêtre—clothed men in the presence of naked women in an idyllic, pastoral setting, which includes a contrast between urban and countryside, a courtier from the city in the distance with a shepherd. Cézanne's *Picnic* is exaggerated; the participants are contemporary yet caricatured and geographically and culturally displaced. Especially in this respect the picture differs from the contemporaneous realism of Manet's *Déjeuner sur l'herbe*, or Monet's picnic theme that goes by the same title.

Roger Fry, Cézanne's first champion for the twentieth century, commented with lucidity on *The Picnic* but would have preferred that Cézanne hadn't painted it:

> *Cézanne at this period believed himself to be a visionary. His imagination, nourished on poetry, aimed at something besides the plastic interpretation of actual appearances. He worked above all to find expression for the agitation of his inner life, and without making literary pictures in the bad sense of the word sought to express himself as much by the choice and implications of his figures as by the plastic expression of their forms.*[3]

Fry was sensitive to Cézanne's conflict. Self-indulgent, he had not achieved art as something beyond self-expression. When looking at his paintings, one sees him more than his art. Meyer Schapiro also addressed himself to this picture:

> *A strange, dream-like atmosphere overlies the ordinary meanings of a picnic here. Above a tablecloth spread out on the grass, on which lie nothing but two oranges—the apparent object of the meditations of the figures—hovers a tall, bent woman with loosened golden hair, a sibyl who holds a third orange in her extended hands, as if performing a sacrificial rite or pronouncing an incantation. She turns her gaze to the frock-coated, gesturing man in the foreground; he resembles the young, prematurely bald Cézanne. In the distance stands a solemn, rigid figure, smoking a pipe, with folded arms like a guard or a celebrant of the ritual; on the left, a man and a woman, dressed like Cézanne and the sibyl, go off into the dark woods arm in arm.*[4]

Schapiro's description is a bit forced to make a point that Cézanne (if that man in the lower right is Cézanne) could not be enjoying the presence of a woman, so hardened in Cézanne biographies is the myth that he was terrorized of women. Schapiro says that Cézanne is the odd man at the party, the one without a woman, and that among the men in shirtsleeves he is the only one in formal dress. But the man Schapiro calls Cézanne is not without a female partner. He is paired with the woman who is standing up, looking at him, yielding two couples around the picnic cloth. And the difference in dress among the men is only that the one resembling Cézanne has not removed his coat.

Not everything about a painting can be reduced to symbolism. While it has been said many times, since the fifteenth century at least, that painters tend to paint themselves, painters are form makers, and to give form to something on a flat surface one needs to establish discontinuities that define a figure and contrast those discontinuities with what is «behind» the figure—what is known as «good gestalt» accomplished by figure/ground definition. Had the man at the other edge of the picnic cloth kept on his black coat, his upper body would be black against black, not sufficiently set off from the distant hill. Some things that a painter does are that simple. Art is optical and also a craft. The man who has taken off his coat, so to speak, with his head resting on his elbow, has yellow hair, but that does not mean that the person he may represent, if anyone, has yellow hair. Had Cézanne had given him black hair, the hair would be invisible against the near-black background, and his face would be a detached mask.

So is one entitled to say that the man has yellow hair any more than, on looking at a black and white photograph of the picture, one can say that everything depicted is, in reality, in shades of gray? One might just as well say that if that man stood up he would be about seven inches tall! Is the hair color of the standing woman in Cézanne's picture actually yellow? The woman at the right and the seated man in the foreground have dark hair; their hair is set off against light ground; where the ground becomes very dark, the seated man's head becomes bald. A black jacket or shirt on the man standing rigidly in the background would just not do. Is the dog in the picture actually a light tan dog, or is it that color because a black dog (keeping in mind that the dog of Cézanne's youth was called, in English, *Black*) would not be set off in color from the dark ground?

One notes in this picture how Cézanne brought the blue of the sky all around the head of the seated woman, setting it off, as he does also in *Idyllic Day*, carefully bringing the green around the seated man's head. Had he not done that, the man's hair would become part of the black shadow, leaving a floating sliver of face. Cézanne had had enough art schooling to paint with visual intelligence, with the basic visualizing concerns of a painter (art as *métier*), rather than having to furnish his theme with a man with golden hair. The light-haired man has been described as having skin as light as his shirt (*à la peau aussi claire que sa chemise*), although he does not, and the smiling countenance fringed with blond hair has caused him to be linked to the *pâle jeune homme dont parle Musset* («this pale young man of whom Musset speaks,» the line taken from Zola's preface to *Mon Salon*, where Zola tells Cézanne how much he has meant to him).[5] Seeded by the primitive, reflexive notion that the similar are necessarily equal, this rhetorical overstatement allows the two men in the picture to be identified erroneously as Cézanne and Zola, symbolically ligatured.[6]

The distance between Manet's *Déjeuner sur l'herbe* and Cézanne's *Picnic* is a measure of how distant Cézanne was from Manet and others of the realist camp who depicted picnics—from Monet, for example, who in 1865 painted a very large, very ambitious *Déjeuner sur l'herbe*. Monet renders casualness in the various attitudes and postures of the figures; this informality is the non-Romantic aspect of naturalism, the uneventful moment of time that is neither specific nor of infinite duration. During the course of a naturalist's picnic, realism can suddenly supplant naturalism when a violent storm breaks out or a bull escapes from the neighboring pasture, as in Daumier's cartoon *The trouble with dining in the too-open air.*[7]

Honoré Daumier. *Désagrément de dîner au trop grand air* (Troubles when dining in the too open air). From Daumier, *Pastorales.*

To make a comparison, in Manet's *Déjeuner sur l'herbe* passers-by disrupt the conversation and a bullfinch just above the group flies by. The picnickers in Monet's *Déjeuner sur l'herbe* could, at any moment, be caught in a rain shower. Time is suspended. No moment of time exists in Cézanne's *Idyllic Day*—neither specific nor non-specific. Nothing has happened, and nothing will happen. The men are given poses of casualness, but their bodies are stiff and stilted; the one facial expression available to the viewer is ponderous, non-specific.

Nor is the sexual gesture of the tree reflected in the water and its counterpoint, the wine bottle, in *Idyllic Day* just a casual allusion, as if the sun at any

Èdouard Manet. *Le Bain* (*Le Déjeuner sur l'herbe*), 1863. Paris, Musée d'Orsay.

Claude Monet. *Picnic*. 1865.

moment might move and change the alignment of reflections. Schapiro wrote of this juxtaposition of the tree and its reflection that is aimed at the paired bottle and glass with the paired sexes, while also saying that such activation of the landscape through vaguely human forms is rare in the painting of the time.[8] This canvas and also *The Picnic* tell us that Cézanne was not ready to relinquish romanticism, symbolism, or the tenacious hold that the classics had on him, justifying, even at this stage, why Gauguin would refer to him as a Virgil perched on a mountaintop.

In the *Picnic*, one man is talking while others listen. In Manet's *Déjeuner sur l'herbe*, the conversation is in the process of being cut off; a direct confrontation has just occurred between Victorine Meurand in the picture and spectators outside it. The vertical curtain-plane of the theater, so to speak, has been punctured; stage-space flows into audience-space; the spectator's space is violated, as when a subordinate talks back, when the privacy of one's fantasy is violated by reality. By contrast, in Cézanne's *Picnic* every person, including the dog, exists in reference to the man in the foreground; even the couple strolling off are securely posed and positioned at the frozen moment when the man speaks. No one is in motion; the action is entirely within the picture; what is seen is as seen by the man who is speaking. Maybe the *Picnic* is just a brainteaser, another rebus, a problem the sibyl is having with dividing three oranges among four people.

In *Idyllic Day*, why are the three women in a separate scale from the three men, the nymphs larger than life (if life is represented by the scale of the men)? As in Giorgione's *Fête Champêtre*, it would seem that the men are not aware of the women; the women are phantoms, not even apparitions in the true cast of nymphs as representing not real women but aspects of nature—aroma, pond mist, breezes. The three men in their separate scale do indeed suggest the triumvirate—Cézanne, Zola, and Baille—as boys on the banks of the Arc. One sees limpid water, blue sky, one of the three is smoking a pipe. But the water it is not the Arc, rather a river extending to a horizon more northerly than Provence, more like the Seine at Bennecourt where Cézanne and Zola updated their adolescence.

This shift in scale seems to reconcile the reality of the three men with the nymphs as fantasy. At times I have thought that, although the picture is Cézannesque, yet strangely so, it is not by Cézanne but, so to speak, *of* Cézanne— that is, done by someone working with him, beside him, one of his painter friends from Aix or from the Suisse.[9]

Manet's *Déjeuner sur l'herbe*, and Monet's too, with recognizable friends as models, are «conversation pictures» of the sort Cézanne had in mind around 1868. Marion reported from Aix to Heinrich Morstatt, a German friend of Marion's in Marseilles, that Cézanne was planning a picture for which he would use portraits of his friends: *In the midst of a landscape one of us will be speaking while the others listen. I have your photograph, so you will be in it.*[10] But neither *Idyllic Day* nor the *Picnic* support the tempting thought that Cézanne actually used portraits of his friends as models. The idea had been on mind for some time. An ink drawing of a satyr holding forth to an audience of nymphs and fawns is an early example. A drawing that dates a bit later than 1878 may be of Cézanne talking while others listen; the listeners may be Pissarro, wearing a Barbizon farmer's hat, Hortense Fiquet, Guillemet, and Pissarro's dog. And several drawings depict friends around an outdoor dining table, smoking, conversing, in some cases a bit inebriated from an excess of wine. In other examples, men and women lounge in conversation on the grassy ground. This allusion to nakedness of people out in naked nature fits to the psychology of the picnic as a sort of spiritual regression to the natural—a back-to-nature impulse, for idyllic days are outdoor days.

The «conversation picture,» whether set indoors or outdoors, has a double meaning: one referencing two or more people—family, friends, any close-knit group—the other an object on which conversation can focus and build.[11] The conversations take place around a dining table, such as Monet's *At the Inn of Mother Anthony* of 1866, or along a path or road where one encounters a friend, such as one finds often in Pissarro's landscapes. Too much art history writing has associated Cézanne's *Picnic* with picnic pictures, the *fêtes galantes* of the eighteenth century, such as Watteau's *Embarkation for Cythera* and his *La Collation*. That is like saying Renoir or Cassatt would never have painted mothers with children had they

Cézanne. Group of friends and a dog, out of doors, one speaking, the others listening. Kunstmuseum Basel. This is not necessarily the composition referred to in Morstatt's letter. In fact, this drawing may have been made in Pissarro's territory north of Paris.

not seen historical representations of the *Madonna and Child*, or that Monet would not have painted a picnic had he not seen Manet's *Déjeuner*. Picnics in the public parks and in the countryside were popular throughout France in the nineteenth century. Magazines, such as *La Mode illustrée*, even had plates illustrating fashions appropriate for picnicking and strolling in parks and along the beach. Any nineteenth-century painter would know how to render couples on a picnic without having had to study eighteenth-century pictures in an art museum.[12] It is always better to search for an artist's inspiration as to imagery in the up-close environment rather than assigning it to remote history. Every cause and effect structure is an arbitrary and hypothetical bracket imposed on a broad continuum of infinite processes, making, as Nietzsche said, a «conception of becoming» out of describable similarities. Cézanne will paint a number of picnic pictures in the 1870s, friends on a picnic blanket, sharing wine; in one a man brings to the group a basket of apples (a traditional gift to friends during late summer). To say that these pictures depend on the artist having seen Rococo picnics would be hardly short of art historical nonsense—forced art history. Rococo picnics were typically of royals and gentry, not in the tradition of villagers and farmers taking lunch in the fields, or; in modern Paris, of ordinary families and friends enjoying and afternoon in the park or countryside. All roads from the 1860s do not lead back to the eighteenth century—some don't lead anywhere.

In November 1866, having sat for a number of dashed-out portraits, Valabrègue wrote to Zola saying that their friend Cézanne had been obliging his friends to sit for portraits he planned to use for a group tableau. *Fortunately, reports Valabrègue, I only posed for one day. The uncle is more often the model. Every afternoon there appears a portrait of him, and Guillemet maligns it with awful jokes.*[13] The referenced uncle was Dominique Aubert, the younger brother of Cézanne's mother, who posed for Cézanne in various costumes and attitudes: monk, lawyer,

Cézanne. Left: Portrait of Uncle Dominique. 1866.
Paris, Musée d'Orsay. Photo Bulloz.

Cézanne. Portrait of a man, possibly Antoine
Marion. 1866. J. Paul Getty Museum.

Turk.[14] But there were others whose images Cézanne most likely painted in Aix and as well in Paris.

Let us recall a few sentences from Antoine Marion's letter to Zola saying that their friend Cézanne, back in Aix, was in the habit of forcing optimism to the point of being ridiculous. *He intends to make a gift of the painting of his friends conversing to the Marseilles museum—nicely framed*, Marion writes, *so the museum will thus be forced to display realist painting and our glory*. Quite a bold statement—»and *our* glory»—for a provincial geology student and dauber to make, as if he understood what it had taken for a Delacroix and a Manet to lead critics to a Promised Land.

Cézanne may have been thinking about how Fantin-Latour's «homages»—*Homage to Delacroix* and *A Studio in the Batignolles Quarter* with Manet at his easel in the midst of friends—had forced the Salon jury and hostile critics to confront artists they despised hanging not from gallows but on the Salon walls. If Cézanne had anything like that it mind, it would point up again how remote he was from the Parisian avant-garde, and how feebly subsisting on compliments and encouragement coming from his family and from friends who were far less in touch with the art world than he was—not one of them a talented painter or knowledgeable critic. It cannot be often enough said that Cézanne's remoteness from the Batignolles group, from Manet, Monet, Fantin, Le Gros, Bazille, and the rest, from all those who defined what Michael Fried calls the generation of the 1860s, and those who will define Impressionism in the next decade (Monet, Renoir), allowed him to evolve along lines that will eventually define not the avant-garde of the late nineteenth-century but the avant-garde that opened onto the twentieth. Cézanne built on his technical faults and emotional frailties with the support of friends who were equally out of touch with the «generation of the sixties.» Cézanne's art carried no cultural load. His greatest contribution to the twentieth century would be his having ridded art of its historical baggage.

40

Courbet, Manet, Monet, and you others who
paint with a knife, brush or broom, you have been
outdone! I have the honor to introduce
your new master—Mr. Cézanne

Almost every painter with whom Cézanne would have aligned his cause, liking them or not, had been by 1870 more than once accepted by a Salon jury, and all had received some favorable press—not only from Zola. One of Manet's paintings, *The Execution of Maximilian*, had been rejected in 1869, but only because of its political imagery—an anti-Bonaparte gesture coming at a time when Napoleon was under fire for abandoning Maximilian and ordering the withdrawal of French troops from Mexico.[1] Even Manet's portrait of Zola—with two strikes against it: the name Manet and the person Zola—had been accepted, and works by Degas, Pissarro, Monet, Morisot, Renoir, and Bazille were also allowed in. As for the 1870 Salon, all except Monet would again see their pictures on the walls. Cézanne alone would be the rejected artist. To make matters worse, he was being also rejected by the other painters, all except Pissarro and the daubers in his small circle of friends. His follies were unappreciated by the other artists, and not at all by Zola, who had come to know that his boyhood friend was a hopeless cause, his blunt tactics out of date. The revolution against officialdom was wearing thin. In the opinion of most of the other realists, Cézanne's personal behavior and dreadful paintings had damaged their cause.

A second reform of the Salon, promising a more democratic jury, had come about for 1870. All artists who had had works accepted in previous salons, medal winners or not, were now eligible to vote for two-thirds of the jury. Accordingly, except for Cézanne, all members of the so-called Batignolles group of artists and their like would have a vote. Although this would appear to have been a victory of sorts, the plain fact of the matter was that the Batignolles painters constituted a tiny block of about eleven votes, while the «everyone else,» with equal voting rights, numbered several hundred. How ingenuous to think that the avant-garde's votes would make any difference. Cabanel and Gérôme still dominated the jury. Daubigny was elected to sit on it, probably to placate landscape painters, but both he and Corot resigned before the jury convened. Manet, Courbet, Millet, and Daumier were unsuccessful candidates, indicating that the modernists of any stripe were far less than a majority among the hopeful. The new policy had the appearance of a democratic vote but was actually very Darwinian. Those who survive as the fittest from previous showdowns with the jury would propagate those who would survive the next round.[2] The results would be no different than in previous years. Manet, whose brushwork skills made him easier to take, would have two canvases accepted. Bazille, Degas, Fantin-Latour, Pissarro, and Renoir had just one work each approved, while Monet, Sisley, and Cézanne were excluded.

Cézanne was not to any extent deterred by yet another rejection. While still in Aix, he had prepared at least one of two very large canvases for the 1870 Salon, surely with the hope of arousing greater commotion and acrimony than had Manet's pictures in the past. One would be the larger-than-life portrait of his friend, the congenital dwarf and fellow painter, Achille Emperaire, the other a naked woman laid out on a divan or bed, the latter known only by the caricaturist, Stock's, rendering of it when making fun of Cézanne's entries.

Cézanne was intent on shocking the jury, shocking the public: there is no way to deny that he was treating the Salon as a freak show. No one could convince me

Caricature by Stock, from *Album Stock*. Parody on Cézanne's two entries rejected by the Salon of 1870.

The annotation at the lower edge reads, «Incident du 20 mars au Palais de l'Industrie ou un succès d'antichambre avant l'overture du Salon.»

This would bear out that, anticipating rejection, Cézanne put on a display in the antichamber, showing his pictures to anyone who dared look. Clearly he was soliciting notoriety in the newspapers rather than acceptance by the jury.

LE SALON PAR STOCK

Incident du 20 mars au Palais de l'Industrie ou un succès d'antichambre avant l'ouverture du Salon

Cézanne. *Potrait of Achille Emeraire*. 1867-68. Paris, Musée d'Orsay. Photo: Wildenstein Gallery, Paris.

Cézanne. An extraordinary portrait drawing of Emperaire. Kunstmuseum Basel.

that Cézanne's intention was other than to be rejected so outrageously as to garner public and press attention, which indeed he got. History records Emperaire in these words: *We still remember him as a man of small stature, a little hunchbacked, with the head of a musketeer of Louis XIII, his saffron-dyed mustache, and who went through life with a cane or an umbrella placed under his overcoat, from behind, in the fashion of a sword.*[3] Most likely Cézanne's portrait of Emperaire aroused greater wrath from the jury than the accompanying nude, considering the vast number of awful paintings of naked women to which the jury was annually subjected when sorting out entries. In reality, Achille had a natural musketeer's head, cultured by long and heavy hair on his head and a thick mustache and goatee, while his congenital dwarfness rendered him very short, with spindly legs and large hands on thin arms. Cézanne painted him while at the Jas de Bouffan, over life-size, seated in the same upholstered chair in which his father had posed for his portrait while reading a newspaper. Emperaire's feet are planted on a foot warmer, a bright red foulard at his neck, dressed in a blue flannel robe open at the knees to reveal long purplish drawers and red slippers. The frank frontality forces the image on the spectators as a confrontation, as Manet had forced the naked Victorine Meurent in *Le Déjeuner sur l'herbe* and the whore Olympia, and with his *Christ Mocked by the Soldiers*, forced the viewer to confront the torture of a Messiah as symbolic of the mocking and jeering of academicians and the press.

Cézanne's bizarre entries provoked immediate notice in the press. Both canvases were promptly rejected but were picked up by Stock, a popular caricaturist, and featured in his newspaper column *Le Salon par Stock*. Stock was probably on hand at the door, or at the jury's deliberations, given an opportunity to sketch the pictures and interview Cézanne, for his rendering of the portrait of Emperaire is fairly accurate in pose and detail, as is his rendering of Cézanne, and his sketch of Cézanne's second entry is a plausible suggestion of what it looked like. Stock introduces Cézanne to his audience, and then quotes what Cézanne purportedly had said to him:

> *Artists and critics fortunate enough to be at the Palais de l'Industrie on March 20th, the last day for the submission of paintings, will treasure the ovation given to two works of a new kind. Now Courbet, Manet, Monet, and you others who paint with a knife, a brush, broom, or any other instrument, you have been outdone!*
>
> *I have the honor to introduce you to your new master: Mr. Cézanne. Cézanne comes to us from Aix-en-Provence. He is a realist painter and what is more, a determined one. Listen to him tell me, with his pronounced Provençal accent: «Yes, my dear Sir, I paint as I see, as I feel—and I have very strong sensations. The others, too, may see and feel as I do, but they don't take risks. They produce Salon pictures. I dare to take risks. Yes Sir, I dare. I have the courage of my opinions—and he who laughs last will have the best laugh!»*

The second canvas in Stock's cartoon features a nude woman, the body coarsely angular, posed not to arouse lust but perhaps to disgust and repel the viewer. Considering Cézanne's choice of Emperaire as a subject for his Salon entry, a combination of his friend's malformed body and Cézanne's grotesque way of picturing and painting him, there is little doubt that the reclining nude was also painted to nauseate the jury. Without making too much of it, the pose of *La Femme nue* can be compared to a drawing by Cézanne of this time, a reclining woman with prominent hips, on a sheet where the same model appears naked and flat on her back—a radical departure from the typical *académie*. The model was

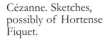

Cézanne. Sketches, possibly of Hortense Fiquet.

probably Cézanne's mistress Hortense Fiquet.[4] I will risk saying that this drawing was a study for Cézanne's entry, or, in any case, related to it.

The painting *La Femme nue* is lost. A few years ago, the Danish art historian Merete Bodelsen suggested it had at one time been in the collection of Paul Gauguin who had a taste for the bizarre. Bodelsen's evidence for this attribution is circumstantial but credible. In November 1889, when the Art Society of Copenhagen organized an exhibition of French and Scandinavian Impressionists, the French section was comprised largely of paintings loaned by Gauguin. The critic Karl Madsen made note of this atrocious nude: *A large picture of an elderly naked woman, painted larger than life by Cézanne, has been excluded from the exhibition, in due respect for Copenhagen's state of innocence. The painting is neither a particularly attractive nor a particularly good one. The elderly woman discloses the sad ruins of her charms.*[5] Madsen describes the color of the nude's body as like that of the dregs of bad claret, with chalky white highlights, but couldn't avoid adding that the brushwork of violent energy and rough swirling contours had the force of a master's hand. The «chalky white highlights» would indeed characterize this picture as by Cézanne, for most of his paintings from 1869 to 1870 are heavily highlighted with white.

Sure knowledge of this canvas evaporates with Gauguin's ownership. He may have brought the canvas back to Paris when he returned from his visit to Copenhagen in March 1891 and deposited it on consignment with the color merchant Père Tanguy, who sold pictures from his hole-in-the-wall shop, including some by Cézanne.[6] Cézanne had also disposed of the portrait of Emperaire— certainly Emperaire himself wouldn't have had use for it. Cézanne may have consigned it to Père Tanguy, from whom he first bought art supplies in 1873, perhaps at times in exchange for pictures; in any case, Émile Bernard, the painter and an admirer of the older Cézanne, claimed having found it at Tanguy's shop around 1890, hidden under a pile of very mediocre canvases. Bernard says that Tanguy told him at the time that he'd had to hide it from Cézanne, who often visited his shop, because he'd sworn to destroy it.[7] Had Cézanne found the *Femme nue* there, he would have destroyed it, too (doing to it as many others would have liked to have done), for after 1875 he shared the same opinion of his 1860s pictures, as had the Salon jurists and critics back then.

The portrait of Emperaire would make its own history, as would Père Tanguy. In June 1891, the *Mercure de France*—by then a supporting medium for modern art—announced: *The House of Tanguy, the agent for the principal impressionist painters, has moved to 9, rue Clauzel. It has, at this moment, a marvelous collection of canvases by Vincent van Gogh, an admirable portrait of the painter Emperaire by Cézanne, still-lifes and landscapes by the same, Guillaumins, Gauguins, Bernards, and so on.* The same year, Émile Bernard, then age twenty-three, being interviewed by the newspaper *Le Echo de Paris*, declared that the only artists he truly admired were Cézanne and Redon; later this year, he wrote to the Belgian painter Eugène Boch, saying, *Tanguy is in dire straits. It you would like the Cézanne—the Emperaire—now is the moment to make your move. The poor devil deserves it, I swear.* Boch purchased the painting and kept it until 1910 when he sold it to the Bernheim-Jeune gallery. Boch's sister wrote of the sale how relieved she was to have the picture out of her sight. To her brother, she said, *I congratulate you with all my heart on the sale of your frightful Mr. Emperaire. This nasty man got on my nerves when in your studio.*[8]

It would appear that the jury's rejection of his portrait of Emperaire did not affect Cézanne emotionally any more than previous rejections. He received a great amount of press—much more than did those who were accepted. On June 7th, 1870, he wrote to a painter friend, Justin Gabet:

My dear Gabet,

It has been quite a long time since I received your letter and I was negligent not to answer it. Now I am redressing the wrong done to you. Anyway, my dear fellow, you must have had news of me from Emperaire about a month ago, and more recently through my uncle who promised me to go and see you, and give you a copy of the caricature done by Stock. Well, I've been turned down in the past, but I don't feel any the worse for it. It is superfluous to tell you that I am always painting, and that for the moment I am well.

There are some very nice things at the exposition I can tell you, and some ugly ones too. There is the picture by Honoré [son of Joseph Gibert, who would succeed his father as head of the Musée d'Aix], *which is very effective and is well placed. Solari has also done a very fine statue.*

Please give my kind regards to Mrs. Gabet and a kiss for little Titin. Remember me also to your father Gautier, the extinguisher of street lamps, and Antoine Roche.

I embrace you with all my heart, dear fellow, be of good cheer,

Ever your old friend,

One might gather from this letter that Cézanne was not chagrined over Stock's caricature, but had passively accepted what he anticipated the reaction to his pictures would be. Nor does the tone of this letter seem the least bit vengeful, as if there were no longer much fire in his belly. He had got what he wanted—press notice, notoriety—but perhaps was at last able to question whether he sincerely wanted the sort of attention that had launched Manet. It is possible that Manet's *Olympia* fomented in Cézanne's mind as a stellar example of an artist becoming famous for having challenged official and public taste and precipitated an uproar that journalists could make hay of, that no one could ignore or forget. Even today, the fame of Manet largely rests on two paintings, *Le Déjeuner sur l'herbe* and *Olympia.* At least in part, if not in large part, Cézanne's burlesque of Manet's *Olympia,* the so-called *Modern Olympia,* was a disrespectful, invidious act that acerbated those whose support he needed. He may have had love-hate feelings towards Manet, whose success-at-failure he tried so vigorously to imitate—perhaps the *Reclining Nude* that Cézanne had paired with his portrait of Achille Emperaire was itself a response to Manet's picture, a crude prelude to the even cruder *Modern Olympia.* By referencing Titian's *Venus of Urbino,* Manet's *Olympia* was too deeply rooted in art history, still too much Venus and not enough whore. Vollard tells us something of Cézanne's distrust of Manet's picture persisting into the 1890s. Purportedly Cézanne said of it, *Une belle tache, pourtant!* (A beautiful blob, nonetheless).[9] Cézanne would refer again to *Olympia* when talking to Vollard about the use of nude models. Vollard mentioned to Cézanne that he'd heard it said that one-day Manet's *Olympia* might be in the Louvre. Cézanne responded wryly, *Come now, Mr. Vollard!* Perhaps thinking of Manet's *Déjeuner sur l'herbe,* where the figures are posed on a riverbank, Cézanne then lapsed into saying to Vollard that he would like to pose nude women on the banks of the Arc...*except,* he says with a jerk*, You understand that women are cows, calculators, manipulators, and they want to get their hooks into me. That's the fright of my life.*

Cézanne didn't actually harbor a phobia of women beyond the typical apprehensiveness that men feel when confronting the feminine. The phrase, «...they want to get their hooks in me,» is overused by historians who find misogyny under every overturned rock. The phrase comes from a context when Cézanne is bragging, digging up all he can to disparage Manet. His words should not be taken literally, and so reverently, as if every remark he uttered were liturgy for preaching. Cézanne had something of Balzac's capacity for *cocasserie* and black humor, even, if not especially, about himself. After saying that women are *calculatrices,* manipulators of men, he tells Vollard a story about Manet getting tricked by a woman, identified in the joke as Victorine Meurent:

Victorine, the woman who had posed for Olympia—Oh, what a virtuous demoiselle she was. And so drôle!

One day Victorine arrived at Manet's. «Listen, Manet, I know a charming young girl, the daughter of a colonel. You should make something of her, since the poor child is down on her luck. Only, you see, she has been raised in a convent, she knows nothing of the facts of life, so it will be necessary for you to treat her with respect and not talk smut in front of her.»

Manet promised to do just that, and asked Victorine to bring the girl to him at her earliest convenience. The following day, Victorine arrived with the daughter of the colonel, introduced her to Manet, and then said to the girl, «Go ahead, my dear, show your pussy to the gentleman.»[10]

41

*The Franco-Prussian War
and the Week of Blood*

In December 1870, the outspoken leftist Louis Ulbach founded the newspaper *La Cloche*. He gave Zola the best chance he'd ever had to take on a broad spectrum of antagonists, free range to roam through art and literature. Protected by the government's recent grant of greater freedom of the press, Zola could join republican attacks on Louis Napoleon's regime, which as rightly as wrongly was being accused by oppositionists of committing acts of skullduggery.

Political skirmishes, warmongering and anti-war mongering, intrigues and scandals, made more profitable news than societal skylarking. Liberal republicans and other revolutionary activists were chronically anti-monarchy with a long-standing reputation for inciting unrest (Cézanne's father was an anti-Bonaparte republican). The long line of Bonaparte rule had been the intellectual's recurrent bad dream for over a hundred years, representing the silencing of open discussion, a powerful military, and club-wielding bureaucracy.

Napoleon III's rule was pro-clerical, aristocratic, reactionary, and yet progressive. Over the past several years, France's economy had thrived. For sound economic reasons, the productive bourgeois and the farmer were favored, of course, over the man of letters: intellectuals neither fight for their country, manufacture, farm, nor pay taxes, and by instinct tend to be anti-government, whatever the government may be at the time. As if prompted by inborn terrier reflexes when sighting quarry of any size, France's intellectual elite unanimously snapped and nipped at the incumbent Napoleon III and the policies of the Second Empire, the empire described by the anti-royalist intellectual Alexis de Tocqueville as *a paradise of the envious and the mediocre.*[1]

For some time, the military and diplomatic conduct of Prussia had signaled the emergence of an expanded and unified German state, a condition that all other European nations had feared since the decline of the Roman Empire. Prussia had defeated Austria and its German allies, and had also taken over parts of Denmark and formed an alliance with Venice. The terms of the Prague Peace Accord had authorized Prussia to create a unified nation, which was in fact accomplished in July 1867 as the North German Confederation. What triggered France to force a war on Prussia was the appearance that Prussia was maneuvering to place a German noble on the vacant Spanish throne. At the Prague negotiations, Napoleon demanded repatriation of all former French land to the west bank of the Rhine, and asked for the annexation of Luxembourg. He got neither. So Prussia, in turn, had reason to fear Napoleon's dream of restoring the ancient border of France. As the threat of conflict beyond saber rattling increased, French politicians were forced to take individual stands, to either negotiate a compromise or start a war to reclaim territory and halt the Prussian expansion into Italy and possibly into Spain. Otto von Bismarck, who headed the new German Empire, could not be ignored.

Louis Napoleon feared Bismarck. As if to forecast his own doom and recapitulate the fall of Napoleon Bonaparte, he claimed to have the mentality of a martyr. Like all true martyrs, he was visionary and ambitious, fanatical in his desire to restore France to its former state of imperial glory, a France that would lead the world. The cult-image of Napoleon Bonaparte still encased him like a suit of armor. But eventually his excessive ambition had to confront the limits of his competence and of France's military strength. His dream of extending France to its ancient Roman borders was of great concern to aggressive capitalists, who just two years earlier had been given the right to form public corporations that could extend beyond national boundaries. The property line with Germany was not consequential for such practical concerns as the global economy, and peace was needed to sustain France's prosperity, especially as the nation's economic growth depended on expansion of trade beyond its borders. France had been enjoying many more prosperous years than recessive ones, so the emperor might have been more confident in keeping France as it was rather than unsettling its foreign relations. Nonetheless one carefully managed plebiscite after another indicated widespread approval of his reign. He seemed confident in public appearances, but when seen up close was rather shaky, hearing only the patriotic majority in his government who called for war. As Émile Olivier said of him in 1870, just before the war broke out, *One is never weaker than when one appears to have everyone's support.*[2]

In July 1870, France declared war and sent an army eastward to engage the Prussians. Within six weeks, those who had proposed a negotiated, conciliatory solution proved to have been right. The French army traveled a long way to confront a formidable enemy in one battle after another with more élan and esprit than munitions and equipment. After a series of setbacks, on September 3rd, 1870 at Sédan, the German army inflicted a crushing blow. The entire French command surrendered in the field. Louis Napoleon was quick to capitulate, having on his mind, perhaps, the decline of France under the dead weight of Napoleon Bonaparte's protracted battles and defeats. He abdicated, bringing the Second Empire to an end.

Parisians refused to acknowledge the surrender: enraged republicans hurriedly formed a government of national defense and a National Guard empowered to recruit troops and defend the city. Subject to the armistice terms, the French army could not come to the aid of Paris, but Paris had been heavily armed with cannons and other weaponry that could be deployed. A huge force of Prussians was dispatched by Bismarck to attack and disarm Paris. The action began in late September; by mid-November, Paris was under a massive siege. The Guard managed to hold out for four months. But the city was soon without supplies, without food; before long, almost every four-legged animal within the German encirclement had been eaten. Zoo cages were emptied into soup pots, children's pets were stewed, and rat pie became a delicacy. Wiser minds knew that the action being taken by Paris threatened a negotiated peace and would drive up the indemnity that Prussian would certainly impose on France. Come March, under orders from the Prussian General von Moltke not to sack or occupy Paris, the expedition force marched victoriously down Paris' broad avenues as a symbolic takeover, and then withdrew to bivouac in the outskirts, doing Paris no more harm.

When the Franco-Prussian war broke out, rather than report on the events of the day, Zola attacked France's history of war making under Napoleonic rule. On July 25th, 1870, the day after the declaration of war, he published the following in *La Cloche*:

> *From China to Mexico, from the snows of Russia to the sands of Egypt, there is not an acre under the sun that doesn't cradle a slaughtered Frenchman, in silent and godforsaken cemeteries, slumbering in the lavish serenity of the countryside. Most of them, nearly all, lie outside some desolate hamlet with crumbling walls that retain memories of terror. Waterloo was only a farm. Magenta had scarcely fifty houses. A tornado swept through these tiny settlements, and the syllables of their names, innocent the day before, acquired an odor of blood and powder such that humanity will forever shiver when pronouncing them.*[3]

Cézanne was in Aix when news of the war took over the country's telegraph lines, scattering perched starlings and the faint of heart. To avoid conscription, Cézanne retreated to L'Estaque, a rather coarse seaside village about eighteen miles down the map from Aix and just short of Marseilles, not wanting anyone but his mother to know where he planned to hide out. He had Hortense, then twenty, travel by train from Paris to Marseilles. The two remained secluded in L'Estaque for several months, occupying a house rented for them by Cézanne's mother. As for Zola, with wife and mother in tow he escaped to Marseilles, using the excuse that Alexandrine was so terrified over remaining in Paris that she would become hysterical. Again completely broke and out of a job—*La Cloche* and other newspapers in Paris having had to shut down during the siege—but with no break in ambition, Zola hoped to capitalize on the public's need for war news. He promptly wrote to Marius Roux in Aix, *How about putting out a small newspaper in Marseilles during our forced absence. It would occupy our time usefully. Without your help, I cannot take the risk. With you, I think it is feasible.*

Roux joined him in Marseilles. They found a financier, deeded him the paper in exchange for his backing, and set to work. The first issue of *La Marseillaise* appeared in November 1870. From the start, they had both marketing and personnel problems—absenteeism and worker demands for higher pay. Ironically, this socialist newspaper on the side of the working man couldn't get enough work out of its composition and printing staff to keep the paper going. The final issue was distributed in mid-December. Even before its demise, Zola had been looking for a way to climb out of his latest hole.

An opportunity came his way shortly after the German advance had destroyed the French garrison at Orléans, and three weeks after the bombardment of Paris had begun. The young Léon Gambetta, then head of the National Defense, and the elder statesman Adolphe Thiers, had escaped Paris by balloon and set up a provisional government in Bordeaux. Functionaries in flocks hurried to this provisional capital with hopes of securing an official position. Zola lost not a minute getting there, too. After several attempts at obtaining a significant role, even an appointment as *sous-prefect* of Aix—his effort denied—he was offered a prefecture position in remote Brittany. He declined that one: though a safe haven, the presence of Zola in primitive, still medieval Brittany would have been a political aberration. When no better offer came his way, Zola served for a while in Bordeaux as secretary to the minister-without-portfolio Glais-Bizoin, who was suffering dementia and performing just an honorary role representing Belgium, so Zola had not much to do beyond making sure daily that his boss still recognized him. In the eye of the storm and feeling agitated, he contacted Louis Ulbach and secured the position of parliamentary reporter for the revived Paris newspaper *La Cloche.*

Although a journalist, Zola could now write in the style of a novelist. And the events of the time were piling up in his head for use in novels he planned to write: future books in the *Rougon-Macquart* series. Frederick Brown offers a deft description of Zola's reports from Bordeaux:

> Zola took his assignment seriously, giving *La Cloche* a vivid account of the issues that set Paris against the provinces, conservatives against republicanism, and moderate republicans against radical ones. When clashes occurred, he analyzed them. When parliamentary debate flagged, he noted talk of the town. When Thier's sojourn in Versailles left Bordeaux free to conjecture about peace negotiations, he evoked the atmosphere of a citywide rumor mill. When he had done portraying major figures, he caricatured squireens in quaint headgear and unfashionable paletots who seemed to have emerged from a time warp for this one momentous conclave. «How many bald pates aglow under the great chandelier I was scrutinizing them just now, studying the countenance of worried land owners.»[4]

At no place in his reporting for *La Cloche* can one detect for certain what side Zola was on. As he'd claimed when defending *Thérèse Raquin*, being a scientific writer, he does not participate emotionally in the text, but remains detached, as if he were a singular audience for a grand drama, a viewer who sees at the same time both the action on the stage and the reaction of the audience. An extract from one of Zola's reports reads:

> *Imagine, if you will, a mortuary chapel. At 2 p.m., dazzled by sunlight, one falls into an auditorium lit by three chandeliers. Red plush seats below, and above on the stage, its curtain raised, a dais with purple bunting set in the midst of drawing-room decor. There is where France will be put to death. One searches dark corners for the hangman. In the loges, many women, a first-night audience. Gloved hands hold opera glasses.*[5]

When news reached Paris that a Prussian army was advancing under orders to take the city by force, most of the artists and writers identified with the avant-garde of art and literature defected. Others, including the core of the realist group, Manet, Degas, Morisot, and Bazille, remained in Paris. Manet's past generations of distinguished military leaders merited his being commissioned as a lieutenant. He was assigned to the artillery corps, ironically under the command of the one artist whose work he most disliked, Ernest Meissonnier. Also assigned to Meissonier's command were Bracquemond, Tissot, Carolus-Duran, and Puvis de Chavannes. Whether all of them stayed in Paris during the assault is not known. Puvis, for one, managed to get out of town, to Saint-Germain. Berthe Morisot, who remained in Paris, said in a letter to her daughters that Manet spent the entire Prussian siege changing uniforms.[6] To Eva Gonzalès, Manet sent a letter by balloon, in which he said, *Degas and I are volunteers with the artillerie canonniers. I expect that on your return you will do a portrait of me in my huge gunner's greatcoat.*[7]

Degas had been assigned to the infantry, but was transferred to the *artillerie* when it became known that he had one bad eye and was too near-sighted to take aim with a rifle.[8] An anecdote told by Berthe Morisot has Degas the wit saying he hadn't yet heard a single cannon boom, but would like to in order to find out whether his ears can take the noise. Degas and Manet were posted to the fortifications north of the *Bois de Vincennes*. Solari, Guillemet, and Guillaumin joined the Guard. Renoir was called up, put in the cavalry and posted at Vie-en-Bigorre near Bordeaux, where, as he later said, he spent his time riding a horse and teaching a young girl to paint. At one time or another, he went to Louveciennes and moved in with his mother. Finding Sisley there, or nearby in Bougival, the two spent their time painting landscapes. Corot had rushed to Paris from his safe haven in Ville d'Avray to offer a lot of money to anyone who would bring cannons to chase the Prussian soldiers out of the *Ville d'Avray* forest—so he could paint without being bothered, one might suppose.

In Manet's letter of November 19th to his wife, Suzanne, safe and secure at

Oloron-Ste-Marie in the Pyrénées, one reads: *A lot of cowards have left here, including our friend Zola. I don't think he will be well received when he returns.*[9] Pissarro, with his family, fled to Brittany, then in December to London; his Louveciennes house was billeted by the Prussian command and made into a butchery. Monet, who'd married Camille just five months earlier, abandoned her and their child; along with hundreds of others escaping in any sort of boat, he sailed across the Channel, making it to England where he met up with Pissarro. Daubigny was already in London, his paintings being handled by Durand-Ruel who had moved over with a large inventory and opened a gallery on Bond Street. Monet and Pissarro's canvases pleased him; he became their supporting art dealer. Earlier, Durand-Ruel had bought a number of Manet's pictures and taken them to London. In December, he would stage his first *Society of French Artists* show, displaying 144 works, including some by Barbizon landscapists, two canvases by Pissarro, and one by Monet. The painter Louis Bonvin, too, had fled to London, while Boudin and Diaz chose Brussels. Alexis and Baille moved back down to Aix.[10]

In a letter to Zola of February 1870, Solari tells of the dullness and depravations of his war experience:

I spent all my time queuing up at the door of butchers, bakers, coal-men—the rest of the time marching and standing at the fortifications. What an existence! Unbelievable the suffering we put up with, the things we ate. Nothing left in Paris but stringy dog meat and black pudding; I almost ate a dog's head, which a butcher was selling as veal. Once the quarter-million sheep that grazed in the Bois de Boulogne were consumed, Parisians dined on rat pie, or, if they had Victor Hugo's means, on bear and elephant slaughtered at the zoo.[11]

Pissarro in London, anxious to hear news of his friends, received at last a letter from the painter Edouard Béliard: *All your friends are well.*

Manet left for the south a few days ago. Zola is staying at Bordeaux, awaiting further events. Guillemet is fine, Guillaumin also. Duranty, the same as always. Cézanne is in the south. Degas is a bit mad, Duranty tells me. I have not seen Fantin, Sisley, or Renoir for some time. Monet, I believe, is in Dieppe or in England. I have no news of your house in Louveciennes. Your blankets, suits, shoes, underwear—as for your pictures, you may as well go into mourning for them since, being admirable, they most likely will become ornaments in Prussian drawing rooms. The nearness of the forest will have saved your furniture from the stove.[12]

Although Béliard has Manet going south, it may have been that he had gone to put his wife, Suzanne Leenhoff, at a safe distance and then returned to Paris. Manet wrote often to Suzanne, the mail sent out of the city by the postal balloon.

On September 30th, he wrote, *It's been such a long time since I heard from you. Some of my letters should have reached you by the balloons that left Paris.*

The Prussians seem to be regretting their decision to besiege Paris. They must have thought it would be easier than it is turning out to be. It is true that we cannot have milk with our coffee anymore; the butchers are open only three days a week, people queue up outside from four in the morning, nothing is left for latecomers. We eat meat only once a day. I believe all sensible Parisians must be doing the same.

I have seen the Morisot ladies recently. They are probably going to leave Passy, as it is likely to be bombarded. Paris these days is a huge camp. From five in the morning until evening, the Militiamen and the National Guardsmen who are not on duty at the fortifications do drills, turning into real soldiers. Otherwise, in the evenings life is very boring. All the café restaurants are closed after ten, and one has nothing to do but go to bed.

On November 3rd, Manet wrote again to Suzanne: *Marie's big cat has been killed. We suspect somebody in the house. It was for a meal of course, and knowing that, Marie was in tears.*

She is taking very good care of us. One does not feel like seeing anyone, it is always the same conversations. Evenings pass very slowly: the Café Guerbois is my only distraction, and that has become pretty monotonous.

I think of you all the time. I have lined the bedroom walls with your portraits. Tell mother not to worry and to make the most of the good weather. We are having torrential rain here, and I am rejoicing in your woolen socks. They have come in very handy, because we are up to our ankles in mud on the fortifications.

On November 19th, Manet wrote to Eva Gonzalès: *No news at all from my poor Suzanne, who must be very anxious about me, though I write to her frequently.*

We are all soldiers here. Degas and I are in the artillery as volunteer gunners. I expect that on your return you will do a portrait of me in my huge gunner's greatcoat Tissot covered himself in glory in the action at La Gonchère. My brothers and Guillemet are in National Guard battle units, waiting to go into action. My paint box and easel are stuffed into my knapsack, so there can be no excuse for wasting my time.

A lot of cowards have left here, including our friend Zola, Fantin, and others. I do not think they will be very well received when they return to Paris. We are beginning to feel the pinch: horsemeat is a delicacy, donkey is horribly expensive. There are butcher shops for dogs, cats, and rats. Paris is deadly sad. When will it all end?

Class distinction shows plainly in Manet's description of the city under siege—for him, meat only once a day, the cafés closing at ten! Paris ranked above all other French cities for per capita consumption of meat, usually taken twice daily by the bourgeois, while the working class spread out their meat in soups and stews lasting all week. And rats were often a survival food for the destitute. Monselet was not the only one asking why it was that dirty rats were not eaten while filthy pigs were. The coopers (barrel-makers) of Bordeaux had made rats a delicacy, skinned, cut in half the long way, grilled and spiced.[13] Manet did not endure more than inconvenience, nor did any of the modernists. The avant-garde suffered only one great loss over the months of the war. In the battle of Beaune-la-Rolande in Burgundy, on November 28th, five weeks before the Prussian army began to bombard Paris, Bazille was killed.

On January 29th, 1871, a general armistice was signed, but not until March 1st did France's chief negotiator, Adolphe Thiers, submit to the final terms of the treaty. There had been little room for negotiation. Bismarck was in a position to dictate terms, but also wise enough to know that prolonged occupation of France would eventually be attritious and that excessive punishment would lead to a future war of vengeance. He knew what he wanted: Lorraine and Alsace. He got them both. And France was constrained to pay an indemnity of five billion francs—an enormous penalty, considering that Haussmann's rebuilding of Paris had, to that date, cost less than three billion.

In February 1871, the provisional government of *La Défense nationale*, headed by its Minister of the Interior, the brilliant strategist Léon Gambetta, convened in Bordeaux. A new government was to be elected, the inaugural sessions held at Bordeaux, away from politicized Paris, and away from Versailles, where Bismarck had established his headquarters (during the occupation, William, King of Prussia, was crowned Emperor of Germany in the *Palais de Versailles'* Hall of Mirrors). By mid-February, Bordeaux teemed with legislators, judges, reporters, lobbyists, and the usual cadre of dealmakers. With the Napoleonic regime demised, Victor Hugo returned from exile and was made a deputy in the new government. On entering Bordeaux, he was met with the cheers of a huge crowd and chants of *Vive Hugo.* That is when Zola rushed up from Marseilles to Bordeaux, when he would become the parliamentary reporter for *La Cloche,* providing daily reports on the debates and sidelights for Louis Ulbach in Paris to work up for publication. He had endless opportunities for sending back juicy reports—intrigues, conspiracies, collusion, violent protests among disputing parties, some so violent as to require intervention by mounted police patrols.

After a General Assembly had been elected and the Prussian hierarchy had withdrawn from the country, although an occupation army remained, the Assembly moved to Versailles rather than back to Paris. This gave the appearance of the government abandoning Paris and threatening the establishment of another monarchy. The majority of the newly elected representatives were monarchists. To a man the republicans were quick to accuse the departed politicians—rightists and monarchists—of bringing on France's humiliation. In the minds and hearts of most Parisians, Paris was France. And that was still true even though the city's population by this time had boiled down to a gelled mass of socialists.

Zola divided his time between Versailles and Paris. Both locations offered daily news. Massive demonstrations against the new government were staged in Paris, the insurgents recruiting even those who were ignorant of the actual events, the workers and the unemployed. Adolphe Thiers, who headed the new government, had good reason to fear Paris, a veritable tinderbox for insurrection. He was still bitter over his overthrow by Parisians in 1848 (the October Revolution). Faced with the potential of another uprising, his first thoughts were to disarm the city's population. He arranged to have all artillery installations withdrawn. Many Parisians, still armed, refused to give up the cannons, especially those positioned high up in semi-rural Montmartre overlooking the city. After stand offs, threats to open fire, women throwing their bodies between soldiers and civilians, and skirmishes that whipped up the crowd, two French generals were slaughtered by a mob. Thiers then withdrew all soldiers from Paris, proclaimed an insurrection, and marshaled the army to assault the city.

Within Paris, on March 28th, 1871, a coalition of socialists elected a governing council and declared Paris a commune, a self-governing island in the Sea of France. This act was impulsive, ill planned, the consequences ill fated. Social issues had not been sorted out from those purely political, and no one in their right mind could have explained how Paris would survive economically when cut off from the entire world, allowed only homing pigeons and balloons for communication. One-third of the population had fled the city when the Prussians approached—most if not all of the upper class was gone; what remained was an unbalanced population, a high proportion of petit-bourgeois and workers who couldn't survive economically without wholesale merchants and the usual array of professionals: bankers, physicians, lawyers. Capitalist leaders, whose businesses reached beyond Paris, were by then in Bordeaux or Versailles, lobbying and negotiating. And Thiers had moved all the ministries and governmental agencies away from the city, even the central post office.

The Commune was a short-lived entity. It survived just 73 days (March 18th to May 28th, 1871). The final week, during which Zola was safely at Bonnières (across the river from Bennecourt) with Alexandrine and his mother, was a voluptuous state of chaos and terror. On May 22nd, Thiers ordered the French army, over 130,000 strong, to punish Paris (a force equal to the Allied manpower of the World War II Normandy landings). After stringing a necklace of cannons around the city, the center was approached by cavalry and riflemen through Neuilly and Porte Saint-Cloud. Most of the assault troops had been brought up from southern camps so as to be without loyalty to Paris and have no relatives among its population.

As the well-trained and equipped troopers overwhelmed hastily thrown-up barricades and ferreted out snipers hiding behind trash and in cracks between buildings along the narrow, debris-clogged streets, communards, bystanders, and the curious who were standing too close were slaughtered by the thousands. It took but a week to put down the resistance in this hell-of-a-place-to-be at the time, where half the population was already near starvation. As the street fighting subsided, arrests and mass executions picked up: over forty thousand accused people were arrested, entire families were shot.

Courbet had played a major role in the Commune. As a friend of Proudhon, who had a large block of supporters in the socialist coalition, Courbet was elected as a people's representative and made president of a general assembly of artists. In the fashion of a true revolutionary with power over life and death, his first act was to call for executions. Symbolically, he lined up and had shot the *École des Beaux-Arts*, the French Academy in Rome, the entire fine art section of the Institute; and after these were abolished from future history, he canceled all medals. None of this would have any effect on the institutions, however, since before any of Courbet's victims fell, the Commune was decimated and Courbet was thrown in jail, heavily fined and slated for exile. What had fallen, however, was the Vendôme column, a powerful symbol of the Napoleonic reign.

Èdouard Manet. Slaughter at the barricades. 1871(?). Budapest, Museum of Fine Arts.

Courbet had instigated and most likely supervised its toppling as a public spectacle. His and Proudhon's friends apparently had sufficient clout to keep his head attached to his body, and while in Ste.-Pélagic prison, he was even allowed to paint pictures, mostly still-lifes.

This week of horror was not a good-guy, bad-guy armed conflict. Little wonder that people like Manet and Zola couldn't decide which side they were on, or why Monet, Pissarro, and Cézanne turned their backs on it, why no artists, other than illustrators, put the horror on canvas. Manet had in mind doing a large painting, but did only a drawing for it and two etchings (one of a queue outside a butcher shop). Meissonier, who had conducted himself admirably during the Prussian invasion, painted a documentary canvas, *The Siege of Paris*. Other than Courbet's commitment to the Commune (for which Manet, and a good many others, would thereafter scorn him), Manet and Degas were the only ones with much interest in politics.[14] Manet's *Execution of Maximilion*, had been the only political painting of significance to emerge from this group. Zola was a fence-straddler: either side would do, as long as he were offered a job and could attack from the left of any issue. Cézanne was so indifferent to such matters as politics and wars that he couldn't even rise to a level of ambivalence.

The Prussians, who had captured the city just three months before, treated the Parisians with much greater compassion than their own countrymen. Some twenty-five thousand citizens were executed—prisoners who had been taken and others who were only accused. Those few days of slaughter, bloodier than Zola could have described, became known as *la semaine sanglante* [the bloody week]. Zola painted a word-picture of what he saw on coming back to Paris from his few days at Bonnières. He supplied this report to *Le Sémaphore de Marseilles,* published on May 27th:

> *I managed to take a walk through Paris. It's atrocious. I will tell you only about corpses heaped high under bridges. Never will I forget the heartache I felt at the sight of frightful mounds of bleeding human flesh thrown haphazardly on the river's towpaths. Heads and limbs mingling in horrible dislocations. Convulsed faces, dead who appeared cut in half, while others had four legs and as many arms. What a dismal charnel house.*
>
> *With warm days ahead of us unburied corpses will breed disease. I do not know if one's troubled imagination plays a role here, but while loitering among the ruins, I smelled the heavy, noxious air that hangs over cemeteries in stormy weather. It all looks like a grim metropolis where fire has not purified death. Stale odors, as of the morgue, cling to side-walks. Paris, which was called the boudoir, or the hostel, of Europe under the Empire, no longer gives off an aroma of truffles and rice powder. One enters the city holding one's nose, as if entering some foul sewer.*
>
> *The Père-Lachaise cemetery...here and there are pools of blood, corpses that no one has taken the trouble to collect. I saw a child of about seventeen, stretched out on a white gravestone, his arms crossed, like one of those stiff gisants of the Middle Ages put to bed on sarcophagi. Nearby, a National Guardsman had fallen on the sharp spikes of a gate, and he still hung there, impaled, bent in two, horrible, like a carcass in a butcher's window. Blood had spurted over funeral wreaths, and on the marble slabs were bloody finger-prints, suggesting that some poor devil had clung to the edge before collapsing.* 15

Pissarro suffered the only loss of artworks affecting art history. On returning from London at the end of June 1871, he recovered only forty pictures out of fifteen hundred.[16]As for the other artists and writers, the war was not much more than a rude interruption. The lower floor of Zola's house had been billeted to domicile refugees, but his furniture and personal items had been moved to the upper floor; nothing was stolen or even damaged.

In Paris, people set themselves to collecting and burying corpses, flushing bloodstains; merchants reopened their shops for business as usual. Investors eagerly grabbed up reparation bonds issued by the government and soon Paris was again under construction. Haussmann's plans went ahead towards completion. In June 1871, Pissarro proclaimed that Paris would soon recover her supremacy.[17] According to Ambroise Vollard, Zola wrote to Cézanne, *Never have I felt so hopeful, so eager to work. Paris is in a state of rebirth. The time for our reign is coming. It is a pity all the imbeciles didn't die, but I console myself with the thought that not one of us fell by the wayside.*[18] Zola ignores the death of Bazille, because he no longer identifies himself with the artists and writers in Manet's circle. He had moved off from associating with them. His «us» meant the naturalists, the likes of Pissarro, Guillaumin, and Cézanne.

Art and literary history in Paris also picked up where it had left off, as if there had not been a war. Having skipped 1871, the Salon of 1872 would come on schedule; another jury, another five thousand entries, another two thousand rejected artists. Zola would visit it and record his impressions:

> *I placidly followed the crowd for three hours, as it led me past all sorts of curiosities, past naked women and well-dressed men who looked at me with a disconcerted air, past Bretons and Provençaux, past colors that made my head throb. When finally I left, rain pelted me. Some ways off, I could see blurrily the Tuilleries, its windows opened wide to a dirty-yellow sky. Two entire years! So many shocks! Yet, here in these halls are the same gingerbread gents and sugarcane ladies, unmindful that 150,000 Frenchmen had been slaughtered since the Salon of 1870.*[19]

By the end of 1872, Zola had renewed his optimism for the future of art. In a *causerie* published in *Le Corsaire* on December 3rd, he spoke of the fateful hour of the war as well chosen by destiny:

> *After every social disaster there settles over the land a sense of stupor, a longing to get back to an untarnished reality. The false platforms on which one has lived are crumbling. One looks for firmer ground to more securely build upon. All great literary and artistic blossoming has taken place either in periods of complete maturity, or after violent upheavals. I confess to hoping that from all this blood and all this stupidity will emerge a massive flow of creativity. And those pariahs of the past, those talents who were denied, that group of naturalists of recent times, will now come to the foreground and continue the scientific movement in art.*[20]

42

I am nearly as lonely as you
and your letters help me to live

When news of France's defeat by the Prussians at Sédan reached Aix-en-Provence, the town anxiously awaited whatever action the government in Paris might choose to take. On September 4th, 1870, a telegram arrived announcing that a new Republic was on the point of being formed. On September 11th, it became official. Another Napoleon had been deposed. On hearing this news, the anti-Bonapartists of Aix went en masse to the town hall and evicted the local government. The incumbent mayor was discharged, portraits of Napoleon III were slashed, and an iron bust of the emperor was tossed into the town's central fountain. Politicians who had lost in the previous election were asked to submit names for membership on the new city council. To that list were added a few others, including Louis-Auguste Cézanne, Baille, and Valabrègue, all three appointed city councilors.

Louis-Auguste, by then seventy-two, was put on the Committee for Finance, Baille on the Committee for Public Works, Valabrègue on the Committee for Miscellaneous Matters.[1] Nominated by his father, Cézanne in absentia was made a member of the Commission for the *École des Arts* and the Musée d'Aix. Zola's name had been mentioned in the local press: *Among the republican candidates from the Bouches-du-Rhône will probably be one of our local citizens, Mr. Émile Zola* (a reference to Zola's attempt to secure a political position as *sous-préfet* of Aix). Of these events, Marius Roux wrote rather whimsically to Zola, who was by then in Bordeaux, *As I observe the revolution marching past, I see in the mob our two friends Baille and Valabrègue. Their exuberance amuses me to no end. Can you fancy those two basket-weavers [francs-fileurs] from Paris sitting on the municipal council, urging military resistance?*

Cézanne, still in hiding in L'Estaque as a defector, was subject to capture and trial by a military tribunal. So there must have been some concern on his parents' and his friends' minds that he had run a terrible risk. Fortunately, Baille and Valabrègue took an active part in the census-taking for the National Guard—a head count of men required to register for the draft—and most likely managed to cover up Cézanne's defection with some success. In January 1871, Zola received a letter from Marius Roux:

Concerning the mobilization of the guard, I have two bits of news for you; one is unpleasant, the other astonishing.

The unpleasant news is that Cézanne is being looked for, and I am afraid he will not escape being found, if, as his mother says, he is still in L'Estaque. Paul did not foresee what was about to happen and was often seen in Aix. He went there quite often and remained one, two, or three days, and sometimes more. It is also said that he got drunk in the company of gentlemen of his acquaintance. He must have—it is even certain—given his address, since the gentlemen (who must be jealous of him for not earning his livelihood) hastened to denounce him and to give information necessary for finding him.

These same gentlemen (here is the astonishing news) to whom Paul said that he was living in L'Estaque with you—not knowing that you were able to leave that hole, and not knowing whether you were married or a bachelor—also gave your name as an evader. On the evening of January 2nd, my father took me aside and told me that he'd just overheard a conscript saying, «Four of us have been ordered to Marseilles to bring back defectors [L'Estaque then lay about fifteen miles from the mid-nineteenth-century edge of Marseilles].» He mentioned some names. Among them, my father told me, were those of Cézanne and Zola. «Those two,» said the conscript, «are hiding in Saint-Henri [a village near L'Estaque].»

I told my father to lend a deaf ear and take no part in any conversation of this kind. The next morning I rushed to the town hall where I have complete freedom of information and was shown the list of evaders. Your name was not on it. I told a friend there, who is a reliable man and devoted to me, what was being said. He replied, «They must have mentioned Zola only because of his association with Cézanne, who is being diligently sought.» At the town hall, nothing officially names you, and among the crowd that bandies Cézanne's name about, I have not heard yours mentioned.

Cézanne managed to remain undiscovered. On February 9th, 1871, Manet, having set aside Zola's «cowardice,» wrote to Zola, who at this time was still a parliamentary reporter in Bordeaux, writing for *La Cloche*:

I am very glad to have good news from you. You have certainly not been wasting your time. Recently we suffered a great deal in Paris. Only yesterday, I heard of the death of poor Bazille. I am overcome—alas; we have seen many people die here in so many ways. At one time your house was being occupied by a refugee family, but only the ground floor; the furniture was moved upstairs. So I think your things suffered no damage. I am leaving soon to join my wife and my mother in Oloran in the Basses-Pyrénées. I am anxious to see them again. I will pass through Bordeaux and perhaps will come to see you. I will tell you then what cannot be put on paper.

Early the following month, March 1871, Zola wrote to Alexis, saying he had not heard a word from Cézanne. A few weeks later, after both Alexis and Zola returned to Paris, Alexis went down to L'Estaque, searching for Cézanne. *No Cézanne here,* he reports back to Zola. *The two birds flew away a month ago. The nest is empty and locked up. I was told by the landlord they went to Lyons to wait until Paris stopped smoking. I am surprised that for an entire month we had not seen Cézanne in Paris. I hope that when you receive this letter you will know more about him than I do.*

Zola responded on June 30th: *What you tell me about Cézanne's flight to Lyons is just a ruse. Our friend merely wanted to throw his landlord off the scent. He has hidden himself in Marseilles, or in some deep valley. I hope to find out where he is as soon as possible, for I am worried.*

> *I wrote to him the day after you left. My letter, addressed to him at L'Estaque, must have gone astray, which is not a great loss. But I am afraid that by an unforeseen set of circumstances it may have fallen into Cézanne's father's hands. It contains some particulars compromising to the son. You follow the reasoning, do you not?*

> *I want to find Paul to have him claim this letter. Therefore I count on you for the following errand. One of these mornings go to the Jas de Bouffan and pretend you are seeking news of Cézanne. Manage somehow to talk to his mother privately, and ask her for her son's exact address.*

> *If you cannot carry through this diplomatic intrigue successfully, go and ask Achille Emperaire, 2, rue Baulezan, telling him that I absolutely must know where Cézanne is staying. Approaching the mother would be better because it is possible that Emperaire is as ignorant of his whereabouts as we are.*

> *That is what I need you to do for me, and now, let me ask for news about you. You wrote from L'Estaque an enthusiastic letter, which proved to me that your heart is not dead to the blue sky and to bouillabaisse, but today you should have something else to tell me. Are you working? That is the eternal question—I will forever ask it. If you return with empty hands, you will be a very miserable man. What kind of a life are you leading? How do you manage, down there in the solitude of the Arc, to simply forget the miseries of the siege and the Commune? I fear that you are sleeping a lot. Remember that Valabrègue has an eye on you.*

Alexis was able to trace Cézanne through his mother. He encouraged Cézanne to write to Zola. He did. That letter is lost, but on July 4th, 1871, Zola replied:

> *Your letter gave me much pleasure. I was becoming worried about you. For four months now we have had no news of each other. Toward the middle of last month, I wrote to you at L'Estaque, then learned you had left and that my letter would not find you. I was just trying to trace you when you rescued me from my difficulty.*

> *You asked me about me. Here, in a few words, is my story. I wrote to you, I believe, shortly before my departure from Bordeaux, promising you another letter immediately on my return to Paris. I arrived in Paris on the 14th of March. Four days later, on the 18th,*

the insurrection broke out, the postal services were suspended, so I couldn't send you a sign of life. For two months I lived in the furnace, night and day the cannons roared and shells whistled over my head. Finally, on the 10th of May, when in danger of being arrested as a hostage, I took flight with the help of a Prussian passport, and went to Bonnières to get over the worst days [of the Commune]. Today, I find myself living peacefully in Batignolles [Paris, near Montmartre] as if I had just awoken from a bad dream. My country house is the same, my garden has not suffered, and I could believe the war was nothing but a farce.

They are printing my novel La Fortune des Rougon. You cannot imagine the pleasure I experience while correcting the proofs. It is like my first piece to come out. After all the shocks, I experience the same youthful feelings that made me await feverishly the pages of Contes à Ninon. It is a pity all the imbeciles didn't die, but I console myself with the thought that not one of us fell by the wayside. We can restart the battle.

Don't wait for months before answering me. Now that you know I am in Batignolles, and that your letters will not go astray, write to me without fear. Give me details. I am nearly as lonely as you and your letters help me to live.[2]

43

When the new Assembly moved to Versailles, Zola returned from Bordeaux to Paris, but made periodic trips to Versailles after the new government had settled in. He was still the parliamentary reporter for *La Cloche*. Paris was recovering. Gatherings of painters and writers at the *Café Guerbois* had resumed. After a time, the core group moved to the *Café de la Nouvelle-Athènes*. But Zola would have little contact with the group, and Cézanne, on returning to Paris, would have nothing to do with them.

Cézanne was thirty-two in March 1871. Zola turned thirty-one in April. Hortense was pregnant, and Zola and Alexandrine had been married for a year. Approaching quickly was the final phase of Cézanne and Zola's youth. Both were in need of structure that could allow limitations to participate in giving form to their work. Cézanne will at last come to terms with art this year, and Zola will find a controlling formula for fashioning a string of novels—serialization on a grand scale. He will challenge Balzac's *Comedie Humaine*, a panorama of French society from the Consulate through the Empire, Restoration, and the July Monarchy. Zola's *Rougon-Macquart* series, as it came to be called, would follow three generations of a family with disparate genes that affect each person according to an inherited temperament.

Corrupt seed comes from the first conjugation when Adélaïde Fouque, an only child of a peasant couple—orphaned at eighteen, her father having died insane—marries an illiterate gardener named Rougon and gives birth to a son, Pierre. Within weeks, this husband dies and Adélaïde is left stranded. She had inherited the bad seed and is subject to nervous fits. Forlorn, in need of company, she befriends an emotionally impervious neighbor, Macquart, who manages to scratch out a living by poaching. A cruel man to climb into bed with, Adélaïde nonetheless does, and in time she bears two more children. Her first-born son Pierre and two bastard children grow up to fill out the novel. Pierre will move on to the next episode.

Zola had had *Les Rougon-Macquart* on his mind since 1868, but it took the Franco-Prussian War and its bloody aftermath to give closure to an idea in need of delimitation. Like Balzac's novels—for that matter, like the *Pentateuch* and Ovid's *Mythologies*—Zola's series would be tied together by genealogies and geography. But there would be differences. Zola was alert to the fact that not only was he inspired by Balzac but that critics might read his books as Balzac warmed over. Defensively, he composed a brief memorandum contrasting the sociology of Balzac with the convergence in his own writing of science and history and the interplay of race and milieu. *My work will be less social and more limited in scope*, he wrote. *I do not plan to present an entire contemporary society but a single family.* He pointed out that Balzac had deployed some 3,000 characters to mirror society—one might suppose in the way a biologist offers thousands of species to map the diversity of organic life—for in this memorandum Zola sets up a Balzacian equation as such, with lawyers and idlers on one side and dogs and wolves on the other. And whereas Balzac was a socialist historian, one could assign to Balzac's writings the histories of religion and royalties—histories involving divine rights and principles, as in law and Catholicism—while Zola's texts would take up laws of heredity and the conflict of unique personality with racial bias: *I don't want to be a politician, moralist, or philosopher. I do not wish to tell men how to manage their affairs, as Balzac does. It will suffice for me to be a scientist, to search for what underlies the behavior of people in society, without drawing conclusions.*[1]

Zola planned the *Rougon-Macquart* as ten novels but he would end up in 1893 with twenty. The first book was *La Fortune des Rougon.* Its serialization had been suspended over the wartime months. Shortly after Paris settled down, it was published as a volume. At the same time, serialization of the next novel in line, *La Curée,* rolled off the press.

In his preface to *La Fortune des Rougon*, Zola says, in so many words, that the Franco-Prussian war, the fall of the Bonapartes, completed in his mind the structuration of the entire series: *I needed it artistically. My scheme is complete; the circle in which my characters will revolve is perfected.* Having disclosed the structure of the series, he then encapsulates it as *a picture of a departed reign, of a bizarre period of human madness and shame.* This sequence of the structural to the pictorial, like the scientist moving from hypothesis to observation, coincides with Zola saying his characters will revolve within the circle, within the scheme—within the structure, which would be the artistic form, justifies his saying, *I needed it artistically.* One can cast back to his letter to Cézanne of April 26th, 1860 wherein he sets down his thoughts about artistic form. *The difference lies in that nameless something*, he writes. *Without form one can be a great painter, but only for oneself, not for others. Form is the conveyance of the idea, and the greater the idea the greater the form needs to be. It is through form that the artist is understood.*

Zola was not original in espousing this idea; it was on many minds as a primary feature of art criticism in the 1860s. Ernest Chesneau had criticized the young realists for their attachment to painting the *morceau*—the piece—while keeping their distance from the larger idea or fullest expression of an idea.[2] In Zacharie Astruc's *Salon of 1867*, one finds the admonition to young painters, *Abandon the detail; enlarge the morceau to become the oeuvre.*[3] The critic Gonzague Privat wrote of Manet's *Olympia* and *Christ Mocked* in the 1865 Salon that if only the public who mocked Manet could know how little it would require to make his too artistic painting readable by them, they would find his art admirable. *Often paint the morceau*, Privat advised Manet, *but be sure to preserve your artistic temperament.* Of this admonition, Michael Fried said, in his astute coverage of the differences between pictures and the tableau, *By artistic temperament, Privat meant the determination not to rest content with the morceau, the fragmentary realist life study of which Manet was a recognized master. Something more was needed, and what made Manet so unusual in Privat's eyes was that he pursued that something more almost too energetically—as if within a single work like Olympia there existed too glaring a disjunction between the realist morceau and the artistic tableau.*[4]

This contrast of the *morceau* with the *tableau* will set off certain Cézanne's paintings from the 1869-71 period when artistic coherence takes over imagery that earlier were pictorial incidents. The dividing line was not sharp, and consistency will take a while. A hint of what is forthcoming from Cézanne can be found in Zola's words. In the preface to *La Fortune des Rougon* he says: *I wish to explain how a family, a small group of human beings, conducts itself in a given social system after giving birth to ten or twenty members, who may appear profoundly dissimilar, one from the other, at first glance, but are closely linked to each other by an affinity. Heredity, like gravity, has its laws.* Zola's key phrases are «linked to each other by an affinity,» and «heredity has its laws.» Laws of heredity agree structurally in this case to the laws of form, or of *formation*; they do not apply to any act of imitation or to plain description or narration. Zola's previous novels, *The Confession of Claude*, *The Dead Woman's Wish*, *Thérèse Raquin*, and *Madeleine Férat*, were not structured or formed texts but stories situated along a story line as plots and sub-plots—stories told, characters described, like illustrations that are mere picturing and not *tableaux*.

This formal weakness in the pre-*Rougon-Maquart* novels had not gone unnoticed by Hippolyte Taine, whom Zola had asked to review *Thérèse Raquin*. Taine was reticent; the hermetic *mis-en-scènes* caused him to say, *There is a touch of lockjaw in the style as there is in the subject.*[5] Readers were denied ways to escape; the novel was potholed, without panoramas that would unify the incidents, the meal just an orgy of morsels. But in the space of time between *Thérèse Raquin* and *La Fortune des Rougon*, Zola reached the level of art called for by Zacharie Astruc: *Abandon the detail; enlarge the morceau to become the oeuvre.* Zola would no longer be writing stories strung out on a line, each connecting its own ending back to a beginning, like a beaded necklace or segmented snake with its tail in its mouth, serialized like a string of fish. He was now able to give form to substance and amplify the *morceau*.

With *La Fortune des Rougon*, Zola comes to a high degree of maturity as a writer, and for the first time someone other than those he had told what to say, or friends whose accolades didn't count, would compliment his writing. He would hear from Théophile Gautier, Edmond de Goncourt, and Gustave Flaubert. On December 1st, 1871, Flaubert wrote, saying, *La Fortune des Rougon is a tortuous and beautiful book. I am still stunned by it. It is powerful, very powerful! What a bold talent and stout heart!*[6] Gautier was more reserved in his praise, less committal, but, considering the source, Zola must have felt pleased with Gautier saying, *He does not have his style down yet. It is bushy and full of creepers, but a master is coming among us.*[7] Zola did have his style down but would never be a «style writer» like Flaubert or Huysmans. He was from the beginning a subject-matter writer. Perhaps because he had envisioned and outlined a string of novels, he was writing into the future, not pressed to put everything between one set of covers, each novel with its own limits yet part of an integrated whole.

Although intense, Zola's *La Fortune des Rougon* is nonetheless finely graded, the paragraphs complete, one not rushing into the next, at times very lengthy but not tedious. And the descriptive passages and connective tissue between them sustain the style of the action scenes. Here follows a sample of what Flaubert would call beautiful in contrast to what he would call tortuous:

But the lovers did not concern themselves with what went on in the Aire Saint-Mittre. They hastened back into their own little privacy, and again walked along their favorite path. Little did they care for others or for the town. The few boards separating them from the wicked world seemed to them, after a while, an insurmountable rampart. They were so secluded, so free in this nook, situated though it was in the very midst of the Faubourg, at only fifty paces from the Rome gate, that they sometimes fancied themselves far away in some hollow of the Viorne, with open country around them. Of all the sounds that reached them only one made them feel uneasy, the clocks striking slowly in the darkness. At times, when the hour sounded, they pretended not to hear, at other moments they stopped short as if to protest. However, they could not go on forever taking just another ten minutes, and so the time came when they were at last obliged to say goodnight. Then Miette reluctantly climbed upon the wall again. But all was not ended yet. They would linger over their leave-taking for a good quarter of an hour. The girl remained on the wall with her elbows on the coping, and her feet supported by the branches of the mulberry tree, which had served her as a ladder. Silvère, perched on the tombstone, was able to take her hands again, and renew their whispered conversation. They repeated «till tomorrow» a dozen times, and still and ever found something more to say. At last Silvère began to scold.

«Come, you must get down. It is past midnight.»

But Miette, with a girl's waywardness, wished him to descend first. She wanted to see him depart. And as he persisted in remaining, she ended by saying abruptly, by way of punishment perhaps, «Look! I am going to jump down.»

Then she sprang from the mulberry tree, to the great consternation of Silvère. He heard the dull thud of her fall, and the burst of laughter with which she ran off without choosing to reply to his last adieu.[8]

Flaubert's compliments to Zola on *La Fortune des Rougon* were given with one criticism: *My only quarrel is with the preface. I feel it mars your work, which is so impartial and lofty. You give away your secret there, and in my poetics a novelist does not have a right to be so candid. I am otherwise without reservations.* How Zola responded, if he did, one does not know. But six years later, on February 19th, 1877, Edmond de Goncourt made an entry in his journal that would have served remarkably as Zola's response had he felt offended by Flaubert:

> *Flaubert attacks—though with tips of the hat to his own genius—the prefaces, doctrines, and the naturalist professions of faith, those with which Zola helps his books to sell. Zola would say something like this in response: «You, Flaubert, inherited a small fortune which allowed you to free yourself from many things. On the other hand, I who have earned my livelihood with my pen, who have been obliged to do all sorts of dubious scribbling in order to survive through journalism, I've retained a touch of the—how should I put it? —of the mountebank. Yes, it is true that, like you, I scorn this word «Naturalism,» and yet I drum it home. For unless things are baptized, the public won't believe them to be new.»*[9]

Zola's preface to *La Fortune des Rougon* tells of the folly of the Franco-Prussian War and the tragedy of *la semaine sanglante* as having provided the final ingredients to complete his visualization of the *Rougon-Macquart* series. The great value of this preface is that, in Zola's own words, it states an intention in advance of doing. It is, in fact, a preface to the entire series.

> *I will explain how a family, a small group of human beings, conducts itself in a given social system after it has blossomed and given birth to ten or twenty members, who, though at first glance may appear dissimilar one from the other, are closely linked by affinities. Heredity, like gravity, has its own laws.*
>
> *By resolving the interactive qualities of temperament and environment, I will endeavor to discover the threads of connection that lead mathematically from one individual to another. And when I have a grip on every thread, and hold the complete social group in my hands, I will show this group in action, participating in an historical period. I will depict it with all its varied energies, and will analyze both the will power of each member and the general disposition of the group.*
>
> *The defining characteristic of the Rougon-Macquarts—the group or family I propose to study—is their ravenous appetite, the peculiarity of our age in its rush to enjoyment. Physiologically, the Rougon-Macquarts represent the slow succession of accidents, pertaining to the nerves or the blood, which befall a race after a first organic lesion. Depending on environmental conditions, this lesion will determine, in each individual member of the race, those feelings, desires, and passions—all the natural and instinctive manifestations peculiar to humanity—whose outcome assumes the conventional names of virtue or vice. Historically, the Rougon-Macquarts proceed from the masses and radiate throughout the whole of contemporary society. They ascend to all sorts of positions by the force of that impulse of essentially modern origin, which sets the lower classes marching through the*

social system. And thus the dramas of their individual lives recount the story of the Second Empire, from the ambuscade of the Coup d'État to the treachery of Sédan.

For three years I have been collecting documents for this long work. The present volume was already written when the fall of the Bonapartes occurred. That event was what I needed artistically, without daring to hope that it would prove so near at hand. It furnished me with the terrible, but necessary, dénouement for my work. My scheme is now completed. The circle in which my characters will evolve is perfected. My work now becomes that of a complete picture of a departed reign, of a period of human madness and shame.

This work, which will comprise several episodes, is already in my mind as the natural and social history of a family under the Second Empire. The first episode, here called «The Fortune of the Rougons,» should, from a scientific perspective, be titled «The Origin.»

Back when Zola wrote *Thérèse Raquin*, he had been exploring his ideas on *tempérament*—for each individual, a distinct personality. This notion of concentrated uniqueness obliged him to develop each character with great precision. Thus each novel, such as *La Confession de Claude*, would stand by itself, unto itself. Had Zola not changed his thoughts about what constitutes the eventual unity of the individual *tempérament* as accounting for everything-in-total that an artist or writer produces, he may not have envisioned the *Rougon-Maquart* (or the other way around), for a theory of temperaments is not a theory of social cohesiveness but the opposite: a theory of differences. The unity and uniqueness of self (as unity of form) takes the place of social or institutional coherence. To express one's personal identity, one's temperament, it is necessary to disassociate from society—be different. The well-worn expression *épater la bourgeoisie* simply meant to cause the public to withdraw by holding up appalling technique or imagery rendered in the most horrifying fashion.

In structuring *Madeleine Férat*, Zola was inspired by the so-called impregnation theory that I mentioned earlier, which held that semen from a woman's first lover would from then on determine the genetics of her children even if impregnated by one or more successive men. As for novel writing, this meant that the author's ideas inseminating the first novel would continue inseminating future novels, even if the characters change. And that would hold as well for artists whose canvases of variable subject matter would be in a signature style. Zola had read and incorporated Dr. Lucas' theories into his notes when planning the *Rougon-Macquart*. He said that to know the history of his characters one needed only to read Lucas' *L'Hérédité naturelle*, where the physiological system that helped to elaborate the genealogical tree of the *Rougon-Macquart* would be found.

Antoine Marion, who had maintained a friendship with Zola as with Cézanne, may have helped promote Zola's interest in heredity, in particular the theory of impregnation. Marion would have known it from his school studies in biology. In an August 1866 issue of *L'Événement*, Zola mentioned a book published by Hachette, *Les Végétaux merveilleux* (Marvels of the Plant World), by his friend Marion, who dedicated one of the *animalcules* (the *Géant de Nématoïdes*) to Zola, dubbing it *le Thoracostoma Zolae*, the «giant» among the nematodes (a tiny organism that lives amidst great masses of marine algae). Marion wrote to Zola, *You were right to have employed the strange physiological phenomenon that I call «the impression of the ovary»—the resemblance of the later born sons of a remarried widow to her first husband This is true for all conditions. I have observed it in animals, in dogs, even more frequently in plants. The pistachio of Provence, a tree well known to you, produces its unique fruit even if pollinated by the térébinthe* [a resinous pistachio tree].[10]

The motif of a successive transmission of semen in Balzac's novels constitutes *La Comédie humaine* that Zola's *Rougon-Maquart* would emulate. Balzac's Valerie, in *Cousin Bette*, adores her husband, who prefers the sluts he finds on street corners and leaves her free to commit her own adulteries. When her husband dies, he is left to rot like a corpse someone forgot to bury. Valerie remarries and also takes on a lover who plots cleverly against the new husband. Aware that his retinue of male black servants carries an African venereal disease, the lover pays a prostitute to perform with one of them so that she will catch the disease; he, in turn, performs with the prostitute to contract it himself, and then passes it on to Valerie so her husband will be exposed through intercourse. Balzac resorts to a similar formula in his novel *Beatrix*: Mrs. Schontz conspires against Mrs. de Rochefide by intentionally contracting a venereal disease and passing it on to her husband. Such contrived passing of venereal disease to take revenge was common in novels. Zola's transmission of his characters' interactions mirrors the sexual act as a flow of body fluids linking generations. But even though both called upon hereditary diseases and flaws to link plots and drive sequences, Balzac's deployment of seminal transmission was not of a Darwin-type, or Lucas-type process, as Zola's was.

The plot of primary impregnation lent a compelling structure to Zola's *Madeleine Férat*. To get beyond the novel that initiates the *Rougon-Macquart*, the theory had to move the genetic proclivities from one generation to another in order to achieve a unity beyond the object and beyond the unique temperament. Taine had proposed that no great novelist lacks a philosophy or system but Zola may not have known Taine had said that. Zola was troubled even by the lack of a coherent theory of modern art. Perhaps he had been thinking about art in terms of the impregnation theory—forecasting a leader who would be the first, the original inseminator for Realism (as Delacroix had been for Romanticism), who would subordinate individual temperaments to the unifying temperament of a master's style. Even in the late 1870s, Zola would lament that no artist of the modernist group had fully achieved the new formula. *The formula is there*, he wrote, *endlessly diffused, but in no place among any of them is it to be found applied by a master. The man of genius has not yet arisen.*[11]

In the sequence from Balzac's novels to what appears as three phases of Zola's progress, almost one atop the other, one gets from the simple passage of semen (Balzac), to the passage of heredity at the first instance (*Madeleine Férat*), to the passage of heredity through generations (The *Rougon-Macquart*) with unlimited possibilities yet frustrated by a flawed or dissident gene that, by its absence or its presence, wars against heredity. It masters the seminal produce and thus controls history. In Zola's string of novels, but not in Balzac's, all of the characters are blood related. It is perhaps not too farfetched to say that every bather composition that Cézanne painted from the early 1870s to the day he died is composed of «blood-related» figures from previous «bathers», that every still-life contains elements from a previous still-life, and so on. This is not to say that the images simply repeat with variations, as in serial painting, or variations on a theme, but that all of the imagery is embodied in one form, a form of infinite possibilities—the *endlessly diffused* applied by a master to a masterful *unity of form*.

The interactive qualities of temperament and environment invoke inheritance as a given condition, or predisposition of self—advantageous or disadvantageous—as well as predilection as the will to achieve or to fail. The will to achieve is one's personal trajectory, variably vigorous or indolent, which comes up against the trajectories of the social force field of attractions or repulsion into which each individual is thrust. Zola's endeavor to discover the threads of connection that lead mathematically from one individual to another would now also deal with phenomenal manifestations, with psychological motivations such as love and hate, desire and greed, that would reflect his characters' relations between forces of the social field and their personal ambitions. In procreation, as in artistic creation, the laws of imitation (replication) and invention are obeyed. In procreation (as in creating art), innateness (*innéité*) comes up against heredity. For Dr. Lucas, equally for Zola, innateness was opposed to heredity—*innée* traits were not those that heredity dictated but what the individual possessed as immune to genetic supremacy. In this sense, the innate was one's individuality, while the inherited would be the *race* from which one cannot escape—and the *milieu* that is fixed in time.

44

*The coming greatness
of Cézanne*

While Zola was engrossed in his *Rougon-Macquart*, Cézanne was still at L'Estaque, where he would remain for about nine months, from July 1870 to March 1871. Still painting small canvases and finishing most if not all of them in a single session, he could have painted anywhere from fifty to one hundred pictures during this stay. Yet only three canvases survive, and only one of these is more than an ordinary picture that most any painter could have done. It is known by the title *La neige fondu à l'Estaque* (Melting Snow at L'Estaque) and at 29x36 inches the largest landscape painting we have from his early years.

Meyer Schapiro offers a splendid description of this picture. He calls it *a remarkable example of a space shaped by intense feeling.*

> *The foreground—the observer's space—is a steep hillside which divides the canvas diagonally in its avalanche descent from left to right down to the sloping red roof, and gives a rushing force to the image. To this downward slope of the hill are opposed the rapid recession of the middle field with it is rising, converging lines, and the immense horizontal sweep of the overhanging gray clouds. From the dark foliage of the tormented black tree at the left starts another movement of trees descending inward on the crest of the hill and merging with the distant horizon in a single rhythm of declining pulse. The foreshortened diagonal lines in depth are parallel to the diagonal profiles in the plane of the canvas; the sinuous contour of the earth—the whole ground of the scene—is repeated in the form of the great tree trunk and in the amazing zigzag of roofs and roads at the right. By these parallels Cézanne unites into a coherent pattern the opposed movements in different planes in depth. The color, too, is a powerful force holding together the near and the far.*[1]

While whatever Schapiro phrases as emotion, such as *rushing force, rapid recession, tormented black tree, declining pulse, sinuous contour, amazing zigzag, powerful force,* can be said of most any picture having such qualities (and too often writers on art believe they've understood a painting because they've described it and transposed the visual imagery into a piece of prose), what emerges from Schapiro's crystalline description of *Melting Snow at L'Estaque* is much more. Schapiro's analysis sepa-

rates pictures from works of art without indulgence in formalism; the qualities of a picture transcend the pictorial to enter into the realm of art. This artistic, rather than pictorial quality appears when Schapiro says, *By these parallels Cézanne unites into a coherent pattern the opposing movements in different planes in depth*, and, *The color, too, is a powerful force holding together the near and the far*. This *holding together the near and the far* is what lent structure to Zola's mature work too. Let me repeat Zola's expression of gratitude for the Franco-Prussian war, saying he needed it artistically; that is, *for his art*. He did not say *for his story*. Then he said of his projected *Rougon-Macquart* series: *The circle in which my characters will evolve is perfected. My work now becomes that of a complete picture.*

Cézanne's masterful painting *Alexis Reading to Zola*, painted at Zola's house in Paris in 1870 or 1871, also has the quality of *tableau*—a work of art on a grand scale in which the pictorial elements, and all means of picturing them, are contained within the structure of the work, the work then having a perceivable quality of totality and wholeness independent of the subject matter but created by the inter-relations of its parts. Here one can distinguish a *tableau* from that which is just a picture, while admitting that a *tableau* can be also a picture. They key to the difference is that «picture» can be a verb, «to picture,» as in saying, «Now picture this,» or, «In my mind, I can picture...» but one cannot make a verb of *tableau*, one cannot *tableau* something. Add to this my insistence that «to give form» to something is not the same as «to make» something, for anyone can make things: birds make nests, bees make honeycomb, bakers make pies, and crocodiles make love. Truly creative acts are not acts of *making*, like making pictures, making music, making out. Nor is form-making just skillful composition, putting things together in some balanced, harmonious, pleasing arrangement. Table settings and flower arrangements may be artistic, but are not works of art. Things nicely composed are not necessarily artistically formed. Forming occurs at the extreme of one's limits, rather than at the moment of one's satisfaction. Only at the extreme can form take shape, as in saying that the mold must press at all points against the cast form. And it's at the variable limits of each artist's capacity to form that individuality sets one artist off from another. Individuality is not enough.

Alexis Reading to Zola shares with *Jeune fille au piano* (Girl at a Piano) certain important traits; for one, the placing of the active person (Alexis reading, the girl playing) to the left side, while to the right is the person absorbed in receptivity (Zola listening, the older woman listening while sewing). This sort of placement corresponds in theater production to the stretch of the open stage; the principal action positioned both left and right so as to utilize the entire space of the stage. The figures of Zola and Alexis are placed within but also set off from a back plane structured by geometric shapes. In Zola's novels, the same effect is accomplished by pairing characters who are near opposites: the Rougons with the Macquarts, the aggressive with the passive, so the tension that gives emotional volume to the story is generated by the stretch of differences. In *Young Girl at a*

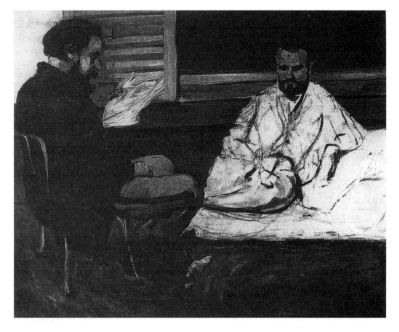

Cézanne. Alexis reading to Zola. c. 1870. Museu de Arte, São Paulo.

Opposite page: Cézanne. *Melting Snow at L'Estaque.* 1870-71. Private collection, Switzerland.

Cézanne. Young girl at a piano (mistakenly titled *Overture to Tannhäuser*). Hermitage Museum, St. Petersburg.

Piano, the stretch that creates visual tension is between the piano and the upholstered chair. The picture plane is horizontal, not receding; the imagery is perpendicular to the viewer. And this can be said also for certain other of Cézanne's canvases from 1869 to 1872, as, for example, *La Toilette Funéraire*.[2] Abandoned in such works as *Young Girl at a Piano* is both a spatial dependence on perspective and the stage-like composition of deep space flanked by close ups, the effect given by the *coulisse*, as in *The Abduction* (*L'Èvènement*) and an earlier version of *Alexis and Zola*. Those two canvases would lead nowhere—audacity and forcefulness not enough to make art—while such paintings as *Young Girl at a Piano* and *Alexis Reading to Zola* forecast the coming greatness of Cézanne as meditative artist rather than impulsive picture-painter.[3]

Yet Cézanne's historians have tried to make Cézanne's *Young Girl at a Piano* into a theatrical mode by giving it the title, *Overture to Tannhäuser*, and larding it with Wagnerianism. The confusion stems from a few letters written between Cézanne's friends in which Wagner's *Tannhäuser* is mentioned. It starts with Guillemet's a letter to Zola of 1867 attesting to Cézanne's higher level of seriousness than playing with regressive mythological themes such as Plutos abducting Persephones, emperors staging orgies, and shepherds winning maidens with a golden apple. He writes that Cézanne would be bringing to Paris a few pictures certain to delight Zola's eyes—in particular, an overture to Tannhäuser in which is a piano is successfully depicted.[4] Several months later, Marion wrote a few lines about this picture to Heinrich Morstatt (the German musician friend obliged to study business in order to make a living, who'd come to Marseilles to serve an apprenticeship. Having come into an inheritance and returned to Germany, Morstatt and Marion kept in touch by letter). Marion says that, among several large canvases Cézanne had started, one was dedicated to Wagner's *Ouverture du Tannhäuse,* the picture referred to probably a more developed version of the one to which Guillemet had alerted Zola:

> *I wish you could see the picture he is working on now. He is once again painting the subject you know about, the Overture to Tannhäuser, but in a completely different tonal harmony. He now uses very light tones, and each figure is carefully finished. There is the head of a young fair-haired girl, both pretty and amazingly powerful. My face is an extraordinary likeness and is also well painted. The entire picture is rendered without that sharpness of color and that somewhat repulsive wildness. The piano is again beautifully painted as in the other version, and the draperies, as usual, are magnificently true. Probably it will be refused at the exhibition, but it will certainly be exhibited somewhere. A canvas like this is enough to make an artist's reputation.*[5]

Erroneously, Cézanne's *Girl at a Piano* is assumed to be *Ouverture to Tannhäuser.* In that this painting would date between 1869 and 1871, the several mentions of it in earlier letters would refer, I believe, only to earlier versions that did not survive. No fair-haired girl or likeness of Marion appear in the picture we have; it is not the one mentioned in the correspondence. The erroneous title given to the canvas, *Overture du Tannhäuser,* has been so overused in the Cézanne literature that what we know about the picture is horribly distorted. Those who talk about that title, rather than the picture, seem unaware that Cézanne did not paint the title but the canvas.[6] Call it *Girl at a Piano* and not much can be made of it; call it *Overture to Tannhäuser* and one can talk endlessly about Wagner, about Baudelaire's response to Wagner, the Wagner Society in Marseilles, Zola's enthusiasm for Wagner as evidenced in a February 9th, 1868 letter from him to Marius Roux, and so on, giving the impression that one is writing about Cézanne's picture.[7]

The pictorial composition of one person doing one thing, such as playing a piano, while another listens or looks on—both completely absorbed—was a common motif among artists that Cézanne knew. Looking at someone doing something that another person sees or listens to, while being completely removed from the scene, is, of course, the baseline of contemplation. Whistler painted an *At the Piano* in 1859—a woman playing while a young girl listens. In 1864, Degas painted a likeness of Manet listening to his wife Susanne Leenhoff playing the piano. I cannot pass up this anecdote: Manet accepted the painting as a gift, but disliking the way his wife looked; he cut the canvas in two. Degas' response: *Would you believe that Manet did that? He thought that Mrs. Manet was not good enough. Can you imagine how I felt when I saw that cut-off half of my picture in Manet's studio? Without wasting a word, I left with it under my arm. At home, I took off the wall a little still life Manet had given me, and attached to it a note: «Dear Sir,» I wrote. «I return herewith your plums.»* Later, when Degas and Manet were friends again—Degas saying, *How can anyone be angry with Manet for long?* —Degas said, *Perhaps Manet was correct! And the plums! How lovely that canvas was! I did a lousy deal that day, because later, after Manet and I had made up, I asked to have my plums back. Well, he'd sold them!*[8]

In 1867, Manet painted a canvas of his wife at the piano, and in 1865, Bazille submitted to the Salon a picture of a young woman playing a piano.[9] About the motif, Bazille said, *I tried to paint to the best of my ability a subject as simple as possible. In my opinion, the subject has little importance as long as what I have to do is interesting from the point of view of painting.* Bazille also said, *the motif of a girl at a piano represents the modern period*—a noteworthy observation, considering that a girl playing a mandolin would represent old-fashioned painting. The home piano was as symbolically and actually modern in the 1860s as a television set would be a century later.

Bazille would not have had Wagner's music in mind; a contemporary girl playing a piano in a contemporary setting is not consistent with nymphs and satyrs playing lyres and flutes in a Lydian landscape that would evoke Wagnerian imagery.[10] While Fantin-Latour was stimulated to paint his dream-like *Venusberg* of 1864 based on the performance of Wagner's opera in 1861 (about which both Baudelaire and Champfleury had written passionate reviews), the Cézanne family salon in Aix was far from Venusberg, and besides, nymphs don't play pianos. (Though not relevant to this historical moment, one cannot pass up another anecdote, a delightful comment made by the critic Félix Fénéon when panning Josephan Péladan's first occult *Rose Croix* exhibition in 1892: *One will never make these exhibitors understand that a painter shows too much humility when choosing subjects already rich in literary connotations, that three pears on a tablecloth by Paul Cézanne are themselves moving and mystifying, while the entire Wagnerian Valhalla, when these artists paint it, is as uninteresting as the Chamber of Deputies*).[11]

From no point of view should *Girl at a Piano* be imputed to Cézanne's interest in Wagner, and nothing in the work suggests that the girl (Cézanne's sister) is playing a score from *Tannhäuser*. These inferences come instead from Marion's friendship with Morstatt acknowledging his friend as musician and as Wagner's countryman.[12] In a letter to Morstatt, Marion says that over one morning of painting Cézanne had almost completed a superb painting called *Ouverture du Tannhäusser*—but we don't know who construed that title even though Marion would be the most likely suspect. In his letter, Marion added, *It belongs to the future, as does Wagner's music*, and then described the picture as *a young girl at the piano, white on blue, in the foreground—the piano magnificently and broadly treated. An old man* [Cézanne's father] *in profile is in an armchair; a young child, in the background, listens with the air of an idiot. The mass is all wild, overpoweringly strong. You have to look at it for a long while.*[13]

Wagner's modern music was of course on many minds in the 1860s. In an essay, *Richard Wagner et Tannhäuser à Paris*, published in April 1861, Baudelaire called Wagner's compositions *le musique de l'avenir* (music of the future). He wrote: *What appears above all to signify the unforgettable music of this master is its nervous intensity, violence in passion. Wagner is now the truest representative of modernism—in whatever subject he treats is a superlatively solemn tonality. Through this passion he adds something superhuman. Everything—wish, desire, concentration, explosion—is felt and realized in his works.*[14]

The nervous intensity and violence in passion was readily associated with modernist painting. While it would not apply to the painters in either Manet or Pissarro's circles, one must not overlook the hundreds of daubers called modernists that did not enter into art history, whose paintings were as unrestrained as those of peripheral Abstract-Expressionists in the New York 1950s. The wildness of this non-surviving version of Cézanne's picture, as described by Marion—the child in the background listening with the air of an idiot—may have stimulated Marion to associate it with the wildness of Wagner's opera, but Cézanne would not have needed Wagner to paint wildly or render an idiotic face. Marion's remark to Morstatt that Cézanne's new version of *Girl at a Piano* is painted *without* that repulsive wildness absolves any need for Cézanne to have read Baudelaire's review with such expressions as *violence in passion* and *passionate energy*, or even to have heard about the review from Zola. It's a fact that Cézanne mentioned Wagner when displaying his friendship for Marion; as a postscript to a letter from Marion to Morstatt of December 23rd, 1865, Cézanne wrote: *The undersigned begs you to accept Marion's invitation. You will cause our acoustic nerves to vibrate to the noble tones of Richard Wagner.*[15] About a year and a half later, again as a postscript to a letter from Marion to Morstatt, Cézanne added: *So we will soon have the pleasure of seeing you again without having to wait for a better world...I press with warm sympathy the hand that no longer defiles itself in philistine occupations* [Morstatt had just come into his inheritance and would no longer be a businessman]. *I had the good fortune to hear the overtures of Tannhäuser, Löhengrin, and The Flying Dutchman.*

It has been recorded that Zola and Cézanne joined Wagner society in Marseilles, but that may only imply that Morstatt had signed them up. We have no eveidence that either Zola or Cézanne actually participtaed in an Wagner event in Marseilles. Anyway, mentioning Wagner, or even worshipping Wagner in a letter, does not mean that the girl at the piano is playing a piece by Wagner, or that playing the piano is a tribute to Wagner. The canvas Marion referred to was most likely a version of the *soirée de famille* (family gathering at evening) that Cézanne mentions in his postscript to Guillemet's letter to Zola of November 2nd, 1866: *I must tell you, however, that, as you feared, my big picture of Valabrègue and Marion has not come off, and that, having attempted a soirée de famille, it didn't come off at all. However, I will persevere, and perhaps another shot at it will be successful.* In the surviving painting, the girl at the piano may be Rose, who was fifteen that year; the woman sewing could be Marie, who was twenty-eight, or even Cézanne's mother, then about fifty; the father is not included, as apparently he had been in an earlier version, although the chair he typically occupied is there.[16]

The title that this picture has been going by represents the art historian's penchant for seeing in Cézanne's pictures what they have in mind about his personality as being excessively temperamental, wild, erotic, and subject to extreme mood shifts. What must be made most important is not how his psychology undergoes change but how his art develops. This picture is not wild, not idiotic, and certainly not Wagnerian. It should be titled *Une soirée de famille*. Cézanne had painted a number of pictures of his family—domestic scenes, such as this one, others of his father reading in an armchair, his little sister Rose reading to her doll, portraits of his uncle Dominique and his sister Marie. As an artist, his family would expect him to paint their portraits, so one cannot isolate Cézanne's reasons for painting them from his being asked to do so. One is reminded of

Cézanne. *Quai de Bercy.: La Halle aux vins*. 1872. A view from a window of an apartment Cézanne rented at 45 rue Jussieu after December 1871. In the following January, Hortense Fiquet gave birth to their son. Photo: Galerie Bernheim-Jeune.

Courbet's frequent visits to his natal home in Ornans, where to please his family he painted neat and decorous portraits of his father and sisters—Zélie's hair ornamented with a wreath of bindweed, Juliette sitting primly in a wicker chair.[17] Degas, too, tells in his letters from New Orleans in 1873, when staying with wealthy cotton-industry relatives there, of being pressed into making pleasing portraits of his host family. *The family portraits*, he writes in a letter to a Danish friend in Paris on November 27th, 1872, *have to be done more or less to suit the family taste, with impossible lighting, with models full of affection but a little sans-gêne, taking you much less seriously because you're their nephew or cousin*.[18] Cézanne's *Girl at a Piano* is not, however, a family portrait of the type described by Degas. Like *Alexis Reading to Zola*, it is a tableau, a painting, not an illustration.

When the high quality of such pictures as *Girl at a Piano, Melting Snow at L'Estaque,* and the *Quai de Bercy: La halle aux vin* of 1871 is overlaid by psychological description, as if, true to Zola's call for art to be nothing but representations of the artist's temperament, Cézanne's pictures can then only be understood by reference to his psychology, as if explaining the art one need only explain the artist. The extraordinary *Quai de Bercy* has been described as a picture of Cézanne's wretchedness. *It is painted in the colors of désespérance, misery, loss of hope*, it is said, the critic ignoring that the date of its execution was mid-winter when the sky over Paris is typically gray, when dampness produces harsh contrasts in a city blanketed with soot, when the plane trees' mid-winter trunks and branches are black and raggedly festooned with dead brown leaves that refuse to drop.[19] In a picture painted in winter, should Cézanne have put a bright sun in the sky, green leaves on the trees, and strewn flowers on the pavement? Onto this marvelous picture all the calumnies that one might muster try to transform it into a document of pain and tribulation.

Look at the picture. Cézanne painted this canvas from a window that looked onto the Quai. It is said that the canvas reflects everything that the penniless and ungrateful house guest Achille Emperaire reports about Cézanne's «miserable» living conditions in this apartment at the time; the picture's genesis is associated with Cézanne's lack of money, apprehension over fatherhood (Hortense was pregnant and delivered their son in January), nagging doubts about his talent, and especially, a deep despondency over again being rejected from the Salon (but there hadn't been a Salon the previous year because of the Prussian invasion).

Does the picture actually tell us anything like that? Let us put this painting into a more sensible context. The *Quai de Bercy* recalls Cézanne's letter to Pissarro of October 23rd, 1866, in which he says, *You are perfectly right to speak of gray, for gray alone reigns in nature*. By «reigns in nature,» Cézanne would have meant that gray unifies the appearance of nature—gray, in opposition to the Rembrandt and Van Dyck browns, the bituminous brown-black tobacco sauce tones that unified Courbet-like and most Barbizon landscapes. Pissarro may have been the first to

Cézanne. Rue des Saules, Montmartre. c. 1866-67. Private collection, New York. Photo: Bulloz.

see the *tableau* quality of Cézanne's *Quai de Bercy*, saying of it in a letter to Guillemet of September 3rd, 1872, *Our friend Cézanne gives us hope. I have with me a painting of great vigor and remarkable strength*.[20] If so, Cézanne's treatment of the scene as unified by gray tones would compare favorably with Pissarro's palette at the time, and also with Monet's, though in different tones and values: Monet tended towards a unifying blue, as did his early mentor, Eugène Boudin.[21] While in London over the previous winter, the persistent fog and rain apparently encouraged Monet and Pissarro to increasingly unify the hues and tonalities of their pictures by effects of weather other than play of sunlight, as typified by Monet's pictures painted in Hyde Park and Green Park, London.[22] Over the latter part of 1860s, and well into the 1870s, both painted landscapes and townscapes during snowfalls and under snow, the imagery unified by prevailing grays.[23]

No people appear in Cézanne's *Quai de Bercy* or *Melting Snow at L'Estaque*. No people appear in the one painting we have of a view within Paris, a street in Montmartre, *La Rue des Saules*, of about 1868, which, when compared to the canvases I am holding up here, show to what extent Cézanne had at last reached status as not merely a notorious dauber but an extraordinary painter.. In fact, other than one surviving example from 1866, in no landscape painting by Cézanne before 1875 do real people appear—real, that is, rather than imagined.[24] This sets him apart from Pissarro and also from Renoir, who remained a figure painter. Cézanne's early letters from Aix to Zola in Paris often describe landscape elements but never the people in the settings. All around Aix were farms, farmers, farm animals—plowing, seeding, cultivating, haying—yet Cézanne speaks only of the river, the ravines, trees, the mountain, the rocks, never of farms. From the mid-1870s comes one painting by Cézanne showing field workers at grain-harvest time, *The Harvest*, which is most likely a copy of someone's painting dating from the same time as when Cézanne faithfully copied Guillaumin's *The Seine at Bercy*. And when Cézanne does paint a farmyard in the 1870s, not an animal or person appears in it.[25] By pulling himself back from subject matter, Cézanne focuses on seeing rather than thinking. As time goes on, he will rid his art of narrative. So rather than assign this absense of people to Cézanne as a misenthrope, fearful of people as if he were a cringing dog, it might be wise to ask wherever he wasn't more interested in art than in the sort of anecdotal or story-telling subject matter on which biographical art historians thrive.

To have content, a landscape must contain something—not just trees or a pond, which are features *within* or *of* the landscape but not *contained* by it. Cézanne's straight landscapes do not enter into sociology, as do those by Courbet, Millet, Daubigny, Rousseau, and Pissarro. His *Melting Snow at L'Estaque* and *Quai de Bercy* have nothing to say about people. His 1870 painting of the railway cutting near the *Jas de Bouffan* is devoid of people or even a train passing through. The landscape is dead silent, just as the trees and clouds in *Melting Snow* are frozen not by the cold but by an infinite duration of the moment. No villager walks on the road, pressing against the wind. In the *Quai de Bercy*, no workmen struggle with the wine barrels. In these paintings, Cézanne represents only the motif, while in Monet's *Road near Honfleur in the Snow*, villagers trudge along the road; in Pissarro's pictures farmers and townsfolk trudge along roads and farm paths, and work the fields; in Renoir's *Heart of the Fontainebleau Forest* a man is communicating with a dog.

What moves in a Cézanne landscape is everything at once or nothing at all, and never just a particular thing, person, or animal; the motion is not a passing moment but a non-bracketed duration. This anti-poetic sensibility is antipodal to Zola's but also complementary. One recalls that in their very early exchange of letters, Zola tried to explain to Cézanne the difference between naturalism, which he then detested, and the poetic towards which he was striving: Zola's words bear repeating: *If one puts in the background a light and nimble girl, one of those peasant maidens of Greuze, tossing grain to a flock of chickens—at that moment, the picture will have poetry.*[26] By the mid-1860s, Zola will have abandoned poetry and fantasies of peasant maidens, and Cézanne in the late 1860s would find no place in his landscapes for people. He had no interest in society or social issues, and would remain until the end of his life the disinterested defector, the uninvolved opposite of Zola, who was a master of describing cityscapes, coalmines, and bedrooms, settings crowded with people and infused with emotion. By contrast, as eloquently voiced by Schapiro, Cézanne's nature existed mainly for the eye, with little provision for desires or curiosity. Unlike the nature in traditional landscape, it is often inaccessible and intraversable.[27]

45

*He scrapes his soup plate,
he even takes his chops in his fingers
and pulls the meat from the bone*

Let us sum up before moving on. Following the Franco-Prussian war, adjustments that Cézanne would undergo from 1872-1874 included insights that his subversive behavior had been working against him, shoving off Zola and denying him a place among those who were moving art into the future. Of the artists of the 1860s who worked to alter the base upon which modern art depended, Cézanne, like Courbet before him, was subversive—not heroically subversive as Courbet thought himself to be, but roguishly seditious. He had fallen prey to zeal and violence rather than commitment and meaningful courage, and his low-grade romanticism had surfaced as a morbid tendency toward self-dramatization. His ambition to subvert the jury has made interesting art history—and him an interesting character—but all it truly accomplished was to screen his unwillingness to confront art on its own terms and to let his art make a case for itself.

In view of his lifetime achievement, it is difficult to accept that over the 1860s Cézanne was a peripheral painter who contributed nothing to the program for modern art as it moved into the seventies. It remains a mistake for art historians to stuff him into the group that centered about Manet, Monet, Renoir, and Degas. Cézanne was outside the circle, and by the late 1870s, when the Impressionists broke up, with Monet and Renoir discouraged, Degas arrogantly depressed, and Pissarro about to capitulate to Seurat, Cézanne was the only one who moved ahead with confidence. His doubts have been misunderstood. They were not symptoms of depression but external signs of an unimpeded determination. A true artist must doubt, because he or she has no real image at hand to assure how the endeavor will turn out. Moreover, in the 1860s, not having a conceptual grasp on art, Cézanne had no secure handle on what he was doing, and no idea what those in Manet's circle were doing. He did not see in the work of Manet, Degas, Monet, or Renoir—certainly not in what Whistler, Legros, Fantin-Latour, and Carolus Duran—that art was undergoing change, but not in the work of those in his own circle: Pissarro, Guillaumin, Guillemet, Emperaire, Coste, Oller, Gabet, a circle that had only widened but not advanced, soon to include hundreds of landscape and rural genre painters. Not until the arrival on the scene of Gauguin and van Gogh would village, farmland, and forest painting take a turn away from the Corot-Millet-Daubigny tradition that, by the end of the 1860s, had finally run its course.

If we believe that Cézanne's paintings of the 1860s were «great,» the work of a genius, then why are they great in our eyes when, in the eyes of Manet, Monet, Degas, Renoir, Bazille, and every perceptive critic of the 1860s, including Zola, they were little more than the hackwork of an ill-mannered dauber? What do we know about art that those artists and critics did not? Let us admit that the «quality» of Cézanne's pictures from the 1860s, with the few exceptions that come about in 1869, is a result of art historical feedback from the twentieth century as much as from Cézanne's late work. To say otherwise would be to claim that Manet, Monet, Degas, and so on did not have an eye for art. From the 1869 year, however, the greatness we now see began to emerge as greatness for his own time.

After the break in time's flow caused by the Franco-Prussian War, it took a while for painters known to Cézanne to reestablish contact. Zola's time was taken up then by writing, and Cézanne's by preparing for parenthood. Biographers have painted a sordid picture of Cézanne's character over these years, 1871 to mid-1872, perhaps to set him up for finding relief under the wing of paternalistic Pissarro, whom he will join in the autumn of 1872. Biographers have depended almost entirely on one biased source for analyzing Cézanne's behavior over these three years, allowing a psychological portrait to be painted by the miserable and ungrateful Achille Emperaire.

Much of what moves through the Cézanne literature as *faux*-evidence of Cézanne's «pre-Pissarro» temperament is extracted from an altercation with Emperaire in late 1871 after Cézanne had returned to Paris from the Midi. One commentator writes, *Crawling out of his wartime burrow at L'Estaque* [note the regression of Cézanne to a species of rodent], *Cézanne did not join the clan* [note the regression of Cézanne to a unit of primitive society]...*Nor, apparently, did he invite the clan to gather around him when Hortense bore him a son* [nor, for that matter, under the same circumstances, did Pissarro, Monet, or anyone else in the *clan* when their mistresses bore children]...*in their dingy flat on the rue de Jussieu.*[1] Cézanne's flat may have been modest but not necessarily dingy. The flat was on *le deuxième étage* (the third floor in America), which typically was the most desirable and often the most expensive rental floor in Paris' days before elevators.

If anyone's house guest after three days starts smelling like aged cheese, one might imagine how Emperaire smelled after being accommodated for six weeks by Cézanne and Hortense (from mid-February 1872 until late March), especially with a newborn baby dominating the household, keeping everyone's sleep on edge over the night. After four weeks of guesthood, Emperaire wrote on February 19th to a friend in Aix, *Paul is badly set up. Also the noise is enough to wake the dead. Because I had no one else to whom I could turn, I had accepted his hospitality, but even if he were to offer me a bag of gold now, I would not stay with him.*[2] Later in March, Emperaire avoids any implication of his own fault when announcing to his Aixois friends that he'd moved out: *I moved out of Cézanne's place, it was unavoidable. I was unable to escape the fate of others. I found him forsaken by everyone. He has not a single intelligent or affectionate friend. The Zolas, the Solaris, all the others, never see him now. He is the strangest creature imaginable.* And to make matters worse, on finally escaping the horror of being Cézanne's guest, Emperaire curses Cézanne for having destroyed the crate in which he'd shipped his belongings from Aix: *Apart from all other blows to my head, I'm now doubly furious not to have for my needs the big crate. I was not present when my luggage was delivered to the rue de Jussieu, and my noble amphitryon host decided to destroy it.* Bad enough to have a houseguest with a luggage crate taking space in a small apartment, Cézanne and Hortense, the latter no doubt expected to do Achille's laundry, must have drawn a line when discarding his big crate.

One might question why Cézanne's biographers take the side of Emperaire, a provincial lost soul of small talent whose fame in Aix would rest on his having sold pornographic pictures to students. Why should Emperaire's opinion of Cézanne prevail as factual—the apartment dingy, the noise unbearable, Cézanne morose and cranky? Cézanne at the time was thirty-three, Hortense was twenty-two, while Emperaire was forty-three, a pitiful half-life creature with every reason to feel sorry for himself and be disgusted with life, while fantasizing that he would visit *the great Victor Hugo*, submit his portfolio to him, and ask that he select from it two pictures for the Salon! Even Rewald sides with Emperaire, saying, *Achille was obliged to return every day to the rue de Jussieu, for it was there that he had to await the jury's answer concerning his entry to the Salon* [he was rejected]. Why couldn't Rewald have said, *Cézanne and Hortense had to put up with miserable Achille returning every day while also coping with an infant's hourly demands?* At every turn of the biographical screw, Cézanne is diminished, always to prove points that, if not embroidered, he would be too plain. For how many days would John Rewald or Frederick Brown put up with Emperaire as a houseguest? And if Emperaire can be believed saying Cézanne was entirely without friends, why not ask why Emperaire had not a single friend in Paris to put him up other than Cézanne?

Cézanne had not abandoned his friends in either Paris or Aix. Nor had they abandoned him. He was exceptionally kind to Emperaire, as he was to others, friendly and loyal, even to Zola who had let him down on many occasions. Before he invited Achille to stay with him, he had written saying it would be a great pleasure to hear from him. Knowing of his friend's financial state, he even enclosed a postage stamp for Achille to use when replying. And in the letter, Cézanne asked

Achille if he was in need of paint tubes, in which case he would send him some. In late January 1872, Cézanne had teamed up with Zola to help Emperaire get free passage to Paris. On January 26th, Cézanne wrote to Achille, *I have just seen Zola, He still needs four or five days before he can give a definite answer. He has tried hard to get a pass for you, but not yet succeeded. Please be patient for a few more days. I need not tell you that I would be very happy to see you. You will be somewhat cramped at my house, but I gladly offer to share my modest quarters with you...I shall meet you at the station with a chariot* [a wheeled cart in days before motor vehicles, too often translated as a wheelbarrow] *and transport your luggage to my house. I live in what used to be rue Saint-Victor, now rue de Jussieu, opposite the wine market, on the third level. If, as I suspect, you have a great load of luggage, take only the necessary things with you and send the rest by freight. I must, however, ask you to bring bed linen, as I cannot lend you any.*[3]

Not a thing is known of Cézanne's life between this falling-out with Emperaire (which would soon be patched up, put back on good terms, Cézanne always being quick to dispense clemency) and his move to Pontoise to live near Pissarro. If Cézanne was without friends over those months, as Emperaire said he was, Zola was no less lacking a social life. One should recall Zola's letter to Cézanne of July 4th, 1871, saying, *I am nearly as lonely as you, and your letters help me to live.* But the critical issue is why Cézanne's historians put Cézanne in the worst light. The answer comes quickly: so he will conform to the mythical preconceptions. At issue is how biographers, scholars, and ordinary gossipers endear readers to a forsaken man. The American painter and pupil of Degas, Mary Cassatt, is an extreme example of source material that Cézanne's biographers pick off the floor. Cassatt set eyes on Cézanne for the first time in 1894 when he was fifty-five and she was fifty. By then Cézanne was a living myth, known only to a few. Cassatt was introduced to Cézanne at a gathering of Monet's friends at Giverny. In a letter to a correspondent in the United States, she wrote:

Monsieur Cézanne is from Provence. When I first saw him I thought he looked like a cutthroat with large red eyeballs standing out from his head in a most ferocious manner, a rather fierce-looking pointed beard, quite gray, and an exciting way of talking that positively made the dishes rattle. I found later on that I had misjudged his appearance, for far from being fierce or a cutthroat, he has the gentlest nature possible, «comme un enfant» [like a child], *as he would say. His manners at first rather startled me—he scrapes his soup plate, then lifts it and pours the remaining drops in his spoon; he even takes his chops in his fingers and pulls the meat from the bone. He eats with his knife and accompanies every gesture, every movement of his hand, with that implement, which he grasps firmly when he commences his meal and never puts down until he leaves the table. Yet in spite of the total disregard for the dictionary of manners, he shows a politeness towards us which no other man here would have shown. He will not allow Louise to serve him before us, in the usual order of succession at the table; he is even deferential to that stupid maid, and he pulls off the old tam-o'-shanter* [the cap that Cézanne often wore in the 1890s], *which he wears to protect his bald head, when he enters the room. I am gradually learning that appearances are not to be relied upon over here. Cézanne is one of the most liberal artists I have ever met. He prefaces every remark with, «Pour moi,» it is so and so [As for me, it is...], but he grants that everyone may be just as honest and as faithful to nature from their own convictions; he doesn't believe that everyone should see alike.*[4]

Aside from the usual way that letter-writers embellish news, this society lady from a Pittsburgh family of great wealth, who refers in the same letter to Monet's maid as «stupid,» hadn't the faintest idea of French table manners of the day. When men gathered informally and dined while conversing, the knife was rarely put down, and the use of one's fingers to eat a chop was perfectly acceptable under the circumstances of Monet's table and even in the best restaurants. Those around the table were most likely all men, and Cassatt, being a painter, was not being treated as a lady. French meals at the time were programmed like theater productions in three acts: entrée, main course, dessert. Table conversation was confined to polite silence or complimentary talk of what was being consumed. Only when the ladies retired to take tea in the parlor and gossip could men light up cigars, tell off-color jokes, and debate political and social issues. Among professionals and the literati, it was common to exclude women from meals so as not to be distracted by needs of decorum and politeness. Charles Monselet, drama critic and author of vaudevilles, made a point of this practice is his 1877 manual prescribing men's manners when dining.[5] Moreover, Cassatt most likely had never seen a real cutthroat with bulging red eyeballs and a fierce-looking beard, but Cézanne was already something of a legend. It must be said too that Cassatt, whose paintings were little more than Impressionism applied to the residue of her academic training in America, abhorred Cézanne's paintings, as she would Gauguin's. In 1910, after the importance of Cézanne had been recognized by Matisse, Derain, Picasso, and Braque, she wrote from Paris to her friend Louise Havemeyer, *The art world here is in a state of anarchy. That idiot Pellerin selling all his fine Manets and keeping his Cézannes works, of which he has a collection containing the very worst—figures really dreadful, neither drawing nor color.» And three years later, she wrote, «Vollard has made a fortune. The taste of the public has been perverted by Gauguin and even by Cézanne.*[6]

In 1872, when Cézanne, Hortense, and their newly arrived baby boy (also named Paul) moved to the village of Pontoise, just north of Paris, Cézanne found a new father in Pissarro, it is said, and like a son at his father's side, at last had a mentor who was both father and supporter. This is where the myth that deprecates Cézanne's father diminishes Cézanne as a self, subordinating his art to Pissarro's. As in the case of Cézanne being *forced by his father* into law school, we are given once again an image of Cézanne as impotent, powerless in his own right, a flaccid boy bowing his head to a father-phallus. It is said that the combination of his parenthood and Pissarro's calming influence took the fire out of Cézanne, cooled him down, brought him at last to emotional maturity. Pissarro has been routinely called Cézanne's surrogate father, a different sort of father than the «old banker» down in Aix.

This flocculent romanticism fits to the standard adopted wild-boy myth—the mythos that lurks in the minds of those who seek reparation for a troubled childhood by finding a new parent. More than anyone before him, Schapiro immured this story in Cézanne's biography, saying that Pissarro was to be more than a teacher to Cézanne, more than a friend, a second father.[7] Perhaps the most contemptuous description of Louis-Auguste Cézanne—even more than Rewald's—comes from Schapiro's interpretation of Cézanne's Ugolino story, to which I devoted an earlier chapter, as Cézanne's wish for his father's death so he would have the financial means to pursue his dream of being an artist. Yet even though supported by his father, Cézanne's dream didn't come to much over the first ten years—no success at all in Paris: not one painting in the Salon, not one picture sold, not one good review, not even by his best friend Zola. Still, the «old banker» kept up with the monthly allowance and welcomed his son home whenever he felt inclined to make the trip. The «old banker» posed for him, provided him with a studio in the family house, welcomed his son's friends to stay over, and surely enjoyed his son's pictures that hung here and there throughout the house. Of Cézanne compared with Louis-Auguste, Schapiro wrote:

> In twin photographs of the painter and his father we recognize an evident opposition of temperament in the faces of the tense, introspective artist and the old self-made merchant and provincial banker, with his shrewd, confident air of the French bourgeois of the old style launched by the Revolution.[8]

In truth we have no «twin photographs» of Cézanne and his father and only one photograph of his father. A character analysis of the type that Schapiro performed on this photograph of Louis-Auguste would be no more and maybe less useful than testing his urine for personality traits. A photograph is one second of life, one second of how one appears, one second of one's personality, usually when blinking or caught off guard. That moment cannot be generalized any more than *a self-made merchant, a provincial banker; an old-style French bourgeois* can ever be a specific individual. Louis-Auguste may have been much of what Schapiro said he was, but what he said was read into, not from, the photograph, just as he had read a wish for the father's death into the Ugolino sketch. Ask why Cézanne is singled-out as the suffering hero and the answer will come as quickly as the formula it exposes. He was the only one among the modernists whose life provided a demonstration, however embellished, of the Oedipal complex and its non-resolution: *hatred for the father, terror of women.* And there would not be another one like him, not Gauguin, not van Gogh, not Picasso, except in the minds of psychoan-alytic-type historians.[9] Cézanne's life story came prefigured, fitted like a glove to intuitional psychoanalysis, a focal point for vicarious emotion, a self-proving case study, and a fill-in-the-blanks psycho-biography.[10]

If Cézanne remembered Pissarro thirty years later as the humble and colos-sal Pissarro—someone to consult, someone like the good Lord—he also remem-bered his real father with veneration. Joachim Gasquet, who knew Cézanne at his advanced age as well as anyone, tells of Cézanne in tears over the destruction of his father's furniture at a time when his sisters were overseeing the sale of the *Jas de Bouffan* following their mother's death, and had seen no reason to keep what was no longer useful. They hauled out and burned furniture that Cézanne and his mother had preserved in Louis-Auguste's room. Perhaps this explains why Cézanne moved the paravent from the Jas to his studio in Les Lauves after his father's death. Of his father's other furniture, Cézanne laments:

> *I would have taken them. Dust traps, worthless things, they called them. And now they have made a bonfire of them. And I, who looked after them like the apple of my eye...the armchair Papa slept in after lunch. The table he did his accounts on all his life. Yes, he had the foresight to provide an income for me. Tell me what would have become of me were it not for that? We must love our fathers. I shall never be grateful enough to mine. I never showed him enough appreciation.*[11]

The statement Cézanne made about Pissarro as a man to consult appears in about every book on Cézanne. It supports the myth of the fatherless son. But nowhere in the secondary literature can one find Cézanne's confessions of love for his father, which threaten the myth, or his having also referred to Pissarro as *an old fool*, even though these statements are equally available in the primary texts.[12] By 1873, Cézanne had known Pissarro for about ten years. Cézanne was twenty-five and Pissarro thirty-four when they met. In 1873, Cézanne was thirty-four and Pissarro forty-three. The nine-year age span between them was not then as great psychologically as a decade earlier—less a father/son age difference than an older to younger brother gap, with Pissarro a friend rather than father. Also disputing Pissarro's tranquilizing effect on Cézanne's passionate subject matter is that all the while Cézanne was with Pissarro at Pontoise and Auvers they painted landscapes; on unpleasant weather days, still-lifes. And from the start, Cézanne was as great a master as Pissarro. Without hesitation, I will rank the certainty of Cézanne's eye and hand, the unifying structure of his *Quai at Bercy*, *Alexis Reading to Zola*, or *Melting Snow at L'Estaque* above any work by Pissarro from the early 1870s. And those pre-ceded their period of work side by side. Pissarro was a subject-matter painter whose paintings were descriptions; they described village life, they described the environs of an industrializing Paris. His and Cézanne's painter friend Guillaumin was of the same mind. He, too, illustrated life in hamlets and the countryside.

The emotional turmoil, runaway passion, which Cézanne was supposed to have gotten a grip on under Pissarro's influence, had never shown up in his landscapes of the 1860s anyway. *Melting Snow at L'Estaque* may be impassioned but Cézanne was painting the effect of weather, not a self-portrait. Winter weather tends to be moody, independently of a painter's mood. Moreover, some landscapes painted after his two years with Pissarro are equally impassioned, such as *The Étang des Soeurs at Osny near Pontoise* of 1877.[13] Nothing painted by Pissarro during the two years they painted side by side can match Cézanne's *Route tournant* or another canvas from 1873, *House of Père Lacroix*.[14]

Cézanne. *House of Père LaCroix.* Pontoise, 1873. National Gallery of Art, Washington D. C. Photo: Bulloz.

Cézanne. *The Turn in the Road* (*La Route tournant*). 1873. Boston, Museum of Fine Arts. Photo: Galerie Bernheim-Jeune. *Below:* Camille Pissarro. *Vue de Pontoise*, 1873. Private collection, Dallas.

Cézanne, center, with Pissarro, right, at Pontoise. c. 1874.

And once Cézanne was back in a Paris studio, not out in the landscape with Pissarro, his imagination again determined much of his subject matter. The separation of the 1860s, as Cézanne's decade of romantic fantasies, sexual frustration, and Salon confrontations, from the 1870s as his decade of order and domestic calm, has spawned a roster of methodological problems. Cézanne's art history is corrupted by insistence on an extreme separation of his 1860s work from that of the 1870s, with Pissarro providing the hinge. Attempts to defend that division betray the usual problem that one encounters when obliged to defend synthetic absolutes. The 1860s decade is forced to close with such pictures as the so-called, mistitled *Courtesans*, in which the woman are dancers putting on their stage clothes. Calling them courtesans is just another way of forcing sexuality upon most everything Cézanne painted. One wouldn't do that with Degas, whose picture of girls preparing for a dance hardly differs from Cézanne's picture.

Left: Cézanne. Dancers dressing, mistitled *Courtesans*. Barnes Foundation, Merion, PA.
Right: Edgar Degas. Dancers dressing.

Were one to end Cézanne's 1860s with a *Murder*, the first version of *Modern Olympia*, an *Autopsy,* and the *Nymph Attacked by a Satyr*. But were we to replace these canvases implicating violence with *Young Girl at a Piano, Melting Snow at L'Estaque, Quai at Bercy,* and *Alexis Reading to Zola,* along with such exceptional still lifes as *Pot vert et bouilloire d'étain,* a very different end of the 1860s would emerge. And if we were to open the 1870s with Cézanne's later *Modern Olympia,* the reworked *Le Festin, An Afternoon in Naples, Battle of the Sexes*, the *Temptation of Saint Anthony,* and yet another *Murder,* a different sort of 1870s would emerge. This is what I mean when saying that artists do not create art history but only the objects

Cézanne. *Le Meurtre* (Murder), 1867-68. Walker Art Galleries, Liverpool.

For every 1860s, pre-Pissarro picture by Cézanne that one would call violent, or impassioned, one can find one that is post-Pissarro.

Cézanne. Woman being strangled. c. 1875. Paris, Musée d'Orsay. Pjoto: Gallerie Bernheim-Jeune.

from which art history is made. Art historians create art history as formalized schema of sequence into which the artist's work is squeezed, style by style, and year by year.

To enforce the cleavage of the 1860 and 1870 decades as a schematic imperative, we are offered these remarks on *Melting Snow at L'Estaque* by Lawrence Gowing, one of Cézanne's most astute admirers, saying that this landscape depicts *the fearful image of a world dissolved, sliding downhill in a sickening precipitous diagonal between the curling pines which are themselves almost threateningly unstable and baroque, painted with a wholly appropriate slipping wetness and soiled non-color unique in his work.*[15]

Now, *fearful, sickening, precipitous, unstable, slipping, soiled*, are powerfully effective words, but more forceful than what they refer to in Cézanne's painting. Gowing's words recall how Cassatt described Cézanne: *cut-throat, red eyeballs, ferocious, fierce-looking*—all overwrought words contrived to impress the reader, like Cézanne scaring Zola with his horror story of the woman in the coach, or entertaining him with descriptions of his baccalaureate examiners.

In her book on Cézanne's early imagery, Mary Lewis says of Gowing's words, *It is hard to imagine a better description. These landscapes convey the same tumultuous world and unsettled passion we associate with the narrative works of the first decade.* But this is only half of her sentence. Lewis is stuck with Cézanne in transition; the second half of her sentence must carry neatly into the 1870s—and it does just that:...*but now the painter's means of expression has become purely formal.* The transition is complete; the descriptive words *become* Cézanne's picture: Gowing's *fearful, sickening, precipitous, unstable* landscape is rendered *by purely formal means*! The bridge to the 1870s has been crossed.

On the other side of 1870, then, how does one account for such coarsely passionate paintings as the *Three Bathers*? One scholar opens his description of this picture saying, A*t the beginning of the 1870s, the period when Cézanne's life submits to important changes caused by the birth of his beloved son, his settling down in the relative calm of the village of Auvers, and his daily collaboration with the serene Pissarro, the violent character of his previous pictures, done with a palette knife for the most part, disappears.*[16] This doesn't make sense. The majority of Cézanne's 1860s paintings done primarily with the knife are portraits, and not one of them is violent. Others painted with the palette knife are exceptionally fine and very quiet, such as *Rue des Saules à Montmartre* of 1867, the still life *Sugar Bowl, Pears, and Blue Cup,* and one of the most placid of landscapes, *The Environs of Aix-en-Provence.* These palette-knife canvases are from the mid-1860s and have nothing to do with any transition to the 1870s. Moreover, a palette knife is not a weapon. It is never used to cut. Painting with a palette knife is like spreading soft butter. From what evidence we do have—and it is very limited—Cézanne did not apply paint with the palette knife after 1867, while both he and Pissarro took up applying paint with the knife again in the mid-1870s.[17]

Cézanne. *Three Bathers.* c. 1874-75. Private collection.

And Cézanne's canvases—the few that we have—that conclude the 1860s are not impassioned or violent; the most truly violent painting; the mid-1860s *Murder* was done with brushes. And besides, much of what can be taken as stylistic changes in Cézanne's painting after joining Pissarro in mid-1872 was already in place during 1870-1871, specifically present in the *Paysage au moulin à eau* and *Les marronniers et le bassin du Jas de Bouffan*.[18]

It is said that, by 1872, Cézanne had turned away not only from the literary

Cézanne. Gang of men assaulting a woman. c. 1876. Art Institute of Chicago.

narratives but also from the compelling romantic fantasies that pervaded his earlier work.[19] This statement goes against the facts. Based on the very few surviving paintings, which are all we have to work with, after 1872 Cézanne painted more themes of violence than he did in the 1860s. In addition to a *Woman Being Strangled* and a *Woman Being Killed with a Dagger*, there are two versions of *The Temptation of Saint Anthony*, two versions of *The Eternal Feminine* (the most emotionally violent imagery he ever painted), *The Battle of the Sexes*, *The Drunkards*, several versions of *An Afternoon in Naples*, and *Medea Slaying Her Children* among others. If one adds watercolors and drawings, the number of emotionally infused and violent themes triples to include such themes as a *Gang Rape*, plus a good many eroticized landscapes with naked female and male bathers. Given that more examples of violent imagery come from the 1870s than from the 1860s (and we have no idea how many more he painted), it is impossible to justify the conclusion shared by many of Cézanne's historians that, in 1872, the accreted vehemence of the first decade was dispelled at Pontoise and Auvers sur Oise under Pissarro's influence.[20] *Alexis Reading to Zola*, *Young Woman at a Piano*, *Still-life with Teapot*, *Quai de Bercy*, *Still life with Pot, Bottle, Cup and Fruit* are the very best that survive from the 1860s. They are as tranquil, unemotional, and composed as any pictures from the 1870s. *Alexis Reading to Zola* and *Young Woman at a Piano* are positively serene.

Of the 178 entries in Rewald's *catalogue raisonné* that he dates any year earlier than Cézanne's move to join Pissarro at Auvers in 1872, only two are of *outright* themes of violence: *The Murder* and *The Abduction*. In one other picture from the second half of the 1860s, a satyr is «attacking» a nymph, but I'm not sure that act should be called an act of violence; if it were, a few hundred other painters from Tintoretto (his *Rape of Lucretia*), to Bernini (*The Rape of Proserpina*) to ten percent of the painters regularly seen in the Paris salons. In Cézanne's *Le Festin* (*The Banquet*) there is some wrestling going on, but whether that is violence or aggressive sexual encounters between consenting adults, I wouldn't be able to say. Cézanne's *Les Voleurs et l'âne* may have a bit of violence at the lower left corner, but that picture is a copy of an illustrated tale that may have no more violence to it than Zola's juvenile story, *Les Voleurs et l'âne*, and it is much less violent than the level-headed Daumier's version of the story. Surely one should not count the copy of Delacroix's *Barque de Dante* as one of Cézanne's violent themes. So, with only a few pictures of violence out of the 178 pictures from the pre-1872 years, from where comes the old ritornello that Cézanne's imagery of the 1860s was violent?

Cézanne's *Women Dressing*, for example, mistitled *Courtesans* and assumed to be from the late 1860s (this picture mentioned earlier, p. 419) is described as *an evocation of savage sexuality* rendered *with bold streaks, crowded space, and crude, slashing figures,* the women's *revealing costumes are like those worn by prostitutes;* the women *flaunt hard, angular breasts,* their postures are *garish and shameless.*[21] Let us set beside this small picture—which, as I said, to my eye does not depict prostitutes at all but dancers getting into their stage clothes, as one sees in Degas' several renderings of the theme—another small canvas, also depicting naked women: *Three Bathers* (p. 421). This picture dates *after* 1870, *after* Cézanne's stay with the sobering Pissarro, *after* his having found domestic tranquility with Hortense (although there is no reason to believe that their relationship hadn't been tranquil all along). So, as the standard line of reasoning says, when addressing this 1870s canvas one cannot speak any longer of *savage sexuality, slashing figures, shameless women,* simply because this canvas was painted *after* 1872, when, as often said, all the violence and eroticism of the 1860s had disappeared. Rathet, of this contradictory picture it is said: *Cézanne had not completely abandoned fantasy and imagination, as in this work, which is overflowing with energy and humor, where three young women (the fourth a ways away) have gathered around a spring, two of them splashing about joyously.*[22] So, after 1872, the *shameless women* become *young women,* while their *savage sexuality* becomes *energy and humor,* and their *slashing* arm gestures become *joyous splashing.* Were one to follow this line of logic, then with *The Eternal Feminine* of about 1876, Cézanne was only being playful when he gouged the eyeballs out of the naked woman on public display, leaving her with bloody eye sockets,[23] and the man and women who are strangling a woman in Cézanne's *The Murder* of about 1874, and the man and woman who are stabbing another woman to death in the watercolor of about the same date, *The Murder,* are not being violent, just having fun, because these picture date later than Cézanne's association with Pissarro.[24] Once one has periodized any historical process, one is stuck with such exceptions and forced into making bad art history. The subjects under study become fitted to their descriptions, rather than the other way around. The diagram takes command of the data.[25]

Cézanne. *La Lutte d'Amour (Battle of the Sexes)*. ca. 1876-78. Private collection, Paris. Photo: H. Roger-Violet

46

*A fantastic figure revealed under
an opium sky to a drug addict*

In 1873, several of the painters known today as the Impressionists formed an organization to plan and stage exhibitions as alternatives to the Salon. By this time a few collectors—or simply, buyers—were purchasing pictures from these painters, creating enough optimism to have them raise their prices. Monet had obtained 1,500 francs for a canvas, while Manet's *Bon Bock*, which had a fine reception at the Salon of 1873, sold for 6,000 francs to the famous baritone Jean-Baptiste Faure, whose art collecting interest was being pushed by the dealer Durand-Ruel. Early in 1874, pictures by Degas, Monet, Sisley, and Pissarro fetched relatively good prices at an auction sale from a collector who had purchased several impressionist works.

To establish independent exhibitions, the painters were faced with having to create their own jury and obliged to put their own Salon fundamentals in place— criteria of choice and which artists to choose. The first exhibition would be the following year, 1874. The first to be rejected by the group was Cézanne.

If Pissarro got past the Salon jury on occasion by saying he was a pupil of Corot, Cézanne would make it into this exhibition solely by the persuasion of Pissarro, the principal organizer, with Alexis the spokesman and promoter, but not necessarily on Cézanne's side. Taking up where Zola had left off, Alexis published an article in *L'Avenir National* on March 5th, the day the official Salon opened, calling for abolition of the Salon jury system and support for artists' individual exhibitions. Monet responded to Alexis' article with a letter published in *L'Avenir National* on May 12th, 1873. This was a contrived letter, intended for the newspaper's readership, saying: *A group of painters, assembled in my home, read with pleasure the article you published in L'Avenir National. We are happy to see you defend ideas that we hold too, and we hope that, as you say, L'Avenir National will kindly give us assistance when the society we are about to form will be constituted.*[1] To Monet's letter when published, Alexis appended a paragraph saying that several artists had already joined in the venture, including Pissarro, Jongkind, Sisley, Armand Gautier, Béliard, and Guillaumin (Cézanne, of course, not mentioned): *These painters,* he added, *most having previously exhibited, belong to that group of naturalists with ambition to paint nature and life in their full and direct reality.*

This 1874 exhibition of the Independents betrayed a growing split between the so-called naturalists around Pissarro, and the so-called realists associated with Manet, who refused to participate. The non-naturalists Tissot and Legros had moved to London by then and could not be persuaded to send pictures. Degas wrote to Tissot, saying: *See here, my dear Tissot, do not hesitate or try to avoid the issue.*

> *You positively must exhibit on the boulevard. It will do you good. It is a way to show your-self in Paris, from which some here say you are running away. And it will be good for us, too. The realist movement no longer needs to fight with the others. It already exists; it must show itself as something distinct, there must be a Salon of Realists. Manet does not under-stand that need. Manet seems to be obstinate in his decision to remain apart. I think he is more vain than intelligent...So forget the money side of the issue. Show your work. Be of your country and with your friends...I have not yet written to Legros. Try and see him and stir up his enthusiasm.*[2]

Cézanne. *Une moderne Olympia.* 1873-74. Paris, Musée d'Orsay. Photo: Bulloz.

Cézanne. *Thatched Cottage at Auvers* (otherwise known as *La Maison du pendu*). 1873. Paris, Musée d'Orsay. Photo: Bulloz.

It was one thing to be rejected by the Salon, another by your comrades in the trenches. Guillaumin was also purged, but Pissarro intervened and managed to have him included anyway. He did the same for Cézanne, who was on no one's mind other than Pissarro's. Even Monet and Degas were opposed to including him. Aside from having little respect for Cézanne as a painter, they figured he would instigate a public outrage, repel the show's viewers, and incite the usual hostile critics. And that is exactly what he did; his intransigence persisted.[3] Although he included two landscapes—as good as he'd ever painted, including the *Thatched Cottage at Auvers*—Cézanne ignored the concerns of his colleagues and insisted on hanging a later version of *Une Moderne Olympia*. The public's reaction to it was what the others feared it would be.

The show had been strategically seeded with artists who had had success at the Salon yet were hardly Impressionists (albeit the term, Impressionism, wasn't yet coined). If viewed today, the show would hardly represent an exhibition of Impressionists as collectively known today, even though some fifty of the two hundred pictures in the show were by the seven painters identified as constituting the core and defining the style. The exhibition was reviewed in newspapers as many as fifty times, supported by a few critics and panned by others. In a letter to Duret, Pissarro reported, *Our exhibition is going well. Itis a success. The critics are devouring us, accusing us of not applying ourselves. I am going back to my work, which is better time spent than reading their comments. Nothing can be learned from them.*[4] While granting that artists should be unyoked from Salon criteria, the minor critic Émile Cardon said, rather snidely, that the *Salon des Refusés* was a veritable *Musée du Louvre* compared with this show.[5]

Most of the favorable reviews served more as attacks on the Salon and the Academy than worthwhile elucidation of what was new and potentially important in the show. Just as it was good journalism to attack the government (agreement, like fair weather, is rarely newsworthy), this opportunity to side with the oppressed would be irresistible to journalists. In the radical newspaper *Le Rappel*, Émile d'Hervilly cited the Salon and the Academy as *the two cripplers of French art*. He wrote that instead of the rhetoric taught at the *École des Beaux-Arts*, the Impressionists' show offered *fresh, gripping works whose generous exaggerations are even charming and consoling when compared in one's mind with the nauseating banalities of the academic routine.*[6] Ernest Chesneau had some reservations about the show, but by now he was committed to its defense, having been the critic-for-hire to write the catalogue text for the Hôtel Drouot auction earlier that year; and Armand Silvestre, who'd been engaged by Durand-Ruel to write the appreciative essay in his catalogue the previous year, saying good things especially about Monet, Renoir, and Sisley, couldn't back off now. Deploying the standard strategy of criticism—saying that if one can't appreciate these painters, it's because one is not equipped to do so—Silvestre put the onus on the viewer: if you don't see it, you're blind; if you don't understand it, you're ignorant. Silvestre wrote, *You need special eyes in order to be sensitive to the subtlety of their tonal relations, which constitute their honor and merit.*[7] And Chesneau, too, had a way out, saying in *Le Soir* that if one does not appreciate such pictures as Monet's *Boulevard des Capucines* now, that's because it is the art of the future. *In a very few years,* he added, *the typical paintings at the Salon will look like the Impressionists'.*[8]

Within this general shift towards modernity, in his introduction to this catalogue, Silvestre may have been the first to detect an art history being created. He proposed a logical line of development and progress leading from Delacroix to Corot, Millet, and Courbet, then to the Batignolles group. Nothing more securely fixes an idea in time than recognition that a connective line from past events to the present anchors it. Art historians depend on it. It's a self-proving logic of historical motion. Academic painting could not entertain history in motion; its criteria for comparison to the past were not what immediately preceded the present. Rather, each moment of the present was compared to a constant remote past, like theology to scripture, philosophy to Plato, natural science to Genesis. What existed before would continue to exist hereafter. The defining characteristic of modern art after 1850, by contrast, was an evolutionary process conducted by a few mutants intruding into an environment that was itself changing, cracked open by shifts in sociology, not unlike climatic and geological traumas that reshuffle organic life—each stage of the advance a logical alteration of the previous stage, as Silvestre had presented it, as Courbet altering Delacroix and Manet altering Courbet.

But in this show it was Cézanne's *Modern Olympia* that brought a large measure of public ridicule beyond the usual judgmental comments. The perennially waffling Jules Castagnary called Cézanne's picture *an example of romanticism without brakes—nature serving only a pretext for personal fantasies that have no meaning to the senses because they are without control and cannot be verified in reality.*[9] The critic Marie-Èmile Chartroule, who signed her review with the pseudonym Marc de Montifaud, commented as colorfully as an Impressionist in drag: *On Sunday the public saw fit to sneer at a fantastic figure revealed under an opium sky to a drug addict. This apparition of a little pink and nude flesh being pushed in an empyrean cloud by a kind of demon or incubi. Like a voluptuous vision, this corner of an artificial paradise has suffocated the most courageous viewers. Mr. Cézanne gives the impression of being a sort of madman who paints in delirium tremens.*[10] Another critic, aghast at what assaulted his eyes, wrote, *Should we speak of Mr. Cézanne? Of all known juries, none ever imagined, even in a dream, the possibility of accepting any work by this man who used to present himself at the Salon carrying his canvasses on his back like Jesus his cross.*[11]

The painter Latouche, serving his turn as a gallery guard, wrote to Dr. Paul Gachet, who'd loaned Cézanne's *Modern Olympia* (apparently Cézanne had left it with him at Auvers): *I am keeping an eye on your Cézanne, but cannot guarantee its safety. I fear it may be returned to you torn to pieces.*[12] The guard's letter was written the day after a lengthy review of the exhibition appeared in the April 25th issue of *Charivari*, penned by Louis Leroy, the perennial thorn in the side of any deviant from the true path. (In this review, Leroy coined the term «impressionism,» which thereafter the artists adopted, much to Leroy's delight).[13] Within the review, which here follows as a nearly complete translation, Leroy remarks that Cézanne's *Olympia* made Manet's *Olympia* look like a masterpiece of drawing and finish. Leroy's review was headed, *Exhibition of the Impressionists*:

> *Oh, it was a difficult day when I ventured into the first exhibition on the Boulevard des Capucines in the company of Mr. Joseph Vincent, a landscape painter and recipient of medals and decorations under several governments. This incautious man had come there without reason to suspect anything so awful. He thought he would see the kind of painting one sees everywhere, good and bad, preferably more good than bad, but not hostile to virtuous artistic manners and good form, not disrespectful of the masters.*
>
> *Upon entering the first room, Joseph Vincent received an initial shock in front of the «Dancer» by Mr. Renoir.*
>
> *«What a pity,» he said to me, «that this painter, with some understanding of color,*

doesn't draw better. His dancer's legs are as cottony as the gauze of her skirts.»

«I think you are being too hard on him,» I replied. *«On the contrary, I find that the drawing is very tight.»*

Assuming that I was being ironical, Joseph Vincent was content with shrugging his shoulders. Then, putting on my most ingenuous demeanor, I very quietly led him before «The Plowed Field» by Mr. Pissarro. At the sight of this astounding landscape, the good man thought that the lenses of his spectacles were dirty. He took them off, wiped them carefully, and replaced them on his nose.

«My God,» he cried, *«What on earth is that?»*

«Can't you see,» I said, *«it's hoar-frost on deeply plowed furrows.»*

«You call those furrows? You call that frost? They are palette-scrapings placed uniformly on a dirty canvas.»

«Perhaps...but the impression is there.»

«Well, it's a silly impression!...Oh, and this?»

«An orchard by Mr. Sisley. I'd like to point out the small tree on the right; it's gay, but the impression...»

«I've heard enough of your impressions; they're neither here nor there. But here we have a view of Melun by Mr. Rouart, in which there is something to be said for the water. The shadow in the foreground, however, is really bizarre.»

«It's the vibration of tone that's astonishing you.»

«Call it the sloppiness of tone that's upsetting me and I'll understand you better. Oh Corot, Corot, what crimes are being committed in your name! You brought into fashion this messiness of composition, these water-thin washes, these mud-splashes in front of which the art lover has been rebelling for thirty years and has accepted only because he was forced to by your serene contumaciousness. Once again, a drop of water has eroded the stone.»

The poor man rambled on this way quite peacefully, and nothing led me to anticipate the unfortunate incident that was to be the result of this visit to this hair-raising exhibition. He managed to sustain, without major injury, viewing the «Fishing Boats Leaving the Harbor» by Mr. Claude Monet, perhaps because I tore him away from dangerous contemplation of this work before the small, obnoxious figures in the foreground could produce their effect. Unfortunately I was imprudent enough to leave him too long in front of the «Boulevard des Capucines» by the same painter.

«Ah-ha!» he sneered in Mephistophelian manner. *«Is that brilliant enough? Now there's impression, or I don't know what the word means. Only be so good as to tell me what those innumerable black tongue-lickings in the lower part of the picture represent?»*

«Why, those are people walking along,» I replied.

«People! Do I look like that when I'm walking along the Boulevard des Capucines? Blood and thunder! So you're making fun of me at last?»

«I assure you, Mr. Vincent...»

«But those spots were obtained by the same method as that used to imitate marble—

a bit here, a bit there, slap-dash, any old way. It's unheard of, appalling, I'll get a stroke from looking at it, that's for sure.»

I attempted to calm him by showing him the «Saint Denis Canal» by Mr. Lépine, and the «Butte Montmartre» by Mr. Ottin, both quite delicate in tone. But fate was stronger than they: the «Cabbages» of Mr. Pissarro stopped him as he was passing by, and from red-faced he became scarlet.

«Those are cabbages,» I told him in a gentle, persuasive voice.

«Oh, the poor wretches, aren't they caricatured! I swear not to eat any more as long as I live.»

«But, it's not the cabbages fault if the painter...»

«Be quiet, or I'll do something terrible.»

Suddenly Mr. Vincent gave a loud cry upon catching sight of the «House of the Hanged Man» by Mr. Cézanne.

At this point, Mr. Vincent becomes delirious. It was not just the opium sky of Cézanne's *Modern Olympia* that crazed his brain but the accumulative effect of the entire exhibition. His brain went into reverse: suddenly Mr. Vincent became enthralled. Leroy tried to bring him back to a rational state of perception: *In vain I tried to revive his expiring reason. But Monet's «Impression, Sunrise» was the last straw.*

Impression indeed! sputters Mr. Vincent. *Since I am impressed there must be some impression in it!—and what freedom, what workmanship! Wallpaper in its embryonic state is more finished than that seascape.*

Leroy tries to find some tolerable features that might restore Mr. Vincent's sensibilities—in Renoir's *Harvesters*, or Degas' *The Laundress*. But Mr. Vincent is too far-gone, his brain is scrambled, he is suffering delirium tremens. *The horrible now fascinated him. The Laundress, so badly laundered, of Mr. Degas drove him to cries of admiration.* Rejecting all concessions, Mr. Vincent then exclaims of Monet's pictures, *They are too finished, too finished; he is sacrificing to the false gods of Meissonier.* Then he calls out, *Talk to me of the Modern Olympia. That's something well done.*

Alas, go and look at it, says the befuddled Leroy. Mr. Vincent does; he sees *a woman folded in two, from whom a Negro girl is removing the last veil in order to offer her in all her ugliness to the charmed gaze of a brown puppet. Do you remember the Olympia of Mr. Manet? Well, that was a masterpiece of drawing, accuracy, finish, compared with this one by Mr. Cézanne.*

His mind having gone completely to pieces, Mr. Vincent then mistakes the gallery attendant for a portrait: *Is he ugly enough?* he asks Leroy. *From the front he has two eyes, and a nose, and a mouth! Impressionists wouldn't have thus sacrificed to detail!*

Move on, says the portrait.

You hear that? Mr. Vincent calls out. *This portrait even talks. The poor fool who daubed him must have spent a lot of time at it.*

And in order to give the appropriate seriousness to his theory of aesthetics, Mr. Vincent then began to dance the scalp dance [imitating an American Plains Indian] *in front of the bewildered guard, crying in a strangling voice, «Hi-ho! I am an impression on the march, an avenging palette knife* [referring to a scalping knife], *the 'Boulevard des Capucines' of Monet, the 'Hanged Man's House' and the 'Modern Olympia' of Cézanne. Hi-ho! Hi-ho!»*[14]

Leroy's column was widely read, even in England, from where Berthe Morisot's mother, concerned for her daughter's welfare, contacted an artist friend of Corot's in Paris and asked that he take a look at the show and report back to her. He did, saying: *I have seen the rooms at Nadar's and wish to give you right off my honest opinion. When I entered I became immediately distressed upon seeing the works of your daughter in those pestilential surroundings. I said to myself, «One doesn't live with exemption among madmen. Manet was right in opposing her participation.» After examining and attentively analyzing the pictures, I did find here and there some fragments of merit, but the painters all have more or less cross-eyed minds.* He advised Morisot to break completely with *the so-called school of the future.*[15]

Vollard says that Cézanne had one sale from this exhibition: *Thatched Cottage at Auvers* (*La Maison du pendu*) sold to novice collector Count Armand Doria for 300 francs.[16] This was the first time to my knowledge that anyone had purchased one of Cézanne's pictures, so this is as good a place as any to question its title. Art dealers, for labels and catalogue entries made up most titles during this era. So one runs risks of misinterpretation when reading any picture by its title. When called *The Suicide's House*, or *The House of the Hanged Man* (*La Maison du pendu*, a prophetic shroud is made to fall over Cézanne's *Thatched Cottage at Auvers* (*Une Chaumière à Auvers-sur-Oise*). To promote the myth that Cézanne's troubled unconscious seethed in violence, such sexually charged titles are used by art historians who interpret pictures by their titles rather than their imagery and read into imagery from outside it, as when *L'Enlèvement* is named alternatively *Le Rapt* (The Rape), or when his so-called *Le Festin* (The Banquet) is called *The Orgy*. While true that *Une Chaumière à Auvers-sur-Oise* (a purely descriptive title) was titled *Maison du pendu* in the catalogue of the 1874 exhibition, it does not mean that Cézanne gave it that title. The title may have been a joke played on him—*the house of the hanged man*, meaning Cézanne's picture, featuring a house, hung on the wall—*le tableau de Cézanne, pendu*—or, the Cézanne is hung. Maybe Cézanne went along with the wordplay, finding it amusing, the attention self-serving. This kind of spoof would not have been at all out of character for Cézanne, or for Renoir, who was not Cézanne's supporter in 1874 and was in charge of the installation. Frankly, it's a more likely explanation than saying that out of some morbid curiosity, or preoccupation with death, Cézanne had set up his easel in front of a house wherein some man had recently hanged himself. Renoir's brother Edmond prepared the catalogue for the 1974 exhibition and most likely made up titles. He was upset with Monet for having sent too many pictures, and for having given them monotonous titles: *Entrance to a Village, Morning in a Village, Departing the Village,* and so on. Frustrated by this lack of poetry, Edmond pressed Monet to come up with a less banal title for his painting of a sunrise done from a window at Le Havre. Monet offered the title *Impression*. Edmond elaborated it to read *Impression, Soleil Levant* (Impression, Sunrise). As I've said, the rancorous critic and master of farcical ceremonies, Louis Leroy, probably used that title to name the Independents *Les Impressionists*.[17]

Claude Monet, *Impression: Sunrise*, 1873. Paris, Musée Marmottan. Photo: Bulloz.

Part IV

IMPRESSIONISM IS DYING

47

*And still we await the
geniuses of the future*

Steered along a trash-strewn path by their rather Machiavellian minds, Cézanne and Zola had traversed childhood to arrive at maturity. After their deaths, they would become famous for what in their lifetime was their notoriety, like the fame of Arthur Rimbaud and Billy the Kid. Zola would be not well thought of over the next several decades, and it would take a new generation of artists to recognize Cézanne's value. The Cézanne of today was made illustrious by myths fashioned around his his personality—from Rewald and Schapiro's father-conflict and terror of women, to Theodore Reff's thesis on Cézanne's constructive stroke assignable to mastering guilt over masturbation, to Sydney Geist calling the brushstrokes phallic, to Frederick Brown saying that, in his old age, Cézanne succumbed to the Catholic church because he still needed a surrogate father. Ignored in the latter context are letters to his son dated a few months before Cézanne's death, in which he had much to say about this «surrogate father,» the priest Father Roux: *Yesterday I was to have gone to see the blackfrock Roux. I didn't go, and that's how it will be to the end. He is poisonous.*

At St. Sauveur [the cathedral at Aix], *the old choirmaster Poncet has been succeeded by an idiot of an abbé, who works the organ and plays in such a manner that I can no longer go to mass, his way of playing makes me positively ill. I think that to be a catholic one must be devoid of all sense of justice, but have a good eye for one's own interests.*[1]

Conditioned as the Western mind is to focusing on originary events and motives—sources of imagery, primary influences, first times—it is difficult to allow people later in life to have experiences that cannot be traced to infancy or youth. Psychoanalysis rests entirely on that supposition: father-son conflict and adolescent apprehension vis-à-vis the opposite sex cannot be allowed to stay in the past. The fact that the entire human society is structured on paternal, maternal, and sibling lines (city fathers, fatherlands, motherlands, sister states, brotherhoods, sisters as nuns, monks as brothers, priests as fathers), makes it difficult to avoid such semantic overlays and intrusions.

In his later books, John Rewald came around to admitting that the picture of Cézanne built up since the mid-1860s was distorted: *It is easy to see how Cézanne became a legendary figure.* Yet Rewald cannot admit that he, himself, was in large part responsible for transferring the early folk-tale status of the myths to art historical scholarship. He writes, *Since Cézanne ceased to exhibit* [after 1877] *his paintings, hidden in his studio, would not bear witness to his sincerity, to his hard and painstaking work.*[2] Yet, even Rewald's phrase *hidden in his studio* is calculated to perpetuate the myth of the aged Cézanne hiding in Aix, avoiding Paris (why couldn't the paintings be simply *stored* in his studio?). And even on the heels of his seeming gesture at dispelling the myths, Rewald goes right on repeating Edmond Duranty's silly story of the fictional artist Maillobert, a mentally deranged painter—*bald, with huge beard, looking at once both young and old, sly and idiotic, a painter of enormous canvasses of naked people, one of a baker and a coal man clinking glasses in front of a nude woman, the figures slashed with white and brown, the canvas painted with a spoon.*[3] Rather than saying that this caricatured painter is not Cézanne (and he is not), Rewald accepts that he is, and then, unmindful that he has just continued the distortion, rather winsomely laments, *Thus the picture of Cézanne continues to be distorted.* He then says, *Cézanne's friends could not deny anything said about him.* Neither could Rewald, who'd become so invested in the myth that he couldn't extricate himself. Not once in his many writings on the artist had he denied that Cézanne was a Balzac'ian Frenhofer, a Zola'ian Claude Lantier, or a Duranty'on Maillobert.[4]

As I said in my introduction, no Cézanne scholar to my knowledge has asked whether at any time Cézanne wept in despair because he couldn't succeed in painting a perfectly beautiful woman, or questioned the logic of Cézanne being afraid that the naked models he didn't keep an eye on would sexually assault him, and so on. One authors offers the predictable conclusion: *Such secondary evidence of Cézanne's struggle to distance himself from the female model did much to promote his legendary image as a blustering but painfully timid provincial whose anxieties about women were never fully resolved.*[5]

One might ask at this point if any man's anxieties about women are ever fully resolved. Mary Lewis, for one, finds evidence of this lack of anxiety resolution in a letter Cézanne wrote in the last month of his life to Émile Bernard, a young painter he'd befriended. Lewis assumes that Cézanne was still suffering anxiety over sexual impulses, still a Saint Anthony-type hermit tormented by lustful phantasms. But Lewis did not give her readers the complete statement that Cézanne made in this letter, nor is the portion she quoted a proper translation from the French. Cézanne wrote:

> *I am always making studies after nature. It seems to me that I make slow progress. I should like to have you near me, for solitude always weighs me down. But I am old, sick, and determined to die painting rather than sink into that degrading senility that threatens old men who let themselves be dominated by passions that diminish their senses.*

Lewis' translation, saying that the sixty-seven-year-old Cézanne swore never to submit to *the debasing paralysis that threatens old men who allow themselves to be dominated by passions that coarsen their senses,* is taken from Rewald's English edition of Cézanne's letters. Rewald badly translated two words in the letter to Bernard: the word *le gâtisme* means «senility,» not «paralysis,» and *abrutissante,* translated by Rewald as «coarsen,» does not mean that but rather «made deadly dull» or «made mentally diminished.» Coarseness is not typically associated with *abrutissante.* Moreover, while the French word *passion* is the same in English, in ordinary daily French speech it does not have the same reflexive linkage to sexual passion as it does in English. In French, *passion* is associated more with enthusiasm, obsession, and fanaticism, with any emotion that is the opposite of passive.[6] By deploying the words «paralysis» and «coarsen,» Rewald made Cézanne «paralyzed» when confronted with «coarse sex.» That helped to affirm that Cézanne's terror of women had stayed with him throughout his lifetime, becoming the fantasies of a dirty old man with diminished mental faculties that regressed him to facing all over again the sexual anxieties of adolescence. Rewald apparently could not resist invoking Claude Lantier from Zola's novel, *L'Oeuvre,* even at this late date in Cézanne's life. The impulse to infuse Cézanne with the temperament of Lantier dictated Rewald's translation. He took the word «paralyzed» not from translating *le gâtisme* but from Zola's notes for *L'Oeuvre,* specifically the passage Rewald had translated as *a sublime dreamer paralyzed in production by a flaw.*

Zola's personal psychology would fare better than Cézanne's when submitted to biographies, although colorful and usually degrading descriptions and caricatures of him would find a joyous audience. As were all bohemian artists and writers, the young Zola was fitted to a type. In 1871, a book that aptly described journalists of his sort was put into circulation by a professor of medicine, entitled *The Influence of Journalism on the Health of the Body and of the Mind.* The author generalized journalists as men ambitious for notoriety, infatuated with themselves and jealous of others, who excite themselves by writing and enjoying the thrills they attain from overstepping boundaries. *They live in a feverish state of pathological excitement, and are dangerous to society because they spread their own nervousness to their readers. By fighting with each other, they win attention as entertainers, while forfeiting dignity. There will always be more respect for authors of books than for the mere journalist.*[7] This is a fine description of Zola, who had known since 1868 that to succeed as a writer he would have to extricate himself from journalism or wind up life as one who had stewed too long in the public soup pot. The reformed jour-

Zola at about the age of thirty-five.

nalist Barbey d'Aurevilly said, *Writing journalism diminishes the writer's faculties, when not entirely destroying them, after having first rendered the writer depraved.*[8]

In 1874, Zola republished *Contes à Ninon* with enough additions to have it titled *Nouveaux Contes à Ninon.* The two editions were like bookends holding a decade of Zola's journalism. In the preface to *Nouveaux Contes à Ninon,* Zola wrote that for ten years he had fed the best of himself into the furnace of journalism, that now, after such colossal effort, nothing remained of what he'd written but ashes. Pages thrown to the wind, flowers fallen to the ground, a mixture of the best and the worst at the same feeding trough. He'd dirtied his hands in the sordid and murky torrent of mediocrity, his love of real values had suffered, seeming so important in the morning but forgotten by the evening. He'd dreamt of creating things eternal but found that he was merely blowing bubbles that the fluttering of a passing fly could burst.

This preface certainly endorsed Zola's commitment to fiction but would not be the end of his journalism. Ten years later, in mid-January 1882, he wrote another preface announcing his decision to close down his journalistic career. *Today I've retired,* he wrote, opening his volume of articles collected under the title *Une Campagne.*[9] *I left the press four months ago, and count on not returning to it—though I've not sworn an oath to that effect.*

As he described it to Magnard in a letter of September 16th, 1880, Zola's journalism was the outward expression of an irresistible need to cry aloud what one thinks.[10] *This has been my passion,* he wrote, *and as a result I'm spattered with blood. Despite grave errors I have made, my voice was heard because of my convictions. Refuse me everything, discuss me and deny me, nothing has prevented me from trying to disengage from literature the heavy hand of political manipulation. If I have done nothing more than that, if I've existed only to kindle literary quarrels, to awaken people sufficiently to heap injuries upon me, well and good. In that case, I feel that every writer, especially the young ones, owe me a debt of gratitude.*[11]

Zola's 1877 novel *L'Assommoir,* wherein his naturalism surfaces like shallow-water sharks, provoked as much scandalized reaction as had his 1860s novels. The crudeness of his language was bad enough, but the book failed to provide the literary left wing with its customary fodder. Zola had not glamorized the poor working class.[12] He'd failed to represent it as the noblest part of the human race, had attributed no flaws whatsoever to the oppressive upper classes, writing like a Victor Hugo of the age of realism and naturalism, in the language of the slums, not only in dialogue but in descriptive and reflective passages. His *style indirect libre* secured homogeneity throughout. He had obliged his characters both to think to themselves and to think aloud in the only language in which they were capable of thinking, with nothing imposed on them from outside their culture—not just afloat in the Parisian Sea but as remote from modern man as Galapagos turtles:

There was a pause. A waiter had just put on the table a huge dish as deep as a salad bowl and full of rabbit stew.

Coupeau, always one for a leg-pull, spoke out with one of his best:

«Look here, waiter. That rabbit came off the floor tiles, it's still meowing.»

And so it was, for a soft, perfectly imitated meow-ing seemed to be coming from the dish. Coupeau was doing it in his throat without moving his lips. It was a party trick of his which always came off, and that was why he never ate without ordering stewed rabbit. Then he purred. The ladies couldn't stop laughing, and dabbed tears from their faces with their napkins.

Caricature of Zola creating his imagery by tossing turds from a chamber pot onto a canvas. The annotation reads, *Le Roman expéri-mental* (the experimental novel). Cartoon by Bourgeois.

Madame Fauconnier asked for the head; she only liked the head. Mademoiselles Remanjou adored the bits of crisp fat. And as Boche was saying that he pre-ferred the «little onions» when they were nicely done, Madame Lerat pursed her lips and remarked:

«Oh, I see.»

She was as desiccated as a hop pole, her working life as monotonous as that of a cloistered nun. She hadn't seen as much as the nose of a man since her husband's death, but all the same she displayed a preoccupation with indecency, a mania about words with double meanings and obscure possibilities which were sometimes so recondite that she alone saw the point. So when Boche leaned over and asked for an explanation of the «little onions,» she hissed into his ear:

«Why...two little round things...enough said, I should think.»

Depravity would have been the perdurable state of Zola's mind had he not expended his passion in fiction where he could puppeteer people he'd created to think and act exactly how he wanted, thus keeping him from burning in the fur-nace along with his writings. Still, twenty years later, when hoping for election to the *Académie Française* or being awarded the *Légion d'Honneur*, Zola was repeatedly rebuffed for having introduced debauchery into literature.[13] If it were any conso-lation to him, he could at least see himself in the company of other notable los-ers: Molière, Beaumarchais, Balzac, Flaubert.

He had lost interest in art and been shunned by French newspapers no longer in need of ink from his poisonous pen, but Zola managed to write a few pieces of art criticism before his final retirement from journalism (from which, of course, he never could completely retire, for he was combative beyond what fic-tion-writing allowed). He had established a friendship with the Russian writer-in-exile Ivan Turgenev (*Tourgueniev*), who was living in Paris at the time. Flaubert introduced him to Zola; in turn, Turgenev introduced Zola to the publisher

Stassyulevich, who commissioned from him a series of essays on modern art for his St. Petersburg newspaper *Vestnik Evropy* (*Le Messager de L'Europe*, The European Herald). In an 1879 essay for this paper, Zola censured Monet's pictures for evidencing a self-complacent sketchiness, saying in so many words that it is easy to be a pioneer, but a more enduring struggle is indispensable for complete victory. Sadly for Zola, his article was re-translated back into French and published in *Le Figaro* under the headline *Mr. Zola has broken with Manet* (the Russian paper had misspelled *Monet*). In this essay, Zola had written, *All the impressionists are poor technicians. In the arts as well as in literature, form alone sustains new ideas and new methods.*

> *In order to assert himself as a man of talent, an artist must bring out what is in him, otherwise he is but a pioneer. For a moment Manet [Monet] inspired great hopes, but he appears exhausted by hasty production; he is satisfied with approximations; he doesn't study nature with the passion of a true creator. All these artists are too easily contented. They woefully neglect the solidity of works meditated upon for a long time. And for this reason it is to be feared that they are merely preparing the path for the great art of the future that is expected by the world.*

When the article appeared in French, Manet was of course offended, and Zola embarrassed. He quickly wrote to Manet, *I read with stupefaction the notice in Le Figaro announcing that I have broken with you, and am anxious to send you a cordial handshake. The translation of the quotation is not correct; the meaning of the passage has been forced. I spoke of you in Russia, as for thirteen years I've spoken of you in France, with solid sympathy for your person and talent.* At Manet's request, this rejoinder was published in *Le Figaro*. But not wanting to add to his embarrassment, Zola did not point out in the rejoinder that he had meant Monet.[14]

In this article, Zola had cast his eyes back to the heroic age, to the Titans and Giants who moved mountains and carried boulders into battle:

> *Alas, with the most passionate joy I would give myself over with ebullience for some great artist. But I can only evoke the brilliance of Delacroix and Ingres, those contumacious geniuses who vanished from the world without betraying their secrets. Those giants left no posterity and still we await the geniuses of the future. Courbet, aged and cast out like a leper, is already following their ascent into history. He too now belongs with the dead, with artists whose pictures, by their power and truth, will last in eternity. Among living artists, there are barely one or two who struggle to raise themselves to the level of those true creators.*[15]

The following year, 1880, when Cézanne enlisted Zola's help on behalf of Monet and Renoir, who'd had pictures accepted by the Salon but hung so badly as to be nearly out of sight, Zola almost did in the entire group. Monet and

Renoir had composed a letter to the newly appointed Minister of Fine Arts asking for better treatment of their pictures. They gave the letter to Cézanne, asking that he pass it on to Zola for possible publication and also to ask Zola for a few comments that would convey the importance of the Impressionists and the interest their paintings had aroused with the public. But rather than use his influence to do that, Zola published three articles in the newspaper *Le Voltaire*, where stubbornly he still called the painters *naturalists*. After a few conciliatory remarks, in very strong words he expressed his disappointment with their temperaments as reflected in production:

> *Many see clearly what they are looking for and one should give them credit for finding it. But in vain one looks for works of art that will bow heads in admiration. This is why the struggle of the Impressionists has not reached its goal. They remain inferior to the level of work that should justify their intent. Stammering, they cannot find the right words.*
>
> *Still, though they can be criticized for personal impotence, they are the true workmen of the century. They have many gaps, are often careless in execution, too easily satisfied, their paintings unfinished, illogical, exaggerated, sterile. They need to work harder at contemporary Naturalism if they hope to put themselves at the head of a movement.*[16]

One is reminded of Zola's early letters to Cézanne in Aix, still vacillating, to be or not to be an artist: *Up to now, you've only had the desire to work, as you've not tackled the job seriously and regularly. What you have done up to now is nothing!*

Zola had not changed much over those twenty years. He wanted artists to continue their assault on a hostile environment—the Salon, the public—not to concede or integrate, but rather to give profundity to naturalism, to socialism, as he was doing then with his *Rougon-Macquart* novels. Zola the indefatigable worker, who could spend an entire year on a novel, writing it only after compiling stacks of research notes (called by Edmond de Goncourt *an engine greased for labor*), could not understand why the painters were so easily satisfied with scanty imagery on tossed-off canvases: *Monet has given in to his facility of production*, Zola wrote. *Too many rough drafts have left his studio. Facility pushes an artist down the slope of unworthy and cheap creation. If one is too easily contented, sells sketches that are hardly dry, one loses taste for works based on long and meditative preparation.*[17]

In order for historians nowadays to defend the Impressionists against Zola, it is necessary to claim that after the mid-1870s he was as blind to quality as the Salon jurists were back in the 1860s when Zola was defending them. But if one can ask, with confidence, how is it possible for an artist to be acceptable one year but not the next (as Zola, himself, had asked in 1868), one might as well ask how it is possible that Zola could see in the 1860s but not later on? In 1896, Zola was asked this question; in *Le Figaro* he responded that back then he was defending the artists, not their art. When he became disillusioned with the artists, their production no longer appealed to him.[18]

As for Zola's role in art history, his support of Manet's, Monet's, and Pissarro's pictures in the 1860s most likely had no effect at all on their eventual success, nor, for that matter, did Baudelaire's support actually push Manet beyond a phase of notoriety. Zola's criticism counts not a bit in Cézanne's achievement and efforts to credit Cézanne with having taught Zola something about art are bootless. That Zola encouraged Cézanne when a youth to abandon Aix for Paris does not figure in Cézanne's art, only in his life as having become an artist. Durand-Ruel would have no need of Zola's promotional articles to motivate his purchase of Manet's paintings in 1872, nor would the collector, Faure, in 1873 when he bought a painting by Cézanne. Faure and Durand-Ruel may have never read what Zola had written about these artists. The success of Manet and the others came after Zola was no longer writing art criticism. And it came not from positive, but from negative criticism that had made the Impressionists notorious and attractive to a different audience than that which had supported Salon painting.

What contribution to modern art did Zola make over the 1860s? After more than 400 pages of this book, the reader expects a conclusion. It will not be forthcoming. A conclusion would conclude nothing but this book. Zola's art criticism cannot be summarized, baled, or neatly packaged. Nor can Cézanne's art of the 1860s, nor can naturalism, realism, impressionism, or modernism. Zola looked for newness in conflict with pastness, newness as fundamental to the dynamics of modernism, for newness extends from newness, propagating it, driving art as linear progression. Gauguin may not have been the first of the modernists to recognize this linearity, but perhaps he was the first to state it more clearly than others who had recognized earlier that each art is appropriate to its own generation. Gauguin said, *The young people who come after us will be more radical. In ten years you will see that we will have looked extreme only for our period.*[19]

Zola was right that the public would eventually come around to accepting the new art, and he was not the only one saying it. Armand Silvestre wrote in 1873 that the moment had come for the public to be convinced, enthusiastic or disgusted, but not any longer dumbfounded. *Manet still belongs in the realm of discussion, but no longer of bewilderment*, he said.[20] And indeed that year, Manet enjoyed his first rounds of applause at the Salon. But if taken as truly meaningful, Silvestre's applause for the public is dubious art history. The public did not come to enjoy Impressionism until the mid-twentieth century, after Impressionism had taken on entirely different meaning than it had in the nineteenth century.[21]

In wording his final criticism, Zola exonerated himself from his earlier support of the artists, bluntly stating what had gone wrong with Impressionism, laying blame on the independent exhibitions and the group's failure to sustain pressure on the Salon. Manet held the same opinion: rather than admitting he had withdrawn, he accused his colleagues of abandoning him. Above all, Zola missed an established structural framework that must follow a revolution's rupture of the system. He couldn't have known that art historians establish such frameworks long after the revolution has passed away. He missed form, the quality of completeness. No one had as yet given form to Impressionism. *The real misfortune*, Zola wrote, *is that no artist of this group has achieved powerfully and definitely the new formula that scattered throughout their works, they all offer. The formula is there, endlessly diffused; but in no place, among any of them, is it to be found applied by a master. They are all forerunners. The struggle of the impressionists has not reached a goal, they remain inferior to what they undertake. The man of genius has not arisen.*[22]

One of the saddest mishaps in modern art history is that Zola died before seeing that the genius he was calling for would be his dearest friend Cézanne. No painter other than Cézanne would take what was scattered throughout Impressionism and reduce it to a formula in the best sense of a word—give it form, that is, release it from ideologies, social commentary, and art history. Manet, a subject painter, had taken the first step by breaking traditions of subject matter: allegory, idyllic landscapes, the nude, even still life, and all in one painting, the *Déjeuner sur l'herbe*. With *Olympia* he wiped out Venus, who'd been for two centuries synonymous with art (Manet's deathbed scorn was for the Cabanel who would go on living and painting, whose silkily painted, audience-sucking *Birth of Venus* won the gold medal in the 1863 Salon when Manet's *Déjeuner sur l'herbe* had been scorned. *That man still has good health*, Manet is said to have mumbled).[23]

If Zola had truly debauched *belles-lettres*, Cézanne's paintings—bizarre, crude, lacking finish—had debauched the *Beaux-Arts*, debauched the aesthetics of the feminine, even that of landscape. Throughout the 1870s and half of the '80s, he continued to submit paintings to Salon juries, only to be rejected every time, even though his days as a subversive artist were over. Only once, in 1882, did a painting of his make it all the way from the door to the wall, and then only because he had been accepted *hors concours*: he'd submitted as a pupil of Guillemet, who was an elected member of the jury that year. And Cézanne, too, hoped to be decorated with the *Légion d'Honneur*. But if his name was ever proposed, it was quickly renounced.

To keep the most brash critics away from the Chambre des Députés, surround it with Impressionist pictures.

In order to double the effect of their pictures on the visitors, the Impressionists fill the gallery with Wagner's music.

«Madame, it would be unwise for you to enter the exhibition. Please stay out.»

«Fancy meeting you here! Don't tell me you are a lover of Impressionist painting?»

«Me! Not at all! But when I go home after having looked at their portraits, my wife doesn't look so ugly.»

48

Let us acknowledge that
Impressionism is dying, the holy
phalanx is no longer up to strength

Painters in Paris who had come through the 1860s with clearly defined enemies—the Academy, the Salon, the Public—lost their vehemence and
passion by 1880. Joined by others who had not experienced the 60s, they
were bickering among themselves, in disagreement over who belonged to the
«group» and discordant over whom would be included in the annual exhibitions
of the Independents. The apostates had become squabbling jurists, no less so
than those of the Salons—self-interested, for the most part, compromising and
making deals. Monet won't show if Renoir doesn't, Renoir won't show if his
friend, Gustave Callebotte, doesn't, Degas won't show if his protégé, Jean
Raffaëlli, is not accepted by the others, while, at the same time, Degas is upset
with Pissarro for forcing the group to embrace his own pupils, Armand
Guillaumin and the upstart Paul Gauguin. Manet won't show at all, having entirely abandoned the notion of independent exhibitions. His success with his *Bon
Bock* at the 1873 Salon had disconnected him from the group. The cover illustration of *Les Contemporains* on the 16th of June that year graphically hailed him as
King of the Impressionists, caricatured as seated on a glass of *Bon Bock* beer as if
defecating in it. And in 1879, a cartoonist limns Manet flat on his back on the
floor at the Impressionists' exhibition: the caption reads, *Mr. Manet, himself, brought
to a nervous breakdown on viewing the Independents' paintings.*

Cézanne did not figure at all in the exhibitions or the disputes. Sensibly, if
not just ambivalent, he stayed away from the infighters (Contrary to popular opinion in the Cézanne literature, this was not because he was timid). His obscurity
kept his name out of the press and off the minds of such young critics as
Huysmans. In the performance world, anyone out of the news for a couple of
years is soon forgotten. In 1882, Huysmans published a book, *L'Art moderne*,
which included his reviews since 1879. He had excluded Cézanne from those
reviews, having taken no interest in him. On Cézanne's behalf, Pissarro protested, saying, *Why is it that you didn't say a word about Cézanne, whom all of us recognize as*

one of the most astounding and curious temperaments of our time, and who's had a great influence on modern art?[1]

Huysmans replied, *I find Cézanne's personality congenial. Through Zola I know of his efforts, his vexations, his defeats when he tries to create a work. Yes, Cézanne has temperament, he is an artist, but in sum, with the exception of some still-lifes, the rest is, to my mind, not likely to live. His work is interesting, curious, suggestive in ideas, but certainly he is an «eye case,» which I understand he, himself, realizes. In my humble opinion the Cézanne-types typify those Impressionists who didn't make the grade. After so many years of struggle, it is no longer a question of more or less manifest or visible intentions, but of works which are full of serious results, which are not monsters, odd cases for a* [medical museum of painting].[2] Certainly Huysmans' humble opinion was largely an implant of Zola's not-so-humble opinion of Impressionism in general, and of Cézanne in particular, for by this time Cézanne was a failure in Zola eyes, an unachieved genius. But so were the others in Zola's eyes, even Manet.

The modern art scene in Paris was not as synchronous as what one gets from art history books that condense events and organize retrospectively what was not yet even enucleated. Modernism was still something of a primordial soup, and there never had been a coherent body of Impressionists—such books as Rewald's *History of Impressionism* created that entity. The conservative critic, Henry Havard, wrote in *Le Siècle* on April 2nd, *Let us acknowledge that Impressionism is dying, the holy phalanx is no longer up to strength.*[3] The *Indépendants* exhibition of 1880 did not include Manet, Monet, Renoir, Sisley, or Cézanne, but rather Félix Bracquemond and his wife, Marie, Armand Guillaumin, and the newcomers Gustave Callebotte and Albert Lebourg. Pissarro added his pupil Gauguin and another newcomer, Victor Vignon. Degas scored heavily by getting his coterie included: Mary Cassatt, Jean-Louis Forain, Léopold Levert, Henri Rouart, Fédérico Zandomeneghi, Charles Tillot, Eugène Vidal, and also Raffaëlli, who crammed thirty-five paintings into the show, even though his academic Impressionism was an embarrassment to many of the old-timers, as, for that matter, was Cassatt's academic style glossed with impressionist brushstrokes.

In January 1881, Pissarro undertook the assembly of another exhibition of the *Indépendants,* but it seems he was left with only one supporter of the common cause, Callebotte, then a thirty-three-year-old wealthy bachelor, a hobbyist boat builder who'd befriended Renoir and Monet, occasionally bought paintings from them, and himself took up painting in the early 1870s. But no sooner had Pissarro and Callebotte started planning who would be included in the show than they, too, were at odds. Callebotte wanted to rid the group of Degas, who had made nasty remarks about Monet and Renoir over their intentions to continue submitting to the Salons. Getting Degas out of the way might encourage them to rejoin the group, Callebotte thought. To state his case, he wrote a very long letter to Pissarro, opening with, *What has become of our exhibitions?*

Here is my well-considered opinion. We ought to continue, but only in an artistic direction. That is our common interest. I ask, therefore, that the show be composed only of those who've shown real interest—you, Monet, Renoir, Sisley, Morisot, Cassatt, Cézanne, Guillaumin, and if you wish, Gauguin, perhaps Corday, and myself. That's all, since Degas refuses to show if Monet and Renoir are included. I should like to know why the public would be interested in our individual disputes. It is naive of us to squabble over who exhibits. Degas has brought disarray to our midst. It is too bad for him that he has such a disappointing character. He spends his time haranguing at the Nouvelle-Athènes, even in public. He would be better off if he were to paint a little more than he does. That he is one hundred times right in what he says, that he talks with infinite wit and good sense about painting, no one doubts (and isn't that the conspicuous aspect of his reputation?) But the real arguments of a painter are his paintings, and that even if Degas were a thousand times right in his words he would be much more right if he stuck to his work. Now Degas cites pragmatic necessities, which he doesn't permit Renoir or Monet. But before experiencing his financial losses, was he any different a person from what he is today? Ask all who've known him, beginning with yourself. No, this man has gone sour. He doesn't hold the high place that he ought to, according to his talent, and though he won't admit it, he bears the whole world a grudge.

Degas claims that he wanted to have Raffaëlli and the others included in the show because Monet and Renoir had reneged and that there had to be replacements. But for three years he's been after Raffaëlli to join us, long before the defection of Monet, Renoir, and Sisley. He claims that we must stick together and count on each other, but for God's sake, who does he bring us: Lepic, Legros, Maureau! Yet he didn't rage against the defection of Lepic and Legros; and moreover, Lepic, heaven knows, has no talent. Degas has forgiven him everything, but no doubt, since Sisley, Monet, and Renoir do indeed have talent, he will never forgive them. In 1878, Degas brought us Zandomeneghi, Bracquemond, Mrs. Bracquemond; in 1879, he brought us Raffaëlli, and others, What a fighting squadron in the cause of realism!!!

If there is anyone in the world who has the right not to forgive Renoir, Monet, Sisley, and Cézanne, it is you, because you've experienced the same daily life demands as they have, and you haven't weakened. You know there's just one reason for all this effort to exhibit—one's needs of existence. When one needs money, one tries to pull though as best one can. Although Degas denies the validity of such mundane reasons, I consider them essential. He has a persecution complex. Doesn't he want to convince people that Renoir has Machiavellian ideas? Really, Degas is not only not an upright person, he's not even generous. As for me, I have no right to condemn anyone for their motives. The only person with that right is you. I do not grant that right to Degas, who has cried out against anyone in whose work he finds talent. One could put together a huge volume from what he's said against Manet, Monet, you.

I ask you, isn't it our duty to support each other and forgive each other's weaknesses, rather than to tear each other down? To cap it all, this Degas, who talks so much and says he wants to do so much, is the very one who has, himself, contributed the least. This entire matter depresses me. If there had been only one subject of discussion among us, that of art, we would have been always in agreement. The person who shifted the subject to another level is Degas. We would be stupid to continue suffering from his foolishness. He has tremendous talent, it is true. I'm the first to proclaim myself his great admirer. But let's stop with that. As a human being, he has gone so far as to say to me, speaking of Renoir and Monet, «Would you invite such people to your house?»[4]

Pissarro refused to agree entirely with Callebotte, even pointing out to him that he, Callebotte, had been one of Degas' recruits. Pissarro then ignored Callebotte and invited Degas.[5] The exhibition was held that year without Callebotte, Monet, Renoir, Cézanne, or Sisley, in an apartment of a building under construction, the rooms jammed with pictures, the light very poor. Pissarro showed twenty-seven paintings and pastels. Mary Cassatt contributed a few benign paintings of children and gardens. Gauguin exhibited eight paintings and two sculptures. Other painters were mixed into the show, which must have come off as an indiscriminate assemblage of antipathetic talents and styles.[6] Refusing to take the show seriously, Degas sent only minor works, mostly sketches and one wax sculpture of the little dancer in a real skirt, her hair tied with a red silk ribbon.

Degas would remain problematical when Pissarro undertook organizing the 1882 show. On December 14th, 1881, Gauguin, still a novice painter and not yet having fashioned himself as exotic, wrote to his mentor Pissarro, *Last night Degas told me he would hand in his resignation rather than have Raffaëlli refused. If I examine calmly your situation after ten years, during which you undertook to organize these exhibitions, I can see that the number of Impressionists has progressed, their talent increased, their influence too. Yet, on Degas' side, thanks to his choices, progress has reversed and is getting worse and worse: each year another Impressionist departs and is replaced by some nullity, some pupil of the Academy. Two more years and you will be left alone in the midst of these schemers.*[7] But Gauguin himself was under pressure to withdraw from the group. Monet hated Gauguin's paintings, saying that the small clique of Impressionists was becoming a huge club open to any dauber, such as the likes of Gauguin and Raffaëlli.[8] In truth, the way things were going, of the original Impressionists, only Pissarro and Berthe Morisot would be left to dance.

Levelheaded Pissarro kept trying his best to calm the troubled waters and pull onto the 1882 raft a less rowdy roster of painters than he'd hauled in the previous year. He was somewhat more successful: when the show opened on March 1st, the exhibitors were Monet, Renoir, Pissarro, Sisley, Gauguin, Callebotte, Vignon, and Guillaumin; Degas was not excluded; he'd declined.[9] Cézanne had been encouraged by Pissarro to send works up from Provence, but so disinterested was he over joining the mêlée that he replied saying he didn't have any paintings available. Morisot also declined, as she was enjoying some success at the Salon and still under the influence of Manet, who refused to be included, continuing to assert that the obligation of a painter was to confront the Salon. Renoir was ill. He was in L'Estaque, where he'd been painting side by side with Cézanne.

Concerned that Callebotte might not agree to being included, Renoir wrote to Durand-Ruel, *I hope that Callebotte will exhibit. I also hope that the ridiculous title «Indépendants» will be dropped. And I would like you to tell those gentlemen who are organizing the show that I am not going to give up exhibiting at the Salon. It is not for pleasure that I do that, but as I told you, submitting to the Salon will dispel the revolutionary taint that upsets me (a small weakness for which I hope to be pardoned). In that I am willing to exhibit with Guillaumin* [whom Renoir considered to be inferior], *I might as well exhibit with Carolus-Duran* [by this time regularly represented in the Salon]. *Delacroix was right,* Renoir continued, *when saying that a painter ought to obtain at any cost all possible honors.*[10]

Renoir was concerned about the company in which his pictures would be shown. He didn't trust the newcomers, especially Gauguin, whom he disliked personally. Nor did he trust Pissarro, who was too obviously promoting his disciples, Armand Guillaumin and Victor Vignon. In turn, Monet refused to exhibit if Renoir didn't, so Renoir was pressed to consent; but then Renoir refused to exhibit if Callebotte didn't. One by one, they wedged each other into the show. Beset by so many disputes, Pissarro was tempted to throw in the towel. Responding to Renoir and Monet's vacillations and the strings attached to their decisions, he wrote to Monet, *I don't understand anything anymore. For two or three weeks now I have been expending great effort to arrive at an understanding with everyone in order to reassemble our group as homogeneously as possible.*[11]

Jules Claretie, who had been tracking the modernists since the mid-1860s, poked jabs at the group's internal spats and bickering, their lack of stylistic coherence. *Some opportunists found themselves among the rebels,* he wrote. *There were squabbles and near squabbles. Mr. Degas, the painter of dancers withdrew, Miss Cassatt followed him out, Mr. Raffaëlli followed her out. These are artists of rare talent whom the Indépendants will be unable to replace. The participants are all people with the right idea but the wrong coloration. They reason well but their vision is faulty. They show the candor of children and the fervor of apostles—of the gray-haired ones, such as Mr. Pissarro.*[12]

Anointed by Zola, the newly ordained critic Joris-Karl Huysmans reviewed the exhibition, regretting the absence of contemporary subjects while bemoaning the excess of landscapes. *The Impressionist circle,* he wrote, *has been too restricted. One cannot deplore too much the diminution of the group that vile quarrels have brought about.* In the next breath, Huysmans recovers enough to hail the benefits of the disputes: *Oh, to hell with it! We abominate each other but march in close ranks against the common enemy. We may even insult each other—afterwards, if we wish behind closed doors—yet we proceed together. It is foolish to scatter one's forces when one fights so few in number against the large crowd. To deny admission to anyone under the pretext of sustaining homogeneity, one fatally arrives at a monotony of subjects, uniformity of methods, and, to say it bluntly, sterility.*[13]

Felix Fénéon, who, like Huysmans, was also just starting out as a critic in the early 1880s, listed in a review what he called *the gallant clan of Impressionists*. Betraying how ill defined Impressionism was by the end of the 1870s, he mentions Manet, Pissarro, Raffaëlli, Renoir, Cassatt (about whom nothing was gallant), Monet, Forain (hardly an Impressionist), Degas, Giuseppe de Nittis (a leech on Impressionism), Morisot, and Sisley.[14] Cézanne's name was not among this assemblage that hardly made sense anyway. In 1886, when Symbolist manifestos brought down the curtain on naturalism in literature and painting, Fénéon published a widely read pamphlet titled *Les Impressionistes en 1886*. He made a history out of the previous two decades, omitting Cézanne and adjusting Manet's role: *During the heroic period of Impressionism, the crowds always saw Manet as first on the firing line. Yet, in reality, the mutation that transformed this bituminous author of Le Bon Bock into a painter of light was accomplished under the influence of Pissarro, Degas, Renoir, and above all, Monet. They were the heads of the revolution of which Manet was only the herald.* In ⁺his book, Fénéon coined the term *Neo-impressionism* to set off from the *Impressionists* the new work of Pissarro and that of Georges Seurat and Paul Signac, heralding the group that Roger Fry, in 1910, would call the Post-Impressionists.

Impressionism has enough characteristics to allow most any definition. Richard Shiff broke them down into four categories: the Impressionists as a social group, Impressionism as a classification of subject matter, Impressionism as a style involving an obvious technique, Impressionism as an artistic goal or purpose.[15] With hindsight, one can make a case for each categorical trait and combine them to arrive at a cooperative definition. Try as one would, Cézanne will not fit to any of Impressionism's categories. I myself am content to define Impressionism as the degree to which the look of any picture resembles one of Monet's.

Part V

THE FINALITY

49

The real history of the avant-garde is
a history of those who escaped from it.
—*T. J. Clark*

The situation with the *Independents* at the end of the 1870s and into the 1880s was not a situation from which Cézanne *fled*, but rather one from which he departed. This beguiling myth of Cézanne's flight into Aix is one more that must be challenged and given a dose of reality. Biographers and historians who suppose that Cézanne suffered the phobias of a recluse, that his move to Aix was a retreat, fail to ask, *from what?* It is easy and more journalistically seductive to say that he was insecure and racked by anxiety, that he couldn't take the heat any longer so he got out of the kitchen—more difficult to acknowledge that he may have been judicious. In view of all the bickering and uncertainty among Cézanne's colleagues in Paris, as the loose assortment of Indépendants further self-destructed, it was not at all that, having been dealt so many blows in Paris, so many rejections and such bad press, Cézanne fled Paris for Aix, where, as Rewald says, he isolated himself, avoiding Paris. Words such as «isolated» and «avoiding» are pejorative. One should credit him, rather, with having some sense as to where modern art was at that moment, where it was headed, or at least where the best place was for him to be.

Timothy Clark said in his *Image of the People* that *the real history of the avant-garde is a history of those who escaped from it, even from Paris itself.* Clark names Stendahl, Géricault, Lautrément, van Gogh, and Cézanne.[1] (The Grenoble-born Stendahl—who, like the young Cézanne, planned to take Paris by storm—reversed the direction of Clark's maxim in *La Vie de Rossini.* Stendahl said there, *Anyone with the slightest energy in Paris was born in the provinces*). Perhaps Cézanne escaped from the avant-garde. Perhaps he escaped from Paris. From our hindsighted position one cannot really tell. How many Abstract-Expressionists of the 1950s remained in New York? How many «escaped» to the Hamptons? Cézanne was a rich man's son who came to Paris and took on a veneer of bohemianism, one of thousands of young men coping with life between adolescence and adulthood. At no time was he a Parisian, nor was he a true bohemian, though at times he acted as one and would refer to himself as one, which was his only alternative to calling himself bourgeois.

Social institutions dictate personal conduct, but not often do these managerial forces regiment artists, whose profession defies definition and is ill fitted by nature to social norms that hinge on gainful employment and a normal family life. Society tends to consecrate non-conformists. The emptiness of their non-materialist status gets filled in with symbols, myths, occultism: artists, gurus, messiahs, philosophers under olive trees, persons touched by some god or fairy, dubbed by a queen; fame conferred upon them by induction into the *Légion d'Honneur* or being given a chair in the *Académie de France*, a noble place to sit. According to Geffroy's memoirs, on an occasion in 1894 when Cézanne was in Giverny visiting Monet, then entertaining friends—Auguste Rodin and Octave Mirbeau among them—Cézanne took Mirbeau aside and blurted, *Monsieur Rodin has no pride, he shook my hand! He, a man who has been decorated by the Légion d'Honneur!*[2]

While Zola had gained fame in caustic doses of notoriety and was the most talked about writer in Paris—and at last earning considerable income from books that sold best when accursed—Cézanne had remained as marginal over the 1870s as he'd been in the 1860s. By 1880, he had come to terms with his own painting and had no need to think of himself as belonging to a group or style (which he'd resisted all along anyway, even in the 1860s). He needed the Provençal landscape, not the Paris of suburban Impressionists, not the Fontainebleau forest of dark and dreary motifs, not the semi-rural vision of Pissarro's urban-edged eyes. Aix was Cézanne's true home and its environs his favorite places to paint. His «seclusion» away from Paris was no graver than Pissarro's at Pontoise, and much less than Degas and Sisley's. As Cézanne grew older, he had less need for Paris, just enough to keep in touch with Zola and a few others he held dear—Pissarro, Renoir, Monet.[3] By 1882, nothing north of Provence even matched Cézanne's palette. Never had he been able to reconcile his personal nature with Paris. Justifiably, his name does not appear in Robert Herbert's book *Impressionism: Art, Leisure, and Parisian Society,* or in Theodore Reff's *Manet and Modern Paris*, where Reff omits Cézanne while managing to find space for one canvas by Pissarro and one by Guillaumin, though neither one was any more urban a painter than Cézanne.[4] Of the many pictures that Cézanne painted while in Paris, only two among the survivors are views within the city, *La Rue des Saules, Montmartre* and the *Quai de Bercy* , the latter a scene of convenience viewed through his apartment window on a wintry day, not a motif he held dear, such as Mount Saint-Victoire.

After 1878, Cézanne was hardly known by anyone in the Paris art world other than by those he had associated with during the 1860s. Because remoteness stimulates deification and enhances myths, it is easy to say that Cézanne shunned people, but this pesky notion that he was a pathological hermit, fearful that someone might touch him, get their hooks into him, is just more biographical balm.[5] One recalls that in Paris, the young Cézanne had quickly made friends with painters he met at the *Suisse*. He had an abundance of friends, as he'd had in Aix, friends of his feather who flocked together, but not Manet, who was culturally remote, not Degas, who deflected friends like water off a duck's back while in his old age going around Paris fulminating against *plein-air* painters. In later life, Cézanne retained friendships with Guillemet, Monet, Renoir, Oller, Pissarro, Alexis, Coste, Solari, and good old Valabrègue, as he called him. Cézanne remained personable, colorful, interesting and entertaining. Through letters he kept up with several friends in Paris. At no time was he a misanthrope. In letters he wrote during his youth, he tended to be doleful and moody, but those are characteristics common to adolescents. And he would retain into old age some boyhood shyness. His modesty was overridden at times by emotional outbursts, but never would he lose his sense of loyalty to friends, or his conversational wit and sense of humor. In 1891, Alexis wrote to Zola from Aix saying, *Cézanne brings a breath of fresh air into my social life. He at least vibrates, is expansive and lively.*[6] Such positive statements are ignored in the literature.

Throughout his later years, Cézanne had a stream of visitors. As he came into his sixties, he welcomed a new generation of acquaintances: Émile Bernard, Joachim Gasquet, Louis Leydet, Louis Aurenche, Charles Camoin, Louis Le Bail, Maurice Denis, and Émile Solari, the son of Philippe. While off and on some of them got on his nerves, his letters to the end of his life display affection and tolerance for young painters and critics who pestered him to reveal his theories—*the clan of intellectuals*, as he called them in a good-natured letter to Vollard, *and good God! of what brand?*[7] He was aware that young artists and critics who visited him in Aix did not see him as he saw himself, their thoughts about him having assimilated the myths of his aggrandized personage; those myths that now dominate his biography were back then in the germ. With one commentator repeating what another has written, the impression is deepened: if Cézanne said, on one occasion and to one person, as he did to Vollard, that he was careful to not let any woman get her hooks in him, by the time a dozen or so others had repeated his words, it became as if what he said was valid for every moment of his life.

One tends to believe what is heard more than once; myths when repeated get stuck to the collective tongue. Many myths of Cézanne's personality issued from the mouths of younger men who encountered him when he was quite old (he died at the age of sixty-seven), and when, as a famous man, he may have been posturing as well as uttering words put into his mouth by those with whom he discussed art theory. Most explanations of his old-age behavior are also tracked back to his youth, as when one takes up Cézanne's church attendance during the final years and fatuously justifies it by Cézanne having had a drawing teacher back in his late teens who was a monk, and to the fact that Cézanne had copied some religious themes when in his twenties.[8] But maturity is not simply cud chewing from youthful grazing, although it may be that humans enjoy swimming because we were once fish. In his late years, Cézanne was much the same as he'd been when younger, still subject to mood swings, as he'd been as an adolescent—so were Manet and Degas—but the swings of Cézanne's late years were not the same ones he swung on when he was a child.

In a letter of January 20th, 1896 to his son Lucien, Pissarro reports that Cézanne seems furious with everyone. *Pissarro is an old fool, Cézanne says, Monet too clever by half, they are all no good (they have no guts), only I have temperament, only I understand how to paint a Red. Oller received one of Cézanne's letters you would have to read yourself to get an idea of his mood. He forbade Oller to enter the house, asking if he took him for an imbecile. In a word, an atrocious letter.*[9] Pissarro didn't know the circumstances of Cézanne's displeasure with Oller. Couldn't it be that Pissarro himself was upset with Cézanne, so much so that his mind dipped back twenty-six years to 1870 when the caricaturist Stock quoted Cézanne as saying, *Yes, my dear Sir, I paint as I see, as I feel—and I have very strong sensations. The others, too, may see and feel as I do, but they don't take risks. They produce Salon pictures. I dare to take risks. Yes Sir, I dare. I have the courage of my opinions.* Pissarro's quotation of Cézanne saying of his painter friends, *they are all no good (they have no guts), only I have temperament, only I understand how to paint a Red*, may not be circumstantial but the eruption of an old grudge he'd harbored or of which he had just been reminded.

On combing through Cézanne's letters, and those of his friends, over the forty-six years since, when twenty, he'd had a spat with Baille, only a half-dozen incidents of disagreeable behavior are recorded (several hundred less than I'd have to admit to over the same number of years)—the one with Emperaire, one with Oller over a misaddressed letter, one with the young painter Louis Le Bail, who made the mistake of barging in on an occasion when Cézanne was sleeping and shaking him awake, one with the brash Gasquet, and apparently one with Pissarro.[10] A few incidents of Cézanne boiling over are about as conclusive of his personality as allowing four or five storms over a period of forty-six years to characterize a region's weather as frightful.

Cézanne's so-called seclusion after 1880 was less psychological than a practical necessity, as it is for anyone who needs time to work. In response to the Italian collector Egisto Fabbri, who had purchased several of his paintings and had written asking for a chance to meet him, to know him in person, saying, *I am aware that you are pestered by many people, and if I should ask permission to come and visit you, I may appear very importunate*, Cézanne's response was coy but sincere. He knew that the image Fabbri would have of him, shaped and colored by myths, might not hold up if he spent much time with him. Cézanne responded: *The number of my pictures to which you've given hospitality assures me of the great artistic sympathy you so kindly show me. I find myself unable to resist your flattering desire to make my acquaintance. The fear of appearing inferior to what is expected of a person who is presumed to be at the height of every situation is no doubt the excuse for one's necessity to live in seclusion.*[11]

By the end of the 1870s, the painters with whom Cézanne identified lived a good distance apart and few of them lived in Paris. Whistler, Fantin-Latour, Tissot, and Legros had settled in London. Zola spent most of his time in Médan. Monet had moved to Vétheuil, then to Giverny. Sisley moved to Sèvres, then to Saint-Mammès near the Fontainebleau Forest. Pissarro spent most of his time in Pontoise. Guillaumin was no longer in contact with Monet, having made friends with Gauguin, who wasn't particularly liked by anyone, and Gauguin spent little time in Paris. So scattered were the artists and writers that an effort was made to organize a monthly «Impressionist dinner» in Paris, but that soon petered out. The situation in Paris just before and soon after 1880, when Cézanne is too often said to have «fled,» offered little encouragement for any of the group to remain in the city. So Cézanne's seclusion was not, in any case, from some group of painters still in Paris, as if the Impressionists were intact and he was off in some wild blue yonder licking wounds. It is hardly relevant that he was not often in Paris.

The naturalist writers were also pulling each other apart while trying to share an umbrella to ward off a rain of symbols. Naturalism had been exotic for a while because it was new. As the 1870s closed, it was looked upon in both art and literature as banal. Symbolist manifestos were on the horizon and would soon engender a new generation of poets and novelists. Art would take over nature, reality would be an internal state of consciousness, the meadow flowers of landscapes replaced by Huysmans' hothouse tropicals, extra-marital affairs inflating to orgies; the temptresses in Saint Anthony's wilderness could now have their way with him. Haussmann's refurbished Paris was the new Babylon, resplendent in night-lighted wickedness. Symbolism would make nature exotic again. But Zola's naturalism would not be deflected in its course. He was a writer for the public domain, not for the small audience of those intellectuals whose works comprise the history of letters and fodder for academicians.

In 1877, Huysmans, Alexis, Maupassant, Céard, and Mirbeau inaugurated the Naturalist School as a sort of memorial to itself. To the first social gathering they invited the innovators Flaubert, Zola, and Edmond de Goncourt. The results were much the same as with the Impressionist's social diners—sporadic attendance and bickering. Goncourt claimed to have invented naturalism, and probably had. His response to Zola's *La Conquête des Plassans*—itself a pretension to the paternity of naturalist writing—was to throw it in a corner. In an effort to pull the rug out from under Zola's feet, Goncourt would insist that he had disavowed naturalism years before.

When Zola's *L'Assommoir*, the seventh volume of the *Rougon-Macquart,* appeared (serialized in 1876 and as a book in 1877), Goncourt accused Zola of plagiarism. Later, in his journal on June 1st, 1891, Goncourt would write: *I gave the complete formula for naturalism in «Germinie Lacerteux.» Zola's «L'Assommoir» was written from beginning to end along the lines laid down in that book. Later, I was the first to abandon naturalism for what the young writers are now doing to fill its place: dreams, symbolism, Satanism, etc. When I wrote «Les Frères Zemganno» and «La Fautin,» in these books I, the inventor of naturalism, tried to dematerialize it long before anyone else thought of doing so.*[12]

As for the painters, most members of the group were now deeply distressed. On turning fifty in 1884, crotchety Degas had already become rather morose, figuring he had become an old man: *One closes off like a door, and not only from friends. One cuts off everything around one and when alone, extinguishes, in a word, kills oneself out of disgust. I was so full of projects. Here I am, blocked, powerless. I've lost the thread.* In time Degas will forsake his colleagues to lead a hermit-like life; after 1886, he did not show any work in Paris, and only a few small pastel landscapes at Durand-Ruel's gallery in 1892. His personality was more extreme than Cézanne's—alternations of timidity and brashness, doubt and displays of excessive confidence. To his friend Evariste de Valernes, he confessed in 1890, *I would like you to forgive me for something that frequently comes up in your conversation and perhaps even more frequently in your thoughts, namely, that I behaved harshly towards you. I was actually being harsh against myself. You will remember this, for you were astonished, and you reproached me for my lack of self-confidence. I was, or must have appeared to be, harsh with everyone, because of a passion for brutality, which can be explained by my uncertainly and bad temper. I ask your forgiveness if, beneath the pretext of this damned art, I have wounded your fine mind and perhaps your heart.*[13]

Yet on the basis of just such limited evidence, Degas, too, has been excessively mythified. As Daniel Halévy pointed out in his introduction to the publication of Degas' letters, *an almost legendary, mythical picture of Degas exists. It is the artist as a recluse, voluntarily leading a churlish life, warding off with his rapid and trenchant replies the indiscretions of the world and of people, even contact with them. By this picture Degas was actually known, admired from a distance, feared from close up, by his contemporaries who thought they knew him, but in reality did not know him at all. In distant outline in the letters reunited in this volume, of this picture there will be no more than an occasional glimpse of that Degas. The reader of his letters is warned not to search for what he will not find. The personage here is not the Degas known to the writers, but Degas himself.*[14]

After 1880, Degas would come to have a very different evaluation of, for instance, Manet, than he'd had in the 1860s, or even in the mid-1870s. He once said to Mallarmé, *Art is a deceit. An artist is only an artist at certain hours by intention. Objects possess the same appearance for everyone. The study of nature is a convention. Isn't Manet the proof of that? Although he boasted of faithfully copying nature, he was the worst painter in the world, never making a brushstroke without the old masters in mind.*[15] Sisley also disassociated himself from his companions and, like Degas, created imaginary problems. He had become irritable, dissatisfied, aggravated—much more than anyone could possibly say about Cézanne.

Continuing this rundown of Impressionists winding down, in his old age, Sisley had a reputation for being suspicious and surly, avoiding new friendships and making life unbearable for himself. Little by little all joy had left his days, except for the joy of painting.[16] When asked who were his favorite painters, Sisley named Delacroix, Corot, Millet, Rousseau, Courbet—not Manet, not Monet, not one of his Impressionist colleagues.[17]

After 1880, Cézanne was, in fact, one of the most confident painters of the group when put in contrast to Renoir, Monet, and even Pissarro. From Naples in 1881, after painting gondolas in Venice, fantasias in Algiers, and boats in the Bay of Naples, Renoir lamented in a letter to Durand-Ruel, *I am still suffering from experimentation. I'm not content, still scraping off. I hope this craziness will have an end. I am like a child in school. The white page must always be nicely written, and bang—a blot! I am still at the blotting stage—and I'm forty!*[18] To the collector Deudon, Renoir wrote, also from Naples, *I feel lost when away from Montmartre. I am longing for my familiar surroundings, and think that even the ugliest Parisian girl is preferable to the most beautiful Italian.*[19] Later in life Renoir recalled that in 1883 a break had occurred in his work: *I had gone to the end of Impressionism and was reaching the conclusion that I didn't know how either to paint or to draw. In a word, I was at a dead end.*[20]

In 1883, Monet destroyed several canvases, tried reworking others, and wrote to Durand-Ruel, *I have more and more trouble satisfying myself and have come to a point of wondering whether I'm going crazy—and I don't know whether what I'm now doing is better or worse than what I did before.*[21]

Pissarro was also distressed about his painting and the grim situation for artists in Paris. In a May 1883 letter to his son Lucien, he said, *I am very disturbed by my unpolished and rough execution. I would like to develop a smoother technique, while retaining the old fierceness.*[22] The following year, responding to a request that he exhibit some of his paintings in his friend Eugène Murer's hotel in Rouen, Pissarro wrote, *I don't believe in the possibility of selling pictures at Rouen, the home of Flaubert, whom they have not yet acknowledged. You may be certain, my dear friend, at the sight of my recent studies the collectors will throw rotten apples. In Paris we are still outcasts, beggars.*[23] Pissarro would then resuscitate himself by joining with younger artists: Gauguin, Seurat, and Signac.

Degas' and Sisley's attitudes and remarks, Renoir's and Pissarro's disappointments, help to establish art history, signaling changes in the sociology of artists, not just their personal psychological predicaments at the time. Claiming that Cézanne's withdrawal from the group was due to some personality flaw, to having been maltreated by his father when young or beaten down by disapproving institutions of art in Paris, is lazy thinking and bad art history. It too obviously evades every question as to the internal dynamics of a so-called avant-garde vis-à-vis social history in motion. It assumes that any artist's withdrawal would be from some state of pleasantness, happiness, and brotherhood.

Of course, any sensible person withdraws from unpleasantness. What makes credible art history are the preponderant conditions for art at the time of the artists' withdrawal, not the conditions of their childhood or a simple turn of life's wheel that shoves them off the stage to make way for the next act.

Cézanne's art can only be understood by the way it entered twentieth-century art. He was not an artist of his time. Over the final two decades of the nineteenth century, Cézanne would rid art of every weak and failing trait of Impressionism—its sentimental and often trivial subject matter, easy techniques, unstructured compositions, superficial emotions, lack of angst, danger, terror. His late work dismantled art's history: the significance of subject matter, the value of manual and technical perfection, perspective, foreshortening; he blocked much of it from continuing. However, he still admired the great masters. A month before his death he would take pleasure in reading the appreciation that Baudelaire had for Delacroix. He wrote to his son, Paul, speaking of a letter he'd received from «a distinguished aesthete, *I can scarcely read his letter. The good man turns his back on what he expounds in his writing; in his drawings he produces nothing but old-fashioned rubbish, which smacks of artistic dreams, based not on the emotional experience of nature but on what he has seen in museums, and more still on a philosophical attitude spouting from an excessive knowledge of the masters.*[24] Again to his son a few days later, Cézanne wrote that he'd been visited by a Marseilles painter, who'd brought along a load of canvases for him to look over and evaluate, and that the visitor had shown him a photograph of a painting by Émile Bernard. *We are agreed on one point*, Cézanne said in the letter. *Bernard is an intellectual constipated by recollections of museums, who can't free himself from the school, from all schools.*[25]

All schools, like all individuals, die. To be immortal, one must step away from oneself, away from the protective security of the self. Cézanne was able to do that. To the next century he offered a way to art as non-style, ahistorical, non-socialized, non-aestheticised, non-contextual. Though all of his late pictures have subject matter, the subjects are there to serve art; beyond that, nothing about them is important—the lack of importance is their importance. Cézanne would rid art even of thought. Of Michelangelo, he said, H*e is a great constructor.* Of Raphael, he said, *He is always tied to the model; when he tries to become a thinker, he sinks below his great rival.*[26]Cézanne offered not a route to follow but a void to fill. He was indeed like the Moses with whom he identified. *Will I be allowed to enter the Promised Land, or like Moses be denied entry?* he asked.[27] He was, in fact, denied entry, but then, true geniuses do not walk through the doors they open. Doing so would be paradoxical.

50

Cézanne's intimate friendship with Zola carried into the 1880s. But so disinterested in art had Zola become, so disappointed on the whole with the Impressionists, he would have nothing to say about his friend's paintings. He did, however, send him a copy of each of his novels as they appeared, and Cézanne responded with thanks and compliments.

Numa Coste, Valabrègue, and Alexis would remain friends to both Cézanne and Zola. Coste, who came into a large inheritance in 1875, had become a mundane conservative painter who showed regularly in the Salon, but was never a factor in Impressionism. He, Zola, and Alexis founded a periodical, *L'Art Libre*, in 1882. On January 6th the next year, Cézanne responded to having received a copy:

> *My dear Coste,*
> *I think it is to you that I am indebted for sending me the paper L'Arte Libre. I read it with the liveliest interest, and with good reason. So I wish to thank you, and to tell you how much I appreciate the generous impulse with which you take up the defense of a cause to which I, myself, am far from remaining indifferent. I am with gratitude your compatriot and, I might say, your colleague.*

On March 10th, 1883, Cézanne wrote to Zola to thank him for sending his latest novel, *Au Bonheur des Dames*:

> *I am rather late in thanking you for sending me your last novel. But here is the extenuating circumstance for this delay. I have just come from L'Estaque, where I had been for a few days. Renoir, who is to have an exhibition of paintings following Monet's, which is now taking place, asked me to send him two landscapes which he had left with me last year. I sent them to him on Wednesday, and here I am at Aix, where snow fell all day on Friday. This morning the countryside presented the very beautiful sight of a study in snow. But it melts.*
>
> *We are still in the country...I will not be able to return to Paris for a long time. I think I will spend another five or six months here. So I remind you of my existence, and ask you to remember me to Alexis.*

Please give my respectful greetings to Madame Zola, also from my mother.

Zola responded on May 20th. His words in this letter, *Do you work? Are you satisfied? Keep up your courage*, sound eerily like those from his letter of twenty-five years earlier, when eighteen-year-old Zola was anxious about his friend still in Aix. *Do you swim? Do you party? Do you paint? Do you play the cornet? Do you write poems? In a word, what do you do?* Zola continues in the 1883 letter with, *You don't mention your return to Paris. I count on seeing you in September, you can pass several days here and we can talk at ease. I have started a new novel. That is my life. Otherwise, nothing new.* One recalls how years earlier Zola had coaxed Cézanne to Paris, always saying how he counted on him.

On May the 24th, 1883, Cézanne responded: *My dear Émile. I will not return to Paris before next year. I have rented a little house and garden at L'Estaque just above the station and at the foot of the hill, where behind me rise the rocks and the pines.*

> *I am still busy painting. I have here some beautiful views, but they do not quite make motifs. Nevertheless, climbing the hills as the sun goes down, one has a glorious view of Marseilles in the background and the islands, all enveloped towards evening to a very decorous effect.*
>
> *I do not speak to you about yourself, seeing that I don't know anything, except that when I buy «Figaro» I sometimes hit upon a few facts relating to men I don't know, thus lately I read a weighty article about the valiant Desboutins* [Marcellin Desboutins, painter and writer, a close friend of Manet who in the 1860s frequented the same cafés]. *I did learn, however, that Gent* [Alphonse Gent, a respected literary critic] *values your last novel highly, but no doubt you know this. As for me, I liked it very much, very much indeed. Do not forget to give my greetings to Madame Zola, and also remember me to Alexis. I press your hand warmly, ever yours.*

At the end of 1883, Cézanne again writes to Zola, thanking him for another book, probably Zola's collection of short stories *Naïs Micoulin*:

> *My dear Émile,*
> *I received the book you kindly sent me. Here is the reason for the delay, which causes me to be thanking you such a long time after. Since the beginning of November, I've been back at L'Estaque, where I intend to remain until January. Mama has been here for some days, and last week Rose lost her child, which was born in September, or October, I think. The poor little thing didn't last long. Otherwise, everything is as usual.*
> *If the good Alexis is not far from you, remember me to him.*
> *I have the honor to salute you, and to renew my thanks for your kind thoughts about me.*

Early in 1884, another book from Zola arrived—the *Joie de Vivre*. Cézanne responds to the gift:

> *My dear Émile,*
>
> *I received the book you recently sent me, the Joie de Vivre, which appeared in Gil Blas—I read some extracts in that paper. Thank you for sending it, and for not forgetting me in the seclusion of my retreat. I should have nothing to tell you were it not that, as I was at L'Estaque a few days ago, I received there a letter from good old Valabrègue telling me of his presence in Aix, to where I ran yesterday, and where this morning I had the pleasure of clasping his hand. We made a tour of the town together, recalling those we had known, but how far apart we are now in our feelings! I had my head full of the character of this country, which seems to me quite extraordinary.*
>
> *On the other hand, I saw Monet and Renoir, who went for a holiday to Genoa, towards the end of September.*

Late in the year, another gift from Zola, this time two books. Cézanne responds with thanks, adding that he hasn't much news about the good old town where he first saw the light of day. He complains a bit about how art is changing—ignorance of harmony, discord in coloration, lack of tonality. After groaning, he says to Zola, *let us cry, «Long live the sun, which gives us such a beautiful light.»*

Over 1885, until April 1886, letters pass back and forth between the old friends. At some point in 1885, Cézanne's heart is distressed over a woman he meets and with whom he has an affair. Zola is asked to help him conceal the liaison, which has put additional weight on his mood, considering that he is still loaded with the problem of hiding Hortense and their son, now twelve years old. Two years later the affair blows over: Cézanne's father, eighty-eight years old in 1886, is finally told about Hortense and that for fourteen years he'd had a grandson, his only son having produced an heir. How he took it, one cannot say. Cézanne and Hortense were married in April 1886 with Cézanne's parents in attendance. A few months after the wedding, Louis-Auguste died, leaving Cézanne with a fortune.

Shortly before the marriage, Cézanne received another book from Zola, this time *L'Oeuvre*. The final letter from Cézanne to Zola, found among Zola's papers, was Cézanne's response:

> *My dear Émile,*
>
> *I have just received L'Oeuvre, which you arranged to send me. I thank the author of the Rougon-Macquart for this kind token of remembrance, and ask him to allow me to press his hand in memory of old times.*
>
> *Ever yours, under the impulse of years gone by.*

The extent to which Cézanne recognized himself in *L'Oeuvre* as the deranged painter Claude Lantier, one cannot know. Cézanne's letter acknowledging the book is written in a different tone than previous letters—formal and restrained, an eloquent expression of sadness. Cézanne must have recognized, on reading *L'Oeuvre*, that his friend no longer esteemed the art they had both struggled for since adolescence. The fictional Claude Lantier was a re-born Frenhofer, but whereas Balzac's *The Hidden Masterpiece* had been a story, Zola's *L'Oeuvre* was all too real, the transparent fictional veneer lacking the opacity of the imagined.

Monet's response to *L'Oeuvre* perhaps summarized how others in the group felt about it. Deploying utmost tact, he wrote to Zola, *You were kind enough to send me a copy of* L'Oeuvre. *I am much obliged.*

> *I have always derived great pleasure from reading your books. This one doubly interests me because it raises questions of art for which we've been fighting for so long a time. I have read it. And I remain troubled, disturbed. You took care that not one of your characters should resemble any one of us; nonetheless I'm afraid that our enemies, the press and the public, may use the name of Manet, or at least some of our names, to prove us to be fail-ures. Surely it was not in your mind to allow that. I refuse to believe it could have been.*
>
> *I have read* L'Oeuvre *with great pleasure, discovering old memories on each page. Excuse me for telling you this. It is not a criticism of the book. You know of my fanati-cal admiration for your talent. But I have been struggling for a long time, and am afraid that at this moment when we appear to be succeeding, our enemies may make use of your book to deal us a knockout blow.*[1]

Zola had had this book in mind for quite a few years. In 1882, having heard the outline directly from Zola, Alexis gave advance reference to it: *A work for which Zola will have less trouble collecting documentation is the novel he plans to write on art.*

> *He will have only to remember what he saw taking place in our circle, and what he, him-self, felt. His principal character is the painter in love with modern beauty, that same Claude Lantier. Zola's plan for this novel is to recount his years in Provence, his early youth which was so unique, so special. I know that he intends to study, in Claude Lantier, the frightful psychology of artistic impotence. Around the character of this central man of genius—a sublime dreamer paralyzed in production by a flaw—other artists will move: painters, sculptors, musicians, writers, an entire band of ambitious young men who've come to conquer Paris, some failing in their pursuits, others more or less succeeding, all of them cases of the sicknesses of art, which are varieties of the prevailing contemporary neurosis. Naturally, Zola will be obliged to make use of his friends, to gather their most typical traits.*[2]

In a letter to his Dutch admirer, Johann Kolff, dated July 6th, 1885, Zola said of his book in progress, *I have begun my next novel, and this novel has, as its milieu, the literary and artistic world. I have once again taken up my Claude Lantier of* La Ventre de Paris [Paris' belly, in reference to the central market *Les Halles*]. *I shall recount my whole youth—I have put my friends, I've put myself in it.*[3] Zola had been interviewed about *L'Oeuvre* by the newspaper *Le Voltaire*. Cézanne may have read his remarks, published on May 2nd, 1886.

Cézanne may have detected his personal presence in the novel, considering that it opens in mid-summer 1862, the year he had come back to Paris to make a commitment to art. He may have noticed, too, that Zola had recreated the inseparables, their wanderings and pranks around Aix-en-Provence (called Plassans in the novel). Baille is defined as one of the three—a young man who abandons art for the bourgeois life. Also deployed as a character is Joseph Huet, who becomes an architect in the novel, as he had in real life, portrayed by Zola as a serious but mediocre petit bourgeois. The young artist at whom Zola and Cézanne tended to poke fun in the early 1860s, Jean-Baptiste Chaillon, also appears, as does Alexis, disguised but nonetheless introduced as a youth from the south who comes to Paris with a handful of poems, and whose father despairs seeing his son sink into bohemian life.

In the character of Claude Lantier, Cézanne would have seen himself portrayed as a distressed personality who vacillates between enthusiasm and gloom, at times so doubting himself as to be suicidal, condemned to never succeed as real geniuses do, never to find an outlet for the full expression of his sensations, his inspiration choked, a victim of romanticism that persistently clouds his vision, with a sub-plot: the chaste man's passion for woman's flesh, as Zola described it. Here looms the temptation to read into Cézanne the character of Lantier—to set Cézanne's clock by how Zola had set Lantier's clock. But one must not confuse refined gold with ore, or reverse the process by which a novelist creates a whole character out of particles of data taken from real characters. Zola had diminished everything Cézanne felt dear: Aix-en-Provence, his youth with Zola and Baille, his painter friends in Paris, and art itself. After 1886, there would be no more contact between the two. Still, it may not have been just the book that broke their bond. Cézanne was completely a Provençal painter now, while Zola was a Parisian novelist. They were as different as they had been since adolescence—no longer joined at the brain stem, not even by «some strange affinity,» but only, as Cézanne said, by impulses that were now in the past.

Cézanne's letter to Zola acknowledging *L'Oeuvre* is the noblest he would ever write—no anger, no display of pain that might distress his friend. But surely Zola knew before having Cézanne's response that he had caused him to suffer. Over the next few years, he would have to depend on mutual friends to keep him informed of Cézanne's well being; their special relationship was irreparably broken. Zola had used up Cézanne's friendship, as he had used people all along his penurious path to fame. Cézanne's love for Zola, and especially his capacity to be forgiving, was much greater than Cézanne's biographers have allowed. The standard reason given for Cézanne's eventual break with Zola is this publication of

L'Oeuvre, but some credence should be paid to Vollard's report of a conversation he had with Cézanne ten years later, in the mid-1890s:

> One day Cézanne showed me a little study he had made of Zola during their youth. I ask him at what moment did he and Zola get on bad terms. He replied, «There never were any bad feelings between us. It was I who ceased going to see Zola. I no longer felt at ease when with him, with his oriental carpets, his servants, and his desk of sculpted wood. It was enough to make me feel that I was paying a visit to a minister. Zola had become a filthy bourgeois [sale bourgeois].»[4]

From what documentation we have, Zola's last knowledge of Cézanne's activities is from the early 1890s, when both were entering their fifties. In February 1891, Numa Coste wrote to Zola:

> How are we to explain that a grasping and hardheaded banker could produce a human being like our poor friend Cézanne? I saw his recently. He's in good health; physically everything is fine with him. But he is timid, primitive, and younger than ever. He lives in the Jas de Bouffan with his mother, who, by the way, has fallen out with the «Ball» [Hortense given the English word «ball,» as in «ball and chain»], who on her part is not on good terms with her sisters-in-law, nor are they on any better terms among themselves. That is how it's come about that Paul lives in one place and his wife in another. And it is one of the most touching things I have ever experienced, to see how this brave boy has preserved his child-like naïveté, forgetting his disappointments in the struggle for life—in resignation and suffering—stubbornly pursuing the work which he does not succeed in pulling off.

In February 1891 (as he'd done back in 1871 when Cézanne was hiding out and Zola was desperate to find out if he was all right), Alexis in Aix wrote to Zola with news of Cézanne:

> Coste, the only one with whom I have any contact, is not digestible every day. Fortunately, Cézanne, whom I rediscovered some time ago, brings a breath of fresh air into my social life. He at least vibrates, is expansive and lively. He's furious about the Ball, who, after a stay of one year in Paris, last summer imposed on him five months in Switzerland, where he found no one understood him except for one Prussian. After Switzerland, the Ball departed with Monsieur le fils. But, by the reduction of her income to half, she's been forced to return to Aix. Yesterday evening, Cézanne left us to fetch her from the station; the furniture from Paris is also about to arrive. Paul intends to put it into a place he's rented on the rue Monnaie, where she will have her rooms. He, himself, does not intend to leave his mother and older sister, with whom he installed himself in the suburbs [at the Jas de Bouffan]; he likes it there and prefers them to his wife. If, as he hopes, the Ball and the shrimp settle down here in Aix, nothing will stop him from going to Paris for half a year from time to time. «Long live the beautiful sun and freedom,» he exclaims.

By the way, no more money troubles for Paul. Thanks to his father, whom he now holds in great esteem—the father who used to say to him, «Look before you leap,» and «Don't be too hasty, take your time and save your strength»—he has enough to live on. He divides his annual income into twelve monthly shares, and then sub-divides each share into three parts, one for the «Ball,» one for the «little Ball,» and one for himself. But the Ball, who is not easily satisfied, constantly tends to overspend her share. Backed up by his mother and sister, Paul now feels strong enough to resist her demands. During the day Paul paints in the Jas de Bouffan, where a workman serves as a model, and where I want to visit him one of these days to see what he is doing. To complete the psychological picture, he is converted, he is a believer, and he goes to mass.

Cézanne remained financially responsible to Hortense, as was Zola to Alexandrine; both Cézanne and Zola were dutiful and affectionate fathers. Alexandrine did not like Hortense, and in Aix Hortense was not appreciated by Cézanne's sisters. So putting her and son Paul up in a separate apartment in town was a handy solution, as Cézanne, in his maturity as when young, enjoyed living at the *Jas* with family, adored by his sisters.

Alexandrine had been unable to bear children, much to Zola's sadness, for he had a powerful paternalistic drive. In 1888, a domestic in the Zola house, Jeanne Rozerot, became Zola's lover; by arrangement with Alexandrine, Jeanne would bear his children. In 1889, a daughter Denise was born; in 1891, a son named Jacques. Zola and Alexandrine stayed husband and wife, living and traveling together, but Zola was obliged to shift from one household to the other so he could enjoy his children. In 1889, when Zola took up residence in Surrey for a spell, Alexandrine and Jeanne (with the children in tow) alternated visits to him.

On the night of September 28th, 1902, Zola and Alexandrine took to bed at their home in Paris after asking their valet to light a fire in the bedroom stove. The chimney did not sufficiently draw. By morning, Zola was dead from carbon monoxide poisoning, and Alexandrine nearly so. Rumors spread that right-wing extremists had assassinated Zola; others held that he had committed suicide. Forensic examinations of the flue and chimney, and chemical tests of the bedroom air managed to offset these suspicions.

Zola's body was placed in a vault in Montmartre Cemetery, and later moved to the Panthéon to lie beside Victor Hugo. Though Zola had been denied the Legion of Honor, the government nonetheless assigned a company of the 28th Regiment to function at his funeral. Fifty thousand people lined the route of his passing through Montmartre. Police and soldiers along the way saluted. Anatole France—with the Dreyfus affair in mind—delivered a speech, ending with:

Let us not pity this man who endured and suffered. Let us envy him. Enthroned atop the most prodigious collection of outrages that folly, ignorance, and wickedness have ever heaped up, his glory attains an inaccessible height. Let us envy him. He has honored his country and the world with an immense body of work and a great act...He was a moment in human consciousness.[5]

On hearing of Zola's death, Cézanne locked himself in his room and wept (he had once told Vollard that though he'd stopped seeing Zola after the publication of *L'Oeuvre*, he could never get used to the thought that their friendship was over). Vollard reports that Cézanne *was in his studio, preparing a palette, when Paulin, who had served at times as housemaid and model, entered, gasping, «Monsieur Paul, Monsieur Paul, Zola est mort.» On hearing this, Cézanne broke out in tears; then motioning that Paulin leave him alone, he closed himself in his studio. From time to time throughout the day, Paulin put her ear to the door, hearing her master weeping and moaning.*

On May 27th, 1906, a bust of Zola by his boyhood friend Philippe Solari was ceremonially installed at the Méjane Library in Aix. Cézanne attended the dedication. Numa Coste, faithful friend to the final days, delivered a eulogy for Zola that would have served as well for Cézanne. Coste spoke of their shared youth:

We were at the dawn of life, swollen with vast hopes, desiring to rise above the social swamp in which petty jealousies, bogus reputations, and sickly ambitions stagnate. We dreamed of conquering Paris, of occupying the world's intellectual home. Here in Aix as youths, and out of doors, surrounded by lonely and barren spaces, by shaded torrents and on summits of rocky escarpments, we forged suits of mail for the titanic struggle. When Zola preceded us to Paris, he sent his first literary efforts to his dear friend, Paul Cézanne, thus letting all of us share his hopes and dreams. We read those letters up in the hills, under evergreen oaks, as one reads communiqués from the first sortie of a military campaign.[6]

Cézanne died on the 22nd of October 1906, having been caught in a cold rainstorm while out in the hills painting. A telegram to his son read, *Come quickly. You dear father is gravely ill.* Zola's body would remain in Paris, while Cézanne's would lie at rest in Aix. In Paris a million people knew Zola's name, while few remembered the name Cézanne. The new director of the Musée d'Aix had vowed that until death did himself part, no painting by Cézanne would ever enter his museum. Well and good—Cézanne belonged not to the culture of Aix anyway, but to its environs. Yet at heart he had not entirely forsaken Paris. There, against all odds, he had become an artist. Earlier in the year of his death, when allowed to exhibit with the *Société des amis d'art en Aix*, he had himself listed in the catalogue as a pupil of Pissarro—to the very end, the guiding light he'd had in Paris since his first days at the *Suisse*.

At the ceremony dedicating the bust of Zola, Coste told his audience that Zola had said, *One thinks one has revolutionized the world, but at the end of the journey discovers that one has revolutionized nothing at all.* Yet Zola and Cézanne were true revolutionaries: one changed the nature of literature, the other the nature of art. Over their lifetime, they had accrued notoriety but not fame. Fame would await their deaths, as fame always does. Glory cannot be made by the glorified. Eminence in fame is what the future constructs from the deeds of past lives. Geniuses are man-made, fashioned by rational minds that follow on the achievements of the usefully insane.

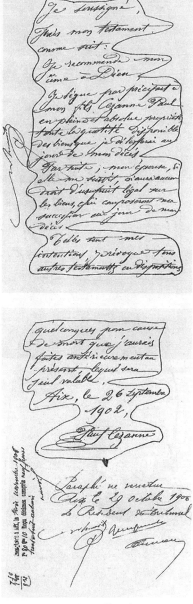

Cézanne's last will and testament.

Cézanne's final studio, at Les Lauves,
Aix-en-Provence. On the wall, a print
of Delacroix's *Death of Sardanapalus*.
Photo: H. Roger Viollet.

Cézanne at the age of twenty.

Cézanne seated in his studio in front of *Les grandes baigneuses*, 1904-06. Apparently a trimmed print of a photograph taken by Emile Bernard in 1904. This print was given to me by Martha Conil, Cézanne's niece, in Aix-en-Provence, June 1964.

ENDNOTES

ABBREVIATIONS

O.C. — *Zola: Oeuvres complètes*. Edited by Henri Mitterand (Paris: Circle du Livre Précieux, 1967), 15 volumes.

Zola, *Correspondance* — General editor, B. H. Bakker (Montréal and Paris: Presses de l'Université de Montréal and Editions du CNRS, 11973-1993).

Rewald, Cat. No. — *The paintings of Paul Cézanne: A Catalogue Raisonné*, 2 volumes. Compiled and annotated by John Rewald with the collaboration of Walter Feilchenfeldt and Jayne Warman (New York: Harry N. Abrams, 1996).

Cézanne: *Correspondance* — *Paul Cézanne: Correspondance, recueille, annotée et préfacée par John Rewald. Èdition révisée et augumentée* (Paris: Bernard Grasset, 1978).

NOTE TO THE READER: For an excellent book on the history and sociology of the decades in Paris spanned by my text, see Rupert Christiansen, *Tales of the New Babylon: Paris in the Mid-19th Century* (London: Sinclair Stevenson, 1994). For a fine essay on John Rewald's style of art history and its influence, see Kermit Swindler Champa, *Masterpiece Studies* (Penn State University Press, 1994), chater 2.

NOTES TO CHAPTER 1

1   *Correspondance*, Zola to Baille, May 14, 1860. Cézanne's letters, some of Zola's and their mutual friends, can be found in several French and English editions. My references are to the letters' dates, not to a specific edition.

2   *Correspondance*, Zola to Baille (Zola quoting Cézanne), May 14, 1860.

3   *Zola, Oeuvres complètes* I, p. 55. See also *Correspondance*, Zola to Cézanne, December 30, 1859 where Zola says, «I have never loved except in a dream, and have never been loved, not even in a dream!»

4   While it is his literary privilege not to, Frederick Brown, *Zola, A Life* (New York: Farrar Strauss Giroux, 1995), p. 311, did not document grounds for saying that «the pun-

ishment François Zola meted out to his twelve-year-old Algerian house boy marked his son forever.» Which was it, the experience or the punishment? We do not know if the boy was punished. Moreover, the adult Zola's fantasy of having sex with a very young girl is not, as Brown says, evidence that Zola still had on his mind the Algerian assaulting his modesty. While making fascinating biographies, such psychological guesswork does not make good art history.

5 For example, Philip Callow, *Lost Earth: A Life of Cézanne* (Chicago: Ivan R. Dee, 1995), p. 29.

6 Paul Alexis, *Émile Zola, notes d'un ami* (Paris 1882).

7 Alfred de Musset, *Rollo*. First published in 1866, later in *Poésie complètes* (1840).

8 Alexis, *Émile Zola, notes d'un ami*.

9 Paraphrased from the description of Musset by Jean d'Ormesson, *Une autre histoire de la littérature française* (Paris, NiL éditions, 1998), p. 144.

10 This is summarized from what in his later years Cézanne presumably told Joachim Gasquet, and also what Gasquet found in Zola's *Correspondance*. See *Joachim Gasquet's Cézanne: A Memoire with Conversations*, translated by Christopher Pemberton, preface by John Rewald, introduction by Richard Shiff (London: Thames and Hudson, 1991), p. 39.

NOTES TO CHAPTER 2

1 Zola, *Oeuvres complètes* XIV, p. 242.

2 Amoury Duval, comparing the situation of artists between 1825 and 1878. I have been unable to locate the original source for this pleasantry.

3 T. J. Clark, *Image of the People* (London: Thames and Hudson, 1973), p. 36.

4 Rewald, *Paul Cézanne*, tr. Margaret Liebman (London: Spring Books, 1950, 1965), p. 13. Rewald writes, "This kind of ostracism to which Cézanne's family was subjected left its mark on Paul Cézanne, who was proud and sensitive, and accentuated his introspective tendencies. Later, when he reached manhood, Cézanne avoided society and found it very difficult to make friends." Rewald make these assertions without much evidence. Cézanne's father may have been shunned by a certain segment of society but so is everyone. Cézanne avoided bourgeois society, but so did about everyone he was associated with, although he enjoyed living with his bourgeois family with all the comforts it afforded. And no evidence whatsoever indicates that Cézanne had difficulty making friends, as my text will bear out.

NOTES TO CHAPTER 3

1 Quoted in Brown, *Zola*, p. 29.

2 Frédéric Mistral, *The Memoirs of Frédéric Mistral*, tr. George Wickes (New York: New Directions Press, 1986), p. 125.

3 *Gasquet's Cézanne*, p. 65.

4 Quoted in Brown, *Zola*, p. 30.

5 Brown, *Zola*, pp. 30-31.

⁶ *Correspondance*, Cézanne to Gasquet, June 3, 1899.

⁷ As many boys masturbated back then with passages from the Bible or the Classics in the other hand as today's youths deploy pornographic pictures. Not surprising, the Greek and Roman classics were under attack by some clerics and other moralists during the 1850s.

⁸ *Correspondance*, Zola to Cézanne, December 30, 1959.

⁹ Even decades later, in the mid-1930s, when John Rewald, as a young German studying in Paris at the Sorbonne, proposed a doctoral dissertation on Cézanne, he was told that no study of an artist later in history than the early nineteenth-century Géricault would be acceptable. But because Rewald was a foreigner and thus not likely to pollute French scholarship, he was allowed to proceed with such a quaint topic.

¹⁰ See Brown, *Zola*, p. 317.

¹¹ *Correspondance*, Zola to Cézanne, June 13, 1860. Mary Lewis, *Cézanne's Early Imagery* (Berkeley and Los Angeles: University of California Press, 1989), p. 27, says that Cézanne was one of the artists who worked on the parade. But Cézanne was twelve years old and a long way from being an artist; he was not even an art student. Many art historians fail to realize that just because a child, or anyone, takes art lessons, that person is not an artist. To say that is like saying that every boy who plays a little baseball is an athlete, that every girl who makes fudge or bakes a cupcake is a chef, that anyone who lays out a floor plan of their dream house is an architect.

¹² Cézanne tells Vollard this in Vollard, *Paul Cézanne* (Paris, 1915), p. 88.

¹³ *Correspondance*, March 7 and March 25, 1867.

¹⁴ Zola in *L'Événement illustré*. See Guy Robert, "Des Inédits d'Émile Zola. Une polémique entre Zola et Le Mémorial d'Aix en 1868," *Arts et Livres*, vol. II, no. 6 (1946).

¹⁵ Zola, in *L'Événement illustré*, July 28, 1868.

¹⁶ For this and more, see Brown, *Zola*, pp. 181-182.

¹⁷ *Correspondance*, Zola to Valabrègue, May 29, 1867.

¹⁸ Brown, *Zola*, pp. 31-32.

NOTES TO CHAPTER 4

¹ This is given by Rewald as a statement that Zola made in the 1880s. John Rewald, *Paul Cézanne*, tr. Margaret H. Liebman (London: Spring Books, 1950), p. 11.

NOTES TO CHAPTER 5

¹ From an Aix newspaper review of Zola's *The Confession of Claude*, 1866.

² *Gasquet's Cézanne*, p. 40.

³ It is not know to whom the other Bs refers. It could be that Cézanne is just multiplying Baille's name as word play.

⁴ *Enfoncé le pion* generally means, "taken pawn," as in chess, but *pion* is also a prefect of sorts, hired to supervise pupils, and can also mean a pedantic person. *Mille*, meaning a thousand, is used in many expressions as meaning just "a lot of," or "many," as in *merci mille fois* (a thousand thanks).

5   *Correspondance*, Zola to Louis Marguery.

6   I think that Cézanne is referring to the Roman poet Caeci'lius Statius (AD 45-c.96) who was known for use of literary and rhetorical devices, hyperbole, and entwined themes; hence Cézanne refers to him as weaver of plots.

7   The *Philippics* were four speeches by which Demothenes attacked Philip II, king of Macedonia. But surely Cézanne means the fourteen speeches Cicero delivered against Mark Antony. Cicero had adopted Demothenes' title.

8   The watercolor probably had had a sort of placard announcing the theme. Both *Senatus* and *curia* refer to the Roman senate—*curia* more to the place of the Senate. Cézanne must have had in mind the *senatus consultum ultimatum*, the ultimate decree of the Senate that condemned Catiline and his co-conspirators to death in 63 B.C. Cicero did not actually slay Catiline but defeated him politically when competing for the 63 B.C. con-sulship. Defeated by Cicero again in 62, Catiline laid plans for a revolution. Cicero managed to get him out of Rome on some mission, and then had his fellow conspirators put to death. Catiline was killed when Antonius marched against him with an army.

9   Theodore Reff, «Cézanne's Dream of Hannibal,» *Art Bulletin* 45 (June 1963), pp. 148-52, see especially p. 149 where one reads, «Cézanne departs from his source, transforming the classical author's urbane irony into a vehement denunciation, and his opponent's silence into a swoon of terror; and here, too, we sense in the exaggeration something of his situation, in which Cicero stands for the righteous father whose anger he fears, and Catiline for himself.» Reff's thesis is preceded by Meyer Schapiro's comments on this poem: «*The Dream of Hannibal*, written in a mock-classical style, the young hero, after a drunken bout in which he has spilled the wine on the tablecloth and fallen asleep under the table, dreams of his terrible father who arrives in a chariot drawn by four white horses. He takes his debauched son by the ear, shakes him angrily, and scolds him for his drunkenness and wasteful life and for staining his clothes with sauce, wine, and rum. These fantasies convey something of the anxiety of the young Cézanne under the strict regime of his father.» Schapiro, *Cézanne*, p. 23.

10   *Correspondance*, Cézanne to Zola, July 26, 1858, and January 17, 1859.

11   As is often the case, Cézanne misspells Latin words, but throughout my text, I correct them, as the purpose of my book is not to point out misspellings with that insidious (sic!). Cézanne's letters, like most anyone's personal letters, are to be received, read, and understood, not graded on grammar and spelling.

NOTES TO CHAPTER 6

1   The expression, "Up your kazoo," is common enough to be used in public without giving thought to its larger meaning, as when President George Bush said in a national broadcast, "...up his kazoo," when referring to what was in store for Saddam Hussein. That expression belongs to his generation as a socially acceptable way of saying, "Up your ass."

2   The French *entreprend quelqu'un*, which ordinarily means, "to work on someone" always implies a result. When used in a sexual context, as in this poem, it means "premeditated seduction."

3   Adolescence is a period of competition. Young males of most any species struggle against others to gain territory and a sex partner. Boys who are bonded for mutual support engage in sexual activities that are preliminary to physical encounters with girls. They strive not to compete with each other except under strictly controlled conditions. A strong older boy will wrestle gently with a weaker boy, while going all out when wrestling with a boy who is stronger. Only later, when required to display one's virility before girls, as, for example, high-school athletes cheered on by scantily dressed cheerleaders, will their full measure of acquired manhood be called on for action. School athletics sustains childhood play, while incorporating competitiveness into the game: fighting to take the opponent's territory, to take away the opponents balls, castrating them, scoring by carrying the ball into their "end zone," by "putting it in," either into a basket (woman) or the hockey net (woman) or scoring a touchdown in the end zone (woman).

4   From here, one might look ahead to the myth that Cézanne dreaded the female nude. But the dynamics of this sort of fear are not so easily determined as to adult behavior. Adults tend to be ashamed of their fanciful daydreams and to conceal them from others, regarding them as their most intimate secrets. Adults would rather confess misdeeds for which they feel guilty than to tell their daydreams and risk feeling ashamed. Psychoanalysts assign the motive to the adult's realization that, no longer a child, the boy is not expected to *play* with reality but *to live it*. Shame is inflicted on children by parents and teachers. As the child matures, that shame is transformed into self-imposed shame (not to be confused with guilt). Parent-induced shame is invariably associated with dirtiness in behavior—soiling one's clothing or uttering dirty speech—for which reason mouth-soaping is inflicted to clean the dirty mouth, like baptism washes away stains of inherited sin. During the transition from adolescence, shame is flirted with: telling dirty stories and showing off erections ease boys along the developmental path to self-censoring adulthood. Shame is a positive feeling when occurring in this growing-up process, for it holds aspects of adult behavior in abeyance until the child is mature enough to act sensibly in the adult world. Intimacy deflects shame. When it comes down to real sexual activity, however, living up to reality is fraught with interpersonal conflict, often dangerous and potentially shameful. So the psychology of child-play is not easy to transform into adult sexual activity without retaining the emotional safety of play. It is preserved in such expressive activity as playing around with one's partner, genital teasing, foreplay, or auto-stimulation as playing with oneself. By sustaining playfulness, the adult strives to recapture the innocence of childhood when playing with toys—not inhibited and not shameful—before biologically motivated parental reprobation dampens the emerging adolescent's sexual urges by assigning them to sin. In this transition from conventional childhood to conventional maturity, deployment of real objects and real situations in play convert to fantasy objects in imagined contexts: the nymph in Cézanne's poem becomes *un objet* the very moment he focuses on her as a sexual object. Such fantasized objects perpetuate childhood pleasures that are offered by real objects, with which very young children play in dead seriousness while imitating adults. Plunging a slide whistle imitates adult copulation. When submissive toys are set to the side at adolescence, the pleasure they had given is preserved in the boy's psyche and remains available for recapture in pleasurable daydreams and play activities that implicate sex and violence. Foreplay and

love play are not just nice expressions to mask what one means but are biologically root-ed in protecting both parties from aggression and readying them for the psycho-mechan-ics of procreative transmission.

Freud proposed that the child does not at first conceal his play from adults, but over time parental censure and punishment forces certain types of play to be shameful, espe-cially any frolic that references sex and defecation. The child learns to conceal that type of behavior from all but his most intimate friends. Intimacy is mutual agreement to behave toward one another without shame, as when an adult lover refers to his partner as baby, or doll, or cookie, when fantasies can be freely exchanged without fear they will be told to others. Children share intimate secrets with each other while hiding them from adults. From an early age, the genitals, places of secretion and excretion, become secret, private parts. Their secretiveness accrues to the meaning of modesty, which is an adult way of moderating shame.

5   *Correspondance*, Zola to Cézanne. December 30, 1859. This complex of fantasy with secrecy will figure even in the adult Cézanne. When the journalist, Marius Roux, a school chum of Zola's, reviewed Zola's first book, *La Confession de Claude*, in early 1867 (the first mention of Cézanne in print), he touched on Cézanne's modesty: *I would give you my opinion of some of his canvases. But his modesty does not permit him to believe that what he pro-duces is adequate, and I do not want to hurt his feelings. I am waiting until he displays his work in broad daylight.*

6   *Correspondance*, Cézanne to Zola, August 20, 1885.

7   Explained in Rewald, *Cézanne*, 1950, p. 119.

8   Rewald, Cat. No. 23.

9   I swiped these titles from John Rewald, *Cézanne, A Biography* (New York: Harry N. Abrams, 1986), p. 40. Rewald also gives them in *Cézanne*, 1950, p. 31. They are actual-ly from Paris Salon catalogues of the time but were typical of titles found in all art muse-ums.

10   For the nymphs, see Rewald, Cat. No. 124; for the tritons, see Cat. No. 122, for the boys at riverside, see Cat. No. 250.

NOTES TO CHAPTER 7

1   As established in my book, *Gauguin's Paradise Lost* (New York: Viking, 1971), Gauguin contrived a signature monogram in Tahiti with his initials P. G. inscribed with-in an O, to be read as Paul Gauguin, a penis set within a vagina. When slurred, in the mind or as uttered, the letters read in French, *Pego*, which was the name Gauguin gave his voraciously libidinal dog. Pego in English is a piece of British merchant-marine slang, meaning prick, cock, or rod that Gauguin picked up while in maritime service on a British vessel. The fact that he associated his person and virile brush with his virile member should escape no one, for it emanates from the fusion of artistic form with the female form. The young Cézanne, on a sheet of attempts to find how he might want to sign his name when he became an artist, fashioned one signature in the shape of the male geni-tals.

2   Théodore Pelloquet, "L'Exposition," *Journal du Salon de 1863*, no. 22 (July 23,

1863). For a fuller quotation of Pelloquet's reaction to Manet's painting, see the context in Michael Fried, *Manet's Modernism* (Chicago: University of Chicago Press, 1996), p. 560, note 20.

3   The expression "April showers bring May flowers" is, of course, a fecundity verse—the Easter eggs of April would hatch in May if not eaten. I am of the age that remembers May Pole dancing throughout my elementary school years. I think we were binding the pole. In my psyche is buried an association at the time of may-pole binding in plaited streamers with a Chinese finger trap, a fiber gadget, also plaited, into which one sticks ones finger only to find it can't be extracted. The plaiting loosens on insertion but tightens on extraction. This device was once a clever condom of sorts to sheathe the erect penis and give extra sensation to the woman. It could not be removed until the penile erection subsided.

4   *Correspondance*, Cézanne to Zola, June 20, 1859. It was clear early on that Cézanne wanted a woman in his studio, not just a muse.

5   *Correspondance*, Zola to Cézanne. June 25, 1860.

6   *Correspondance*, Zola to Cézanne. March 3, 1860.

7   *Dingue*, as the basic word in this play with the sound, may be *dingus*, one of the many Provençal slang words for "penis."

8   *Correspondance*, Zola to Louis Margery, March 9, 1859.

NOTES TO CHAPTER 8

1   Cézanne's horror story is a daydream. Like in sleep-dreams, dream-matter arises from infantile and early life conflicts, but daydreams are to a great extent controlled by conscious wishes. In most cases, the desired object—wealth, success, heroism, recognition, fantasy woman—is either attained or within one's grasp, as is the graspable woman in Cézanne's story. Hence daydreams, unlike sleep-dreams, can be made up and endlessly repeated with alterations, changes of characters, revised endings. A horror story needs the sort of ending that Cézanne gave his. The story could not allow for his conscious wishes to be gratified: cuddled and suckled at a breast, possessed by the woman he wishes to possess, for the woman in the coach is a projection of his mother who must die as both object and objective of sexual desire. Daydreams of this wish-fulfilling kind are usually scripted by what the daydreamer has read or been told, even when stimulated by workings of the unconscious. The split between the modest, nurturing and mothering wife, who is a bore, and the *femme fatale* of Cézanne's story—the woman in the coach—was a common literary motif at mid-nineteenth century, of passion bringing both pain and pleasure. Regarding the bountiful examples of the *femme fatale* in the disguise of a virtuous woman, Balzac writes in *Le Peau de chagrin*: "In Paris alone do we meet such creatures whose candid faces are as pure and tender as the petals of daisies but who harbor the deepest depravity and subtlest vices—a species of denial, lacking a heart, which punishes tender souls for wanting to experience the very feeling of which they are deprived." But it was not only in Paris that such apparitions roam; they are harbored in virtually every male mind and are the subject of erotic journalism. Cézanne and Zola were alert to the world outside their readings, to the storytelling of their social environment in

newspapers, magazines, and as local gossip. And they were also aware of the opposite of the fatal woman: the angel of purity featured in thousands of nineteenth-century engravings and church publications—children of Mary, sweet and virginal, in the image of Mary the immaculate mother, nourishing breast and undefiled sex. Cézanne will sublimate such fantasies in his paintings, while Zola will expand and elaborate them in novels. The polarity of sublimation and embellishment will, in time, distinguish, though by no means entirely, the difference between their respective achievements. Literature and real life teems with variations on this syndrome fusing terror and passion—of the deadly breast in this case, the poison apple, whether kissed or bitten. Gauguin, when in Martinique, is warned by an onlooker that a melon he is about to eat had been crushed on a woman's breast and would surely poison him (Wayne Andersen, *Gauguin's Paradise Lost*, p. 46). Balzac, in *Le peau de chagrin*, deploys the breast of the angelic yet sexually voracious Pauline. Banished by her lover Raphael, Pauline finds him in his bedroom. She confronts him; he confesses his philandering. Furious and feeling vengeful, Pauline rushes to her room to commit suicide—she will give him the ultimate denial of her body by destroying it. But Raphael comes to her room and to dissuade her from dying sets about vigorously to satisfy her sexually. But in his weakened condition after years of debauchery, he dies in the effort. As he expires, he regresses to infancy; he bites Pauline's breast. And when the butler enters and tries to tear the dead Raphael from Pauline's embrace, as if cradling an infant in her arms, Pauline yells: "What are you doing? He's mine. I have killed him.".

Cézanne's phrase, "Most likely I will break my neck," is the standard fate of boys who climb recklessly up trees, ladders, and vines when attempting to conquer terror, save maidens, and be respected as men. Zola, too, will deploy the metaphor of a broken neck when acknowledging potential punishment for his literary efforts. Neck and penis coincide in the male psyche, each extending from the body and furnished with a head; in French, *cul*, meaning tail, and *cou*, meaning neck, are not remote in the psyche from the female and male sex organs, respectively.

2   *Correspondance*, Cézanne to Zola, July 26, 1858.

3   Schapiro, *Cézanne*, 1952, p. 23.

4   Baudelaire's translation of Poe's poems was published in 1856. *Histoire extraordinaire* (Tales of Mystery and Imagination).

5   So persistent is this motif in French Catholicism that in 1972, at Chartres Cathedral, I witnessed a catechism class of young girls being taught to conquer temptation of the flesh by resisting demons, to never question the word of God but to submit without question or else suffer the entrance of Satan into their bodies. These girls had just come from an art class of sorts, having painted a huge paper mural depicting a girl on a castle turret casting down demons, like a Juliet on her balcony with a knife, slashing at climbing ropes, sending a swarm of Romeos to crash on the cobbles, breaking their necks (penises).

6   Rewald, Cat. No. 240, for example.

NOTES TO CHAPTER 9

¹   Rewald states this throughout his many books on Cézanne. See his comment at *Correspondance*, Cézanne to Zola, November 17, 1858. This is said also by Meyer Schapiro: "We know of a prolonged struggle with his powerful father whom he feared greatly and who destined him, as his only son, for the family bank, sending him to law school against his wishes," *Paul Cézanne* (New York: Abrams, 1952, 1962), p. 22. But nowhere in actual documentation have I found evidence that Cézanne feared his father beyond what is typical for growing boys responding to parental discipline and advice. Louis-Auguste should hardly be condemned for having his son's best interests in mind, such as a future, when a career as an artist hardly meant having a future. Of course, the universality of «father fear» does not reduce the signicance of it in Cézanne's case. I am objecting only to the extremes to which the «conflict» has been carried in Céanne biographies—such extremes appropriate to novels but not to art history.

²   The coincidence of the word *droit* is pointed out by Theodore Reff, "Cézanne and Hercules," *Art Bulletin* 48, no. 1 (March 1966), pp. 35-44.

³   For these examples, see Reff, "Cézanne and Hercules," p. 37.

⁴   Prodicus' celebrated allegory was included in school editions of Xenophon's *Memorabilia*. Cézanne and Zola may have come upon a passage in Musset's *Rolla*, reading: *Hercule, fatiqué de sa tâche eternelle, s'assit un jour, dit-on, entre un double chemin* (Hercules, worn out by his eternal tasks, came to rest, it's said, at a crossroads). And in Cicero's *De officiis*, Hercules comes up in a discussion of the ways one chooses a career. This contrast between the imaginative and the practical life, implied in such interpretations of the Hercules legend, comes through the ages in many and various forms, even showing up in Schiller's *Ideal and Life*, where Hercules bears every toil on earth until life's mournful close, when the mortal part of him is forsaken and the godly part is taken to Mount Olympus. For more see Reff, "Cézanne and Hercules," p. 35; Cicero, *De officiis* I: 115-21. Frederick Brown, *Zola: A Life*, p. 318, note 8, made the interesting observation that the antithetical brothers in Zola's *La Conquête de Plassans* (Serge and Octave) call to mind the myth of Hercules at the crossroads wondering whether to take the path of pleasure or of duty.

⁵   *Correspondance*, Cézanne to Zola, December 7, 1858. See Zola, *Correspondance*, p. 162, note 3, where the authors propose that *Pitot* was a nickname for a supervisor at the Bourbon, and that Zola's poem, *Enfocé de pion*, features the same person. This seems a bit far-fetched, as *pitot* was also in general use as a term for a rather pitiful, lazy student.

⁶   *En relisant tes lettres de 'l'année dernière, je suis tombeé sur le petit poème d'Hercule entre le vice et la vertu.*

⁷   *O Droit, qui t'enfanta, quelle cervelle informe*
Créa, pour mon malheur, le Digeste difforme?
Et ce code incongru, que n'est-il demeuré
Durant un siècle encore dans le France ignore?
Quelle étrange fureur, quelle bêtise et quelle
Folie avait troublé ta tremblant cervelle,
O piètre Justinien des Pandectes facteur,
Et du Corpus juris impudent rédacteur?
N'était-ce pas assez qu'Horace et que Virgile,

Que Tacite et Lucain, d'un texte difficile
Vinssent, durant huit ans, nous présenter l'horreur,
Sans t'ajouter à eux, causes de mon malheur!
S'il existe un enfer, et qu'une place y reste.
Dieu du ciel, plongez-y le Gérant du Digeste!

8   *Tu sais que de Boileau, l'omoplate cassée*
Fut trouvée l'an dernier sans un profond fossé,
Et que creusant plus bas des maçons y trouvèrent
Tous ses os racornis, qu'à Paris ils portèrent.
Là, dans un muséum, ce roi des animaux
Fut classé dans le rang des vieux rhinocéros.
Puis on grava ces mots, au pieds de sa carcasse:
'Ci-repose Boileau, le recteur du Parnasse.'

9   In some stories, in a fit of madness inflicted by Hera, Hercules kills his wife and children. To make amends he is condemned to perform the twelve labors. Should one plunge into the depth of Cézanne's psyche, one might find that the decision to undertake law studies could have generated a feeling that he'd killed his marriage to art-as-woman and the babies his copulation of the art-muse would produce. Artists and poets alike experience such pregnancies and deliveries: in French, the issuing of a baby or a book is expressed with the same words and phrases. On the publication of his first book, Zola says he feels as if he has just given birth to a child. The expression is almost too common to cite examples. Still, Cézanne says in a letter to Numa Coste towards the end of November 1868, "A poet must always be pregnant with some Iliad, or rather with a personal Odyssey."

10   As a professor at MIT for twenty years, where every entering student is an "A" pupil out of high school, and most students are aimed in the career direction of their father, I have had any number of occasions to observe intentional failures by young men who resist by showing they are incapable to achieve what their father has in mind.

11   *Charles* Baudelaire: *Letters from His Youth*, tr. Simona Morini and Frederic Tuten; ed. Enid Starkie (New York: Doubleday & Company, 1970), p. 75. Letter of August 3, 1838.

12   In my draft, I spelled this "canons," which, like a "Freudian slip" might be called a "post-modern slip."

13   This expression is usually taken as having been said by Cézanne's father. The expression was so commonplace, however, that it should not be associated with one instance or an originator. See Rewald, *Cézanne*, 1950, p. 13 where he says Cézanne's father said it. I suspect that Rewald got the expression from Zola's letter.

NOTES TO CHAPTER 10

1   Meyer Schapiro, *Cézanne*, 1952, p. 23.
2   Reff, «Cézanne's *Dream of Hannibal*,» *Art Bulletin* 45 (June 1963), p. 149.

3   From the Goncourt journals, to be discussed later.

4   This poem will be given in its entirety in a later chapter.

5   *Correspondance*, Cézanne to Zola. January 17, 1859.

6   Reff picks up on the Latin expression used by Cézanne: *Infandum, Infandum* (unspeakable! shocking! abominable!) as alluding to the ancient Aeneas' melancholy reply to Queen Dido's entreaty, thus giving the word extreme historical weight. But it's unlikely that Aeneas would have used that expression. It is often used by Cézanne, as in his letter to Zola of July 9th, 1858, when among the pleasures he would like to discuss with him, such as hunting, fishing, and swimming, he adds love, and then quickly says, *Infandum, let us not broach that corrupting subject.* Surely the expression was a commonplace among schoolboys immersed in the classics, who, like Cézanne, enjoyed showing off their knowledge of Latin phrases, as many academic scholars still do as adults.

NOTES TO CHAPTER 11

1   Ugolino descended from a noble Tuscan lineage. In 1275, he conspired with son-in-law Giovanni Visconti to elevate the Guelphs to power in Pisa. In 1285, he and Visconti took over the Pisan government. Three years later Ugolino turned on his partner and conspired with Cardinal Ruggieri to oust the Visconti. That done, and wanting Pisa for himself, Ruggieri in turn betrayed Ugolino, took control of Pisa, and with the aid of the newly empowered Ghibellines hunted down Ugolino and imprisoned him and his male descendants (who might inherit their father's noble rank) in the Tower of Hunger. They were put away in June 1288. Kept alive for several months, perhaps on bread and water to lengthen their suffering, the doors to the tower were locked shut one day. They starved to death in February 1289.

2   *Tête de veau* and *tête de porc* were, and still are, fairly standard fare for country diners. The boiled head would be placed whole on a platter for serving. Typically, the father would do the carving and family members would call out their preferences, such as *Pour moi la langue...Moi, je prens une lèvre,* and so on. A head on the platter would not, in itself, be at all strange for a family dinner in Cézanne's era.

3   *Correspondance*, Cézanne to Zola, beginning of July 1859.

4   Kurt Badt, *Die Kunst Cézannes* (Munich: Prestel-Verlag, 1956). English translation: *The Art of Cézanne*, tr. Shiela Ann Ogilvie (Berkeley and Los Angeles: University of California Press, 1965). Meyer Schapiro, «The Apples of Cézanne: an Essay on the Meaning of Still-life,» *Art News Annual* 34 (1968); reprinted in Schapiro, *Modern Art: 19th and 20th Centuries* (New York: Braziller, 1979), pp. 1-38. Schapiro looked ahead to Cézanne's still-lifes of skulls, in particular to a picture painted in the 1890s of a young man—who Schapiro would want to call Cézanne's own son, also named Paul—seated at a table on which a skull rests on a stack of books. Rewald, Cat. No. 825. *Jeune homme à la Tête de Mort*, 1896-98. According to Joachim Gasquet, the model was the son of a local farmer. See *Gasquet's Cézanne*, p. 52.

5 I am generalizing this point made by Schapiro in «The Apples of Cézanne,» *Modern Art*, pp. 29-30. Schapiro connects this scenario with Cézanne's later still-life elements— apples, pots—as a coherent choice of a family of objects. He associates this ordered

household of objects in Cézanne's mind, and on his canvases, with the family dining table—a congregation of kinfolk; the fruit as vague references to women, to breasts and bellies if differentiated downward, or condensed as maternal presence as *au sein de la famille* (in the bosom of the family). Baudelaire, among other romantics, had also associated choice of subjects with the artist's psychology, with Delacroix in mind—whose imagination, Baudelaire said, was akin to the poet who conceives objects as virtual human presence: *Le style, c'est l'homme; mais ne pourrait-on dire avec une égale justesse: Le choix des sujets, c'est l'homme* (Style, that is the man; but one can say with equal justification: the choice of subjects is the man).

6   Meyer Schapiro, «The Apples of Cézanne,» *Modern Art*, p. 29.

7   Kurt Badt, *Die Kunst Cézannes*, p. 68. My quotations and paraphrases that follow are from the English edition (trans. Shiela Ann Oligive), *The Art of Cézanne*, with Badt's discussion of the Dante sketch running from pp. 97-107.

For another interpretation of this drawing, see Theodore Reff, «Cézanne: The Severed Head and the Skull,» *Arts Magazine* LVIII (1983), pp. 84-100.

8   *Correspondance*, Cézanne to Zola, June 20, 1859.

9   Claude Lévy-Strauss, in the introduction to *Le totémisme aujourd'hui* (Paris: Presse Universitaires de France, 1962).

10   *The Journals of Eugene Delacroix*.

11   Reproduced and discussed in Albert Elsen, *Rodin* (New York: Museum of Modern Art, 1963) p.37.

12   Elsen, *Rodin*, p. 43.

NOTES TO CHAPTER 12

1   Adrien Chappuis, *The Drawings of Paul Cézanne, A Catalogue Raisonné* (Greenwich, Connecticut: New York Graphic Society, 1973), Cat. No. 46. The notes read: *How is this fine to be proportioned...14. Only the galleys entailed no fine: all the others, one. —The fine was intended to reimburse the cost of the trial. The penalty of a fine is essentially divisible...—2ndly. Restorable; if an innocent man has been convicted his money can be refunded. —Equitable and appreciable. I.e., it can be proportioned according to the income of the delinquent. How is this fine to be proportioned..."* See Rewald's comments in *Cézanne, A Biography* (New York: Harry N. Abrams, 1986), p. 19.

2   The screen remained at the family home for forty years. After his father's death in 1886, and his mother's death in 1897, the family property, the Jas de Bouffan, was sold in 1899 to settle the estate, and Cézanne moved the paravent to his newly constructed studio at Les Lauves, a district on the edge of town.

3   The paravent is illustrated in Èmile Bernard's 1925 book, but his book, and Rivière's, too, were assembled some sixty-five years after the proposed date of the screen. The pictorial side of the paravent has been extensively restored; there is no sure way now to analyze what would have been the original brushwork. And recently the screen was enhanced for the market by being given a new title, *Environs de Aix-en-Provence*, but nothing in the imagery justifies that description, not even the mountain in the distant right side—which Rewald sees as resembling Mont Sainte-Victoire, although it does not.

Elements of the screen appear in the background of a few paintings by the mature Cézanne, but this only means that he had the screen in his studio, salvaged by him from the Jas de Bouffan after his mother's death and the sale of the estate. He may have kept the paravent intact over the years, aside from its practical use as a screen, because it was important to his personal history. The screen's practical use may have been reason enough for not discarding it.

NOTES TO CHAPTER 13

1   Brown, *Zola*, p. 310.

2   Goncourt, *Journal* II, pp. 1134-35 (May 5, 1876). Quoted by Brown, *Zola, A Life*, p. 310.

3   Goncourt, *Journal* II, p. 1059 (April 4, 1875).

4   Paul Seymard, who became a lawyer, died in 1936 apparently without knowing that he had bested the famous Cézanne with this Justine.

5   *J'y vis derrière je ne sais buisson, je ne sais quel gens, faisant je ne sais quoi, et, je ne sais comment, aiguisant je ne sais quels ferrements, qi'ils avient je ne sais où, et je ne sais en quelle manière.*

6   Charles Baudelaire, "Le Salon of 1846," Part XIII. "On Ary Scheffer and the Apes of Sentiment," in *Art in Paris 1845-1862*, tr. and ed. Jonathan Mayne (Greenwich, Connecticut: New York Graphic Society, 1965), I have condensed Baudelaire's text to suit my purpose.

NOTES TO CHAPTER 14

1   I will make use of this stanza later in the context of Cézanne's poem, *Hannibal's Dream*.

2   Even as a fully-fledged adult, Zola will dream of sex with a very young girl who is not yet a woman. «Yes, it scares me,» Goncourt reports him as saying: «I see myself hauled trembling before a jury.» Goncourt, *Journal* II, pp 1221-22 (January 28, 1878). But that fantasy is too common and widespread to make anything of it special to Zola.

3   *Permets-moi de pleurer sur l'écrivain qui meurt en toi; je le répète, la terre est bonne et fertile: un peu de culture, et la moisson devenait splendide. C'est ne pas que tu ignores cette pureté dont je te parle; tu en sais peut-être plus que moi. C'est qu'emporté par ton caractère, chantant pour chanter, peu soucieux, tu te sers des plus bizarres expressions, des plus drôlatiques tournes provençales. Loin de moi de t'en faire un crime, surtout dans nos lettres; au contraire, cela me plaît. Tu écris pour moi, et je t'en remercie; mais la foule, mon bon vieux, est bien autrement exigeante; il ne suffit pas de dire, il faut bien dire. Maintenant, si c'était un crétin, une croûte qui m'écrive, que m'importerait que sa forme fût aussi déguenillée que son idée. Mais roi, mon rêveur, toi, mon poête, je soupire quand je vois si pauvrement vêtures tes pensées, ces belles princesses. Elles sont étranges, ces belles dames, étranges comme de jeunes bohémiennes au regard bizarre, les pieds boueux et la tête fleurie. Oh! pour ce grand poête qui s'en va, rends-moi un grand peintre, ou je t'en voudrai. Toi qui as guidé mes pas chancelants sur la Parnasse, toi qui m'a soudain abandonné, fais-moi oublier le Lamartine naissant par le Raphaël futur. Je ne sais trop où je suis. Je voulais te rappeler en deux lignes ton ancien poême, et 'en demander un nouveau plus pur, plus soigné. Je voulais te dire que je ne me contentais pas des quelques vers que tu m'envoies dans chaque*

lettre; te conseiller de ne pas quitter entièrement la plume, et, dans tes moments, de me parler de quelque belle sylphide. Et voilà—je ne sais trop pourquoi—que je me perds, que je dépense futilement le papier. Pardonne-moi, mon vieux, et contente-moi; parle-moi de l'Aérienne, de quelqu'en, de quelque chose, en vers, et longuement. Bien entendu, après to examen, et sans entraver en rien tes études au musée.

⁴ *Zola, Oeuvres complètes,* XV, p. 892.

Son regard incertain qui, vague, par moment,
Sans paraître rien voir, caresse doucement,
Son pas harmonieux, sa démarche légère
Qui semble dans un vol se détacher de terre
Sa taille qui se plie au vent comme une fleur,
Me la firent dans l'ombre, en poète rêveur,
Prendre pour une fée, une vierge sereine,
Et surnommer tout bas du nom d'Aérienne.

⁵ This was, and still is, a common belief, promulgated by the Church and the military. The need to retain sperm as energy was but one way to restrain boys from masturbating.

⁶ *Correspondance,* Cézanne to Numa Costa, November 1868.

⁷ Paraphrased from Brown, *Zola,* p. 80.

⁸ See page 00 for additional texts on *L'Aérienne.*

⁹ *Correspondance,* Letter No. 25, p. 195, note 3.

NOTES TO CHAPTER 15

¹ *Correspondance,* Zola to Cézanne, February 5, 1861. The high tension Zola experienced from repressed and unrealizable instinctual goals did not result in quiet boredom, often mistaken as laziness, but actually a blend of narcissism and depersonalization equivalent to fluctuations between surges of self-esteem and ego-defeating moods. Zola managed to survive the boredom of late adolescence by having a fertile imagination and an ability to dissipate anxiety through daydreams. He offset tension by meditation on the outside world, by compulsive eating and smoking, gratifying substitutes for whatever one craves, companion activities to the productive discharge of one's instinctual urges.

² Dante, *L'Infer* V: 121-123. But Zola was recalling the phrase from reading Alfred de Musset's *Le Saule: Il ne pire douleur/Qu'un souvenir heureax dans les jours de malheur.*

³ *Correspondance,* Zola to Cézanne, June 13, 1860.

⁴ One has here a forecast of how in 1878, following the financial success of his novel *L'Assommoir,* Zola will furnish and decorate his house at Médan after his books amassed wealth—antique tapestries, oriental rugs, antiques, bric-à-brac, stained-glass windows.

NOTES TO CHAPTER 17

¹ This flies in the face of historian-novelists who would prefer that, with a few effects stuffed in a pillowcase, Cézanne had shinnied down a bed sheet out a bedroom window and hopped a passing freight train. Apparently John Rewald felt himself caught

short, for he wrote sarcastically that Louis-Auguste accompanied Paul only because he happened to have some business matters to attend to in Paris, but Rewald couldn't find a grain of proof for that, nor is there any support for Rewald's opinion that the reason for Louis-Auguste's capitulation to Cézanne's move was his son's «reproachful glances, brooding silence, and barely contained rebellion.»

2   G. du Maurier (London: Trilby, 1895), the chapter «Chez Carrel» (alias for Gleyre). See also a studio described by Edmond de Goncourt in *Manette Solomon*, (Paris, 1866), Ch. V.

3   In *«L'Art dans une démocratie,»* quoted by A. Alexandre, J. F. *Raffaëlli* (Paris, 1909), pp. 31-32.

4   Reported in E. Faure, «Renoir,» *Revue Hebdomadaire*, April 17, 1920.

5   This would be Adolphe Yvon, who may have been a student of Paul Delaroche.

6   This would be Isadore Pils, who will be elected to the Academy in 1869. See «Notice sur M. Picot, July 24, 1869,» in *Académie des Beaux-Arts: Séances publiques*, Vol. XV (1864-1870).

7   Due to the difficulty in reading handwriting, in Rewald's different publications of Cézanne's letters, Gudin is spelled Gubin. Gudin was a fairly successful painter and at least by the end of the 1860s a member of the Academy. Muller was also a member. Glaise was a favorite among collectors of sensual subject matter. I can find no record of Hamel. Gérôme and Cabanel were not yet members of the Academy but were highly acclaimed. Both would become members in 1863.

8   Paul de Saint-Victor, «Salon de 1857,» *La Presse* (August 11, 1857).

9   Paul Mantz, «Salon de 1857,» La Presse (August 11, 1857). An excellent book on Meissonier is Marc J. Gotlieb, *The Plight of Emulation: Ernest Meissonier and French Salon Painting* (Princeton: Princeton University Press, 1996). See also the catalogue of the *Ernst Meissonier: Retrospective*, curated by Philippe Durey and Constance Cain Hungerford, Lyon: Musée des Beaux-Arts (March 25-June 27, 1993); also Michael Fried, *Manet's Modernism* (Chicago: University of Chicago Press, 1996), p. 245.

Few nineteenth-century artists achieved in their day the honors awarded Meissonier. His career spanned five decades. Born in Lyon in 1815, he died in Paris in 1891. A regular exhibitor at the Paris Salon from the mid-1830s, medal winner throughout the 40s, by the 1850s Meissonier had been hailed as the leading genre painter of his generation. In 1864 his Salon entry was singled out as the supreme experience of the modern French School (it sold in 1890 for the highest price ever paid for a work by a living artist). But even though in 1889 Meissonier was the first artist to be awarded the Grand Cross of the Legion of Honor, all along his palm-strewn route to fame adverse critics pelted him as ruthlessly as Courbet or Manet had endured. Earlier in his career, Delacroix had proclaimed him the incontestable master of the epoch and Théophile Gautier admired him, but by mid-century the lure of Meissonier's technical perfection and charming subject matter attracted only passive eyes. His misguided devotion to the means of painting, one critic advised, was the ultimate consequence of a school committed to the theory of *art for art's sake* in neglect of profound ideas. «One doesn't say,» this critic adds, «that a Meissonier painting is beautiful, rather one says it's well done.» So, by the 1860s, Meissonier, the «king of easel painting,» whose quailing aspiration was to emulate great art of the palace and cathedral, was but one among an outdated lot whose paintings were designed to embellish the walls of bourgeois apartments. «God of the bourgeoisie,» proclaimed Zola, summing up Meissonier's place in the pantheon.

10   I've taken the liberty of revising this letter. Otherwise, from Rewald's editions it would appear that the first half of the letter was written after the second half. It cannot be true that on the day Cézanne said adamantly that he was going back to Aix, Zola talked him into doing his portrait. The portrait was already in process before then. So I put this sentence in the past tense.

11   From this letter Rewald derives a set of conclusions not supported by what Zola says. Rewald writes: «As we can see from Zola's letter, Cézanne did not work during the sittings exclusively but even more after the model has left.» How does Rewald know that Cézanne worked *even more* after the model left? Cézanne says only that he wanted to retouch it. Rewald also says, «While the model was there, he studies color and expression, only from time to time does he touch the canvas.» Nothing in Zola's letter says this. From where is Rewald getting his information? Rewald also says, «Once the model has left, Cézanne really began to work.» From where did he get that? And Rewald says, «Apparently the presence of a living person disturbed him and hindered him up to a point from working during the sittings.» This is the sort of hyperbole that fouls Cézanne's biographies. See Rewald, 1950, p. 24.

12   If the *Suisse* was like its later counterpart, the *Académie de la grande chamière*, where in 1962 I worked a few sessions before the model, the place was a den of mediocrity, the environment raunchy and boisterous, the models regularly jeered and crucified, and many so-called students working there were older men relaxing after a days work at jobs by gazing at a naked woman, fantasizing while tracing the same lines they had drawn a thousand times.

13   E. Viollet-le-Duc, «L'enseignement des arts,» *Gazette des Beaux-Arts* (June 1862). A longer translation will be found in Rewald, *Impressionism*, pp. 22-23.

14   Both quotations will be found in Rewald, *Impressionism*, p. 65.

NOTES TO CHAPTER 18

1   *Correspondance*, Zola to Louis Hachette, May 20, 1862.

2   Earlier known as *La Bibliothèque bleue de Troyes*, the most popular books of the eighteenth and nineteenth centuries, usually distributed by peddlers.

NOTES TO CHAPTER 19

1   Monet to Bazille, September 1968. Poulain, p. 130.

2   George Moore, in his mid-twenties, was a rather colorful and entertaining ass that offended the Café Guerbois artists, even destroying a portrait of himself that Manet had painted because it was not flattering. Degas despised him. Moore's *Reminiscences of the Impressionist Painters* (Dublin, 1906) should be read with caution. See Rewald, *Impressionism*, pp. 401-402.

3   On Cézanne's friends in Aix during the 1860s, see «Une lettre de Cézanne à

Joseph Huet,» Provincia, *Bulletin de la Société de Statistiques et d'Archéologie de Marseilles*, No. 2, 1937. Also Bruno Ely, «Cézanne, l'École de dessin et le musée d'Aix,» in *Cézanne au Musée d'Aix* (Aix-en-Provence, 1984).

4   See, for an example, John Rewald, *Studies in Impressionism* (New York: Harry N. Abrams, 1985), p. 68, note 1.

5   Pierre Cogny, *Le Huysmans intimé de Henry Céard et Jean de Caldain* (Paris: Nizet, 1957), p. 127. See more by Brown, *Zola, A Life*, pp. 125-127. The face bears a close resemblance to photographs of Alexandrine, even though the photos are of her at a later age.

6   From Zola's novel *Madeleine Férat*, published as *La Honte* (Shame) in Autumn 1868, the art historian Jean Adhémar constructed a speculative but tantalizing case for identifying the novel's heroine—a young woman without family, of loose morals, torn between her first lover and the man who marries her, the two men having been intimate childhood friends—as Alexandrine. J. Adhémar, «Le Cabinet de Travail de Zola,» *Gazette des Beaux-Arts* (November 1960), p. 297. See also A. Laborde, «Trente-huit Années près de Zola—La vie d'Alexandrine Émile Zola,» Paris, 1963; and Rewald's discussion at Cat. No. 75.

7   Daime had been the canal company manager in Aix and had supported her efforts to get legal aid from the company to sue for a share of the company. Protesting was Jules Migeon, whose interests would be better served if Émilie's case went against her. It was Migeon who claimed in his protest that Émilie's financial interests were tied in with Daime's, and that they were involved in an illicit love affair. No documentation tells us what Zola's mother's daily life was like—why as a young and attractive widow she did not remarry. Émilie may have transferred to Zola her ambitions to restore her deceased husband's financial losses, reminding him of the imperatives of money. Young as she was, it may have been emotionally difficult for her to accept that, in time, Alexandrine would share the modest quarters she had with her son. It is believed by some Zola scholars that she resisted allowing Zola to marry Alexandrine, which could explain why the marriage was delayed until Zola turned thirty, when by law he was not required to furnish parental approval. Colette Becker has established that the Civil Code then in effect required that a son obtain parental permission to marry before the age of thirty.

8   A few months later, Zola, under the pretext of reviewing a book, *Histoire de Jules César*, took up again the myth of providential man. *Salut public De Lyon* rejected the review. Zola included it in *Mes Haines*.

9   See Rewald, Cat. No. 165.

NOTES TO CHAPTER 20

1   *Le Moniteur*, April 24, 1863. On the emperor's visit to the Palais de l'Industrie, see Ernst Chesneau, «Salon de 1863,» *L'Artiste* (May 1, 1863).

2   Ingres, quoted Amaury-Duval, *L'Atelier d'Ingres*, ed. E. Faure (Paris, 1924), p. 211.

3   Étienne Delécluse, in *Journal des Débats* (May 7, 1831).

4   Étienne Delécluse, in *Journal des Débats* (March 14, 1839).

5   Boudin to Martin, September 3, 1868, in Jean-Aubry, *Eugene Boudin* (Paris, 1922),

p. 70.

6   While Zola will enter into this process and be a force promoting it, Cézanne will hold back. At times he will try to fall in step with the avant-garde that was actually accommodating bourgeois society by moving in the same direction, but on the whole, Cézanne represented the branch of the dualist avant-garde that protects its boundaries as art—art kept internally to itself. The social classes that will eventually support his art, as an art for the public, were not in place during the nineteenth century. Both the advance of Impressionism in the 1870s and the backlash against it in the 1880s, when naturalism lost ground against a surge of symbolism and spiritualism, hardly affected him. And it did not affect Zola, simply because, after the mid-1870s, he did not move in the direction of the avant-garde; his audience was expanding horizontally rather than ascending.

7   See Theodore Zeldin, *France 1848-1945: Taste and Corruption* (Oxford: Oxford University Press, 1980, pp. 119-120.

8   Théodore Gautier, «Salon de 1837» (March 8, 1837). Cited by Rewald, *Impressionism*, p. 21.

9   J. Champfleury, *Histoire de l'imagerie populaire* (Paris, 1869), p. xii. In 1857, Champfleury published a collection of his short pieces in a volume titled *Le Réalisme*. He was much respected by Manet, who included him among the personages in *La Musique aux Tuileries*. Fantin-Latour included him in his grand tableau, *Homage à Delacroix*.

10   Ernest Chesneau, «Salon of 1863,» *L'Artiste* (May 1, 1863).

11   J. Castagnary, «Le Salon des Refusés,» *L'Artiste*, August 1, 1863.

12   Philip G. Hamerton, «The Salon of 1863,» *Fine Arts Quarterly Review*, October 1863.

13   Z. Astruc, «Le Salon de 1863,» May 20, 1863. Quoted in Rewald, *Impressionism*, p. 83.

14   Z. Astruc, «Le Salon de 1863,» May 20, 1863. Quoted in Rewald, *Impressionism*, p. 83. Impression is, of course, a mark on an imprint made or inflicted on something or someone. Émile Deschanel, in 1864, explained that the word «style» means «the mark of the writer, the impression of his natural disposition in his writing.» For this and a rich discussion on the topic of *«l'impression,»* see Richard Shiff, *Cézanne and the End of Impressionism* (Chicago: University of Chicago Press, 1984), Ch. 2, «Defining Impressionism and the Impression,» pp. 14-20, and Ch. 3, «Impressionism, Truth and Positivism,» pp. 21-26. See also an important discussion by Albert Boime, *The Academy and French Painting in the Nineteenth Century* (New York, 1971), Ch. IX, «The Aesthetics of the Sketch,» pp. 167-184. I remind my readers, however, that I do not regard any discussion of «impression» or «tempérament» dating later than 1870 as useful to my text, as the meanings underwent transformations when uttered retrospectively.

15   Louis Etienne, «Le Jury et les exponants» (1863).

16   Théophile Thoré, *Salons*, 1863.

17   Jules Castagnary, «Salon of 1863,» reprinted in *Salons*, 1892.

18   Viollet-le-Duc, «L'Enseignement des arts,» *Gazette des Beaux-Arts*, Vol. XII (January-June, 1862), p. 135. On the teaching reforms of 1863, see Albert Boime, *The Academy and French Painting in the Nineteenth Century*; Albert Boime, «The Teaching Reforms of 1863 and the Origins of Modernism in France,» *Art Quarterly*, n.s., 1 (Autumn 1977),

pp. 1-39; Shiff, *Cézanne and the End of Impressionism,* pp. 70-78. Much of the debate over originality during the 1850s had to do with the withdrawal from romanticism and the difficulty in finding the right way to speak of naturalism and realism. No single source can tell us when and how the arguments were formulated. For Corot, it was necessary to interpret nature with naïveté and personal sentiment, which had led him in earlier years to submit to the first impression of a landscape and to capture the effect in his studies, his oil sketches. For Courbet, imagination in art was in knowing how to find the most complete expression of an existing thing, but never in creating the thing itself. Cf. Linda Nochlin, *Realism and Tradition in Art 1848-1900* (Hammonsdworth and Baltimore, 1971), pp. 35-38. Nochlin has important things to say about this, especially about the difference between romantic *naïveté* and realist *sincérité.*

[19]   Ludovic Vitet, «Les art du dessin en France,» *Revue des deux mondes* (November 1, 1864), pp. 74-107. For more on this see Boime, *The Academy and French Painting,* pp. 174-184, and Shiff, *Cézanne and the End of Impressionism,* pp. 71-75.

[20]   In 1863, Théophile Thoré, *Salons of W. Bürger,* Vol. 1, (Paris, 1870), p. 421.

[21]   Edouard Manet, *Reasons for Holding a Private Exhibition* (1867).

[22]   Duranty's complete text in English is reprinted in Charles S. Moffett, *The New Painting: Impressionism 1874-1876* (Geneva: Richard Burton, 1986), pp. 37-47. In this same volume, see Shiff's essay, «The End of Impressionism,» where on p. 71 he writes that *vérité* was often used by critics in conjunction with *naïveté* and *sincérité.*

[23]   When the status of the sketch aroused controversy in the late 1820s, the government of the July Monarchy proposed a series of public sketch contests to demonstrate an accepting attitude towards the wider community of artists. Even back then, the relaxation of technical skill had allowed an authentic proletariat of painters to emerge and demand representation, a situation not unlike what would develop in the 1860s.

[24]   Boime, *The Academy and French Painting in the Ninetieth Century,* pp. 166-181—a fine chapter on the *première pensée,* the sketch, originality, and so on. Boime's text suffers just a bit, however, from an excess of data, quotations, references, and so on, from much too broad an historical base—from the early nineteenth century to the twentieth, from France to England, and so on. No one back then knew that much. The comments made by Monet, for example, are retrospective—his memory from the 1880s of what he felt in the 1860s cannot be accepted as evidence of what he actually felt in the 1860s, having in the meantime read books and articles and reviews that put words in his mouth and elevated to the status of principles what may have been, twenty years earlier, nothing more than vague hunches. Artists rarely know what they are doing at the time they do it. I have tried in this book to not go beyond what Zola and Cézanne would most likely have read, known, been aware of, etc.

[25]   For more on this, see Wayne Andersen, «Border and Frontier, Definition and Prestige: L'Art à sa Fin,» *The European Legacy,* Vol. 1, No. 8 (1996), pp. 2274-2279.

[26]   Delacroix, «Lettre sur les concours,» *L'Artiste,* Vol. 1 (1831), p. 50. Reprinted in Delacroix, *Correspondance générale,* ed. André Joubin, Vol. 1, (Paris, 1936-38), p. 268. See Boime, *The Academy and French Painting in the Nineteenth Century,* p. 119 (pp. 115-121) for a thorough discussion of the official practice of the sketch.

[27]   See Alfred Sensier, *La vie et l'oeuvre de Millet* (Paris, 1881), Vol. I, p. 214.

[28] Baudelaire, «The salon of 1859: Letters to the editor of the *Revue française*» (1859).

NOTES TO CHAPTER 21

[1] See Michael Fried, *Manet's Modernism* (Chicago and London: University of Chicago Press, 1996), p. 259.

[2] I develop this topic more thoroughly in my *Picasso's Brothel* (New York: Other Press, 2001).

[3] P. de Saint-Victor, in *Hommage à Cézanne*, ed. F. Desnoyers (Paris, 1886). Cf. Rewald, Impressionism, p. 18.

[4] *Zola, Oeuvres complètes* X, p. 735.

[5] Charles Baudelaire, *The Exposition Universelles*, p. 125.

[6] Charles Dickens, *Les Grandes Espérances and Oliver Twist*.

NOTES TO CHAPTER 22

[1] Printed almost verbatim in «Faits divers,» *Le Moniteur universel*, November 23, 1865.

[2] In *Psychology of Love*, Freud concluded that the fantasy allows the harlot to be symbolically the man's mother, who falls like an Eve when the son realizes that his mother is a sexual creature rather than an eternal virgin. Typical of his structural methodology, Freud assigns the rescue to a first cause and first instance, while ignoring that the urge to rescue is broadly based in human psychology and integral to the larger complex of instincts for biological survival. Most girls dream of being rescued, and what is a honeymoon other than a bride who is bridled, mounted, and ridden off by a groom (Get it?).

[3] Quoted by Brown, *Zola*, p. 308.

[4] Pajot seems to identify Zola with Claude, for he used *tu etc. etc.*

[5] Cabronne denied doing that, but the story stuck and was well known to most everyone in France in the 1860s. The expression, *faire un Cabronne* is a polite way of saying, «shit on...». But *merde* in French has never been as strong a word as its English equivalent. Even young French children today are as likely to say *merde* as American children would say, «damn.»

[6] Barbey d'Aurevilly, 1972, p. 121.

[7] *Quoi qu'il en soit, la donnée de l'ouvrage n'est pas immorale. Ce que l'auteur s'est proposé, c'est de dégoûter la jeunesse de ses liaisons impures où elle se laisse entraîner sur la foi des poètes qui ont idéalisé les amours de la bohème. M.. Zola donne à ces poètes un énergiquentique: «Leurs maîtresses,» dit-il, «étaient infâmes; leurs amours avaient toutes les horreurs des amours du ruisseau; ils ont été trompés, blessés, traînés dans la boue; jamais ils n'ont rencontré un cœur et chacun d'eux a eu sa Laurence qui a fait de sa jeunesse une solitude désolée.» Il faut donc tuer les Laurence, puisqu'elles nous tuent notre chair et nos amours. A ceux qui sont affolés de lumière et de pureté, je dirai: «Prenez garde; vous entrez dans la nuit, dans la souillure.» A ceux dont le cœur dort et qui ont l'indifférence du mal, je dirai: «Puisque vous ne pouvez aimer, tâchez au moins de rester dignes et honnêtes.» C'est la moralité que Claude tire lui-même de sa confession. Je ne pense donc pas, Monsieur le Garde des Sceaux, que*

l'ouvrage intitulé La Confession de Claude doive être poursuivi comme contraire à la morale publique.

NOTES TO CHAPTER 23

1   Delacroix's *Barque de Dante* was acquired by the state from the Salon of 1822. Until 1874 it was housed in the Musée du Luxembourg, then transferred to the Louvre. For a complete bibliography and discussion of Cézanne's copy see Rewald, Cat. No. 172. Rewald dates the copy c. 1870, while Lawrence Gowing and Robert Ratcliffe assigned it to 1864, and Lionello Venturi had dated it 1870-75. In my opinion, it is the same canvas as the one mentioned in Cézanne's letter, which he had not yet retouched. Because Cézanne retouched certain pictures sometimes years later, there is no reason to hypothesize a later copy.

2   Roger Fry actually said, «Cézanne counts pre-eminently as a great classic master. We may almost sum him up as the leader of the modern return to Mediterranean conceptions of art-his saying that 'he wished to do Poussin after nature' is no empty boast. Cézanne then was a Classic artist, but perhaps all great Classics are made by the repression of a Romantic.» Fry, *Cézanne, A Study of His Development,* 1932, p. 87.

3   In 1962 I found high up on a shelf in one of Jean-Pierre Cézanne's closets in Paris a cardboard box containing a few things not discovered by previous archivists, and not known even to Jean-Pierre. Among the things was Cézanne's wallet, the contents of which I published as «Cézanne's *Carnet violet-moiré,*» *The Burlington Magazine,* CVII (1965), pp. 313-318.

NOTES TO CHAPTER 24

1   Zola depends heavily on Taine's innovative ideas, which Prosper Lucas' text supported. Lucas, a theoretician of heredity, stimulated Zola's series of novels, which contrasted the genetic properties of the two family branches. Over 1847 to 1850, Lucas published segments of an enormous study, with perhaps the longest book title in the history of writing: *Traité philosophique et physiologique de l'hérédité naturelle dans les états de santé et de maladie du système nerveaux, avec l'application méthodique des lois de la procréation au traitement général des affections dont elle est le principe; ouvrage où la question est considérée dans ses rapports avec les lois primordiales, les théories de la génération, les causes déterminantes de la sexualité, les modifications acquises de la nature originale des êtres et les diverses formes de névropathie et d'aliénation mentale.*

On this subject in a larger context, see Shiff, *Cézanne and the End of Impressionism,* p. 20, who writes, «The conclusion to be drawn from the writings of Deschanel, Littré, Castagnary, Caussy, and others is this: an art of the impression (or of sensation) may vary greatly from artist to artist, in accord with the individual's physiological or psychological state or, in other terms, with his temperament or personality. Whatever truth or reality is represented must relate to the artist himself as well as to nature. Indeed, one might say that the artist paints a self' on the pretext of painting nature.»

2   Zola may have in mind at this date the long review of Flaubert's *Madame Bovary* by Valéry Vernier that appeared in the opposition paper *La Revue de mois* in March 1863.

3   Taine sets this forth in his *Essai sur les fables de La Fontaine* (1853).

4   Zola cites three of the anti-materialist «*spiritualists*» who admit to the existence of a soul and insist that thought is not a product or even a function of the brain. Jouffroy was a professor at the Sorbonne and the Collège de France; Maine de Biran and his colleague Victor Cousin were professors at the Sorbonne.

5   Émile Deschanel, *Physiologie des écrivains et des artistes*, p. 335. *Dans ce qu'on nomme les oeuvres de l'esprit, tout ne s'explique pas par l'esprit. Mais aussi, à plus forte raison, tout ne s'explique pas par la matière.* I'm accepting «spirit» is the closest I can get in English to the French *esprit*.

6   The reference is to a letter from Zola to Valabrègue of July 6th, 1864, discussing *La Genèse*, a composite of three poems on the subjects of science and philosophy.

NOTES TO CHAPTER 25

1   Zola to Valabrègue, February 6, 1865.

2   On this and the larger picture of authors and publishers, see John Lough, *Writer and Public in France* (Oxford: Clarendon Press, 1978), p. 333 *passim*.

3   I am following Brown's discussion in *Zola*, p. 161.

4   Brown, *Zola*, p. 161.

5   P. Mantz, «Le Salon de 1863,» *Gazette des Beaux-Arts* (June 1863). For Zola's attack on Offenbach, see his *causerie* of October 3, 1869 in *Le Figaro*.

6   To the extent that Zola was aware of economic hierarchies in literature, he had forsaken poetry, which was still regarded as writing *par excellence*, untainted by commerce. During the Second Empire, poetry was at the summit of the hierarchy, consecrated by the Romantic tradition that had flowed into the writings of Gautier and Baudelaire. Poetry's readership is primarily other poets. At the low end of the hierarchy was theater, which was subordinate to the values and whims of the general public. Poetry and theater pivot around the novel, with poetry the least mercantile and theater the most, while inversely, poetry is the most sanctified and theater the least. The novel had acquired its status from the writings of Balzac, Stendahl, and Flaubert, while remaining associated with mercantile literature, still tied to journalism by the *roman feuilleton*. More than anything, this tie to commercialism will cleave Zola from Cézanne as to their professions when Zola finally succeeds as a novelist. Painting is necessarily an activity limited to unique works, hence more noble than the novel and more consecrated by the bourgeois. But, insofar as avant-garde painting has, like poetry, a restricted market and is not for public consumption, it cannot satisfy the demands of a large audience. Zola will break the novel free from the serial, but only when substantial earnings permit publication of bound books reaching a very wide audience. For more, see Pierre Bourdieu, *Les Règles de l'art* (Paris: Editions du Seuil, 1992), trans. Susan Emanuel, *The Rules of Art* (Stanford: Stanford University Press, 1995). See the chapter «The Emergence of a Dualist Structure.»

NOTES TO CHAPTER 26

1   Oller's Biblical battle scene was perhaps as much a gesture towards conforming to Salon subject matter as Edgar Degas' *Medieval War Scene*—Degas' one and only historical painting and first Salon entry.

2   Quoted in Hamilton, *Manet and His Critics*, pp. 189-90.

3   *La grossièreté n'est pas la force, non plus la brutalité n'est la franchise, ni le scandale la réputation.* Nadar, *Jury au Salon de 1853* (Paris, 1853), not paginated.

4   Alfred H. Barr, Jr., «Cézanne d'après des lettres de Marion à Morstatt: 1865-68,» *Gazette des Beaux-Arts* (January 1937). Letter dated Summer 1867. Barr's article is translated and published by Margaret Scolari in *Magazine of Art* 31 (May 1938), pp. 288-91.

5   Rewald, cat. r., p. 93.

6   Barr, Marion to Morstatt.

7   Letter from Madame F. to J. L. Le Coeur, June 6, 1866 in *Cahier's d'Aujourd'hui*, January 1921.

8   Ironically, a hostile critic to Manet's *Olympia* referred to Olympia as a rotting corpse. See Yve-Alain Bois and Rosalind E. Krauss, *Formless: A User's Guide* (Cambridge, MA: MIT Press, 1997), p. 15, note 13.

9   «*Le jury,*» April 27, 1866. This essay was followed by *Le moment artistique* (May 4), *M. Manet* (May 7), *Les réalistes au Salon* (May 11), *Les chutes* (May 15), *Adieux d'un critique d'art* (May 16).

10   Odilon Redon, in his «Le Salon de 1868,» *La Gironde*, May 19, June 9, July 1, 1868, would also use the term «moment.» «It is impossible not to recognize the exact hour at which Mr. Daubigny has been working. He is the painter of a moment, of an impression.»

11   Zola, «M. Manet,» *L'Événement*, May 7, 1866.

12   Michael Fried astutely summarized Zola's criticism: «Not only *is* Zola unsympathetic to painting that relates to earlier painting [as Manet's *Olympia* to Titian's *Venus of Urbino*], not only do the topics of Frenchness and schools of painting leave him cold, not only is his use of the term *tableau* without the least connotation of achieved unity, there is also in his writing not a jot of interest in absorption [reflective viewing]; in short, his art criticism stands amazingly detached from discursive commentary on painting. His unshakable conviction that considerations of subject matter, composition, and expression have no bearing on questions of art was the basis of his originality as a critic—it was, to put it badly, what enabled him not to be put off by Manet. But it is also his peculiar limitations as a guide *to* the pictorial culture of the 1860s, which took all those considerations extremely seriously.» Zola's ill-informed notion that true art does not acknowledge its subject matter was, as Fried says, not an original and fecund insight but an endowed myth that would lead art criticism down the path of a disinterested formalism. Michael Fried, *Manet's Modernism* (Chicago: University of Chicago Press, 1996), p. 248 and notes 129-133.

13   Zola, *Mon Salon, Écrits*, pp. 148, 134.

14   This principle of literature still prevails among many French critics. The most recent I've come upon is Jean d'Ormesson, *Une autre histoire de la littérature française* II (Paris: NiL éditions, 1998). *S'il fallait résumer en deux mots l'image que nous nous faisons de la littérature, nous dirons: la plaisir et le style. Ils ne cessent de se mêler et de s'entrecroiser. Les plaisis: les*

histoires, l'intrigue, les personnages, la surprise et la gaieté, l'intelligence et la hauter, le souvenir et l'espérance. Tout cela n'est rien et ne peut rien être sans le dieu mysterieux qui règne sur les mots et qui donne son statut à la littérature.

[15] Sainte-Beuve, *Madame Bovary, Causeries du lundi* (Paris: Garnier frères, 1851-1862), XIII, p. 76].

[16] Charles Coypel, «Dialogue de M. Coypel, premier peintre du Rois sur l'exposition des Tableau dans le Salon du Louvre en 1747,» an extract from *Le Mercure de France* (November 1751). Quoted in Thomas E. Crow, *Painters and Public Life in Eighteenth-Century Paris* (New Haven: Yale University Press, 1985), p. 10. Though dealing only with the eighteenth century, Crow's book has considerable significance for understanding the Salon and the Salon's public in the nineteenth century.

[17] Zola, *Mon Salon*, 1866. *Écrits*, p. 60.

[18] Zola, «Édouard Manet» (1867), *Écrits*, p. 99; and «Édouard Manet,» *Mon Salon* (1866), *Écrits*, p. 60. For more, see Shiff, *Cézanne and the End of Impressionism*, pp. 31-31.

[19] Émile Zola, *Mon Salon* (1866).

[20] Eugène Delacroix, «Questions sur le beau,» *Revue des Deux Mondes*, 2nd ser. 7 (1854), p. 313. For this in a larger context, see Shiff, «The End of Impressionism,» in Moffett, *Impressionism*, p. 74.

[21] Valabrègue to Marion, April 1866, in M. Scolari and Alfred Barr, Jr., «Cézanne in the Letters of Marion to Morstatt: 1865-1868,» *Magazine of Art*, February, April, May 1938.

NOTES TO CHAPTER 27

[1] Jules Claretie, «Deux heures au Salon de 1865,» *L'Artiste* (May 1865). Reprinted in *Peintres et sculpteurs contemporains* (Paris, 1873), p. 109.

[2] Paul de Saint-Victor in *La Presse* (1865).

[3] Théophile Gautier, *Le Moniteur universel* (June 24, 1865).

[4] *Le Charivari* was founded in 1832 by Charles Philipon as a daily satirical pamphlet. Daumier and Gavarni were its most noted cartoonists. The magazine launched attacks on the July monarchy and the bourgeoisie. After a few decades of obscurity, it resurfaced during the Second Empire when it extended its coverage to include politics, literature, and drama.

[5] L. Leroy in *Le Charivari* (May 5, 1865).

[6] The reference is to Manet's *Episode d'un combat de taureaux.*

[7] I have taken some liberties quoting Leroy's script because certain words and expressions in his day, and in his language, do not seem so funny today. So I have substituted cultural equivalents.

[8] *Mes Haines*, May 7, 1866

[9] *L'Événement* (May 7, 1866).

[10] Zola, *Mes Haines.*

[11] This is from his article «Proudhon et Courbet,» reprinted in *Mes Haines.* Cf. Rewald, *Impressionism*, p. 143.

[12] Zola, «Une nouvelle manière en peintre, M. Édouard Manet,» *La Revue du XIXe*

Siècle, January 1, 1867, also in Zola, *Édouard Manet, étude biographique et critique* (Paris, May 1867). *Écrits*, pp. 101-02. For a larger discussion of Zola's statements on Manet from a somewhat different point of view than mine, see Shiff, *Cézanne and the End of Impressionism*, pp. 93-95.

13   Zola, *Mes Haines*, p. 98.

14   Zola, «Le Salon de 1866,» reprinted in Zola, *Salons*, ed. F. W. J. Hemmings and Robert J. Neiss, *Société de Publications Romanes et Françaises*, 63 (Paris: Minard, 1959), p. 71.

15   Zola, *Mon Salon*, in *L'Événement*, April 27-May 20, 1866.

16   Bazille to his parents. April 16, 1866. Daulte, p. 52.

17   Zola, *Mon Salon, in L'Événement*, April 27-May 20, 1866. Also included in *Mes Haines*. Although I would like to, I can attach no significance to the fact that Zola ends his final Salon with Pissarro, and a century later, John Rewald opens his *History of Impressionism* with Pissarro.

NOTES TO CHAPTER 28

1   See R. Walter, «Cézanne à Bennecourt,» *Gazette des Beaux-Arts* (February 1962).

2   Translation by John Rewald, which I have slightly modified.

3   Rewald, Cat. No. 97. R. Walter, in the *Gazette des Beaux-Arts* (February 1962) identified the sitter as the father of Madame Dumont—père Rouvel—with whom Cézanne and his friends lodged at Bennecourt.

4   See Rewald, Cat. No. 97, where Laurence Gowing disputes that this canvas was painted out-of-doors. But if Cézanne cut down the canvas and painted out the remaining background, it would appear to have been painted indoors. See also Rewald, Cat. No. 83, where a landscape background seems to have been painted out.

5   The word *un cheveu* in Cézanne's letter would mean «a single hair» but his handwriting is not easily transcribed. I am assuming he meant *un cheval*.

6   As identified by R. Walter, *Gazette des Beaux-Arts* (February 1962), and «Aux sources de l'Impressionisme Bennecourt,» *L'Oeil* (April 1988), pp. 32-33.

7   I cannot avoid linking this setting to the black forge of Zola's novel *L'Assommoir* where, in one of his most dazzling erotic scenes, Zola has a passionate Gervaise watching Goujet rhythmically laying on hammer blows while the boy Étienne fans the fire with bellows.

8   See below, p. 00.

9   Letter from the spring of 1865, in Poulain, p. 50.

NOTES TO CHAPTER 29

1   Rewald, in *Paul Cézanne Correspondance* (Paris, 1937, p. 101, note 1. *Les obstacles que le père de Cézanne croyant devoir élever à la carrière artistique de son fils avaient rendu celui-ci très sévère contre ses parents et ainsi s'explique le passage ci-dessus.*

2   In the role of big brother, he also may have had sexual feelings towards his sister. It would be exceptional if he didn't, particularly towards Marie, who was two years younger: at her age between thirteen and fourteen, she would have come into blossom

and sexual awakening about the same time as Cézanne did at the age of fifteen to six-teen. Most likely, Cézanne's first look at female nakedness was at his sisters, whether inad-vertently or when peeking, and if he needed an image of a live naked girl to accommo-date his fantasy when masturbating, Marie was an opportune resource. About 1859, when in an agonizing need to find an outlet for his dammed up libido, Cézanne had composed a poem entitled Marie. This poem was private, written on the back of an unrelated draw-ing. Was this Marie his sister, or some other Marie? The name was common, and was, of course, the name of the Virgin Mary.

> My gracious Marie
> I love you, and I beg you
> To save the written words
> That your friends send to you
>
> On your lovely pink lips
> This bonbon will easily glide
> It passes through many things
> Without spoiling their color
>
> That lovely pink bonbon
> So nicely shaped
> In a pink mouth
> Would happily enter.

POÈME
Ma gracieuse Marie
Je vous aime et je vous prie
De garder les mots d'écrit
Que vous envoient vos amis.

Sur vos belles lèvres roses
Ce bonbon glissera bien,
Il passe sur bien des choses
Sans en gâter le carmin.
Ce joli bonbon rose
Si sentiment tourné
Dans une bouche rose
Serait heureux d'entrer.

3   I believe that Cézanne is talking about literature here, not about painting.

4   In 1867, Marius Roux had attempted to promote Cézanne in Marseilles, and had exhibited one of his pictures in a shop window. Valabrègue reported on the public's reception of it: «the onlookers stupefied. I think that if the painting had been on display much longer, the show would have ended with the crowd breaking the window and destroying the picture.»

5   As in Zola, «Édouard Manet,» *Mon Salon* (1868). *Écrits*, 100-103, 142.

6   A piece of lore, perhaps factual, tells us that when Monet was in the forest at Chailly, near Barbizon, in early 1866, desperate to finish his huge 165 x 59-inch *Déjeuner sur l'herbe* in time for the Salon, Courbet passed by and offered to help, adding, to Monet's regret, plenty of last-minute black. It is said that this was the primary reason Monet cut up the canvas, salvaging only two parts. Another piece of lore: in the 1850s, or maybe the 1860s, there was purported to be a Bitumen School of painters that convened over summers at Pont-Aven in Brittany. As the story is told, one summer the *École Bitume* mounted an exhibition during a week of extremely high temperatures. Over one night, with the doors closed and heat building up inside, the paint melted and slid downward off the canvases, to be found the next morning as puddles of tar on the floor See Andersen, *Gauguin's Paradise Lost*, p. 42.

7   Even today, brown suits and brown shoes are worn by less than sophisticated men. Consider Frank Zappa's proclamation: «Brown Shoes Don't Make It.»

8   Too much has been made of Cézanne's habit at the *Suisse* of placing a pure black and a pure white cloth at the model stand, for that was common practice in teaching studios; between the black and the white students were to adjust their values, as still today when professional photographers say that a perfect print must have somewhere on it a pure black and a pure white, otherwise it will appear washed out.

NOTES TO CHAPTER 30

1   Vollard's information was not from Cézanne but probably from Antoine Guillemet, who would also be a key source of information for Zola's fabrication of *L'Oeuvre* (Guillemet, two years younger than Cézanne, lived to the age of seventy-eight and was in touch with Vollard up to the end. Wanting to connect these non-existing pictures with certain canvases of the 1870s that have also been titled *Un Après-midi à Naples* (though not by Cézanne), Rewald assigned a certain Cézanne watercolor to 1866-67, saying it is a study for one of the 1867 paintings, *Le Punch au Rhum*. In this watercolor one sees a naked woman and an equally naked man, both sprawled on the floor, the man smoking his pipe; a fully dressed, servant-type woman enters bearing in her outstretched hands a tray on which rests a pot. That pot alone may have been enough for Rewald to associate this picture with the title *Le Punch au Rhum* and connect it with the pictures described by Vollard and titled by Guillemet. But surely this watercolor is one of several pictures from the 1870s that bear the title *Un Après-midi à Naples*. *See Rewald, Cat. No. 34*. Rewald's stylistic analysis to support the mid-1860s date is not at all convincing. The titles—*Le Punch au Rhum* and *Un Après-midi à Naples, Le Vidangeur*—belong to the mid-1860s but all of the images we have by Cézanne that correspond to these titles date to the early 1870s. Three versions of the *Afternoon in Naples* exist today as paintings, and there are also a few drawings (Chappuis 284-286). The setting for each is a *cabinet particulier* (private room) in a brothel or the type of cabaret that provided private rooms for amorous rendez-vous. One very small canvas (Rewald 289), just a bit larger than 5 X 9 inches, depicts a debauched couple sprawled on a bed; from the left a female waiter rushes in with a tray of refreshments; at the right is a round table holding bottles; above the table one can make out a parrot. In another version (Rewald 290), the man and woman

are in a post-coital conversation following a passionate bout that knocked over a chair and put the bed covers in disarray. A servant enters the room bringing food and drink to the couple. In yet a third version (Rewald 291), the couple seem again to be relaxing, although like the mirliton of yore, the woman has an aspect of aggressiveness in her pose and the props are rather exotic: a North African servant, Rococo vases, a mirror at bedside for self-voyeuring. All of the elements in these three versions—private spaces set off by heavy curtains, food and wine service, a parrot on a stand, vases for flowers—and even cats, which appear in a couple of Cézanne's drawings related to this theme, are standard accouterments of the nineteenth-century French brothel, and still today. This *cabinet particulier* theme was made popular in the 1870s by Jean-Louis Forain, who was well known for descriptions of the sensuous life of Paris. In 1883, Huysmans singled out a watercolor of a man, a woman, and a servant in a *cabinet particulier* to typify Forain's imagery. [«Exposition des Indépendants,» *L'Art Moderne*, 1883; reprinted in Huysmans, *L'Art Moderne*, Paris, 1929, pp. 122 ff. Cf. Gustave Geffroy, «J.-L. Forain: L'Homme et l'Oeuvre,» *L'Art et les Artistes*, Paris, N.S. IV, 1921-22, pp. 54-58. See Joseph C. Sloan, Jr., «Religious Influence on the Art of Jean-Louis Forain,» *The Art Bulletin*, XXIII, 1941, pp. 199-206]. Cézanne was acquainted with Forain. In a letter to his son of August 3rd, 1906, touched by having received a message of kind thoughts from Forain, he wrote that their acquaintance went back a long time, «to 1875 at the Louvre.» A recollection after more than thirty years had passed, it may be that 1875 is a generalized date; their acquaintance may date earlier. Cézanne told Vollard that when he first met Forain, he was very young, that «the little bugger already knew how to render fabrics.» Forain moved freely in the Impressionist circle at least as early as 1871. [See Claude Roger-Marx, «Les peintres de la vie de société—Forain,» *L'Amour de l'Art*, XIV, No. 3 (March 1933), p. 54. Forain's chronology, especially of his early work, is not at all clear. Stylistic evidence would date *Le Vieux gentilhomme* to as early as 1872. His career began in the second half of the 1860's. By 1870 he was taken by Degas' style and followed it closely until after 1875 when he leaned toward the style of Manet. It was precisely around 1872 that Degas achieved, especially in the costumes of his ballet dancers, the harshly luminous effect that appears in the Forain, and began rendering his studies in long, loose lines like those in Forain's background. See, respectively, *Musiciens de l'Orchestre* of ca. 872 and *Danseuse aux Cheveux longs* of 1872-74 in Lillian Browse, *Degas Dancers*, Boston, n.d. (1964), Nos. 5 and 25]. Forain's *Le Vieux gentilhomme* (translatable as The Dirty Old Man) is remarkably similar in content-structure to Cézanne's theme: an old man slouched in an armchair being smothered by an excited ballet girl, looks up to see a female servant entering with a tray of food and drink. Even the arrangement of characters from left to right—servant, female, male—corresponds to the order in Cézanne's *Afternoon in Naples*, and in two of his three canvases the woman is holding the man down. The attitude of the servant in one of Cézanne's pictures is rather the same as in Forain's; and in one of Cézanne's examples appears an armchair of the same type as the one in Forain's, and in the same position. It is tempting to connect Cézanne's *Afternoon in Naples* with Manet's *Olympia*, for Manet's picture also has a servant bringing something—flowers, in this case—to a prostitute, and a cat appears in a couple of Cézanne's drawings of this theme. Rewald sees the cat and concludes reflexively that it had come from Manet's *Olympia*, as if there were no other cats in Paris. (Rewald, Cat. No. 291. Rewald is referring to Chappuis 286 and Rewald, *Acquarelles*, no. 35). One is tempted to also implicate Courbet, for the spiral-based table with a parrot hovering over it (made out more clearly in the drawings, Chappuis 278, 280), will be found in his *Woman with a Parrot*, one of Cézanne's favorite mental pictures. But by this time, Cézanne had a repertoire of images in his head; such resemblance to figures or objects in other artists' pictures are worth no more than a passing glance, or a nod. It makes no sense whatsoever to say, for example, that the side drapes in *Afternoon in Naples* can be traced back to Vermeer, because Vermeer deployed them for settings of intimacy, when such drapes were commonplace in Cézanne's own milieu—to partition off sleeping areas in a small apartment, to partition side shows at the fair, to establish private spaces in brothels, to close off supplicants in confessionals. Cézanne's *Une Moderne Olympia* of 1869 also has the characters and props of *An Afternoon in Naples*: man, nude woman, servant, and in the same order from right to left, also a spiral pedestal table with food and spirits and a heavy curtain on the left. The exotic servant, a negress wearing a long skirt hung from the hips, has been compared to the servant in Delacroix's *Femmes d'Alger*. (Suggested by Reff, «Cézanne's Dream of Hannibal,» p. 151). For other bibliography, see Rewald, Cat. No. 291. In my lecture at the Museum of Modern Art, «*Cézanne's Bathers*,» for the «Cézanne, The Late Years» exhibition at the Museum of Modern Art, New York, October 1977, I showed that the poses Cézanne deployed for his figures in the *Afternoon in Naples* pictures, and others, including the so-called *Baigneur aux bras écartés* (Rewald, Cat. Nos. 252, 253 255, 369-370 and Chappuis, Cat. Nos. 378-89 were based on his use of Rubens' *Hero and Leander*, available in the print room of the Louvre as an engraving by Heinrich Vorsterman. All of the foregoing will be found in my forthcoming book, *Cézanne and the Eternal Feminine*.

2   Zola's notice appeared in *Le Figaro* (April 12, 1867).

3   Gasquet may have enhanced Zola's remark about the appropriateness of carrots when having Cézanne say (though most likely he didn't), «Isn't a bunch of carrots, painted simply in a personal way, worth more than the École's everlasting slices of buttered bread, that tobacco juice painting, slavishly done by the book.» *Gasquet's Cézanne*, p. 68. I cannot accept as useful the assumption that Cézanne had one or more pictures n the *Salon des Refusés*. Rewald found that in the 1863 Salon there was indeed a canvas titled *Pig's Feet*, entered by a painter known only by the name Graham. See Rewald, *Impressionism*, p. 266, note 6.

4   Zola strikes close to Baudelaire with the remark about philosophy. In an essay perhaps written in 1859-60 but not published until after his death, Baudelaire argued against the intrusion of philosophy in painting. But he may have espoused his thoughts on this in other contexts and not necessarily in writing. He referred to *L'Art philosophique*, as defined by Chevanard and the Germans, as art that was destined to replace books, a return to the infancy of the race, a monstrosity that has unfortunately attracted talented artists. C. Baudelaire, *Oeuvres complètes*, «*L'Art philosophique*,» p. 1100. Zola does not deny that Cézanne had something in the 1863 Salon, which would have been the Salon des Refusés. This may be the only evidence, however, slight, that Cézanne did exhibit then even though his name does not appear on the exhibition's checklist of exhibitors.

5   Zola, «Mon Salon,» in *L'Événement*, April 27-May 20, 1866. Reprinted in *Mes*

Haines.

6   *...élonge aussi parfait de moi-même.* Jamot-Wildenstein-Bataille, *Manet*, Vol. I, p. 82.

7   This publication did not materialize.

8   Émile Zola, «Edouard Manet, étude biographique et critique,» *Écrits sur l'art*, p. 155. *Quand you embrassez d'un regard toutes les toiles à la fois, vous trouvez que ses oeuvres diverse se tiennent, se complètent, qu'elles représentent une somme énorme et de vigueur.*

9   G. Poulain, *Bazille et ses amis* (Paris, 1932), p. 208.

10   This passage combines remarks from two letters.

11   Duranty to Zola, 1878; see Auriant: «Duranty et Zola,» *La Nef*, July 1946.

12   Vollard, *Cézanne*, 1915, p. 30. The descriptive word with which Cézanne refers to the Guerbois group is *salauds*.

13   Taking the event literally caused Rewald to associate it with Cézanne as a bohemian who dreams of being dirty (the passage is actually from Zola's notes for *L'Oeuvre*). Not willing to interrogate Rewald's silliness, Mary Krumrine spices her text with it in *Cézanne: les années de jeunesse*, p. 31.

14   Cited by Vollard, 1915, p. 35.

15   In Léger, *Caricatures*, p. 32. See Klaus Herding, *Courbet*, p. 22.

16   For this statement by Count de Nieuwerkerke see J. C. Sloane, *French Painting between the Past and the Present* (Princeton: Princeton University Press, 1951), p. 49, note 13.

17   Émile Porcheron, *Le Soleil* (April 4, 1876).

18   Haussmann, *Memoires*, II, 570-72.

19   *Le bougre, il af...le pied au c...des Beaux-Arts.* Vollard, *Cézanne*, 1915, p. 36.

20   *Les Aixois lui agacent toujours les nerfs, ils demandent à aller voir sa peinture pour ensuite la débiner; aussi a-t-il pris avec eux un bon moyen: «Je vous emmerde,» leur dit, et les gens sans tempérament fuient épouvantes.*

21   *Il paraît que le sieur d'Agay, ce jeune Fashionable que tu sais, rentre un jour dans le Musée Bourguignon. Et maman Combes l'y dit, «donnez-moi votre canne, papa Gibert ne veut pas de ça.» «Je m'en fiche,» dit l'autre. Il garde sa canne. Gibert pater arrive, il veut faire une scène, «je t'emmerde» lui crie d'Agay. Authentique.*

NOTES TO CHAPTER 31

1   Baudelaire, «The Salon of 1859,» *Art in Paris, 1845-1862*, ed. and tr. Jonathan Mayne (New York: Phaidon Publishers, 1965), pp. 198-99.

2   F. de Lasteyries, «Review of the Salon of 1864,» *Fine Arts Quarterly Review* (January 1865). Quoted in Rewald, *Impressionism*, p. 18.

3   See A. André, *Renoir* (Paris, 1928), p. 57.

4   Baudelaire, «The Salon of 1859,» *Art in Paris, 1845-1862* (New York: Phaidon Publishers, 1965), p. 197.

5   Baudelaire, «The Salon of 1859,» *Art in Paris*, p. 194.

6   Astruc, *Le Salon intime: Exposition au boulevard des Italiens* (Paris, 1860), pp. 99-101. See Michael Fried, *Manet's Modernism*, pp. 170-174, who deploys more of Astruc's comments in an important discussion of the hierarchy of genre.

7   P. J. Proudhon, «Qu'est-ce que la propriété?» (1840). Quoted in Theodore

Zeldin, *France 1848-1945*, Vol. I (Oxford: Clarendon Press, 1973), p. 147.

[8]   Charles Baudelaire, «The Salon of 1859,» *Art in Paris, 1845-1862* (New York: Phaidon Publishers, 1965), p. 195.

[9]   Pissarro once exclaimed with surprise at how much a client was willing to pay him for a pure landscape, one with no figures in it at all. Even in the late 1870s, the writer Joris-Karl Huysmans would deplore the large number of straight landscapes being exhibited by the impressionists. On critical antagonism to landscape, see Fried, *Manet's Modernism*, pp. 168-174.

[10]   There were, of course, other criteria, in that the presence of Ingres and Delacroix was to demonstrate the scope and excellence of French painting to an international audience. When Napoleon III purchased a landscape painting by Corot in 1861, his motivation was not to simply acquire a work of art but to demonstrate, by his purchase of a landscape, that his taste was magnanimous and democratic—an emperor for all people. It is said, however, that his son was an avid collector of Barbizon pictures.

[11]   This remains true even today. Few landscape painters rank high on the list of major artists. And one finds the same plight for landscape designers, who are to architects what dental technicians are to dentists.

[12]   Honoré Daumier, *Das Lithographische Werk*, ed. K. Schrenk, 2 vols. (Munich, 1977).An excellent essay on this subject is by Nicholas Green, «Rustic Retreats: Visions of the Countryside in Mid-nineteenth-century France,» in *Reading Landscape: Country, City, Capital* (Manchester: University Press, 1990), pp. 161-176. See also G. Simmel, «The Metropolis and Mental Life,» *Cities and Societies*, eds. P. K. Hatt and A. Reis (Glenco, New York, 1961), pp. 635-46. For specific relevance to art history, see T. J. Clark, *The Painting of Modern Life: Paris In the Art of Manet and His Followers* (London, 1984), pp. 97-102.

[13]   Daumier, *Bon Bourgeois*, Plate 27.

[14]   Daumier, *Bons Bourgeois*, Plate 32. *Pour une belle vue, voilà une belle vue...*

[15]   Daumier, *Bons Bourgeois*, Plate 8.

[16]   For a rich discussion of the «problem of the tableau,» see Fried, *Manet's Modernism* pp. 267-280. Fried gives the background for the term in the eighteenth century, and then proceeds to deal with it in the work of Delacroix and Courbet, then in paintings by Manet and his immediate colleagues. I too have kept *tableau* in the French because its English translation as 'picture' doesn't fit the bill. I use «picture,» «canvas,» «work,» and so on without special meaning, except when I say «picture-painting,» or «picture-painter,» or «merely a picture,» in which cases I mean a pictorial presentation that does not have the quality of a *tableau*.

[17]   Degas to Rouart, December 5, 1872. *Degas Letters*, p. 27.

[18]   For an interesting discussion of Proudhon linking Géricault directly to Courbet, and perhaps to Manet, see Fried, *Manet's Modernism*, pp. 94-95.

[19]   Zola's statement can be traced all the way back to Martin Luther saying that each individual must establish an independent relationship with God, which equals God seen through the medium of an individual temperament.

NOTES TO CHAPTER 32

1   Bruno Ely, 1984, P. 183.

2   Henri Loyrette in *Cézanne* (1996), Cat. No. 12, p. 102.

3   Lewis, *Cézanne's Early Imagery*, p. 163.

4   I am referring to a painting that Jacque Lipchitz alerted me to in 1962, the picture owned by his brother.

5   Georges Rivière, *Paul Cézanne* (Paris, 1923), pp. 46-47, 198.

6   Rewald, Cat. No. 121. The entire matter of when and why Cézanne signs certain pictures is open to question. Rewald has been wrestling with this question for years. He offers the most complete coverage of the problem at his Cat. No. 259. See also his Cat. Nos. 298, 312, 315, 316, 327, 328, 329.

7   Rewald, Cat. Nos. 327-28.

8   Anyway, someone other than Cézanne added the signatures in red paint at a later date, perhaps just before the Hôtel Drouot sale of the Zola estate. One of the «signed» pictures from the Vollard archives, a portrait of an unidentified man, has a signature in red majuscules, *P. Cezane 65*, spelled with only one *n*. Rewald says of this, *Short of space, Cézanne spelled his name with one n only.* That conclusion is not acceptable. Rewald continues: *but the fact that the artist also wrote his name in this fashion under a childhood sketch has led Chappuis to lengthy considerations on this subject.* In his catalogue of Cézanne's drawings, Chappuis tells of a book found posthumously in Cézanne's sister's possession with a portrait sketch in ink adorning the title page, beneath which is scrawled in pencil *Cezane*—here too with but one *n*. Chappuis says that the image is *the first self-portrait by the painter known to us,* and he assumes without question that the «signature» in pencil is in Cézanne's hand. Surely it is not. And if that inept sketch is in fact a self-portrait, it would date about 1857-1858, by which time Cézanne's penmanship would have displayed the usual elegance of French script as one sees in his letters.

9   Rewald's list of signed paintings as to category is as follows: paintings given to friends, Cat. Nos. 74, 75, 116, 121, 122, 521; paintings loaned for exhibition, 139, 202, 259; paintings sold to a collector, 292, 189, 191. But Cézanne also exhibited Cat. No. 225, and gave some pictures to friends that were not signed.

10   Vollard, *Cézanne*, 1915, p. 134.

11   Rivière, 1923, pp. 46-47. Rewald, 1936, P. 70.

12   Zola, *A New Way of Painting.*

13   J. Meier-Graefe, *Paul Cézanne*, trans. J. Holroyd-Reece (LOndon, 1927)].

14   Zola, *A New Way of Painting.* Much effort has gone into justifying why this picture would have been a gift to Zola. It has even been argued that the mountain in the background of the picture, and the apparent river in the foreground, allude to Mont Sainte-Victoire and the Arc river, which would have reminded Zola of his youth in Provence, swimming and fishing with Cézanne, thus endearing him to the picture. But the mountain bears no resemblance to Saint Victoire, and the river, if there even is one in the picture, is undefined.

15   Chappuis, *The Drawings of Paul Cézanne, A Catalogue Raisonné* (Greenwich, Connecticut: New York Graphic Society, 1973), Cat. No. 12.

16   Reff considered and rejected this identification in favor of *Pannini's Banquet,* also in the Louvre («Cézanne's Dream of Hannibal,» *op. cit.,* p. 152 and note 38). For other

Cézanne copies after Veronese's picture see Chappuis, *The Drawings of Paul Cézanne*, Cat. Nos. 28 and 29.

[17] Nebuchadnezzar does, however, have much to do with rich food and wine, and also with excesses of every sort. See the *Book of Daniel* 1:5-16.

[18] Lewis' statement (*op. cit.* p. 182) that «Both Flaubert and Cézanne could have been aware of the account in Daniel of another magnificent feast, that of Belshazzar,» implies that the *Book of Daniel* features two feasts. But it does not.

[19] The association of Cézanne's *Le Festin* with Veronese's picture has been made by many writers. See the bibliography at Rewald, Cat. No. 128. In the 1860s Cézanne made several sketches copying details of Veronese's picture (Chappuis, Cat. Nos. 00).

[20] G. Geffroy, *La Vie artistique*, VI (Paris, 1900). In my opinion, the best description of this painting is by Fry, *Cèzanne*, 1932, pp. 10-13. The only indication of Rubens' style appears in the later state of the canvas, which would, of course, be the modified canvas that Cézanne delivered to Vollard in the 1890s. Elsewhere I will show that the Rubens-type nude in *Le Festin* is derived from a nereid in Ruben's *Hero and Leander*, which Cézanne did not know until after 1872. Andersen, *Cézanne and the Eternal Feminine*, in press

[21] I am not convinced that the servant in the foreground, coming into the pictorial space is a black man, as Rewald says (Cat. No. 128), nor do I find this figure sufficiently reminiscent of the black woman in Delacroix's *Femmes d'Alger* to merit even mentioning. Reff connected the painting to Cézanne's poem, *Songe d'Hannibal*, in «Cézanne's Dream of Hannibal,» *Art Bulletin* 45, June 1963, pp. 148-152, but I do not see a connection.

[22] See note 132 and its references in Albert Boime, *Thomas Couture and the Eclectic Vision* (New Haven and London; Yale University Press, 1980), p. 629.

[23] The Flaubert passage reads, *The king eats from sacred vessels, then breaks them.* Mary Lewis says, *The exactitude with which Cézanne rendered the Flaubert passage—with such additional details as the broken and scattered crockery on the banquet table—clearly establishes that Cézanne's primary debt was to his literary contemporary.* But neither in Flaubert's text nor in Cézanne's picture is broken and scattered crockery on the banquet table. Nothing on the table in *Le Festin* is broken. The four small golden colored plates are neatly arranged along the table's edge, the vase on the table is upright and perfectly intact. Only at the lower left does anything appear in disarray (other than the revelers): some empty platters and depleted jugs, which indicate that food and wine have been consumed (even in Manet's *Déjeuner sur l'herbe*, an empty and overturned vessel appears).

To tie Cézanne's picture to the whole of Flaubert's novel, Lewis says, *Like Flaubert, Cézanne has deliberately emphasized the idea of temptation in his orgy scene. In the story the vision of Nebuchadnezzar's copious wealth was so enticing that the envious saint took on the persona of the king, only to become «instantly sick» and seized with a craving to «wallow in filth.»* But this is Lewis' interpretation of Flaubert's words. No one is sick in Cézanne's picture, nor is anyone wallowing in filth. Should one be out looking for Flaubert's details, such as dining on low couches, diners crowned with violets, revelers sick of excesses, one can find them in Couture's *Romans of the Decadence*, but that canvas was painted years before Flaubert's novel. Lewis continues: *Cézanne augments the theme of temptation in his painting by manifesting Nebuchadnezzar's riches with frequent touches of golden-yellow paint and by adding a sinister, undu-*

lating serpent in the lower right corner. The serpent serves as both a motif of sin and betrayal and an ominous mirroring of the curves of the tempting female forms above. Had Lewis looked through a line-up of Cézanne's paintings from the mid-1860s into the 1870s, she would have seen a number of them with his preferred yellows—Naples Yellow, Chrome Yellow, Yellow Ochre Light—and nowhere in his use of these yellows do they symbolize wealth. Calling Naples Yellow «golden-yellow» cannot convert it to gold. Moreover, the sinister undulating serpent that Lewis sees in the lower right of *Le Festin* is not a snake at all but the undulated, serpentine hemline of the woman's red dress just above it. At some point in the process of painting this picture, that portion of the woman's dress got a smear of pigment over it, obliterating the fabric while not entirely obscuring the hem. The blue fabric just to the left of the large ewer on the table, and in other pictures by Cézanne, similar undulations edge hemlines.

24 Nebuchadnezzar's madness would also find its way into Flaubert's *Education sentimentale* (1869) as a monumental painting of the *Feast* that the ill-mannered artist Pellerin cannot complete in the style of Veronese. One is tempted to find here a connection of Pellerin's ambition to Cézanne's *Le Festin*, which is equally ambitious and sufficiently within Veronese's style to be associated with the Venetian's *Noces de Cana*.

25 Edward King, *My Paris: French Character Sketches* (Boston, 1868), p. 1. Boime suggests that Pellerin is modeled on the character and manners of Couture («vicious tongue, inordinate pride, who harangues the realists»). Boime, *Thomas Couture and the Eclectic Vision*, p. 629, note 135.

26 The reader is reminded of the titles given Cézanne's pictures: *Un Après-midi à Naples* (for low-class men) and *Un Nuit à Venise* (for the traveling diplomats and businessmen). The «night in Venice» motif was a commonplace reference to lovemaking in Venice, as illustrated often in pornography.

27 Alexis de Tocqueville, in a speech before the Chamber of Deputies, January 27, 1848. See *The Art of the July Monarchy* (Columbia and London, University of Missouri Press, 1990), pp. 45-46. See also Mark Traugott, «The Crowd in the French Revolution of February 1848,» *American Historical Review* 93, No. 3 (June 1988), pp. 638-653. The most comprehensive study of Couture's canvas is Boime, *Thomas Couture and the Eclectic Vision*, Chapter VI.

28 The works by Martin mentioned here are discussed and illustrated in William Feaver, *The Art of John Martin* (London: Oxford University Press, 1975).

29 «Période autoritaire du second empire,» *Gazette des Beaux-Arts* 71 (1968), pp. 303-48. Cf. Zeldin, p. 124.

30 Rewald, Cat. Nos. 143, 145, 146.

31 This small canvas depicting Lot and his daughters came on the market recently, authenticated by Lawrence Gowing as an early Cézanne from about 1861. This picture is not by Cézanne—not onto or through any screen of Cézanne's mind was it projected. It is simply of his time and milieu, a rather banal example of a biblical theme rendered as provincial pornography. Rewald also assigned this work to Cézanne, but as a picture from the mid-1860s, claiming it fits to the style of other figures from that time, such as the 1867 *L'Enlèvement* (The Abduction). Rewald supported Gowing's opinion by comparing the coloration to Delacroix's *The Death of Sardanapalus*. But many painters emulated

Delacroix's brushwork and colors, so such comparisons are not at all useful, and having been so often made are less than interesting. Rewald found the painterly qualities of this picture truly amazing. He admired *the volume of the female nude* and *the compositional mastery with which the three legs are assembled.* Gowing marveled at *the roundness with which Lot's daughters separate themselves from the Venetian shadows around them.* But these marvels that evade response to the subject-matter point not towards but away from the young Cézanne, who couldn't have drawn that assemblage of three legs so skillfully without imagery to copy from. And it would be difficult to find anything in his letters to Zola during these years to support Cézanne having firsthand knowledge of such a sophisticated, accurately depicted sex act at a time when he shied away from any girl he encountered, such as the elusive Justine. The picture is described by Mary Lewis as a mirror of Cézanne's psychological state when he painted it: *The vehemence of the brushwork suggests the artist's violent attitude towards the sexual image...beneath its boisterous surface, lurks a mood of dark terror that has explicit roots in both the romantic conjunction of sexuality and violence and aspects of the painter's own, sometimes tortured sensibility.* But the evidence does not hold up: the picture's darkness is due to nighttime, not to the painter's mood. The surface of the canvas is not at all boisterous. And if there is any act of violence in this picture, it would be sexual violation on the daughters' part, for after coaxing their father to drink beyond reason, they are raping him.

[32] One can never know how many pictures his family demised after his death. Widows and other relatives of artists tend to destroy offensive works along with other objectionable items left behind by a deceased husband or father—pictures of girlfriends, address books, love letters, diaries, pornography. Museum curators in the nineteenth century were at times culpable of such laundering, wishing to purify the sanctified dead, such as the destruction of Turner's and Ingres' pornographic drawings.

[33] George Moore published two books of recollections: *Reminiscences of the Impressionist Painters* (Dublin, 1906), and *Modern Painting* (New York, 1898).

[34] How true this is one can hardly tell from the scattering of the tale in the literature, but most likely Cézanne would have wanted to destroy early works that represented a period of his life he had just left behind him.

[35] Rewald, Cat. No. 12.

[36] On this, see Rewald, *Cézanne*, 1950, p. 13.

[37] Rewald, *Impressionism*, p. 326.

[38] Two fragments of Manet's demised painting exist, one, *Toreos in Action*, in the Frick Collection, New York; the other, *The Dead Toreodor*, in the National Gallery, Washington, D.C. Too much is made of Cézanne destroying canvases. I was with Mark Rothko one afternoon in 1965 when he had been asked by an art dealer to authenticate an early, unsigned painting. Rothko ripped it up, saying it was a fake. Later, while in a bar, he admitted to me that it was by him, with the excuse, «An artist has got the right to improve the quality of his early work.» I was with Pierre Soulage in the early 1960s when he was cleaning his studio. He rolled up and put in the trash at least twenty canvases that didn't satidfy him. Also in Paris at about the same time, I stopped in at Leon Golub's studio during a rain storm. On entering, also in Paris, I stamped my wet feet on a painting, and yelled, «My God! Leon, I've just ruined one of your pictures.» Leon laughed and said, «Wipe your feet on it. It failed.»

³⁹ Monet was threatened by creditors at this point and feared his canvases would be seized and sold. As he perhaps did not want to be known any longer by the earlier work, he chose to destroy what he could. Some remaining works were seized and sold at auction in lots of fifty at 30 francs per lot. The number may be exaggerated, as stories about famous artists usually are. Rewald (*Impressionism*, p. 166, note 27) accepts the count, saying it is verified by R. Gimpel, «At Giverny with Claude Monet,» *Art in America* (June, 1927).

⁴⁰ In an essay on authenticity, the connoisseur Walter Feilchenfeldt, a co-editor of Rewald's catalogue of Cézanne's paintings, bluntly appraised the problem of attribution. He wrote: *Cézanne's principal dealer, Ambroise Vollard was probably at times on the verge of bankruptcy. Paintings brought to his gallery were looked at through the eyes of a dealer who felt that there was no profit in wondering whether a work was genuine or not. One has to be aware that after 1895, Vollard obtained works by Cézanne not only from the artist's son but also from artists and other Paris art dealers.*

Vollard picked up a good many pictures from the painter-friend of Gauguin, Émile Shuffenecker, who had been associated with several van Gogh forgeries, also provided Vollard with Cézannes, as did Dr. Paul Gachet and his son (also named Paul).

⁴¹ Vollard, *Cézanne*, 1915, p 48. For more on this see Richard Shiff, «Cézanne's Physicality: the politics of touch,» in *The Language of Art History*, ed. Salim Kamal and Ivan Gaskell (Cambridge: Cambridge University Press, 1991), p. 133. Also Wayne Andersen, «Cézanne's *L'Eternel Feminin* and the Miracle of her Restored Vision,» *The Journal of Art* (December 1990), reprinted in Andersen, *Cézanne and the Eternal Feminine* in press.

⁴² After studying many of the attributions depicting motifs, such as those in the Pontoise and Auvers area that Cézanne was known to frequent, Gowing said, *many painters in the 1860s used a palette knife to lay on paint, and also tended to paint when out with others, so even landscape motifs were shared.* Lawrence Gowing, in *Cézanne* (London: Royal Academy of Arts, 1988-89), at No. 10. Gowing points especially to Rewald, Cat. No. 53, that the style was common to several painters at the time. As for Rewald, Cat. No. 59, from the Paul Gachet collection and titled, apparently by Gachet, *Guillaumin sur un arbre*, is clearly from the mid-1860s but Cézanne was not at Auvers with Guillaumin until 1872—and besides, on what basis can the strokes of paint under the tree be seen as the figure of Guillaumin? Even Rewald says, «There were many down-and-out painters at Gachet's, and this work could be by most any one of them.»

From the entire 1860s, of roughly 158 paintings in all categories of subject matter, Cézanne signed only six canvases, and only three bear a date. But one must not be naïve about authenticating works by a signature or date; it is easier to paint a signature and a date on a canvas than to fake an entire picture. Hundreds of canvases throughout the Western world in museums and private collections, by unknown and often mediocre landscape and hamlet painters, now bear signatures of the marketable masters. As the saying goes, not without merit, «Over his entire lifetime, Corot painted two thousand pictures, of which three thousand are in the United States.»

⁴³ The inventory of the Gachet collection, prepared by Gachet's son, is on deposit with the Louvre, but under embargo until the year 2011. In the early 1930s, when

Lionello Venturi was preparing his monumental catalogue of Cézanne's paintings (now superseded by Rewald's), Gachet's son refused access to canvases claimed to be by Cézanne—wouldn't even allow them to be photographed, thus obliging Venturi to depend on a handwritten list with descriptive titles. Most of these pictures were acquired later by the Wildenstein Gallery and put into the market. I will add that compilers of catalogue *raisonnés* are put under great pressure by galleries such as Wildenstein and Rosenberg. Lionello Venturi's catalogue of Cézanne's paintings, *Cézanne: Son art, son oeuvre*, 2 vols. (Paris: Paul Rosenberg Editions, 1936), was financed and published by the art dealer Paul Rosenberg, and John Rewald was not out from under the Wildenstein power base when preparing his revised and updated catalogue. It is difficult for any art historian, whose research resources often come from wealthy and influential collectors, as well as from museum directors and curators, to de-classify a painting and cause thereby great financial loss to the dealer or owner—even risking a law suit.

[44] Rewald, Cat. Nos. 63, 62, 64, and 65, respectively.

[45] A portrait of a woman, long thought to be Cézanne's portrait of his mistress Hortense, was found showing up in the background of a painting that Guillaumin did of his own studio interior, framed and against a wall among other of Guillaumin's pictures. Back in 1970, I associated the overall impression of this portrait with the soft-media technique of Pissarro and Guillaumin, which led Rewald to search for this picture through the *oeuvre* of each painter. See Rewald, Cat. No. 180, and Wayne Andersen, *Cézanne's Portrait Drawings* (Cambridge, Massachusetts: MIT Press, 1970), Cat. No. 31, pp. 14, 75.

[46] Cézanne's son furnished Vollard with pictures that were left at the *Jas* and at Cézanne's studio. These could have included canvases left with Cézanne by friends with whom he painted in the area, especially because when visiting him they would stay at the Jas.

[47] Albeit that the provenance is Cézanne's son, who was neither an expert nor knowledgeable about his father's early work, and eager to profit from his father's legacy. Cézanne's widow, Hortense, had no interest in her husband's career, and made no effort to be a responsible executor. His grandson, Jean-Pierre, authenticated a number of spurious drawings as by Cézanne.

[48] See Rewald, Cat. Nos. 86, 88.

NOTES TO CHAPTER 33

[1] Rewald, *Paul Cézanne*, 1950, p 69.

[2] An undated letter in the collection of Dr. F. Emile-Zola: *Vous m'avez dit d'être franc avec vous et de vous tenir au courant de l'impressions de votre roman sur le public. La vérité la voici: on trouve cela très pâle, bien écrit, de bons sentiments, mais embêtant. Vite vite arrêtez les frais.* Cited in Zola, *Correspondance*, p. 455, note 8.

[3] Henry Houssaye, the son of Arsène Houssaye, writing under the pseudonym Georges Werner, in *La Revue du XIXe siècle*, December 1, 1866.

[4] One recalls Zola's approach to Manet: he had idealized Manet's pictures to the point of abstraction, seeing in them no action, no conception of an idea, no character:

«You wanted a nude, and you took Olympia, the first to come along. You wanted bright, luminous passages, and the bouquet served your purpose. You wanted black patches, so you added a black woman and a black cat.»

5   Jules Antoine Castagnary. The history of «realism» in nineteenth-century France is too large a topic for me to delve into. The reader is referred to Gabriel P. Weisberg's essay «Early Realism» in *The Art of the July Monarchy, France 1830-1848* (Columbia and London: University of Missouri Press, 1990), pp. 101-115. Also to Léon Rosenthal, *Du romantisme au réalisme: La peinture en France de 1830 à 1848* (Paris: Macula, 1987), Ch. *«Vers le réalisme.»* Gabriel P. Weisberg, *The Realist Tradition: French Painting and Drawing, 1830-1900* (Cleveland: Cleveland Museum of Art and Indiana University Press, 1980); and Gerald Needham, *Nineteenth-Century Realist Art* (New York: Harper and Row, 1988).

6   Ferdinand de Lasterie in *L'Opinion nationale* (June 20, 1868).

7   On the role of caricature promoting Courbet's name recognition, see Klaus Herding, *Courbet: To Venture Independence*, tr. John William Gabriel (New Haven and London: Yale University Press, 1991), pp. 182-187. Herding writes, «In the long run, it was largely due to the caricaturists that a sensibility for Courbet's innovations emerged at such an early date and became so widespread. Behind their back, and with their inadvertent aid, the art they so detested experienced its breakthrough. Facing backwards, like Don Quixote, the caricaturists unwittingly broke a lance for modern art» (p. 187).

8   Edouard Manet, *Reasons for Holding a Private Exhibition.*

9   *J'interroge l'avenir et je me demande quelle est la personalité qui va surgir assez large, assez humaine, pour comprendre notre civilisation et la rendre artistique en l'interprétant avec l'ampleur magistrale du génie.* Zola's oratorical sign-off from criticism has been taken as a virtual paraphrase of Baudelaire's conclusion to the Salon of 1845. Charles Baudelaire, *Art in Paris 1845-1862*, trans. Jonathan Mayne (London, 1970). Anthony Janson, in an essay «Corot, Tradition and the Muse,» *The Art Quarterly* (Autumn, 1978), pp. 294-315, consolidated several passages from Baudelaire's «The Salon of 1846» to arrive at the following, which gives a larger context for Baudelaire's statement, «It is true that the great tradition has been lost, and that the new one is not yet established.» The fragments of the quotation will be found in *Art in Paris*, pp. 46, 66, 97, 115-16, 119. «Romanticism is the most recent expression of the beautiful. That's because of its entirely modern and novel quality of which Delacroix is the latest expression of progress in art. He is heir to the great tradition—that is, to its breadth, nobility, and magnificent compositions—and a worthy successor of the old masters. He has even surpassed them in his command of anguish, passion, and gesture! It is really this fact that establishes his greatness. Take away Delacroix and the chain of history is broken. It slips to the ground. Doubt has led certain artists to beg the aid of all the other arts. Doubt, or the absence of faith and of naïveté, is a vice peculiar to our age. The life of our city is rich in poetic and marvelous subjects. We are enveloped and steeped as though in the atmosphere of the marvelous. But we do not notice it.» I do not agree that Zola needed Baudelaire to arrive at his own perception or wording. If anyone's, it would be Horace's statement, as I've suggested.

NOTES TO CHAPTER 34

1 *Celui-là sera le peintre, le vrai peintre, qui saura arracher à la vie actuelle son coté épique, et nous faire voir et comprendre, avec de la couleur ou du dessin, combien nous sommes grands et poétiques dans nos cravates et nos bottes vernies. Puissent les vrais chercheurs nous donner l'année prochaine cette joie singulière de célébrer l'avènement du neuf.*

2 Zola had taken on art's officialdom and the hooting public like a warrior—a man of the streets rather than the boulevards. Baudelaire had taken jabs at the Academy while heroizing the noble past. It shouldn't be passed off lightly that Baudelaire's modern artist exemplar was not Manet but Constantin Guys, one among many illustrators whose art was essentially commercial, just as today when the imagery of commercial artists is considerably more modern than paintings by fine artists. Baudelaire's direct and determinate influence on Manet and other painters has been exaggerated in the literature on modernism. Only a reflexive, tradition-bound propensity to subordinate visual art to literary sources would assign Baudelaire to the role of Manet's exclusive guide in the discovery of modern urban life as a source of subject matter and stylistic innovation. The modernism that blossomed in Manet's paintings was underway while Baudelaire was still a student in the *lycée*. See Theodore Reff, *Manet and Modern Paris* (Chicago: University of Chicago Press, 1982), p. 13. Reff remedies this overstatement somewhat by saying what made Manet's images of Paris specifically modern, rather than merely contemporary like those of his predecessors, was how the images were shaped by Manet's own vision and values, as well as by the modernization of Paris effected by Haussmann and the modernism advocated by Baudelaire. But Reff still credits Baudelaire for advocating that without Baudelaire Manet would only have painted a merely contemporary Paris rather than a modern one.

I do not trust the statement made by Antonin Proust (*Edouard Manet: Souvenirs*, Paris, 1913, p. 7) as Reff does, that as a *lycée* student in the mid-1840s Manet had rejected Diderot's dictum: «When a people's clothing are mean, art should disregard costume,» by asserting bluntly, «That is really stupid, we must be of our time and paint what we see.» Proust's recollections of what Manet was supposed to have said at different times came into print many years after Manet had died. Typically, authors of memorial and appreciative biographies tend to enhance the juvenile brilliance of their subjects.

3 Clark, *Image of the People*, p. 124.

4 Clark, *Image of the People*, p. 124.

5 See a very interesting essay on this subject by Mary Lewis Shaw, «Discourse of Fashion: Mallarmé, Barthes, and Literary Criticism,» *SubStance, a Review of Theory and Literary Criticism*, XXI, No. 2 (1992), pp. 46-53.

6 «Le peintre de la vie moderne,» *Le Figaro*, November 26, 28, 1863. Reprinted in Baudelaire, O. C., p. 1163.

7 See this in context in Clark, *Image of the People*, p. 127.

8 Veronese green, a pigment that Monet used, was easily recognized by artists and critics back then.

9 Veronese in his time was known for having dressed his figures in a mix of historical and contemporary costume as one sees in . «The inclusion of modern fashions and, most probably, of specific portraits underscores what we might today call the contemporary relevance of his pictures.» David Rosand, *Painting in Seventeenth-*

Century Venice, revised edition (Cambridge: Cambridge University Press, 1997), p. 125.

[10] As reported by P. Burty in C. Roger-Marx, *Eva Gonzalès* (Paris, 1950).

[11] Vollard, 1915, p. 34.

[12] If any comparison is in order, it could be to Boudin's rendering of fashionable women's dress in 1869. See for example, *La Princesse de Metternich sur la Plage de Trouville*, 1869. Illustrated in color in Jean-Arbry, *Boudin*, p. 83.

[13] The sources for Cézanne's imagery as from *La Mode illustré* was discovered by Mark Roskill, «Letter to the Editor,» *Burlington Magazine* (January 1974), p. 46. Vollard mentions Cézanne's use of popular magazines for models. In the context of Cézanne's difficulty in getting models to stay «on the pose,» etc., Vollard writes (p. 102): *Alors, dans certains moments d'exaspération contre la malice des choses, il arrivait à Cézanne de se rabattre sur les images du Magasin Pittoresque, dont il posédait quelques tomes chez lui, ou même sur les journaux de modes de ses soeurs.*

NOTES TO CHAPTER 35

[1] Boudin to Martin, May 4, 1868. This quotation is adapted from Rewald's: *Impressionism*, p. 189.

[2] *Les Mystères de Marseilles* was published in 1866 *en feuilleton* in *Le Messager de Provence* on March 2, May 14, May 23, August 29, September 19. It was then issued by *l'imprimerie Artauld* in three volumes over June to October 1867.

[3] See D. H. Pinkney, *Napoleon III and the Rebuilding of Paris* (Princeton, New Jersey: Princeton University Press, 1958).

[4] *Le Globe*. O. C. X, p. 726, 735.

[5] Baudelaire, «Salon de 1846,» *Curiositiés Esthétique. Oeuvres complètes* (Paris, 1923), p. 196.

[6] See Brown, *Zola*, p. 174.

[7] Baudelaire, *Salon de 1859*, p. 159.

[8] For a thoughtful discussion of the Goncourt's *nouvelle histoire*, see Peter Burke, «Elective Affinities: Gilbert Freyre and the Nouvelle Histoire,» *The European Legacy* 3, No. 4 (July 1998), pp. 1-10.

[9] Théophile Gautier. The introduction to his *Mademoilselles Maupin* (1835). *Il n'y a de vraiment beau que ce qui ne peut servir à rien.*

[11] C. Baudelaire, «The Exposition Universelle,» p. 124.

[12] Brown, *Zola*, p. 27.

[13] C. Baudelaire, «The Exposition Universelle,» p. 124

[14] Èmile Zola, «Exposition Universelle 1867: Nos peintres au Champ de Mars,» in *Salons*, 112-13. For more in a fuller context, see Vivien Perutz, *Èdouard Manet* (Lewisburg: Bucknell University Press, 1993), Chapter 1.

[15] Odilon Redon, «Le Salon de 1868,» *La Gironde*, May 19, June 9, July 1, 1968.

[16] On the role of Taine in nineteenth-century art, see the extensive discussion in Shiff, *Cézanne and the End of Impressionism* (Chicago; University of Chicago Press, 1984, 1986), pp. 39-46 and where indicated in the index.

[17] Taine to Zola. March 2, 1866.

[18] Castagnary, «Le Salon de 1868,» reprinted in *Salons*: 1857-1870 (Paris, 1892), Vol. 1, p. 254.

[19] Théophile Gautier, *Le Moniteur Universal*, May 11, 1868.

[20] E. and J. de Goncourt, *Manette Solomon* (Paris, 1867). I've had to distill this quotation from a long, complex, mannered, and at times nearly incomprehensible speech, but with confidence that it expresses the true thought of the Goncourts at this time.

[21] *Réponse au rapport sur L'Ecole Impériale des Beaux-Arts* (Paris, 1863). See E. Chesneau, *Le Décret du 13 Novembre et l'Académie de Beaux-Arts* (Paris, 1864), and C. Clément, «L'Académie des Beaux-Arts et le decrét de 13 Novembre,» *Etudes sur les Beaux-Arts en France* (Paris, 1865).

[22] Baudelaire, p. 148.

[23] Bazille. Letter to his parents (Spring 1869). Poulain, p. 147-148.

[24] Zola, «Notre peintres au Champ de Mars,» *La Situation* (July 1, 1867). Reprinted in *Zola: Salons*, edited F. W. J. Hemmings and R. J. Neiss (Paris and Geneva, 1959), pp. 107-115.

[25] J. Champfleury, *Les amis de nature* (Paris: 1860), Ch. 1. Quoted in Rewald, *Impressionism*, p. 42. I have modified the translation.

NOTES TO CHAPTER 36

[1] Zola to Arsène Houssaye, Paris, 12 February 1867. *Zola, Oeuvres complètes,* letter 161

[2] Émile Zola, *Thérèse Raquin*, tr. and with an introduction by Leonard Tancock (London: Penguin Books, 1962), pp. 13-14.

[3] Sainte-Beuve, *Causeries du lundi* (Paris: Garnier frères, 1851-1862) XIII, pp. 346-63.

[4] For these passages from *Thérèse Raquin* I am using the translation by Leonard Tancock, with thanks. When appropriate to my own text, I freely paraphrase Zola's.

NOTES TO CHAPTER 37

[1] Zola, *Correspondance*, II, p. 122.

[2] Zola, *Correspondance*, II, p. 124.

[3] I've borrowed a few passages from Frederick Brown's more complete coverage of Zola's 1868 journalism, pp. 176-177.

[4] *Zola, Oeuvres complètes.* XIII, p. 207.

[5] *Zola, Oeuvres complètes.* XIII, p. 117.

[6] *Zola, Oeuvres complètes.* XIII, p. 117. Zola seems to be prognosticating «Cats.»

[7] *Zola, Oeuvres complètes.* XIII, p. 132.

[8] *Zola, Oeuvres complètes.* XIII, p. 196-97.

[9] The novel was *Madame Freinix*. See Brown, p. 178.

[10] Jean Boric, «Zola et les mythes ou de la nausée au salut,» referred to in *d'Émile Zola, sa vie, son oeuvre, son époque...*, ed. Colette Becker et. als. (Paris: Editions Robert Laffont, 1993), p. 238.

---

11 Brown, *Zola*, p. 185.

12 Brown, *Zola*, p. 185.

13 I am paraphrasing Brown's succinct summary of the novel, *Zola*, pp. 184-85.

14 Zola, *Correspondance*, II, p. 165. November 14, 1868.

15 Brown, *Zola*, p. 186.

16 *Zola, Oeuvres complètes*, pp. 768-769.

17 *Zola, Oeuvres complètes*X, pp. 768-769.

18 *Si the roman a pour objet la peinture des moeurs contemporaines, il faut avouer que ces maladies morales, ses cachemars persistants, ces soumissions de l'instinct charnel et de l'idée fixe sont rares. A mon sens, l'avenir du roman consiste dans l'histoire de la volunté combattante et victorieuse à travers le pêle-mêle social et les défaillances de l'animal surmené. Vous avez le sens de la vérité, et je crois qu'en jetant les yeux autour de vous comme moi vous reconnaîtrez celle-là.* Quoted in *Dictionnaire d'Émile Zola, sa vie, son oeuvre, son époque...*, p. 238.

NOTES TO CHAPTER 38

1 The line, «Being alone I take my chances at the café,» has been taken as evidence of Cézanne's debilitating shyness. On the contrary, it meant that he was without a woman down there—his girlfriend Hortense was in Paris—so with some difficulty he entered the café to make a pick up. Most men share that apprehension, which is not so much shyness as common sense. Men suffer many rejections when hunting women.

2 John Rewald said that Cézanne was so thoroughly distressed at this time that he failed to date his letters. On the contrary, it would seem that Cézanne was very content at home in Aix, that he had many friends. Rewald should have been content with the fact that, like the date on a painting, the exact date on a letter is not as important to a correspondent as to an archivist. Not to mention that Cézanne sometimes wrote letters over several days.

3 Alexis, *Emile Zola*, pp. 90-91.

NOTES TO CHAPTER 39

1 My quotation is from Brown, *Zola*, p. 187.

2 Rewald, Cat. No. 173. See Rewald's notes for the date of this picture. Either overtly or covertly rendered, all of these stock images of non-clinical, benign voyeurism can be found in Cézanne's early paintings, and often in later ones. Voyeurism is a loaded word with negative connotations and invariable assigned to men as visually violating women. This silliness deprives women the right to take pleasure in looking at any object of sensual pleasure. Pleasurable looking should not be called voyeurism, even if the pleasure is secret. And not all looking is a gaze, which by American academics is a rather meaningless translation of the French *le regard* that has become an academic affectation, with few using it knowing what it means. *Regader* simply means «to look». One may gaze over a crowd, but one looks at a person. When a woman returns a man's «gaze», she looks, not gazes, at him. Lovers don't gaze into each other's eyes; they look. Victorine Meurent, in Manet's *Dejeuner sur l'herbe*, is not gazing; she's looking, and her spectators do

not gaze at her but return her look. Lot's wife didn't turn to gaze back at the city; she looked back. Gazing is again to grazing. A cow grazes the pasture, but eats grass.

3 Fry, 1927, p. 9.

4 Schapiro, *Cézanne*, 1952, p. 34.

5 The reference is to Alfred de Musset's *La nuit de décembre*, in *Poésies complètes* (Paris, 1923) pp. 317-322.

6 Krumrine in *Cézanne: les années de jeunesse*, 1859-1872, p. 37.

7 The trouble with dining in the too-open air. Daumier, *Pastorales*, Cat. No. 108D.

8 See Schapiro, *Cézanne* 1952, p. 21.

9 At Rewald, Cat. No. 85.For this painting there exists a drawing attributed to Cézanne and said to be astonishingly close to painting. I find it astonishingly distant. In the drawing the scale of the three men is the same as the scale of the three nymphs, and the five figures over the left portion of the picture plane are remarkably unified, whereas in the painting they are disjointed, especially the nymph with upraised arm that seems entirely outside the grouping, outside the setting even. In my opinion, this drawing is not a study for the painting, but rather a copy of the painting with the painting's compositional anomalies corrected, the elements brought into a unity of form. The drawing is mechanically executed; the lines and hachures are not searching because everything in the composition already exists, needing only to be copied. There is a much more precise association as to scale and closeness of the women to the men, as if the women were in fact companions, if only in Cézanne's imagination reflecting those fantasies of his early adolescence when he and Zola dreamed of muses coming into their lives.

10 Marion to Morstatt, 1868.

11 See Mario Praz, *Scene di comversazione* (Rome, 1971), tr. *Conversation Pieces: A Survey of the Informal Group Portrait in Europe and America* (University Park, Pennsylvania, 1971), Ch. 6, «The Family Group in an Outdoor Setting.» Also Mark Roskill's discussion of this in landscape settings, *The Languages of Landscape*, pp. 93-97.p. 93-97.

12 Moreover, it is not that the *fête galante*, as depicted in Watteau's *La Collation* evolved into the casual picnic. If the *fête galante* were to evolve into anything, it would be a lawn party set up by royals and the very wealthy. Picnics rendered by Manet, Monet, Cézanne, were more closely related to the peasantry—farm workers having lunch in the fields, when women and children come with picnic baskets to join the men. I offer an extensive analysis of the picnic in a book that I will soon submit for publication: *The Picnic and the Prostitute: Manet's Art of the 1860s*.

13 *Correspondance.*

14 See the surviving examples in Rewald, Cat. Nos. 102-111.

NOTES TO CHAPTER 40

1 Napoleon III was made to bear the blame for the surrender of Archduke Maximilian, whom he'd installed as emperor of Mexico, only to withdraw the French troops rather than face the advancing forces of Benito Juárez. Maximilian was obliged to surrender and on March 19, 1869, was executed by a firing squad. On February 7, 1869, Manet was indirectly warned in an article in the *Gazette des Beaux-Arts* that he had better

not try to show his painting in the Salon: «M. Édouard Manet has painted the tragic episode that brought our intervention in Mexico to a close. The death of Maximilian has still not been officially accepted as history, since Manet has been informed that his picture, which is in fact excellent, would be rejected at the next Salon if he insisted on presenting it.»

2   The so-called avant-garde of art history books dedicated to the 1860s in France embodies about twenty or more artists, while only nine (Manet, Degas, Pissarro, Cézanne, Monet, Renoir, Sisley, Bazille, Morisot) merited a chronological listing and separate bibliography in Rewald's *History of Impressionism*, the standard college textbook since its publication by the Museum of Modern Art in 1961. Yet, in the Salon of 1863 were 2,980 other artists, of which perhaps two or three hundred, or even more, evidenced in their work similar characteristics to those now classified as the proto-Impressionists. Those artists, like the crowd that would press through the galleries, are imaginary entities essential to art historical refining, just as tons of crushed rock is essential to refine gold. It is too prevalent in art history books written by those who champion the so-called modernists, and heroize the martyred among them, to castigate the Salon jury while assuming uncritically that every painter who fits to linear art history should have been accepted.

3   From the *Encyclopédie Départmentale des Bouches-du-Rhône*, cited by Rewald, *Studies in Impressionism*, pp. 63-64. In 1983 the Municipal Council of Aix-en-Provence named a street after Achille Emperaire.

4   Venturi, Cat. No. 1227 suggested it was Hortense Fiquet. See also Andersen, «Cézanne's Portrait Drawings from the 1860s,» *Master Drawings*, V. 5, No. 3, 1967, p. 274, where I identify the woman as her. Chappuis, at Cat. No. 82 does not agree with me, but he mistaken calls the sheet «academy studies.»

5   Karl Madsen, Merete Bodelsen, *Burlington Magazine* (May 1962), pp. 208-09.

6   For a larger discussion of this, with bibliographical citations, see Rewald, Cat. No. 140.

7   E. Bernard, «Julian Tanguy, dit le Père Tanguy,» *Mercure de France* (December 16, 1908), p. 609. Rewald, Cat. No. 139. See also Wayne Andersen, *Cézanne's Portrait Drawings* (Cambridge: MIT Press, 1970); Wayne Andersen, «Cézanne, Tanguy, Chocquet,» *Art Bulletin*, IL, (June 1967).

8   All of this information on the fate of Cézanne's portrait of Emperaire will be found in greater detail at Rewald, Cat. No. 139.

9   Vollard, *Cézanne*, 1919, p. 34.

10   Vollard, *Cézanne*, 1919, pp. 36-37. *Allons, ma belle, montre ton casimir au monsieur!*

NOTES TO CHAPTER 41

1   On France's economy, see the admirable historian of French politics, economics, and sociology, Theodore Zeldin's, *France 1848-1945* (Oxford: Claredon Press, 1973), Vol. I, particularly pp. 504-505.

2   Quoted by Zeldin, *France 1848-1945*, p. 505. Ollivier, after the fall of Napoleon II rallied to Thier's cause and formed a cabinet in 1870 to transform the regime.

3   Zola, O. C. XIII, p. 303. Quoted in a richer context by Brown, *Zola*, p. 195.

4   Brown, *Zola*, pp. 209-210.

5   Brown, *Zola*, p. 210. Translation Brown.

6   Berthe Morisot to her sister Edma, February 21, 1871. In Denis Rouart, *Correspondance de Berthe Morisot* (Paris, 1950), p. 48.

7   Manet to Eva Gonzalès, in Claude Roger-Marx, *Eva Gonzalès* (Paris, 1950).

8   Berthe Morisot, in a letter to her daughters dated October 18,

8   Berthe Morisot, in a letter 1870, in Rouart, *Correspondance de Berthe Morisot*, p. 44. (Degas suffered problems with his eyes throughout his lifetime).

9   Manet includes Fantin-Latour as a deserter, so the second sentence of my quotation actually reads, «I don't think they will be well-received when they return.»

10   Some art historians who protect the morality of their subjects try to justify the exodus of these artists. Paul Tucker, «The First Expressionist Exhibition in Context,» in Moffet, p. 110, says, «Most of the Impressionists had a patriotic streak. Degas, it will be recalled, had volunteered for the National Guard. And even though Monet and Pissarro had gone to England to avoid the war, both expressed concern about their country.»

But there is a mile of difference between expressing concern about your country after having deserted it (Monet also deserted his wife and child), and staying to fight for your country because you love it. Moreover, if Degas had not volunteered, he would have been inducted, as Manet would have been. I confess to having great reservations about the way Paul Tucker brings so much political matter into the context of the first Impressionist exhibition in 1874. That Monet painted a few pictures showing some reconstruction in the Paris area doesn't say a thing about his patriotism. The Franco-Prussian war aroused only the most negligible feelings, and it doesn't make sense to invoke it in the context of Impressionist painting.

11   Correspondance, II, p. 278.

12   This letter is quoted from the partially unpublished original found among Pissarro's papers. See Rewald, *Impressionism*, p. 258. My text differs somewhat from Rewald's, but only in writing style. N. B. Could this person be François Auguste Biard, 1799-1882, a French painter referred to by Degas in a letter of Dec 5, 1872?

13   Zeldin, *Taste and Corruption* (London: Oxford University Press, 1980), p. 399.

14   I am not sure of how interested Degas was. He does say, in November 1872 while in New Orleans, in a letter to Lorenz Frölich, «Politics! I am trying to follow those of my native France in the Louisiana newspapers. They talk of little but the super-tax on houses, and they give Mr. Thiers their expert advice on republicanism.» *Degas Letters*, p. 23.

15   Mitterand, *Zola journaliste*, p. 147. Brown, p. 221. I have contracted the text to what I feel gives my readers a sense of the whole.

16   Pissarro to Duret, June 1871, in A. Tabarant, *Pissarro* (Paris, 1924), p. 20. The 1500 number is most likely an exaggeration.

17   Pissarro to Duret, June 1871. A. Tabarant, *Pissarro* (Paris, 1924).

18   Cited in Rewald, *Impressionism*, p. 264, as a letter from Zola to Cézanne dated July 4, 1871. Actually, Zola's words are to be found in Vollard, *Cézanne*, pp. 32-33, where Vollard has Cézanne telling him about his and Zola's activities during the Franco-

Prussian war. I have taken my quotation from two places in the dialogue—the first: *Zola terminait sa lettre en me pressant de rentrer, moi aussi: Un nouveau Paris est en train de naître...c'est notre règne qui arrive.* The second: *Je vous aurais montré un passage ou Zola se désolait de ce que tous les imbéciles ne fussent pas morts.*

19 *Zola, Oeuvres complètes,* XII, p. 909.

20 Zola, «Causcric du dimanche,» *Le Corsaire* (December 3, 1872), in Zola, *Salons,* ed. F. Hemmings and R. Niess (Geneva and Paris, 1959), p. 25.

NOTES TO CHAPTER 42

1 Continuing his attack on Cézanne's father, Rewald says that Louis-Auguste failed to attend all the meetings, and so on (Rewald doesn't mention the fact that cowardly Cézanne, hiding in L'Estaque with a girlfriend, failed to attend a single meeting).

2 Vollard, *Cézanne*, 1915, p. 32, quotes a discussion with Cézanne about his and Zola's activities during the Franco-Prussian war. This letter figures in the description that Cézanne gives of Zola's tribulations. He says to Vollard that he wished he'd kept the letter. By some circumstance the letter did survive. See the French text in Rewald, *Cézanne,* (Paris: Flammarian, 1986), p. 91.

NOTES TO CHAPTER 43

1 RM II, pp. 1736-37.

2 This aspect of 1860s art criticism has been given special attention by Michael Fried who brings great intelligence to bear on the problem as dealt with in the critical writings of Thoré, Castagnary, and others. *Manet's Modernism,* (Chicago and London: University of Chicago Press, 1996), especially pp. 276-280.

3 Cited in Fried, *Manet's Modernism* p. 279.

4 Fried, *Manet's Modernism,* p. 271 and notes 16-17.

5 Quoted in *Thérèse Raquin* (Paris: Garnier-Flammarion, 1970), pp. 53-54. Cf. Brown, *Zola,* p. 160.

6 See Brown, *Zola,* pp. 232-33.

7 RM, I, p. 1541. See Brown, *Zola,* p. 232.

8 I have but slightly altered the translation by Ernest A. Vizetelly in the Continental Classics series, *The Fortune of the Rougons* (Gloucester, Alan Sutton Publishing, 1985), pp. 212-13.

9 I am indebted to Brown, *Zola,* p. 233, note 1, for this passage from Edmond de Goncourt's journal, and also for use of his translation, which I have altered just a bit.

10 *Vous avez très bien su employer cet étrange phénomène physiologique que j'appelle impression sur l'ovarie lui-même (resemblances des derniers fils d'une veuve remariéeavec le premier mari). La chose est exact sur tous les rapports. Je l'ai observé pour les animaux chez le chien; puis fréquemment encore chez les vegetaux. Le pistachier de Provence, arbre que vous connaissez bien, produit des fruits particuliers lorsqu'il est fécondé par le térébinthe.*

11 Zola, Le naturalisme au Salon. *Le Voltaire, June 18-22 (three articles), 1880.* In E. Zola, *Salons* (Geneva, Paris, 1959), pp. 233-254.

NOTES TO CHAPTER 44

1   Meyer Schapiro, *Paul Cézanne* (1952, 1962), p. 38. Schapiro's commentary on this painting is beyond doubt the best. He draws a connection to Manet's art: «[Cézanne's] taste for cold black, cold white and gray, seems natural to Cézanne's mood; but this taste presupposes Manet's elegant and impassive art of which the tones and directness of vision have here been put to emotional use and strangely transformed.»

2   Rewald, Cat. No. 00.

3   Stable forms transcend the moment. Unstable forms do not, because the moment itself is unstable. The artist's sense of form is what sustains the artist's art in contrast with the illustrator's art. If the painter simply records on the canvas something seen, even in his head, the work remains a picture. Stories can be pictured, and one can write stories about pictures. As for a tableau, a work of art, one can write a story only about the subject matter, not about its structure, which at best can be described. To merely see the story that any picture tells, is to transfer the imagery from picture to viewer, a process of ordinary seeing that has no more connection to art than taking snap-shots, or cavorting has to professional dance.

4   Guillemet to Zola, 1867 (pre-September).

5   Marion to Morstatt, September, 1867.

6   I am referring to such unfounded conclusions as this one given by Lewis: «Both were intended as tributes to Wagner and were entitled *L'Ouverture du Tannhäuser*.» But there is no evidence whatsoever that Cézanne attributed this theme to Wagner or titled the picture. Lewis says of the picture that it is indebted to Dutch genre painting simply because «this type of quiet, intimate family scene is often found in paintings of Dutch interiors.» It would seem from this sort of grotesque teleology that Cézanne would have never thought of painting a quiet, intimate family scene unless he had seen Dutch genre painting. No consideration is given to the fact that Cézanne's home life was one of intimate family scenes every day. Dutch painters did not invent domesticity, not even the motif of one person playing a musical instrument while another listens. Nor can I buy any argument that Cézanne's *L'Idylle* of about 1870, or any other of Cézanne's pictures, were inspired by Wagner's staging of *Tannhäuser*, or that Cézanne saw himself as the troubled hero Tannhäuser struggling between the flesh and the spirit. Lewis, *Cézanne's Early Imagery*, p. 139 and 188-192.

7   In the catalogue of the exhibition *Cézanne: les années de jeunesse, 1859-1872*, 1988, Gowing bring the entire speculative mass down to a certainty, even saying that the girl in the picture is actually playing an overture to Tannhäuser (*Cézanne mettait sans doute en même temps la dernière main à un tableau montrant sa jeune soeur Rose au piano du Jas de Bouffan, jouant L'ouverture de Tannhäuser*), p. 26. In the same place Lewis devotes several pages to the theme, saying that it is a «realistic picture» (*un tableau réaliste répresentant une jeune femme au piano, dont le titre L'ouverture de Tannhäuser, en ferait un hommage à l'oeuvre tant controversée du compositeur*), but the rest of her text and the roughly twenty-five footnotes related to it are about everything except the picture (pp. 48-50 and notes 30-56). In this same catalogue Mary Krumrine deploys the same title and renders a similar treatment to Cézanne's *Temptation of Saint Anthony* and *Le Pique-nique* (The Picnic), with entangled interpretations,

reading into the personages of Cézanne's pictures not only Cézanne but Cézanne's sister Marie along with Hortense, Zola, Baille, even Eve, and makes flimsy associations of the context with Zola's *Thérèse Raquin*, with Frenhofer from Balzac's *Le Chef d'Oeuvre inconnu*, and the *pâle jeune homme dont Musset parle*. I wouldn't know how to start untangling her assumptions that confuse similarities with sameness (pp. 35-39).

8   Vollard reports this story as one that Degas had told him. The relationship between Manet and Degas was actually close, and the story rings true to their personalities. I quoted the story, with slight changes in the translation, from *Degas Letters*, ed. Marcel Guèrin, tr. Marguerite Kay (Oxford: Bruno Cassier, 1947), p. 262.

9   This would be Bazille's first effort to get a picture past the Salon jury. Anticipating the picture would be rejected, he said in a letter to his parents that he was also about to paint a still-life of fish, figuring that sort of subject matter would be accepted. If both are rejected, he adds, I will sign with both hands a petition requesting an exhibition for the refusés. As anticipated, the *Girl at a Piano* was rejected; the *Still-life with Fish* was accepted. See Poulain, p. 63, and Rewald, *Impressionism*, p. 108, 134.

10 Corot's medal-winning, *Morning: Dance of the Nymphs* of 1850, was another picture that would represent for Bazille not modernity but the past, for it was known how much Corot depended on traditional ballets and instrumental music to inspire such fanciful bacchanalian rituals in heaven-on-earth settings. See Hélène Toussaint, *Hommage à Corot* (Paris: Orangerie des Tuilleries, 1975), p. 82.

11 Félix Fénéon in *Chat Noir* (March 19, 1892).

12 At this time, Marion was a student in the natural sciences. Morstatt became the head of a music school in Stuttgart, and Marion became a professor of biology at the University of Marseilles and also director of the natural history museum.

13 Alfred H. Barr, Jr., «Cézanne in the letters of Marion to Morstatt, 1865-1868,» *Magazine of Art* (May 1938).

14 See the discussion and a more substantial Baudelaire quotation at Rewald, Cat. No. 149.

15 Rewald, *Correspondance*.

16 Rewald has suggested that the two females may be daughters of Dominique Aubert, Cézanne's uncle. The straight-backed floral-patterned armchair appears in two other pictures: full-length portraits, one of Cézanne's father and the other of Achille Emperaire that Cézanne submitted to the Salon of 1870 (Rewald, Cat. Nos. 101, 139).

17 Clark, *Image of the People*, p. 36.

18 Degas to Lorenz Frölich, letter of November 27, 1872. *Degas Letters*, ed. Marcel Guèrin, tr. Marguerite Kay (Oxford: Bruno Cassier, 1947), p. 22.

20 Pissarro to Guillemet, September 3, 1872, in *Bailly-Herzberg*, Vol. I, p. 77. Rewald surmised that *Quai de Bercy* was the picture to which Pissarro refers (Rewald, Cat. No. 179), for in Pissarro's letter the picture is not identified. Lorette takes it as a certainty.

21 See, among others, Boudin's *Les Quais du Port de Trouville*, ca. 1865. Reproduced in G. Jean-Aubry, *Eugène Boudin* (Paris: La Bibliothèque des Arts, 1968), p. 49.

22 Daniel Wildenstein, *Claude Monet* (Lausanne-Paris: La Bibliothèque des Arts, 1974), Cat. Nos. 164-65.

23 Wildenstein, *Monet*, Cat. Nos. 254, 255, 257, among others. For Pissarro, *The Gisors Road, Pontoise* and *Old Road to Ennery, Pontoise*, among many others. Grays were also used by Boudin as the unifying tone, following the prevailing gray, usually blue-grays of weather, as in his *Le Port du Havre* of ca. 1864. Reproduced G. Jean-Aubry, *Eugène Boudin* (Paris, 1968), p. 29. Tonal painting has a history in French landscape painting extending back to the 1830s, especially in the work of Théodore Rousseau. See the fine essay by Ptra Ten-Doesschate Chu, «At Home and Abroad: Landscape Representation,» in *The Art of the July Monarchy: France 1830-1848* (Columbia and London: University of Missouri Press, 1990), pp. 116-130.

24 Rewald, Cat. No. 88, *Mur de Jardin*, has a man walking rather awkwardly on a path, but this canvas is among those in the general style of how Cézanne painted at the time, and is not necessarily by Cézanne. Vollard's claim that he purchased this canvas from the Zola sale cannot be confirmed, as the picture does not appear in the sale's catalogue. Likewise, Rewald, Cat. No. 233, *Un Peintre au travail*, is probably not by Cézanne. The subject, a painter seen from the back, is identified by Rewald as the dauber Justin Gabet, simply because Vollard bought the canvas from Gabet. It could have been painted by any of the picture-painters in Gabet or Cézanne's circle.

Such pictures as Rewald, Cat. Nos. 244, 245, 246, where figures appear fishing or relaxing along a river, were painted in the studio and are essentially subject paintings, not landscapes. Rewald, Cat. No. 205, *La Seine à Bercy*, where workers appear, is a copy of painting by Guillaumin, while Rewald, Cat. No. 301, *La Moisson*, where field workers appear, is, in my opinion, a copy of an as yet unidentified source. Gauguin owned this canvas and copied it in turn.

25 Rewald, Cat. No. 389, *Cour d'une ferme*.

26 *Correspondance*, Zola to Cézanne, March 25, 1860.

27 Schapiro, *Cézanne*, 1952, p. 14.

NOTES TO CHAPTER 45

1 Brown, *Zola: A Life*, p. 275.

2 *Correspondance*, pp. 141-142.

3 Rewald, *Studies in Impressionism*, the chapter «Achille Emperaire and Cézanne.»

4 Mary Cassatt, Letter to Mrs. Stillman. A. D. Bellskin, *The Graphic Work of Mary Cassatt* (New York, 1948), p. 53.

5 Charles Monselet, *Lettres gourmandes. Manuel de l'homme du table* (Paris, 1877). Such manners of men when without women at the table are not confined, of course, to Paris in the mid-nineteenth century. Even in 1964-66, when I was a member of the Art Historians' Dinner Club, consisting of professors above the rank of Assistant Professor from Harvard, MIT, Brandeis, and Wellesley, meeting at Harvard, women were excluded, even those who were full professors. In 1967, women were allowed in. Dinner conversations changed remarkably, and within a few months the club disbanded.

6 These quotation are given by Rewald at cat. no. 507.

7 Schapiro, *Cézanne*, 1952, p. 26.

8 Schapiro, *Cézanne*, 1952, p. 26.

9   For this, see my book, *Picasso's Brothel*

10   Schapiro had, I believe, a strong sense of identity with Cézanne, more than with other artists he dealt with. Partly this was due to his interest in Freudian theory and psychoanalysis, party with his own psychology which had, I suspect, a strong oedipal component: a need to overwhelm, to bedazzle, show off. Yet he kept Cézanne in a passive state, as when saying, «Cézanne submits humbly to the object, as if in atonement for the violence of his early paintings.» *Cézanne*, 1952, p. 27. On Schapiro's psychological investment in his writings, see my *Freud, Leonardo da Vinci, and the Vulture's Tail* (New York: Other Press, 2001).

11   *Gasquet's Cézanne*, p. 38. I have somewhat contracted Gasquet's text.

12   For «the old fool» remark, Pissarro says that in a letter to his son Lucien dated January 20, 1896. See *Correspondance*.

13   Rewald, Cat. No. 307. See also *Cour d'une ferme*, Cat. No. 389.

14   Rewald, Cat. Nos. 00, 00. *Thatched Cottage in Auvers* is generally known as *La Maison du pendu* (House of the Hanged Man), but as my text bears out, Cézanne did not give it that title.

15   Lewis, *Cézanne's Early Imagery*, p. 196. Lawrence Gowing, *Cézanne, The Early Years, 1859-1872* (London: Royal Academy of Art, 1988), p. 166.

16   Cat. No. 38, p. 153.

17   See Rewald, Cat. No. 307, *L'Étang des Soeurs à Osny*. For Pissarro, see L. R. Pissarro and L. Venturi, *Camille Pissarro* (Paris, 1939), Cat. No. 300.

18   Rewald, Cat. Nos. 158 and 183.

19   Lewis, *Cézanne's Early Imagery*, p. 203.

20   Lewis, *Cézanne's Early Imagery*, p. 207.

21   Lewis, *Cézanne's Early Imagery*, pp. 197-203.

22   Cat. No. 38, p. 153. Henry Moore, who owned this picture, said of it «Not gamins, not girls, but large women, fully flowered, like mothers.»

23   See Wayne Andersen, «Cézanne's L'Eternel Feminin and the Miracle of her Restored Vision,» *The Journal of Art* (December 1990).

24   Rewald, *Les Aquarelles de Cézanne*, No. 39.

25   The problem of this excessive estrangement of the 1870s from the 1860s can also be laid to Lionello Venturi's and John Rewald's narrow descriptions of Impressionism, especially the works included in the first so-called Impressionist exhibition in 1874. Recognizing some small differences between the pre-Franco-Prussian War and post-war decades, they reinforced them to become big differences. Lionello Venturi, «The Aesthetic Idea of Impressionism,» *Journal of Aesthetics and Art Criticism*, I (Spring 1941), pp. 34-45. Rewald, *Impressionism*, p. 330-338. I am following the argument made by Shiff, «The End of Impressionism: A Study in Theories of Artistic Expression,» *The Art Quarterly*, Vol. I, No. 4 (Autumn 1978), pp. 338-340. Rewald wrote, «Rejecting the objectivity of realism, the Impressionists selected one element from reality—light—to interpret all of nature...light seen directly or immediately, rather than objects in space seen indirectly.» As Shiff has pointed out, Rewald took that insufficient observation from an eyewitness, Jules Castagnary, who wrote at the time that the new term Impressionists should define those who render not the landscape but the sensation produced by the

landscape. Castagnary was not talking about Cézanne, but about Pissarro, Monet, Degas, Morisot, and Sisley. Castagnary had nothing good to say about Cézanne. And Rewald did not quote all that Castagnary had to say about the others. Castagnary also said that the Impressionists departed from reality to enter into complete idealism, which Shiff (p. 338) correctly gave as his meaning not a world of universals lying behind the world of appearances—behind reality—but a world of individual ideals, sensations, and imagination, a world associated with the aims of the earlier Romantics. The Impressionists, Castagnary had concluded, differ from their predecessors only in the exaggeration of the sketch-like technique. Jules Castagnary, «L'Exposition du boulevard du Capucines,» *Le Siècle* (April 29, 1874). Reprinted in Hélène Adhémar, *L'Exposition de 1874 chez Nadar* (Paris, 1974), not paginated.

NOTES TO CHAPTER 46

[1]   Monet to Alexis, May 7, 1873. Letter published in *L'Avenir National* on May 12, 1873.

[2]   Degas to Tissot, undated, 1874. *Degas Letters*, pp. 38-40.

[3]   An important, relevant essay is by Steven Eisenman, «The Intransigent Artist, or How the Impressionists Got Their Name,» in Charles Moffet, *The New Painting, 1874-1886* (Geneva: Richard Burton, 1986), pp. 51-57. Eisenman's text, however, cannot be allowed to backtrack into mine since his start-off date is 1874. I am using the word-form «intransigent» as a descriptive adjective, applicable to Cézanne from about 1865 to 1873, while later on, or about that time, it becomes a descriptive noun, the alternative name for the Impressionists of the 1870s as discussed by Eisenman.

[4]   Pissarro to Duret, May 5, 1874.

[5]   Émile Cardon, April 29, 1974.

[6]   Cited by Paul Tucker in *The New Painting*, p. 106, where can be found a more complete survey of press response to this show than I have need to include here.

[7]   Armand Silvestre, April 22, 1874.

[8]   Ernest Chesneau, «Au Salon,» *Le Soir* (May 9, 1874).

[9]   Castagnary, April 29, 1874.

[10]   Montifaud (May 1874), pp. 310-311.

[11]   Émile d'Hervilly, L'Exposition du Boulevard des Capucines, *Le Rappel*, April 17, 1874. Cited in Rewald, Impressionism, p. 328.

[12]   Latouche to Dr. Gachet, April 26, 1824. In *Le Docteur Gachet et Murer* (Paris, 1956), p. 58.

[13]   Louis Leroy, «L'Exposition des impressionistes,» *Charivari* (April 25, 1874).

[14]   Leroy's text is quoted in Rewald, *Impressionism*, pp. 318-324. I have modified the translation and deleted a few sentences that are not essential for my use.

[15]   Quoted in Rewald, *Impressionism*, p. 325.

[16]   Rewald, *Impressionism*, p. 334: «It is known that Count Doria purchased Cézanne's *Maison du pendu* for 300 francs.» The sale is mentioned in Vollard, 1915, p. 38. At some later date, Cézanne's patron Victor Chocquet traded with Doria his *Neige fondu á L'Estaque* for *La Maison du pendu*.

¹⁷ Louis Leroy, «L'Exposition des impressionistes,» *Charivari* (April 25, 1874). The application of the word «*impression*» to aspects of art had been around and in use for a very long time before this event.

NOTES TO CHAPTER 47

¹ Letter his son dated August 15th, 1906.
² Rewald, *Cézanne*, p. 142.
³ Edmond Duranty, «Le peintre Louis Martin,» *Pays des Arts* (Paris, 1881, pp. 313-350. Probably written in the late 1860s. Published posthumously.
⁴ The Musée d'Orsay's exhibition, *Cézanne: les années de jeunesse, 1859-1872*, the first devoted to Cézanne's work of the 1860s, should have dampened a century of feasting and merriment over the caricatured Cézanne, but instead took a grand opportunity to indulge in it. Among the essays by Lawrence Gowing, Mary Louise Krumrine, and Mary Tomkins Lewis, one finds Krumrine ravishing Duranty's story of Maillobert. While admitting that the impersonation was a rather cruel caricature, Krumrine nonetheless offers what she accepts as substantiation: gossip among the Batignolles painters. «The legend was in part true,» she writes. «He was as violent as gentle, as timid as fierce,» and then she repeats the same physical description: «his overcoat stained green from mildew, his trousers too short, his agitated nervousness having become a tic that he threw malevolent glances all about him, that to Manet he refused his hand, saying I would shake your hand, Mr. Manet, but I haven't washed in a week,» and so on. From that opening to her essay, Krumrine sees Cézanne through Zola's eyes, fixated on the fictions of *L'Oeuvre* and *Thérèse Raquin*. The informative essay by Sylvie Patin, «Amateurs et collectioneurs des oeuvres de jeunesse de Cézanne,» does not figure in my critique. Mary Louise Krumrine, «Les écrivains parisiens et l'oeuvre de jeunesse de Cézanne,» Musée d'Orsay, *Cézanne: les années de jeunesse, 1859-1872* (Paris, Éditions de la Réunion des musées nationaux, 1988), p. 31.
⁵ Lewis, *Cézanne's Early Imagery*, p. 197.
⁶ I find it strange that in this age of gender sensitivity a young woman like Mary Lewis would repeatedly use the expression «old man» when referring to Cézanne in his late years, just as Rewald and other repeatedly called Cézanne's father «the old man,» or «the old banker.» Men using the expression «the old lady» might not fare as well in academic writing.
⁷ I. Druhen, *De l'influence du journalisme sur la santé du corps et de l'esprit* (Besaçon, 1871), see pp. 20-21. I have partially paraphrased expressions by Zeldin fused with those of Druhen. Neither had Zola in mind, however. See Theodore Zeldin, *France: 1848-1945: Taste and Corruption*, the chapter «Newspapers and Corruption.»
⁸ Barbey d'Aurevilly, *Les Oeuvres et les hommes: Journalistes et polémistes* (1895), Cf: Zeldin, pp. 156-158.
⁹ Published by Charpentier in 1882.
¹⁰ Zola, *Correspondance*, letter no. 00.
¹¹ I am paraphrasing from several of Zola's statements.

[12] Translation by Brown, *Zola*, p. 00.

[13] Cf. René Peter, «Zola et l'Académie,» *Mercure de France* CCXCVI (March 1, 1940), pp. 572-73.

[14] See F. W. J. Hemmings, *Emile Zola: Critique d'art*, introduction to Zola, *Salons*, pp. 28-31. Translation by John Rewald (slightly modified by me) in Rewald, *Impressionism*, p. 426.

[15] Zola, «Nouvelles artistiques et littéraires» *Le Messager de l'Europe* (July 1879). Reprinted in E. Zola, *Salons* (Geneva, Paris, 1959), pp. 225-230. Quoted in Rewald, *Impressionism*, p. 426.

[16] Zola, «Le naturalisme au Salon,» *Le Voltaire* (June 18-22, 1880). Reprinted in Zola, *Salons* (Geneva, Paris: 1959), pp. 233-254.

[17] Zola, «Le naturalisme au Salon,» *Le Voltaire* (June 18-22, 1880). Reprinted in E. Zola, *Salons* (Geneva, Paris: 1959), pp. 233-254.

[18] Zola, «Peintre,» *Le Figaro*, May 2, 1896.

[19] Paul Gauguin, Letter to Émile Shuffenecker, May 17, 1885. See Rewald, *Impressionism*, p. 496.

[20] In the introduction of the Durand-Ruel catalogue, Rewald, *Impressionism*, p. 302.

[22] Émile Zola, «Le naturalisme au Salon.» *Le Voltaire*, June 18-22 (three articles), 1880. In Zola, *Salons* (Geneva, Paris, 1959), pp. 233-254.

[23] See Rewald, *Impressionism*, p. 476.

NOTES TO CHAPTER 48

[1] Pissarro to Huysmans, quoted from a draft dated May 15, 1883. See Rewald, *Paul Cézanne*(New York, 1948), p. 129.

[2] Huysmans to Pissarro, (late May 1883). See Rewald, *Paul Cézanne*(New York, 1948), p. 129. I have modified a few words in Rewald's translation. The «medical museum» referred to is a museum of anatomy founded by Dupuytren.

[3] Henry Havard, «L'Exposition des artistes indépendants,» *Le Siècle* (April 2, 1880). For other reviews, see the full coverage by Charles Moffett, the chapter «Disarray and Disappointment,» in Moffett, *The New Painting*, pp. 293-214.

[4] Callebotte to Pissarro, January 24, 1881. Found among Pissarro's papers and published by Rewald, *Impressionism*, pp. 448-449. Translation by Rewald, but I have taken some of the rambling out of it to make the text more readable.

[5] Pissarro to Callebotte, January 27, 1881, in Janine Bailly-Herzberg, *Correspondance de Camille Pissarro*, 1865-1885 (Paris, 1980), p. 145. For a detailed coverage of this exhibition, see Fronia E. Wissman's chapter, «Realists Among the Impressionists,» in Moffett, *The New Painting*, pp. 337-369.

[6] For more on this exhibition, see Rewald, *Impressionism*, p. 449.

[7] Gauguin to Pissarro. Published in Rewald, *Impressionism*, pp. 466-67.

[8] See Rewald, *Impressionism*, p. 447.

[9] I am discussing here only one of the exhibitions of the Indépendants. For an excellent, comprehensive account of all the exhibitions, see the essays by Richard R.

Brettell, Hollis Clayson, Steven F. Eisenman, Joel Isaacson, Ronald Pickvance, Richard Shiff, Paul Tucker, Martha Ward, and Fronia E. Wissman in *The New Painting: Impressionism 1874-1876*.

[10] Renoir. Rewald, *Impressionism*, p. 469.

[11] Rewald, *Impressionism*, p. 468.

[12] Claretie. In *Le Temps*, reprinted in Claretie, *La Vie a Paris, 1882* (Paris, 1883). Cf. Rewald, *Impressionism*, p. 472.

[13] Huysmans. Reprinted in Huysmans, *L'Art moderne* (Paris, 1883), pp. 285-301.

[14] F. Fénéon, «A l'exposition d'Édouard Manet,» *La Libre Revue* (April 1884), p. 105.

[15] Shiff, «The End of Impressionism: A Study in Theories of Artistic Expression,» *The Art Quarterly*, Vol. 1, No. 4, 1978, pp. 343-349. See also Boime, *The Academy and French Painting in the Nineteenth Century*, pp. 170-172. For the various Impressionist and Symbolist interpretations of Cézanne, see Shiff, «Seeing Cézanne,» *Critical Inquiry*, Vol. IV, No, 4 (Summer 1978), pp. 769-808.

NOTES TO CHAPTER 49

[1] Clark, *Image of the People*.

[2] *Correspondance*, p. 236. One should take note of the similarity of this joke on himself to Cézanne purportedly saying to Manet, «I would shake your hand but I haven't washed in a week.»

[3] For an overview of Cézanne's withdrawal, see Shiff's' chapter «The Cézanne Legend» in *Cézanne and the End of Impressionism*, pp. 162-174.

[4] Robert Herbert, *Impressionism: Art, Leisure, and Parisian Society* (New Haven, Yale University Press, 1988). Theadore Reff, *Manet and Modern Paris: One Hundred Paintings, Drawings, Prints, and Photographs by Manet and His Contemporaries*, an exhibition at the National Gallery of Art, Washington, D.C. (Chicago and London: University of Chicago Press, 1882).

[5] Another tirelessly repeated statement about Cézanne's «timidity» is his fear that someone would get their hooks into him (*peur de grappin*). This comes from a very mild sentence in Vollard, *Cézanne*, pp. 100-101: *En entendant ce grand peintre se complaire à des enfantillages de cette espèce, et en le voyant accepter, de prime abord, toutes choses, sans aucun examen, des observateurs superficiels se sentaient volontiers la tentation d'user à leur profit d'une telle «naïveté»; mais, quand Cézanne s'était ressaisi—et il se ressaisissant toujours—il sortait bec et ongles, et, débarrassé de l'intrus, il pouvait placer triomphalement sa phrase favorite: «Le bougre, il voulait me mettre le grappin dessus!»*

[6] Alexis to Zola,

[7] *Correspondance*, Cézanne to Ambroise Vollard, January 9, 1903.

[8] Reff, «Cézanne, Flaubert, St. Anthony, and the Queen of Sheba,» *Art Bulletin* 44, no. 2 (June 1962), p. 114.

[9] Pissarro, *Correspondance*, p. 241.

[10] *Correspondance*, Cézanne to Francisco Oller, July 17, 1895. For the conflict with Le Bail, see *Correspondance*, Cézanne to Louis Le Bail, 1898.

[11] *Correspondance*, Letter to Fabbri, May 31, 1899.

[12] Edmond de Goncourt, *Journal*

[13] Degas to de Valernes, October 26, 1890. *Degas Letters*, pp 170-172.

[14] *Degas Letters*, pp. 5. I have not followed the English translation, which is rather wordy.

[15] From Berthe Morisot's notebook. See M. Angoulvent, *Berthe Morisot* (Paris, 1933), p. 76. Rewald, *Impressionism*, p. 568.

[16] A. Alexandre. *Introduction to the catalogue of the Alfred Sisley sale*, Galerie Georges Petit, May 1, 1899.

[17] Rewald, *Impressionism*, p. 576.

[18] Rewald, *Impressionism*, p. 462.

[19] Rewald, *Impressionism*, p. 462.

[20] As told to Ambroise Vollard, *Renoir*, Chapter III.

[21] Monet to Durand-Ruel, December 1, 1883. Venturi Archives, v. 1, p. 264. Rewald, *Impressionism*, p. 488.

[22] *Pissarro, Letters to his son Lucien* (New York, 1943), letter of May 4, 1883.

[23] Pissarro to Murer, August 8, 1884. Tabarant, *Pissarro* (Paris, 1924), p. 48.

[24] *Correspondance*, Cézanne to his son, September 13, 1906.

[25] *Correspondance*, Cézanne to his son. September 26, 1906.

[26] *Correspondance*, Cézanne to Charles Camoin. December 9, 1904.

[27] *Correspondance*, Cézanne to Vollard.

NOTES TO CHAPTER 50

[1] Monet to Zola, April 5, 1886, pp. 151-152.

[2] Paul Alexis, *Emile Zola, notes d'un ami* (Paris: Charpentier, 1882), pp. 121-22. The classic and unexcelled study of Zola's *L'Oeuvre* is Robert J. Niess, *Zola, Cézanne, and Manet* (Ann Arbor: University of Michigan Press, 1968). Also recommended is Theodore Bowie, *The Painter in French Fiction* (Chapel Hill: University of North Carolina, 1950).

[3] See Niess, p. 256, note 4.

[4] Vollard, *Cézanne*, p. 132. *Il n'y a jamais eu de facherie sentre nous, c'est moi qui ai cessé, le premier, d'aller voir Zola. Je n'étais plus a mon aise chez lui, avec les tapis par terre, les domestiques, et l'autre qui travaillait maintenant sur un bureau en bois sculpté. C'est avait fini par me donner l'impression que je rendais visite a un ministre. Il était devenu (excusez un peu, M. Vollard, je ne le dis pas en mauvaise part!) un sale bourgeois.*

On the furnishings of Zola's study, see Jean Adhémar, «Le cabinet de travail de Zola,» *Gazette des Beaux-Arts* (November 1960).

[5] Alfred Bruneau, *A l'ombre d'un grand coeur. Souvenirs d'un collaboration* (Paris: Charpentier et Fasquelle, 1932). For a more complete text of Anatole France's speech, see Brown, *Zola*, pp. 795-76. Anatole France would become the first president of the Société littéraire des Amis d'Émile Zola. Anatole France's reference to the Dreyfus affair was also a cause of considerable protests over the interment of Zola with such honors. Dreyfus was a Jewish military officer wrongly accused of treason and imprisoned. Zola took it upon himself to publish a very strong protest, titled «J'accuse» in the newspaper

L'Aurore on January 13th, 1898. Some 300,000 copies were sold within a few hours. Zola's key line was «My nights would be haunted by the specter of the innocent man, who is atoning, in a far away country, by the most frightening of tortures, for a crime he did not commit.» Having erased the line between personality and politics, having absorbed unto himself the condemned man's misery, Zola set a standard for the «engaged intellectual.» He was surely aware that for his arrogance the anti-Semite public would himself put him on trial for slandering the court, which was huge. And indeed he was. Dreyfus was eventually released after a military review of his case. One should regard this defense of Dreyfus as in the same spirit of the young Zola's defense of artists against the judgments of the Salon jury.

6   Quoted by Rewald, *Paul Cézanne*, p. 211.